I0777290

THE CHAOS SPIRAL

ADAM "DOC" BRACKIN

The Chaos Spiral © 2023 Adam L. Brackin

www.adambrackin.com

ISBN: 978-1-959544-02-9

FÆROS PUBLISHING
Austin, TX

This edition distributed through Ingram

Cover & interior art by Randall Worley

FÆROS PUBLISHING is an imprint of Wootton Major Publishing, LLC

www.woottonmajorpublishing.com

For Ian

Author's Note

The "Arab Spring" was a revolutionary wave of violent and non-violent demonstrations, protests, riots, coups, and civil wars in North Africa and the Middle East. It began on December 17, 2010 with the Tunisian Revolution, which sparked a wave of upheaval through 2011 and beyond. The Syrian civil war, the Kurdish Spring, and the Iraq War would deeply change the modern Arab world. Many contested locations now lie in ruins, their people scattered across the world.

At the time of writing, many regions and borders in this area remain closed or disputed. There seems no end in sight to the power struggles being fought over these ancient lands. These places continue to ferociously guard the deeply significant mysteries that have lain hidden there for many millennia.

The following is a work of fiction set in the summer of 2010, just months before these lands slammed their doors shut to the west. All scientific studies, art, research, locations, and theories referenced herein, however, are a matter of academic record.

*   *   *

The Proto-Sinaitic alphabet is a variant of the Phoenician alphabet and a precursor to biblical Hebrew and perhaps all other Semitics. Like the Phoenician alphabet, the "Old Hebrew" alphabet contains 22 letters, all of which are consonants. The language is described as an abjad after its first four letters, a term coined by Solomon Birnbaum in 1954.

Name	Pictograph	Meaning
Aleph		Ox/strength/leader/God
Bet		House / "in"
Gimmel		Foot/camel/pride
Dalet		Tent door/pathway
Hey		Lo!/Behold!/"The"
Vav		Nail/peg/add/"And"
Zayin		Plow/weapon/cut off
Chet		Tent wall/fence/separation
Tet		Basket/snake/surround
Yod		Arm & hand/work/deed
Kaf		Palm of hand/to open
Lamed		Staff/goad/control/toward
Mem		Water/chaos
Nun		Seed/fish/activity/life
Samekh		Hand on staff/support/prop
Ayin		Eye/to see/experience
Pey		Mouth/word/speak
Tsade		Man on side/desire/need
Qof		Sun on horizon/behind
Resh		Head/person/first
Shin		Eat/consume/destroy
Tav		Mark/sign/covenant

PROLOGUE

Ras-Shamra Ruins. Ugarit, Coastal Syria. April 2010. Aarons.

Self-proclaimed biblical archaeologist Wyatt Aarons had just started a video log on his little corporate laptop when muffled shouts from the guards told him something was very wrong. His blood ran instantly cold with the little echoing pops of gunfire from the maze of passages beyond. Far worse, only moments later the ruins went completely silent.

Aarons quickly and unceremoniously stuffed the papers and artifacts he had been working on into a well-worn leather satchel. Laptop abandoned, he hefted the bag to his bony shoulder, cringing a little at how the ancient tablet fragments clacked together amongst his dirty underwear. But there was no time to do it differently.

This was one of many linked chambers used in ancient times by the Canaanite kings as library storage. Once, this place had held hundreds of clay tablets, carvings, jars, and other things now long turned to dust. It was a complicated room, but not huge, and there was only one door. The portable lampstand the treasure hunter used to catalog his discoveries did not cast much light either.

One corner of the room had crumbled long ago in some forgotten disturbance. Aarons lurched towards this dark corner and ducked between two thick support columns. He cringed again as his pack smacked against one of the pillars, then plunged deeper into the shadows. He clambered up a pile of rocks and debris, dragging the bag behind him. He was no young man anymore, but decades of work in inhospitable areas of the world had kept him fit and wiry. *Please, let it be enough,* he prayed.

Effectively blind, his foot slipped on a loose stone. A small rockslide cascaded down below him. It sounded like thunder to his ears. A moment more and he reached the damaged ceiling. Angry yelling started from somewhere nearby. It was not English. Aarons hesitated for only a breath, then hauled the bag up. He rooted around and dug out a small leather-bound journal tied closed with a strap. His hand went back in for a small but sturdy red and yellow prepaid mailing envelope, one of several he kept for sending things back to the States. He shoved both deep into the leg pocket of his cargo pants, whispering a blessing upon whoever invented functional legwear. With a deep sigh of resignation, he flipped the pack closed and thrust it as far over the debris as he could reach. It vanished between the rubble and the edge of the mass of collapsed roof-stone. It wasn't the best hiding place ever, but it would have to do.

Aarons half-fell, half-slid back to the floor. He patted the book through his pant leg, praying that he had not made a terrible mistake. No, he had to have faith. The tablet fragments were too large and fragile to mail to himself, but the journal...

Suddenly, the invaders were there. Even from the shadows, Aarons could see the three young men's matching military garb. Camo pants and jackets, emblematic armbands of their faction, black masks that covered all but their eyes, and AK-47s older than any of them. Standard para-military garb in the Middle East. They spoke in the rushed and excited manner of adrenaline-fueled teenagers with machine guns and an agenda. This part of the world was filled with such lost boys. But they were still kids. It hurt Wyatt Aarons' heart.

As it was in the days of Noah...

One intruder planted himself in the only doorway. The other two split and began a careful search of the room, rifle barrels probing the shadows behind the supporting colonnade on each side. Aarons' heart banged in his chest and his mouth tasted of coppery fear. He was quickly running out of options. He was pinned, so any advantage the dark corner was giving him would only last a few more seconds.

One man passed close enough to the lampstand for Aarons to see the details of his armband. He recognized the symbol instantly: a black raven. It was a symbol he could never forget, and it could only mean one thing: This was personal. They had come for him.

His cold fear ignited into hot anger.

At that moment, deep within the mound of Ras-Shamra, Wyatt Aarons knew what God had led him there to do. And no bloodthirsty revolutionaries with a vendetta were going to stop him from doing it.

Aarons picked up a small stone and threw it across the darkness towards the lamp. He missed, but the stone cracked against the far wall and bounced a few times. All three men whipped their heads towards the noise and away from his side of the room. It was enough.

He burst from the shadows flailing like a frightened animal, knocking the nearest soldier onto the dusty floor. He spun past the second before any of them realized what was happening. His attempt to wrench away the man's large weapon failed, but he found himself in the narrow passage beyond the chamber regardless.

Aarons kept going.

A hail of gunfire echoed behind him, drowning out the confused and angry shouts of the men. Pieces of the ancient stone wall broke away and bits of flak stung him in the shoulder and arm.

He did not stop even when he emerged into the hot, moonlit ruins. The Syrian night hit him like an oven. Too dry for sweat, and not so much as a Mediterranean breeze this night. Even the stones remembered the day's inferno. Aarons knew these twisting trenches and roofless rooms better than anyone. The chances of outrunning his assailants outright were slim. It would be even worse above the half-excavated city, assuming he didn't run into any more of their brothers on the way out. No, he'd stay in the sunken moonlit hallways and find another way. He darted through a narrow passage and ducked behind fallen columns. Several minutes later, he had worked his way out of the labyrinthine complex.

Aarons made a beeline for the silhouette of trees that marked the edge of the tiny town called Burj al-Qasab. He plunged into a real alleyway as soon as he was able, sticking to the shadows as he wove his way through like a thief. He didn't stop until he finally collapsed against the wall which held the town's only mailbox.

He glanced at the red "Syrian Post" box with Arabic and French translations. Completely useless of course. Syrian mail wasn't very reliable, and all packages had to be assembled in front of a postal officer. But next to it was the shiny new courier dropbox that would save him. He had arranged for this private box to be picked up every week by an international shipping company based out of a less paranoid part of the world.

The scrapes where the flak had grazed him ached. His arm had gone numb and his other hand was beginning to tingle too. He gently touched his shoulder, the sharpness of sudden intense pain surprised him. His hand came away entirely too bloody. He looked closer and immediately understood. Between the adrenaline and the darkness of the night he simply hadn't recognized the bullet wound for what it really was.

A wave of dizziness passed over him. One side of his shirt was soaked with the sticky redness.

Oh. Time for a new plan then.

Wyatt Aarons wasn't worried. He was chosen, and he'd been delivered this far. He was months, perhaps weeks away from solving the single most important archeological mystery in the history of the world. And if there was one thing that Wyatt Aarons knew, it was how to improvise. A plan began formulating in his mind. He knew just the man for this job. Aarons just hoped his old friend would be more open-minded and forgiving than his pursuers. He gave it about even odds either way.

He emptied his pockets and stumbled towards the mailbox.

Praise God. Miraculously, he still had a pen.

I

M40 Motorway. Buckinghamshire, England. David.

David Evans stared out of the bus window, his heart pounding for more reasons than he could count. Unfamiliar cars and trucks zoomed by on the wrong side of the freeway. This was the M40 "Motorway," and the Airline "Coach" was the easiest way to Oxford from Heathrow Airport.

Motorway? Coach? Yes, he was in England, a parallel world. And he felt excited, nervous, and completely alive!

Except that everything possible had gone wrong. His grandfather, Arthur Evans, was supposed to have picked him up over an hour ago at the airport, but hadn't shown up. If that wasn't trouble enough, David's phone had stopped working as soon as he left America behind. The mobile phone company had promised his international plan would work automatically, but the not-so-smart-after-all-phone had gone deaf and dumb when he got here. It informed him:

No Service

Here! Here was England. And that was unimaginably amazing.

Being without social media or texting felt incredibly weird. David was truly alone, and completely winging it. But then, what in the last few months hadn't felt weird since that letter from Oxford? He'd first applied to the University Fine Arts Program to study digital photography over a year ago on kind of a whim. But he remembered the day his letter had arrived like it was still happening.

*   *   *

David was roleplaying with his friends around the dining room table when the doorbell rang. In an era when nobody rings doorbells anymore, it startled them all out of their goblin battle. David doubtfully opened the door. The mail carrier needed a signature for certified mail.

"That sounds like fun," she said, looking past him into the large dining room.

"Yea, we're trying out *Pathfinder*," he blurted. "The scenario is pretty epic so far, but I'm pretty sure our wizard is going to get clobbered before he gets anywhere near the center of the Labyrinth." His throat went dry. Why had he said that? When he got nervous, David's imagination always took over for his brain. There were plenty of geek girls in the universe, but the mail carrier was probably not one of them. "Um, it—it's a game," he tried to explain. "Like… Dungeons and Dragons?"

"Neat." She winked at him and tore the signature slip away. "I'm jealous. D&D just hasn't been the same since Fourth Edition."

David clenched his eyes closed and grimaced as he shut the door. He'd been out-geeked by the mail girl! Well, maybe it was for the best. She was too tall for him. Most girls were.

He stared blankly at his friends in the other room shaking dice and howling at some good—or really bad—roll. The guys were the same sort as him, though they were all older, and definitely shaggier. He'd always had older friends. They had beards. He had an electric razor he used about once a week. That was just the way it was.

"What was that all about?" one of the guys called over. "Strike out again?"

David ignored the jab. "It's from Oxford University," he said with mock-ceremony and his best fake English accent. He tore it open as he returned to the table and froze. "I—I guess I got in."

*   *   *

There had been a video interview and a million other steps afterward. The big thing was that while he had gotten in, it was under conditional status, pending a formal final interview in August. It technically meant they could still turn him away if they wanted, right at the start of term. He had no real backup plan and nowhere to live yet, but he tried not to think too hard about it. He had the whole spring and summer to figure it out. No pressure!

But then… spring betrayed him. The whole thing was a fuzzy time-lapsed blur. David got his passport, a bank card, and a one-way ticket. Everyone congratulated him, sent him money, and his mom even threw him a going-away party the likes of which the old Evans house hadn't known in two generations. That's when he'd been given his new smartphone. The best ones had full-sized touchscreens and HD cameras now, and his parents had splurged on the top of the line.

"An investment in his education," his mom said. His dad hadn't even complained about the cost much. It was an amazing gift. Third gen and a full thirty-two gigs of space. It did nearly everything his expensive camera gear and laptop could do, and people were making more and better apps every day. 2010 was a good time to be alive.

At some point, his mom made arrangements with David's Grandfather Evans. He was some kind of professor at Oxford, but the man was pretty much a complete stranger to David. He was an aloof family legend. The hermit, the scholar, the mysterious ex-adventurer, and world traveler. David imagined he was going to like the old man. The few short conversations with him had given David the impression that Dr. Evans was clearly brilliant if a bit scatterbrained. And now David was going to live with him for a few months until, his mom had said, "You can get yourself established." Whatever that was supposed to mean. David's imagination ran wild with what might lie ahead. Excitement mixed with fear, mixed with mystery.

Almost the first thing he'd done was google his grandfather's name to see if there was anything about his mysterious archeological career or maybe a more current picture. The results had been weird—down the rabbit hole weird. He'd swiped down past stuff about ancient civilizations, labyrinths, and other myths. He tapped through a few of the hits without really reading them, then closed the browser. Clearly the wrong Arthur Evans, but it had made for a fun status update.

> My Grandfather Evans is so mysterious that the Internet thinks he discovered Minotaurs. Can't wait to meet him.

*   *   *

David sighed as the bus zoomed along on the wrong side of the highway. His mind was wandering again. Grandfather Evans hadn't shown up in London. David had sat in that terminal for an hour, constantly scanning the room for a vaguely familiar nose or set of lips. He'd fought the urge to go outside and look around for Big Ben. And he'd even grabbed photos of the pigeons who had snuck inside the terminal. *Go birds!*

Finally, before one hour became two, he'd gone rogue.

First, it had been a visit to a money changer for some fake-looking British Pounds. Then, resolving to spend some of this Monopoly money, he strode up to the bus terminal ticket counter and bought a ticket for the next "coach" heading to Oxford. Adulting complete, he'd ordered a tea from the coffee shop, savored the irony, and waited for the bus in style.

Now, looking out the bus window, he watched a comedically small car zoom into the fast lane on the wrong side. Who knew what adventure lay ahead? It could be literally anything. Obviously, he'd have to find his grandfather and figure out why he hadn't shown up at the airport. Maybe figure out how to get his phone working and try to call him again? Barely two hours in the country and he already had two quests. *Excellent.*

On a whim, he pulled up the photos on his phone, scrolling till he found the series he wanted. Supposedly, pictures of David being held by his grandfather when he was a baby existed, but his mom hadn't been able to find those pictures anywhere. So, David had extended the search for family photos to a place he was forbidden to open: the family's antique leather steamer trunk stored in the attic. The one he'd always thought of as the "Mystery Chest." But all he'd found there were even older Polaroids—photos of a much younger Dr. Evans from his archeology days. These pictures were on David's phone now.

He hadn't told his dad.

His parents rarely fought, but the worst time David could remember had been something about that old chest and Grandfather Evans. David had sneakily rummaged in that trunk off and on for years. It was full of cracked and faded photos of people he didn't recognize. His favorite had always been a cigar box full of sepia images of some lady in front of things like Egyptian ruins, old airplanes, and mountains. She looked like Amelia Earhart or Carmen San Diego or somebody. The name "Judi Bell" had been scrawled on the box, but he had no idea who the woman might have been. He'd always liked the unusual spelling of it though. The Mystery Chest was full of bizarro stuff like that.

As the bus zoomed along its way on the wrong side of the road, David smiled at the digital versions of those faded Polaroids from the Mystery Chest. One showed a group of men at an archaeological dig in the 1980s. There was a hill behind them with white lines crisscrossed on the ground for some archeological purpose. He zoomed in on one man with his arms crossed and his foot on a small rock. It was a little blurry, but he could still make him out. He was short like all Evans men, but basically a slightly different model of his dad all the way down to the scowl. On the back of the photo, one word had been scrawled:

DOOMSDAY

So weird.

With London well behind him, David checked his phone's settings again. Oddly, even though Heathrow didn't have Wi-Fi, the bus to Oxford did. More backwards, and worth a try! He logged on easily and a few dozen notifications popped up on his screen. He started by sticking his earbuds in and hit play on an audiobook he'd been listening to. Then, pulling up a messenger app, he settled into his seat to chat with his friends for the next hour. They must be wondering what had happened to him, it was nearly nine o'clock in the morning!

But strangely, hardly anyone was on. He refreshed the app once before it hit him. The phone had magically adjusted the time to the correct local one, six hours ahead of Dallas to Greenwich Mean Time. Actual GMT.

Time Zone: (UTC +00:00) London

Everybody he knew was asleep, except for a few extreme night owls. To them, it was still only three in the morning. Because, duh. But he didn't feel tired at all. What was all this stuff about jet lag then?

He closed the app and looked out the window at a squat little catering truck. It had a strange-looking phone number with too many digits written on the side. An alien language. The phone numbers here were backwards too. He took a picture of the truck and posted it to Twitter. His tweets were picked up by Facebook and reposted there for him automatically.

> Greetings from backwards England. My phone is on
> strike, but buses have Wi-Fi *#thestruggleisreal*

He emailed his mom to let her know he'd landed and that all was well just in case she didn't see his post or if his dad missed the joke. She'd get one or both in the morning. Till then, he was on his own. No need to worry her with the details.

He went back to his audiobook and watched the cars go the wrong way on the freeway for the next hour. Yep, England was backwards. And David was loving every fantastic backwards second of it.

II

Mansfield College. Oxford, England. Arthur.

Dr. Arthur Evans, tutor of ancient literature and languages and Oxford University fellow, fumbled with the buttons of his brown sportscoat. He quickly crossed the meticulously manicured circular green of the Mansfield College courtyard, hoping no one would notice. The strictly enforced rule was that one wasn't permitted to walk on the croquet field except when playing a game, but Evans was in a rush, and most students were gone for the summer anyway.

It was imperative that he make it to the train station before the tourists from London arrived and crowded out the streets in their typical summer droves. He had no idea how early that might happen on a May Saturday in Oxford, despite having lived there for most of his life. It was his habit to sleep in on Saturdays, and he was a creature of deep habits. He glanced at his wristwatch and noted the time.

Good lord, it was nearly ten? Not good. It encouraged him to pick up the pace.

Evans was generally spry and in far better health than most Texas-born men in their mid-sixties. But Evans' bones still ached when the temperature dropped. Summer or not, Oxfordshire was much closer to the Arctic Circle than the U.S., and it was still a bit chilly in the mornings yet. Especially when it was cloudy, and it was always cloudy in England. Evans had never managed to fully acclimate to English mornings. Reading late and sleeping in was Evans' idea of a life well-lived.

Abandoning his jacket's impossible buttons, Evans straightened his muffler, reset his fedora, and tried to focus. This morning was a highly unusual situation that would not be solved by his usual rituals and stubbornness. That was why he'd dug out his personal key to the garden gate and cut across the college grounds instead of going the long way around the block. He puffed towards the porter's lodge by the front entrance, grumbling at the memory of the phone call some months ago that had started all of this.

*   *   *

It was the ringing that startled Evans awake. His hand shot out to search the bedside table for his glasses or the phone, whichever his fingers should happen to find first. The phone won, but not until after he knocked a short stack of books to the floor. Squinting at his antique alarm clock, he noted the time as just past 4:00 a.m.

Groggy and quite unused to rude midnight calls, he hauled the receiver up to his ear and grunted a monosyllable. As a long-time widower who had permanently taken up residence in England many decades ago, he had no idea who might be trying to call him at such an impossible hour.

"Hello?" a faraway voice asked.

"Hello, this is Arthur." He yawned, scratching his chin through his gray beard. It was time for a trim again.

"Yes, Arthur! This is Karen, can you hear me?"

"I suppose so. Sorry, who is this?" It was an American accent. Woman, obviously.

"Oh Arthur, thank goodness I finally got through. It's Karen Evans, Joe's wife." Her slow and annunciated voice was far away, but his tired brain forced the pieces together. *Karen Evans? Ah yes.* His daughter-in-law. Something must be deeply wrong. Had someone died?

"Listen, I apologize for the late hour there, we have been trying to reach

10

you for a few days now. It keeps saying your voicemail is full and we weren't able to leave any messages."

"Messages?" He blinked. "Oh, I don't really do messages." *This line has voicemail? Odd.*

"Oh, I see. Okay, Arthur." Was she laughing? Evans straightened his wool pajamas and wiggled himself into a better position.

"Listen, Arthur, we have some good news!"

"News? What news?"

The details followed. To Evans, the information sounded incoherent. There were random detached facts about somebody's grandson and some kind of visit to England. The university was involved. No one had died.

"Thank you for telling me," he managed, noting that he also sounded rather detached himself.

"Actually, Arthur, that isn't the whole reason I'm calling." Karen suddenly sounded different. Was she nervous? He disliked talking with nervous women. They made him, well, nervous also. "We were hoping that David could stay with you for the summer?" There was an awkward pause. Evans waited it out.

Who the devil is David?

Suddenly it clicked, and he realized what Karen was talking about. For a moment it was 1976 again, and Evans was a fresh widower with a six-year-old son Joseph and an offer to stay on at Oxford as a tutor. He'd made the difficult decision to place Joseph in an American boarding school then, but his boy had always been quite smart, and the issue had resolved itself. Maybe the Boarding Academy would take little David too? It felt like a lifetime ago. Someone else's lifetime.

Karen was saying something about colleges and interviews in August, then a question he didn't catch.

"Arthur? Are you still there?"

"What? Yes. Blast it, Karen, I'm not sure what you expect from me." It sounded more selfish than Evans had meant it to. "What I mean to say is that I haven't talked with Joseph in..."

The reality startled him as he realized he didn't know how many months, or perhaps years, it had actually been. He and Joseph had voiced their differences over the years, but Karen tended to tamp that down. The fact that they would foist their son off on him for a summer after all this time had never occurred to him. He started again.

"I can't take care of a little boy Karen. I'm a cranky old man. I live in an efficiency behind one of the Colleges, for goodness' sake."

"Arthur!" She was no longer laughing, and she was most certainly not nervous. "David is coming to Oxford for college! He's been accepted into a bachelor's program to study art. He's nearly seventeen. He will be having his final interviews with some of the colleges and needs a place to stay while he's there. We want you to show him around, not adopt him!"

There had been more to the call, and others after that. During the next months, Evans ate much crow and promised to behave himself. It wasn't often that he lied to women, especially those he truly liked, but sometimes one had to make exceptions to these things.

*   *   *

As Evans slipped through the door to the mailroom which served as Mansfield's porter lodge, the more technical aspects of the arrangement slipped away. They were replaced by the task at hand. Simply, he was supposed to be in London right now picking up David and he was terribly late.

Understandably, Evans had experienced difficulty getting to sleep last night, so he had taken his phone off the cradle. Then this morning, his typically reliable alarm clock had failed. So, he'd accidentally overslept like any other normal Saturday. Realizing it, he'd tried to call, but the boy hadn't answered his phone. Evans wasn't sure what else to do. Thus, this was no normal Saturday. It was a fiasco.

"Good morning, Professor." The first-shift porter clearly didn't know Evans that well. He was young, red-haired, and spoke with an Irish lilt, a testament to the truly international flavor of the twenty thousand plus university students here.

"Just a tutor," Evans said automatically. "Not a professor." Oxford was a college town to be sure, but a deeply medieval one, and many traditions remained. One did not study for a degree at Oxford University as much as "read" for one. To that end, things worked very differently overall. Per tradition, only the heads, chairs, and deans were called "professor." Evans had never quite achieved that level of prestige, though being an Oxford don in any form was nothing to sneeze at, certainly.

"Certainly, Dr. Evans. My apologies," the college porter said with a chipper smile. "If you are looking for your post, the morning delivery hasn't come yet, but you do have a package that's been here a few days."

The young man set a small red and yellow mailer covered with stickers and stamps onto the platform of the Dutch door that separated them. He was clearly happy to be rid of the thing. He hopefully eyed the overstuffed mailbox behind Evans' shoulder where the seasoned tutor directed his University-related mail so that he could check it at his leisure. Or ignore it entirely, as he more often did.

"What? Oh, yes thank you," Evans replied. "And call me Arthur, please."

He absentmindedly picked up the heavy-duty envelope but forced himself to stay focused on why he was there. Evans was perfectly aware he had never quite mastered the art of polite English conversation. Try as he might, it was hard to shake the deeply rooted American spirit in him. His grandfather had been a man of culture from Hertfordshire, greater London to be precise. But Arthur M. Evans had been born and raised as a second-generation Texan in the family's old modern-style house near Dallas that Joseph and Karen now owned.

Some said Evans was a brilliant lecturer who knew the ancient world like he'd been born there. Others, that he was anything from absent-minded to rude. But the truth was, Dr. Evans just didn't feel like six and a half decades on this planet was long enough to understand how individual people could be so inconsistent and emotional all the time. Case in point, when his young wife had died unexpectedly in the mid-70s, he'd simply poured himself into his work and never looked back. Such a course of action seeming the sensible thing to do. And Joseph had certainly been no worse for it.

Evans still missed Elisabeth dreadfully. Sometimes he could almost see her there, walking with him in the ancient streets of Oxford as she had so many years ago. Her, never aging or growing older than her mid-thirties, while he passed into his fourth, fifth, and finally sixth decade. He was hardly recognizable to himself in the mirror anymore. Elisabeth Evans was the only one who had ever really understood him. She had also understood his love for all people in general, and his difficulties with individuals in particular. The very idea of meeting Joseph and Karen's boy made him twitchy.

The boy! No distractions, he reminded himself. He cleared his throat and pushed his glasses up to his nose. "Actually, I was wondering if you could tell me when the next train to London runs? I'm supposed to pick my grandson up at the airport this morning, and I think I may be running late." It was a polite lie of the English variety. He knew darn well he was late. He was also grumpier than usual, and he was trying to compensate.

"Certainly, Arthur. Might I recommend one of the Airline coaches instead perhaps? They leave every thirty minutes on the hour and half past, so it's easy to predict, and they are direct to Heathrow." The porter looked unfazed by the urgency of the situation.

Evans set the package he was holding back down on the Dutch door ledge and looked at his watch again for emphasis. The porter eyed the mailer dubiously, then grabbed the bus schedule from his wall and scanned it.

"Though I suppose if you make haste, one will come through High Street in just a few minutes. It's the second stop on the line."

Evans hadn't thought of that! He didn't hesitate. Turning to go, he began a "Thank-you-very-much," but the porter cut him off.

"Sir, your package?"

Evans quickly shoved the thick envelope into his coat pocket, ignored the man's further protestations about the rest of his mail, and hurried out the door.

He momentarily considered grabbing his bicycle from among the dozens on the rack by the gate but dismissed it. Aside from the difficulty getting it onto the bus with him, if he cut through the Turf Tavern to St. Helen's Passage he might just—but no, the Turf wouldn't open till when? Eleven? He'd have to do Radcliffe Square and hope the tourists hadn't taken it over yet. He began to jog briskly down Mansfield Road towards Broad Street.

It had only taken the Texan transplant a few days to learn to navigate Old Oxford, but even after decades of living there, Evans still discovered new shortcuts and passageways from time to time among the innumerable lanes and courts of his little medieval town. Ducking down New College Lane to the twisting Queen's Lane walking path wasn't particularly difficult or hidden, even the tourists sometimes knew to do it. It was the quickest way to High Street at this time of day. Or so Evans hoped. If he hurried, he could be at the High Street bus stop in less than five minutes.

Evans hurried.

III

International Waters, Pacific Hemisphere. 35,000 ft., Eastbound toward Los Angeles. Mel.

When she was in Beijing, Melanie Chen sat in the most powerful office in one of the world's largest corporations. Mel was one of the ten richest women in the world, but she rarely thought about it that way. She avoided going to Beijing as much as possible, and very rarely ever sat in that office. Mel much preferred the office she took with her, in a jet that was in every way that mattered an identical twin of the American president's *Air Force One*.

It was in this mobile office above the clouds, that Mel Chen thumbed on her monitor and cued up the reports waiting for her. It was her habit to watch these while she drank her tea. She ceremoniously selected and measured an appropriate variety for the antique teapot that was often part of the little ritual. Mel always prepared her own tea. It helped her think.

Mel was the CEO of a corporate empire bigger than the gross domestic product of most countries. But one small slice, a wholly-owned subsidiary called Mao Sien, was the only real thing she cared about. The rest bored her immeasurably. The name basically meant "Adventure Company" in English, her little joke. Its purpose was one thing and one thing alone: To pursue various para-archaeological ventures that no other institution would have dared waste time or money on. Melanie Chen found, bought, and sold true-myths and miracles wholesale. This was her true passion. To find the lost cities of the world, the legends, the impossible places, and things hidden in the depths and buried long ago.

She smiled to see that Wyatt Aarons' weekly status report was up first today. It was late. He hadn't sent one for almost two weeks, the first reports he had ever missed in his time with the company. It was unlike Aarons to miss his camera time. The file called to her, but her tea was ready. She poured the piping hot *Da Hong Pao* from the old vessel into a matching cup.

Oolong-style teas are not particularly uncommon. But according to one legend, the mother of a Ming Dynasty emperor was cured of an illness by a certain tea, after which he sent great red robes to clothe the four bushes from which it originated. Recently, one of Mel's teams had confirmed that some of these original gnarled and twisted bushes still grew on a rock in the Wuyi Mountains, reportedly dating back to the even earlier Song Dynasty. Mel had paid upwards of $35,000 American for this particular batch. While admittedly delicious, what she truly savored was the taste of the legend. It was superb.

Mel never shied from using her massive leverage and resources to get what she wanted. She hired away the best of the best in every imaginable field. She even had employees from unorthodox disciplines like paleo-archeology, forensic geology, and epigenetics. By side-stepping the normal categories, she had successfully plowed past government roadblocks, academic peer review, and popular opinion. Mel found and conscripted those individuals able to connect the dots between presumed fiction and actual historical finds. These individuals were her human computers.

In this same way, Mel had finally snagged Wyatt Aarons, the charismatic and—in certain circles— famous biblical archeologist. And one of her favorite human computers to keep tabs on. Aarons was a one-man team, not including his locally hired guards. He had never quite fit into the Mao Sien family dynamic, but she had still watched every one of his reports personally from day one. She loved his silly southern drawl and his ridiculous snow-white van dyke beard and handlebar mustache. But truthfully, Mel deeply admired the man for his decades-long track record of finding "unfindable" religious relics and doing the seemingly impossible. He had done it for over a year now under the Mao Sien banner. In fact, it had taken her that long to finally convince him to build a proper team moving forward. That team was scheduled to meet up with him this week, as it happened. Yes, he was coming around.

Mel frowned. Something was strange about this video. She noted the urgent tag one of the handler techs had placed on the file for her and double-checked the date stamp. The video had been processed today, but the raw data was recorded over two weeks ago. This was last week's report, but something had delayed it. She took the teapot to her glass-top desk and hit play.

Mel watched the recording, poured herself another cup of *Da Hong Pao*, then immediately watched it again. The third time, she picked up a stylus and took notes, embedding them in the file. She transcribed with care the details of Wyatt's words to the camera, the precise timestamp of the off-camera gunshots, and even the length of the dead air before the three masked gunmen entered the far end of the room and started their search. She slowed the feed down and looped the video. In quarter speed, the wild-eyed Aarons flung himself out of the room, physically shoving the men aside. The militants shouted and gave chase, and the ancient room emptied.

Mel considered the fact that the rest of the file was nothing but an empty room. A few hours of nothing, according to the tech's notation. The loop started again, Aarons bursting from the shadows as before. Hours of an empty room obviously meant that the recording had not been turned off. She wasn't surprised given what was on it. Then, after the battery of the archeologist's laptop ran down, it would have shut itself off abruptly without uploading anything to the satellite. Plus, there was a lot of stone in those ruins. Aarons had been forced to take the laptop to the excavated parts for the internal sat-phone modem to connect, then wait for the upload to finish.

What did not make sense was why she now had the video at all. It was likely that the next time it powered up, the computer would have automatically connected and uploaded the file. But who had plugged it in and turned it on? And from where? Certainly not from the depths of the palace ruins. She took a sip of her tea.

There were several possibilities, but none of them were very encouraging. If the gunmen had come back for the laptop, it had been later. Many hours later at least. That didn't make sense. If Aarons had escaped, come back later, charged the laptop, and sent the file; then why had he not contacted her, requested extraction, or sent an addendum to the file? Wyatt Aarons would have reported in. She already knew he hadn't, but she double-checked the logs to be sure.

Nothing. No, this file's late and automatic delivery seemed more like an accidental upload of some incompetent thief due to the failsafes built into her software. Wyatt Aarons was missing, or worse. She had to consider the very real possibility that her man was captured or lying dead somewhere in coastal Syria. What had the invaders wanted? Clearly not research. A high-profile kidnapping? It wouldn't be the first time she'd dealt with that. It never ended well for the kidnappers. Who were these men? And why no ransom demand?

She opened a communication window and waited for the video chat to connect with one of her people on the ground. "Tie me into the human resources database index."

"Which one?" The heavily accented man on the other end replied, barely glancing up. "Mao Sien employee? Master holdings Employee?"

"No," she said flatly, "I want everything. Build me a Boolean index. But kindly save me a step and set up a filter on your end first. Flag anybody who has ever had any connection at all to Mr. Wyatt Aarons of the Ras-Shamra dig and prioritize by that."

The man snapped to attention. "Yes, ma'am." His eyebrows told her that he was pleased and intrigued by this order. Rarely did she request such a large and tricky search, but her people liked a challenge. If they didn't, she didn't hire them.

The window disappeared. Behind it, the loop of Aarons wrestling past his assailants still played. She watched his mop of white hair and ridiculous Dr. Livingstone khaki uniform disappear up the murky stairway in jerking slow motion. The dark man with the distinctive para-military garb slowly rotated away and fell to the ground.

A new detail caught her eye. She paused the video and zoomed in on the image of a bird the man wore on his shoulder armband. Adrenaline surged through her. The legend was true then! Mel needed no image search to confirm what she already knew about that emblem. Even in the washed-out colors of this grainy low-light pixelated image, she recognized a black raven on a red and white background when she saw one. These were no ordinary guerilla freedom fighters then. And they were quite far from home.

When in doubt, always rely on the human computer.

"Excellent," she said aloud, then drank off the last of her costly tea. "Perhaps we can kill two birds at once then."

Her monitor chimed, signaling that the connections she had requested were available. She now had access through her array of private satellites to the massive index of "persons of interest" her people maintained and curated for times like this.

Even with the limitations she'd set, the POI list was massive and growing exponentially. A decade ago, a similar search would have taken hours, even from the mainland. She loved technology. She swiped through a few of the top names but nothing interesting jumped out at her immediately. She needed a way to narrow the search.

She adjusted tactics and opened a little spider program some of her best IT people had recently coded up for her. Every second of every day, humans uploaded more information to the internet than existed in the American Library of Congress. Something was out there that would lead her to Aarons.

Correction: Someone.

Mel needed a new human computer. Someone with the right connections, history, and knowledge to get inside Wyatt Aarons' head and track him. To see what nobody else could. It might be anyone, but it had to be just the right someone. She entered her new variables and ran the program. This part might take some time. Humans could be slow. She could wait. The entire internet was working for her now.

IV

Holywell Street. Oxford, England. Arthur.

As Evans rounded the corner past the King's Arms Pub onto Catte Street, he could already see crowds gathering in front of Oxford's iconic Radcliffe Camera for the first walking tours of the city. Worse, it looked like another blasted street fair was happening down Broad street. Tents lined the road below the high and intricate façades of pale-yellow Cotswold limestone.

Evans sighed. He was surrounded by bumbling bodies in tourist garb taking bad photographs, and he only had a few short minutes left. Public transit did not wait for anyone in England. Evans needed that shortcut right now. His eyes shot to the old Hertford skyway that joined two parts of Hertford College at the second story. He grunted and darted under this Bridge of Sighs, as it was often called, and on through to New College Lane. The narrow and twisting passage was little more than a cobblestone alleyway so he risked a jog, listening for any bicycles that might come his way. Huffing down the path, he congratulated himself for successfully avoiding the circular "Rad-Cam's" crowds.

Many things in the old city had secret nicknames. Well, open secrets at least. And Evans knew most of them. As a tutor, he had held contracts with many of the autonomous thirty-eight colleges and six permanent private halls nestled in among the twisting stonework passages of the medieval college district. He had been variably employed in every corner of his city at one time or another. But, knowing his way around its mazelike alleys and hidden paths was a plus for other reasons too. He was now making record time to the High Street bus stop, so that was something.

A horrible thought occurred to Evans. He would likely be spending his afternoon touring a curious teenager around his city instead of his usual habit of spending Saturday reading at the Ashmolean museum. When they inevitably came walking back this way, would the young man care that the Hertford Skyway was referred to as the Bridge of Sighs because of its supposed similarity to the famous *Ponte dei Sospiri* in Venice? He doubted it.

Perhaps the lad would be more interested in a related funny story, like the legend that many decades ago, a survey of the health of students was taken, and as Hertford College's students were the heaviest, the college closed off the bridge to force them to take the stairs, giving them extra exercise. Thus, the pun in the name. Evans tried to imagine young David laughing at his joke, but realized he had no idea what the boy even looked like, having not seen him since he was a baby. Well, except for Karen's regular holiday cards, but whoever made a study of those? He managed a vague image of his son Joseph at about the same age. No image of David came.

Besides, Evans knew from personal experience that if the Hertford College bridge was not used, the students actually climbed fewer stairs, so the legend had to be false. Or was that his rational academic mindset making him stuffy again? Maybe he would skip that part. Or, he could just explain it. That's what tutors did after all, did they not? Engage in the ancient art of explaining things? He sighed, picking up the pace.

He considered other possibilities for entertaining the boy. Perhaps the old Oxford Castle on the hill? Historians had made a discovery recently, adjusting the age of the fortress's old Saxon tower. The scandalous date possibly eclipsed the age of the Saxon tower attached to St. Michael at the North Gate—currently considered the oldest in the city. Evans' best friend Father Matthew had been cordially doubtful. And Evans had been cordially doubtful that the discovery at the fort would have any impact whatsoever on ticket sales of the St. Michael tower admission, or the adjoining gift shop which the church also oversaw.

Yes, Evans could start with the Saxon Tower at St. Michael, and give David one of the best views possible of the old city proper. Also, Matthew's church was the current City Church of Oxford. That counted for something, right? Fascinating trivia. Best of all, Matthew would let them go up without paying like the tourists.

Oh, but the tourists. No, not the tower. At least not on the weekend. Perhaps that Harry Potter walking tour they give? Ugh. Same problem. Besides, he never read modern children's books and wouldn't be a very good companion to the boy, he feared. Evans was floundering.

Part of the problem was that despite his four decades living in Oxford, Evans had never properly played tourist. He'd been far more interested in the ideas of the people who had lived, studied, and died here. Philosophers the likes of Thomas Hobbes, Walter Raleigh, and John Donne. Some of the great writers like Samuel Johnson and Jonathan Swift. And who could forget the influence of revolutionary poets like Oscar Wilde and Percy Shelly? Not to mention the scientists. Edwin Hubble and Richard Dawkins had challenged whole paradigms of thinking that had simply been accepted as unshakable before they'd come along. Even opposites like Margaret Thatcher and Michael Palin had walked these streets as students. Yet, despite Evans' decades of access to the great libraries here, he'd barely scratched the surface of these more modern minds. No, his mind thrived in the libraries and museums of his ancient city. Who had time for tourism?

It was a true conundrum, but it would have to wait. He had arrived. Evans emerged from the alleyway and spotted the bus already parked a few lampposts down. He was too late! With mere moments to get aboard, Evans discarded whatever decorum he was still trying to preserve and waved his arms, yelling to the driver to wait for him.

Everyone on the sidewalk stopped and stared at the crazy old American as he flailed past. He ducked his head and charged forward, his coat flapping back and forth as he ran. Something in his pocket slapped against his upper thigh, but he didn't stop to think about it. With adrenaline pumping, Evans grabbed the exterior handrail and flung himself into the doorway of the bus. He'd made it!

The driver's seat was empty. A few of the passengers stifled a giggle or two, but Evans just leaned against the inside steps red-faced and uncomfortable.

A long moment later, the driver stepped in behind him with a wry smirk and a wink. "Need a lift on the coach mate?" he asked with that special breed of gravelly sarcasm reserved by London cabbies and airport bus drivers in an otherwise extremely polite society.

"Uh, yes, thank you," Evans muttered between breaths. He searched his wallet for a fifty Pound note while the man used the onboard kiosk to print a ticket receipt. Evans snatched his round-trip ticket and headed towards a seat in the back where he could disappear.

"Excuse me," a young and clearly American voice behind him called out. "Grandfather Evans?" Evans turned. A young man of about his same height stepped into the bus and eyed him questioningly.

The teenager had on worn tennis shoes and faded blue jeans, with a tee-shirt sporting some kind of Asian cartoon character. Over this was a light blue hooded jacket, unzipped. In one hand, the youth clutched an ultra-modern cell phone. His other hand was tightly tucked under the straps of a fat backpack slung over his shoulder. A white headphone cord extended from one ear to a clip, then over to the phone. The other one dangled nearby. Other than his brown curly hair needing a trim, he seemed a fairly clean-cut and typical all-American kid.

There was no mistaking it though, if the slight Texas accent hadn't given it away, the young man had Karen's piercing green eyes. And like a ghost from Evans' past, the boy was every bit the spitting image of Joseph as a teenager. He looked more like one of Evans' students than the kid he had been picturing. Regardless, this was most certainly David.

Evans must have gaped like a fool as he sized the boy up, because after a moment the teen followed up with, "I'm sorry, but you are Arthur Evans aren't you sir? I recognized you from your archeology pictures." The teen motioned with his phone hand, apparently showing him something. Indeed, the screen was lit up with some kind of old photo. Returning to the front of the bus, Evans recognized the photo immediately. Though cropped, it was a picture that had been taken of him at his old Turkish research site in the early 80s: a past life that he had long ago abandoned and thought successfully buried. This teenager must have been born a solid decade and a half after this picture was taken, yet his comfortable familiarity with its existence made Evans squirm.

Suddenly Evans felt like an old man staring through a window in time. Though he would have preferred better words, he fell back on one of his automatic catchphrases instead. "Pleased to meet you, I'm Arthur." He extended a hand, but David didn't have one free, so Evans simply clasped the boy on one shoulder. A gesture he'd used on many a student at graduation, or after notice of their successful exam marks.

"Um, okay Arthur. I'm David."

They stood awkwardly for a moment, Evans unsure what to say next to his new ward. The entirety of the English language had momentarily left him.

David rescued him. "We should probably get off the bus?"

As they stepped out, Evans noticed that the crowds had taken over everywhere now. He supposed it didn't matter which way they went. They would all be equally horrible and would just have to deal with it.

It occurred to Evans a few minutes later, that the driver had kept the rather substantial change for the ticket he had needlessly purchased. It was clearly the beginning of a dreadful day.

*　　　*　　　*

"So, yea, I'm sorry I couldn't call you, my phone stopped working when I landed," David said as they hurried through the canyon of medieval façades.

"Phone? Oh, quite right. I suppose things are different on this side of the pond. Though, I don't really do technology or the cellular phones. I have enough trouble keeping to my business without all that nonsense." Evans stopped walking. "Wait a tick, where is your luggage?"

David swallowed a grin. "I don't have any bags." He shrugged his overstuffed backpack onto the ground. "Just this."

Evans grunted in approval and relaxed a bit. He straightened his coat and turned on his heel toward a stone archway that led away from the street. The boy hefted his bag and tried to follow.

"Oy, watch it!" a local woman protested as he nearly clipped her baby stroller with it.

"Sorry!" David called to her and put his backpack on properly. He slipped his phone back into his pocket and matched Evans' pace as best he could. The woman mumbled something about American tourists Evans didn't catch. He sighed and slowed his walk for David to catch up, but the boy was standing stalk-still.

"Wow," David breathed, eyes filled with enchanted wonder. "That's the Rad-Cam! Hey Arthur, is this Radcliffe Square?"

Evans lifted an eyebrow. This often happened when people saw one of the iconic places in Oxford for the first time. They had slipped from the medieval storefronts where the busses landed, into a wide yellow courtyard of dreaming spires with its ornamented cylindrical reading room squatting in the center. The boy had done his homework then, good.

Evans smiled weakly and darted forward, hoping to find a quick reprieve from the massive crowd that constantly moved and swirled around on the uneven cobblestone streets and narrow passages. "Yes, it is," He called back. "If you ever get lost, just ask for it and then head north. My flat is just up the road there."

David still didn't follow though. He turned instead to look at the thirteenth-century tower sculpted spire of the University Church of St. Mary

22

the Virgin. "The pictures on the internet just don't do this place justice!" the boy declared, then in complete disregard of his statement, like the tourist that he was, he held his phone high to take quick pictures of everything himself. Evans closed his eyes and sighed as people pushed past him on all sides.

"Is your, uh, *flat* where we are going?" David asked, finally trotting up beside him. He was clearly amused by Evans' use of the English word for an apartment.

"Oh, good lord, no," Evans proclaimed. "The pub and a pint first, I should think." He could already see the corner of the King's Arms. He had no intention of passing it by twice in one morning.

"Pub? What, like an English bar?" David laughed. "Arthur, I'm sixteen!"

"Are you?" Evans asked, missing the point entirely. "Fabulous. Then let them know you are with me but remember that only I can order alcohol for you." He stopped short. "Unless you are hungry. Are you hungry? They may have the grill up, I'm not sure what time they..."

But David had fallen behind again. He was inexplicably pointing his phone at the Bridge of Sighs, then spun to point it again at the sculpted busts atop the stone and iron fence of the Sheldonian Theatre. *What on earth?* Evans sighed again. At least he wouldn't have to play tour guide all day.

V

The King's Arms Pub. Oxford, England. David.

David sipped at a tiny glass of Coke while his grandfather—that is to say "Arthur"—clutched his decidedly larger pint of *bitter*. He held it close like an old friend.

The stuff Arthur had was dark. Really dark. And it smelled more like bread than anything else. This amused David, and he wondered if maybe things he'd heard about American beer being "bad" from his gamer friends were truer than he'd realized. Arthur hadn't actually drunk any of it yet. David wondered if he was even planning to. He glanced at his phone for the time. Yep, barely 10:30 in the morning. His grandfather was one interesting guy.

Down the rabbit hole we go!

After a few minutes of awkward silence, Arthur excused himself and went to the men's room. "Toilet," the sign said, pointing downstairs. England was amazingly weird. And apparently, pubs weren't too bad either, because he had a Wi-Fi signal in here too. David thumbed through the pictures he had just taken, selecting which ones were share-worthy. Most of them were average, but some were pretty good.

David had studied every iconic image of Oxford for months as both an art lover and a future student hopeful. He knew most of them now, but this was different, he was here. He hadn't realized how close these things all were to one another. Every part of him wanted to run out and touch the ancient buildings and take pictures of it all and post them for his friends to see. David was exploding with excitement, and Arthur wanted to sit in a bar?

David had never imagined his grandfather might drink. David's dad, being the sort of evangelical protestant minister who didn't drink, meant that David had never really been around alcohol. His mom had given up her evening glass of wine when they'd married. That was true love, David supposed.

Frankly, David didn't have any major vices that he could think of, unless you counted being a gamer, and he knew people that thought that way. He was pretty boring in real life. But in his "other lives," he'd played every role from an orc barbarian to a wise old wizard. Come to think of it, Arthur kind of reminded him of a modern Gandalf. With a shorter beard. And a much more practical hat.

Undeniably, this was no ordinary bar though. David took a selfie, making sure to get a good angle on the tavern, and posted it. The whole pub was like something out of *Lord of the Rings*. Wood floor, offset levels, and little hidden rooms with paneled walls. Wooden tables and benches. Not chairs; benches. He half expected a squat hairy dwarf and a poncy elf to come through the door at any moment with strange tales of a dragon's treasure hoard and a semi-predictable plot hook. None did. Instead, Arthur returned from the bathroom, grunted, and sat down.

The old man wriggled a bit, then promptly stood back up. He took his jacket off, fumbled in the pocket, and extracted a folded mailer envelope covered in stickers, then just stared at it like he'd discovered an old sandwich from last week. David held in a laugh. The guy was hilarious to watch. Apparently satisfied, Arthur tossed the little package onto the table. Having found the source of his discomfort, he replaced his coat and sat back down to resume cuddling with the mug of black stuff he wasn't drinking.

"What's that?" David asked, mostly just to get some kind of conversation going. He motioned towards the little package with his phone.

"What's what?" Arthur glanced around the room for whatever David might have meant, then saw. "Oh, that? I have no idea. Came in the mail this morning."

"Well, I mean it's obviously a package. But aren't you going to open it?" David was still trying his best not to laugh. He wasn't sure how Arthur might take it.

"Be my guest." Arthur's smile was detached but genial. He seemed to be relaxing a bit.

Out of curiosity more than anything, David slid the thick envelope over to himself. It was strange. Over the foreign stickers and ink stamps was a whole other layer of little stickers and markings. And that flowing script almost looked like Elvish. Maybe it was Arabic?

The once red and yellow mailer was stained and dirty. David guessed it had been around for a while and tossed between postal bins here and there. It had Arthur's name, but what was really strange was the address, or rather the lack of one. The thing had only been sent to the University at large and then made its way to Arthur the hard way around. There was a big fat sticker with signatures and initials of at least three different campus offices. *Campus?* Was that even the right word for a city like this?

David slipped a finger under the lip of the seal and popped it open. More like a theme park, only with dark beer.

Ooh! And fish and chips. Yes!

David set the mailer down and smiled up at the server who had just arrived at the table. A massive batter-fried fish fillet as long as his forearm leaned against an enormous pile of French fries. English fries? Maybe that's why they were called chips. There was also something that looked like a dab of wasabi, which surprised him.

"Care for some tomato ketchup or HP, luv?" the server asked.

The only thing that David could think of that HP might stand for was "hit points" but he doubted that's what she meant.

"Uh, sure?" This was fun.

A moment later she brought two bottles to the table, one with the prominent letters HP on the label. He poured a big gob onto his plate. It was better than steak sauce, whatever it was, and whatever it stood for. David decided he liked pubs.

He was halfway through the best flaky battered fish he'd ever eaten when he noticed that Arthur had emptied the little mailer. He was thumbing through a small leather-bound book with pages full of hand-written script. Dog-eared pages and little bookmarks stuck out at odd angles, and David spotted something like drawings on some of the pages. His interest sparked. Arthur flipped through it too quickly to be reading, but he looked as white as a sheet and a little sick. His pint still sat untouched and now entirely forgotten.

"Arthur? You okay?" David mumbled, mouth full of fries.

His grandfather shut the book and slipped it into his pocket, then folded the mailer package and put it away too. "Certainly. Completely fine. Just some research from an old colleague of mine, that's all."

David nodded as if he understood. He might have said something, but his mouth was full again.

The wasabi wasn't. It was some kind of mashed peas. Really good too. He wished he had about ten times more of it than this little dab. He picked up his phone and opened the internet browser to find out what the point of mashed peas with fried fish was, but Arthur started talking again, as much to himself as to David. The little book was back in his hands.

"But... but... this is a bunch of stuff and nonsense!. Ramblings of a man I knew years ago. Goes by the name of Aarons. I'd know his deeply out-of-context Bible quotations anywhere. Called himself a 'biblical archeologist' among other things. Eventually, we had—well—a disagreement and parted ways. I came back to Oxford. As I understand it, Wyatt went fundraising around the American south to finance expeditions to search for the Tower of Babel or some-such fool thing. He went on to claim, well—that is, he made a lot of outlandish and unsupportable claims."

There was a momentary lull and Arthur started flipping through the book again mumbling under his breath about the Aarons guy and something about Syria. David let his eyes drop back to his phone and thumbed in a search on "Aarons, biblical archeologist" for fun. The result was so surprising he nearly fell off the bench. He swallowed the food in his mouth so hard that it hurt.

"Like how he found Noah's Ark?" David blurted.

"Yes, exactly," Arthur said dryly, without looking up. Then his head jerked up, a fire in his eyes. "Wait a tick. How the devil do you know that? What exactly did Karen tell you?" The old man stopped and softened as if he remembered who he was talking to suddenly.

David silently lowered his phone to the table, sliding it past his half-eaten plate of pub food and the mostly drunk Coke, right next to Arthur's untouched pint of beer. Arthur needed only a quick glance to understand. On the browser was one of the many hits of articles, images, and videos that David's quick internet search had revealed.

NOAH'S ARK FOUND!

The title proclaimed. Below it, the unabashedly sensationalized article began:

> Renowned biblical archeologist Wyatt Aarons confirms his original findings at the Noah's Ark site in

It went on, but it was not flattering. Embedded in the text was an eerily familiar black and white image of David's young grandfather and other men standing in front of a large hill-like structure. The same weird white lines stretched across it in a grid pattern, just like the old Polaroids. Same moment, different camera?

David watched nervously as his grandfather scanned the article emotionlessly. He grunted, then slid the phone back.

"David—" he started, his voice serious and stern, his expression hard and intense and more laser-focused than David had imagined the absent-minded professor could be. It scared him a little.

"I'm sorry!" David blurted out. "I didn't mean to, uh—" David broke off. He didn't know what he didn't mean. He wasn't even sure what he'd done. He just sensed he had stumbled into some kind of family taboo. He had a sudden memory of his father telling him to stay away from the old steamer trunk many years ago, making him promise never to get into it up there in the attic. Of doing it anyway sometimes… and then immediately doing so all over again when he got admitted to Oxford, going through every page and paper looking for a better picture of Arthur but only finding weirder ones. Of exploiting the Mystery Chest for years on end every time he made a new friend, by taking them up to the attic just to impress them with made-up stories about how his ancestors used to be pirates.

Fantasy pirates back then. Fantasy castles and pubs now. And here was a man he barely knew, casting a spell of shame upon him. An angry wizard. Not Gandalf, but Saruman.

"Just forget it," Arthur said abruptly, holding up a hand in peace. He then used the hand to grab his mug, and took the first actual drag of his beer, draining it almost halfway. It was kind of impressive really.

David ate in awkward silence and finished his now cold fish and soggy fries. They didn't taste as good anymore, and the HP steak sauce wannabe had a weird aftertaste. The coke glass was too small and he had to order another one at the bar. He didn't realize that they didn't do refills and had to pay for it. He felt like a dumb kid and he had the tiniest ache of missing home suddenly. His adventure was souring way too soon.

David's mind was reeling. He wanted to slay Oxford so bad it hurt, but honestly, he had no idea what that even meant. Everything familiar was an ocean away. He felt alone and nervous. His imagination took over and he shoved the darker thoughts away. He'd focus on his mysterious grandfather who received secret journals from old partners. His friends would get such a kick out of that if he did it right.

He picked up his phone and tentatively unlocked it. Arthur was nose-deep in the journal again. A few more patrons had drifted into the pub and were chatting loudly. It gave the illusion that other things were happening around them and that it was perfectly normal for the two Evanses to be ignoring each other.

David skimmed the rest of the article until he got to the bottom, paying close attention to each of the images. He found no more mention of his grandfather nor any clue as to what the former partners' disagreement might have been about. He held his finger on each image and saved them to his phone's photo directory anyway, as was his habit with interesting tidbits, memes, and whatever else he wanted to hold onto.

At the bottom of the article was the iconic "Tweet" share button among the other social media icons. David smiled. He tapped the icon and the screen shifted to his Twitter app with a URL shortcut for the website embedded. He quickly typed two messages in quick succession:

> Have infiltrated fantasy castle town. Granddad Evans
> wants me to call him Arthur. Might need to call him
> Merlin though. (1/2)
> He gets super-secret journals from an Indiana Jones-
> type named Wyatt Aarons. Both possibly wizards.
> Taking quest for much needed XP. (2/2)

Then, as an afterthought, he snapped a picture of the sauce on the table. David's new wizard loomed behind, looking over his glasses with a deep scowl into the little journal. It was too perfect. He tweeted the image with a caption.

> Have looted HP potion. Use with caution as it drains
> mana over time. White wizard seeks counterspell.

David smiled to himself. Just a little joke between him and the rest of the internet. Arthur didn't have to know about it.

Or at least, he hoped Arthur wouldn't ever know about it.

VI

International Waters, Pacific Hemisphere. 35,000 ft., Eastbound toward Los Angeles. Mel.

Thousands of miles away on another continent, a series of nodes on a massive cloud server automatically handed off a few million packets of encrypted information to a large data center located in Hong Kong. It was just one small rivulet in the constant stream of data that flowed through the world-wide-web.

Within that rivulet, a Twitter account was quickly flagged by a digital spider. The little program was borrowing the computer array's resources for a complex Boolean search it was assisting on behalf of a very powerful anonymous user, half a world away. The information was processed, filtered, indexed, and forwarded, then the spider moved on.

Fractions of a second later, the information itself passed through several high-level systems before being vetted and admitted into the Mao Sien company intranet. It was shunted aside for a few seconds while the system ran a cross-reference to the massive high-security POI database. The data was given a predictive importance rating along with a growing index of similar data. This triggered a new connection, and with the importance threshold reached, the data was automatically flagged, logged, and forwarded via private satellite to the in-flight mobile desktop of CEO Melanie Chen.

The screen chimed, informing Mel of this new high interest hit on her near real-time search. She brought up the results. It contained a log of internet activity from an IP address in England. An Oxford pub to be precise. The content was somewhat innocuous. It was from a Twitter account with a series of tweets, links, and various images with corroborating metadata. These had been posted over the last hour by an American teenager who had just arrived in the country, evidently to visit his grandfather.

That was fine. It was what the facial recognition software in the POI database told her about the image of an older man holding a little journal that made it significant. And then there was the smoking gun.

> He gets super-secret journals from an Indiana Jones-
> type named Wyatt Aarons...

Mel tapped through to the man's file. Dr. Arthur M. Evans of Oxford was already in the Mao Sien database as a person of interest to the company, thanks in part to his former connection with Wyatt Aarons

There's my human computer, she thought. Soon, Dr. Evans would join her staff, and after that, they would find Wyatt Aarons.

An old notation from her HR headhunters indicated that there had been difficulty in trying to recruit Dr. Evans in the past. It seemed the man lived off of the grid somewhat. That wouldn't be a problem for her. And she would be overseeing this one personally, starting right now.

With a few keystrokes, Mel had a very different personnel file open. Mel had an employee almost everywhere that mattered. There was an operative already in place in Oxford—relatively new, a bit young, and more than a bit unconventional, but otherwise would do just fine. She liked unconventional. The man had come with the highest possible recommendation. Mel knew how to be very persuasive, and that didn't always mean money. Every trap required the right kind of bait, after all. According to the file, this operative had required a certain lifestyle. She had provided it, with all its eccentricities, leading someone in HR to nickname him "Mr. Suit." This made Mel smile.

There was much to do and little time to do it. She would need to repurpose the team that had been set to meet up with Aarons, not to mention find better security options. Ah, but she was getting ahead of herself. This development called for a fresh pot of tea. She glanced at a nearby screen that showed the hour in every zone in the world and noted the time in the UK.

English Breakfast it was then.

VII

Keeble College. Oxford, England. Mr. Suit.

In a small residential room at one of Oxford's more modern dormitories, a man stirred from sleep. His work phone chimed in the nearby student desk. He forced himself up, head throbbing, and staggered naked the short distance across the blurry room. Few knew the number of his work phone. Whoever was texting him, it would be important.

He knew he should not have stayed out so late last night, but the temptations of this city were sometimes too great for him to resist. He had neglected his duty and now cursed his luck. But at least the text was coming this morning and not last night. He glanced at the time and swore aloud. *This afternoon.*

He picked up the little mobile and flipped it open, rubbing the blurriness away. What he saw made him instantly sober up.

Time to clock in

The company. An assignment! He quickly typed his reply.

Proceed

The naked man opened the nearby closet and surveyed himself in the built-in sink's mirror. He was in his mid-twenties now and well-built. His handsome Middle Eastern features, short black hair, and olive skin were a consistent draw to the ladies. Particularly the American college girls. They especially loved his tattoo, and inevitably wanted to show him theirs. Such young women thought he was dangerous and safe all at the same time. A fantasy he afforded them.

They were half right.

He did not remember the name of the girl he had met last night. He wasn't sure he had asked. It didn't matter, it hadn't gone anywhere this time. The possibility of failure was half the fun. Aside from a little redness in the whites of his otherwise dark and piercing eyes, he looked fine. Like any other graduate student who had stayed on for summer studies and partied too late. But then he was no ordinary student. Again, only half right.

The student room he called his own was small but served his simple needs. Nearly every Oxford dormitory room was occupied by someone year-round. Even during the summer months, they were let to all sorts of people. He had found these accommodations quite amenable amid the various waves of tourists, professional academics, and conference-goers. He had met the most interesting people since coming to England. Not one had ever met the real him.

The phone buzzed again. The details of the job followed. A local man. A bit of recon regarding a book. *Easy.* Then the name came. He raised his eyebrow at that, but what he needed to do became crystal clear. At least he wouldn't have to look up the man's address.

The naked man made his bed, showered, cleaned his teeth and face, and meticulously trimmed his close-cropped beard. The chilly water felt very good today, but he was already wide awake. He stepped to the other side of the little closet and pushed his immaculately pressed shirts to one side. He prided himself in purposeful neatness, having sworn off tee-shirts years ago. He did own one pair of $200 weekend jeans, but they were for those same American girls. Part of the costume.

He would not need his regular wardrobe today, however. He withdrew instead a suit carrier, took it to the bed, and laid it out. He slowly unzipped it and extracted the expensive tailored suit his generous employer had provided for such occasions. He wore it only when he was working. His skin tingled into gooseflesh at the thought of putting it on today.

This suit was too valuable for casual wear, no matter what the ladies might think. Not that he needed that kind of help. He slipped the shirt on first, buttoning it most of the way up. He then slid into the suit trousers, savoring the feel of the expensive material against his skin. He had chosen Italian silk. He had chosen well.

The well-dressed man walked over to the built-in bench by the window. He set aside one of the seat cushions and with his forefinger, popped open the lid to the hideaway storage below. It was a simple board, under which he kept some of his less used things. The English were very efficient with their space, he had always admired that. He drew out a gym bag and unzipped it, pushing aside a towel and various other items. This revealed the three passports, a bundle of cash in each respective currency, and a weapon and vertical shoulder holster he knew were there. His go-bag.

The sleek Hungarian-made FEG was not a large gun, but it was easy to hide and would serve his purpose. Loaded, safety on, just as he had left it.

The man slipped his arms into the concealed carry holster and tucked the gun away. The holster was a personal gift from a very important man. The weight felt good at his side. Part of him now. The man in the suit was a small part of a very complex network. He was rewarded very well to be this, and he had just been activated. Whether or not he shared the ideologies of his employer was irrelevant. Rich fools could believe what they wanted.

The man in the suit replaced the bag and the cushion as they had been. He walked back to the bed and shrugged himself into the suit coat, making the weapon disappear. Finally, he slipped the phone into his coat and smiled. His transformation was complete. It was time to go to work.

He scooped up a shiny red motorcycle helmet and a pair of polarized sunglasses, hesitating for only the briefest moment before slipping a second phone into his inside breast suit pocket.

A minute later, the man in the suit crossed the college green towards where his Ducati Multistrada 1200 S Sport stood locked and chained. Another magnificent gift from his employer. He almost felt bad keeping secrets from them.

Almost.

VIII

Dr. Arthur Evans' Residence. Oxford, England. Arthur.

This day—*this month*—was a total fiasco.

The boy David had been here less than a few hours, but already he was nosing into the one topic that Evans had tried his hardest to put behind him. He'd spent the better part of three decades successfully burying his dealings with that skunk Wyatt Aarons. Now, out of nowhere, the man was trying to drag Evans back into his deluded world where "faith" trumped evidence. That was simply not going to happen.

But David had used that blasted smartphone to search for Wyatt's name on the internet. It wouldn't have been hard to find, Evans realized. It was one of the reasons he had chosen not to keep up with the technology, unlike many others of his generation. It was just a matter of time now before the boy knew everything. The very thought made him cringe.

Evans glanced at his old faded armchair where David had tossed his backpack and sighed. He'd sent the younger Evans to the Mansfield College Porter with a note to get a spare key. The boy had barely even stepped into the flat, but his backpack was already invading Evans' armchair. His *only* armchair. Evans lifted the overstuffed bag to the floor with a grunt, then plopped into the tatty upholstery. It was the most comfortable chair in the world, having conformed to his hindquarters over the decades. Being home was somewhat calming at least.

Evans looked around his tiny three-room flat. The most notable feature of the oddly triangular dwelling was the inordinate number of books that he had amassed. Evans had always been obsessed with information and had compiled a small personal library to that end. Having quickly used up the meager built-in shelving available in the humble flat, he'd allowed his collection to spill over into any and all other available spaces, starting with the baseboards. Evans had never bothered to invest in bookshelves. It would have been impractical to some degree. Well, technically it would have been highly practical, but he reasoned that the cost of a bookshelf was better spent on a book. Or better yet a stack of books. Certainly, more so than some functional pieces of wood.

This method had served him well until he'd run out of space in the anteroom. So, he'd simply continued the collection in the bedroom the same way, and when that ran out of room too, he'd filled the kitchen. Not a problem, since he rarely cooked. This process had taken years. Decades even. A lifetime. The effect of this was that no corner of his little oddly shaped home was without books. Stacks and rows along every wall, crevice, and space. It was an eccentric book-lover's dream. He knew where every book in his collection could be found because layer upon layer of it was chronological, based upon when he'd added the book to his collection.

His home was a physical representation of his mind. Neither one was a good place for a teenager.

Evans had no idea what he was going to do next. His was a quiet existence. There was one small bed, one chair, a table with a surface he knew was down there somewhere under the texts, but only one stool to go under it. This whole thing was a fiasco. Yes, that was the right word.

Good lord, but I've become an eccentric old man!

His memory wandered to the little cottage on the edge of town that he and Elisabeth had taken when they were first married. It had all been promise and hope back then. He with a respectable lecturing position and possibilities of more someday, once he'd proved his stripes. It had been her excellent tenure at the Ashmolean Museum that had afforded them the luxury of the tiny house. Elisabeth had done up the nursery for baby Joseph in the classic English style, and it had all seemed so perfect. The biggest problems had been choosing a color scheme and working out the maternity schedule with the museum. Those years had been the best ones of his life. Elisabeth's joy of having a child and the way she balanced motherhood with her job were memories he treasured. The time before the chaos brought about by Wyatt.

Evans suddenly had a foreboding feeling that this quiet existence would be coming to an end soon too. For starters, he would need a cleaning lady to come around. Kids were messy. Old men were messier. This place was already at maximum mess. He looked around again at the collection of books he had amassed and sighed again, audibly and with purpose. He loved them all, but he knew that a book could not love you back. Neither could a University, he supposed. No matter how much you loved it first.

The thought of books and his old partner made him realize that the little journal was digging into his hip again, wedged against the old armchair. With a grimace that was as much imagined as genuine discomfort, he extracted it from the coat pocket. It came open at a later point than he had been browsing before, the last written page in fact. Wyatt had almost filled this entire book with his mad ramblings.

But this entry was different. It made the hair on Evans' neck stand on end. It was hastily written and sloppy, still recognizable as Aarons' elegant handwriting, but he had broken from the clean lines of his normal entries and written in large hasty strokes. At the bottom, the page was smeared with brown dried something, and at the edge a smudged thumbprint of the same something. It looked like blood.

If this wasn't bad enough, the message itself sealed it. It was a personalized message from Wyatt to him. And what a horrible thing it was too. Mostly because it contained what might arguably be interpreted as an apology.

> *Arthur, you were right about Nûh and the tree after all.*
> *I had proof but it is hidden away.*
> *Can't go on without your museum's collection.*
> *The path is real, but I'm being watched and hunted now.*
> *I'm sending you this journal so you will understand.*
> *"As it was in the days of Noah," eh?*
> *It's time we were vindicated for Doomsday.*
> *The alphabet is the place to start.*
> *I'll meet you in Dilmun when it's safe.*
>
> *—Wyatt*

Dilmun? Wyatt was after the lost city of Dilmun? It couldn't be. Evans' mind retreated from the idea in horror. For the briefest of moments, his interest had been piqued. But in one swift wave, all of Wyatt's crazy came rushing back. Wyatt was a madman if he was looking for Dilmun now, after everything that had happened. After finally getting his farcical Noah museum on Doomsday Mountain greenlit by the Turkish Government itself, there was nothing to gain by it except a return to mockery and public shaming. Wyatt's ventures had always reeked of cheap marketing and glossy commercialization, designed to appeal only to "the faithful" and bolster American Evangelical support for his endeavors, but why now?

Evans was startled out of his analysis by a knock on the door. David returning no doubt. But no, it was too soon. That meant the boy had either gotten lost on his way to the porter, forgotten something, or some other bother. Either way, it meant he wouldn't have the spare key he'd been sent to fetch, and Evans would probably be required to intervene. Evans extracted himself from the chair and opened the door. He was surprised to see not his grandson, but a well-kept Middle Eastern man in a very nice suit smiling broadly at him.

Evans' flat was sunken a half-story into the ground. The steep steps leading down from the road meant that there was a distinct lack of standing room for callers at his front door. Plus, the little old doorway required one to duck to enter and exit the flat, meaning it was too short to stand behind without ducking ridiculously low, even for him. Thus, Evans usually found himself in the little front garden, uncomfortably face to face with his disturbers of the peace. He enjoyed his awkward flat, which often reminded him of a Hobbit hole, but there were moments it inconvenienced him. Like now for example.

The caller had solved the space problem by retreating up the first two stairs and leaning against the iron railing. This was great for him, but it meant Evans was now looking up at the man in silhouette from below.

"Uh, yes? How can I help you?" Evans asked gruffly.

"Pardon me, sir. You are Dr. Evans, are you not?" The man's British English was good, but there was an undertone of accent there. It reminded him of something, but he couldn't place it.

"I am. Call me Arthur, please."

The man in the suit smiled. He removed his polarized sunglasses with practiced grace and thrust out his hand. His eyes were piercingly black and uncomfortably intense. Evans realized he was still holding the journal, so he shoved it back into his pocket and met the stranger at the steps, shaking his hand noncommittally.

"Certainly, Arthur. I do apologize for the intrusion." The man smiled widely again, then launched into his pitch. "I was wondering if I might have a moment of your time? There is an important matter that I wish to discuss with you. I represent a consortium of professional interests who hire the best and brightest talents in Oxford for various types of academic pursuits. Our goal is…"

The man continued, but Evans didn't need to hear the rest. It was one of *those* pitches. This sort of thing was common here, and Evans had developed a nose for sniffing out the type of organization the man was representing. There was nothing inherently immoral about the idea of a tutoring center or conference based in Oxford. It was a city just like any other. *Except, it isn't.* It was ancient, steeped in history, and full of prestigious and revered institutions. But that was precisely the issue. The very name of "Oxford such-and-such" commanded respect and attention. Academics and non-academics alike all over the world knew it. To attend a conference "in" Oxford, to present a paper "in" Oxford, or to speak to an organization "in" Oxford was worth the price of the plane ticket just for the CV bullet point. This was because most people didn't think past the name to ask whether or not the institution, conference, or tutorial center was truly affiliated with the University "of" Oxford or any of its Colleges, as opposed to simply having the opportunistic fortune of being conveniently located in the city of the same name. Regardless, much like academic real estate, there was still a certain pomp that came with having the word Oxford on one's list of accomplishments. It was all about location, location, location, as they say.

Evans couldn't have cared less, frankly. After four decades and change in his city, first as a student, then alumnus, and now University don, he had developed a penchant for dodging such inquiries. It was just dumb luck that this caller had found him at home instead of his office up at the museum, as was his regular habit for a Saturday. Oh, how he longed to be there right now. But for this David situation, he would be.

"I'm sorry young man," he interrupted. One of the perks of being an American was the double standard that allowed him to be rude. "But I'm not looking for any additional contracts right now. Good day to you." This last he punctuated by ducking backward through the little green doorway of his flat, throwing the latch, and leaning against it with his whole body and a great exhalation of relief.

Evans had barely caught his breath when he was physically jolted by more knocking. He jumped back and spun as if the door had bitten him. *What the devil?* This guy had some nerve!

"I'm sorry!" he shouted at the door. "But I have said good day!"

"Hey, uh, Arthur? It's me," David called through the door. "Should I just use the key then, or what?"

Evans relaxed and collapsed into his chair. He watched as the sanctity of his home was violated by his own spare key. Awkwardly, David pushed the door open with one foot.

"You decent? The, uh... The key works."

Evans beckoned the teen in. David stooped past the threshold into the little three-sided living room filled with the books of Evans' life. The boy's arms were overloaded with mail.

"I brought you your mail. Where should I put it?"

Total fiasco.

IX

Dr. Arthur Evans' Residence. Oxford, England. David.

Arthur was making tea. David hoped it would be as good as the tea he'd had at the airport. Killing time until his grandfather came back in the room wouldn't be hard, the place was a library. He took a picture to post, then realized he didn't have a connection.

A thin layer of dust and a thick layer of books on every shelf and surface reminded David all the more of a wizard's library, in no way dispelling his fantasy from earlier. Undoubtedly, Arthur liked bachelorhood and had a mad obsession with really weird books, but no obsession with organizing them. David scanned the stacks for fantasy, sci-fi, or any kind of genre fiction really, but there was a distinct lack. The only fiction was really old. Some of the books even looked like they'd been printed in the 1800s or something.

David decided he liked this room. He had read more fan-fiction and pulp fantasy than he cared to admit. The stuff he'd brought with him on his phone was just the tip of his collection of audiobooks, eBooks, and PDFs he had archived. Some people, like his mom, played Farmville. When he wasn't playing tabletop games or doing photography, David downloaded, listened to, and read as many novels, game manuals, and sourcebooks as he could manage. His dad insisted that listening to an audiobook "wasn't actual reading." His mother shushed him and let David do it his way. Suddenly, Arthur's "flat" with its rows and rows of books stacked high against the floorboard felt very comfortable. Did David have that many titles too? He'd never counted. His collection was way easier to carry around though.

Arthur came in balancing a tray with a fine china teapot and two matching teacups and saucers. He set the tray down on a little end table, the only surface that was noticeably clear of books. David watched the old wizard drop into his cushioned throne and pour tea for them both. Arthur didn't ask what David wanted in it, he just poured milk from a tiny little pitcher before handing it over. *But, when in Oxford...*

David plopped to the floor and took a sip. It was amazing. It didn't even taste like tea. Certainly, not the syrupy sweet iced tea that he was used to back in Texas. This reminded him more of hot pancakes, or maybe fry bread from the State Fair. Weird, but good weird. He felt himself relax a little more. Suddenly his eyelids felt very heavy.

Out of nowhere, Arthur surprised David by speaking. "Well, I suppose we should talk about Wyatt Aarons' journal."

A jolt of fear shot through David. He looked up at Arthur nervously, afraid that once again he had violated some dark family taboo. But the old man gave him what was meant to be a reassuring nod. David was wide awake now, his pulse thundering at the mere mention of the mystery book.

"Listen, David, I'm a grumpy old man and we didn't get off to the best start. It's just that when it comes to your father, we don't always—." The room went cold. David stared into his tea while Arthur struggled to finish his sentence. He abandoned it instead. Arthur suddenly looked like the tired one, and David pitied his grandfather a little, though he couldn't really say why.

"What I mean to say, David, is that I know you will get the world's version of the story from that infernal phone of yours eventually, so I thought that you had better hear my side first. I'm not the best at tea and talking, but let's give it a go regardless. What do you say?"

David grinned widely, tucked his foot under his leg, and grabbed his teacup. "Sounds good, granddad," then fake-coughed and quickly added, "Arthur." He leaned back, expecting to find the wall, but displaced some books and sloshed tea on his jeans instead.

Arthur didn't notice. With a firm nod and a guttural, "Mmm-hmm," he extracted the journal and began flipping through its pages.

David sat up straight and didn't try to move again.

"Ah, here it is. You are going to be an Oxford man soon, so look at this and tell me what it means to you." Arthur held the journal out to David, open to the last written page.

The paper was stained and a bit smudged, but David read it. The handwriting could have been nice, except it had been written too shakily. The hands of an old man with bad eyesight maybe? The words themselves were ominous and strange.

> *Arthur, you were right about Nûh and the tree after all.*
> *I had proof but it is hidden away.*
> *Can't go on without your museum's collection.*
> *The path is real, but I'm being watched and hunted now.*
> *I'm sending you this journal so you will understand.*
> *"As it was in the days of Noah," eh?*
> *It's time we were vindicated for Doomsday.*
> *The alphabet is the place to start.*
> *I'll meet you in Dilmun when it's safe.*
>
> *—Wyatt*

David read it twice, but nothing made sense. His curiosity quickly turned to confusion.

"Okay. I don't get it. What does it mean? Somebody's after Dr. Aarons?" Arthur shrugged noncommittally, so David tried again. If it was a test, he was failing it. "'The days of Noah.' That's from the Bible, right?" It wasn't really a question. Because, duh.

This time Arthur nodded. "Gospel of Matthew. 'As it was in the days of Noah, so it will be at the coming of the Son of Man.' Christ said it, predicting his second coming as I recall."

"The second coming? So, Doomsday is what, the end of the world?"

"Well, yes. Wyatt always was a bit of an end-times Revelation nut, but it's more than just that. Start at the top."

David read it a third time. "Okay, so what does Dr. Aarons mean by 'Nûḥ and the tree?'" He looked up from the little book hopefully. Arthur was resequencing a short stack of books on the end-table in some way that only made sense to himself.

"Oh, well that's an easy one," Arthur supplied absentmindedly. "Nûḥ means Noah, and the tree is the Tree of Life. And for the record, it's *Mr.* Aarons. Wyatt never took a degree."

David processed this. "Tree of Life? Like Adam and Eve?"

"I should think so. Aarons likely means the Tree of Life from the Eden account in *Genesis*."

"And Noah? Like Noah's Ark, Noah? Is *Nûḥ* his Hebrew name?"

Arthur frowned, but not at David. "No, *Nûḥ* is Arabic. Well, a phonetic transliteration anyway. Aarons isn't referring to the Moses tradition."

"Well, of course not," David laughed. "Moses's Ark and Noah's Ark aren't the same thing, everybody knows that. One's a big boat and the other is a little box they kept the Ten Commandments in."

"What?" Arthur crossed his arms and leaned back into his chair. "Oh bother. That's not what I meant at all." He huffed in apparent frustration, as if not sure how to explain. "I'm sorry. I sometimes forget how little people actually know about Noah. I mean, there is so much more to the flood myths than the tale recorded in *Genesis*. I was referring to the fact that *Genesis* is one of the books ascribed to Moses." Now Arthur looked like a fish, thanks to the glasses riding low on his nose.

How little people know about Noah? Flood myths? Books "ascribed" to Moses? David wasn't sure what Arthur was getting at. Pretty much everybody knew about Noah and the flood, didn't they? And David knew as much about Noah's Ark as anybody, being a minister's kid and all. His dad Joe was a somewhat well-known religious writer on top of being one of the education pastors at the big church downtown. You picked stuff up as a preacher's kid.

Plus, David personally had nearly seventeen years of Sunday school under his belt. And sure, he knew the first section of the Bible was written by Moses. His whole class had memorized the Bible book names by section in vacation Bible school as a little kid. Jews called the ones written by Moses the Pentateuch, the whole thing was the Torah, and Christians called it all the Old Testament. Jesus quoted from it all the time. Believers knew it was true. What more was there to know?

"The thing about the Flood," Arthur attempted, scratching his gray beard as if to coax the words out, "is that it's about the end of the world. It's an apocalypse. Or rather, an apocalyptic warning to people that this sort of thing is possible. Can happen, has happened. That is the warning part, you see?"

David didn't see.

"'As it was in the days of Noah' is more than just a First Century prophecy about the end of the world. It's a very old idea. One of the oldest ever. The idea behind it is that if the world gets too chaotic and evil again, God might just wipe us out, and call an end to it. Or in the Christian tradition, that the messiah will return. Of which John was pretty clear, that is not a happy day. It's the 'End of Days,' to be precise."

"John? Like the *Book of Revelation*, John? I thought we were talking about *Genesis?" Backwards, again.*

"Right. End of the world, end of days, and so forth. Just like all the other apocalypses that happened before."

David waited for the punchline. *Other apocalypses?* What was Arthur talking about?

"Um, Arthur, are you saying that Mr. Aarons truly thinks the world is going to end soon?"

The old wizard was completely stoic. "Well, yes."

"But why? What does doomsday have to do with the Flood? That happened a really long time ago, and God promised not to do it again. Big rainbow or whatever? I mean, what exactly did Mr. Aarons find in the Middle East? Should we warn somebody?"

"What? Goodness no." Arthur furrowed his brow. "Oh, I see now. We've muddled it already." He made a noise like a horse that turned into stammering and then finally soured all over again. But he also must have realized he was needlessly overcomplicating the topic. He set his jaw in frustration. David suddenly had a feeling that maybe they weren't even talking about the same thing.

Finally, Arthur cleared his throat and tried again. "I might as well start from the beginning." Then leaning his head back to stare at the wooden slats of the ceiling, he began his tale. A medieval bard now. "In September of 1960, a young man named Wyatt Aarons—whom I suppose was about as old as you are now—read an article in LIFE Magazine about a boat-shaped formation in the mountains of Ararat."

Wait. 1960 was the *beginning* of Noah's Ark?

David decided not to interrupt.

Arthur slurped at his tea and continued. "The article's title was 'NOAH'S ARK?' in all capitals, and a big fat question mark calling into question its own assertion. The text began with the phrase, 'Boatlike form seen near Ararat!'" Arthur gestured with his free hand in a sweeping arc, painting the invisible headline in the air as he spoke.

Suddenly he straightened up, distracted by some long-lost memory. He looked around the room as if he could somehow find the thought on one of the bare walls above his stacks of books. David watched him stand, cross to the obtuse corner of the triangular room and carefully remove the row of books from atop a dark trunk. Arthur stacked the first set precariously onto another row that was already too high, but they managed to stay. He then flung open the chest and rummaged around in it, pulling out odds and ends, various shoeboxes and envelopes, a cigar box, and yet even more books, all while looking for something David could only guess at.

With a shock, David realized where he had seen such a trunk before. It was an exact duplicate of the Mystery Chest at home. This surreal coincidence reminded David that his house had been in the family for five generations. He had never asked his dad about the details. Had Arthur lived there as a boy? As a young adult before moving to England? Who had lived there when David's dad was a kid at boarding school and Arthur was here in Oxford?

Suddenly David was back in his parents' attic, nine years old, with the contents of the Mystery Chest strewn all around him. He'd often done this while his mother spring cleaned and organized the five generations of junk collecting dust up there... Until the one time his father came up and discovered this activity. His dad's anger hadn't been with David though. It was directed toward his mom. The fight was seared into David's little mind. When David thought of marriage arguments, this was the moment that came up in his head. It remained the only time he'd ever heard his father swear, and the anomaly that reminded him how great his parents usually got along.

But this time, seeing the trunk in such an unexpected place, something tugged at his memories. A detail in his brain refreshed by his recent and much stealthier search of the Mystery Chest while looking for some good pictures of Arthur. With his dad away on one of his many promotional book-signing trips, David had casually cataloged the full contents of the Mystery Chest in anticipation of his upcoming move to Oxford. David had examined all the clothes, the stone samples, and the strange old equipment, but as the old and new memories of rifling through the Mystery Chest collided, he suddenly thought of a detail that he had not pieced together before. There were the old Polaroids of course, including those of Arthur and Mr. Aarons by the dirt mound, and then the really old ones of the woman by the stonework wall. His eyes flicked back to the cigar box on Arthur's floor. But the cigar box just like that one had not been there.

The Judi Bell box had been a deep cigar box of old letters, opened, stacked in order, and neatly folded. Along with the letters were those old pictures of the Amelia Earhart-looking lady in front of planes and stone walls and the like. But *inside* each of the letters was a single picture of her as a hauntingly beautiful little girl, whose face he had never forgotten. Flipping through those little pictures, young David had watched the girl age from a baby to a toddler to a teenager. She was a ghost from some long-forgotten past. He'd always thought that set of sequential pictures of Judi to be strange but interesting. Enough to never forget those details. Except that he'd only just now realized they had been missing.

As a kid, he'd avoided reading the stack of letters entirely. They'd obviously been love letters from somebody named Gertrude to her "Dearest Leonard," so he'd skipped them as any self-respecting kid would. He would have read every word of those love letters now, but that was the thing, wasn't it? That the cigar box full of love letters and pictures hadn't been there this last time, and he just hadn't noticed. Only now it seemed to be screaming at him as obviously as, well, a teleporting trunk. Had his dad taken them? It was yet another mystery to add to that chest.

David's meandering thoughts were cut short. Arthur resurfaced from the trunk with a glass frame and a proclamation of, "Aha!" He closed the trunk loudly, handed the frame to David, then sat back down to his tea like the Mad Hatter.

David stared at the object in disbelief. In one sense, the ordinary frame held nothing more than a faded full-page magazine clipping. On it was a small bit of text under a large black and white image of somewhat inscrutable undulating forms. But the sensational title was just as Arthur had described:

NOAH'S ARK?
Boatlike form is seen near Ararat.

The article was like something from a parallel world, or maybe those old supermarket tabloids. So then, David's adventuring grandfather's mysteries were stranger even than he had imagined. Way stranger.

X

Broad Street. Oxford, England. Mr. Suit.

The man in the fancy suit texted word of his success to his employer and waited patiently for a reply. Any moment the stand-down order would come through, and he would go back to being just a grad student again.

He waited, leaning casually on his expensive bike. Its helmet hung on the bike's handlebars, ready for his next move. He was parked near a little café on the south side of the street the locals simply called "The Broad." It was the most probable path between Dr. Evans' flat and the Ashmolean Museum, where the tutor was known to spend most of his time on Saturdays. But today, something was interfering with Dr. Evans' usual schedule, and the man in the suit hated not knowing what it was.

He patiently sipped on a French-style coffee in a takeaway cup to give him a little jolt of caffeine while he waited. Coffee, tea, and beer were as old as any tradition in Oxford. Each in turn serving the student, the gentleman, and the professor, depending on the time of day—or so the joke went.

It was no joke that the oldest coffee houses and pubs in Oxford had been some of the earliest student common rooms. Pub stood for "public house" after all, though few had rooms with beds to let-out anymore. As a result, more than a few secret societies and study groups had cropped up in the world's coffee houses and pubs throughout the ages. In the days when British imperialism had run the world's economy, a steady stream of coffee and tea had arrived at this university town from every corner of the world.

The man glanced down at his oversized takeaway cup and black plastic lid. It had never stopped. Students were students in any era and nothing without their caffeine. Nor had the induction of youth into secret societies and brotherhoods stopped. This amused him. Western men knew nothing of true brotherhood or family.

Remember who you are. Remember what you are. His silent mantra, given to him by his great mentor.

Today, he pushed the aphorism away. He was having too much fun. This particular cup he held, proclaimed its own authenticity. It assured him in bold advertising that the coffee inside was fair-trade and organic, and that the cup itself was both made from recycled materials and likewise recyclable.

Western guilt in a cup, he mused.

One of Oxford's numerous and varied street fairs was in full swing. Always the major pedestrian thoroughfare, today Broad Street was an open-air market. Canvas and aluminum pop-up stalls had been thrown up in front of the stained yellow and gray stone of the street's medieval façades. According to the various posters around town, the theme of this one was "Arts and Crafts." This also amused the man in the suit greatly. All manner of contemporary handcrafted items and so-called "art" overflowed from the portable stalls. Student work and amateur Western pop culture abounded.

The impromptu fair reminded him of the real street market in Şırnak, the insignificant town in far-eastern Turkey where he was born. He recalled the deep smells of rich foods and piled spices sold from ancient stone stalls in a market far older than the mere medieval porticos before him.

As an orphan—some might have called him a street rat—he had done whatever it took to survive. Early on that had meant stealing, but he'd quickly realized that his social skills were a much better way of getting what he needed. A merchant would remember and beat a child who stole, but he would remember and feed a child who helped. Winsomeness had taken him far. Certain benefactors had enabled him to move to Istanbul as a teenager, go to school, learn proper English and the traditional subjects, and take real jobs. He'd even been given secret jobs that his particular skill set afforded him. He could be very persuasive, and what were people if not complex clocks to be studied, understood, and manipulated? That had been one of his first lessons as a boy.

The Turkish Air Force said he was one of the best pilots they had ever trained, but he grew bored with that life and abandoned it. He took a new name, and when he had mastered the cons of one city, he moved on to the next. Studying, learning, fighting for this cause and that, but always growing stronger, and never staying in one place for too long. Until finally he had been sent here to Oxford to watch, wait, and learn. He hadn't minded. He liked Western culture best, and his most ebullient benefactors had even arranged this fun and highly profitable little corporate spycraft job.

The man in the suit smiled. His part of the world had been fighting important holy wars over magnificent Persian palaces when this place was still a lowly ford in the river where farmers made their oxen cross. Here, the scant inhabitants had barely scratched out a living in the mud when not fighting off invading barbarian Saxons with crude farm tools. Long before that, his people had been the first to form cities. It was the same everywhere. Food first. Then protection. Then finally the art, culture, and luxury came.

But not stories. The stories had been with mankind from the beginning. Stories were power. The keepers of knowledge and secrets were the truest powers of all in this world. He kept many secrets. This was something his current employer failed to understand. Mao Sien would have all secrets exposed for its gain. But the company was a means to an end for him. The truth was that the deepest secrets of this world were simply inaccessible to most Westerners. Even when they knew right where to look, they often preferred superficial imitations to the real thing.

People see what they want to see, he reminded himself.

Real markets were the lifeblood of the oldest communities of this world. Not pop-up fantasies for rich little student artists. He had accomplished much in his life by recognizing how to see past people's masks and learning how to use them. He crushed his empty coffee cup and tossed it into the trash a few meters away. An American man in a sports Jersey congratulated him on his "three-pointer" as he walked past. His little girl was wearing an "I'm a Disney Princess" tee-shirt. He thanked the ignorant fool politely with a grand smile and a slight bow. *If he only knew.*

The man in the suit often passed the time by analyzing the strands of wide-eyed tourists milling down the road. They were always searching for various historical sites, food or drink, and an overall good time. He loved to people watch, and under normal circumstances, he would have been more than happy to select some of them and help them achieve their goals of fun and memory. To his personal gain, obviously.

Such people are resources to be consumed. Another lesson from his teachers.

He smiled at an attractive cookie-cutter blonde as she passed by him. She wore too-tight cutoff shorts and a brand-new oversized Oxford University sweater. The girl had misjudged the English weather and attempted to compensate with her credit card. The same story played out a dozen times here every day. *Ah, Americans!*

Some other time, perhaps. He was working.

It had been no work at all to find Dr. Evans at his little college flat. There was nothing about this town's workings that he did not know, nothing he did not know how to find out. He knew a porter or a groundskeeper in nearly every College and had made friends in surprisingly high positions, but all they knew about him was whatever he wanted them to know. Mostly, he watched and remembered.

People are clocks to be studied.

Dr. Evans was an interesting fellow. The tutor's Saturday habit was to have a lie-in, spend the afternoon at the Ashmolean Museum where he kept an office, and then dine at Mansfield before returning home. Thus, perfectly willing to perform a little burglary if necessary, the man in the suit had gone straight up to Dr. Evans' little flat in broad daylight. By a stroke of luck, the old man had not only come to the door but was holding what could only be the Aarons Journal.

After all, how many books could one man own?

Fate was smiling on him today. Though frankly, it was all a bit of a letdown. He enjoyed picking locks and going where he was not meant to be. The itch would pass; there would be other days to indulge his skill. He relished the adrenaline rush when he was working, but he was also a very cautious man. Unnecessary risks were not his style. He laughed aloud at this.

Oh, the lies we tell ourselves!

Thus, with a harmless tale about a local organization he had blown Dr. Evans off. More half-truths. He'd then reported back to his employer, saying with confidence:

Item confirmed with high
probability

Finally, the reply came. It surprised him.

Acquire it.
Digital delivery is
expected in 6 hours.

But it also exhilarated him. He had not expected them to encourage such nefarious actions. Instructions on how to digitally deliver it followed. He hesitated, not wanting to appear weak or indecisive, while at the same time not willing to risk misinterpreting his employer's expectations either. He had more information than they knew he had, but he still must consider his real agenda before he started kicking in doors or making armed threats. Should he retrieve the little book by open force? Was true violence an acceptable part of the equation? His employer was asking him to take unnecessary risks.

Currently, Dr. Evans was oblivious to him, but that could change very quickly. And being outed would cause much bigger problems for him than failing this little task. He considered various possibilities for how to lie to the company, but it proved to be unnecessary. His other phone rang, the one his employer did not know about. Where a number should have been, it simply said:

UNKNOWN CALLER

"Speak," he demanded.

"Does Dr. Evans have the journal yet?" asked a familiar male voice. It was slightly distorted as if the connection were being routed from very far away or by radio. Odd, since his true mentor was a man not afraid to use his voice or speak plainly. Adrenaline instantly coursed through the man in the suit. His mentor always seemed to know when to call just when he needed him most.

"Yes, my mentor. I saw him with it."

"Good. Be alert. Stick by your phone. I don't have to remind you what the real threat is right now."

"Understood. But, as you feared might happen, my employer also knows about the journal."

"Already?" The man on the line's tone was thick with disbelief. "Then things are twisted together more than I realized. How she found out about it so fast I have no idea, but that changes things, son. You need to stay on Evans and that journal every second till this thing plays out."

His mentor's opinion of the company had always been clear, but there was something more there this time. He'd never said "she" before. Was his employer female? Interesting detail. He filed it away for later use.

"With apologies, there is more. I am expected to hand a copy off to the company tonight."

There was a long pause. "Well, then I suppose you will have to steal it," the voice on the phone decided.

"As you wish," the man in the suit affirmed, but the caller had already disconnected.

This job was getting complicated. Complicated could be messy, and the man in the suit hated messes. Still, he was going to enjoy what came next.

XI

Dr. Arthur Evans' Residence. Oxford, England. Arthur.

Evans watched as David carefully scrutinized the framed artifact from his long-buried past.

NOAH'S ARK?
Boatlike form is seen near Ararat.

"Is it real? I mean, is this article true?" David was practically whispering.

"Well, yes. But it's complicated." Oh, but how to explain without sounding like a crazy man? Evans decided to stick to the facts. "The *LIFE Magazine* readership ate the story up of course. It all started when a Turkish army captain who was routinely examining aerial photos of his country spotted an oddity. It was on a mountain, twenty miles south of Ararat."

"Wait. Near Ararat? Not on Mt. Ararat?" David already looked confused.

"Near the mountain that is popularly considered the biblical resting place of Noah's Ark, yes."

David opened his mouth to say something but didn't. Evans felt himself slipping into tutor mode. It helped.

"So, because this Turkish captain fellow caused a buzz, soon an expedition including American scientists set out for the site. Then, when *LIFE* got wind of their plan, well, they wrote an article about it."

"This one."

"Right," Evans Affirmed. "And as you can see, the article features that blurry black and white picture which admittedly contains a somewhat boat-shaped form about 500 feet long."

David scrutinized the old black and white picture and shrugged. "If you say so, Arthur. It looks like an amoeba or tree bark to me."

Evans snorted. "The article essentially made the expedition a global phenomenon."

"Meaning that it really didn't matter what was there or what they actually found?"

"Precisely. Very good, I wish all of my students were as intuitive."

David smiled. "Dad says I'm a quick study. Mom always said it's why I finished each of my classes so fast."

Evans nodded slowly at him. Joseph had always been quick too. Come to think of it, the boy had cited it as the root of his boredom and discipline problems at the boarding academy back in the day. Evans pushed the silly memory away.

"So, what did they find? I mean it couldn't have been the Ark or we'd all know about it, right?"

"Funny you should say that. So, as it happens, at about 7,000 feet above sea level is a place called Durupinar, roughly translated as 'Doomsday Mountain.'

Now David snorted. "Really? Again, with the end of the world stuff?" Then, "Oh! Doomsday! Like an apocalyptic flood that kills everybody, doomsday!"

The boy was starting to connect it up. The story of Noah was a story about the end of the world. Just not *this* world.

"Essentially, yes." Evans stuck his lips out and looked over the rims of his glasses with a steely glare at Joseph's son.

"But what did they find?" The boy would have been on the edge of his seat, had he been on a seat at all instead of the floor.

"Well, up there, amid crevasses and landslide debris, the investigative team found a relatively clear grassy plateau. It was shaped like a double-pointed ship and rimmed with steep packed-earth sides. Its dimensions were close to those given in *Genesis*."

"Close? How close?"

Evans smoothed his beard and paraphrased from memory. "'The length of the ark shall be 300 cubits, the breadth 50 cubits, and the height 30 cubits,' that is to say, about 450 by 75 by 45 feet, depending on if you think Moses converted to the Hebrew cubit or stuck with the Egyptian cubit he was probably educated on."

"Huh? What's an Egyptian cubit? Is that like metric?"

Evans allowed one tiny chuckle out. "Well, that's as good a metaphor as any. Moses was adopted by Pharaoh's daughter, you may remember. *Mesu* means 'son' in ancient Egyptian you see."

David looked dubious. Perhaps he knew the more common etymology of Moses as *Mo-uses*, meaning "saved out of the river," and thought they were in conflict. They weren't of course. To an ancient Egyptian, birth was all about being drawn from a mother's waters, a sort of ancient Egyptian pun perhaps. Evans decided not to get sidetracked.

"Anyway, the 1960s team made a quick two-day survey, decided that it was a rock formation covered in a layer of dirt, and declared there was no evidence the object was man-made. And that was pretty much the end of it. While one scientist in the group did say nothing in nature could create such a symmetrical shape, nobody was willing to fund a follow-up excavation."

"So, it really was just a rock formation or something then?" David sounded rather disappointed.

"Well, that's where I come in. Some fifteen years later, just after Elisabeth—I mean your grandmother—passed, I was working as a brand-new Humanities lecturer at the college. I was doing relatively well for myself professionally, but I was having, well, a difficult time." Evans cleared his throat and pushed away what was now a torrent of memories. Suddenly self-conscious, he glanced up. David smiled encouragingly.

"Right. It was during that time that I received a letter from one Wyatt Aarons. He claimed he was a biblical archaeologist who was leading an expedition to Turkey. He aimed to investigate the Doomsday Anomaly for the first time since the original team had gone. I of course asked him why he wanted me, but he said he needed an ancient language scholar on the team who could translate any early pictograms and cuneiform he might find. Since that was my particular specialty and we translators don't often get offered fieldwork, well, I let his obsession become my distraction for quite a while.”

Evans finished off his tea in one gulp and prepared another cup. David pulled out his phone and brought up some photos. The boy's digital collection of the old dig pictures had grown during their time at the pub. The thought gave Evans a quick shiver.

“So, this is you and Mr. Aarons then?” David held the digital photo on the phone up for Evans to see, Wyatt's little blonde beard and broad smile making him look like a carnival barker, gloating in front of the Doomsday anomaly.

Evans swallowed. “Yes, that's us,” he admitted. “That was a picture taken during one of the later magnetic experiments. Those white lines behind us are where we laid out markers when Wyatt got a hit with his machinery. They said the metal detector was getting hits about three feet below the dirt.”

“No way,” David laughed. “You actually found stuff there?” The importance of that detail seemed to stun him for a moment. Evans simply shrugged and sipped his tea. David was enjoying this. Evans was too, he realized.

“Arthur, what are you saying? Did you actually find metal and wood? Was it really a ship?”

Evans considered his options. The boy's inquiries at the pub had been a shock initially, but at least here at home, they were alone. He understood where the boy's curiosity was coming from, but it didn't change the reality that this kid Evans barely knew was probing into events that he had literally not spoken with anyone about for decades. Blood or not, Evans didn't know why he was telling his grandson any of this now, but something about it felt right. He felt... lighter, somehow.

David held his empty cup out for more tea. Evans obliged, emptying the pot for him, but this time forgetting to add the cream and sugar. Then, to Evans' surprise, he answered the boy's question.

“That nincompoop Wyatt certainly thought so. But keep in mind, the Turkish government never would permit us to dig. We mostly had to make do with the scraps we could find strewn about the site. Certain so-called ‘experts’ back home said it was petrified wood due to the abundant volcanic soil or somesuch, and still others swore there were identifiable planks, cross-planks, and iron rivets hammered in hot. Nonsense of course. Carbon dating of various samples came up with conflicting dates, but most were less than a thousand years old. They said it was probably due to various types of site contamination. In retrospect, it wasn't very scientifically done at all, but I cannot take the blame for that.”

“Because you were the humanities guy?”

“Because I was the humanities guy.” There was a little smile-smirk with his snort-laugh this time. He felt the wrinkles forming up along the edges of his eyes and mouth. It felt strange to be chortling with the young Evans. "Wyatt was always convinced that we would find something like an ancient written record that proved the biblical Noah story. As far as he was concerned, I was there to fact-check such a find against the biblical record and debunk the other sources."

"Other sources? What kind of other sources?"

"Other flood myths, of course."

"There are other flood myths?"

"Oh my, yes. When I was still a graduate student, I published some papers about them. Aarons got hold of one and that's why he contacted me. The fact is that there are over six hundred or so known flood myths throughout various cultures. And from every corner of the world. The *Eridu Genesis*. The Mesopotamian *Atra-Hasis*. The Hindu *Manu and Matsya*. China's *Gun-Yu Myth*. Hawaii's *Nu'u* tale. Even Native Americans have one."

"Really? How come I didn't know that?"

"Many people wonder the same when they find out. Most who do know, especially those who choose to believe the Noah version is seminal, like to pretend the others don't exist."

"Why? Is it because they contradict each other?"

"Oh..." How to explain? "Well, they're wildly different. The size and shape and method of the so-called 'ark' is different in every tale. In some, it is a high mountain or ancient bunker of sorts. In others, it is a god, demigod, or man who saves some variety of living things, seeds, or other people by building a boat. In some versions, it is the gods who are angry with mankind for being too loud. Everything from frogs, snakes, fish, and dragons play a part—either causing the deluge or helping mankind survive it. The landing place is almost always local to the story, and the details are central to the culture telling it. In truth, the only real unifying factor is the flood itself. But I digress."

David looked confused and doubtful. It was a look Evans knew well as a tutor. He decided to clarify with an example.

"One of the oldest versions is the Sumerian tale, which is part of the *Epic of Gilgamesh*. A personal favorite. Some of the more recently discovered lines I helped decipher for the new Oxford translation a few years back." Evans let his pride sneak through a little on that one. "Cuneiform is one of my specialties, I'm one of a few hundred people in the world who can read and understand most forms of it."

"Really?" The boy's eyes were huge. "But hold on Arthur, I know that I've read *Gilgamesh*, and I don't remember reading anything about Noah's Ark in there."

"Well, certainly there is. The *Epic of Gilgamesh* is arguably the oldest surviving written story on Earth. The earliest versions are from somewhere between 2750 and 2500 B.C. It comes to us through Ancient Sumeria, in the fertile crescent. Babylonia if you like. The later contiguous epic version was written on twelve mostly rectangular clay tablets in a cuneiform script called Akkadian. The tale chronicles the legendary adventures of the historical king of Uruk, the great and brave epic hero of the titular Gilgamesh."

"Wait, Gilgamesh was real? I thought he was a mythical character."

"Well yes, both. He was even deified after he died. But mythical does not mean false, David." The boy held up a questioning finger, but Evans pretended not to notice. "So then, King Gilgamesh is searching for the secret to eternal life. Thus, he hunts down an important man named Utnapishtim, who had saved humanity and animals by building a boat. As a reward, Utnapishtim was granted immortality by the gods and a beautiful walled garden in which to live." Evans was talking louder now and with full flourish and gesticulation.

Suddenly, David made the connection. "Oh wait, I do remember some of that! It was so different from the real Noah, that I guess I never thought about it that way."

Evans soured a bit at David's choice of words but did not shrink back. "Yes, most people don't. But we should." He glanced at the section of his beloved books where several *Gilgamesh* translations stood. "It's probably the precursor to the Hebrew version, a story they may have even picked up in the Babylonian exile, along with all the other *Genesis* cross-overs. Though, that little detail probably wasn't covered in Karen's homeschool curriculum." It sounded more accusatory than he had intended. Evans tried to backpedal. "Besides," he tried, "what were you doing reading the *Epic of Gilgamesh* at your age? It's typically freshman college curriculum, is it not?"

"Actually Arthur, I love reading," David shot back. The boy's gaze flicked to Evans' private library that surrounded them. "I did Honors English all the way up and I read *Gilgamesh* a few years ago just for fun."

To Evans' surprise, David waved a thumb in the general direction of his *Gilgamesh* volumes. A coincidence, certainly.

"But I also took some classes at the community college last year for dual credit, and I read it again then."

"Really?" Evans was genuinely impressed, though he'd happily have words with any college professor who neglected to relate *Gilgamesh* to other flood myths. Perhaps it had been a religious objection? People were complicated about religion.

"Well, good for you then," he added. *Had that sounded sarcastic?* Evans hoped not. He cleared his throat. "So then, you will of course remember

Dilmun." David didn't, so he explained that too. "Dilmun is the name of Utnapishtim's garden. It is where Gilgamesh ultimately finds him."

"Wait, are you saying that Mr. Aarons wants you to look for Utnapishtim's garden, like Gilgamesh in the story? And he wants to meet you there?"

Evans shrugged. "More a city than a garden by the time it went missing, but why split hairs."

"That's bonkers." David was absolutely right, it was. "So, what's this 'days of Noah' stuff about then?" David had picked up Wyatt's journal again. "If that's not the doomsday he's talking about, then what is Mr. Aarons saying?"

"Well, David, I suppose that Wyatt believes the world is reverting. That things are chaotic and sinful enough for the second coming." At the moment, Evans didn't feel inclined to argue the first point. Though truthfully, he didn't believe Wyatt's conclusions for a second. "It's his style." *Helps with the fundraising too,* Evans didn't add.

David processed this. "Okay. And what does all of this have to do with Noah and a tree?" David asked. "What was it you were right about?" He handed the journal back to Evans, his finger on the related line:

Arthur, you were right about Nûh and the tree after all...

Evans leaned forward and plucked the journal from him. For the briefest moment, David looked exactly like little Joseph again. Evans felt a wave of panic and fear wash over him. All his old ghosts were coming to haunt him today. To his great surprise, an imaginary Elisabeth crossed her arms and shook her head at him in disappointment. An echo of not-so-imaginary Karen chewing him out in their recent conversations.

"We want you to show him around, not adopt him!"

And then Aarons with his blasted book, and his "you were right" non-apology. No, the day was much too young for all of this. He needed to try to recover some of his Saturday. He needed his office at the museum. Maybe do some research or translation. Perhaps starting with that ridiculous journal.

"That, David, is a very complicated question," Evans sighed. "Would you care to visit one of the greatest museums in the world to try sorting it? My office is there, and there are things I'd like to accomplish—today, if possible."

What he most wanted to accomplish he realized, was a complete debunking of Aarons' journal before filing it in the trashcan. He just hoped he could distract David long enough to do it.

"Sure," the boy said, beaming.

"Very good. To the Ashmolean then."

After all, what better distraction to an aspiring young art student could there be than a proper English museum? Evans could think of none.

XII

Ashmolean Museum. Oxford, England. David.

David was surprised and a little disappointed when Arthur grabbed a complimentary museum map and handed it to him. As an afterthought, Arthur snatched the map back and unfolded it. He then stabbed at a grayed-out room on the fourth floor with a pen from his lapel and scribbled down a barely legible door code. The whole scenario did not bode well.

"I'll be right there for the rest of the afternoon," Arthur said cheerily, "but consider all of this your starter course." He motioned towards the nearest gallery full of glass cases and unidentified objects. "The building itself is an architectural masterpiece, thanks partly to recent renovations. Nearly every gallery has some sort of natural light flowing into it."

Arthur's pride in the Museum stood every bit as tall as the massive Roman columns they had passed through when entering. He sounded like a starry-eyed tour guide, but he clearly did not intend to play the part. Instead, he whisked off in the other direction, towards a surprisingly tall and ultra-modern white marble staircase. From where he stood, David could see up into the higher floors and galleries. One wall was almost entirely glass and walkways. On another, an open balcony crisscrossed with the stairs and glass railings. This place was bigger on the inside.

"Don't overlook the Heberden Coins in the basement," Arthur's voice echoed down from somewhere. "It is much too often overlooked, I'm told."

Coins in the basement, right. David didn't wait for Arthur's disembodied voice to assign any more homework. He felt a little duped. What was all that about solving the mystery of Noah and the tree then? Gilgamesh? Mr. Aarons? Maybe David had misunderstood. Arthur was a bit scatterbrained, but this felt different. His wizard was up to something.

David folded the map roughly and shoved it into his hoodie pocket. He took a deep breath and decided to re-embrace his own adventure. His grandfather's eccentricities aside, David loved museums! And what kind of amazing things must there be in an English museum of art and archeology? Dark Age knights? Anglo-Saxon castles? He aimed to find out, tour guide or no tour guide. It was quest time. And who knows, maybe he'd find Noah, Gilgamesh, and the Tree of Life anyway! If the key to understanding Mr. Aaron's weird journal message was here, David would find it.

He checked his phone and to his delight, the museum had free internet for guests. He snapped a selfie and boasted to the world that he was about to get some culture. It was well past time to catch the people up on his exploits!

Delving into one of the rooms at random, he found himself in an L-shaped gallery full of Greco-Roman sculptures. He felt a little twinge of guilt, looking at so many life-sized naked people all at once.

Or should that be 'nude'?

In his senior year, David had taken a dual credit art history course alongside English Lit. He recalled the interminable PowerPoint slides of countless façades, vases, sculptures, and paintings shown in every class. And the naked people were never naked, but always "nude." Or so his professor had insisted. But the slides had never seemed to live up to her enthusiasm. Now, standing in front of real pieces of art, it occurred to David that all that in-class stuff had been information directed at him about the art somewhere else. A rational study of countless pieces and movements and cultures, but not the same as standing here among actual stones worked by ancient hands.

He felt completely overwhelmed. Up close and personal the statues looked bigger. He'd never thought about that. Life-sized? No, they were even bigger than that. His pulse quickened. These sculptures seemed more real than he had imagined marble could be for some reason. He could feel the people here. They were beautiful, perfect. He could see their veins, muscles, sinew, and hair. Seriously, how do you sculpt hair? It was crazy. He wasn't alone at all, from a certain point of view.

David barked a laugh at this that echoed in the tall bright room. These figures weren't real at all. Half of these "people" were statues of mythological Greek and Roman gods, and those had never been real. Yet, in their own way, these idealized stone creatures were truer than a living person who neglected or abused his own body. And much longer-lasting. Even the statues missing limbs and heads had all outlived their possibly ugly, pudgy, or awkward sculptors—people who'd had their own human problems and died long ago.

David wasn't sure what he was getting at, but it felt like something important was just out of reach. It excited him. He scrutinized every piece and read every plaque and sign in the room, trying to dig it out. His imagination took over, filling in the missing parts. A hand here, a foot there, even the occasional head.

There was a second sculpture room, so he went in. Here was a torso of a wounded Amazon man with no arms, legs, or head. Why? Was that the best one they had found? He read the placard and discovered that at one point it had been restored, but recently those parts had been removed "for authenticity." That made him laugh again. Nearby, he saw a funerary bust of a doctor and his wife sculpted together. Had they died together? They didn't look very happy about it. He casually wondered what a Roman doctor did and googled it. Slowly, one after another, he began to sense how each piece told a story about itself, its subject, and in part its creator too. And in a way that no textbook or enthusiastic professor ever could.

Then, tucked away in a corner, he stopped short at a tiny piece he would never forget. He blushed a little at the shy Venus holding her hand in modesty while shielding her son Cupid from—what? Him? But what was he supposed to do, not look? It was art after all, and she wasn't any more nude than the rest. Or was she?

Then it hit him: She was naked. In and among all of the nudes, she alone was self-conscious and ashamed. Scared too. It vaguely reminded him of something, but he couldn't place it. He stood there for a long time, forgetting to read the placard entirely, imagining various things that might be the source of her fear.

A noise made by other visitors in the next room snapped him out of it. Now it was his turn to feel self-conscious, and a little silly. David took a picture and moved on. How long had he spent in just the ancient sculpture rooms? He'd never thought of art quite this way before, and definitely not in class. Was this what Oxford was? What higher education was meant to be? He filed it away to ask Arthur later. He felt exhilarated by it, just as he also felt it already slipping away from him. He strained to remember something—anything— from the art class, but no grand epiphany came.

David wandered from room to room in a daze, only to find himself crossing from the Roman era to the Egyptian period effortlessly. This place wasn't what he'd expected at all. He gave up on reading the displays and lost himself in the various eras. He completely forgot about medieval suits of armor or castle knights. It was like trying to drink from a fire hose. There was no way he could take in this museum in a whole summer of Saturdays. He was an accidental time-traveler bouncing around in the whole of history way too fast.

He stood in a daze over an ancient model of a ship. He discovered something called the Aegean Empire. He was surprised to find a whole other gallery of Classical sculptures and busts that he and Arthur had walked right past when first coming in. He stood for the longest time over an ancient board game collection. They even had dice made of bone, a full chessboard, and something resembling backgammon. He craved to know the rules. How fun would it be to roll up a character with those dice? To strategize over that board, or learn the rules to a game that was thousands of years old.

After some time wandering the galleries, David was shocked to discover that he had become entirely disoriented. Not only had he walked all around the fourth floor without spotting anything that looked like offices, but somehow, he'd accidentally made it back to the third floor again—at least according to the signs. Was this museum built on a hill? He didn't think so. He searched for a familiar room but came instead into a whole new string of small unfamiliar chambers. There were old paintings, and then fine china, and some kind of furniture display. It didn't even feel like the same museum.

When David finally pulled out his map to figure out why he was lost, he had to laugh. The first floor was the second floor, and the "ground floor" was where they'd come in. *So, when Arthur said fourth-floor office, he'd essentially meant fifth? Weird.* England was a different planet.

David decided to let the elevator sort it out. He held his finger over the "+4" button but paused. He punched the button marked "-1" instead. Arthur's basement coin room.

He was surprised to find it much more than that. A large sign announced a "Crossing Cultures" theme. Displays gave information about the development of ancient reading, writing, and textiles as well as money from throughout the ancient world. The ancient coins alone crossed nearly all eras. David managed to lose himself entirely in the people and places that the little bits of metal represented.

He stood for a long time fixated on the coin of King Offa of Mercia, a kingdom of Anglo-Saxon England. He'd found his castle knights after all. According to the sign, Offa had been a powerful Christian king who came into conflict with the Church. But he managed to persuade the Pope to split the archdiocese to support him and his legacy. It had apparently worked since his son had coins here too. Some of Offa's coins also carried images of his wife, Cynethryth. *"The only Anglo-Saxon queen ever depicted on a coin."* Clearly, King Offa did things his own way. Quite the interesting guy. A Protestant and proto-feminist before his time, sort of.

David snapped another picture. Medieval Europe was the time and place in history closest to the fantasy worlds he read about and played tabletop games in. Yet when it came down to it, David knew next to nothing about the real history of the period. And he wasn't going to learn it today. David's brain wasn't even remotely full, but his feet were starting to hurt. With regret, he left the room.

Around the corner, he was surprised and very happy to find both a high vaulted café and a little gift shop. They hid them in the basement? Well, when in Oxford… He decided to visit the café first to rest his feet and fill his stomach. A sign announced that it was teatime, which amused him greatly. He ordered the largest sandwich they had and conquered it like a barbarian defeating a dungeon boss. After that, he went to the gift shop to search for loot.

*   *   *

A few minutes later, David was scanning the gift shop for a shirt to add to the three he'd brought with him when he realized that the girl behind the counter was watching him. She wasn't much older than David, and she had a nice smile. To his horror, he heard himself ask where the tee-shirts were.

"I'm not sure we sell shirts," she said, apologetically. "Shall we have a *squizz?*" Her accent was different. Not quite Australian, but no local Brit either. David had no idea what she was proposing, and apparently it showed.

"Sorry!" she said, a little embarrassed. "I mean, shall we look about?"

David grinned and her smile came back. They searched the little shop high and low for a shirt but found none. "It's my first day solo," she pretended to whisper. "Student placement summer job. Don't tell anybody, but I have no idea what I'm doing yet."

"It's my first day in Oxford," he pretend-whispered back. "I feel exactly the same way."

They laughed at this and also about the Ashmolean's lack of marketing foresight regarding wearable advertising. David bought a thick softcover souvenir museum guidebook from her instead. He was excited to know that he could take the whole museum home with him. And an actual paper book too. Arthur would certainly approve.

"Have you been around it all yet?" the girl asked.

She means the museum, he realized stupidly. "Yea, it's great," he said, a little too enthusiastically.

"Oh, that's a shame. I'm off work now. I was about to go *have-a-squizz* upstairs myself." This last she laid on super thick, then lightly took her bottom lip between her teeth. She was messing with him. David cracked another smile. He and the gift shop girl laughed at their new shared joke. True enough, another museum employee had come in at some point and fastened on a nametag, he was now logging in to the cash register. David hadn't even noticed.

"Fancy going 'round again anyway?" She said conspiratorially, then went back to biting her bottom lip. She was looking straight at him with a burning intensity. Her eyes were crystal blue. "After a *cuppa* though. I'm *knackered.*"

Cuppa? Knackered? David had never met anybody like this girl before. He liked it. *Houston, I have made first contact with an alien species. Please advise.*

"Around the museum?" he managed. "Have you not ever seen it?" This idea surprised him.

She laughed and poked him in the rib. "Course I have, silly. Dozens of times. I'm at Oxford for Art History." She shook her head and laughed like it was the most obvious thing in the world. "I reckon working here'll be paradise."

Suddenly, everything beyond the walls of the museum fell away, and his feet didn't hurt anymore. David realized he did "fancy going 'round again." A great deal in fact. He said so.

"Ever heard of King Offa?" she asked him, hooking her arm around his and dragging him back into the coin room.

Her name wasn't Cynethryth, thank goodness. She was Emma, and she was a proud and feisty New Zealander. Later, David would fondly remember that she smelled of raspberries, roses, and pencil shavings. He remained David from Texas who hadn't refreshed his deodorant in a day. But evidently the former was much more interesting than he had imagined, and she either didn't notice or was polite enough not to mention the latter.

XIII

Von Bothmer Reading Room, Ashmolean Museum. Oxford, England. Arthur.

Evans felt much more balanced and in control now that he was in the little corner that he fondly called his office. The Von Bothmer was a private top-floor reading room that required a code to enter. Given that he had the only key to the roll-top desk shoved in said corner, it was an arrangement that worked for him. It certainly kept the visitors and solicitors at bay. Students too, should any be so bold. They could knock on his flat all day and never find him up here. He only needed a few square feet for his modest research anyway.

Thanks to some old family connections, Evans had a standing reservation to use the room when it was not otherwise booked for an event. It was an exception that few knew about, and he took advantage of it whenever he could, Saturdays especially. Plus, the museum was one of the few places where Elisabeth still seemed to linger. Before the recent remodeling, he could almost see her walking the halls sometimes, admiring the ancient exhibits, or setting up a new one. She would've loved this newer Ashmolean. She had been a part of the museum. And the museum was as much a part of Evans as any other thing, be that his books at home, his tutoring work, or—well, actually that was about it. But sometimes, Arthur just missed his old stuffy dark museum, and lately, he just hadn't seen his imaginary Elisabeth roaming the halls as much.

Evans took a deep breath and pushed the melancholy away. He had spent the afternoon probing Wyatt Aarons' journal. He found it quite satisfying to identify some of the ridiculous man's most outrageous alleged "facts" and "conclusions" that he knew could easily be debunked with proper research and fastidious scholarship. He'd pulled a little worktable over to his corner and was now fully ensconced behind books and binders to the point that he could no longer see over them. Language references, mostly. And while his library could have also been helpful, the reality was that he had most of the material there internalized. When dealing with a set of hypotheses as reliant on "magical thinking" as Wyatt Aarons' journal, there was no point delving deeper.

David had been wandering the museum all afternoon, much longer than Evans would have predicted. And thanks to the national policy of Britain's museums to make their general exhibits free for all, it hadn't cost him tuppence. Even the expansive and renowned National Museum in London was this way, and the Ashmolean was of course no exception.

Truly, the greatest museum system in the world, Evans thought with pride. He was aware that many modern nations felt differently, but to his mind, many thousands of the world's treasures had been rescued and preserved during more turbulent times by the British museum system. And in a way, it had rescued and preserved him too, thanks to Elisabeth's memory in this place. She would have loved the modern, light-filled Ashmolean.

Evans sighed and returned to his task. Over the last few hours, he had determined that Wyatt Aarons' journal consisted entirely of entries written over the last few months. It surprised him how much better Wyatt's bookkeeping had become over the decades since they'd worked together in the early '80s. There were still glaring errors of illogical assumption, bad procedure, and swaths of religious drivel, but it seemed that most of the basic facts and rudimentary translations of the ancient texts checked out. Clearly, Wyatt had been struggling with it for a while.

But Evans had known what he was looking at instantly. The cuneiform in the journal was not the traditional Sumerian Akkadian of *Gilgamesh*, but a very different language called Ugaritic, similar only in appearance. It was specific to a tiny coastal region in Syria but incredibly important to the study of ancient languages. Like everyone whose doctoral work involved Semitic languages, Evans had studied Ugaritic in his graduate work. But unlike any of his colleagues, he had veritably mastered it by the end of the term. It was a life-changing time because it had opened up both Hebrew text and cuneiform on a new level.

Regardless, the first entry in the journal picked up in mid-thought process, practically in the middle of a sentence. It supported what Evans had suspected, that it was merely the most recent in a long line of many journals. The near entirety of this one seemed obsessively focused on newly found tablets and various artifacts from Syria where he had recently holed up. No wonder this work had ended up in Evans' hands. Wyatt wasn't just searching for evidence of Utnapishtim anymore—he was straight up looking for a more complete *Atra-Hasis*, discovered less than a century ago right where the old buzzard was digging. It could be no coincidence.

The whole thing gave Evans an uneasy feeling deep in his gut. For hours now, he had been slogging through the journal that had resurrected this foolishness about the old Doomsday expeditions in the first place. He was ready to be done with it. His stomach growled. He'd missed lunch, and now it was closer to suppertime. But despite himself, Evans couldn't tear himself away. He still marveled at the rubbings and transcriptions that Wyatt had put onto these pages. They were wonderful.

Assuming they were authentic, of course. That was always the trouble with Wyatt Aarons. The man had always acted as though "peer review" meant praying for what to write and asking the Holy Spirit where to dig. Plus, based on the wear and tear and occasional coffee stains, Evans had a pretty solid guess that the journal had been written under the same sorts of conditions that he had always known Wyatt to keep his notes. Horrible ones.

Evans knew that he and David had much more important things to do, but he was almost done reading the blasted book. He somehow felt that once he put it aside, the matter of getting David settled would be altogether easier. His plan was to put him up in one of the college rooms until he could figure out a more permanent solution, but he also knew that they were often booked well in advance. He might have to call in a favor or two. Plus, it was Saturday. Evans should have done it weeks ago, but he had been so dreadfully busy, procrastinating with research. He still was, technically. But surely David would find him soon and force him to get on with it.

He carefully parted the stack of books on the desk, making a narrow embrasure through which he could spy on the only entrance. The room was empty. Even the familiar on-duty attendant had gone home for the day. Evans grudgingly returned to the pages of the journal as the least discomfiting of the two royal pains the day had brought him. Looking over his glasses, he re-immersed himself into his former partner's dig notes.

This particular page was one of Wyatt's very last entries. On it was a clear pencil rubbing of part of a tablet that had cracked apart at some point in its long history. *What deplorable technique!* Delicate tablet fragments like that had been destroyed by idiots with softer tools than a pencil. Any archaeologist worth his salt would have tagged, photographed, and cataloged this fragment, in case the other half or another copy of the text was ever found. As many as two million cuneiform tablets had been excavated in modern times, less than one hundred thousand of which had ever been cataloged, properly translated, or published. A respectable number of those translations Evans had even done himself. Not that there had been much fanfare about it. Was it any wonder the remainder were still unaccounted for, with fools like Wyatt doing the digging?

He didn't notice anything spectacular about this rubbing compared to the others in the journal. The cuneiform looked to be of a rarer and older variety, likely a transition stage, but nothing to write home about. Cuneiform was one of the earliest written human languages after all, and it had undergone several changes throughout its three-thousand-year history of use. He did a quick translation of the first few lines, yawned, and turned the page. More of Wyatt's distinctive handwriting meant the start of a new entry. No, not just a new one, it was the last one. It faced the blank page that separated the journal proper from the hastily scrawled message at the end of the book. The blank page had a dated label like the other drawings and rubbings, but evidently Wyatt hadn't finished the job before his troubles caught up with him.

Evans read the entry as carefully as all of the others, but this time Wyatt's words lashed out at him from the page, mocking him. Evans could practically hear the Southerner's Kentucky-fried drawl as he reread the self-styled biblical archeologist's entry:

> *4-16-10: Last night I prayed for an hour under the stars of Canaan, and today the Lord led me to a new tablet fragment that I'm confident will be the key to locating Dilmun. It matches up with yesterday's piece perfectly. The original tablet was broken in half, but both parts are preserved. Even with my little knowledge of the writing, I recognize some of the symbols. I'll need to find a translator who can do it right. If only I could somehow convince Arthur to help! His Evans collection is the key to all this. I only pray that he will be more open-minded about the Lord's work after all this time.*

Evans' throat went dry. So, this is why he had been on Wyatt's mind. It could even explain how Wyatt had managed to translate some of this stuff. He'd probably used some of Evans' old work to do it. The entry was the typical

Wyatt Aarons™ brand of crazy that Evans remembered. Aside from his blind faith mixed with arrogant pig-headed foolishness, if it wasn't doomsday prophecies, mystical ancient knowledge, or medieval secret societies, it was praying for miracles. Evans thumped the journal in bitter satisfaction. He extracted his handkerchief and blew his nose triumphantly, considering the facts.

For starters, despite what Wyatt seemed to think, Ugaritic was not symbolic. It was most similar to Ancient Hebrew in that it was phonetic, a unique blending of the two styles of writing based on sounds instead of symbolic meanings. Most likely the language had come into being as cuneiform was passing from the scene and alphabetic scripts were making their rise, a bridge from one to the other and very important for the development of both. Wyatt never did know what he was looking at, and it seemed clear that Mr. Aarons was still fabricating what he wanted to be true.

But more to the point, nothing Evans had written, translated, or transcribed had ever made it into any sort of "collection." Unless something was on display in that ridiculous Noah's Ark Park "visitor's center" they had eventually built out on Doomsday Mountain without his knowledge. That was possible. Lord only knew what sort of nonsense they had plastered on the walls out there. Evans had no intention of ever visiting that cinderblock shed on a hill, but it was no British National Museum, that he was sure of!

Evans sighed in contentment. Here was the smoking gun he had been searching for all afternoon—evidence strong enough to be done with it. How ironic that Evans' own failure to contribute anything lasting to his museum's collections would be the thing that shone the light on Aarons' foolishness. No Evans had contributed anything meaningful to a museum collection in nearly a century. He smugly looked through his book slit at the door.

He had already burned too much daylight on this fool's errand. It was an afternoon wasted, but at least he wouldn't have to waste any more time on Wyatt Aarons. If he was going to install a teenager here in Oxford, it was time to stop procrastinating. He would call on the evening porter and reserve David an efficiency starting tomorrow. Tonight, they would need a roll-away mattress, some groceries, and perhaps a cooking pan if his new little Evans was going to—

Little Evans? Why had he just thought that? *Oh, dear lord. It couldn't be. Could it?*

As Evans' brain caught up with his grouchy subconscious, the blood left his face so abruptly that he nearly fell out of his chair. He picked up the journal and reread the same entry, the impossible truth filling his mind with a deep and foreboding dread.

Then, flipping to the last page with the stains and hasty scribbles:

With a horrible sinking feeling, Evans flipped again to the rubbing of the broken tablet and squinted over his glasses at the jagged edge. His heart dropped to his feet. Feeling an overwhelming need to stand, Evans staggered away from his little writing desk. He accidentally kicked his old wooden chair some distance across the floor and in the same moment, overcompensating, braced back against the desk, causing half of his book embrasure to topple loudly onto the floor.

No Evans has contributed anything meaningful to a museum collection in nearly a century!

It wasn't *Evans'* museum collection, it was *his museum's* collection. Wyatt wasn't talking about Arthur's own translation research, but about a collection every bit as familiar.

If anyone had been in the room, they might have thought Arthur was having a heart attack.

He wasn't ruling it out just yet.

XIV

Ashmolean Museum. Oxford, England. David.

Emma was a whirlwind tour guide. David headed for the elevator and Arthur's office, his head spinning.

This time, he knew to go to the real "fifth" floor to look for Arthur, and mashed the button marked "+4". The doors slid closed around him. David pulled out his phone and unlocked it. Emma's freshly entered contact info popped onto the screen. He couldn't remember ever having so much fun with somebody he'd just met. She told him more about the Egyptians than he could have imagined, and he told her all about his recent insights into mythological marble gods, community college, and even his phone dramas.

She likewise confessed a particular affinity towards the Venus sculpture and told him everything she knew about it. She even mocked the pose for David—fully clothed thank goodness—while he took a picture. Not that he needed one. It would be a while before that image left his head. Emma seemed to know everything there was about the British museum system. She told him that they needed to go to London to see the "big one," and have curry at a place she knew of on the next block over.

David had been still working out the logistics of what all that even meant when she suddenly told him that she was taking him to the closest phone outlet tomorrow morning to get his connection sorted out. She proclaimed, "It's a date then!" before he could even answer.

Yep. Whirlwind! Also, "date?" Was that more New Zealander slang, or did it really mean… *"date?"* He'd never been on a real one. And certainly not on a Sunday morning. The idea terrified and exhilarated him simultaneously. What would his dad think? *Probably best not to mention it.*

As the doors slid open on the top floor, it occurred to David that he had learned literally nothing about Gilgamesh, Noah, or the flood. He leaned against the wall, pulled out his new guidebook, and flipped to the index to see if he had somehow missed it despite doing basically the whole museum twice. Nope, not a thing. Had the museum just been Arthur's distraction? If so, it had worked.

David sighed and shoved the book back into his jeans. Perhaps his grandfather's secret past with Wyatt Aarons went too deep for a single day of prying to unearth. David turned the corner into a distinctly more administrative hallway. The walls were lined with awards and posters proclaiming various former museum projects, upcoming special collections, and past grants. He hardly noticed them, until one grand poster caused him to stop short. On the glossy print was a massive Minotaur, and under it a bold proclamation.

THE SIR ARTHUR EVANS ARCHIVE PROJECT

The Arthur Evans archive consists of the archaeological records and papers of Sir Arthur Evans. Much of these relate to his travels in Crete and excavations at Knossos.
The Ashmolean has been working to catalogue and improve public access to this unique archive since 1997, with assistance from the J. Paul Getty Trust.
For more information, see the Digital Archives Project at www.odl.ox.ac.uk/collections/evansKnossos.htm

David read it three times, his confusion turning to amazement, then teenage exasperation. *Sir? As in knight?! I can't even!*

Arthur had some serious explaining to do.

*   *   *

David stomped down the hallway and found the door to Arthur's office. The sign said it was some kind of reading room, but it was secured with a keyless door handle, so it had to be the place. David unsuccessfully mashed in a few possible interpretations of the code Arthur had scribbled down before he heard the click and the door allowed him in.

Arthur sat behind a huge stack of books at a comedically small desk. It irritated David that his grandfather had not come and opened the door for him. He hadn't even noticed David come in, but David was confused, frustrated, and hungry for answers.

"Arthur, are you some kind of knight?" he demanded.

The old man looked up at him with surprise from a massive old book, finally realizing he was there. But something wasn't right. Arthur looked pale, sick even. The old wizard's coat was off, and his shirt untucked. His hat was on the floor and his hair stuck out in about twelve directions, only adding to the overall look of quiet feverish intensity.

"Uh, Is everything okay Arthur?" David asked. He was still scowling, his arms crossed, but his voice showed genuine concern.

"I—actually David, no, I don't think it is," he whispered, flipping back and forth between two pages of a little book held open inside the larger one. "Wait a tick, did you say 'knight'?"

David nodded nervously, his angry courage swept away in an instant by his wizard's magic debuff.

"Yes, that's good! Let's start there," he croaked. "Come with me."

Arthur tossed the journal deeper into the mess on his little desk, thumped the big book closed, and charged towards a door identifying itself as "Off-Display Collections."

"It's high time you learned about the family skeletons, David," he said, holding the door open in a surprisingly gentlemanly way. Dr. Evans was back in tutor mode again.

David shook his baffled head and charged in after him.

Other than the meager safety lighting and what little else spilled through the only door, the museum's archives were kept in the dark. With practiced steps, Arthur dodged and weaved past the gigantic shelves piled high with all sorts of wonders that David could only guess at. The whole room smelled like a bookstore and an attic all rolled in together, like secrets and treasure.

David calculated each step with extreme precision so as not to knock some priceless artifact onto the floor. Arthur plunged forward, first past some modern aluminum shelving, and then into the deeper darkness. These were the older archives, characterized by wooden shelves and top-to-floor drawers with faded labels. It was like some lost treasure hunter's vault from one of David's games. He wondered if that wasn't exactly what it was, in fact. Arthur had just said "family skeletons," after all. In this place, David could believe that Arthur might have meant it quite literally. A thrill of excitement passed through him, any anger over Arthur's oddities momentarily forgotten. Now they were getting somewhere!

Then, rounding one corner and another final one, Arthur stopped so fast that David bumped into him and had to apologize.

"It's fine," Arthur whispered as though he was in church. "Go on, please, read it." David realized his grandfather was gesturing to a huge and very heavy-looking wood and glass display case. Arthur turned and switched on an old floor lamp. It did little to help illuminate the deep shadows of the storeroom.

David searched Arthur's face, then turned to the massive case for the possible meaning of his wizard's directive. His eyes darted from one end of the dusty displays to the other, slowly adjusting to the darkness. The glass top cabinets were filled with countless volumes of notes, fat little clay tablets, and other small artifacts. They all looked really old, and the glass was dirty. Massive shelves full of leather-bound books dominated the back wall. Arthur slid his massive book home among a whole row of other volumes just like it.

"What is all this?" David asked, even as he spotted a bronze label riveted to one of the cabinets.

ARTHUR EVANS ARCHIVE, CASE 1A

"Wait, is—is this stuff yours?"

"Oh goodness no," Arthur said. "At least, no more mine than yours." He pointed up to the wall, where an enormous oil painting of a stuffy-looking mustachioed nineteenth-century gentleman hung just above the first case. On the elaborate wooden frame was a tarnished bronze plaque.

SIR ARTHUR JOHN EVANS

[8 JULY 1851 – 11 JULY 1941]

KEEPER OF THE ASHMOLEAN MUSEUM, 1884-1908

"Meet the infamous 'Little Evans,' David."

"Little Evans?" David had no idea what Arthur was getting at.

"Just a nickname of course. That esteemed gentleman is your Great Uncle Arthur." There was pride in the old man's voice. "Or rather, my Great Uncle Arthur. My namesake, if you hadn't guessed. I'm not entirely sure what that makes him to you."

"That's, um, a lot of greats."

"Yes, quite right. He's the reason they let me come up here so often. Well, that and Elisabeth's persuasiveness back in the day. Sort of a polite legacy of looking the other way for our family, I suppose you could say. You see, the museum wouldn't be here if not for him."

"I see." David didn't see. "So, I think I've heard of him before, but who was he? Like, a famous knight or something?" Something tugged at the back of his mind, remembering the internet search for his grandfather he had performed on the bus that had failed so gloriously. *Oh yeah—wrong Arthur Evans.*

Arthur frowned as if he thought David might be playing a trick on him. "Right, then. I shall show you."

XV

Off-Display Collections Room, Ashmolean Museum. Oxford, England. Arthur.

Evans was taken aback. How could David not know he was related to the great Sir Arthur Evans? He'd certainly drilled the fact into Joseph over the years. Evans needed to remedy this oversight immediately. He switched on an enormous magnifying lamp looming over a nearby examination table.

"First, I think Wyatt might be on the trail of something regarding the more enigmatic Minoan scripts, but he can't go further without all this." Evans motioned to Sir Arthur's archive all around them.

"That sounds neat," David said, but his tone betrayed that he had not understood half of what Evans just said. "And the Minoans are something Uncle Sir Arthur worked on?"

Had Joseph truly kept these things from David so completely? Evans couldn't even begin to fathom how that could be.

"Worked on?" He replied, faking a chuckle. "Oh no David, Sir Arthur discovered the Minoan civilization. The man uncovered whole pre-cuneiform pictograph and script language families. Why, he rigorously excavated, studied, and cataloged them most of his professional life.”

David's eyes went wide. “Wow, okay. So, what exactly is a ‘pre-cuneiform pictograph language family’ then?”

Evans paused for a moment pursing his lips. He censored himself from a rude comment about that information being readily available on David's earlier tour of the museum. Again, the thought of a grumpy Karen tempered his words. Instead, the seasoned tutor nodded once, straightened up, and cleared his throat. “Ah. Well, let's begin at the beginning then.”

Evans turned to a nearby antique storage cabinet filled with large, tray-like drawers. He drew one out as far as it would go and gestured for David to take over. “Release the catch on that drawer and extract it,” he instructed. “Yes, like that. Now, bring the whole thing extremely carefully over here to the exam table.”

David did as he'd been told. The tray was heavier than he expected, but he managed it. And no wonder, given it was literally full of ancient stones. Meanwhile, Evans reached over to the side of the table and extracted four latex gloves from a small box. He handed two of them to David, who grinned cartoonishly and stretched the gloves over each hand with a snap.

“Now, what do we have here?” Evans prompted. “Take it slow and be detailed. Talk it out.”

With a deep breath, David gingerly picked one of the stones up with his gloved thumb and forefinger. He held it up to the magnifying glass. The boy was touching history and he knew it. That was very good.

“There are little pictures on them,” David said with awe. “A boat? They are all kinds of different colors, and there are duplicates of some of the shapes. This is some kind of cow, and those have a man on them. Is that, like a deer or something?”

“Good,” Evans complemented. Then he waited. It took David only a moment to realize that Evans was expecting him to keep going. He picked up another few he'd passed over the first time.

“Uh, so this one is like a stalk of wheat or maybe a leaf? And this one is... some kind of swirl?”

The boy needed a nudge. "Ah," Evans said, stretching the word out to about four syllables thick with mystery. "That, David, is one of the most ancient symbols in the world. Variants of that spiral shape are found on every continent. It almost always means the same thing: the unknown, confusion, chaos, and nature. The proverbial snake in the grass ready to strike. But at the same time, it reminds us of the opposite: order, truth, culture, and a clear path forward. A line to walk and guide us through life. Above all, it is the great and ancient struggle between order and chaos. It's also the womb from where life originates and ultimately the labyrinth we must all navigate to find the divine path to truth through an otherwise chaotic world."

"Wow, that's intense," David said breathlessly. "I think I get that symbol."

Evans' morning cascaded down around him in a swirl of memory and frustration. He was tutoring his grandson from Texas. The boy was to be staying with him for the summer. Evans was a grumpy old widower who enjoyed his routines. He had one chair, one bed, and more books than floorboard at his flat, and this boy's mother had thrown it all into a tailspin with one phone call. Yes, Evans also understood that little symbol quite well. Frankly, he would challenge anyone on the face of the planet not to comprehend this representation of the basic human condition.

David set the stone down and looked to Evans for a clue as to what to do next. He graciously obliged. "So, can you deduce their function?"

"Well, they look like they might be semi-valuable gemstones to me, but I guess they could just be colored quartz or something. I don't see any holes like beads would have, so I'd say they aren't from a necklace or whatever. They are all pretty much ovals and circles. Some have two sides, and others have three like a deflated football, maybe?"

Evans stood by with the brooding intensity of a proper Oxford don but said nothing. He waited the boy out and watched as David thought of something, then picked up a few of the stones again to check his idea.

"Some of these have more than one carving on them. Could they be dice?"

Evans pursed his lips. "Not bad. No, these aren't dice, though you aren't the first to think it. You are right that they are not jewelry either, that's well spotted. These are called seal stones, they are sort of like signet rings or metal stamps used by leather craftsmen."

"The kind kings used, to seal up messages with candle wax?"

"Well, essentially, yes. Except these stones were used by merchants rather than kings, and they likely never saw any sealing wax the way people think of it. These were pressed into wet clay and an impression was left, making early writing. These were used on tablets and jars."

"Wow, kind of like a printing press?"

"Well, yes actually," Evans said, thinking it over. "But as far as we know, the use of ink on skins and papyrus didn't come about for nearly two thousand years after they were using this technology. And that's probably because this system worked quite well. One of the great errors of our modern age has been to believe that in order to build palaces, keep genealogies, or have myths, a civilization first needs a system of writing for recording their deeds. But that's modern folly. Ancient man was much better at remembering and retelling stories than we give him credit for. It is a rare skill these days, but the world has been largely illiterate for most of history. Oral tradition was the norm in most places for many millennia."

"I don't know, I think I'd just prefer a pencil," David joked.

"Ah, but with a pencil, you have to know how to read and write. Therein lies the brilliance of this technology." Evans felt himself getting into it now. "Let's say you are an ancient sailor who has brought your boat full of goats out to an island in the Mediterranean. When you get there, a buyer decides to take thirteen of them from you. He pays you with valuable stones, or perhaps metal coins."

"Like the ones in the basement."

"Indeed." Evans was pleased that David had taken his advice to visit the Heberden room. "So then in our example, you the goat seller are either handed thirteen stones with a goat symbol on them, worth one goat each of course, or a dozen all sealed up in a jar along with one extra placed in your hand. At which time you would give your buyer...?"

"The thirteen goats. Okay, so why a jar?"

"Right. Well, it's not a modern jar. More like a small clay pot, you see, an urn of sorts. It is prepared in advance with the valuable stones inside, and on the outside pressed into the clay before it was fired—"

"The symbols from the stones," David interrupted. "It's a piggy bank."

Evans hummed a vague approval. "I suppose so. But a record of the transaction also. You could open it by breaking it, or simply keep it as a larger denomination for next time."

"Heh. Ancient receipts." David evidently liked this.

"Over the centuries the custom shifted from trading with valuable stones to the much easier to carry jars full of stones. Then, to the much safer sealed jars of stones marked with their contents, until finally, somebody realized that they didn't need to exchange the heavy jars of stones at all but could simply use a clay tablet to press the stones into instead."

"Debit cards. Nice."

Evans was doubtful of the over-strained analogy but continued the lesson. "Well, that's not the end of it. Over time the symbols evolved from pictographs of goats, heads, and stalks of grain into more abstract shapes. Harder to remember for the common man, meaning literacy was required to use it, but overall easier to write if you didn't have the right seal stone handy."

Evans opened up a case further down the aisle that was not part of the Sir Arthur Archive. He brought a fragile-looking clay tablet to the exam table. It was entirely filled with lines and marks.

"See these lines? This is the end result. Well, nearly—give or take a few centuries. We call this cuneiform writing. Each of these hash marks was made by the same tool—a blunt reed for a stylus. Note the wedge shape at the end of each line marking direction."

"Now this I remember studying in art class," David said with pride. "Basically, the old pictures and Egyptian hieroglyphs or whatever evolved into this style of writing. It then evolved into our modern letters, right?"

"Not bad," Evans said. "In time, Western scribes ditched the notion of representing objects with pictures and narrowed the symbols down to a few dozen that represented sounds instead. Except that Akkadian cuneiform has nothing to do with Egypt, any more than it has to do with Crete. And the modern alphabet is a direct decedent of the Semitic alphabet, not cuneiform. Through the Phoenicians, to be precise. It's why we call it phonetic."

David's face fell. Evans wasn't being critical of the boy, he was just being overly blunt again. He proffered a weak smile to his grandson. David squared his shoulders and nodded in understanding.

"Don't feel bad David, most people don't think about how far away things were in the ancient world. Today it's a day trip to hop the ferry across the Channel, have lunch in Le Touquet, then still be back in time for supper—but in the ancient world, the edge of the Mediterranean was functionally the outer edge of the world."

Evans' flat Earth joke fell flat, but David sailed on. "*Mediterranean* means 'middle of the Earth' though, right?"

"True," Evans confirmed, "but that was a Roman perspective. Thousands of years and many nautical advances later."

David nodded, but Evans wasn't sure if it meant he knew this, or if he was just taking in new knowledge.

"Back then it was very normal for each area along the coast to evolve its written language separately, simply because so few used it. Kings mostly. Not to mention maths. Some used base ten, the number of fingers on our hands. But others like the Greeks, just a relatively short distance away by our standards, developed a base six system."

Maths? David mouthed. Evans pretended not to notice. "Uh, yea. Well, I'm glad we don't do the base six thing anymore then."

"Oh, but of course we do." Evans scratched his beard. "Look at the sixty seconds, in each of the sixty minutes, along the twelve hours of a clock face, and you adopt the Greek mentality."

"Huh. I never thought about that. No wonder clocks are so weird."

David was a good pupil. Evans could tell that the boy was filing all of this away. Like most people, he'd simply had no idea that modern life was so ancient, but this was where Evans lived every day.

"So, that's interesting and all Arthur, but what does it have to do with these seal stones and our great, great, whatever uncle? Not to mention Mr. Aarons."

"Oh, quite right. Thank you, David." Evans had been enjoying going down this particular ancient rabbit trail so much that he had entirely forgotten to make his point. He leaned in conspiratorially and whispered the rest. "It's quite the scandal, really."

XVI

Parks Road. Oxford, England. Mr. Suit.

The man in the suit was furious.

He had watched Dr. Evans and the boy walk past him towards the museum hours ago. Immediately, he'd doubled back to the old tutor's flat, confident that there would be plenty of time to search it. The lock he picked easily, but when he stepped inside, he stopped short. Never in his life had he seen such an outrageous and haphazard collection of books in one little place as that of Dr. Arthur Evans.

The man in the suit had now wasted entirely too many hours carefully combing through the endless volumes before finally concluding that the Aarons journal was simply not there. The old man still had it on him.

Touché, Dr. Evans.

This was a big problem, and it felt too much like failure. His employer had a reputation for being unforgiving of staff who failed to deliver. And, as his mentor had also informed him, she was desperate and time was short. There was a very real chance that the wrong people were beginning to figure things out. The man in the suit needed solutions now. This situation was a setback to his assignment for the company, but that was nothing compared to his desire to please his mentor.

Remember who you are. Remember what you are.

As of now, his target suspected nothing. But every moment that passed increased the chances that the peculiar scholar would accidentally hand over the information in the journal, or otherwise do something incredibly foolish with it. Wyatt Aarons had sent it to his old partner for a purpose after all. If Dr. Evans got any crazy ideas about all that, then everything could change in an instant. None of those possibilities were acceptable.

The man in the suit shrugged his shoulders angrily as he mounted his motorcycle, as much to reposition his coat as to feel the gun holstered at his side. It calmed him slightly, reminded him that he had options, had control. Everything would be fine. He knew where Dr. Evans was—where he always was on Saturday afternoon.

In his little museum.

XVII

Off-Display Collections Room, Ashmolean Museum. Oxford, England. David.

"What kind of scandal?" David could taste his curiosity like a real thing. He'd no idea he was related to a famous person. It was like his dad had intentionally been hiding this Uncle Sir Arthur guy from him his whole life. But why? He had a feeling Arthur was about to tell him.

"Well, first you need to understand, David, that Sir Arthur was a distinguished scholar any way you take it. But our esteemed great uncle was something of a loose cannon in his day. At the time, the Ashmolean was little more than a storehouse for other museums. It can legitimately lay claim to origins in the 1600s as a natural history museum, but the building and collections were nothing like the art and architecture pieces you saw today. All that changed about a century ago, courtesy of our Sir Arthur."

David was intrigued. He nodded thoughtfully as Arthur continued.

"As you see from his portrait there, Uncle Arthur was the curator of the museum for nearly a quarter century. He eventually became a well-recognized, practically infamous, professor of prehistoric archeology at the university in 1909."

"How is that a loose cannon? Sounds pretty legit."

"Ah! I'm getting to that, but a lot of it ties to his nickname."

"Little Evans?" The words still stung a bit.

"Yes, indeed." Arthur leaned in secretively, even though there was nobody else in the room. "You see, Sir Arthur wasn't always 'Sir' Arthur. He began in the shadow of his father, John Evans. John was one of the first great archaeologists and collectors ever, in a time when very little value was given to the practice, sadly. Those coins downstairs? Many of them were John's. Not to mention the Anglo-Saxon jeweled Ixworth Cross and Tostock Buckle, among others."

David was surprised. He'd missed those last things in his earlier walks of the museum too. Maybe they were in here somewhere?

"Point being," Arthur continued, "It was 'Big John' Evans who was President of the Society of Antiquaries, and thus an ex-officio trustee of the British Museum."

"That's the one in London," David said confidently. *Thank you, Emma!*

"Yes. Big John was a small man with a big reputation. He held dozens of titles and laurels including honorary degrees and various institutional positions of respect and authority. It made him extremely well-known throughout the world. Thus, when young Arthur went into the family business, it's perhaps no surprise—"

"He got known as *Little* Evans. Oh man." Seemingly, Evans men had been short for generations. David understood it all too well. Arthur nodded his sympathy too.

"But it was Sir Arthur's interest in ancient coins and the writing on stone seals from Crete that lured him to the island in 1894."

"You mean these ones?" David looked again at the seal stones with even more amazement than before.

"Some of these very ones," Arthur affirmed. "Sir Arthur's early adventures brought him up against the crumbling Ottoman Empire. He was jailed as a spy and even thrown out of that part of the world more than once. Only when the empire was finally ousted from Crete could he dig. And dig he did!"

David could imagine it all as clearly as if he was there. Great Uncle Sir

Arthur, a small brown-haired aristocrat with a magnificent nineteenth-century mustache, plus entourage, sailing to Crete. The adventuring museum curator, oblivious to international relations and diplomacy, storms the beach with tents and equipment borrowed from the British army, and even runs the Union Jack up a flagpole. The locals must have thought that England had invaded.

"So, why is all this stuff hidden away up here, Arthur? Shouldn't it be in the museum for people to see? There was a sign in the hallway that mentioned something about showing the Evans archive. But nobody is going to see it up here."

Arthur paused and cleared his throat. "Oh, well, the museum can only show about twenty percent of its collection at any given time. The rest is stored off-site, or in dozens of other rooms like this, and rotated out to the floor from time to time." He smiled weakly. "Alas, good Uncle Arthur can't stay out on display permanently."

Arthur clearly took deep pride in his Uncle Sir Arthur, yet there was a sadness in the way he was telling the story too. But over what? It wasn't that David thought Arthur was lying, but for some reason, he felt like his grandfather wasn't telling the full truth either. He decided not to mention it. Arthur was finally opening up and he didn't want to ruin it.

"So, what happened next with Uncle Sir Arthur? And what does it have to do with Mr. Aarons?"

"Ah, well, the year following his big Crete trip, Sir Arthur wrote a book called *Cretan Pictographs and Prae-Phoenician Script*. Then, during a lecture shortly thereafter, he suggested that the Mycenaean civilization of the Greek mainland might have had its very origins in Crete. It caused quite the controversy at the time."

"Really? Why?"

"I suppose that modern Greek folks didn't particularly want to be from an island they were none too fond of. Everything we know about the people of Crete was colored by the ancient Greeks, and those stories weren't flattering. The Myceneans were their enemies, likely their conquerors, and ultimately their usurpers. But their stories of the 'big island' have lived on. Even to this day."

"Oh." David chuckled. "So, what did Uncle Sir Arthur do about it?"

"About the only thing he could. He set out to prove his theory. Uncle Arthur purchased a promising tract of land, and after a year of digging, he'd unearthed palace ruins covering nearly six acres. The size and splendor of his findings indicated to him that the Palace of Knossos had been an ancient cultural capital."

"But Arthur, none of that sounds scandalous at all. It sounds like an impressive find. Even his dad had to be proud of him for all that." Suddenly, David felt connected to the past in a way he'd never known before. He understood and was even starting to share in the deep pride his grandfather held for his famous uncle, these stones, the archive, and even the whole museum. But he still felt like Arthur had barely scratched the surface of some deeper truth that lurked in this dark treasure room of his grandfather's Great Uncle Sir Arthur.

"Well yes, it was quite impressive. Except for two things. First, Big John had financed the purchase of the land. There would always be the awkward matter of repayment for that loan, which was never quite settled. Second, and most important, Sir Arthur made one terrible blunder in his work. It nearly destroyed him, the field of archeology, and the Evans name once and for all."

David leaned in. This was finally getting good.

XVIII

Off-Display Collections Room, Ashmolean Museum. Oxford, England. Arthur.

Evans saw David's eyes become saucers.

"What exactly did Uncle Sir Arthur do that was so terrible?" the boy demanded. The trap was set. His new 'Little Evans' was about to learn a hard lesson.

Evans lowered his voice to a conspiratorial whisper. "At the Palace of Knossos, the multi-chambered floor plan reminded Sir Arthur of the Greek stories of the Minotaur's Labyrinth he had devoured in his youth. He immediately associated everything he was uncovering with the legendary King Minos."

"What, like the story of," David screwed up his face, forcing the knowledge to come. "*Theseus and the Minotaur*? Where Poseidon curses the king, and his wife has a bull-man for a son, so he hires a guy to build this crazy maze and feeds his enemies to him?"

Evans smiled sheepishly. "Something like that. It sounds like you've read the children's version, but that's essentially the core of it."

The boy looked at him sideways, but Evans decided it might be best to leave it there. He considered the earful he would get if Karen learned that on their first afternoon together, Evans had taught young David the full X-rated version of the story. The Minoans had indeed worshiped bulls, as symbols of virility among other things. As such, one of Daedalus' first inventions was supposedly a hollow but anatomically correct bronze cow. This strange commission was from Minos's wife Pasiphae—Greek goddess and witch-queen of Crete—so that she could climb inside and conduct her much desired "interview" with a Cretan bull. All in order to conceive the Minotaur. Poseidon was more of a side-note frankly. Perhaps they would save the discussion of sex cults, bull worship, and witchcraft for another day.

Evans cleared his throat and refocused. "Sir Arthur went so far as to name his civilization at Knossos the 'Minoans,' you see."

There was a pause while David took this in, his face betraying his realization. "Oh, I get it. Uncle Sir Arthur was wrong, wasn't he? They weren't really the Minoans at all?"

Evans nodded conciliatorily, "That's right. At least, not the sort of Minoans the Greeks told stories about. You see, David, Sir Arthur was digging for mythology. Myths are what bind each civilization together. It is how we differentiate ourselves from other cultures. Myths are central to how we define the human experience and explain away the terrible and mysterious things that we cannot understand. But myths aren't objectively real in the Newtonian sense either."

"Huh?"

"*Myth* is not a dirty word, David. We must take them seriously. Just, not literally."

The words hung in the air like the darkness around them. David was laser-focused. He was clearly processing things out. Evans kept going, if for no other reason than to avoid silence. There was no turning back now. "You see, David, as soon as Sir Arthur started looking for Minotaurs and labyrinths, everything he saw became interpreted through the lens of that subjective opinion. For example, what he called King Minos's 'Horns of Consecration' was merely a very well-known symbol for the horizon in ancient Egypt. Which is probably exactly what it meant to the real ancient 'Minoans' as well." Evans put his thumbs together to form a loose W with his hands, demonstrating the shape. "Sir Arthur fell prey to a phenomenon called *confirmation bias*. Finding evidence for a preconceived theory. Bad archeology abounds with examples of it."

David swallowed. "But Arthur," he said, hesitantly. "I thought you said

Egypt was really far away?"

Evans made a noncommittal gesture. "Well, Crete is a lot closer to Egypt than it is to ancient Mesopotamia, where that Akkadian cuneiform I showed you originates." He paused, leaning in close. "But I'll concede the point since it's even closer to Greece."

The corners of David's mouth twitched. "Okay."

"Notwithstanding," Evans went on, "Sir Arthur doggedly stood his ground in his belief that his Palace of Knossos corresponded to Greek Mythology to varying degrees until the day he died. But he could never really prove he was right, any more than his opponents could prove him wrong. To some, he was little more than a laughing stock and a crackpot." A strange feeling of *deja vu* tugged at Evans. He ignored it.

"Well, that's not okay! Why would they do that to him?"

"Why would they...? No, no, it's the other way around entirely. It's called academic integrity, David. It's the cornerstone of modern knowledge. One cannot simply advance any line of thinking one finds appealing or fascinating until it's eventually disproven. Enlightenment is about casting light with known facts, not about blindly stabbing around in the dark."

"Huh. So, why would he even do that, then? I thought everybody knew that the Greek gods weren't real. I mean, it's called mythology for a reason, isn't it? Study of myths."

This was the chance to set the hook that Evans had been waiting for, and he didn't hesitate. "It's not always that simple David." He turned to Sir Arthur's old glass cabinet and opened it, carefully extracting a small tray of clay tablets. "Here, help me with these."

David took the tray to the table and set it in the light of the magnifier then went back for another as directed. With palpable excitement, the teen began carefully examining the tablets in the first tray one by one.

"What are these? They look different from the cuneiform. Really different. More like letters."

"Yes. This is an early form of Mycenaean writing. Something he called Linear-B Script. Sir Arthur had always hoped to decipher it and some of the other forms he found, but the truth is that he never could make his translations stick." He pointed to a very different set of tablets in the second tray. "And this even rarer pictographic form he called Linear-A. Sir Arthur's dig at Knossos eventually yielded some 3,000 of these clay tablets, which he never translated. He ran out of money and time and was eventually forced to come home."

"Oh," David said. "That stinks."

"Indeed." Disappointments always stank. "Well, that brings us to 1884 when, as I said, the museum was about to be closed, the whole place in shambles. The first curator had died, leaving his assistants in charge for nearly a decade. Frustrated collectors were ready to pull out of Oxford entirely. Others were, understandably, unwilling to invest. That's when our unemployed Sir Arthur stepped in."

David raised an eyebrow.

"He was consulted by a museum assistant to locate some missing volumes that he'd written about and they had subsequently misplaced. So, with his career in danger of dissolving, our uncle found himself in the right place at the right time, and with the right qualifications. Thus, in 1884, Arthur J. Evans became the Keeper of the Ashmolean."

"What, they just put him in charge because they lost some books? That's... kind of hilarious."

"They did. Now, keep in mind that it was a defunct old taxidermy museum with no backers or funding. Something of a stuffed Dodo bird itself, if I might be so bold. Perhaps the unemployed archaeologist with the crazy ideas seemed to be a good fit for them. Perhaps he was meant to be a scapegoat. Who really knows?"

"So, what did he do?"

"Well, Sir Arthur did the only thing he felt he could, I suppose. He threw himself into the job with his usual reckless abandon. The first thing he did was to re-brand it as a 'Center for Art and Archeology.' Aside from a few trinkets in the basement, there were no such items here though."

"Heh. That's some spin."

"Quite. Not to mention, it was the world's very first university museum. Something that had simply never been done before."

David's attentive interest was palpable. This was going well.

"Consequently," Evans continued, "if Sir Arthur was going to get donors and backers for the new direction of the museum, he realized he'd have to go first and set a good example. That's why he packed up the thousands of tablets, his notes, all of his priceless Minoan artifacts, and set aside his translation research. He then donated the entire collection to the museum. He even started a big public relations campaign to bring in scholars and tourists. It began with a grand inauguration where he laid out his grandiose plans for all to see. And lo and behold! Donors and art collectors started contacting him."

"Oh wow. So that's why he never translated it all." David picked up the old tablet and held it up to the light again.

"That's right. Fortunately, most of Linear-B has been translated now. A lecture that the rather old Sir Arthur delivered in the 1930s eventually inspired an amateur linguist named Michael Ventris to work on the script.

There was a theory that it might be an early form of Hellenic. Based on this, Ventris and his team were able to crack it. Today we know that Sir Arthur's so-called Minoans were the Aegean people. The first great European civilization to emerge in history."

David's face lit up with recognition and surprise. "Wait, Emma and I spent like half an hour at that big Aegean display today. Those were Uncle Sir Arthur's Minoans? Didn't they basically turn into the Myceneans? You know, sculpture, mythology, democracy, all that?" Evans nodded distractedly. "So, Uncle Sir Arthur was right. The Minoans actually did become the Greeks!" David was nothing less than exuberant.

Evans frowned. He had meant to lay a trap for David and inadvertently walked right into it himself. "Well, yes. Sir Arthur was right—in a way. No evidence has ever been uncovered that links the Minoans to the myths of King Minos or the Minotaur, or anything more than theories about the Labyrinth in Knossos. But the Greek connection to the Minoan people is quite real. Culturally at least. And that's likely thanks to the celebrated goat merchant we began with. Sailors were the true ambassadors of ancient culture. Crete had a mighty navy, and the entire ancient world had a longstanding relationship with the Mycenean Greeks in the north."

David looked dubious.

"You have to understand David, that while the ancient Myceneans were still basically barbarian hordes, the Aegeans of Crete were building magnificent palaces with flush toilets. They traveled the Mediterranean from one end to the other, selling their art and fine goods to every other major port and civilization. Knossos was the first truly great city in the world, positioned right smack in the middle of the Mediterranean. They gave birth to European civilization as we know it, then they inexplicably disappeared, practically overnight. It is still one of the great archeological mysteries of the ancient world. Many theories abound: earthquakes, a plague, a military conquest, but we don't know for sure. Eventually, their Mycenean cousins took over the island and even rebuilt some of the palaces. But they never reached anything like the technology and sophistication of the Cretan Aegeans. We don't know why."

"Well, okay. But what happened to Uncle Sir Arthur? That can't be the end of it. When did he become a 'Sir'?"

Evans considered that for a moment. "Over the course of a few decades, Sir Arthur doggedly pursued his investigations. He even returned to Crete and helped to place all of Mycenae in a proper historical perspective. Those seal stone pictograms are the earliest script in Europe. A Pre-alphabet. Sir Arthur discovered three full stages of writing, the most ancient Western scripts.

Minoan pictograms, Linear-A, and also Linear-B. He did all this at the foot of the first throne of Europe, the imposing natural stone-carved 'Throne of Minos' at Knossos. For this and more, he was knighted in 1911, as is I suppose, rather obvious."

"Wow." David seemed genuinely impressed. "He did a lot for archeology." This wasn't going at all as Evans had hoped.

"Yes, yes he did. But I think you missed my point, David. Sir Arthur went to his grave believing the Palace at Knossos was the legendary Minotaur's labyrinth simply because of the bull imagery abounding there. To the workers, it was the face of the devil, but to him, it was a divine sign. And while there, he lost any reservations about the Minos myths not being true. He forgot that the Minotaur is a Greek myth, not an Aegean one. It was propaganda of a later century and culture, designed to make an old enemy look bad. No more a man of science, Sir Arthur became an idealist and dreamer. His unrestrained imagination got the better of him and very nearly destroyed him. It took his entire life to overcome his early mistakes."

David offered no opinion on the statement, just an expression of open curiosity. It was now or never, so Evans took the opening to drive his point home.

"So, regardless of his ultimate successes David, Sir Arthur remained guilty of one grave and unforgivable sin, which forever haunted his career and his legacy."

David still said nothing, staring at him blankly. It was frustrating.

"Faith, David!" Evans blurted. "Uncle Arthur was a man of blinding faith. His example should remind us that when we allow our hearts to overshadow our minds, it brings about bad scholarship every time. That's what happens when we trust in dreams and fairy tales like Uncle Arthur did. As Wyatt Aarons does. When we chase mythology, we make fools of ourselves. Biblical legends and myths are no different. When we go looking for them, we will always find them!" Evans could feel a cold sweat on his brow. He had pushed too far, and he wasn't talking about Sir Arthur anymore.

David turned away, peeled off his gloves, and laid them on the table. Looking back, he gave Evans a slow sympathetic nod of understanding, but his next words were surprising.

"I don't know, Arthur," he considered. "Never dreaming about anything at all sounds to me like a terrible way to live your life. I mean, having an imagination is important."

Evans didn't know how to respond.

"Mr. Aarons found something, didn't he? Something that connects to Uncle Sir Arthur's research. And you know what it is." It felt like an accusation. Scathing in its truth. "Something important. Isn't it?"

Evans was out of ideas. He knew he couldn't put this off anymore, he just had to figure out how to go about it in a way that wouldn't tear his family apart. Not again. Not this time.

"Yes, David. I think so," he sighed, resigning himself to the horrible conclusion he had come to earlier. "And I think it is somehow connected to Sir Arthur, Noah, and that blasted mountain in Turkey."

Wyatt Aarons' final words tumbled around in his head:

"As it was in the days of Noah," eh?
It's time for us to be vindicated for Doomsday.

"But, er, how about some dinner first?" Evans' stomach was in knots. He needed to buy himself an hour or two to think.

Much to his great relief, David agreed. But as they left the darkened storage room for the fluorescent security lights of the empty museum corridor, Evans could have sworn he noted a horrible twinkle in the boy's eye.

XIX

Mansfield College. Oxford, England. David.

The two Evanses had spent more time talking about the ancient world than David realized. As they cleaned up and put away Uncle Sir Arthur's archives, David grabbed a few digital pictures of the various artifacts—Uncle Sir Arthur's original notes, and several tablets that interested him, translated and untranslated alike.

David soon discovered that Arthur was happy to continue the conversation about ancient people and languages while walking the three blocks to Mansfield College. But he decided not to bring up Mr. Aarons or the journal again until Arthur had a full belly.

To David's surprise, Mansfield College served dinner in a beautiful gothic chapel. It was complete with ornate woodwork, column arcades, a hand-chiseled dark oak chorus, and stained glass. This last, he quickly found out, was Arthur's personal favorite. The beautifully colored windows did not depict Christian saints, but great figures with historically significant minds. The late afternoon sun diffused colored light into the old chapel gloriously, from all along the clerestory above the vaulted nave. It was an odd juxtaposition of science, art, and religion that sent David's imagination racing, even if it did seem a little irreverent. Or was that the point?

As David stared up toward the vaulted ceiling in wonder, Arthur took great delight in explaining that as the early religious emphasis waned among Oxford's colleges, many repurposed their chapels for other purposes. Currently, Mansfield was using theirs for summer dining purposes. David felt a pang of sadness about that, but he wasn't sure why. It's not like there weren't other churches around; they'd passed by dozens of others just today.

"Next, we have Desiderius Erasmus of Rotterdam," Arthur was saying, pointing with his fork at one of the stained-glass scholars. His mouth was full of buttered potato.

"And who was he?"

"Well, Erasmus was called 'the crowning glory of the Christian humanists,' for one. He was famous for using humanist techniques to work on texts. He even prepared important Latin and Greek editions of the New Testament, which raised questions that would be influential in the Protestant Reformation and Catholic Counter-Reformation."

"Humanist? Isn't that another word for atheist? Was he some kind of anti-church rebel or something?"

"Well, in his own way, I suppose he was. In today's way of thinking, he'd be better classified as more of a proto-Protestant. He was in fact a most devout priest. You see, medieval humanism was quite different from how we use the term today. Nowadays, *humanism* refers to a post-modern philosophy that promotes the value, agency, and potential of being human. But humanism was born in the Middle Ages as a movement that advocated critical thinking and evidential reasoning. It was a means to resist uncritical acceptance of authoritarian dogma or traditional superstition. That would include atheism, by atheism's own reckoning, I suppose."

That sounded like double-talk to David. He passively pondered if Arthur was a humanist, modern or otherwise. He sure didn't act like the card-carrying Evangelicals David had grown up around. Could you be a modern humanist and a believer? He didn't think so. Arthur continued talking, hardly even coming up for breath.

"Middle Age humanists sought to create a population that would be able to speak and write with eloquence and clarity. They would thus be capable of engaging in the civic life of their communities, even persuading others to virtuous and prudent actions. They wanted this accomplished through the study of what they called the *studia humanitatis*."

"The study of humans?"

"Very nearly. Though it was extremely radical and revolutionary then, today it's just known as the humanities. It was grammar, rhetoric, history, poetry, and moral philosophy. Their opponents feared it would destabilize and collapse their entire civilization and bring about the apocalypse. They weren't far off, truth be told. Erasmus is one fellow to blame if you don't like having an English class. But the fact is, the late medieval notion of a popular education ended their feudalistic way of life. It wasn't cataclysmic or immediate, but it was fairly universal. That's what the word *universitas* means, after all, 'universal unity in thought.' It's no coincidence that Oxford began in the pre-dawn hours of the Enlightenment." Arthur gestured around himself as if to present David with the whole city as Exhibit A of his argument.

"Wait a minute, Arthur. Are you saying that the Renaissance was the end of the world? Like the flood was to Noah?" His heart thumped a little faster at the risk of mentioning Noah again, but Arthur didn't seem to notice.

"In various forms and locations, yes. For Middle Age Europe at any rate. We don't call them the Dark Ages because it was dark back then; rather, it's a slight on their way of life. Renaissance propaganda. So's the word *Renaissance*, frankly."

"Renaissance means *rebirth*, right? That doesn't sound bad at all. It sounds good."

"Ah, then I see the propaganda has worked. Rebirth implies a recovery from death. Death, dark, middle—it's all a deep insult to the old ways. Frankly, theistic feudalism worked rather well, all things considered. Until it didn't anymore. Until we became too 'enlightened' to be comfortable with its implications."

"Wow, Erasmus caused all that?" David glanced up again at the stained-glass scholar in awe.

"Well, he certainly helped. As I said before, there have been many apocalypses throughout human history, and most are precipitated by an enlightenment—some more bloody than others. And only some have been caused by man. The others were so-called acts of God, a reassertion of natural chaos like in our mythical flood of Noah. Still others remain mysteries, like the downfall of the Minoans."

David felt a tiny shiver at Arthur's willingness to discuss Noah and the Minoans again. Still, he would have to tread carefully.

Arthur popped another tiny potato into one side of his mouth. "You see David, when societies get too chaotic they are subject to a cosmic wipe-out. It's what the word *apocalypse* literally means. It's an unveiling, a revelation of truth. It's a synonym for enlightenment. In the case of Erasmus, a new way of life was created by destroying the old way of life. Suffering and betterment ensued."

"Revelation? Like the book?" It was the wrong end of the Bible again, but at least they were narrowing in.

"Well, yes, somewhat. John's Revelation is considered to be in the genre of apocalyptic literature. It's as much to do with the knowledge gained as to the supposed end of days. In that sense, an apocalypse has happened to every society ever. Even our own, by some definitions. I suppose we could say that one recurring theme in *Genesis* is that God didn't want to operate in cataclysm anymore. He promised that His punishment would fit the crime. Or in the case of Moses' Hebrew audience, the covenant. Either way, it's a philosophical framework Erasmus likely appreciated."

Score! David sized up his wizard as he chewed. "So, Noah's society got too chaotic?" he ventured.

"Well, yes, certainly. In many ways, the Noah myth is simply the second volume of the Adam and Eve story. The archetypal first people seek enlightenment, accidentally damning humanity to separation from God. The inevitable return to chaos comes in the flood of Noah, who then becomes the new Adam of a sort. A redo. *Genesis* One tells us that the world was made from a formless void. A better translation of the word is chaos. The creation myth and Noah myth are inextricably linked."

Creation myth? Noah myth? Did Arthur think that all the stories of *Genesis* were just myths? David picked a different question he already knew the answer to. "But Arthur, Adam and Eve didn't go looking for enlightenment, they were tempted by Satan. They ate fruit from the Tree of Life and disobeyed. Original sin entered because they sinned and that's why creation fell, right?" *Sixteen years of Sunday School for the win!*

Arthur smiled awkwardly. "No, that was the other tree in the Garden. They were allowed to eat from the Tree of Life. It was the Tree of the Knowledge of Good and Evil that was forbidden. And the tempter was something called a chaos serpent. It wasn't until the Middle Ages that scholars connected the chaos serpent with the Devil canonically. All as a part of the very same Middle Age Enlightenment that Erasmus helped ignite. But even so, Lucifer—another medieval moniker for Satan—means *bringer of light*. As in, enlightenment and knowledge. It's all quite logical, really."

David considered this. It felt like everything he said today was wrong. The serpent wasn't always seen as Satan? Man, his grandfather had some weird ideas. He was pretty sure that there was a passage somewhere about Lucifer falling from Heaven. He filed it away to look up later.

"Regardless," Arthur continued, "the seeker of enlightenment always struggles with the same thing: He falls in love with his own ideas and becomes stuck in them. To avoid that trap is the real enlightenment. To realize when one is in error.”

“Tree of Knowledge,” David realized. “Wow, okay.” Something else to look up and confirm later.

“Of course, Erasmus is also the name of the campus cat.”

“The cat?” laughed David, nearly launching a bit of potato across the chapel.

“The cat. They tend to cycle through the scholars every few decades as the felines lose their ‘tenured chair,’ so to speak.”

“You mean they name the next college cat based on the stained-glass windows when one of them dies?” Arthur did a fair imitation of a bobblehead doll. “That’s funny.”

David sized up his grandfather intently as the servers took his empty plate. The old man was in a better mood, his hunger for food seeming satisfied. But David’s hunger for knowledge was not even remotely sated. He decided to risk it. “So, Arthur, it’s after dinner. What was the great discovery you made with Mr. Aarons’ journal, and how does it connect to Uncle Sir Arthur exactly?”

Arthur cleared his throat and swallowed his last mouthful of potato a little sooner than he should have. This required him to reach for one of the glass bottles of water on the table.

“Ah, yes indeed,” he finally coughed, as he fumbled around for the journal in his coat pocket. It wasn’t there.

David reached into his hoodie pocket and extracted the little book. “You, uh, left it on your desk. I thought you might need it.”

Arthur blinked a few times, then mumbled a word of thanks and something about his head being attached. He peered over his glasses, flipped to the last journal entry, and read it aloud for them both:

> *4-16-10: Last night I prayed for an hour under the stars of Canaan, and today the Lord led me to a new tablet fragment that I’m confident will be the key to locating Dilmun. It matches up with yesterday’s piece perfectly. The original tablet was broken in half, but both parts are preserved. Even with my little knowledge of the writing, I recognize some of the symbols. I’ll need to find a translator who can do it right unless I could somehow convince Arthur to help. But his Evans collection is the key to all this. I only pray that he will be more open-minded about the Lord’s work after all this time.*

David felt his excitement rise. So, Mr. Aarons actually was looking for

Gilgamesh's Dilmun. He'd found something but apparently still needed key information from the family archive, which Arthur knew so much about. But which part of it? There was a lifetime of finds up in that storeroom. Thousands of tablets across three languages, many of them still untranslated. What David had seen today barely scratched the surface of the Minoan artifacts. He reached for his phone. And what could the real Noah have to do with any of it? He had a weird image pop into his head of a Minotaur stalking along inside Noah's Ark as the storms raged. Arthur pulled him back from his wild imaginings.

"So, do you remember what I said about Linear-B?" he asked.

"That some guy in the thirties managed to translate it and prove Sir Arthur was right about the Greek connection?"

David bit his lip. That was more sarcasm than he usually allowed himself. He was letting his tiredness and impatience with Arthur get to him. He suddenly thought of his dad. If stubbornness was a family trait, then he was beginning to understand where it came from. Arthur let the little jab slide though.

"Um, yes. Well, the thing is that Linear-A has never quite given anyone as much luck. In fact, not many people realize that some of the Linear-A tablets went missing, and all we have is Sir Arthur's transcriptions of many of the originals."

That seemed like a big deal to David. Arthur kept going though, confirming exactly what David had just concluded.

"At first, I thought Wyatt meant me in his entry. But clearly, he means Sir Arthur and the notes that he took eleven decades ago about the original Minoan tablets."

"You mean these?" David held out his phone, displaying photos he'd taken earlier of the pages from Uncle Sir Arthur's notebooks.

Arthur took the phone. "Yes, like those." He pointed to one of the old Linear-A tablet transcriptions. "And you recall that this language is more primitive than the Linear-B."

"More like pictographs, I think you said?"

"Precisely. It has always been theorized that Linear-A is a transition between the pictographs like those on the seal stones and Linear-B. Sir Arthur went to his grave swearing it. But the reality is that they are just too different. Even given enough time for the language to evolve, experts agree that the syntax and structure of Linear-A don't seem to match the latter." Arthur made to demonstrate with one of the photos, but the phone had already snapped to black. He set it down on the table in front of him instead.

"Like how the Greek base six in the clock and calendar is different from our normal base ten?"

"Well, yes, I suppose so, in a way. Some have suggested that Linear-A is the true Minoan language, while Linear-B is from the Mycenean conquerors who took over the island, but I can't reasonably say. Linear-A and B aren't among my specialties. I can't read Linear-B nearly as well as I can read Sumerian or Ugaritic cuneiform. And I couldn't even begin to decipher Linear-A any better than the others who have tried and failed over the last century. Or at least, I thought I couldn't."

"What do you mean?"

Arthur opened his mouth to answer but was cut off by a shrill noise between them. It echoed loudly throughout the little repurposed chapel. One of the wait staff gave Arthur a dirty look. The noise came again before David realized what was happening.

David's defunct smartphone was ringing. He snatched it up and answered it before a third ring could disturb the peace any worse than it already had.

"Hello?" David whispered into it, ignoring the stares from all around. The impossible voice on the other end made no sense.

"Uh, Arthur," David whispered across the table, looking over at Arthur in bewilderment. "It's for you."

XX

Beaumont Street. Oxford, England. Mr. Suit.

The man in the suit charged up the stone stairs to the immense glass door that marked the entrance of the Museum and stared in disbelief.

ASHMOLEAN MUSEUM OPENING HOURS

10am–5pm Tuesday–Sunday (Closed Mondays)

ADMISSION IS FREE

This was becoming a fool's errand. It was just past five now. The iron gate was down, and the entire premises were locked tight. Breaking into a major museum was not something the man intended to add to his performance today. Even if Dr. Evans was pulling a late workday in there somewhere, no museum night-guard in his right mind would let him through those doors now.

He swore in three languages and spat, then returned to his motorbike. He was better than this, but he was also out of time and options. He slid his helmet on and gunned the Ducati to life. He subconsciously shrugged his shoulder again, the feel of his gun lighting up the deepest parts of his brain, a nervous twitch now. This surprised him.

No, he was in control, a man who acted, not reacted. As a mindful and calculated act, he took in a deep breath and exhaled slowly, letting himself feel the smooth silk of his suit. It was an eastern meditation technique he had learned from one of his old teachers as a child. That had been a long time ago. Was Oxford making him soft?

Remember who you are. What you really are. The mantra centered him.

He could still use this mess. All of it. The fruitless break-in, the boy throwing off the schedule, the old man's penchant for said schedule. But he would have to find Dr. Evans sooner rather than later if he was going to make this new plan work. The others were counting on him. He made his decision. He killed the bike and locked it. Leaving it here meant that he could move more stealthily. That is what he needed now. That, and some good luck. Dr. Evans always ate at the Mansfield College dining hall on weekends. It was a gamble worth taking.

He hated being rushed. This could get even messier before it was done. Much messier.

*   *   *

Ten minutes later, his gamble paid off. As he passed like a shadow through the main gates of Mansfield College, he noticed three things.

First, the porter was not one he knew, reducing his chances of recognition from at least one source. Second, a small group of students played croquet in the round central court, providing a nice distraction for anyone who might otherwise be paying attention. And third, Dr. Evans was exiting the old chapel and talking loudly on a mobile phone.

This last, he had every intention of listening in on. His time was already up, and Dr. Evans' time was about to be.

XXI

Mansfield Road. Oxford, England. Arthur.

Evans stepped quickly into the Mansfield College courtyard and held the miniature *Space Odyssey* monolith David called a phone up to his ear. It was like talking into a bar of soap.

"Yes, hello? Are you still there?"

"Dr. Evans?"

"Call me Arthur. Who is this?"

"Wonderful. This is Melanie Chen. Call me Mel. Please apologize to your grandson for the use of his phone. I noticed that it was not working properly, so I took care of it." The perfect Queen's English on the other end surprised him. Perhaps she was Chen by marriage?

"Okay," he faltered.

"More to the point, how are you faring this afternoon, Professor?"

"Just a tutor," he said automatically.

"Quite right," she agreed. "The college hasn't seen fit to endow you with proper laurels, have they? That is a shame. In some countries, you would be called professor simply based on your education and experience, instead of some arbitrary medieval meritocracy. Perhaps we can fix that."

Evans was taken aback. Who was this woman? He was failing at social interaction after a dozen words. This was why he hated phones.

"My understanding is that you have in your possession a journal written by your old business partner Wyatt Aarons. Tell me, have you by chance been contacted by Mr. Aarons otherwise?"

"Uh, no. I must admit I haven't seen or heard from Wyatt in decades. I'd like to keep it that way, frankly."

"Ah, I see. Well, you should know that he has spoken favorably of you on more than one occasion. He said I should recruit you for our work, and I quote, 'no matter the cost.'"

"I see," Evans lied.

Mel Chen laughed. It sounded like a wind chime. "Professor Evans, you haven't been very keen about our offers so far. My best recruiters tell me that you are a difficult man to persuade. Even with some of our more flattering proposals."

There had been offers? A vague memory tugged at him of a series of calls from some company some months back with silly talk of adventure and archeology, a promise of fortune and glory and other nonsense. He'd given it about as much stock as it deserved.

"You have to understand professor, that when I say no matter the cost, that means something. I'm familiar with your work, and I know your history. I also know what you believe about Wyatt Aarons' work. But things have changed. I want that journal, but I need you more."

"I'm sorry, what? I don't—"

Evans wanted dreadfully to hang up the phone, but something told him that this Mel person was not someone to simply be hung up on. His mind was torn between the impossible things she apparently knew and how best to end the conversation as quickly as possible.

"What I mean to say, Mel, is that you have me at a disadvantage. Who are you, exactly?"

"How foolish of me. Obviously, you wouldn't know. Wyatt Aarons works for me, professor. He is the visionary who has been leading my research in Ugarit for the better part of a year now. He is mere weeks away from a major discovery that will change the world forever."

Wyatt, a visionary? Evans' opinion of the woman dropped a few notches.

"My company is called Mao Sien. We specialize in finding the unfindable. Perhaps you've heard of us?"

That name, Evans recognized. It was a company regularly under fire from experts and serious academics. Mao Sien was a terrible waste of funds with a reputation for the incredulous and their methods were highly suspect, scientifically and academically. Oh yes, he'd heard of them. Associating with them was a death sentence to a legitimate career, and his was already in sufficient tatters, *thank you very much!* Evans had decided long ago that he wasn't taking any more chances with idealistic weirdoes. Not even filthy rich ones. Wyatt Aarons may have found himself a corporate sponsor for his nonsense, but for him, Mel's would be a very quick bubble to burst.

Ms. Chen continued with the excitement of a schoolgirl. "Dr. Evans, my company is responsible for remarkable things. I'm sure you know of the 'Hobbit Fossil' discovery on Flores. Or perhaps the Paleolithic flints in the 700,000-year-old deposits at Pakefield we helped finance? That find has pushed back the earliest known human occupation of Britain by something like 200,000 years, you may know."

Evans didn't know. He also didn't care. *Hobbits? Really?* He grunted noncommittally and let her keep talking.

"Regardless, you should know that we have built a team for the second phase of our research in Ugarit. We are in desperate need of someone who can read and translate ancient cuneiform and Semitics. I would also have you examine some of the other ancient tablets Mr. Aarons has found."

"Huh, good luck with that," Evans laughed. "There are about five hundred people in the world who can read cuneiform, and most of them are completely nuts. They are the guys in tinfoil hats on public access television who think aliens built the pyramids and Atlantis was the ancient word for America." Evans didn't bother to hide his sarcasm.

Mel laughed like he'd told a good joke. "I know, Dr. Evans. That's why I want you." Evans remembered the politely oblivious Mao Sien recruiters a little more clearly now. Every few months when they had managed to get him on the phone, he would politely—or perhaps not so politely—decline their offer. He usually just cited schedule conflicts and college responsibilities. But it would take an act of God to drag him back out into the field on some wild goose chase for Hammurabi's lost tablets, or King Aeëtes' golden fleece, at the behest of some smooth-talking madman. Or in this case, madwoman.

"Ah," Evans croaked. "Now, come to think of it, didn't your people tell me that you are in the process of cataloging and dating the Paleolithic mounds of pre-Columbian America for the very purpose of finding Atlantis in the Mississippi or some such thing?"

"Indeed we are. We have found compelling evidence of a pre-Celtic— perhaps Phoenician—presence in North America as far back as the last Ice Age. Over five hundred artifacts. Though, it may be the Mississippian Cahokia Mounds in Illinois that you are thinking of. If you like, I could make available—"

"Hogwash. I'm a man of letters, not fantasies. I no longer have any interest in chasing legends."

"Yes, Dr. Evans, I know. That is why, when Wyatt Aarons sends his field notes to you instead of his employer, I take notice. I would love to tear him apart for that one, but things have become complicated. Mr. Aarons has gone missing, Professor. So now, it seems that I also need a team leader for the final phase of our operation. An important position, and you are the most qualified person for the job."

There was a pause while what she was saying began to sink in. This was no recruiter. This woman ran the company, which meant he was talking to a multi-billionaire. She was smooth too. He found himself strangely intrigued by her words, especially the part about tearing into Wyatt. It was an opportunity to ditch this silly book and get paid for it besides. Old desires buried deep were working their way up to the surface. Then, one detail hit him like a brick.

"Wait. Wyatt is missing? What do you mean by 'missing,' exactly?"

"Dr. Evans, I've read your work. You have the journal; you also have the skills I need. My Dilmun team leaves out of Paris tomorrow, and it is short a leader." The chimes were gone. Chen was deadly serious. "I need someone to lead that team and find Wyatt Aarons. Name your price."

"I don't—" Evans stammered, flabbergasted. Was this woman bribing him? He fell back on the safe thoughts that he knew so well. "I'm just an ancient literature and language tutor, Mel. I'm not who you think I am. Not anymore. And I'm certainly no Wyatt Aarons. Legends and myths are enjoyable fireside reading. Often, they are windows into the thinking of an ancient world. But such stories mustn't be seen as shortcuts for amateur archeologists who don't know the difference between feigned or embellished history and the real thing."

He thought of the grand portrait of Uncle Arthur at the Ashmolean, but it was replaced by the image of his Elisabeth. He could see her hurrying across the Mansfield Quad, skipping towards him with some happy news or another about the museum, or little Joseph, or new yellow curtains for the cottage. *Am I losing my mind?* He blinked. *No—only a student.* But his heart beat a little faster regardless.

Ms. Chen was talking again but he missed it. "—but perhaps, Dr. Evans, it is time to remember who you once were, and take back what was stolen from you? You are my only choice to lead this expedition. No one else knows what you know, nor can anyone do what you can do." She paused to let him process this until, thick and slow, she sank the hook in again. "Name your price, Professor." *Ridiculous line.* She might as well have been a queen promising half her kingdom, but Evans believed her.

He suddenly felt like the fabled mathematician Sessa, having just shown his new invention, the game of chess, to the King. According to the story, the ruler was so pleased that he gave the inventor the right to name any reward for his new game. The clever man asked the king for something quite odd. For the first square of the chessboard, he would receive one grain of wheat, two for the second one, four on the third one, and so forth, doubling the amount each time. The arithmetically clueless ruler accepted the inventor's offer. He was offended by his perception that the inventor was asking for such a low price but ordered the treasurer to count and hand over the grain regardless. However, when the treasurer took more than a week to calculate the amount of wheat, the ruler demanded a reason for his tardiness. The treasurer then gave him the result of the calculation and explained that it would take more than all the assets of the kingdom to give the inventor the impossible reward.

Mel Chen waited for an answer. Evans considered the fate of Sessa the mathematician. In some much later variants, the inventor was rewarded, or even became the new king. But in most versions, the story ended with the inventor being beheaded. Ancient Eastern morality tales were not like Western fairy stories.

Evans glanced toward the door he had exited. David leaned against the entryway, the little chapel not quite big enough for a proper vestibule. The boy was yawning and shaking fatigue away, quickly becoming the victim of jet lag. With his hands shoved solidly into the pockets of his hoodie, David blinked at Evans with imploring puppy-dog eyes, still not yet understanding the nature of the call, or why his phone was working at all. Technically, Evans didn't either, but he still didn't care.

"There are complications Mel. I'll have to decline your very, uh, generous offer. Again. I'm sorry." It was a half-truth. This was a deal with the devil no matter how you sliced it. While something about today had sparked an old fire, the reality was that Mel Chen's so-called "visionary," that weasel Wyatt Aarons, was the last human being on the planet that Evans wanted to have a conversation with, much less to waste time tracking down. Whatever foolhardy pursuit Wyatt had engaged in was his own mess. It was highly likely that he had been thrown into some Turkish prison again, or was squatting in an American embassy and laying low.

"All right Dr. Evans, I'm sorry too," Mel stated matter-of-factly. "If you change your mind in the next twelve hours, this is my personal number, direct to me. Good day, Professor."

"Yes, good day, and thank you for your—" but the call had ended. Melanie Chen was obviously not one for wasting time once the decision was made.

For a brief moment, Evans wondered if he had made the right decision. But as he looked across the field to where the little group of twenty-somethings was playing croquet, he threw his doubts away. He was taken back forty years to an evening not unlike this, and a game not unlike that one, where he had been soundly beaten by a young woman named Elisabeth, a woman he'd just met at the Museum earlier that day. The memory grounded him. Suddenly, Evans felt free. He had made Karen a promise, and all day long he had felt trapped by it. But now, it had become his escape. It was time for the Evanses to finish their family talk. He also needed a pint, possibly two. The Bird and Baby seemed an appropriate choice.

"'We don't want any adventures here, thank you!'" he quoted aloud.

"What's that, Arthur?" David said, stepping up to take his phone.

"Hmm? Oh, nothing David, nothing. Just something a wise little Hobbit once said to a certain disturber of the peace."

Hobbit fossils indeed! What stuff and nonsense.

XXII

Chinese airspace. Westbound at 36,000 ft. Mel.

Mel fumed. She paced from one end of the cabin to the other, gripping her mug tight enough to choke a snake. Her young employee in Oxford had utterly failed to do his simple little job. The overconfident graduate student in his silly little suit was a mistake. His inability to accomplish even this small task was most vexing. He had been highly recommended by someone she respected deeply, an oddity of a different breed, but still one of her oldest advisors. Practically an uncle. Family. But this "Mr. Suit" was proving to be more appearance than competence.

She rarely got these things wrong, but something was wrong with the man in the suit. It bothered her not knowing what. Were his secret-agent delusions getting in the way? Fancy clothes and fast bikes were all part of what his recruitment profile had suggested, so she had supplied them.

Megalomania in her people usually wasn't a problem. She bottled and sold all flavors of eccentricity regularly. The various peculiarities of her employees were part of their usefulness more often than not. Which was largely why this circumstance bothered her all the more. She didn't like reading people incorrectly, and she realized now that she had sized up Dr. Evans wrong too. Emotions always changed the equation; perhaps she had missed something? She sipped from her masala chai latte and assessed the situation. Her anger was getting in the way. She needed to set it aside and think logically. Anger caused people to do such irrational things.

The tea helped. She went over everything again. With time running out, Mel had decided to talk to Evans personally. Due to a clever service network hack and a phone hijack, she'd co-opted the visiting grandson's inoperable phone for the call. Much easier to do when you own the satellites. The side-benefit would be easy surveillance and a direct line to Evans if she wanted it, but that likely wouldn't matter now. In three sentences, she'd discovered what she needed to know.

Yes, he did have the journal.

No, he didn't' know where Aarons was.

And worst of all, he was not the man he had once been.

In this situation, Mel's mind had been the key, and some things you just had to do yourself. *Above all, trust the human computer!*

Evans' cowardice surprised Mel and even disarmed her a bit. It was a shame. He was nothing like Wyatt Aarons. She had suspected that the allure of the legend wouldn't be enough for Evans, given the man's history and public shame in his early career. But she had never anticipated that the Oxford don would turn down an opportunity to make a name for himself, live in luxury, or even take a higher position. Evans was undoubtedly a fool, but fools and cowards were also easy to manipulate. It just required a different approach.

No, she was being unfair. She was still angry, and Evans was no fool. She took a step back and examined her anger, a self-analysis of the variety she sometimes applied to her people, rarely to herself.

Mel was exasperated that her employee in the suit had failed her.

She was frustrated that she hadn't turned her plane around eight hours sooner.

She felt betrayed by the reality that Aarons hadn't trusted her with his important notes, instead of a man who hardly knew him anymore.

And she was infuriated that Dr. Evans hadn't taken her bribe.

Ah, there it is. Mel had simply never known anyone who couldn't be bought. She wasn't used to dealing with such a fanatical level of – what? Stubbornness? Resolve? like Dr. Evans had exhibited. She jealously wanted that unwavering quality on her new team. A leader who would send her the key information, not some old partner from decades prior. One who couldn't be bought. Yet, such fanaticism was also highly suspicious. It would be very difficult to trust Dr. Evans at all now. The irony was scathing.

Mel felt empowered by this new set of insights. She had ordered the pilots to turn around and start flying westward, but she still couldn't get her feet on the ground in England for at least eighteen hours. By that time, the new Dilmun team would already be in-route to Ugarit, and her only real option was to meet up with them there. A team that was still leaderless, and without the benefit of Aarons' secret notes, would have to recreate his work from square one. Delaying the team would be difficult, if not impossible. And there were other factors, including military factors, regarding the Syrian government. She needed Evans on that plane, journal and all. She needed all her human computers to align, to network, to function as one, but she was simply out of time. Mel was about to add that fact categorically to the list of things she was angry about when suddenly the solution presented itself. A thread that could pull all of these problems together.

She wasn't thinking rationally because emotions changed the equation.

Anger causes irrational action!

Yes, it was a possibility, but it would mean burning resources. No, it meant burning a potential family member. As well as taking a big gamble on someone else's anger. She hated gambling. She much preferred to cheat. She eased into her chair and pulled up a communication screen, text only. Her last few messages of the conversation with Mr. Suit appeared. She tightened her mouth at the nonsense spy lingo that she had been using to accommodate his little fantasy.

Item confirmed
with high probability

Acquire it.
Digital delivery is
expected in 6 hours

Item remains on him.
He is off his routine

She consulted the asset's file and quickly composed a final message to the haughty little boy in the suit. A match to set the house on fire, and a little splash of petrol to help it burn.

You have failed.
Your employment is terminated.
Your portfolio is burned.
Your passphrase invalidated
We will arrange for the collection of
your vehicle, mobile, and company
apparel shortly.

Passphrase. Portfolio. What nonsense.

That done, she opened another message window to a very different employee in a very different location: Mr. Suit's handler, the man who had first recommended him. Her father's old friend. Her uncle. True family.

Your Mr. Suit is sacked.
I'm pulling you out of
retirement like you wanted.
Use him, please.
Motivate Arthur Evans.
Plane leaves tomorrow
out of CDG. Be on it

The reply came in less than a minute.

Whatever you say Kiddo. Don't you
worry about another thing

XXIII

South Park Road. Oxford, England. Arthur.

The Bird and Baby wasn't the closest pub, but it was Evans' personal favorite. Walking off a good meal in anticipation of a good ale was one of the few things he did impulsively. Truthfully, he had that impulse quite regularly in the evenings and always on Saturday, especially after a full course of English hospitality from one of the college dining halls. Tonight though, Evans had the ominous feeling he had forgotten something.

"Arthur!" Evans whirled. Why was David shouting? "Are you even listening to me right now?"

Evans blinked. He hadn't been at all. He tried to confess it but stood stupidly with his mouth producing random syllables instead. The boy was ranting and angry for some reason.

"I mean, if you know something, then why wouldn't you want to help? What is it you are afraid of? Is it me? This Mr. Aarons guy? What aren't you telling me? It seems like every time you are just about to explain to me what he figured out, something happens."

Evans was taken aback. Why was this happening? David was shouting in the street like a madman.

"First, there's all this stuff about you finding Noah's ark on some mountain in Turkey, which you still haven't told me the whole story about. Then, you said it had something to do with the *Epic of Gilgamesh*, the Tree of Life, and ancient flood stories, but instead of telling me what you meant, you ditched me in a museum that it turns out our great-great-whatever uncle Sir Arthur basically started!" All of this was true, but David didn't stop there.

"You promised to explain how that all connects to that crazy journal, but instead you got a call on a phone that doesn't work, and isn't yours, from somebody who, what? Made you some kind of job offer? What are you Arthur, some kind of international spy? I'm tired of distractions. The phone is off." He pulled it out of his pocket for emphasis. "I'm listening. I'm full. And I don't need a coke, or a beer, or a museum tour. I'm not moving another step until you tell me what the heck is going on!"

David had stopped at a little concrete barrier meant to deter bicyclers from taking the walking-only footpath. He now stared at Evans crossly. The modern-style flats to the right stood in stark contrast with an old residence nestled up against the high perimeter wall on the left. Old and new façades, staring each other down for dominance. A multi-generational game of chicken, played out in architecture. *Hmph!*

Evans suddenly missed Elisabeth more than he had in a very long time. He needed the wisdom of a wise mother. She would have been a phenomenal grandmother. What would she want him to say to her grandson? Evans honestly didn't know. He was horrible at this grandfather thing. He could see Elisabeth standing there with the boy, her arm around him, comforting him.

Him? Why him?!

Evans was the one that needed female wisdom now, not the boy! Then the reality struck him. Evans was wrong and his young grandson was right on every count. Evans had been terribly difficult, irresponsible, and selfish.

"Remember how angry you were when you came home from Turkey?" The imaginary Elisabeth's expression seemed to say. *"How alone and scared? How hurt? Do you remember that?"*

Evans said as much. Or at least, he started to. "I'm sorry," he began. "I'm not used to having to care for someone—" That wasn't right. That sounded wrong. "I—" he began again but choked on the words. He was having trouble seeing.

"David, this isn't the American college system, and I'm not Karen," he managed. David was glaring at him with laser focus, looking for meaning that hadn't come to him yet. "What I mean to say, David, is that I'm not a homeschool teacher. This is Oxford. I'm a tutor at a very old English college with very old traditions. Things are different here. We read for degrees, we don't study for them." David shook his head. He still wasn't grasping the point. "David, my boy, don't you realize the importance of everything you just said? Don't you realize what you've done today? Everything you've already learned? How much can you expect to take in after just one day? Yet, look at yourself." There was an awkwardness as the two Evanses stared each other down. "Don't you see, David? You've been learning all day long."

A glimmer of realization crossed David's face.

Evans pounced on it. "Your whole world became a little bigger today, didn't it? Is history's timetable a little more real? The foundation of a thousand lifetimes of work was dumped out in front of you, and you took it. Or rather, it has taken you, unless I miss my guess. Uncle Arthur's love of the past is calling to you."

David nodded. It was quick, almost imperceptible, but enough.

"Well, me too," Evans stated. "Anew, I mean." He cleared his throat and juggled the journal out of his pocket. "And it's all because of you, and a very strong desire not to make a fool of myself over this mad journal." His glasses slid down his nose, but he left them there, flipping furiously to the end and the last completed rubbing that Wyatt Aarons had made. "Here," he squeaked.

Evans handed David the book. His thumb again marked the place where Wyatt Aarons had so sloppily transferred the first half of his discovery. The boy sighed heavily and took it, tossing his hood back and squinting at the little pencil rubbing.

"What am I looking at?" David demanded. "It's cuneiform, right? Like the one you showed me at the museum?"

Evans found his voice again and used it. "Essentially, yes. But to be more precise, Ugaritic cuneiform, a language that came into being as the old Akkadian cuneiform was passing from the scene and alphabetic scripts were making their rise."

David stared at him as if he'd spoken in Ugaritic, but he was fairly sure he hadn't.

"This language is phonetic. It uses an alphabet with only a few sounds askew of our own. All Semitic alphabets are rather well understood in academic terms. Ugaritic took a team of Rabbis a relatively brief time to crack, once they realized the phonetic connection to Hebrew. Once one learns the basic symbology, even Arabic and Hebrew are fairly easy to jump between, assuming you can speak it."

"Yea, okay. Great. So, then, what does it say?"

"What? Oh, nothing important at all frankly. It's a list of gifts to a noble lady of some sort, perhaps a princess. Probably part of some longer peace treaty and one of a set of tablets if I had to guess. That's not the point."

"Alright Arthur," David growled. "What is the point then?" He glared at Evans suspiciously. At that moment, Evans would have given even money for the teenager either throwing up his hands and charging off in disgust or taking to shouting at him again. But Evans would have lost those bets because David did neither. He only stood, waiting.

"Look at the very bottom of the rubbing, my boy. Along the broken edge. Look closely. I missed it the first time too."

Slowly, David scrutinized the faintly pencil-marked page again, angling the book to catch the early evening light. Evans didn't need to look, it was burned into his memory now. The pencil rubbing of the three-sided fragment ended in a diagonal break, but at the bottom point, there was one incredible detail. A sliver of pictograms crammed tightly together like a dozen other tablets and fragments he had shown David earlier that day. Then, Evans saw the light of recognition in the boy's face as he focused on the jagged bottom inch or so of the rubbing.

"These ones…"

"Yes?" Evans held his breath.

"It's not Ugaritic. Not even cuneiform, it's pictographs." With every word, the boy's agitation was dropping away like sand from an hourglass.

"Do you recognize them?" Evan's prompted.

"Actually…" David pulled out the phone again and watched it slowly power back up.

Was the moody teen avoiding looking at Evans on purpose? After a long uncomfortable moment, David started swiping wildly through the images of the tablets and transcriptions he'd taken earlier.

Then finally, "Yea, okay. They look a lot like Uncle Sir Arthur's untranslatable Linear-A language from Crete."

"Precisely. That little snippet is Linear-A. And it shouldn't be there."

"Okay. So what? Why does it matter?"

"David, do you know what the Rosetta Stone is?"

David's attention snapped up. "It's a translation stone that has some different languages on it. And because of it, we know how to read hieroglyphics. They keep it in a museum in London. It's kind of a big deal."

"Ancient Greek, Demotic script, and Ancient Egyptian hieroglyphs, yes. It's a stele inscribed with a decree issued at Memphis, Egypt, in the late second century B.C. on behalf of King Ptolemy V."

"Okay. So what? You said this stuff didn't have anything to do with Egypt."

"What? No, you misunderstand me. I'm not talking specifically about Egypt. But even cuneiform was decoded only because of the discovery of the Behistun Inscription, which was written in three languages. Old Persian, Elamite, and Akkadian. It was translated through a very long process, by multiple linguists, but it was translated. It's how this process works."

"What?" David screwed up his face. His exasperation was back. Evans was muddling it all up again.

"I only bring them up as parallel examples, David. It doesn't matter. But listen, if I'm right, then Wyatt may have bumbled into one of the greatest archeological discoveries since the Rosetta Stone or the Behustin Inscription."

Saying it aloud made Evans feel hollow and full of fire at the same time. A furnace of ambivalence. He channeled the energy into his legs and began walking again. He wanted to close the gap between himself and that drink. The sooner the better.

"After the discovery of the Ugaritic texts, the idea that Israelite beliefs came from foreign civilizations in Mesopotamia was abandoned. The tablets showed that people living there in Canaan during biblical days were quite literate. It was an important revolution in thinking since the oldest manuscript evidence for the Hebrew Bible at the time dated to roughly 1000 A.D."

David came up beside him. "A.D.? As in after the New Testament? Arthur, that doesn't make any sense."

"It may surprise you to know that most of our ancient texts are copies of even older texts. Parchment and papyrus simply don't last very long at all. A handful of centuries at best. Well-crafted and preserved tablets last for millennia. Even the recently-famous Dead Sea scroll jars contained only badly decaying organic materials from the third century B.C. They've been slowly piecing them back together like a giant jigsaw puzzle for decades. The much older *Ketef Hinnom* scrolls are made of silver, so they survived well. Once we figured out how to unroll them, that is. The oldest things we have are the oddest things it turns out. Clay does pretty well, all things considered." He was rambling. To his surprise, David was listening to every word.

"Wait." Excitement leaked into the boy's voice as he figured it out. "You think this tablet rubbing might be a Rosetta Stone for Linear-A? You think that Mr. Aarons has found a way to translate Uncle Sir Arthur's untranslatable language." It wasn't a question, it was another accusation. "No wonder you think Mr. Aarons' discovery is so important. Imagine what else his translation tablet might unlock. Like maybe there's an untranslated Old Testament in Linear-A archived in Uncle Sir Arthur's cabinet somewhere and we don't even know it?"

The very thought made Evans prickle with the possibilities before he forced it all away. But it was too little, too late. David saw it, and the boy's face flooded with surprise, then worse, blasted *compassion*. With a sly smile, his grandson stepped forward, dropping his voice to a whisper.

"Arthur, you wanted to take that job." Still not a question, but the accusing tone was gone. "Only, you're worried that you'll end up like Uncle Sir Arthur, or worse, like Mr. Aarons. Because you don't want to jump out there on nothing but faith and a few sketchy clues."

Evans didn't answer. Partly because no question had been asked of him, but mostly because yet again, he knew the boy was indisputably right.

XXIV

"Arthur, stop," David called.

Arthur didn't stop.

"Do you honestly think this tablet rubbing might be the key to translating Linear-A?" David jogged into step behind the insufferable old man. His legs were already aching from all of the walking they had done today, but Arthur was still outstepping him two to one. "So, how's that possible? You said they were like a thousand miles away from each other before when I said basically the same thing! Wouldn't somebody have found other evidence before now? You said Sir Arthur found over three thousand tablets."

"Yes, I am aware. But I also said that the East coast of the Mediterranean—modern Syria—was the center of the world. And Ugarit is a lot closer to Crete than most of those other places." Arthur was keeping his voice low. "Besides, even the Rosetta Stone was found on a stroke of luck. Though probably erected in some Egyptian temple originally, it is assumed to have been moved during the early Christian or medieval periods. It was in point of fact used as building material in the construction of Fort Julien, near the town of Rosetta in the Nile Delta. That is where it was rediscovered in 1799 by a Napoleonic soldier, and also where it gets its name. It was a fluke that unlocked ancient Egyptian for us, David."

"Really? I didn't know that." The passage narrowed, but not so much that they couldn't walk abreast.

"Yes, well, if that Linear-A tablet truly did come out of where Wyatt claims he found it, then not only was he right, but Sir Arthur was right too."

"I don't follow, Arthur. Right about what?"

"Sir Arthur always believed that the ancient myths were true. Wyatt did too, or rather, the biblical ones. If this tablet is real, and if we can find the other half Wyatt says that he found but never made a rubbing of, and if it does coincide with the above text as a translation in Linear-A, then it means nearly everything we know, or think we know, about the ancient-world origins of ancient languages and writing could be wrong."

"That's a lot of 'ifs' and a big fat 'maybe,' Arthur. Why do you even say that?"

"Simple. If it is all true, then we might be looking at a missing link between what are thought to be two completely discordant language family groups. If that's the case, then even Wyatt Aarons' theories that all the ancient languages stem from the same source just might be true too."

"Wait, are you talking about the Tower of Babel? Where all the languages split when they were building a tower to God?"

Arthur soured. "That's what Wyatt believes, yes. But scholars today call this theoretical original language, for which there is some evidence, 'Proto-Indo-European,' because they don't yet know when or how it split. Regardless, even though there are other languages in the world that share no linguistic commonalities with Proto-Indo-European and could not have branched from it, Wyatt firmly believed we'd eventually find proof of a common single origin for all languages. He called it 'the language of Adam and Noah,' a sort of Proto-Semitic in his view, which is of course ridiculous. But more importantly, he was also convinced that the popular oral tradition theory of *Genesis* was wrong."

"The what?"

"The idea that stories were passed from Adam to Moses across fourteen or so key generational storytellers. Wyatt has always believed that this must have also been accompanied by a written language. He had me scour the ancient texts for anything with a connection to the biblical flood myth. I even looked into the stranger traditions like the Jewish Kabballah and Apocryphal books, even though all those originate far too recently to offer any real bearing on the question. I wrote out summary translations of it all for him. As I said, it's what he took me to Doomsday Mountain for in the first place. To find and decode something, anything, written by Noah or his sons. He was obsessed with it."

"Wow, I didn't know that was a thing." David knew that something called Kabbalah existed in Jewish tradition, but he didn't have a clue what it was. He had a vague recollection of hearing about there being certain non-biblical Jewish spells and golem magic, but if he was honest, David knew way more about fictional D&D spells and the rules for summoning one of its four elemental golems than he did about any kind of historical Jewish mysticism.

"Certainly it is. After all, it ultimately comes down to this. If you believe *Genesis* is literally true, then logically you must either believe the earliest Bible stories were passed down from generation to generation from eyewitnesses, or else *Genesis* was dictated by God to Moses or one of his contemporaries."

"I've never really thought about it that way, but I've always believed that the Bible was written by God." He paused, uncertainty creeping in. "Co-written? You know, whatever it's called?"

"Of course you do, David," Arthur said bluntly. "Because that's exactly what Joseph and Karen taught you to believe." David opened his mouth to argue, but Arthur softened. "Listen, none of the early stories in *Genesis* are set in Israel. They are all Mesopotamian. Every one of them, from Adam to Abraham. Even Job. All of them must be considered through the lens of Hebrew adaptation. The Ugaritic and Akkadian stories are the same in many ways. But when we look at all three side by side, it triangulates the myths because they are all Semitic. Noah was Mesopotamian. Abram was. Moses too. *Genesis* is simply not the modern-style history textbook that many modern Americans seem to think it is. It's a near certainty that those stories are far older than can be accounted for by a mere fourteen generations."

David considered this for a moment. He hadn't ever thought about *Genesis* that way either. "Like how everything we know about the people of Crete came through the unflattering lens of Greek propaganda?"

Arthur brightened. "Yes. Good connection."

"But Arthur, if you think that Mr. Aarons has discovered something important, then why didn't you take that job offer? It sounds like a big opportunity."

Arthur stopped and stared at David with uncomfortable intensity. He sucked his teeth for a moment then sighed. "Because David, I promised Karen I'd look after you, and I've been doing a rotten job of it. You are in the greatest city in the world, about to begin the greatest days of your life. I wouldn't dare steal that chance from you."

David believed him. It was the first crack of warmth he had seen in his grandfather's stoic façade. Without warning, he felt flooded with love for the old man.

"Besides," Arthur huffed, looking away. "Archeology is never about treasure hunts, it's about knowledge. And the greatest center of knowledge in the world is right here."

It was an ironic choice of words because as David looked around in wonder, he could no longer see the tall spires and ancient walls of the colleges. The twisty passage was walled in on both sides by simple gray stones and paved with cobblestones down the center. The place was eerily cut off from all connecting roads because of an illusion with the s-curve bend. David could neither see the path behind them nor the path ahead for more than a dozen steps either way. Even the trees from beyond the wall covered the walkway like a tunnel. And where the sky did peek through, it was only the swirling clouds of overcast Oxfordshire. A little tile sign cemented into the wall identified the place as the Lamb and Flag Passage.

"Wow, it's like we are going out of the world and into Narnia or something," His voice echoed in both directions. "When I was a kid, I read every word of *The Chronicles of Narnia* a dozen times. They were my favorite. Mom first read them to me before bed when I was little. A chapter each night by the fireplace. I always begged for more."

"Funny you should mention Narnia, David. Did you ever hear of a writer's group called the Inklings?"

David shook his head, his curiosity sparked.

"*Narnia*'s author, C. S. Lewis, was a member. Just ahead are the two pubs where the Inklings met up most often. The Lamb and Flag, just ahead. And beyond it, the Bird and Baby, which is precisely where we are going."

"No way!"

Arthur chuckled. "Welcome to Oxford."

The spell was broken by the footfalls of a well-dressed olive-skinned man coming along the path behind them, followed closely by a laughing couple chattering in German. The man adjusted his expensive suitcoat and quickly passed them by, focused intensely on a glowing flip phone. The couple stopped for a long moment to stare at a tourist's map the woman held, then erupted in laughter anew before turning back the way they'd come.

"Let's get moving, David," Arthur said. "We're almost there. It's Saturday, so the pubs will be standing-room-only soon. The sun sets quite late here in the summer, but the real weirdos will be out and about before we know it."

XXV

St. Giles Street. Oxford, England. Mr. Suit.

The man in the expensive suit hurried out of the narrow pedestrian passage. He had nearly had them, but Saturday night in Oxford was a crowded mess. Fortune had smiled on him twice now: First when he eavesdropped on the company's offer of employment to Dr. Evans, and then again as he passed them in the passage.

Regarding the former, Dr. Evans had turned the company's offer down. Clearly, fortune and glory meant nothing to the old man. That detail was interesting, and it made his job much easier. As for the latter, Dr. Evans and the boy were headed to a pub. Where better to pick a man's pocket? He knew of no pub named 'Bird and Baby' in Oxford, but it had to be close. Pubs were everywhere in this city: One never had to walk far to find one. He glanced at the sign over the door to the Lamb and Flag before walking past. He knew the place well.

The man in the suit scanned both sides of the busy St. Giles thoroughfare. The namesake chapel to the north bisected and forked the road. To the south, he could just see the Martyrs' Memorial sticking out of the ground like a church steeple splitting the other end. Countless shops and entryways lined both sides of the road, with more than a few pubs as candidates. The hustle and bustle of an early summer Saturday evening in Oxford was already in full swing.

It would be only seconds before Dr. Evans and the teenager emerged from the passage. If the old man hadn't just recognized him as the solicitor who came to his door earlier that day, he likely would put it together the moment he realized he was being followed. No, the best chance was to beat them to this pub they had mentioned and have a "coincidental" meeting. That meant staying ahead of them. But where? He didn't know this 'Bird and Baby.' That in itself was strange.

His mind was whirling. He was having trouble staying focused. Only minutes before, a text had come through from the foolish woman he worked for:

Employment terminated

It was fine. He was done playing her silly little spy games. The corporate fantasy had been nice, but he answered to a higher order anyway. If his so-called "boss" couldn't recognize his talents and have patience enough to let him finish the job his way, then he would be done with them. He was done with them. With her.

The eastern company had bought his western lie. He wore new identities at his leisure like he wore his tailored Italian suit. This corporate woman wanted to take back his motorcycle, his phone, and his steady paycheck? Fine. He could do without these luxuries. But he was keeping the suit. He'd earned it. Besides, now that he knew a woman was in charge, he was glad to be done with her and her ridiculous company.

His personal phone buzzed in his pocket. He swore. Picking a direction at random, he hustled away from the Lamb and Flag Passage exit.

"Speak," he spat, mashing the green button.

"The company fired you, huh?" The voice said. "You have a problem."

"Yes. But I'm working on an alternative solution." Even as he said it, he saw the tutor and the boy emerge from the passage and turn right towards the northern crosswalk. He had guessed wrong and was now behind them.

"They will be coming for that journal some other way, you realize?"

"I'll have the book within the hour," he told the caller, "but there are other factors. Dr. Evans just turned down an offer from the company. A very generous one, I would guess."

"Really? Well, that complicates things, but I'm not surprised." His mentor's voice was laced with amusement. "Well, the rest of the plan is working, and your ex-boss is playing right into it. Either way, I need him. I'm moving forward on my end, so get it done. Don't worry about collateral. Stop thinking about the company or anyone else. Just get Evans on that plane. Forget subtlety. This is much bigger than you and your coursework."

"I understand. It's not as if I can take the degree anyway."

"No, I'd think not," the man on the line chided. "Now, don't screw this up. If you do, more people are going to die. Don't forget where your real loyalties lie, boy."

Things were getting messy again. He needed a clean solution that would work to his advantage. One that wouldn't betray his true loyalties or tip his hand to anyone else. A solution that likely didn't exist.

Remember who you are. Remember what you really are.

"I remember," he growled into the phone.

As the man in the suit hung up, he noticed a trio of smarmy-looking guys walking toward him. They were taking up the whole sidewalk and closing fast. He stepped aside, but not before one of them danced sideways and bumped into him with a jutting elbow. The punk's phone flew from his hand and skidded across the concrete into the gutter. A newer model, mostly glass.

"Hey, my phone!" He exclaimed, throwing his hands in the air.

Another swooped and picked it up in one smooth motion. "Oy! It's broken mate." The glass screen was visibly cracked and very badly damaged. More so than one quick fall ever could have inflicted. "You'll have to pay him for that."

The man in the suit sneered. He knew this scam. There was a time when he might have tried such a con himself. The unwitting tourist or businessman accidentally "knocks" the expensive-seeming but already-broken phone to the ground. He feels guilty. He forks over some of the cash that travelers almost always carry, and if he is lucky, he is only out a few hundred bucks, having bought off his guilty feelings. If the mark isn't so lucky, well, the group might just relieve him of the rest of his cash a few minutes later. Especially if said traveler happened to bumble into an alley without witnesses.

"Work another street," he spat, turning away from the small-time thieves.

"Hey! You can't just walk away after breaking my phone." The other two were all nods and affirmations. The whole thing was badly rehearsed.

The man in the suit turned back smoothly and stared the street thug straight in his pock-marked face. He lifted his lapel lightly, revealing the gun underneath. The scammer instantly deflated. His companions fell silent too. "I assure you," the man hissed, "I can." The little street gang stumbled over themselves, backing away with blustering profanity and insult.

The man shrugged his coat back into position. He had no time for pathetic amateurs, but they had given him an idea. He whirled and scanned the road for Evans and the boy, relieved to see that they had not noticed the little disturbance behind them. They were crossing the median past the little church's cemetery. But if they were crossing, then that meant the Bird and Baby must be somewhere on the other side. Perhaps down one of the connecting side streets?

The man in the suit breathed deeply, centering himself. Too many times today he had needed to refocus. This would be the last time. He was already formulating a new plan, one that just might work to his advantage in all regards after all. It was tricky and dangerous, but even the company woman wouldn't be able to complain about this one if it worked. Not that that mattered.

Remember who you are. Remember what you are.

The man in the suit was already darting across the middle of the busy street when he saw it.

'Bird and Baby' indeed!

Dr. Evans was clever, but it was time to end this childish nonsense.

XXVI

St. Giles Street. Oxford, England. David.

David and Arthur exited the Lamb and Flag Passage through an archway so tiny that David would never have found it, coming from this side of it. Slipping past a pub of the same name, David now found himself on the sidewalk of a busy, rush-hour-fueled street that seemed way too modern to be in Oxford. They came to a series of crosswalks that made no sense, even for backwards England.

The little cars, trucks, and countless motorcycles weren't going slower due to the proverbial rush hour, but faster. The street crossed over itself here, splitting and converting into one-way roads while also funneling the speeding cars into three directions at once. All without so much as a street sign. It was split by no less than three medians at the widest part, and somehow parking was a part of this. Try as he might, David just couldn't sort it out in his head.

"You need to look right when you cross the street David," Arthur said helpfully. "The cars won't hesitate to run you down. The English aren't as polite when they get on the road, I think you'll find."

David nervously looked both ways twice anyway, before stepping out after Arthur. "These cars are so small though, I'm not even sure it would hurt." The quip fell flat on Arthur.

The sidewalk curved around an old church graveyard. It looked ancient, somewhere where spirits might haunt on certain nights of the year or zombies rise on a foggy evening. Beyond the low stone wall were two thick trees and a dozen lichen-covered graves. But the real oddity was an indeterminably old pattern of sunken stones, peeking through the churchyard's grass. It looked like the foundation of some long-abandoned medieval maze. With a start, David realized that that's exactly what it was. Oxford was so insane.

David's entire day had been a confusing maze, thanks to Arthur. David wasn't exactly mad at his grandfather anymore, but he hadn't fully forgiven him just yet either. He truly had learned more in one day than he could have imagined learning in a whole summer of Saturdays, but he still felt tricked slightly. Arthur seemed to be able to put him under a spell over and over again. The man was infuriating, stubborn, closed-off, and entirely too difficult to communicate with. But there was something about the guy that David just couldn't turn away from.

His wizardly grandfather was—well, *cool*. And completely weird. Even now, Arthur was still rambling on about birds and babies. He was a brilliant teacher and simultaneously bonkers.

"So these Inkling guys wrote their stuff in this pub then?" David offered, hoping to reenter the conversation.

"Well, no. Not as such. But the Bird and Baby lays claim to several interesting literary connections. It was always one of my favorites as a student."

David wasn't sure Arthur was going to finish the thought, so he encouraged him. "What kind of connections?"

The old man looked over at him as though he had only just realized David was there. "Oh, well, for starters, the authors J.R.R. Tolkien and C.S. Lewis were probably the most illustrious members of the club. They and fellow writer-friends met up weekly for their legendary discussions and readings of each other's work."

"The Inklings were a writing club. Right, you said that."

"Well, more of a reading and drinking club really. It's just that what they read was their own work, mostly. The story goes that Lewis read from the pages of *Narnia* while Tolkien read from his stories of Middle-Earth, but that's the real fantasy. The dates simply don't match up. They'd had a falling out by the time Jack got around to writing about his magic Jesus-Lion."

"Jack?" David decided to ignore the lion in the room. Er, road.

"A nickname. Lots of those to be had in Oxford. Rad-cam. Bridge of Sighs. The Inklings called Lewis 'Jack' and Tolkien 'Tollers', and the pub itself they nicknamed 'the Bird and Baby', a moniker that comes from the coat of arms hanging over the door, and a pun on the pub's real name, you see?"

"Its real name? But Arthur, Bird and Baby is what you've been calling it."

"What? Oh, quite right. I suppose I have." The old man chuckled. "There it is right there. See?"

David looked to where Arthur pointed. A three-story yellow Elizabethan façade proudly boasted a massive coat-of-arms depicting an eagle dangling a baby from a cloth in its talons, much like the proverbial stork. Under it was the actual name of the pub: Eagle and Child. The image instantly reminded David of a certain giant eagle who aided the escape of two Hobbits in the final scenes of the most recent Peter Jackson film. He mentioned this to Arthur.

"Is the sign where Mr. Tolkien got the idea?"

"Interesting theory," Arthur said. "Of course, the original sign from Tolkien and Lewis's time now sits over at The Kilns, Lewis' restored home. But the image is similar enough. I suppose we must add it to the list of literary mysteries that will likely never be solved. At least until some unknown letter to one of Tolkien's friends or editors turns up and declares his inspiration."

"Does that ever happen?"

"More often than you might think. Frankly though, while I do find the Inklings quite fascinating, the reality is that I frequent the Bird and Baby most often because it triangulates perfectly with the Ashmolean and my flat. With all due respect to Tolkien and his work with languages, I much prefer the proper ancient epics to the modern ones."

"Oh I don't know, the movies are pretty great."

Arthur snorted. "I wouldn't base my theories on anything you see in silly film adaptations."

"Well, maybe you'd like the extended edition?" David's gaming group had marathoned the long-form version of the Jackson trilogy more than once. It was a twelve-hour commitment, well worth it in his opinion.

"You do realize, David, that the real 'extended edition' of *The Lord of the Rings* runs some twelve hundred pages, including appendices and maps?"

Evans was deadpan serious. David was holding back a laugh.

He matched his grandfather's tone. "Very good Arthur. I solemnly swear to read it again soon."

"Therein lies the true danger of any translation or adaptation, you know," Arthur mused. "The original meaning is often lost or obscured, changed and warped for the new audience or reader's bias. Besides, I'd far sooner trust to the wisdom found in the pages of a book than some Hollywood mogul's version on a videotape."

David lost it. "'Videotape'? Arthur, when was the last time you actually saw a movie?"

Arthur considered this but didn't have a chance to answer. Cars were honking. Some businessman ran across the northbound half of the street from the median and very nearly got himself taken out by a little black taxi and a motorcycle in quick succession.

"Good way to die there, David. What did I just say about looking left?"

"Actually nothing," David mumbled under his breath. He walked in step behind Arthur the rest of the way, still trying to figure out the logistics of crossing the street in a place that's backwards but forked into one-way streets, and where the rush-hour traffic actually rushed.

Out of nowhere, the same swarthy businessman who had bolted across the road popped out of the doorway, grabbed Arthur's arm, swung him into the shadows against the pub wall, and pulled out a gun—all in one swift motion. Arthur stood stupidly with his hands raised at shoulder-level in complete shock. His hat had come away and his hair was doing the mad scientist thing again. In stark contrast, the gunman's meticulous hair and beard communicated his severity of intent before he even spoke. But there was a smirk there too, dripping with derision. He was enjoying this.

"I don't have much money," Arthur stammered. "But whatever cash I have is yours."

The man laughed. "I'm not mugging you, Dr. Evans." His honeyed words came in lightly accented British English. "But you will give me the book now."

David bristled. How did this man know Arthur?

"What book?" Arthur wondered aloud. Then he straightened. "I know you. You were at my home and in the passage. You've been following us."

At that, the man smiled impishly and stuck the gun out sideways toward David. A woman passing by gasped and ducked into the building. Another passerby recoiled as if he'd seen a snake.

"You have three seconds, sir," the gunman growled.

Without breaking his gaze at the other man, Arthur reached into his suitcoat, clearly expecting the journal to be there, but his pocket was empty.

David knew why. Mr. Aarons' journal was still in his pocket. He'd never given it back after looking at it in the alleyway. It was his one chance.

The man in the suit's eyes flicked down to Arthur's hand with a smug smile and he opened his mouth to speak, but in that moment of diverted attention, David acted. Like lightning, he dove forward, grabbed the gunman's arm, and wrenched it toward the sky. The pistol went off like a thunderclap. Confused and frightened pedestrians screamed and hit the ground out of pure reflex in both directions.

The gunman yanked the pistol higher and away, but David went for the low blow. He brought his knee up hard into the attacker's groin and watched the man crumple to his knees, then collapse against the pub wall clutching his manhood. A low squeal barely escaped his clenched teeth, but the gun clattered away and bounced into the street.

David stood in triumph, not sure what came next. He crouched down casually and picked up Arthur's hat for him. His heart was still beating out of his chest. Arthur hadn't moved, but his lips were moving, even though no sound came out.

"Wha—?" David stammered. His ears were ringing too.

"I said run, David!" His wizard pantomimed loudly at him.

David blinked at Arthur uncomprehendingly, then glanced at the fallen man, the pub, and finally back to his grandfather. Then, finally understanding, David turned on his sneaker's heel and did as he'd been told. In a flash, he took off down the street.

To his surprise, Arthur was keeping pace right beside him.

XXVII

St. Giles Street. Oxford, England. Arthur.

Evans could feel the adrenaline coursing through his veins, competing with the six and a half decades of life he had managed to survive on this rock. If not for his regular habit of biking and walking, he doubted he would have been able to catch up to the teenager regardless of how much pizza and video games the teen might himself be struggling against. Even so, the sprint was a challenge.

"Arthur, who was that guy?" David shouted. He already sounded out of breath. Evans wondered how long they could keep this pace up. Not long he'd guess. They had run south on St. Giles right to where it narrowed and became Magdalene Street. They were just now coming up onto the entrance to the Ashmolean where they had spent their afternoon.

"I never saw him before today!" Evans shouted back.

"Arthur, he knew your name!"

"He came to the flat this morning with a bad sales pitch. He passed us by in the Lamb and Flag Passage a few minutes ago too. He's been following us." Hearing it again made it sound no saner.

Evans considered veering right to the museum and safety. It wouldn't be the first time he'd pestered the after-hours guard to let him in for private access to his office. But it also meant they might have to wait in the courtyard for a few minutes. And that would be the antithesis of the safe destination he desired. No, they needed to be where people were, as horrible as that sounded. Saturday night crowds in Oxford? That wouldn't be a problem.

Evans darted around a fancy red motorcycle someone had left parked in front of the Museum and ran on. They rushed past St. Mary Magdalen's medieval cemetery where innumerable bicycles were perpetually chained to the fence.

Evans' sides started to burn. He longed for his own forsaken bicycle chained up at Mansfield, congratulating himself on his habit of keeping a regular fitness routine. Evans took himself mentally to that place he went when he needed to push through pain in the name of health. It was an ironic discipline he'd never quite mastered, and it didn't work now either. Evans had always much preferred a nice bracing walk or lazy ride in the countryside, to doing laps at the 8-lane Rosenblatt pool or sprinting or, god forbid, a marathon. He tended to stay away from anything that was too grueling. A frenzied run from a mad gunman down the center of town, for example.

Oh, but the gun!

"David, did you grab that gun?" he gasped.

"Uh, no!" David shouted back and thrust out his hand anyway. At the end of it was Evans' favorite hat. "You said to run. Besides, it's illegal to carry guns in England, isn't it?"

The absurdity of this struck Evans. Just like a Texas youth to know the obscure gun-carry laws of a foreign country, but not know which way to look when crossing the street. "There are times David," he gulped, "when one should probably make exceptions to such rules. Perhaps this is one of them?" He snatched the fedora and crammed it onto his head.

"Yea, I'll try to remember that for next time, Arthur," the boy shot back, sarcasm not withheld. "Till then, where exactly are we going?"

The truth was, Evans had no idea where to go. The summer sun wouldn't set for another few hours or so at least. Cover of darkness was not an option. People were everywhere, but they needed a real tourist hub to get lost in. He surveyed locations on the map in his head, ruling them out one by one. If they kept going south, they would end up on Cornmarket Street. That eventually led to either Queen Street or the junction where the A420 to Bristol dumped the busses full of tourists into High Street. But Evans doubted he could make it that distance without collapsing onto the road.

The internet-loving teenager had also dropped to a steady jog. There was simply no way they could keep it up, they needed to stop. Perhaps he could make it one more block to Market Street? If they headed for the crowds of tourists inevitably milling about the historic covered market, they would be able to shortcut through it. The underground maze of meat and produce stalls was perfect. They need only get past the food and specialty shops and exit directly onto High Street, or maybe even cut through Golden Cross and back out to Cornmarket to lose their pursuer. Assuming they were still being pursued at all?

As if in reply, Evans heard the whine of a high-end motorcycle tearing towards them down Magdalene.

"It's him!" David shouted, glancing backwards.

Had the man stolen a motorbike? They could never make it to Market Street now. Evans didn't have the breath to waste on a reply. Instead, he darted left through a crowd that was just starting across Magdalene. He flew past Boswells department store in a flash, and with renewed urgency headed east down the south side of the always-crowded Broad. Only foot traffic was allowed there. It could work.

To his horror, the motorcycle careened through the crosswalk behind him, sending screaming pedestrians diving for the sidewalk. The rider banked a tight left, nearly colliding with a parked Tesco truck before threading the three-foot vertical traffic barriers. The Evanses were out of time. Ahead of them was more than just the crowd of tourists Evans had hoped would be there. He had forgotten about the street fair on the other end of the Broad. It meant that the usual crowds were magnified, and dozens of opportunities to dodge behind a stall had just presented themselves! If they could make it to them, they might be able to lose this madman.

A loud pop and a crash made Evans duck reflexively as a bullet shattered a store window behind him. His hopes suddenly turned to fear. This crazy gunman was shooting into a crowd of three hundred people? Who was he? The shield Evans had hoped to find in the crowd was suddenly an unacceptable option. If this psychopath injured or killed some innocent bystander, he'd never forgive himself. Evans couldn't help but steal a glance over his shoulder. People were dodging out of the way of the motorcyclist left and right, but he still had to stop and start every few feet, waving at the confused and frightened crowd with his gun until the herd parted. For every yard the gunman progressed, more curious onlookers wandered haphazardly into his path.

Unfathomably, many in the crowd seemed to believe this was some kind of performance show related to the festival, lifting their children onto their shoulders to watch the stunt. Others were taking pictures with their phones. The good news was that the gunman hadn't pulled the trigger on the crowd. If the window had been a warning shot, maybe there was a chance for them to slip away after all? Evans felt pulled in ten directions at once. He had to act, and it had to be now.

He tapped a store of energy he hadn't believed he had and dashed towards the edge of the crowd. He ducked behind the first row of arts and crafts booths. His loafers were biting blisters into his toes and heel and his brown sport coat flapped back and forth against his elbows. His hat tried to leave him, but he slammed it back onto his head and charged forward nonetheless. It was the second time today he'd found himself running through the streets of his city. It was an unsettling trend.

With the massive stonework façades of Balliol and Trinity Colleges hemming the north side of the street and nothing but tiny row shops to the south, there was not so much as an alleyway for them to duck into. He had found his crowds, but now Evans and David were no better than cattle trapped in a box canyon. The sidewalks were a mere philosophic construct at this point.

Everywhere Evans looked were stalls full of crafts and a great swirling sea made up of people's heads and bodies and arms. There were shops, but ducking into one of them would be suicide since most didn't have back doors. And those that did, opened into all manner of closed courtyards or twisting private back alleys that often led nowhere at all. Evans didn't know most of those private passages, and even if they did manage not to get turned around, they could still most certainly be cornered and shot.

Evans realized he was thinking in circles. They couldn't outrun the motorcyclist in the open, nor could they leave the safety of crowds. His head throbbed with exertion and he felt tingly and dizzy all over. He was going to pass out. He needed a compromise. An indoor crowd that wasn't alive. A forest maybe? A hedge maze perhaps? This was nonsense of course. Such things did not exist in downtown Oxford. Then he saw exactly all of that at once.

Spotting a small break in the crowd, Evans darted across to the north side of the street. He pushed past some startled pedestrians, forced himself toward his targeted storefront, and stumbled blindly through the unassuming blue double doors of No. 50 Broad Street.

"This way, David!" he called back without stopping.

Someone behind the counter called out that the store was closing in a few minutes. Evans only hoped they had that long. He bounded down the stairs leading to the basement and flung himself around the bend. An innumerable number of bookshelves stretched out below him. He had lost himself among them countless times, although never to hide from a gunman.

"We did it!" Evans rasped. His breaths were jagged and coarse and quickly degraded into a fit of coughing that caused him to collapse into a padded reading chair.

When he finally recovered his breath a little, Evans glanced around to get his bearings. He was in the little alcove between the historical maps and the classics section, only one among the many others in the bookstore's cavernous basement. Evans had found his indoor crowd, forest, and maze all in one. And while he treasured books, he would also not lament one taking a bullet if an innocent stranger were spared instead. Or himself for that matter. That part of his impromptu plan had been a success. What he had utterly failed to notice was that David was not down here with him. In fact, he realized with a shock, he had no idea at what point he had seen the boy last.

XXVIII

Blackwell's Bookstore. Oxford, England. Arthur.

In 1966, Blackwell's Bookstore opened the ten thousand square foot Norrington Room, named for a former president of Trinity College. This was appropriate, as the room extended under the College's quad, and had once been a part of it. Evans had often quoted the statistic that the subterranean room boasted five kilometers of shelving, contained over 160,000 books, and had long since merited an entry in the *Guinness Book of Records* as the largest single room for selling books in the world. Now, for the first time, it seemed entirely too big and entirely too full of bookshelves.

"David?" Evans croaked, as loudly as he dared. He was forced to clear his throat and cough into his hand a few times before trying again. A handful of shushing floated over the shelves to him from the few remaining bibliophiles and last-minute shoppers, but he ignored them. Having already drawn attention to himself, he risked a louder cry. "David! Where are you?" There was no response. "Devil take it," he added.

Had they been separated by his haste? Had the crowds somehow split them? Or could the unthinkable have happened, and perhaps the gunman had hit his mark after all? Evans felt the bile rise in his throat at this. He forced himself to stagger from the chair. He had to find the boy, and fast. But instead, a wave of dizzy nausea came over him and the room dipped.

"Apologies sir, but we are closing now." The voice of a young woman the next aisle over caused Evans to turn his ear, but it was the reply that turned his blood cold.

"Yes. Thank you very much." The Middle Eastern man's tone was sweetly venomous.

The woman moved on, but Evans was about to be found out. He darted away from the voice towards a short aisle perpendicular to his, a T-junction between the classics and another section beyond. Evans hoped the maneuver would allow him to creep away, but it was too late. The suited gunman had a light sheen of sweat on his face but was otherwise unfazed by the chase.

Evans knew he had nothing left to draw on. He needed a nap, a pint, and a do-over on the whole day and he wasn't going to get any of it. He lunged for the only thing he could reach, an end aisle display. Promotional signs and a sculpted copper bust of the author accented a half dozen thick brown hardcovers. He sloppily threw one heavy volume at the man, who effortlessly sidestepped it. Evans threw another, and another until the man's gun was in his face again.

"The journal," The man growled. "Now."

The gun was a matte gray Evans noted. Gunmetal gray, he supposed. Nearly the same color as the man's suit. His nails were expertly manicured, and on his wrist, some sort of tattoo peeked out from the tailored sleeve. It was an odd juxtaposition with the suit, but he never had understood young people's strange affinity towards body art.

Evans was about to die, and his mind was wandering.

"I—I don't have it." It was the truth. David must have held on to the journal, he suddenly realized. Seriously, what was it supposed to be? Some kind of bird? A chicken perhaps? Tattoos were such silly vanities. Evans simply didn't understand the point of them.

His overdressed pursuer swept most of the remaining books from the end display onto the floor with a cascade of thumps and thuds. The man's face was the picture of cold rage. "The journal!"

"I swear to you, I don't have it!" Evans was yelling now too. He tried backing away from the man down the short aisle. He was trapped by too many books. Well, if he had to die somewhere, at least it would be among friends.

The gun fired. Someone screamed and there was a great shuffle. In the underground hollow of the vast bookstore basement, even that substantial number of bookshelves was not enough to dampen the echo of the shot. Again, Evans' ears rang, and he staggered and tripped backward, half-sitting half-falling onto his hands and rear. He opened his eyes and checked himself for holes or blood, but there was neither. The man in the suit had either fired a warning shot or was a phenomenally terrible aim.

The gunman zeroed the weapon in again, closing the distance with only one step. "I can't give you what I don't have," Evans pleaded, scooting backward on hands and rear away from the weapon. His voice sounded like a shout from the far side of a lake. "I gave it away!"

It instantly occurred to him as he said this that perhaps he was endangering David with these words. But it also dawned on him that if the man had overtaken the teen, then he would have found the journal and broken off the hunt. *David must still be okay!*

"That is, er, I hid it!" he lied, somewhat unconvincingly. "And good luck to you ever finding it!"

Evans bumped back against the perpendicular shelf on this side. The short aisle ended in another T-Junction. What was wrong with parallel rows anyway? Libraries did just fine with them. Did the store think that if the customer got lost in a maze, they would be inclined to buy more books? Come to think of it, that had worked on him. But then, getting lost was exactly what he needed right now. And nowadays he knew this literary maze as well as anyone. Without thinking, Evans rolled sideways, scrambled to his feet, and doubled back along the parallel short-aisle towards the wrecked end display where he had started. It was madness and a terrible strategy, but it was all he had at this point.

It took only a second to reach the pile of fallen books and round them. Evans stopped short. To his surprise, the man in the suit had barely moved at all. The gunman was three short steps away with his back turned and creeping toward where Evans had been, listening for clues to his prey's movements. Improbably, Evans had the jump on him. It was a long shot, even crazier than his first plan, but he took it.

The scholar snatched the copper sculpture from the wrecked display and lifted it over his head. It was lighter than he expected and nearly flew up and out of his hands. At the sound, the gunman whirled, but before he could react, Evans charged forward and brought the bust down on the attacker's head. With a sickening crack, it caved in, a cheap plaster imitation sprayed with metallic paint. It was enough though. The gunman crumpled to the thin carpet, his olive face buried in what remained of the hollow head. The fine suit was covered in plaster dust, and his arms and legs splayed out in all manner of undignified directions.

Evans spotted his hat and quickly moved to retrieve it. As he reached out, his eyes fell on the bullet hole in the cover of a lone volume of a gilded 50th-anniversary re-release of *The Lord of the Rings*.

"Well, cheers and good day to you, Tollers," Evans gulped, tipping his hat to his late colleague.

Turning back to the matter at hand, he saw that the man in the suit was still out cold. Evans needed to know more about this intruder. He took a chance and quickly searched his assailant's pockets for a wallet or some kind of ID. There were two cell phones, nothing more. *Who needs two cell phones?* He tossed the infernal technology aside, then as an afterthought pulled the handkerchief from his coat pocket and shakily wiggled the gun from the man's hand. He stepped in no way lightly on the gunman's wrist as he did so, at about the place where he had that strange chicken tattoo.

Ah, but the tattoo was of a blackbird. That was slightly better. The foreshortening from the business end of a gun had only made it look squat and wide. Most logical. Yes, that's what he needed now, rationality. With that little mystery solved, he slipped the pistol into his coat pocket and scanned the room. The clerk who had been there a few minutes ago had made herself scarce. He needed to summon the police before the tattooed burglar awoke. Perhaps they were even on their way, given all that chaos on the street above.

Burglar? An odd word choice. Why had he thought that?

An old memory bubbled to the surface. Evans snapped his attention back to the tattoo. He had seen a tattoo like that before. He reached up and touched his eye, the pain of a right hook coming back to him as freshly as the day he'd failed to dodge it. A quarter century of forgetting finally being pried away by these long minutes of adrenaline-fueled panic.

That was no blackbird tattoo. It was a black *bird tattoo*. A raven. Arthur's blood ran cold, the weight of the gun in his pocket tugging his coat askew. Again, Wyatt's words came to him:

> *I had proof... but I'm being watched and hunted now...*
> *"As it was in the days of Noah," eh?*
> *It's time for us to be vindicated for Doomsday.*

With a start, Evans suddenly understood Wyatt's meaning. He'd "had proof," something good enough for the raven-tattooed men to take notice even after all these years, just like in their time at Doomsday Mountain. In their shared "days of Noah."

The truth whirled around him with nauseating vertigo. Thirty-odd years ago, Evans had been successfully frightened away while Wyatt blundered on. And now Wyatt wanted them to finish what they had started—except he was missing now, in hiding, captured, or maybe even dead. But Wyatt believed he had real proof this time. Some Linear-A translation tablet that would unlock that mysterious alphabet and somehow prove Evans' original theories about the Mesopotamian flood myths, Nûḥ, *Atra-Hasis*, and *Gilgamesh*'s Dilmun. Could it really be that after a lifetime of searching, Wyatt Aarons had finally managed to succeed at something of real historical merit? It would be an earth-shattering find, no matter what.

It should have exhilarated the ancient language expert. *Real vindication, after all this time?* If Mel Chen had it her way, it could mean a full resurrection of his career, and everything he and Elizabeth had ever dreamed of. But instead, all Evans could focus on was that raven tattoo peeking out at him from a gray suitcoat sleeve.

That tattoo changed everything. The police would be no help at all. After three decades of hiding from the past, his precious Oxford was no longer safe.

Oh, dear lord. I'm being watched and hunted too!

XXIX

Municipal Police Station. Erzurum, Turkey, 1985. Arthur.

Dr. Arthur M. Evans, up-and-coming young lecturer at Oxford University, was becoming increasingly flushed and irritated the more he stewed about their situation. The Turkish police cell smelled like a cross between a stable and a dirty bathroom, and looked even worse. Though to be fair, Evans was fairly certain the smell was being accentuated by their personal body funk. Either way, his eye hurt like it was going to fall out, and his pride wasn't much better off. As he looked at his business partner with his one good eye, Evans forced himself to swallow the anger. He was choosing steely silence over wrestling Wyatt to the ground and choking him, or something equally satisfying.

In complete contrast, the thirty-something Kentucky native across from him was smiling and having the time of his life. His slightly crooked teeth were somehow perfectly white despite not having been brushed in days. Mr. Wyatt Aarons, crusader for biblical truth. Hero of the faith to churches all across the American South as a famed amateur 'biblical' archeologist. Champion Evangelical. Noted discoverer of the fossilized remains of Noah's Ark!

Not to mention an insane liar. That snake-oil salesman smile was why they were in this mess now. That, and the man's insatiable desire to dig where he shouldn't, permits or not.

"We'll stay on 'em like stink on a skunk 'till they give us the permits to excavate," he had often said, explaining that it would, "all work out," and they'd, "cut through red tape eventually."

Except they hadn't. In fact, nothing about the prior few days had gone to plan. The whole thing pretty much stank in Evans' opinion, from the shocking reality brought on by the geology report earlier in the week to the discovery of the break-in at the hotel on what was supposed to be their last night in Dogubeyazit.

And what does one do when thugs break into your room and steal your things? Go to the closest town with police, of course. Only, the officers hadn't believed the American men's story about the three dark-skinned, turbaned burglars with bird tattoos on their forearms. Nor did they care that these same men had stolen the Americans' identification, travel papers, and what little cash they'd had left. Even the shiner Evans had presented as evidence was not enough for the lawmen to be swayed. Not to mention that the thief's sucker punch had allowed the men to get away clean, making Evans' attempts at heroics fairly worthless. His was still swollen and purple.

Add to all of this that the plane they had pre-paid for was going to leave without them in less time than it took to get back to Istanbul, and it was pretty hard for Evans to imagine a worse scenario. "Stink" was the right word all around.

"You look mighty deep in thought there, my friend," Wyatt said in his thick Kentucky gentleman's accent. He'd been watching Evans brood from the other side of the cell for a while.

"And you are smiling like a circus clown," Evans replied with sweet sarcasm. "You do realize they consider us two American criminals with no papers or money? We're in a literal Turkish prison, thanks to your antics!"

"This isn't a prison, Arthur." Wyatt laughed, a twinkle in his eye. "It's just a police holding cell. You will sort out our paperwork and everything will be fine." Wyatt was at it again. Did he ever stop? Evans merely shook his head in disbelief.

"I will sort it out?" He couldn't believe it. "I'm not talking to you, Wyatt," he said firmly, crossing his arms. "You've been making that red tape argument for years, yet here we are anyway. We could be detained here for months for all you know. I have a course to teach back at the university that I'm unavoidably late for now."

Evans had not mentioned the telegram from Oxford. They had denied his request for an extension on his field-work sabbatical, beyond the start of the 1985 Michaelmas term. Not that it was terribly surprising. Evans had already used all of his allowed leave on these blasted trips, and he was well into docked-pay territory. His upcoming review was on shaky ground for sure.

"I might lose my position thanks to you, Wyatt."

"Won't happen. I had a vision. Soon, they'll beg you to stay on."

"Another one?" Evans pulled his hat low and leaned back against a yellow-brown patch of wall he hoped was slightly less filthy.

"Yes. It was magnificent, Arthur."

"Uh-huh. And what did the Almighty reveal to you this time Wyatt? Is there a key to the cell door under your bench? Or perhaps an angel is going to come to break us out?"

Aarons laughed. "I wouldn't know anything about that." He scratched his blond head with two dirty fingers. "But what stories do you remember about Babel? Maybe something from the Zohar?"

"Pardon? As in 'Tower of—'?"

"What else?" Aarons placed his hand over his heart and leaned in close, the picture of humility. His eyes were that intense steely gray which made Evans so uncomfortable, but there was nowhere else to look. "I know where it is, Arthur." His voice was little more than an excited whisper.

"God told you where to find the Tower of Babel?"

"Yes! Well, what's left of it. I had a dream."

"Uh-huh, I see." He had moved up to thick patronizing sarcasm. "Wait, you had a dream or a vision? Which was it?"

"I'm serious Arthur. You should have more faith in our work. If we will just trust in God, he will lead us to all the great ancient biblical sites. The truly faithful may not need proof, but we are going to give it to them anyway. Think of the symbolic importance of Babel—it's just like what's going on in the world now. The Lord is preparing something big for this final generation. You'll see!"

"Yes, yes." Evans had become incredibly bored with this end-of-days nonsense. "'As above, so below,' and all that. I'm familiar with your nutty mantras, Wyatt, but you can't puppet God. And stubbornness is not synonymous with faith.”

“We are going to find it in old Babylonian records. I know it, we just have to go to Ur.”

“Ur? In Iraq? Do you have any idea what you are suggesting? No. Forget it. I’m done.” The finality of Evans’ own words surprised him.

“What do you mean?” Aarons laughed, but Evans was done laughing. “Just imagine how many more will strengthen their faith when they see the real-world evidence for the things in the Bible! Then they’ll know that Scripture isn’t just some myth, but real, literal history! Just like the ark, we will find Babel next! Then who knows where that will lead?”

“No, Wyatt. I’m through.” He waggled a frustrated finger at his ridiculous cellmate. “When we get out of this cell, I’m going back home to teach my course at the University and grovel to my superiors. I’m going to have afternoon tea at my lovely new flat. I’m going to patronize the very first pub I see, and lord willing I’ll get more translation work from the museum. Consider this my verbal resignation from our little duo of alleged biblical archeology. Your proverbial reach has overstepped your literal grasp this time, Wyatt.” He punctuated this with a swoop of his fist and a determined nod.

“Oh Arthur, you don’t really mean that.”

With these words still echoing in the cell, the rest of Evans’ private thoughts spilled forth.

“They warned you not to dig, Wyatt!” he bellowed. “But you just had to do it, didn’t you? It didn’t matter if you had the permits or not. You were so absolutely convinced you found the Ark up on Doomsday that nothing else mattered. Not the law, not credible archeology, not good science. And now, somewhere deep down you realize that it’s all falling apart. The metal analysis, the carbon dating, it’s all saying you are wrong. Even our American geologists are telling you that you screwed up. So, it’s onto the next wild adventure for Wyatt Aarons. Well, I’m done by god! Good luck with it. I’m out.”

“Come now Arthur, I can see you are upset. And I understand why! Let’s talk about it later, after you calm down.”

Evans sat in silence for nearly an hour, arms tightly crossed and hat pulled low. He felt more frustrated at himself for not keeping his cool than anything. Finally, a giant key turned in the groaning iron door and a policeman motioned him out. Evans left Wyatt peeking into the hall until the door slammed shut again.

It was even hotter in the station than it had been that morning. The officer was dripping sweat from his dark brow and had long pit stains on his shirt.

“Your tell-phones call is connect,” the man said from somewhere behind his massive black mustache.

He motioned to a battered wooden desk piled high with folders, on which was a rotary phone from circa 1950. The receiver lay next to the base. The officer had set it there after finally being able to connect on Evans' behalf.

"Which number were you able to connect to?" Evans asked.

The policeman simply cocked his head and smiled thinly, plopping down in front of a noisy radial fan. Evans tried again, holding the receiver in one hand and gesturing with the other, over-pronouncing each syllable so that the officer might better understand.

"Is this the university?"

No good. The officer pulled a rag and wiped his forehead, then began rolling up his sleeves in front of the fan. Evans sighed and mimicked the gesture with the back of his hand, then wiped the sweat onto his stained and torn blue jeans. He put the greasy receiver to his ear, careful to avoid his swollen eye.

"Hello, this is Dr. Arthur Evans speaking internationally from Turkey. To whom am I speaking please?" There was a slight delay while his voice traveled the wires halfway around the world and the reply did the same.

"Dad?" came the surprised voice. It sounded tinny and very far away, which of course, it was. Apparently, having no luck with the university, the operator had tried the other number Evans had given, the boarding school in Texas where his teenage son Joseph lived. "What's wrong, Dad? What have you done this time?"

Evans shouted so that the boy could hear him better. "Joseph, just listen. We've gotten into a little bind here in Turkey. I need you to have the university wire the Turkish government some documentation. Is your headmaster with you?" An interminable pause, then an irritated affirmation. "Okay, good. Now write this down and do as I say precisely. I'm going home to Oxford, but my passport and all of my cash were stolen. I also need them to wire me some money, and I need him to inform my supervisor—"

"Oxford isn't home anymore, Dad," the boy cut in gruffly. "I'm not sure it ever was." The infernal long-distance delay was frustrating, and Evans had already lost his train of thought. Before he could work out a response, young Joseph's sigh crossed the six thousand intervening miles. "Are you in any real danger?"

"What? No, not at the moment. But there's no telling how long this will all take from my end if you don't help speed it along. Now, don't interrupt. The university needs to know I'm going to be late for the start of term. I need you to call them and tell them where I am." There was a series of clicks. "Joseph? Joseph? Are you there?" The sudden lack of static was telling. Evans toggled the switch a few times, but the line was quite dead.

"Sorry sir," the officer shrugged. "Phones is, eh, very bad."

But Evans knew better. Joseph had hung up.

"It's fine. Tell me though, do you have more than one holding cell here?"

The officer motioned to the far side of the room, but Evans didn't look. He was distracted by a new detail, now visible on the man's forearm.

Curious, Evans thought. *That raven tattoo must be a popular one around here. I wonder what it means?*

XXX

Blackwell's Bookstore. Oxford, England. Arthur.

Evans snapped out of his freshly exhumed memory with a jolt. With hardly a breath to spare, he ran up and out of the bookstore, dodged past the now-familiar motorcycle, and aimed for the street corner out of pure habit. It was due north to his flat, but he dared not go straight there.

Straight ahead was the King's Arms, where he had so recently sulked about tiny inconveniences amidst awkward family issues as David enjoyed his fish and chips. Why couldn't he focus? Evans dodged across the street and into the pub, collapsing onto a bench at the unused end of a table just as a couple was vacating it. A bit of luck, as the pub was standing room only and swarming with its Saturday evening crowd. Evans lapsed into another ragged coughing spree, just hoping he hadn't been spotted.

The approaching police sirens a moment later did not calm him as he might have hoped. He watched out the window as they put up a police line, the motorcycle now part of their investigation. Just where had the suited gunman gone exactly? Not knowing gave him a chill. Evans worked a hand into his coat for some beer money, then tugged it out guiltily. He smiled to the other pub-goers in what he hoped was a professorial and innocent manner of the sort given out by one who does not have a gun in his pocket.

Every second he wasted here could spell danger for David, but Evans had no way to warn him, and the man in the suit could easily be watching the street from the crowd of curious bystanders. Grabbing the gun had been foolish. He didn't even have the boy's number memorized; it was on the bedside table at home. Evans needed a beer or possibly three, a better plan, and the boy's phone number. *In that order.* He resolved to begin this strategy immediately.

*　　*　　*

With his heart rate stable and his stomach full of liquid courage, Evans judged that the man in the suit had been given a wide enough berth. Sufficient time for the gunman to flee the crime scene at least. He only hoped that the man in the suit had done just that. As for David, Evans could only pray that the boy had gone to ground somewhere safe since he had completely failed to protect him. Karen was going to wring his neck.

Evans felt old. Not just because of getting winded earlier, or because of the boy and his technology. No, it was deeper than that. He lived and breathed for his medieval English town, but it had always felt new and alive to him compared to the ancient texts he'd built his life on. Dusty old tablets and long-dead colleagues had been his companions for some forty years now. After the cancer took Elisabeth, he'd fully retreated into that ancient world, courtesy of Wyatt Aarons. Then after that foolishness imploded, he found his sanctuary right where he had left it. Embracing his somewhat diminished role as tutor and nestling into dark corners of libraries, occasionally working as a translator for the museum... it had all been—easy.

And now, with David's chaotic arrival, harsh light had flashed into his happy little corners. Oh, but what a horrible thought it was too. Old memories long suppressed were now threatening to overwhelm the comfortably stuffy life he had built for himself. Perhaps even destroy it.

'Enlightenment' and 'apocalypse' are synonyms, after all, he reminded himself as he drained the last of his mug and wiped the foam from his beard.

He was, of course, being entirely unfair to David. Truth be told, Evans was reasonably pleased with the job Joseph and Karen had done. The youngest Evans was smart and clever and had not suffered from his unorthodox home education, evidently. At least, not any more than Joseph had as a boy.

It had been a difficult decision to send young Joseph to the boarding academy, but it had not been the terrible and damaging thing his strong-willed son had often accused him of. Joseph's character and self-worth had done just fine! He'd attended a respectable Texas seminary, married well, and even took charge of the Dallas homestead when Evans' own father passed. Even better, Joseph had unmistakably produced a bright young man who would do just fine at Oxford. Time would sort the rest out.

Evans pushed away the sliver of doubt that had been dogging him for so long and silently complimented himself instead. Clearly, his decision about Joseph and boarding school had been for the best. David was living confirmation.

Only, there was no guarantee any of it would happen now. Not with the raven-tattooed men after him too. This Wyatt Aarons thing was a ghost that needed to die. Karen would want it. Elisabeth would have made him do it. And David deserved it. He would go home, call the boy, then they would meet somewhere safe. After that, they would do the sensible thing and visit the police to give testimony. Perhaps Evans would even call this Mel Chen person and offer her the journal. Let her people deal with the silly gunman and his raven-tattooed brothers. Everything would be fine.

With a calmness he didn't expect, Evans extracted himself from his reverie and his booth. He slid out the side door and went the long way around the block to the Mansfield College gates to retrieve his bicycle. Then he rode straight across the croquet field and exited by way of the side garden to his flat. Evans threw the latch on his green door and charged to the back room without bothering to turn on the lights. He grabbed his phone off the cradle and fumbled around for the scrap of paper with David's number on it. He dialed the international digits as quickly as his old rotary would allow.

The ringing seemed to go on forever, then finally, "Arthur is that you?" The boy's voice sounded muffled and strange.

"David? Thank the lord. Where are you, what happened?"

There was a loud gulp on David's end. "I'm not sure Arthur. I looked back and you were gone. That motorcycle guy took off down a side street and shot out a store window. I thought we'd lost him but then I couldn't find you. I hung out for a while till the cops showed up, but eventually I just started walking the same way we'd been going and wandered around for a while looking for you. Are you okay?"

"I'm quite fine, but you need to get off the street immediately. That was no random attacker, but it will take some time to explain."

"No problem. I'm actually in a KFC now, eating something called a Cajun Boxmaster Meal, it's like the weirdest thing I've ever had. I mean, I get the chicken breast, but there's a hash brown, cheese, and what they call Cajun Sauce, all wrapped in a tortilla thing. My friends at home are all laughing about it on Facebook."

Evans couldn't believe his ears. KFC? Facebook? David was safe. And he was already eating again? The boy had a hollow leg. Regardless, Evans relaxed in a place he didn't know had been tight. He closed his eyes and allowed himself a deep breath, centering his thoughts on the city he knew so well. The teen must have kept going to where the road became Cornmarket Street, taken a side street, then eventually doubled back down by where Ship Street met St. Michael. Quite logical.

"Perfect!" Evans exclaimed. "I want you to walk quickly across the road and go to the church of St. Michael at the Northgate. Ask for Father Matthew Williams. Tell him I sent you. He's my dearest friend and you can trust him implicitly. He's a hopeless optimist, but he's a good man."

"Okay. At the north gate of what, exactly?" David's mouth was full of Boxmaster again.

"What? Oh, no. That's simply the name, it's a throwback to when the old city had a wall. St. Michael lays claim to the oldest tower in the city, which was just inside the old walls back around 1050 or so— You know what, never mind. Just head for the dirty great old rectangular tower across the street. You can't miss it. Only don't try to go in through the visitor center, go around and knock three times on the big wooden door on the opposite side. I'll be there as soon as I can, but I need to get some things in order first. Do you still have the blasted journal?"

"Yea, of course."

"Good. Oh, and David, tell Matthew to lock all the doors. I have my own key, so have him let absolutely no one else in but me, no matter what." Evans swallowed hard. "Not even the police, understand?"

"Um, okay, Arthur," there was doubt in the boy's words. "Be careful?" Evans was pretty sure that was supposed to be his line.

"Yes, you too," he managed. "I'll explain everything when I get there. Now, hurry on!"

Though he seriously doubted he could ever say so to Karen, this summer guardian thing was not at all as it had been advertised. *"No trouble at all,"* he seemed to remember her saying. *Hogwash!*

Evans left a few more quick phone messages to tie up loose ends with his summer tutoring schedule, then headed for the door. As he stepped into his unlit living room, something caught his eye. A book, distinctly out of place in the middle of the floor. He took one hesitant step toward it but needed to go no further to immediately recognize it. Lodged in the hardbound volume was a bullet, threading the iconic golden ring on the cover of *The Lord of the Rings: Fiftieth Anniversary Edition.*

Evans' blood ran cold. All lingering doubts left him. The message was clear: his cozy Oxford sanctuary was no longer safe. There was only one option now. It was time for that deal with the devil.

XXXI

St. Michael at the North Gate. Oxford, England. David.

David lightly knocked, then pounded on the large wooden doors of St. Michael at the non-existent North Gate. He could hear real pipe organ music inside, but the door was locked. He cringed when the music stopped in mid-chord, an angsty note echoing and fading away.

A sign posted here clearly indicated that this entrance was for worshippers only. It directed tourists to the now-closed glass entrance he'd passed on the other side. But the worship times listed didn't include Saturday night either, so he'd had to knock just as Arthur told him to.

After a few moments, a frizzle-haired lady opened up and began to inform him of the same information as on the sign. He felt bad but interrupted her anyway.

"Excuse me, ma'am? I need to speak to Father Matthew, please. My grandfather Arthur sent me here. There's been some trouble and he said I should come to St. Michael."

The woman's face soured. "Arthur? Arthur Evans?" Obviously, she'd met him.

It took a minute of explaining, but David soon found himself standing in a gorgeous old church. To David, it all looked very Catholic, much like the chapel at Mansfield, though less ornate overall. It was a strange mix of new and old. Towards the back was a little wood-adorned church library and office, tucked behind the wooden stairway. The floor-stand sign read, "Oxford's oldest Saxon tower." The stairway was also accessible from the dark ultra-modern giftshop visible through a glassed-off archway.

But the frizzle-haired lady went the other way. She threw the latch on an ornate wooden door, led David to the front of the sanctuary, and then through a decidedly normal-looking one. They stepped a few centuries into the future and David found himself in a little social area with an attached kitchen. It could have been a tiny fellowship hall from any of the hundreds of American churches in the southland that David's father had spoken in when he was a kid. The anachronism of it all amused him greatly, but he also felt strangely at home.

In this room sat a hairy giant. The man looked to be somewhere in his thirties. He wore a black shirt and tan slacks, and he lounged in a hideously upholstered and comedically oversized easy chair that he somehow still spilled out of. He had a fluffy light brown fleece of a beard and a head of hair to match. He was reading an old book, a pot of tea within arm's reach. Apart from the hair color, he could have passed for Hagrid's younger brother in a *Harry Potter* film.

Hagrid's brother glanced up, pulled his reading glasses off, and smiled warmly. "I say, Annie, what sort of interesting fellow have you brought me this time?" Father Matthew's rumbling accent betrayed his mixed Scotch-English heritage.

"This young man has quite the line, Father. He claims to be your Dr. Arthur's grandson. I thought perhaps you'd like to have a chat with him?"

The priest's face broke into a massive smile. "I see. Well, hallo to you, young man. It is quite lovely to meet you. Heard absolutely nothing about you." The mischievous giant winked. "I suppose we should brew ourselves a fresh pot of tea then."

Sixty seconds later the pot was on and the organ music was back.

"I quite enjoy reading a good book while Ms. Annie practices. Tell me, have you ever had occasion to read the *Father Brown* mysteries?"

*   *   *

David was on his third cup of tea when Father Matthew finally stopped asking him questions about the day's events. The priest leaned back in his chair placidly, hands laced behind his head, deep in thought. The leather journal lay on the desk, small and forgotten. Even reclining, the priest loomed over everything. Everybody was tall to David, but this barrel-chested Englishman was at least six-foot-six.

"So then, our esteemed Dr. Evans is supposed to have found Noah's Ark on a mountain in Turkey, is he? Who would have guessed it?" His voice was full of bemused wonder. "It seems to me, David, that you have done a fine job of unraveling the longstanding riddle that is your grandfather. It's taken me a decade to learn what few secrets I have about him, but you seem to have wormed out a number of his deeper ones in the better part of a day."

David was pretty sure that this wasn't true. He still had about a million questions for Arthur. Questions about everything from his time with Mr. Aarons, to details about the Doomsday Ark, to how the *Gilgamesh* and Uncle Sir Arthur stuff all fit in with the journal. But he got Father Matthew's point. The half-giant priest was easy to talk to, and clearly, the closest thing to a best friend the old wizard had. David was intrigued by that idea most of all. He was bursting to ask Matthew a few of those million questions about Arthur right now. Then, before realizing it, one slipped out anyway.

"Father Matthew, do you have any idea why he and Mr. Aarons might have stopped working together?"

"I couldn't say," Matthew said flippantly, then opened one eye and raised one bushy brow. "But I could take a cracking good guess, I'd wager." David didn't hide his smile. "Your grandfather has a bit of a bee in his bonnet when it comes to *Genesis*. Perhaps you noticed?"

"Yea, he called it mythology at the museum. He got all worked up about the Minotaur's maze and Uncle Sir Arthur."

"Ah, so he gave you the full backstage tour of our esteemed Ashmolean, did he? Rightly so. I should have known. He threw quite the fit when they took down the old Minoan display some years back. He complained about it endlessly. As I recall, your grandmother had much to do with the creation of that room. It was getting a bit faded and tatty though. Can't properly blame the staff for wanting to take it down after all those years."

David's hours exploring the museum alone, and then again with Emma, cascaded over him. Arthur had mentioned that the Sir Arthur archive was out on the floor at one point, but the idea that his Grandmother Elisabeth had somehow been responsible for it hadn't occurred to him. He tried to imagine his young grandmother walking and working the rooms they'd been in, but all he could picture was art history geek Emma strolling through the modern layout. A strange sadness and longing whispered to him, but then it was gone.

"So, Arthur doesn't believe in the Bible then?"

"What? Where on earth did you get that idea? He most certainly does. Though he may not express it the same way as you or I."

David's face asked the question for him. The priest nodded sympathetically. "Shall I relay to you the Dr. Evans biblical manifesto—in brief, if you don't mind? I daresay I shall mangle it, despite the many, many times I've endured it during our chess matches, but I'm game to give it a go."

Arthur plays chess? David's expression must have betrayed him once again, for Matthew released a hearty barrel-chested guffaw.

"Apologies, David! Your grandfather and I long since decided that life is too short to speak of serious matters without a healthy distraction." He reached over to a nearby shelf and extracted a large handmade wooden rectangle. David recognized the checkered inlay of a folded chess board immediately. "Tell me, am I right in thinking that you also enjoy the game?"

David could not reply fast enough. "Oh, yes sir! I love them all." In no time, each hand-carved piece was in its starting place and the miniature battle simulation began.

"Arthur would likely put it something like this," Matthew said, after a few opening moves. "First, we must never apply a literal interpretation to that which is intended solely as a metaphor. Second, Scripture is not God's direct word to man, but man's exploration of God through literature." The Englishman did not attempt Arthur's homegrown Transatlantic accent with its hint of Texas drawl, but he did inject a bit of grump.

David bit his knuckle and laughed. "What's that even supposed to mean?"

"Well, David, I suppose it's tied up in Arthur's belief that first and foremost, the Bible isn't a book so much as a library. And each individual 'book', as we think of it, is often a further collection from various genres, we might say. Be that poetry, letters, stories, biography, and so on."

"Okay." David processed this and marched out a pawn. He considered Arthur's little apartment full to the brim with books but wasn't sure how the dots connected yet. "So, what's wrong with that? Sounds fairly legit."

"Well, nothing is wrong with it in particular. It's quite sound really. The Bible is the foundational library of knowledge for all of Western civilization. I suppose it's more a question of authorship. You see, Arthur sees Holy Scripture as authoritative, but not necessarily 'inspired' in the way American Fundamentalists would have it."

David's dad would have had something to say about that one. Pastor Joseph Evans' latest book had been all about the inerrancy of the Bible. His dad had spent months researching the Chicago Statement of whatever-it-was, interviewing various contributing authors and other experts while traveling a lot. It had done well. Another bestseller even, but David hadn't read it. His dad's interests were not really his thing. He already believed in the Bible, so he'd assumed the book wasn't meant for people like him.

"So, Arthur just takes the parts he wants from the Bible? That doesn't seem very respectful."

"Oh, no-no-no my boy! Arthur would never do that."

The force of Father Mathew's correction surprised David. A knight came out to shore up his defenses. "Arthur goes the other way with it. You see, to your grandfather, the Bible is much like the holy books of the ancient Egyptians, or the greatest myths like the *Epic of Gilgamesh*. First and foremost, he sees each individual book as a particular form of literature, warts and all."

David was puzzled. *The Bible has warts?* And how could it be like other holy books? Those other religions were all wrong!

"Arthur is entirely comfortable with the idea that the Bible contains allegory and allusion," the priest continued. "To him, Adam and Noah are archetypes, and we shouldn't read them literally, but for whatever purpose the original author presumably intended given his ancient audience."

"Is that the metaphor part? Like, he's saying we have to read for the symbolism and not take it too literally?"

"Quite right. When I've caught Arthur reading the Bible, it's almost always been in ancient Hebrew or a copy of the Talmud. And sometimes, it's some non-canonical one-off. The man tried to pass off a verse from the Book of Enoch to me some months ago as legitimate. I swear he did it with a wink and a grin, just to see if I was paying attention." Father Matthew shook his great shaggy head in amusement. "Fortunately, I was. You truly must know your onions when you converse with that man."

No kidding, David thought as he parsed all that in his head. He considered his private lecture at the museum. Apparently, Arthur had wanted him to know the whole history of the Minoans before he would answer a simple question about Mr. Aarons' journal. Yet, David still wasn't sure where he was supposed to sleep tonight. He half expected it to be the floor of Arthur's apartment on a bed made of books. Or, maybe he'd need a lecture on architecture and the history of bed construction first.

"But, your grandfather is neither a fool, nor a coward," Matthew continued, releasing his queen onto the center of the board. "He's not afraid to walk right up to the confusing parts of the Bible and punch them around a bit. Once you get used to it, it's quite fun to watch. He's rather good at what he does. Check, by the way."

David definitely wasn't used to it yet, but he was beginning to see how what Matthew was saying must be true. He was also curious about what a 'Bible wart' looked like. "Like how?"

"Well, perhaps we can take our friend Noah as an example."

"Yea, Arthur mentioned that there were other versions of that story. He said the one Moses wrote was just one out of four hundred ancient flood myths or something."

The priest's casual smile turned mischievous. "Did he say the word wrote precisely?"

David thought about it. "No, I guess not. I don't know. Why?" He moved his king out of danger for the moment.

"Ah, because you have just given us an even better example than what I was thinking. Arthur would be the first to tell you that in all probability, Moses never wrote anything. His was an oral culture."

XXXII

Parks Road. Oxford, England. Mr. Suit.

The man in the suit watched from the shadows as Dr. Evans mounted his bicycle and rode off. The well-seasoned tutor was weighed down with two bags, but he managed it without weaving back and forth too much. His destination was irrelevant. The bags told the man in the suit everything he needed to know. He allowed himself a tight smile no one would see.

The man in the suit reached into his pocket, wincing at his throbbing wrist and the memory of Dr. Evans' rather direct means of relieving him of his gun at the bookstore. *What is it with this man and books?* The thought made him smile a bit more. The old fellow had some spirit after all, and there was more to this Dr. Evans than it appeared. Still, he was going to miss that gun.

The man in the suit was also beginning to wonder if his splitting headache would go away with sleep, or if he had a genuine concussion. Either way, pretending to be knocked out had been the easy part, allowing himself to become injured only slightly less so. It was the endangerment of the suit that had been the most difficult, but it seemed to have come away from the little deception no worse for wear, other than a few spots of plaster dust.

No time for pain. I am working for a higher purpose now.

He took a deep breath and popped a small handful of pain pills he'd snatched from the tutor's medicine cupboard. He pocketed the rest, extracting one phone, then the other. Good, the company phone had finished its factory reset. He popped it open, pulled the sim card, then crushed it into the pavement. It was as much for himself as for practical purposes. He didn't want to take any chances that his former employer might be tracking him beyond this point.

The other phone he used to call in his success.

"How did it go, my boy? Did you set the trap?" The man asked him.

"I was forced to improvise, but Dr. Evans now believes he is no longer safe. He will take that company job now. By tomorrow, he should be on his way with the journal."

"Risky, but not horrible. I'll have better control over the situation once he's on that plane. It won't be long now till all the pieces are in place. Until then, we can't risk losing the upper hand, not even for a day. We need to keep the pressure on, and I want you there to do it."

There? So he was finally being pulled back with the others then. Loyalty now cemented, he'd be keeping his target close. That changed a few things. The man's mind reeled as a thousand possibilities adjusted in his head.

"Come in through Aleppo. You'll be harder to track from there. Call one of your brothers, steal a plane, just do whatever it is you do. Work your magic."

A jolt of fear and excitement went through the man in the suit. Just who did the man on the phone think might be tracking him, precisely? He knew better than to ask those sorts of questions.

"You know, you're doing surprisingly well, boy," the caller continued with just a hint of sarcasm. "I never doubted you for a second. Call me when you hit the ground. I'll know more then." And with that, the call ended.

The man in the suit exhaled. He hadn't realized he was holding his breath. So, his adventures as a graduate student in England truly were at an end. His particular skills and talents must be needed if he was being extracted after this long. There were certainly dozens of qualified men who could get to Evans faster. *None better, though,* he realized, given his familiarity with the situation.

The man chided himself for his selfishness. He must do this if he was to accomplish his real job. Like a clock, things were now set in motion that could not be undone. *Remember who you are. Remember what you really are.*

But in all truth, the idea of continuing this little game thrilled him. Booking a flight was the obvious choice. Still, airport security was always such a pain for men who looked like him. He would much prefer to be the one behind the plane's control stick than stuck in a passenger's seat, but it wasn't practical. There was no going back now. It was time to begin his real job, the one that could only end in death.

Dr. Evans had helpfully disposed of the gun for him. He would have to find a new one when he arrived in Syria, but what he needed now was access to the net. A borrowed smartphone would do. Everything else was in his go-bag, but that wasn't far away at all. Nothing in Oxford ever was.

It occurred to the man in the suit that his favorite nightclub was not terribly far either. It had a Roman theme to match its ancient architectural bones. Plus, it attracted the most hedonistic and uninhibited as a side-effect. Lots of rich girls with smartphones there.

People are resources to be consumed, he reminded himself. *Societies are but clocks to be studied and made to work to my advantage.* Had the very man he had just received his new orders from not taught him this so many years ago? Where would he be now if not for this reality?

The man in the suit had always wondered who he could go home with while wearing his magnificent suit. And since technically he was not working for the company anymore, that needn't be a concern. The possibilities were endless. This was his last chance for Oxford nightlife and he decided to find out. One wasn't supposed to sleep with a concussion anyway, right?

He tossed the former work phone into a nearby trash bin.

Ah, the lies we tell ourselves. The pills were already kicking in.

XXXIII

St. Michael at the North Gate. Oxford, England. David.

David sat rooted at Father Matthew's desk. He was drinking in every word from his grandfather's best and possibly only friend. He was also waiting for the priest to decide where to place his bishop.

"Now, before we go any further, in the interest of full disclosure, I should probably tell you that I'm something of an expert on scripture myself."

David laughed. Sitting in the Anglican priest's office, surrounded by religious books, hymnals, and church icons, it seemed sort of obvious. A few of said books had even been authored by Matthew. David could just make out part of a title about '*The Heavens*' and something or other about '*God and the Cosmos.*'

"I'm good with that," David said, shifting a rook.

"Right then," the priest continued. "So, back to the topic at hand. Arthur is correct that Moses was from an oral culture. The stories passed to him and on through him had authority from their respective 'tradents,' authority upheld by the community. They were steeped in what to them was family tribal culture."

"Wait, Arthur said that most of the ancient world didn't write stuff down, so a 'tradent' would be what, an author, but in an oral culture?"

"Essentially, yes. More like an authorial tradition. Come to think of it, 'tradition' would be of the same root etymologically. I'll spare you a lookup in the OED, though Arthur might not be so lenient. As I recall, 'trader' is also a word-cousin, but then, not my area frankly."

"So, Moses relied on the old stories for what he wrote. Got it."

"Erm, not precisely. And certainly not according to Arthur."

"But obviously, somebody wrote *Genesis*. I mean, it exists. We have it."

"Ah." Matthew cleared his throat awkwardly. "I unquestionably agree with you, but that is the meat of it isn't it? Arthur does not think that there is enough evidence for written authorship by Moses. He argues that the languages Moses could have written in did not include Hebrew as we know it, as that language wouldn't exist for several more centuries. Thus, at least the earliest stories, and quite possibly much more, must have had many tradent contributors by the time they were finally jotted down. One common argument even contends that the Hebrew Bible went largely unwritten until the time of the Babylonian Exile." Matthew's queen moved again.

"Wait, you're saying Moses might have just collected and retold the *Genesis* stories without ever writing them down? Like a bard?"

A one-shouldered shrug and a non-committal head bob was the priest's reply.

A vivid image of a fantasy bard popped into David's head, fluffy pantaloons, stockings, lute and all. The character class had a bit of a stigma to gamers as being a throwaway support character, but David liked playing bards. It was fun to roll for "bardic knowledge" and try to improv a poem or song on the spot.

Knowledge. Tradition. Tradent. Trader? The thought took him suddenly back to the goat merchant with the seal stones who had been the harbinger of writing by Arthur's account. Coins, words, writing, authorship of stories, travel to other lands—he felt the connections forming in his head. There had to have been commerce and cultural exchange between ancient Israel and other countries, that was obvious. But some people argued that Moses didn't know how to write Hebrew? That was nuts.

"Father Matthew, wasn't there a Jewish king who pulled out a bunch of old scrolls and freaked out because they weren't following God's laws?"

Matthew lifted one bushy eyebrow and pulled the passage out of his brain. "'And Josiah raised money to repair the temple, and during the repairs the high priest Hilkiah found the Book of the Law.' I say David, well spotted. It has been argued that Hilkiah's discovery is the source for Deuteronomy. The name means 'second law,' if you care to know. Perhaps I'll point that one out to Arthur one of these Sundays. It's certainly pre-exilic, and a direct reference to Mosaic Law."

David had picked up a lot over the years traveling around with his parents to all those churches, but he'd never met a pastor anything like Matthew before. David repositioned a knight. "So Arthur thinks the Bible is just an old collection of made-up stories?"

"Well, I wouldn't sell him too short on that one. I've heard him call it the greatest collection of stories, history, and wisdom of all time. And rightly so.

But where he and I differ is that I still firmly believe the Holy Spirit had a hand in the formation of it from the get-go. All through its various iterations, edits, revisions, compilations, being gathered up into collections, and so on. Whereas, Arthur prefers to look upon the Bible's various parts... rather separately."

David squinched his nose questioningly. Father Matthew leaned in, lowering his voice to a stage whisper. "He scoffs a bit at the later canonization process. Says calling something 'scripture' based on a popular vote is ridiculous nonsense. I have attempted to convince him that by his own argument we've always done that, though not through an ecumenical council. And certainly not with the purpose of closing the canon, as they eventually did."

"Ecumenical?"

"Oh, apologies." He leaned back and found his regular voice again. "It means, the representation of several different Christian churches. Though I daresay that medieval scholars would have defined it somewhat differently. My reason for mentioning it is simply that Arthur says scripture is, and always has been, more of a living document. Every time we translate it, we change it a bit." The priest smiled mischievously and used his queen to take David's now unprotected bishop.

David wondered for about a millisecond what his dad would have to say about that one, then realized he already knew. "But not in any meaningful or theologically significant way, right?"

His dad's words, coming out of David's mouth? Now that was weird. But Matthew's subtle nod revealed that the priest agreed. David could practically hear his dad's mega-church back home starting a prayer chain about the weird ideas 'Anglican religion' was starting to put into their pastor's son's head. Or were these just Arthur and Father Matthew's ideas?

"So, what does all that mean, then? Why even trust the Bible? If there was no author, how would we know people didn't just make stuff up?" David's knight took Matthew's queen, much to the priest's surprise.

"Well David, I suppose some believers find great comfort in knowing that God's people have been in the business of guarding and curating His word since long before the respective books were collected into the Holy Bible or even written down."

David wasn't so sure. He seemed to remember that Moses went up the mountain and God dictated. Or was that just the Ten Commandments? His dad had always insisted that God was the 'author' of the Bible and that settled it, but for some reason, David thought of Wyatt Aarons' journal entry too:

Mr. Aarons was certainly in the dictation-from-God camp. But according to the internet, the guy wasn't just some hypocritical Bible-thumper—he lived by his visions. David could imagine what that must be like, and he kind of admired the biblical archeologist for it. Even if he could never tell Arthur that.

And with that, something clicked.

"So, you think Arthur left Turkey because Mr. Aarons believes in the Bible literally? Because he said God was telling him where to dig or whatever, and Arthur basically couldn't take it anymore?"

"That would be my wager, yes. But he's never told me about his Mr. Aarons. So that particular wound must go quite deep. I only know Arthur's scars. Every generation of students tries to get under their tutors' skins, but I never could with Arthur. Perhaps that's why we are good friends now. This Wyatt fellow must have hurt him rather badly, I'd guess. And it seems clear to me that Noah's Ark has become your grandfather's dragon." Matthew repositioned a rook to protect his lonely king.

"Yea," David said, laughing at the mental image. So much about Arthur was slowly falling into place. His secrecy, his gruffness, his eccentric quirks. David's old wizard had a dragon? Maybe Arthur was Gandalf after all.

Great sympathy for Arthur suddenly bloomed in David for the grandfather he'd never known. He imagined what it must have been like for Arthur, a lifetime of theories burned to the ground by both church and academia because of one adventure early on. And all because he had worked with a renegade man who interpreted the Bible differently than he did. Or was there more to it? A career derailed because of Arthur's hope in proving a myth true, perhaps?

That might also explain his grandfather's strange ambivalence towards Great Uncle Sir Arthur. Arthur had indicated a great love and admiration for his eponymous uncle, yet he had also shown that strange resentment towards Sir Arthur's passion for myths and faith in stories. Maybe Arthur saw it as some kind of family trait, a tendency to get over-excited and chase myths at the expense of rigorous scholarship. But without that excitement, without imagining what might be, how would anyone have the passion to undertake the tedious work needed to uncover the truth?

A thought bubbled up in David's head from earlier in the day, a question that had gone unanswered coming back to him. "So, Father Matthew, if Mr. Aarons was taking the Bible literally, then why were Arthur and him looking on some obscure Turkish foothill? Doesn't *Genesis* specifically say that the

Ark landed on Mt. Ararat? That's a pretty big mistake for Mr. Aarons, wasn't it? Arthur said Doomsday was like twenty miles away, or something."

"Interestingly, that's one of the things this Mr. Aarons could have easily gotten right. Have a careful look at *Genesis*, chapter eight." He nodded once at a nearby leather Bible with gold-edged onionskin paper.

David motioned an 'I got it' with his phone and pulled the verse up there instead.

"It says, 'The water receded steadily from the earth. At the end of the hundred and fifty days, the water had gone down, and on the seventeenth day of the seventh month the ark came to rest on the mountains of Ararat.'" David stared at it silently for a moment, processing what he had just read as if seeing it for the first time. "Wait, 'mountains'? I never noticed that before. What's it mean?"

"Well, for starters, it means that most people who care to try, are probably looking in the wrong place for the Ark of Noah. The snow-capped mountain peak we call Ararat likely wasn't even there when Noah was around. Much less named 'Ararat.' It's a volcano, and it's a relatively new one in geological terms."

David pondered this. "Volcano? Father Matthew, if Arthur didn't tell you any of this, how do you know?"

"I know my science." The mischievous smile was back.

"That seems kind of random for a, you know—"

"For a man of God?"

"Well, yea, honestly. If you don't mind me saying it."

"I don't mind a bit." Matthew sat up and straightened his shirt. "David, it's not often that a student changes their course of study at Oxford, but it does happen from time to time. I am one of those cases. My calling as a minister came late, but it came all the same. At the time, I was in a very different program and already had two diplomas under my belt. I was studying the heavens in a very different way."

"You switched your major? Like, changed degrees?"

"Yes." He smiled widely. David was reminded of a proud barn cat producing a mouse.

"From what?"

"Cosmology. Astrophysics, I believe you'd call it."

David couldn't help but laugh. "You went from space science to religion? Wow. That's quite a jump!"

"Interestingly, it hardly is when you get into it." He nodded sideways to the bookshelf where his grouped titles stood. This time, a mere flicker of a smile appeared behind his fluffy facial hair.

"But science and religion are total opposites," David protested.

"Ah, there is where we will have to cordially disagree. They are only opposites if one starts by thinking that the Bible is a science book. I assure you, it's not. The Bible is a narrative. And like all narratives, we have to read the beginning as influenced by the ending. The Bible is no mere collection of short stories—it's an interlinked library with innumerable cross-references and a plot that spans well more than two millennia. A great deal more, if you consider the events of the *Genesis* epics historical. Either way, it's quite the remarkable text."

David found he agreed with that much at least. "And Arthur doesn't think the first part of *Genesis* is historical?"

Father Matthew made a deep and thoughtful rumbling growl.

"'It's such a strange old book,' I've heard him repeat. 'Just why has it outlasted castles and kingdoms?' I really can't say what he believes in his heart, I'm afraid."

David nodded. He liked this man, though why Arthur did was still a mystery.

"The gospel of scripture and the gospel of creation are quite harmonious if one takes the time to learn the language of each," Matthew added, going back to his earlier point. "It is an egregious error to consider science and scripture as the opposing sides of a battle, or some complex interplay of pieces in a never-ending game of chess." The priest motioned to the board between them.

David realized that he hadn't moved in some time. "Oh, sorry!" He repositioned his queen. "Checkmate."

"Oh, I say. Well played, David. Shall we go again?"

XXXIV

St. Michael at the North Gate. Oxford, England. Arthur.

Evans fumbled with his keys, then walked his bicycle through the church door. Muted conversation and a soft glow came from the direction of Matthew's little office, but otherwise, the building was dark and still. Evans stepped toward the conversation and paused. Through the doorway he could see Wyatt's journal and the priest's antique chessboard, both pushed aside.

The latter was abandoned with a checkmate in David's favor, he noted. Evans couldn't recall the last time he had managed to beat Matthew at chess. The priest played four to five moves ahead. He could never seem to get more than one or two moves out in front of the man on his best day.

Matthew glanced up at Evans knowingly, but David didn't notice. The boy's attention was rooted in his phone again.

"What kind of inconsistencies?" David said without looking up.

Evans scowled quietly, but Matthew winked at him before returning his attention to David. Evidently, their conversation had been going on for some time now. Evans knew his best friend's tells well enough. He had taken tea and lost at chess with Father Matthew Williams nearly every Sunday afternoon for the past decade. Evans had found him to be a well-read man of faith who believed strongly in miracles, mankind, and the scientific method, pretty much in that order. And while Evans was well aware that he did not see eye to eye with his old pupil on many aspects of their shared subject, the tea and bracing comradery were always good.

And apparently, the scientist-priest could bait an inquisitive Evans of any age, and he was enjoying this fresh opportunity to do so.

"Let us visit the flood story properly," Matthew suggested. "Chapter seven says, 'And the waters prevailed so mightily on the earth that all the high mountains under the whole heaven were covered. The waters prevailed above the mountains, covering them fifteen cubits deep.' Fifteen over. Let's remember that."

Evans had always envied his former student's flawless memory when it came to quoting long literary passages.

"That sure sounds like a scientific fact about the flood to me." David defended. "If not, then what is it?" Evans stiffened. David was taking the bait.

"Yes, perhaps. But before we consider where the 'prevailing waters' might have come from, or who took the measurements atop all of those various 'mountains,' perhaps we can agree that God created the laws of science too? Would you agree that natural science simply should not be used to explain something super-natural, nor should we try?"

"Well, yea sure," David said hesitantly. "But dad says that scientists are way too biased about stuff anyway. They don't use good scientific methods or whatever. They make tons of assumptions like about how many billions of years old the world is, or that there can't be miracles, so there can't be a God. You know, that sort of thing?"

Joseph's words, coming from David's mouth. Evans felt his own mouth curl sourly.

"Some men of science are biased and jaded, yes, but that doesn't mean we should just discard the gospel of creation. We must be careful to remember what the Bible is, and what it is not," Father Matthew responded evenly.

Evans couldn't see David's face, but he reasoned that the teen looked perplexed, for Matthew smiled and tried a different approach. "Perhaps you've heard that Einstein said, 'God does not play dice with the universe?' I daresay most people don't understand the intent of the quote."

"It means that Einstein believed in creation, doesn't it? That God, uh, 'fine-tuned' the universe when he made it, not some random roll of the dice?"

They've explored the fine-tuning argument? Oh, good lord.

"A common assumption. But alas, Einstein was almost certainly an atheist. His point was to say that the universe is quite deterministic and measurable. He was dismissing quantum mechanics as an entirely bizarre theory that he could not endorse. Quantum physicists propose that there is a world of tiny particles behind everything, governed by randomness and probability." Matthew was getting into it now. This was the space-priest's wheelhouse.

"Einstein was being sarcastic?" David's tone was incredulous.

"Somewhat, yes. Einstein was using 'God' as a metaphor, and therein lies the danger of metaphors at large. We might more accurately quote him when he wrote in a letter, 'I do not believe in a personal God and I have never denied this but have expressed it clearly. If something is in me which can be called religious, then it is the unbounded admiration for the structure of the world so far as our science can reveal it.'"

"See?" David's tone shifted to something closer to exasperation. "That's exactly what I'm talking about. And science says that Einstein's theories were right, doesn't it? Atomic bombs work, and E still equals MC squared last time I checked. So, like, what was he worried about?"

"It has been said, that science doesn't say anything, David. People do."

Score one for the priest. David looked at Matthew sideways. Evans had been about to clear his throat and announce his presence, but something kept him from it. Matthew wasn't usually so blunt. Could it be that the priest might have finally met his match? Young or not, if "kid-internet" could repeat his tricks from the pub earlier, he might just have a chance against him. Sorely vex the religious scholar, if nothing else, and that would be worth watching from the peanut gallery regardless. Evans leaned against the doorway and smoothed his beard, curious how this would play out. He began to keep score in his head. The priest was up by one.

"My apologies David, that was uncalled for," Matthew soothed. "Permit me to try again? In one sense, Einstein was well within his rights to reject the tenets of quantum theory. He was a theoretical physicist, and as such, his theories required the consistency of the cosmos for the math to balance. He was greatly bothered by his observations of the universe. In complete contradiction to his predictions, it seemed that something was overcoming the effects of gravity and pushing everything in creation farther away at an ever-increasing rate. These observations have long since been affirmed now, but we still don't know how it all fits together."

"Affirmed by other scientists, you mean. Isn't dark matter, like, some big unsupported theory to make the math work?"

Score one for David.

"Yes indeed," the priest chuckled. "But let us not be too hasty in dismissing Einstein's professional choices. He lived in a time when the world believed the universe was static. Only, his advanced mathematical theories kept coming up with a most frustrating result. His calculations predicted our expanding universe, and this was a problem. He adjusted his math to fix the problem. We call it, dark energy and dark matter. He called it the cosmological constant. I'd simply call it confirmation bias."

"Yea, Arthur talked about that. It's when you look for results that support your theory instead of the other way around. But what was Einstein's bias?"

Evans smiled. The boy didn't miss a tick.

"Simply that an eternally static universe doesn't need a creator. Whereas a universe that banged into existence a few billion-odd years ago would necessarily require one. A universe with a beginning requires a beginner."

Score two for the priest. Uh-oh!

"Banged? What, like the Big Bang? But that's an atheist theory that goes against the Bible."

"Ah! Well, you see David, it didn't start out that way. In fact, atheistic scientists feared the Big Bang at first. Until propaganda swung the argument to their side." The priest leaned in close, a confession of his own to make. "For what it's worth, I have no problems believing in the Big Bang. I just know who made the bang."

David laughed at this, shaking his head. Evans wondered what Joe and Karen would say if they could hear this coming from a fellow Protestant and man of the cloth. He was suddenly thankful that they were an ocean away.

"In fact," Matthew continued, "one of the great ironies of modern scientific endeavors is that the faithful often make these wonderful discoveries about the universe which support theism, only to have them appropriated by those who would pit science against faith in some silly imagined war. For example, Galileo's heliocentric theories were welcomed by the Church and funded by his friend the Pope until the political landscape changed. He was asked to affirm that the Church had authority over such matters and to stop teaching his theory until it could be tested."

"Wait, really? I thought he was tried as a heretic and burned at the stake or something?"

"No, no. Nothing so drastic as that. He was put under comfortable house arrest and died naturally as an embittered old man."

"You're kidding? That's crazy."

"You see, Galileo was warned, but he simply didn't stop. He allowed his pride to give voice to his work. He wrote parodies with obvious satires of living men he didn't like. He engaged in what was considered a bad scientific method by his peers even then. And in many ways, he was more of a stargazer and a theorist than he was an astronomer. Alas, he could prove nothing. A brilliant man, certainly, but also a phenomenally stubborn and difficult man. And bombastic to boot. Eventually, he was ruled a suspected heretic by the inquisition, but it wasn't for his scientific theories. 'Martyr for science' is not the true lesson to be learned from Galileo."

"Wow. I had no idea."

Score another. What was that? Four? It didn't look good for the kid.

"So, what is the lesson, then?" No frustration from David, just admirable curiosity.

"Simply that Galileo had an attitude problem, which the Church was trying to address the best way it knew how. Einstein lived in a much different era—practically our own—and was not bound by any church as his sponsor or financier. But his problem was the same, ultimately. Both men had a heart problem and valued their pride over humility before God. As do we all, from time to time."

"Wait. Are you saying that Einstein fudged his math so that he could avoid dealing with the possibility of God creating the universe?"

Matthew shrugged noncommittally.

"See, that's exactly what I'm talking about! That's like, academically dishonest or whatever. It's disgusting." There was that frustration. *Another one for the boy, regardless.*

"Well, let's not be too unkind to Einstein. He indeed proposed his cosmological constant to allow for the repulsive form of gravity he thought he needed. But he followed the best theoretical understanding and experimental evidence available to do it. Equally significant is that he later removed it from his equations. It simply didn't seem necessary for the universe or his math to function. Before the end, he regarded his invention of the cosmological constant as his biggest blunder. So perhaps he agreed with you."

And another to the priest.

"Wow. I didn't know any of that stuff." David glanced at whatever was on his phone. "But, if I'm remembering right, isn't dark energy a current theory still? I mean, if the Big Bang really points to God, and I'm not saying it does, then why should people care what's in Genesis at all? Isn't the point of the Bible to tell us how God made the world in seven days and the real way the flood happened?"

Scratch that. Score one for the boy. Evans suddenly wasn't sure who he was rooting for in this argument.

Father Matthew chuckled. "Well David, the truth is that even good science explains neither myths nor the Bible away. Science is a tool that can be misapplied, or applied badly, but we could say the same about sacred texts. The Bible also requires us to use our brains and our imagination in tandem. Let's look again to Noah, shall we? This time, read Genesis 7:19-20 in a different version. Perhaps something marked as an amplified or expanded translation?"

David consulted his phone, fiddling with the settings on his Bible program. After a minute or so he began to read. "'And the waters have been very mighty on the earth and covered are all the high mountains which are under the whole heavens. Fifteen cubits upwards have the waters become mighty, and the mountains are covered.'" He stopped short. "Wait, that's really different from what you quoted a minute ago. Fifteen cubits isn't enough to cover a mountain, is it?"

"The current understanding scientifically is that ocean levels worldwide rose a few hundred feet between eight thousand and six thousand years ago. It is attributed to the melting of the Ice Age by many climatologists. So, in that regard, there was a worldwide flood. Even more so than a mere fifteen biblical cubits. Though it would have taken many generations, you realize. And one's conclusions depend greatly on how one interprets the data. Some argue that this same rise occurred in periodic spurts. Eighty centimeters there, a meter here. It's hard to know for sure."

David changed the settings on the phone again and came up even more dissatisfied. Matthew interlaced his fingers over his stomach and smiled understandingly while David swiped and scowled at his phone. "But, what...? Why?" David finally said, giving up the search. Point and match to the priest.

"It bothers you that biblical verses that appear to convey scientific facts are not clear, does it? It did me too. For years. Decades even. It took a lengthy gazing at the stars for me to reconsider things. But I finally surmised that a rational mind has in many ways more to do with personality than faculty. The greatest mistake is believing that what we think we know is absolute."

"Lucifer," David said.

"I beg your pardon?" Matthew lifted an eyebrow.

"You know, 'Bringer of Knowledge?' Arthur said that the temptation to know more is the basic human problem. I forget how he put it exactly, but the idea was that societies fall when we get too enlightened."

"Ah, yes, I see," the priest whispered, a twinkle in his eye. "Before Satan fell out with God, he fell in love with himself. Perhaps he even believed he was right. Yes, science and scholarship can be like that. I daresay Einstein would have done well by employing a bit more trained imagination, so to speak."

"So, it wasn't that Einstein lacked imagination," David's gears were turning at a blurring speed. "Just that he used it to make his logical theory fit what he wanted it to be?"

The priest paused, considering his words. "When either reason or imagination is out of balance, there is great potential for causing problems."

"So then, we need to train our hearts and our minds together?" David probed.

"Quite right! It's not unlike your esteemed Uncle Sir Arthur in that regard."

"How so?"

Evans eyed the priest suspiciously. It would be just like Matthew to muddle the groundwork Evans had laid down for the boy only just this afternoon.

"Well, Sir Arthur Evans was one of the first great pioneering archeologists. He developed and employed new techniques and opened up a previously-unknown civilization in ancient Crete. He merely got a bit high-spirited, letting his imagination run away with him regarding the Minotaur's maze. Or so Arthur's version of the story goes, anyway."

It was odd for Evans to hear Matthew say this as if he weren't standing in the doorway.

"Arthur's version?" David wondered.

"Well yes, we all have our versions of legends and myths. And there is not a more mythical archeologist than Sir Arthur Evans."

Evans felt his hollow chest full of ambivalence smolder threateningly again.

"Mythical? But Father Matthew, Uncle Sir Arthur was a real guy, not some Indiana Jones."

Matthew laughed raucously. "Unquestionably! Many myths and legends are, don't you know. And all are true in one sense or another. That's the point of them, after all. Powerful stories are capable of changing lives and shaping whole cultures. There's a bit of Sir Arthur in every Hollywood adventurer, I'd lay wager. The world of myth is not a place of things, it is a place of ideas. Nor is it a place to perceive, quantify, or understand objectively, but a place to act. It's why we moderns have turned poor Galileo into a martyr. The truth is far less interesting than the myth."

"'Myth is not a dirty word.' That's what Arthur meant?"

The priest leaned in again with a mock whisper, as if telling the greatest secret in the world. "C. S. Lewis once called Christ the 'true myth', if you can believe it." He leaned back with a creak, his point made, waiting.

David sat, saying nothing. Evans felt his cheeks and neck getting hot under his merciful beard. It was time to step in, and he did so quite literally. But one foot was all he managed before Matthew spoke again.

"As for our little mystery with *Genesis* chapter seven, your grandfather would probably say that it's just an idiomatic translation difference. When we look at the earliest texts we have, it can be interpreted either way. So, we must ask whether the now-mysteriously-missing waters literally raised the Ark some five and a half miles above sea level—as would be required by current mountain heights—or, perhaps even more strangely, were the mountains in Noah's day only fifteen cubits high? Which would be about, what? Seven meters, Arthur?"

David turned so quickly that Evans was surprised he didn't suffer whiplash. Arthur's eavesdropping was over, but so was their private discussion.

XXXV

St. Michael at the North Gate. Oxford, England. David.

David was overwhelmingly relieved to see that Arthur was okay. *How long has he been standing there?*

"Ahem, yes. Fifteen cubits are roughly seven meters," Arthur stammered from the doorway. "Closer to eight, if you use the Egyptian cubit. Not that it really matters. Twenty-five feet is barely a hill, much less a mountain."

David had done as he'd been told, but it had been hard. Now, seeing his backpack next to Arthur, he had a strange feeling that maybe things weren't over after all. At least his weird European phone charger was in there. The little smartphone had endured quite the day too.

"I'm relieved you are okay, David," Arthur said, echoing David's own feeling. "And you, Matthew, seem to be enjoying his company."

"Indeed I am!" the priest exclaimed. He rose from his chair to clasp Arthur's whole forearm in a massive two-handed shake, much to Arthur's obvious discomfort. "Why have you never told me about your brilliant protégé before? Is it because his arguments are better than yours?" Then offhandedly, "He certainly plays a better game of chess."

David blushed a bit. He'd felt a little bad after the third game in a row of destroying Matthew, but strategy games were kind of his thing, after all. Letting somebody win was too much like cheating, so he never did it.

Arthur ignored his best friend's playful ribbing. "Can I assume, that based on the topic of conversation, you have updated Matthew on our situation?"

"That he has," the priest interjected. "And if you don't mind me saying so Arthur, I'm a bit envious that you never took me on a chase through town with a wild gun-toting motorcyclist in pursuit of a mysterious journal from your old archeology partner. What was his name again?" He glanced from Arthur to David and winked.

"Wyatt Aarons," Arthur grumbled. "And I assure you, though I may not have been in communication with the man in three decades, he has caused me enough trouble in one day to make up for it."

Father Matthew let out another hearty barrel-chested laugh that rocked his bookshelves. David cracked a smile, and even Arthur had to shake his head at the oddity of the situation.

"So, what do we do now Arthur?" David asked. "Did the cops get the guy chasing us?"

"Well, I don't know," Arthur admitted. "I have many things to tell you both. But first, Matthew, we would very much like to stay here for the night."

This surprised David. Were they really in that much danger?

"This isn't a monastery, Arthur," the priest countered. "I was about to lock up and go home to Mrs. Williams' steak and kidney pie when David and I began our interesting conversation. Where exactly do you plan to sleep?"

"I don't really expect to at all," Arthur replied, extracting the pistol from his coat pocket with his handkerchief.

Matthew tensed at the sight of the weapon, but David couldn't have been more surprised if it had been painted orange.

"Now, first things first. If I could borrow your phone for a moment, David? And I'll take the journal back too, if you please?"

David unlocked and handed it over, then deftly caught the journal as Father Matthew tossed it over. Both of them stared wordlessly at Arthur as he deciphered exactly how one made calls on a phone with no buttons. He finally connected to one of the recent incoming numbers.

"Hello, Mel? Yes, it's Arthur Evans. I have thought about it and am prepared to name some terms. First, I'm going to need to get to Paris quickly if I'm to make that flight in the morning. Oh, and I have two assistants coming with me."

Father Matthew and David looked at one other, eyebrows at peak elevation. The priest lifted a finger and started shaking his head furiously. David began stammering vowels. Arthur maddeningly turned towards a bookshelf, pretending not to see them.

"Helicopter? Sounds dreadful. No, no, It's fine. We'll be at Wolvercote by sunup. Next, for my compensation which you mentioned earlier, I'm thinking expenses covered and a reasonable day rate. I've had to cancel my tutoring contracts for the summer, you see. I'll get back to you with a proper total later if that's all right. I don't want to end up like Sessa."

Father Matthew looked at David. The priest's face had gone completely pale. David was at a complete loss. This was not the Arthur he thought he knew. Even more significantly, the priest seemed to be thinking the same thing. Arthur kept going.

"Yes, that Sessa. Inventor of chess. Never mind, it's not important. Third, as I believe I mentioned, things are a little complicated right now. So we will require a full scholarship and stipend for my youngest assistant, starting next term here at the university, specific college yet to be determined. Non-negotiable, I'm afraid."

David's mind raced. Oxford tuition wasn't cheap. His parents were going to flip.

"Excellent. Finally, we'll need a respectable donation for the purpose of restoration and upkeep to the church of St. Michael at the Northgate."

It was Matthew's turn to splutter in confusion, whispering Arthur's name over and over to no avail. Arthur glanced over his shoulder to scowl and wave him into silence.

"Good, thank you. Yes, a series of letters to those ends would be very helpful indeed. Oh, and one more thing. You should be aware that a well-dressed Middle Eastern man tried to kill us today and take the journal for himself. I don't know what your current security level is, but—"

A pause, David could almost hear Ms. Chen's rapid reply. Then, "Ah yes, ex-special forces sounds quite satisfactory." Another pause, and finally, "To you as well Ms. Chen. Thank you for understanding, I shall look forward to meeting the team tomorrow."

Arthur handed the phone back to David, who ended the call for him, oblivious to the gaping stares from both his grandson and his best friend.

"Now, where were we? We have about nine hours to prepare before we must meet the company helicopter. Ms. Chen said she would be sending an email, one of you will need to access that. Also, perhaps call up those Linear-A notes and tablets you photographed earlier? Matthew, do you have a chalkboard we can use? Oh, and before I forget, I assume your passport is in this bag somewhere, David? You will most definitely need it when we get to Syria. Matthew, I presume you'll need to go home and collect yours?"

The dam broke all at once. Both David and Matthew unleashed a torrent of excuses, questions, and arguments at Arthur. He looked at them for a moment, his face stoic, entirely unreadable. Then, something in his expression shifted, cutting them both off. With a purse of his lips and a little wave towards their respective chairs, Arthur communicated everything. David's grandfather, the mysterious and enigmatic world traveler, Dr. Arthur M. Evans of Oxford, was going back into the archeology business. And this time, he was the one in charge.

Mr. Wyatt Aarons didn't stand a chance.

XXXVI

Chinese Airspace. 36,000 ft., Westbound towards Syria. Mel.

Mel smiled and dropped a few hand-rolled jasmine pearls into her teapot. The little spheres plinked nicely and formed up in a circle before she poured the boiling water over them. She stood watch as they unfurled in unison, their higher function in life playing out just for her.

As she had hoped, the man in the stuffed suit had acted out. Rather badly in fact.

We make such terrible decisions when we are angry.

Her second plan had worked, and Evans was hers now. The man she pulled out of retirement to motivate Mr. Suit had been one of her father's oldest friends till the day he died. Her remarkable uncle dug inside Mr. Suit's mind better than she ever had. This did not bother her. Mel was the real puppetmaster. And Mr. Suit had similarly motivated Evans. Eventually, all things came into alignment for her purposes. Dominoes falling. Networked minds working as one. Mel dumped the liquid and poured more hot water. The second pouring of jasmine tea was always better. No need to drink the first one.

She was the matriarch of this big corporate family. Its employees were her children. Mr. Suit had utterly failed to understand this, and so had needed to go. The good of the whole and the function of the human network required it. She had underestimated the vain young man's selfish streak at first, just as she had underestimated Dr. Evans' noble one. She wouldn't make either mistake again. The Dilmun team was leaving in a few hours, and she would have all of the right human computers on board, and most importantly, that journal. On her plane's current course, she could meet the team in Syria just a few hours after they were settled in. The timing was acceptable. No need to second guess her earlier decisions.

And yet, Mr. Suit had still been the key to securing Dr. Evans. It pleased her that her strange gamble had worked. Only a few short hours after flatly refusing, Dr. Evans was begging to lead her team. Mel knew Dr. Evans' true motivations now. In the end, Dr. Evans' price had been quite reasonable. College tuition for his grandson, an endowment to a church, and his personal expenses covered. It was hardly more costly than Wyatt Aarons had ever been to her. Even with Evans' two tagalongs, he had severely undersold himself. "Research assistants," he'd called them? Very cute. Quite convenient for him to bring his leverage with him, though.

She still didn't know if she could trust Wyatt Aarons' old partner, but whether he fully understood it or not, Dr. Evans was working for her now. Her newest human computer. He would need access to the team data and a standard expense and travel account. The easiest thing in the world, a few clicks and done. Soon, images of the journal would be delivered into the hands of her people, they would scrutinize them and pass their findings on to her.

Tea first, she reminded herself. The Jasmine-infused tea leaves swirled and swayed as she poured, then drank deep. *Dance, little ones, dance.*

XXXVII

Cornmarket Street. Oxford, England. Arthur.

Evans held firm to his decision to go. It surprised him how quickly Matthew agreed to come along. The priest made some calls and went home, locking the Evanses in.

As promised, Mel Chen emailed an encrypted and password-protected link to a massive project folder. Fortunately, because of her earlier mechanizations of David's phone, the boy was able to access the email for him. It included dossiers of the three people already on the Dilmun team and scads of other material. This meant that it was absolutely no good to Evans whatsoever. It seemed barely readable as he squinted and tapped at the comedically small screen. But David seemed to experience no such problems with the infernal device, so Evans let him keep that job.

Over the next hour or so they transferred the top points of the digital files to a little spiral notepad until jet lag finally claimed David. As the boy slept in Matthew's old padded reading chair, Evans scoured the journal for more clues but he didn't find anything new.

Well before sun-up, Father Matthew met them in front of St. Michaels with a little black taxi. The cabbie took them to the outskirts of town, where a company helicopter was supposed to pick them up. Matthew was wearing his priest's collar along with black jeans and a sensible shirt. If his best friend had decided to treat this like a missionary journey, Evans decided not to fight it. At least Matthew had a reasonable duffle bag and not a suitcase. Enthusiastic as he was, Evans had always admired his friend's sensible side. It was perhaps why they got along so well.

"I'll have you know that neither Mrs. Williams nor the bishop were particularly happy about this little call-to-adventure," Matthew said. "Especially given the late hour and last-minute nature of it all. I only hope he keeps a sermon prepared for such occasions, else he'll be pulling from one of the books this morning."

Matthew's face betrayed him though, Evans had never seen such an extraordinary grin on the happy-go-lucky priest's face before. He was already having fun, and they hadn't even left Oxford yet. Besides, while Mel's donation hadn't hit the church's account just yet, it was sizable, and the bishop was no fool.

"And I imagine that the congregation will have quite the surprise too," Matthew said. "I've been doing a series on integrity and consistency in hopes of bolstering attendance. Not the best object lesson, I'm afraid."

Evans did not reply. David snickered at the jibe, and that was sufficient. Those two could keep each other company while he worked. They complimented each other well. And now that they were both here beside him, he was glad of it. It all seemed right somehow with them along. Evans wasn't operating on rational thinking alone anymore, and he was going to need help coping with that.

It only took a few minutes to arrive at the prescribed lane and field. Instead of the commercial craft Evans had expected, a lightweight military-issue helicopter was waiting for them. The two front-mounted machine guns and RAF insignia were a pretty good tip-off. The bearded and traditionally dressed Middle Eastern taxi driver gave them a fleeting glance pregnant with questions. Evans could only shrug. Mao Sien was better connected than he'd imagined.

Evans smiled weakly, grabbed his satchel, and slid out of the little car. "Let's go, David."

As an afterthought, he tipped the man. The driver smiled politely but was clearly unimpressed with the amount. He mumbled to himself in Arabic as he performed a sloppy three-point turn and drove away.

Their pilot emerged. He was dressed in military flight gear but smiled in welcome and waved them forward. Minutes later, they were lifting into the air, watching long-haired sheep scatter to the far ends of the field.

"David, can you see that graveyard there?" Evans shouted into his noise-canceling headset and mic.

Falling quickly away was a misty cemetery filled with upright stones. It lay beyond the edge of the pasture, framed in the distance by a little road lined with Cotswold cottages. The faintest hint of sunrise drew the gravestones out from the deeper shadows.

"Yea?" David shouted back, looking up from his phone.

"That's Wolvercote Cemetery, it's where Tolkien and his wife are buried."

"Really? Neat."

"Yes, I'll have to take you to see it sometime. The inscriptions are quite nice. Besides, his voluminous work saved my life recently, the least I could do is pay my respects when we return."

"When will that be, Arthur?"

It occurred to Evans that he had absolutely no idea.

"I was supposed to go shopping with Emma later," David continued, "but I guess that won't be happening. I'd kind of like to make sure she knows I didn't stand her up. Do you think I can get a signal up here?"

Emma? David's mention of the name rang a faint bell, somewhere in the back of his mind. Who was this person? Evans was about to ask when suddenly they were all thrown back into their seats as upward movement shifted into forward thrust. Evans had been across the English Channel many times, by ferry mostly. He had flown in through Charles de Gaulle Airport more than once in his younger days, and exactly once had tried the Chunnel train, swearing that one off permanently. But never had he made the trip this quickly or dramatically. He grabbed the edges of his chair, for whatever good that might do.

"How fast can this thing go?" David shouted into his microphone with clear delight.

"About three-ten Kph," said the voice from the front. He had a classic Londoner's inflection with the overlay of a no-nonsense RAF type, which Evans supposed he was.

"How long will it take to get to France, then? Like eighty minutes?"

"Eighty-three, mate. Good guess. We couldn't ask for clearer weather. You'll spot the Channel straight off."

Evans allowed himself a smirk. David sat poking at what looked to be a calculator program on his phone. It was no guess—the superphone had struck again.

As the thunderous whir of the propellers rocketed them across the dark fields and hills of the English countryside, Evans clenched his teeth tight and his eyes tighter. There was no going back now. It was time to finish what he had started over thirty years ago.

In the field below and far behind them, an imaginary Elizabeth blew him a kiss and waved goodbye.

Or, more accurately, no one did anything at all.

XXXVIII

Mao Sien SA-342 Gazelle helicopter. 14,000 ft. Eastbound over the English Channel toward France. David.

About twenty-four hours ago, David had been on a plane heading towards England for the greatest adventure of his life: college. His mysterious grandfather had been little more than a family legend, and Oxford a castle town of adventure and possibility. The man and his hometown had exceeded his wildest expectations.

Suddenly though, as the sleek little helicopter rocketed across the sparkling English Channel towards France, the reality of what was happening hit David like a ton of bricks. How would his parents react? Was a scholarship enough to calm his father down from what would almost certainly be unabashed rage toward Arthur for this abduction? His mother would be worried out of her mind. Ugarit wasn't some Mediterranean beach resort, it was modern-day Syria. *Syria!* The U.S. had been sanctioning that country for literally David's entire life. And he was going there on what, a tourist passport? In a military helicopter! This was some field trip.

The truth was, David still barely knew Arthur at all. The last day hadn't helped, either. David may have come to understand the old man a little better, but he still held on to the possibility that his grandfather was completely nuts. The man now had terrorists or whatever coming after him from some discovery thirty years ago? Just what had he and Mr. Aarons found on that Doomsday Mountain? David's imagination sparked into a lightning storm of possibilities. You don't go chasing down a stuffy old professor after half a lifetime for an insignificant hill in the middle of nowhere. More than ever, David felt sure that his grandfather had found something earth-shattering. It was the only thing that made any sense. And now, they were on the hunt for Mr. Aarons' next big discovery!

And what about Emma? David was supposed to be meeting her for coffee and an expert tour of the city in just a few hours. He'd sent her a stream of messages to let her know the crazy things that were happening, but she hadn't responded yet. Soon, he might be out of range and not get her reply at all. David wasn't clear about what this Miss Chen person had done to his phone. Sure, he'd paid for the international plan before leaving the U.S., but it hadn't worked—until it had. And she'd made that happen. *How? What kind of power and influence does a person like that have?* He considered googling her, but something about doing it on the phone itself made him nervous. He now felt like his super-phone wasn't entirely safe anymore. That alone made him feel kind of violated, and maybe a little mad.

As the sunrise turned the English Channel to liquid fire, David could see the coast of France in the distance. They were flying parallel to it, almost due south, near the beaches of Normandy where the Allies had stormed France to push back the Nazis. They were all tourist beaches now. A very different world back then, he supposed. The context of a shoreline made him realize how fast they were going. The roar of the blades above him beat the sky into submission, slicing them forward on what seemed a sheer force of will alone. It was exhilarating. This was the way to fly!

Without warning, the helicopter turned slightly into the sun and flicked them over the shoreline. In moments, it was all patchwork shades of green and brown with little provincial towns sliding by underneath them. They were too high and fast to make out any real details. But David couldn't shake the feeling that it was all just a big mural and that if he looked away, he would find himself back at the Ashmolean staring at a model landscape, or back home commanding a miniature army in a tabletop battle scenario. This truly was the shortest way to Paris. Too bad it was only for a layover at Charles du Gaul airport. David wouldn't get to practice his amateur French or see anything iconic. Like in London, it was going to be all planes and busses and down to business. This was no sightseeing tour. He felt a little frustrated by it.

This was supposed to be his big summer of adventure, but never in his wildest dreams had he imagined this. "Getting settled" in Oxford was impossible now. Arthur didn't even know how long this Syria trip was going to last. What if they didn't find Mr. Aarons right away? Would they just come back in a few weeks, regardless? Would David still get his scholarship? And more on point, what if David missed his interview before the start of term? Or what if the University needed to get in touch with him? Imagined scenarios of the many and varied ways it could all go wrong cascaded through his head. So much had changed since his small worries from yesterday. Finding the absent Arthur, a misbehaving phone, tasting proper tea. It all seemed so petty now. Had it only been a day? It felt like a week.

As the helicopter slowed for their approach to Paris, David realized he'd been wrong about one thing at least. Looming large in the distance beyond the Napoleonic era rooftops of the city was the unmistakable silhouette of the Eifel Tower. Even from this distance, the massive steel structure jutted out like a finger daring anyone to dismiss it as just a nineteenth-century broadcast tower.

C'est impossible! He snapped a dozen pictures to post later.

It soon became clear that the helicopter was neither as expected nor as welcome as it could have been. As the private military vehicle circled, the pilot argued about the details of their landing in rapid French with the air traffic control tower. David had gotten through Spanish III with his mom, but his occasional experimentation with French language software was not much help for this torrent. Obscenities hadn't been covered, and there seemed to be more than a few of those. David could almost hear a slight echo of his father from a hemisphere away through the furious accusatory tones of the men on the radio. *"My father took our son where?!"*

The pilot's mic crackled and brought David out of his imaginings. "We are cleared to land now. Please stay where you are until we've stopped spinning and someone collects you. You'll all be walking across the tarmac straight to the company plane from here, I'm told. The French don't want to have to deal with us or our employer, it seems. I would consider that a bit of luck, all things considered."

Minutes later with bags in hand, the three adventurers sprinted across the tarmac towards a company jet complete with boarding stairs. David considered the passport tucked away in his bag. The French authorities weren't even going to check it? *Just who is this Mel Chen person?*

A cold shiver started at his head and went straight to his toes.

But it might have just been the chilly morning air of Paris in May.

XXXIX

Mao Sien private jet. Charles de Gaulle Airport tarmac. Paris, France. Arthur.

Evans let David climb the boarding stairs first. The youth stepped through the door of the plane and stopped short. Evans all but bounced off his overstuffed backpack. Once inside, Evans immediately understood why. While the exterior looked much like any other small commercial plane, the interior had undergone significant upgrades. If not for the oval windows and the long tunnel-like curve of the plane's ceiling, Evans would have easily believed they'd accidentally stepped into a high-tech ultra-modern VIP lounge.

Eight plush leather easy chairs faced one another in an elongated ellipse. Each one had a small collapsible worktable and a private screen on a swivel arm. Glancing left as he stepped into the space, Evans also noticed a huge flat-screen monitor on the front wall. There were other unsettling gadgets he could only guess the use of, all bolted down and secured in place. Airplane cabin or not, this was a top-end board room meant for world-class passengers. It was quite horrible.

Four people already occupying the cabin offered polite greetings to the new arrivals. The little spiral notebook with simplified notations of the personnel files was keeping the Aarons journal company in Evans' coat pocket. All he needed was a little time to study said notes, and fortunately, the flight would provide that.

The seven team members were joined by a flight attendant from another room who began helping to stow bags in little compartments toward the back.

Seven passengers? Was that right? Already Evans' notes were failing him. He had understood the team to be six, including himself, David, and Matthew.

Something was off. Usually, in these cases, it was his math, but three plus three wasn't exactly advanced calculus.

As Evans tried to puzzle it out, the plane jerked backward, signaling it was ready to find its runway. He grabbed his hat with one hand and reached for a plush leather seat back with the other to avoid stumbling. No announcements on this flight, then. Matthew charged in with a broad smile. Then it was all shaking hands and nodding heads and "Lovely to meet you."

David looked around once then plopped into a chair next to the only female team member. This was the young anthropologist, Evans remembered. She put down the book she was reading and greeted David with a surprised smile and a perfect Castilian accent. "Hola. ¿Cómo estás?"

David hesitated, then haltingly fumbled over the syllables of a reply: "Yo-es-toy-bien. ¿Y-tú?"

The Spanish girl didn't hide her bemusement, but she played along. The rest was an exchange of "Spanglish" that surprised Evans, David stumbling through perfectly fine American words and being schooled in the "correct" pronunciation by the other. Most Texans studied Mexican Spanish out of practicality, but for some reason, he hadn't expected Karen's homeschooling to be so thorough. It wouldn't do David much good where they were going, but at least the boy had an ear for more than one language.

Evans puckered his lips thoughtfully over this teenager who was grinning like a fool and turning beet red, then looked again at the young woman. Her dark wavy hair, light brown eyes, and lightly tanned skin perfectly complimented her accent. She had an athletic build accentuated by tight clothes that looked brand new. She had done some shopping in Paris yesterday, he'd wager. She also understood the function of makeup. So many of Evans' students didn't.

Admittedly, it had been a long time since Elisabeth had passed, but Evans certainly wasn't dead yet. *If perhaps a little out of practice with the female of the species... okay, a lot.* But clearly, his grandson wasn't dead either. No wonder he was turning colors and grinning like a ninny. The young woman was gorgeous and hardly much older than David. According to her file, she'd acquired her first Ph.D. at the age of sixteen. Her second, he didn't recall offhand, but it was somewhere in his spiral notebook. A beautiful and brilliant European, just like Elisabeth.

A dull memory of grief tugged at Evans. He'd missed Elisabeth a little more than usual lately. This thing with Joseph's family had brought some of that forward. Maybe that was why he had been seeing her so much more often. Not to mention, he was starting to have what could only be thought of as grandfatherly feelings for David. That was not good at all. If he wasn't careful, he could lose his objectivity over silly human emotions, and that would be unacceptable. Despite their unusual situation, he and the boy seemed to be getting along reasonably well. It would be a shame to muck it up with complicated feelings as he and Joseph had somehow done for so long.

"You must be Dr. Evans?" An Asian man in his mid-forties diverted Evans' attention. "I am Dr. Ken Lee, very pleased to meet you, sir." He spoke in heavily accented words but helpfully annunciated them very slowly if a little oddly.

"Ah, yes. Um, I'm not entirely sure who everyone is yet," Evans replied with a little wave. He realized with embarrassment that he had been bracing himself against the man's chair since the plane started moving. "What is it you do? I don't think I got all the files." He staggered a bit and pulled out the notes he had made on his spiral notepad. He looked over his glasses for a page in the notepad where he might have written about this Dr. Lee person, but he already knew such a page did not exist.

Lee chuckled. "I understand the confusion. I am a practitioner of traditional medicine. You would say, 'alternative medicine,' maybe. Not one of your team's scholars." he bowed his head slightly. "However, very pleased to make your acquaintance."

"Really?" Evans said without looking up, flipping through more pages than he remembered having made.

"You might be surprised at how many doors it opens. I have treated the Aitolia, I consult for both Great Leaders in Korea, and I regularly see various influential persons in China, including the President."

"Great Leaders?" Evans realized he was being quite rude by not looking at the man. He slipped the notebook back into his pocket and focused on Dr. Lee. "Do you mean of North Korea? How did you manage that?"

Lee chuckled. "Simple. I am North Korean. Pointedly, that is where I am headed. Miss Chen has been generous enough to let me tag along on this flight for the first part of my journey. So, I must also thank you for allowing me to share your comfortable seating."

Relief and confusion washed over Evans. He didn't have notes on the man because he was not on the team. Also, being from the closed country of North Korea was a very good answer to how he could meet and treat its communist dictators. Though Evans did wonder exactly how Lee was able to cross over the closed border so casually when Western cameras weren't even allowed in.

Before he could probe further, an old man who had been hovering hard like the helicopter they'd just left inserted himself into the conversation. "And I'm Ryan Pitman, geomorphology!" the man bellowed. He toasted Evans with his ginger ale. He had a southern accent, grown in one of the Carolinas.

Nothing so deep-fried as Aarons', but greasy enough to put pause to one's portions. At least he had a reasonable fashion sense. Evans was fairly sure he owned the same sports coat at home.

"You're our new team leader, huh?" the old man accused him.

"Yes, that's right," Evans said. He didn't need his notes to know this man, though Pitman's appearance now surprised him. The rockhound was about a decade older than Evans, but time hadn't treated him well. The guy was all teeth and wrinkles. Wiry, shriveled, hairless, and blotchy skin that looked like old shoe leather, Pitman looked more like an Egyptian mummy than a scientist. Yet, for a man in his mid-seventies, Pitman presented with almost childlike excitement. Evans afforded him a polite smile.

"Well then, commander," the fossil joked, "The medicine man you've just met, and Señorita deMata is welcoming your young assistant over there." The anthropologist looked over and wiggled her fingers politely, but Pitman didn't stop. "And the good rabbi, our ancient religions scholar, is the hairy one on the end with the yarmulka." The dismissiveness with which Dr. Pitman spoke reminded Evans of why so many of his European colleagues considered Americans to be impolite.

At the mention of himself, the man in the traditional kippah hat looked over and gave a quick nod. "I'm pleased to meet you Dr. Evans, Yosef Ibrahim at your service. I am looking forward to working with you." Evans instantly recognized the throaty and flat Israeli accent of a native Hebrew speaker. Admittedly, the man's traditional facial hair and sidelocks had been a pretty big giveaway, regardless of Pitman's tactlessness about it. Matthew had found a seat across from the rabbi and they were already chatting away, so that was something.

"Likewise, I'm sure." Evans nodded back, trying not to sound too patronizing. He often felt he came across this way to religious scholars. It wasn't personal. Evans disliked blind faith, and discovering whether or not such people were hostile to his more rational ideology was often unproductive and uncomfortable. Not everyone could be like Matthew, after all. It was one of the key reasons he'd wanted his best friend along. Matthew's gleeful optimism notwithstanding, Evans valued the priest's longsuffering patience with him. Not to mention his scientific pedigree.

Evans forced a smile on the Jewish scholar's behalf and shifted to face Pitman directly. "I remember you, Ryan. You worked with Wyatt on Doomsday after I left. As I recall, he touted you as one of the foremost biblical geomorphologists in the world." He tried to keep the sarcasm out of his voice. To be fair though, it was likely true, given that Pitman was probably the only 'biblical geomorphologist' in the world. "I read your book back in the '80s,"

Evans offered amicably. "The evidence you provided for a flood using cores from the Black Sea was what first turned Wyatt towards your work."

"Guilty as charged!" Pitman was smiling from ear to ear. "I was wondering if you'd remember me, Doc. My lab was the one that analyzed all those rock samples from Doomsday you and Wyatt sent back to the States."

Evans knew for a fact that Pitman, like himself and the others here, had a terminal degree. In his case, a Ph.D. in the study of the features of the surface of the Earth, earned even before Evans' time with Wyatt. But if nicknames were this fellow's southern way of being friendly, Evans could let it slide. "Doc" was better than "Commander" certainly. He didn't recall Dr. Ibrahim's file designating the professor of religious studies as being an ordained rabbi either. More likely, the Israeli scholar had been given the nickname by Pitman, who seemed to revel in the power of name-giving. It was an ancient right of kings, and Pitman seemed to think he was Nebuchadnezzar. But then, 'rabbi' simply meant 'teacher,' so perhaps the nickname was truer than Pitman realized.

Evans forced a smile. "Actually, Ryan, I was the one who recommended you to Wyatt. He hired you on before our last trip was even over. You and I missed each other by mere months, but I spent three days in a Turkish jail cell because of those drill cores. Wyatt didn't have permission to dig them, it turned out."

Pitman's expression tumbled into sly bemusement. "Well, now." He dragged the 'well' into about three syllables as only a southerner can. "I would say I'm sorry, but I didn't have anything to do with that." The old man laughed. He was the only one.

Evans snorted. "Oh, don't worry. I blame exactly one man for that fiasco, and I'm glad it happened. Wyatt and I parted ways after that. But you worked with him for a number of years, did you not?"

'Glad it happened?' Why had he just said that? It couldn't possibly be true.

"I certainly did," Pitman said. He had a whimsical lilt Evans thought odd. This man was strange. "I suppose one could argue that I still am. After all, isn't that our purpose here? To find Wyatt and Dilmun all in one swoop?"

The others had stopped talking and all eyes were on Evans. Fortunately, the jet reached its runway and the plane lurched to a stop. Pitman sat. The engines whined, the lights dimmed, and the flight attendant made a quick pass to grab their empty glasses. Evans used the moment to situate himself in the empty chair by Dr. Ibrahim and fumbled around for the seatbelt. He had never flown in a sideways board room before. It was unsettling to say the least, and they were still on the ground.

Evans dearly hoped he had dodged Pitman's question. He didn't want to air his personal conflict with Aarons to strangers. Opening up to David yesterday had been a fluke, off-guard by family pressures and a moment of weakness. But here, Evans needed to be a strong leader, not a babysitter. He closed his eyes and took a long breath.

"You know, Doc, you're still wearing your hat there," Pitman teased.

Does the man never stop talking? Evans flicked his eyes open, gave him a weak smile, and reached to his head. At that exact moment, the plane shuddered and lurched again. The fedora slipped out of Evans' fingers and rolled awkwardly to the other side, settling near Pitman's feet. With one swift move, the old man swiped the hat from the floor and put it on his bald blotchy head.

"Perfect fit," he said with a skeletal grin meant to signal it was all in sarcastic fun. "Darned shame." He then tossed it frisbee-style back across the cabin. To Evans' great surprise, he caught both the attempt at humor and the actual hat.

Are you sure your head isn't too big? he stopped himself from saying and settled for a weak smile back.

That's when it hit him. Wyatt had hand-picked this team, not Mel Chen. Evans glanced at the young woman chatting up David, and the Hebrew scholar laughing with Matthew. The tagalong Dr. Lee had settled back into his chair with his eyes shut. Pitman just kept grinning like a ninny. *Oddballs, every one.* Exactly what he would have expected from Wyatt.

Leading this team was going to take everything Evans had.

Maybe more.

XL

Oxford Railway Station. Oxford, England. Mr. Suit.

A well-dressed Middle Eastern businessman in an expensive Italian suit placed his gym bag into the overhead compartment of a train headed towards London. Inside the bag was a change of undergarments, some toiletries, an empty concealed-carry holster, a crimson passport, and a stack of American cash. Spare change compared to the real money he had in international accounts, but American money was welcome everywhere.

He put the passport and a short stack of cash into his inside jacket pocket and winced. This time it was not because of any pain in his hand or head, but because of the plaster dust visibly smeared on his lapel. He could kill Evans for hurting his wonderful suit. The lump on his head would heal, and his bruised hand would feel better in time, but this suit and his pride were inextricably linked, and he hadn't had time to visit a dry cleaner.

As promised, everything had been arranged for him overnight. The name on the airline ticket matched one of the aliases that had been prepared by his brothers for times like this.

Remember who you are.

Just like he'd hoped, Dr. Evans had seen his tattoo. The tutor now understood the stakes and was fleeing the country with the help of the man in the suit's former employer. The scholar's plane would be taking off any minute, which meant that the trap was set.

People are clocks to be studied. Resources to be consumed.

And as for the man in the suit himself? Well, he was just an important businessman on his way to Aleppo to conduct important work. He'd never been a billionaire playboy before. It suited him. Too bad it didn't come with a corporate line of credit anymore.

The man relaxed into the empty seat below, just as the train began moving away from the station. He practiced his new name in his head. He couldn't count how many other names he had used in the past. It was better not to try. He wondered offhandedly if the Thames Valley Police had put the pieces together yet. They would track his impounded motorcycle's papers or find his prints or some other detail, then descend upon his old room like dogs— assuming they hadn't already. The little room had served him well, but that time was over. He was someone else now.

Remember who you are, he reminded himself.

Remember what you really are.

It is time to fulfill your vows.

XLI

Mao Sien private jet. Charles de Gaulle Airport tarmac. Paris, France. Arthur.

Evans had never quite gotten used to flying. The bigger the plane, the greater his unease. Arthur M. Evans, Ph.D., knew full well that there were well-founded logical truths that made a winged metal behemoth fall up and away from the solid ground. He was perfectly aware that there was no such thing as magic, and the opposing forces of lift and drag and whatnot were not miracles. But even if it wasn't miracles, he still had to remind himself every time that these fundamental principles of physics were woven into the very fabric of the universe. Still, this particular reality was always a little easier to swallow with a few drinks. And he hadn't had one today.

Suddenly, a dark cloud of doubt came over Evans, clawing and scratching its way into his mind with an almost animal panic. What was he doing here? What good could possibly come out of all this adventuring? The business with the gunman had to be some big coincidental misunderstanding. It was likely not even related to this trouble with Wyatt Aarons. He was an old man! Why hadn't he just talked to the Oxfordshire police after all? Silly panic was no reason to— Oh, but the engines were going again. Was it too late to get off?

As if in answer to his question, the plane shuddered and lurched down the runway for take-off. Still no announcement from the captain, just thrust fighting drag. Lift was not yet a challenge to gravity, but the threatening roars of intent were unmistakable.

Evans watched David stagger against the movement like some beach bum in a 1960's surfing film of the sort he'd never bothered to watch because he'd been too busy reading for a degree. The youth had changed his mind about his backpack and was dragging it back to his seat. Laughing, he half-danced, half-floated to his seat. He said something Evans couldn't hear to deMata, his white headphones swinging wide before he caught them with one swift motion of his free hand.

David crammed his fat bag under the seat somehow. The young lady anthropologist met his goofy grin and whispered something they both cackled at. David buckled in just as the engines roared to full power, and the plane rocketed down the runway. The teenager was having the time of his life, the spirit of adventurous youth strong enough to drown out any fear of the unknown. Little miracles of opposing forces.

Evans closed his eyes and resigned himself to his fate. His enthusiastic grandson chatting with a girl replaced the image in his mind of the young Wyatt Aarons sitting across from him in that Turkish prison cell, chattering away about Ur.

He felt the plane's massive wheels break contact with the ground. Gravity relinquished its hold on the multi-ton hunk of metal. The complex interplay of thrust, lift, and drag drew the plane up into the sky against all common sense, ready to span the length of the Mediterranean in a handful of hours. It was mind-boggling.

Yet, out of all these mysteries, one bobbed up to the surface above all the others.

Why do dealings with Wyatt blasted Aarons always have to start with bloody miracles?

*   *   *

As the company jet leveled out to its cruising altitude, Evans still had not stowed his hat. He fumbled with it for a few minutes, then finally settled on pulling it low over his face. He hadn't slept properly since his lie-in yesterday and was now completely off of his sleep cycle. Given that they were about to jump ahead a handful of time zones anyway, he fully intended to nap in the luscious chair.

Various murmurs of conversation were cut off by a mechanical chime as the big screen at the front of the room flickered to life. It was obviously time for a safety video of the sort every seasoned traveler had memorized. He braced himself for three minutes all about seat belts and emergency exits and oxygen masks. But like the other formalities of commercial flight, that feature too had been done away with. Instead, the oversized head and shoulders of Mao Sien CEO Melanie Chen appeared and spoke.

"Hello, team!"

Everyone else snapped to attention, including Matthew and David. Various responses were uttered from around the cabin toward the screen. This was no mere recorded message. Mel was live video chatting from a corporate office somewhere, and apparently, she could see them too. The thought of that made him suddenly uncomfortable. He jerked himself straight and his blasted hat plopped off onto the floor again. Fortunately, it stayed near his feet this time, and he used his heel to push it out of sight.

Evans was finally face-to-face, albeit virtually, with his new employer. He hadn't bothered to trim his whiskers this week. He could feel hat hair sticking up in multiple directions too. The deep cloud of doubt threatened to slice back into Evans' mind. Had he made a terrible mistake? What exactly had he gotten himself into? But he pushed the feelings away with practiced ease, remembering the sequence of events that had led him here. The tattooed men had come for him. Oxford was not safe. There was nothing to be done about the hair. This was his choice. He was in charge. This was his moment of vindication.

He realized with horror that this notion was precisely what Wyatt had said in his scrawled note on the last page of the journal. But Wyatt Aarons could be hanged. It was the real scholar's turn.

"Good morning," Evans said. He was the last one to reply, so he did it with what he hoped was a punctuating firmness. The nap would have to wait.

XLII

Chinese Airspace. 36,000 ft., Westbound towards Syria. Mel.

Mel Chen spoke to the camera on her desk with calculated grace and poise. Thanks to a complicated setup on the other end, she could see each of her elite passengers quite clearly. Their faces appeared across multiple pop-up windows on her concave array of screens, while her image was transmitted to them in near real-time between two aircraft almost a quarter-turn of the world away from one another. Technology was a wonderful thing.

"I presume you have all made your introductions to our leader, Dr. Arthur Evans," she began reverently. She already knew the answer obviously, she had watched them do it. Her first lie.

"He had the distinguished honor early in his career of working with Wyatt Aarons long before any of us. As some of you already know, we are at a critical stage in our quest for Dilmun. However, Mr. Aarons' last report from Ras-Shamra was recorded over two weeks ago but only recently uploaded. We do not yet know why." She kept her expression reverent for now.

"We have confirmed, however, that Mr. Aarons' Syrian guards were attacked by Kurdish guerilla rebels far outside their normal territory. We now know that Mr. Aarons uncovered an important clue as to the physical location of Dilmun and placed it in his notes." This was the second lie.

Aarons had never reported these things, nor mentioned his secret journal

to her. The actual content of it was mere guesswork but based on Evans'
expression she knew she'd hit the mark. Mel hid her reaction and switched
her tone from worshipfulness to chipper excitement. An actor following the
script.

"That clue is now in Dr. Evans' hands. He has kindly agreed to lead the
expedition moving forward. Your objective is to locate Mr. Aarons by
continuing his hunt for Dilmun."

The particulars of Dr. Evans' recruitment were less lie than omission, but
there was no need to make things difficult for the man.

Yet, Mel couldn't have him keeping secrets from her, either.

Those necessary details outed, she continued. "Your plane has been given
clearance to land at Bassel al-Assad International Airport, on the coast of
northern Syria. You will be transported to the Ras-Shamra ruins, ten
kilometers north of Latakia, in armored military vehicles. You will be escorted
the entire way by our personal security team." Right on cue, she pulled up a
little map that illustrated everything she had just said, highlighting the
important locations.

Mel had a very profitable partnership with various first-world
governments to provide troops and equipment in the Middle East.
Consequently, her assets had been given high levels of access to military-grade
equipment. And why not? She had one of the largest private armies in the
world. You can't run a global fuel empire without one. The Americans loved
to hire her well-trained human assets in places like Iraq and Afghanistan. It
helped them to pretend their presence was much less, citing only the
"deployed" rank and file troops in their public reports and media releases.

She had a similar deal with Russia. They were quite happy to let her people
staff various "secret" bases that weren't supposed to exist. Even the Syrian
President was eager to contract her people and shore up the eastern border.
Their presence meant that her Western-trained troops helping the U.N.
efforts in Iraq could now bolster its westerly neighbor as well. Pulling a small
squad over to the coast for this little operation was a no-brainer. Aarons had
hired locals to guard his tent while he worked. Mel was bringing in a highly
trained military presence to avoid that vulnerability, and Syria was paying her
to do it. It was a win-win for everybody.

The animated map retreated, and Mel continued her virtual briefing. "If
all goes well, and the city roads are clear, the drive will take less than twenty
minutes. Commander Raskolnikov has command of all things military and
will take care of everything in that regard. I recommend you take this time to
express and aggregate your various hypotheses regarding Dilmun to build
upon Mr. Aarons' overall findings to date. Get to know one another. You will

all be working together for some time."

Mel leaned in close to the camera. It was a trick she had learned for making herself seem more imposing during these necessary virtual video chats. She looked slightly left, a motion that made no sense from her perspective. She knew though, that it would give the impression her giant face was looking directly at Dr. Evans from the viewpoint of everyone watching the big monitor in the plane's cabin. Lie number four.

"Dr. Evans, I have given you access to Mr. Aarons' video entries, including his final report which I have personally annotated. These are his last recorded actions."

At that, she hit play and let the important first few minutes of the Aarons video log do what even she could not. She watched their faces as the little crackles of gunfire caused Aarons fear. They all held their breath when he dodged into the shadows for a long and tense minute. She smiled at the gasps from her passengers as the masked men entered and searched for him. The cabin stared in horror as he burst forth moments later from the columns at the edge of the screen and wrestled his way into the dark passage beyond the door. The militants raced out behind him, then more chattering gunfire marked the end of the clip.

No further lie was needed. She had them.

Mel stopped the video before anyone could respond, again leaning in to address her new team leader personally. "Dr. Evans, I look forward to taking your first report in person. I will be arriving on-site soon after your team is settled. Thank you one and all for this. You are each the best at what you do by far. I predict enormous success from this expedition. Dilmun is within our grasp at last and finding it will change the world."

And with that, she disconnected. The journal was outed and now there would be questions. Better to let Evans handle them. It was important for establishing his authority, and for everyone to believe he was in charge. Most importantly, she needed Dr. Evans to believe it himself. He would now be forced to talk about the journal, and if he was later discovered to be holding information back, then she'd know that Dr. Evans couldn't be trusted. It was still quite possible that he was colluding with his old partner. She would know soon enough.

She left the spy cameras running, recording every angle. Mel wanted to get some sleep before arriving in Syria tomorrow. And Mel Chen always got what she wanted.

XLIII

French Airspace. 33,000 ft., Eastbound towards Syria. David.

Everybody was focused on Arthur. He looked a bit like a cornered cat.

"Well, Doc, how about you let us see this journal with the mysterious clue to everything?" It was the old guy named Dr. Pitman. He was the sort of person who considered himself clever and assumed everybody else did too. At his words though, David tensed. Mr. Aarons' suspended discoveries were the purpose of this expedition and the secrets in the journal were not going to be secrets much longer. But something about the way Dr. Pitman said it seemed more like an accusation than a question.

Arthur cleared his throat. "Yes, of course." Then, looking over his glasses, "This is Wyatt's last entry." Arthur read it aloud slowly and clearly, just as he had done for David at dinner the night before.

> *4-16-10: Last night I prayed for an hour under the stars of Canaan, and today the Lord led me to a new tablet fragment that I'm confident will be the key to locating Dilmun. It matches up with yesterday's piece perfectly. The original tablet was broken in half, but both parts are preserved. Even with my little knowledge of the writing, I recognize some of it. I will need to find a translator who can do it right. The Evans collection is the key to all this.*

Arthur stopped there, satisfied to leave out the part where Mr. Aarons had hoped Arthur would be willing to help. David noted that he had skipped over a few words about Arthur's overall attitude in the middle there. Maybe it was brevity, or maybe it was a touch of embarrassment on Arthur's part. Either way, David smiled to himself a little. He also couldn't help but notice, that while not technically a lie, it was Mr. Aarons' last official journal entry that Arthur read, not the note directly to Arthur with the stuff about Noah and the tree and vindication for Doomsday. David wondered if his wizard was going to share that part with the team at all.

"Wyatt means the Ashmolean's Sir Arthur Evans Archive," Arthur continued as if it were the most obvious thing in the world. "David and I have now thoroughly reviewed that material and taken note of artifacts which pertain to our investigation."

We did? With a start, David realized that yes, they effectively had. Though not exactly in the way that Arthur made it sound. David had dozens of photos from the archive, maybe more. Was Arthur going to sit on the Linear-A stuff then? He hadn't mentioned the whole Rosetta Stone parallel. Or was he just being, well, Arthur? David didn't have a clue, and whether Arthur planned to elaborate or not, the conversation was jump-started sufficiently without it. Three voices spoke all at once while Arthur returned the journal to his pocket. David tried his best to track them, pulling up the team personnel files in his head.

"Dilmun is going to be well hidden, it's long been sealed from mankind's ability to find." Dr. Pitman, the biblical geomorphologist. *Because that's a thing, apparently? Very cool.*

"Find it? It's ancient mythology, obviously." Dr. Catalina Lopez deMata, the Spaniard anthropologist with a great accent. "No different than the legends of Arcadia or Mt. Olympus. Science tells us that the people who predated the Mesopotamian revolution came to the area looking for safety and food." Dr. deMata was super brilliant and attractive enough to be distracting. She'd told David to call her Cat, and he had been doing that, though nobody else seemed to be.

"A tablet? I would be very interested in finding that. If we consult and cross-reference the ancient texts..." Yosef Ibrahim, religious expert, and rabbi besides.

This went on for another few seconds until Arthur held up his hands like Moses at the red sea. The cabin fell silent almost immediately. It was kind of impressive, though Arthur looked a bit surprised it had worked. A polite cough broke the silence, followed by a new voice.

"Apologies all, but I'm afraid I'm at a disadvantage. What precisely do we mean when we say Dilmun?" Father Matthew. Anglican priest, science guy. *Socially fearless.*

"Ah," Arthur said, grabbing onto the conversation thread and running with it. "Well yes, that is a good place to start. Let's define the objective of Aaron's search and proceed from there. I presume we are all familiar enough with the *Epic of Gilgamesh* to functionally recall the main points?"

Quick nods all around, including from Father Matthew and himself. Even Dr. Lee showed mild interest. Except for Cat, who paired a sarcastic nod with a soft snort of amusement, hardly more than a breath.

In their short conversation, David had mentioned that he'd come to Oxford to prep for his entrance interview, and she quickly jumped on the topic with tips and advice. She'd launched into her own experience doing pretty much the same thing nearly a decade ago. David knew he was a young and gifted applicant, certainly. But Cat had been a child prodigy. Though she didn't look it, she was barely three years older than him. Now, with one Oxford Ph.D. down, she was working on another in Paris. Dr. "Cat" deMata had been tapped for the Ras-Shamra team because of her work on ancient Mediterranean cultures. These facts stirred something inside David. He felt childish with no more degrees than the high school diploma his mom had printed from the family desktop.

But Cat's tolerance for myths seemed low, a feeling David found concerning. He was reminded of his conversation with Father Matthew about the very real and simultaneously "mythical" figures of Galileo, Uncle Sir Arthur, and Einstein. He wondered what Cat might say about that idea. But then, he just might get the chance to find out. Like Ms. Chen had said, they were all going to be spending a lot of time together. David again wondered what his dad might have to say about that idea.

Arthur cleared his throat, pushed his glasses up, and began a well-practiced lesson. "As you likely know, *Gilgamesh* is an epic poem recorded in Akkadian. The copies we have are on clay tablets, surviving from ancient Mesopotamia, and it's often regarded as the earliest surviving work of great literature."

"Written work, you mean?" Rabbi Yosef inserted. "We must not discount the oral traditions."

Arthur gestured an ascent. "Of course. Again, defining terms is important. I was thinking of the birth of literature as the written word, though that's debatable." The Rabbi seemed to accept this with a gracious nod as Arthur plunged forward. "Far be it from me to discount the oral traditions of a species that very likely story-told ourselves into existence." With a start, David realized that Arthur was talking about humans. *Story-told? What's that even supposed to mean?* Just when David thought he was starting to figure his grandfather out, Arthur said crazy things like that.

As if that wasn't weird enough, suddenly Cat was agreeing with Arthur. "Yes! Fireside theory. Early primate brains evolved to use language and recognize emotions. Over time, our faces became more expressive and our language more complex, because our ancestors discovered fire and were able to sit around it every night telling stories."

David was perplexed. Were they seriously talking about human evolution? And were Arthur and Cat saying that stories were a part of that process? He looked over to Matthew on the other end of his row of seats for help, but the priest was entirely engrossed in the conversation, his hands folded innocently in his lap. He sat soaking it all in like a school lecture. David decided to do the same.

"Something like that, yes," Arthur said. "Though I think we'll pick up a few hundred thousand years later Dr. deMata, if you don't mind."

There were a few polite chuckles. Cat shot Arthur a sarcastic smile. David simply leaned back slowly into his chair. A moment later, Arthur scratched his beard and continued the lecture.

"What some of you may not know, is that the literary history of Gilgamesh begins with five Sumerian poems about 'Bilgamesh,' which is the proper transliteration of the original Sumerian. The historical man Bilgamesh was a king of Uruk in the Third Dynasty of Ur, circa 2100 B.C. These independent stories were later used as source material for a surviving combined epic known as the Old Babylonian version of *Gilgamesh* a few centuries later. Only a few tablets of that have survived, but the later standard version dates from sometime between the thirteenth and tenth centuries B.C. It bears the title *Sha Naqba Imuru*—that is, 'He who Saw the Deep-Unknown.' We have approximately two-thirds of this longer, twelve-tablet version, first discovered in the 1850s. It was finally published some twenty years later, causing quite the scandal in academia."

"Yes, I imagine so," the Rabbi said with a chuckle. David didn't get the joke. He opened his mouth to ask, but Arthur had moved on.

"I suppose it's worth mentioning that the only version of the story ever found outside of Mesopotamia is the *Atra-Hasis* tablet, unearthed only a few decades ago. It's short, fragmented, and describes the hero character only as 'Atra-Hasis,' which means 'Exceedingly Wise One.' It has a few nice parallels to *Gilgamesh*, though really it's only notable in that it was found at Ras-Shamra."

David felt a surge of adrenaline at this. Wasn't Atra-Hasis one of the myths Arthur had mentioned yesterday? He wracked his brain to remember any details but came up short.

"And that's where we're headed," Dr. Pitman declared. "Canaanite port city and place where your Noah knock-off was discovered. Wyatt found a new chamber in Ba'al's old pagan temple archives, and he's been digging up all kinds of things."

For the first time, David saw real curiosity from Cat. "A new chamber? That is most interesting."

"Yep. Aarons prayed about it, and God told him where to find it," the geomorphologist said smugly.

This time, when Cat scoffed, Arthur joined her. Clearly, there was a wide range of faiths and beliefs in the room. David couldn't tell if Dr. Pitman was mocking Mr. Aarons or merely stating facts.

"Regardless," Arthur continued, "it is the second half of the *Gilgamesh* epic that concerns us. Experiencing grief over the death of his best friend and adventuring companion Enkidu, the titular king undertakes a long and perilous journey to discover the secret of eternal life. He eventually learns from the divine alewife Siduri, a brewess and goddess of fermentation, that the 'life, which you look for, you will never find.' She tells him that when the gods created man, they kept the secret of life and left us only death. Though I suppose between evidence of his great building projects, his literary account of Siduri's advice, and what he tells us about the immortal Utnapishtim and the Great Flood, Gilgamesh's fame survived his death anyway."

Father Matthew politely cleared his throat again, causing Arthur to look his way. "Thank you, Arthur. Now that's cleared up. Dilmun?" A subtle social nudge.

Arthur blinked. "Oh right. So then, facts first. Dilmun—or Telmun, depending on the dialect—was an ancient Semitic-speaking country. It is mentioned throughout Mesopotamian literature from the third millennium B.C. onwards. It is regarded as one of the oldest civilizations in the Middle East. The precise location of the capital city for which it is named is lost, but there are clues. Dilmun is described as a paradise and a port city. And according to Babylonian texts, it's where people lived after surviving a great flood."

Some of this David knew, though he took note of the new details. Arthur seemed to be enjoying having a full audience, even if some of them already knew it too. Dr. Pitman was sucking a lemon, but Cat was nodding now. Yosef was unreadable, and Father Matthew was laser-focused, soaking it all in like a sponge. Dr. Lee was just enjoying the show.

"Of interest to us is that Gilgamesh's quest essentially culminates in Dilmun both geographically and narratively. It is there that he has his conversation with a very old sage named Utnapishtim. Similar to the biblical Noah, Utnapishtim tells how he built a multi-chambered ark by the command of an assembly of gods. He loaded it with animals, and along with his family and a few others, survived a great and ancient flood."

David's curiosity spiked again. *Others? As in, not Noah's family others?* That was new. But even stranger was that this team really was looking for the city from the Gilgamesh flood myth. But why? David still didn't know what a biblical archeologist like Mr. Aarons could have to gain from it. It didn't make any sense. Was that the scandal Arthur had spoken of?

"The obedient Utnapishtim was granted immortality," Arthur continued. "So, when Gilgamesh finally turns up, he gives him a long and pronounced speech about enjoying life, seizing the day and so forth. Being so old, Utnapishtim is now incredibly wise, you see, and thus able to teach Gilgamesh the meaning of life despite the reluctance of the gods to share this secret with mankind. After much badgering, Utnapishtim finally tells Gilgamesh that there exists a box-thorn plant that restores life and grants eternal youth, but it could only be found at the bottom of the sea.”

“If only that were true,” Dr. Pitman grumbled. He might have been talking about the idea that age imparted wisdom, or just wishing aloud for a magic plant that restored youth. David couldn’t tell.

Cat jumped in too. “What you call badgering was Utnapishtim’s wife telling him to do the right thing. Without her around, Gilgamesh would have failed.” Then she wordlessly mouthed to David, shaking her head in pantomimed disbelief, *“Men.”* It was slow and derisive, like a foul obscenity. David wasn’t sure how to take that, so he smiled and shrugged. He didn’t know her well enough to know if she was joking or not, and David didn’t want to step on any gender-based landmines so early in their friendship.

Arthur cleared his throat and went on. “Missing the point and thinking himself clever, Gilgamesh binds stones to his feet so he can walk on the bottom of the sea.”

“The point?” Pitman interrupted again. “What point? I can’t keep up with all this symbolic nonsense.”

“Well, it’s a morality tale.” Arthur sounded frustrated. “A good life need not be an eternal one, is what Utnapishtim has been trying to say. And as Dr. deMata has pointed out, his wife persuades him to give in to Gilgamesh’s demands. Utnapishtim fails to convince him that eternal life does not a good life make.”

Dr. Pitman looked doubtful. Cat gave a little nod to Arthur.

“So anyway, Gilgamesh manages to obtain the plant and heads toward home, excited to find out if it works. Unfortunately, when he stops to bathe, a snake smells the plant and steals it, shedding its skin and turning young again as it departs. Gilgamesh weeps at the futility of his efforts because he has now lost all chance of immortality. He returns home to Uruk, where the sight of its massive walls prompts him to praise this enduring work to the ferryman of the dead. And to become a lifelong fan of architecture, presumably. Ultimately, the *Sumerian King List* records that he reigned for some hundred and twenty-six years, which isn’t too shabby by any count.”

The room was silent. David had sat quietly the whole time while the others took turns frowning at various elements, and now there was a shared reverence at the end. *Like a moment of silence at a funeral.* He had to admit that the *Gilgamesh* story was epic, as good as any tabletop RPG he’d ever played. Yet he felt dissatisfied, uncomfortable, even twitchy, though he didn’t know why.

Finally, Father Matthew spoke up. “Thank you, Arthur. As our friend Yosef has pointed out, that is quite the scandal."

David couldn't take it anymore. "What scandal?" he blurted. "It's just an old story. We find out where this ancient city of Utnapishtim's was, find Mr. Aarons and we go home. You know, like Gilgamesh did? So, why is that a scandal?" He looked around the room at the scholars staring at him. "I mean, what am I missing?"

"Ah, I see," Arthur said. "Quite rational of you, David. How can I put this?" He paused for only a moment to scratch his beard some more. "You'll recall that I mentioned the *Epic*'s first modern translation was published a century and a half ago? Well, that translator's name was George Smith, and he did not publish under the ancient original's title, *He Who Saw the Deep-Unknown*. You see, Smith knew his nineteenth-century Western culture well, and knew the problem the story would cause if he simply released it as-is. So, he came up with a rather creative solution to minimize the damage."

"What? Did he change parts of it or something?"

"Oh no, nothing so academically dishonest as that. He simply published it under the rather misleading title, *The Chaldean Account of Genesis*."

"*Genesis*? Oh, I get it. Utnapishtim. Noah. Back to Flood stuff again. Ark, animals... So what?"

Arthur stared at David blankly for just a moment. "Oh, I understand the difficulty now. No, no. It's not just Utnapishtim, it's the whole package, don't you see?"

David shook his head. For the thousandth time in two days when Arthur thought he was being clear, David did not see.

"David, Utnapishtim is like Noah certainly, but it's more than that. Utnapishtim's tree of immortality, it's the Tree of Life. And he and his wife lost access to it by making a bad choice at her behest. The snake, well, we might just as easily call it a chaos serpent. It's every dragon or serpent that's ever been in literature causing trouble. The cat-bird-snake that devours, destroys, tempts, and deals death. And as for the place where Utnapishtim lived, well that—"

David saw it. He felt ridiculous for having missed something so completely obvious. It had been staring him in the face from practically the first moment Arthur and he had talked about Mr. Aarons' journal.

"*Nûḥ means Noah, and the tree is the Tree of Life*," Arthur had said as David sat cross-legged in the wedge-shaped apartment full of books, spilling tea on his blue jeans and trying to figure out how to get along with his eccentric old wizardly grandfather a million years ago yesterday.

"It's a garden," David squeaked. "Dilmun was a garden." *Because, duh.*

Arthur nodded, as did Yosef. Cat bit her knuckle and suppressed a pained groan at David's expense. Dr. Pitman held nothing back and openly guffawed, while Father Matthew knit his brow in sympathy.

David finished the thought. "So Mr. Aarons is looking for the Garden of Eden?"

"Yes, David," Arthur confirmed, uncharacteristic compassion rising in his voice. "Wyatt isn't just looking for some mythical ancient garden. He's been looking for *the* mythical ancient garden. And now, because of him, so are we."

XLIV

Heathrow International Airport. London, England. Mr. Suit.

"If it's just the one carry-on, then you are all set," said the delicious little English girl behind the airport check-in desk. She tucked a freshly printed boarding pass inside the red passport of a man who didn't exist.

The suave Middle Eastern businessman in the expensive Italian suit smiled innocently at her and plucked the paperwork away. All too easy. On some other day, he might have seen her as a mark, a pretty conquest, a challenge. But not today. He was technically unemployed, but nevertheless working.

Remember who you are. Remember what you are.

The airline counter girl was looking at his lapel. He glanced down. "Sorry, you have a little—" She pointed, then brushed at his chest. It was a bit of plaster dust from under the collar he had missed. An excuse to touch him.

"Ah, thank you," he said. "Difficult finding good cleaners these days."

He faked a perfect smile, grabbed his bag, and stalked away. He brushed at his shoulder with some futility before he finally ducked into a men's room to hang the coat up properly. He had no coat hanger. He looked around, finally settling on hanging the jacket from the back of a flimsy toilet stall door hook. He felt bile rise in his throat. It was beginning to feel like amateur hour. He was better than this.

A man came past with his two small boys trailing behind him, twins. They had fire-red hair like their father. All three spoke with a northern lilt. "Come along," he said. "Let's not keep the ladies waiting. We don't want Mother to get cross."

The man in the suit agreed. *Family first, always.* And never allow Mother to get cross.

Remember who you are. Remember what you are.

He glanced at his phone to check the time. He had a short wait, but Dr. Evans' plane should be far from Paris already. Dr. Evans had slid right into the trap like a frightened animal. He had enemies on that plane, though he was almost certainly oblivious to it. Either way, it was out of the man in the suit's hands.

He took a deep breath and focused. He'd have his part to play soon enough. For now, there was the ridiculous gauntlet of airport security-theater to run and a boarding gate to find. Then there would be nothing to do except enjoy the amenities of his flight. After all, one always met the most interesting people on an airplane.

People are tools. Resources to be consumed.

The man in the suit replaced his coat and strolled out of the bathroom feeling much better.

XLV

The Mediterranean Sea. 33,000 ft., Eastbound towards Syria. David.

"So, could Eden actually still exist?" David asked the cabin at large.

The atmosphere in the plane felt a little more relaxed to David now. The plane had leveled out to its cruising altitude, so drinks and brunch had been served. The original overall tension of Miss Chen's rather shocking video had also leveled out somewhat.

"I suppose it's possible," Arthur said, noncommittally. He seemed more relaxed now. Plus he was onto his second bottle of beer, so that was probably a contributing factor. "The search for Eden is hundreds, even thousands of years old. The Crusaders, Marco Polo, even Christopher Columbus, and most of the other explorers of the New World looked for Eden. They did so from Asia to Africa to America and everywhere in between. Most concluded that it simply doesn't exist anymore."

The reaction from the others was mixed, ranging from a smug smile from Cat to a few nervous chuckles, a huge eye-roll from Pitman, and one wry smile from Father Matthew like the cherry on top. Matthew had to be well aware of Arthur's position on the matter, but all he was showing the room was priestly restraint.

"Possible?" Dr. Pitman laughed and looked with shocking intensity from Arthur to David. "Son, I seem to recall one of your grandpa's papers arguing for its existence rather strongly."

David smiled politely but didn't say anything. Arthur fidgeted, his calm waters disturbed by the geomorphologist's verbal stone.

"You cited those same *Epics of Gilgamesh* if I remember in that paper, didn't you Doc?"

Arthur cleared his throat, straightened his coat, and smiled awkwardly. "*Epic.* The stories of King Gilgamesh together form one epic collection. And that essay you refer to was written a very long time ago, but the thesis centered around connections between the *Atra-Hasis* and *Gilgamesh* accounts, rather than the biblical ones. As I said, it remains the only other pure version of the ancient Babylonian flood story found outside Mesopotamia, but it dates to the much more recent eighteenth century B.C., meaning it's newer than *Gilgamesh* by centuries. The part of my essay about Dilmun was more of a footnote."

"Oh, pardon me!" Dr. Pitman exclaimed, laying a hand to his heart mockingly. Then, thumbing his chest, "Geologist!" It was all sing-song sarcasm, as if that somehow excused him from being polite.

"Eden," Arthur said hesitantly, "is a somewhat complicated study. It has been convoluted by multiple faiths and a somewhat unrealistic reliance on various contrary literary elements."

"Like the Bible?" David blurted, thinking of what Father Matthew had told him about Arthur's view of scripture.

"Well, yes. First and foremost, the biblical book of *Genesis* is a collected epic myth too, but let's not start there."

"Not start at *Genesis*?" Dr. Pitman hooted. "Oh do tell, Doc, this should be good."

Arthur ignored him. "There are many descriptions of Eden throughout the written works of man. The Mesopotamian words for Eden—*edin* in Sumerian and *edinu* in Akkadian—both mean 'open plain' or 'uncultivated land.' While in Hebrew, *adhan* means 'to be delighted', or some might say 'place of delight.'"

The Rabbi agreed with one blinking bow and a wry little smile.

"The Greek *paradeisos*," Arthur continued, "means 'wall-around,' and the Persian *pairidaeza* means 'enclosed parkland.' Both have obvious connections to our English word *paradise.* Other etymological clues point to a hedged-in, protected, walled garden, orchard, or enclosed park." He was slipping into full-blown Oxford tutor mode again, despite being buckled into an airplane seat.

"The problems arise when we begin to examine the individual ancient texts to compare them. For example, Eden has been described as being located at the center of the earth, which as you'll recall is also the Latin meaning of *Mediterranean*. Any comparison, of course, relies on considerable anachronism."

David smiled at this, remembering his conversation with Arthur about the same thing.

"Nearly every ancient literature or mythology contains some sort of reference to 'the navel of the earth,' which any respectable scholar will tell you is an ancient claim that man's first home is a sort of natural and spiritual center of the world. It's an umbilical image, which arguably still survives in our talk of 'Mother Earth.' However, if modern ideas are allowed to pollute the question of location, we might as well start our search at the North Pole!

"Less ambiguously, some ancient sources put Eden on a high mountain valley somewhere in the Lake Van region, an area that is essentially thousands of rolling hills full of such vales and dells. Still other sources seem to indicate that Eden was in a place called Eridu, and it was the land Abram's people left as described in early holy texts. Or, we could just as easily try to triangulate it with the land of Nod, where Cain was said to be exiled. It's where we get the phrase 'East of Eden,' you see. Ultimately, though, it's a very old mystery. The oldest, maybe."

At this, Cat jumped in. "I cannot understand why you call it a mystery. The *Genesis* account is obviously a metaphor for Neolithic Migration dressed up in religious overtones by later generations." No one took the bait, so she continued. "Ancient stories are little more than embellishments by superstitious cultures, trying to explain the world around them. Your allegorical story of Adam and Eve is comparable to the transition from a hunter-gatherer society into an agricultural and technological one. Neolithic inhabitants, probably Indo-Europeans, would have moved out of their 'paradise,' likely due to adverse weather conditions or the melting of the ice age."

David gulped. Cat was saying stuff that made his stomach twist, but there was something compelling about her passion. She reminded him of an elvish warrior princess or something from one of his tabletop games. Foreign, mysterious, brilliant, fearless.

"I couldn't have summarized the Neolithic migration theory better myself," Arthur agreed. "It's a fairly good bet overall. The name *Adam* quite literally means 'mankind,' and there is an archetypal quality to the biblical version that is most satisfying. Two trees, one that gives life, one that gives knowledge. The latter is forbidden, yet necessary for man to have free will and a chance to advance culturally. In the ancient world, the idea of civilization and order was often portrayed as male, while the idea of chaos, nature, and the unknown was portrayed as feminine. Adam and Eve personified."

The faintest hint of a scornful smile tugged at the edge of Cat's glossy lips, but Arthur missed it. She cupped her hands around her mouth, forming a pretend bullhorn, then blurted in an exaggerated stage whisper, "That's what happens when men control the narrative!"

Arthur blinked several times. "Hmm. Quite so. It's probably no coincidence that more recent anthropological theories have claimed that the feminine influence is the driving force behind civilization. Plus," he continued, "If an early human population retained any memory of its origins, it would have first been through oral myths. Pictographs and hieroglyphs eventually emerged, then cuneiform, and finally phonetic *abjads*. The biblical origin stories were written down much later than some would like to think. Early man's brain simply did not work as ours does. They spoke in stories for thousands of years before our modern empirical systems of classification and thinking were contrived. There is good evidence that these oral stories retained their essential essence for some twenty-five thousand years or so in certain cases."

"Hogwash." Dr. Pitman screwed up his face like a troll. "You talk like everything except the Bible is authoritative evidence about ancient man. You haven't bothered to mention that Genesis gives us not only a detailed description of Eden, but also detailed instructions on where to find it." He stuck four fingers in the air for everyone to see. "Four rivers," he said with punctuating finality and a hint of a smirk. "And as for your alleged 'archetypal quality,' if Eden is a metaphor for a bunch of farmers learning to plow, then why in the world would that be theologically significant?" Pitman looked meaningfully at Matthew, who sat and smiled back, innocent as a saint, refusing to be dragged in.

"Bah," Arthur spat, "too often, biblical scholars try to award Moses a posthumous doctorate in science, giving him anything from a degree in quantum physics to laurels in advanced genetics. Modern frameworks ascribed to ancient thinkers don't do us any blasted good. The natural world does not operate according to the attributes of a biblical God. Sunshine and rain are not just, they fall on everyone equally. Death is not merciful, it is the end result of the basic entropy that permits the universe to function. Science is an absolutely terrible lens for understanding Genesis." He took another drag from his beer.

Pitman's face somehow screwed itself into even more of a disgusting twist of wrinkles. "You can't just cherry-pick what parts of the Bible you want to call real. Either it's true, or it isn't. It's that simple. Take it or leave it."

"I take what I can prove is real," Cat asserted with absolute finality, that smug little smile tugging at the corner of her mouth again.

Out of the corner of his eye, David saw Father Matthew raise a bushy eyebrow at Arthur. Whatever the question was, David couldn't read it. It occurred to him that the barrel-chested priest was loving all of this to his bones.

Arthur cleared his throat. "My apologies, Ryan," he said with hard-mustered sincerity. "Actually, *Eridu* literally means 'four rivers,' and that 'holy text' I mentioned was Genesis. So, I think we will find no great conflict with the biblical account. It states that the four rivers were the Gihon, winding through the land of Cush; the Pishon, flowing through gold-rich Havilah; the Hiddekel—that is to say the Tigris—flowing east of Ashur; and the Perath, which in most translations is called the Euphrates."

He paused, waiting for Dr. Pitman to comment, but the old man simply waved his hand and said in a sing-song, "Oh no, do go on, please. You're the boss, Doc."

Arthur hesitated, then continued. "People have been looking for the Gihon and Pishon for ages. They simply don't exist anymore, if they ever did. Moreover, trying to use *Genesis* as a verbal treasure-map is just plain sloppy scholarship."

Without missing a beat, Cat took up the argument. "All bodies of water shift. Riverbeds and coastlines frequently change and are renamed. There is no evidence that the Tigris and Euphrates of today are the same ancient rivers as those written of in the ancient world."

Arthur nodded at this, waggling a finger at her.

"Check a map, little lady," Pitman countered, his argument now shifting to her. He gave her one of those smiles old people reserve exclusively for young people who know too much for their own good. "The rivers of Eden run between modern Iraq and Iran. There have been opposing militant superpowers pressing in on those riverbanks since the beginning of recorded history. If you need a metaphor, then war is a pretty good 'flaming sword,' if you ask me. So maybe, we'll finish up our little mystery at Ugarit and then head on over to the fertile crescent! Eh, Doc?"

Arthur grunted noncommittally. Matthew finally spoke, using his scripture-quoting voice. "'After He drove the man out, He placed to the east of the garden cherubim and a flaming sword flashing back and forth to guard the way to the Tree of Life.' Genesis 3:24."

"Land between the Rivers." David blurted. "*Mesopotamia* literally means, 'land between the rivers.'" Cat slipped David a low and subtle palm, which he promptly gave five to.

David hoped that Dr. Pitman wouldn't think "the kids" were ganging up on him. He liked Dr. Pitman in a weird sort of way. His southern accent and Bible-thumping attitude were something David had seen a lot of in churches. Most guys like him were good people doing what they believed was right. Plus, it was clear that the retired scientist had spent decades in Mr. Aaron's wake, assisting the biblical archeologist and his adventurous expeditions.

"Even if the modern Tigris and Euphrates were the right rivers," Cat practically yawned, "The location of the Gihon and Pishon is entirely guesswork. There is absolutely no proof for these theories. The Fertile Crescent is a big place and we do not exactly have an ancient map to go from."

David didn't like the way this argument was going. As he looked at the rock expert, something wasn't right. Where a moment ago he had been in a foul disposition and arguing for a scriptural Eden, Dr. Pitman now seemed to be smiling in the face of Cat's more rational approach to the legends. Not just smiling—gloating.

"And that, señorita," Dr. Pitman said smugly, "is where you're wrong. There is proof, and Wyatt sure did have a map to Eden!"

The cabin was silent as everyone waited for the man to explain. He was all smiles, but his calm expression didn't match his posture. He had his ginger-ale in one hand, the other clutching his armrest in a death grip. He leaned over toward Cat like a snake coiled to strike.

"I should know—I'm the one who gave it to him." He paused, letting his eyes roll skyward and placing his hand over his heart with intentionally dramatic flair. "With a little guidance from Heaven, you might say."

XLVI

The Mediterranean Sea. 33,000 ft., Eastbound towards Syria. Arthur.

Evans sat looking at the information from Pitman's private screen, somehow mirrored onto the big one at the front. For over an hour, the man had hijacked Evans' casual discussion with a well-prepared presentation. The old turkey had no fear of technology, evidently. Another strike against the man, as far as Evans was concerned.

Only now, the lecture was ratcheting up into something more akin to an interactive argument. All historical and literary approaches to Eden were long forgotten. Pitman had dramatically and pompously explained the modern miracle of satellite imaging. He had been working with Wyatt out of Mao Sien's London office to coordinate a high-resolution scan of the Middle East, Mesopotamia, and the rivers in question. Dozens of spectral images and heat-map-this or digitally-enhanced-that pictures from space had been put up on the screen and everyone's questions were answered in turn. Evans didn't pretend to understand the science, but he did know an ancient riverbed when he saw one. *"Guidance from Heaven," my foot! More like pictures from space, you old goat!*

At first, Evans had trusted that the seasoned scientist could be brought on board with a little objectivity. Yet the man seemed all too eager for pretentious arguing, and Evans had never done well with openly difficult people. Worse, it was clear that the sun-baked twit had spent decades with Wyatt, with every manner of nutty faith-based ideas fueling one another's fire.

Three decades ago, Pitman's lab had been instrumental in Evans' wake-up call by outing Aarons' fallacies using science and reason. Evans had no idea why the glorified geographer had decided to join Wyatt's work afterward. Frankly, Evans wasn't sure he even cared to know. Pitman sounded more like Wyatt every time he opened his mouth. *Three decades away from academia doing privately-funded, agenda-driven research is enough time for anyone to go soft.*

But the worst of it was that Evans was deeply compelled by the information now being presented. It was scientific, rational, and completely un-Wyatt. If it was real, and assuming Evans understood what he was seeing, Pitman had managed to focus his search down to two hot spots. The first was at the head rivers of the Tigris-Euphrates, and the other was literally below the waters of the northwestern end of the Persian Gulf. That is to say, beyond the delta of the same rivers at a point under the sea.

In both cases, Pitman had found evidence with his satellite images of ancient riverbeds, the idea being that these rivers flowed at a time when the world's ocean levels were much lower. To Pitman, this meant before the biblical flood, but regardless it was astounding work, and frankly brilliant. Evans could only wonder why none of it was in Wyatt's journal or the digital information Mel had sent him. Was it possible Mel didn't know about it?

And that's when the bottom fell out of the conversation. Space pictures led to speculation about the age of the rivers, which quickly spiraled into questions about the age of the Earth, which then became an evolution versus creation debate. To Evans' great surprise, Pitman was a young-earther as well as a biblical literalist. Suddenly it all made sense. This man was one of those rare geologists who flew in the face of all conventional scientific wisdom.

No, not geology, he reminded himself, *Geomorphism.* Pitman was no rock-licker, he was a glorified cartographer being led by his narrow self-affirming viewpoint. The man glossed right over not only the mountains of data supporting an ancient earth and the Big Bang, but the very fossil record itself. Young-Earther geologists were a rare breed, but if Pitman was genuinely ignorant of the scientific methods used in geology-at-large, perhaps anything that contradicted his six-to-ten-thousand-year-old creation narrative was simply ignored or twisted into confirmation bias. *No wonder Wyatt likes him!*

As for deMata, at first, Evans had wondered why in the world Aarons had put the young atheist on the team at all. Then, it occurred to him that Wyatt hadn't known Evans would be here. Dr. deMata was supposed to be the ancient Mediterranean cultures expert. But it was a bad fit. According to the personnel file Mel had sent, deMata didn't do translation or linguistics, and her scholarship regarding Crete hadn't been anything to do with Sir Arthur, Linear-A, or Knossos. She had focused her work at a palace altogether on the southern side of Crete. The Phaistos Palace was a site completely bereft of legal records or other writings altogether. Judging by its title, one of deMata's dissertations had been an attempt to debunk Minoan artifacts as modern fakes, rather than any sort of real scholarship that could help with a Linear-A translation tablet. Leave it to Wyatt Aarons to research an ancient country and get everything he possibly could about it wrong.

Evans honestly felt a little bad for the girl. He feared she wouldn't have much to do on this trip. At least David was along to keep her company, and they seemed to be hitting it off just fine. If he had to guess, David's budding attraction to art and archeology was probably already displaced by a healthy teenage attraction to the artful anthropologist.

Evans forced himself to tune back into the conversation. DeMata and Pitman were now arguing over the science behind the flood and ice age theory. They'd been at each other's throats for practically the entire presentation. Her, defending the scientific pillar of knowledge, him standing firm on "biblical truth," and "plain readings."

"I think there is plenty of evidence to support the idea that the flood was total, and the mountains were covered," Pitman said. "I see no reason why many of the formations we see today could not have been made by tectonic stress during the flood, given the earth-shattering forces described in Genesis."

Yep, he sounded just like Wyatt. It was exhausting. No wonder they'd chosen to work together. Evans wanted to think that somewhere along the line Wyatt had brainwashed the old geezer, but he knew in his gut it wasn't true.

"Consider this, Señorita," Pitman said. "When I was a much younger man, I had the opportunity to raft down the Grand Canyon. What I saw opened my eyes to the reality that a worldwide flood clearly must have happened at some point in the world's history. Now, some scientists would say that sediment over hundreds of millions of years deposited around the fossils and rocks, then was slowly carved out by an even slower process by a tiny river. But others, such as myself, understand that the evidence points unambiguously to a worldwide cataclysm. The Grand Canyon was probably formed in a few months as vast amounts of sediment were laid down and compressed by the flood, then the canyon we know today was carved out in mere weeks as the Great Plains emptied back into the Pacific. That's enough proof for me, and it's just one example."

The scientific prodigy was shaking her head in complete disbelief. "Some scientists? Try all. You cannot expect us to listen to this," she gestured at the presentation on-screen, "when you want to ignore scientific data and the conclusions of scholars worldwide! Objectively, there is not enough water on the planet to fully cover the all the land on earth. It would take a miracle to do that."

The young scientist's sarcasm was palpable, but still, Evans could tell she was holding back. He empathized. Any idiot could look at the Grand Canyon or the like and see that the layers of earth there weren't laid down in a single event.

Then again, maybe not any *idiot.*

Pitman was all smiles and patronization. "And what's wrong with miracles? But I don't think we need one. As I was saying, young lady, there is a relatively popular theory among biblical scientists that your missing waters were and perhaps are once again stored up under the earth's crust. Also, *Genesis* tells us that at one time a great deal of it existed in a layer of atmosphere we no longer have. Then, through a some natural process, that moisture was released, causing the flood precisely as described in scripture."

"What natural process?" She challenged. "And where did all of this theoretical water go?"

"Well, it would have to be stored back under the crust, wouldn't it? Or boiled off into space. Frankly, we don't know just yet by what process the moisture was recollected or precisely where such reservoirs might be, but various foundations around the world are working on it. This is not a small-time operation. Billions are invested every year to demonstrate the scientific accuracy of the Bible and combat the groupthink the world has been fed as real science."

Evans rubbed his forehead. This man was giving him a headache. He'd had his fill of "biblical scientists" three decades ago. They twisted facts to fit their narratives, and when that failed them, they punted to miracles. It was a straw man fallacy made into a lifestyle. And it would take a miracle to salvage this conversation.

"*Genesis* chapter one plainly says there were 'waters above the sky,'" Pitman blustered on. "And it doesn't seem to be there anymore, which is very telling!" He motioned with one hand over the other, demonstrating something inane. Then he motioned a great gush of fingers from underneath, punctuating his point. "Chapter seven states that the 'fountains of the great deep burst forth' at the same time that the 'windows of the heavens were opened.' Such an event would inevitably shift the tectonic plates and create new mountains." He steepled his fingers into mountains and waved all doubt away in a grand gesture. "What the floodwaters didn't kill, the ensuing earthquakes and tsunamis surely would, wouldn't you say?"

"'Fountains of the deep' and 'windows of the heavens,' yes, I have heard you," she sassed.

Technically Matthew had said it, scripture always at the ready but remaining otherwise neutral. He'd said nothing besides the occasional Biblical quotation. Did Pitman even know the priest was a scientist yet? Evans admired his friend for waiting to weigh in. He would have to thank him later.

"But still, you cannot explain why this would be," deMata insisted.

"The simple answer is that God made it that way. As I said, irreducible complexity like that found in the bombardier beetle or the eyeball is profound evidence that there had to be a designer. And real science is the tool which helps us determine these things."

The conversation was now lapping itself.

DeMata mumbled something in Spanish Evans didn't understand—modern languages weren't his department. David went wide-eyed and a shade redder.

"We can all look at the same data," Pitman said with finality, "but the conclusions—well, those are largely steeped in our paradigms. And that, my friends, is the key to understanding how to interpret the data. As for me, the Bible says it, I believe it, and that settles it. That's faith, my friends! Anything else is just defiance against God."

Evans cringed. There it was. The old turkey was openly feeding his own confirmation bias. Pitman blustered on with more of the same. Something about his particular paradigm being right because it was written in *Genesis*.

But Evans had already stopped listening again.

*   *   *

Later, the lights of the upper cabin were dimmed and many of the passengers wound down to read or sleep. Rabbi Yosef turned to Evans from the next chair and softly cleared his throat. Evans realized that he had not heard the man in the seat next to him say a word for hours.

"Dr. Evans, perhaps it would be a good time to speak about alternative Dilmun theories? How is your ancient Hebrew?"

Evans smiled. Semitic languages were his bread and butter, and his ancient Hebrew was superb. He said as much.

"And your Proto-Hebraic?"

"What's Proto-Hebraic?" came a voice from behind Evans' chair.

He turned and saw David standing behind them, one of his white headphones dangling. He had just returned from the lavatory and was taking the long way around to his seat for some reason.

"Sorry, Arthur. What I mean is, can I join you guys for a while?" Yosef smiled and gestured for the boy to stay.

"Thanks." David's voice dropped to the merest whisper he could manage over the constant rumble of the plane. "I think Cat is kind of flirting with me, a little."

Evans was astounded. Even he had known that. What he couldn't imagine was why David would possibly not want a brilliant and stunning young scientist fawning over him. What teen wouldn't? She wasn't that much older than David at the end of the day. But then, Evans never had been able to understand what made people tick. Modern young people especially. It's why he'd stuck to ancient literature and language for all these years. Such were the true mysteries of the universe. The boy would figure it out eventually.

XLVII

"Certainly, Dilmun cannot be real unless it is *Hayden* by another name," Rabbi Yosef said.

David assumed that meant *Eden*, but he didn't want to interrupt just yet. *Ancient Hebrew maybe?* He added that to his ever-growing list of questions.

"This, I commend," Yosef continued. "But there are many differences between the Torah and the old stories of the East. The most important is that Yahweh is not present in them. This indicates which one is the true source of knowledge from the oldest traditions, and we must not confuse them."

There was an awkward silence. David jumped on it. "Do you mean that *Genesis* came first, and so the right version to look at? Like Dr. Pitman was saying?"

Arthur visibly winced but said nothing. His fist was firmly lodged in his hairy cheek while his elbow dug deep into the armrest of his plush seat. David sat cross-legged in front of them on the floor, his body forming a triangle between Arthur and Yosef at one end of the two oddly mirrored semicircles of seats.

"No," the Rabbi clarified, "I mean that the written text, whenever it was first written, is layered with deep explanations and even deeper truths. It is said that Father Moses transmitted this received tradition to Joshua, who in turn passed it on to the Levites, priests, and rabbis throughout the generations. This tradition contains the complete meaning of the books you call *Genesis*, *Exodus*, *Leviticus*, *Numbers*, and *Deuteronomy*. Commonly known to us—"

"—As the *Torah*," David finished with a smile. "I'm David," he said, thumbing his chest.

Rabbi Yosef smiled back. "David? A kingly Hebrew name," he said with a nod. "I am pleased to meet you." Yosef put the accent on the second syllable of his name, making it sound decidedly more Hebrew. He talked with his hands, and his enormous gray beard lent him a Santa Claus quality that was hard to shake. But for his blue dress-shirt and yarmulke that belied it, he might have done well in an American mall somewhere, accent and all.

"Moses himself instituted that the scroll would be read regularly in places of worship. Today we read from the Torah four times a week. Shabbat morning, Shabbat afternoon, and on Monday and Thursday morning. This is important—critical. But it is incomplete."

David was perplexed. What was this man getting at? Was he also saying that *Genesis* wasn't the oldest source? That didn't seem very... orthodox.

The rabbi read the question on David's face and chuckled. "Do not worry young man, I am not saying anything against the words of God. Only that together with the written law, *Torah*, and traditional commentaries, *Midrash*, there was transmitted to Moses a very rare oral tradition which explains every aspect of the written law."

"Oh, I say, Yosef, are you referring to Kabbalistic studies?" It was Father Matthew, from the seat across from Yosef.

The Rabbi tipped his head agreeably. This was enough for Matthew to unbuckle and join David cross-legged on the floor. The two holy men had been chatting off and on across the aisle since Matthew sat down. Beard-care alone had provided a good ten minutes of conversation.

"The tradition of *Kabbalah* is somewhat cryptic and requires much explanation, does it not?" The priest probed as he made his bulk comfortable.

Arthur had mentioned Mr. Aarons had an interest in Kabbalah stuff, but David hadn't expected it to come up. Based on the duck face Arthur was making, he hadn't either.

"This is true," the Rabbi agreed. "Included in the oral tradition is the *Kabbalah*. The very same tradition programmed into Adam, received by Abraham, and now largely incorporated into the written Torah body." The Rabbi's pride was evident.

'Programmed?' David thought. *What does that even mean?*

"It is taught that Moses received four levels of interpretation on every aspect of the Torah," Yosef continued. "These four levels are called *Pardes*, meaning 'an orchard.'"

"Orchard?" David asked. "Like a garden of fruit trees? Because *pardes* sounds a lot like *paradise*. Like Arthur was saying before."

Yosef nodded, but Matthew spoke. "Well remembered, David. And as I recall, the tradition also implies that there must have been an unbroken line of family members who possessed knowledge of the mystical tradition, starting with Adam and his sons."

"Also true," the Rabbi agreed. "The transliterated Hebrew for the word *Pardes* are the letters *P-R-D-S*, an acronym, and indeed the true origin of the word *paradise*. The letters stand for four words: *Pshat*—the simple meaning. *Remez*—allusion, or what is hinted at in the text. *Drush*—the instructive interpretation. And finally *Sod*—the mystical dimension. The very idea of Edenic paradise is embedded in the reality of multiple interpretations and hidden depths of meaning, including secret sacred knowledge."

The Rabbi held his hands out as if it couldn't be clearer, but David had no idea what the man was getting at. He started to ask, but not before Arthur inserted his opinion.

"The *Kabbalah* is not mainstream to Jewish belief." The grumble came out of one side of Arthur's mouth, the fist never moving. "It is a rather niche discipline."

"Yes, yes, but Dr. Evans—"

"Call me Arthur."

David suddenly flashed back to another conversation with Arthur. His frustration-fueled argument in the middle of the Lamb and Flag Passage. *"If you believe* Genesis *is literally true,"* Arthur had said, *"then logically you must either believe the Bible stories were passed down from generation to generation from eyewitnesses, or else that* Genesis *was dictated by God to Moses or one of his contemporaries."* Was Rabbi Yosef claiming to have proof of the oral tradition theory?

"You correctly call *Kabbalah* 'niche', Arthur, but is not the Methodist, the Baptist, or indeed the Anglican or Roman Catholic, a Christian who believes in the same *Yeshua HaMashiach*?"

"The same what?" David asked. As probably the only Evangelical Protestant and pastor's kid in the cabin, he wasn't too sure about the direction this seemed to be going. He'd known some Universalists and even had a Roman Catholic friend take him to a Mass or two, but he had never quite swallowed the 'separated brethren' arguments. His dad always said that the problem with any group claiming to be "the one true church" was that it was no different from being modern Pharisees. He also said that Christians spent way too much time arguing about theological points when it was easy to just read the Bible and find out what it had to say about the matter. He'd even written a whole bestseller about it.

But Yosef was using words David had never heard, and David was fairly sure weren't in the Bible. The idea of an oral tradition seemed kind of heretical. Cultish, even.

"*HaMashiach*, David. The *Messiah* or, if you prefer the Greek, how about the *Christos*?"

"You're talking about Jesus?" It surprised David to hear a Jewish Rabbi talking this way.

"*Yeshua bar Yosef*, yes. That is 'Jesus, son of Joseph.' *Yeshua HaMashiach* is 'Jesus Messiah,' or again, if you prefer the Greek, *Iesous Christos*."

"Is that the Hebrew translation? Of his name, I mean?" David asked. It sounded vaguely like Spanish to his ear.

Matthew chuckled, and a grunt emanated from somewhere inside Arthur. David turned toward his wizard, thinking maybe he should feel embarrassed by his own question, but he kept it in check. This was important stuff, and he wasn't going to be ashamed of not knowing something three older scholars clearly knew.

Arthur cleared his throat. "The English name *Jesus* is derived from the Latin *Iesus*, a transliteration of the Greek *Iesous*. The Greek form is a rendering of the Hebrew *Yeshua*, a variant of the earlier name *Yehoshua*."

What? David was speechless. *'Jesus' wasn't Jesus' name?*

Matthew raised a finger thoughtfully. "*Yehoshua* precisely means 'Yahweh is salvation', if I recall Arthur's lessons correctly."

David was fairly certain there was some humility in play there.

"Yes, *Joshua* was a common name in the New Testament era," Arthur confirmed. "The Joshua of Exodus was a key figure who apprenticed under Moses. He was the military and spiritual leader of Israel during the Canaanite conquests. Walls of Jericho and all that."

Rabbi Yosef was visibly pleased by this. "You see, we are already unified in mind and spirit about a great many things. The *Kabbalah* is not so strange once you study it."

"That's *Kabbalah*?" David marveled.

"Christian *Kabbalah*, yes," the Rabbi assented. "A divergent, but important distinction."

"Rabbi, are you a Christian?" David gaped in disbelief. He'd heard of 'Jews for Jesus' and that sort of thing before but had never met one. Yosef simply blinked and nodded once.

"Except that all of the *Kabbalah*, regardless of divergence, is probably a medieval tradition with no real claim to the oral tradition of Moses." It was Arthur, ruining the moment again. "I'm confident that the *Kabbalah* teaching is no mere denominational diversion. Its researchers struggle to provide a provenance that goes back further than the Middle Ages. That's a problem."

Matthew and David looked at him questioningly and then exchanged a worried glance. Arthur seemed oblivious to how offensive he'd sounded. He fished his hat from under his chair and crammed it low on his head, signaling that he was intending to take a nap. So that was conversation over for Arthur, then.

"Problem?" Rabbi Yosef was laughing cherubically, again in Santa mode. "Why Arthur, I'm shocked. Are you suggesting that you would require written evidence for an oral tradition to feel secure about it?"

Arthur peeked out from under his hat. "No sir, I am not. It's just that— well, it's more complicated than that, and we both know it. Everyone in this room knows it."

David was pretty sure he didn't. Arthur motioned to the rest of the cabin, where Pitman sat brooding over something on his laptop and Cat sat curled with her legs tucked under herself, book in hand but nodding off in the luxurious leather seat. Even Dr. Lee had been dozing for some time now in the chair at the far end. With everybody tuned out, it wasn't a very convincing visual of Arthur's point.

Again, David thought of Arthur's words in the Lamb and Flag Passage. *"Either the Bible stories were passed down from generation to generation... or else* Genesis *was dictated by God to Moses."* Did Arthur believe in the dictation-from-God thing after all? Or was his reaction against this *Kabbalah* stuff to do with something he and Mr. Aarons had argued about long ago? David's wizard was acting strangely, even for him.

"Actually," David interjected, "Just yesterday Arthur was talking about the oral tradition of Noah, and that—"

Arthur cleared his throat, purposefully cutting him off with an expression that David had only ever seen on his father Joe. One-part warning, two-parts total disbelief. It only lasted a moment, then softened. But it was enough. Understanding passed between the two Evanses. Arthur hadn't read Aarons' private words aloud to the team, and he was guarding back other things too. David needed to trust him.

Arthur faked a smile and turned back to the Rabbi. "I apologize, Yosef. David has reminded me. I did not mean to impugn your expertise. I didn't think before I spoke. It was quite rude of me."

"Forgiven. Forgotten," the jolly man laughed. "No offense should be taken where none was intended."

Yosef was strange, but his friendliness was contagious. The laugh spread first to Matthew, then David, and even a weak smile made it to Arthur, much to David's relief.

"Besides, if you truly require such proof, I can provide it." The Rabbi's tone was conspiratorial, almost menacing but for his smile. "Come closer, David. Allow me to show you something interesting."

David paused, looking to Arthur for permission. Seeing his grandfather's brooding shrug of abandonment, he came around to the side of the chair next to the strange Rabbi so he could better view the screen. Yosef then pulled up an image that David vaguely recognized. It was cross-like, but with interconnecting lines connecting across eleven circles, making it look more like a cut diamond.

"Let's begin with the Path of the Flaming Sword, shall we?" the Rabbi pointed to the big diamond shape. "This is the *Etz haChayim*, the Kabbalistic

Tree of Life."

David felt a chill run down his spine. Mr. Aarons' journal mentioned a tree of life, and now there was more than one kind? That was interesting.

"These circles are the *sephirot*. They are stations. The lines connecting them are paths. You may think of them as connections between higher modes of thinking and being, and thus eventually to holiness and God."

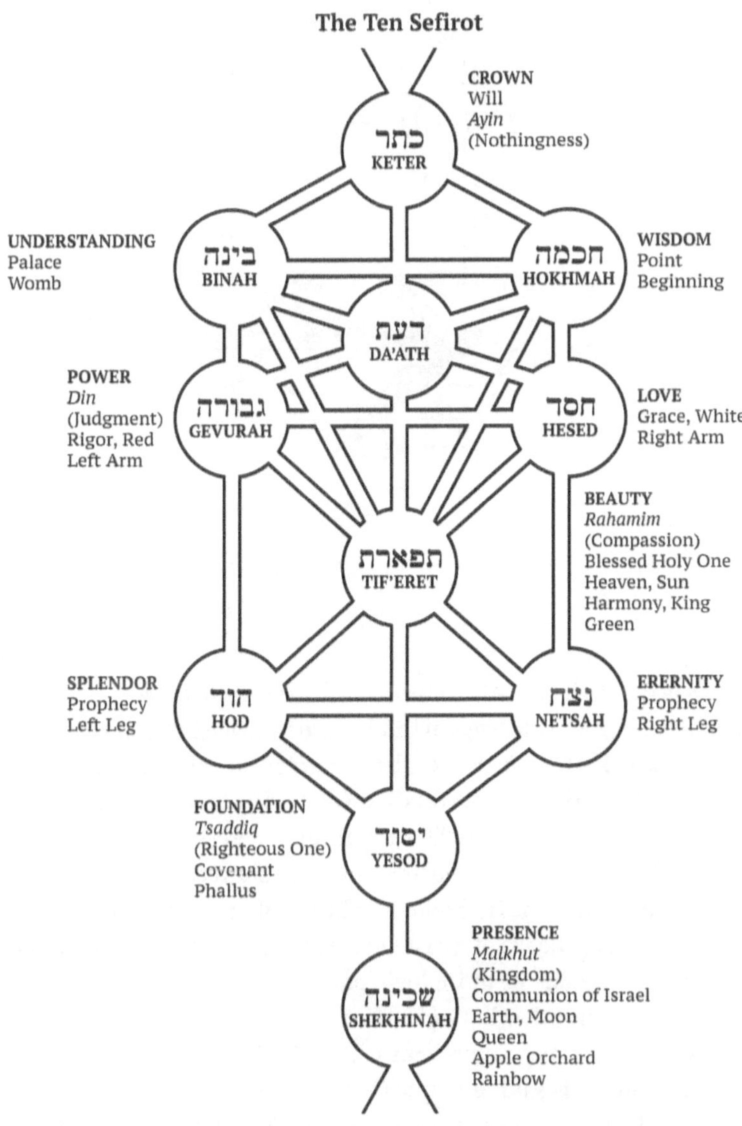

Yosef called up a drawing tool and traced a zigzag from top to bottom, touching every circle on the way.

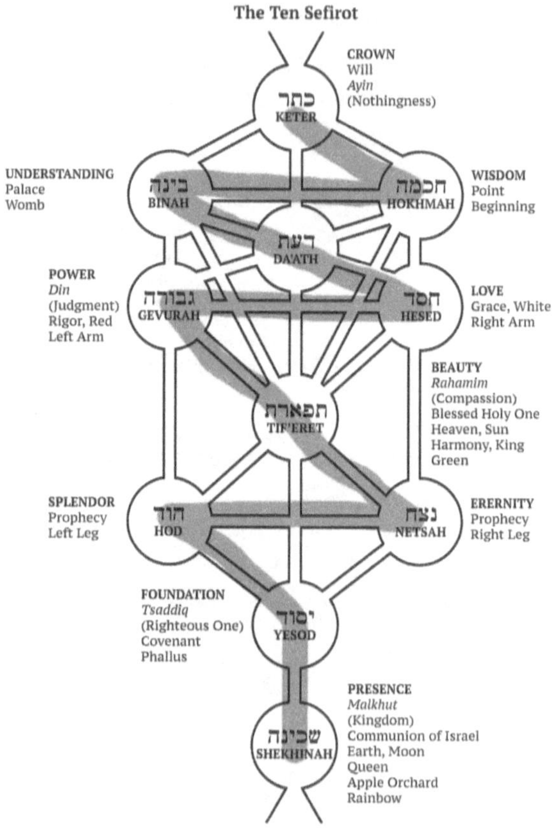

"This is the Path of the Flaming Sword," Yosef explained. "It is an ancient discipline for engaging in ways of thinking so that one's prayers can be aligned with God's will. Each *sephirah* is to be meditated on and achieved in sequence. When done correctly, such meditation will bring about a change in the state of one's being. It's not unlike the stations of the cross during passion for the orthodox Christian, for example, though much slower. A lifetime, even."

David was intrigued. He had never heard of any of this before. The only Sephiroth he'd ever heard of was a *Final Fantasy* villain. "It looks kind of like a maze. Or maybe one of those logic puzzles where you have to draw a line from one end to the other but only touch each circle exactly once."

"This pattern is also sometimes called the Lightning Flash," Yosef said, tracing it again. "It is said to mimic God's very act of creation. Starting at the topmost circle, translated as the *Crown*, we move down through each of the others in turn. To reach the bottommost circle of Earth, one must pass through such elements as *Beauty, Mercy, Victory, Love, Power,* and *Splendor.* Doing so, our line also crosses the *Abyss Threshold,* the dividing line between God and his creation, here."

He drew a horizontal line bisecting the interior circle under the top three. The line went right through the fourth circle.

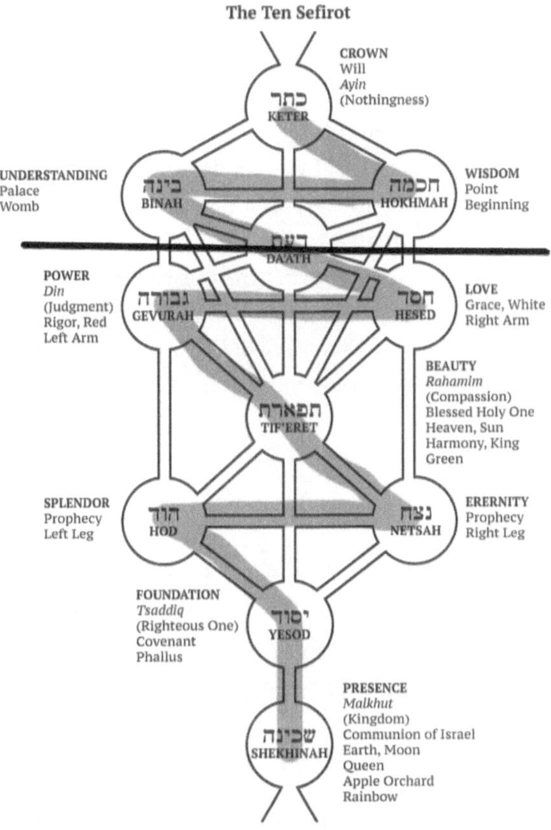

"And this David, is *Da'ath,* the hidden *sephirah.* Care to speculate its name in English?"

David shook his head. He didn't have a clue where this was going. Most people his age had never actually read the *Old Testament.* He had, except for some of the *Deuteronomy* and *Leviticus* stuff, but aside from some vague similarities in the terminology none of this had been in his version. Had it?

"Knowledge," Yosef whispered. "This is the *sephirah* of knowledge and power. It is the *Elohim.*" As quickly as he said it, the Rabbi tapped an undo command and the horizontal line disappeared.

David blinked. He was sure Yosef thought this was meaningful, but somehow it just seemed like a fancy graphic organizer for memorizing stuff. His mom had used similar visuals in their years of study together. Albeit, usually for plotting out literature, not for explaining quasi-mystical religious stuff.

"And most importantly," Yosef said with a flourish, pointing to the topmost circle. "This is the holy city of the divine king. The starting point of the journey. And it is always said, 'as above, so below.'" He traced the path one more time. "This teaching is the key to all real magic, to understand that in each order of things, there is a connection to the higher and lower orders also. In us, in our society, in God, and even in our legends. Thus it is by meditating and acting in unison with God that we can be instruments of his will."

David wasn't sure what to say, but it was better than mind-mapping Shakespeare for sure. And really, really weird. Was this guy genuinely talking about real magic? Maybe Arthur wasn't the only wizard here after all. The old tutor offered no commentary—it looked like he had fallen asleep. David smiled sheepishly at the self-proclaimed *Kabbalah* magician. It didn't faze Rabbi Yosef a bit. "So... how do we do all of that?"

XLVIII

The Mediterranean Sea. 33,000 ft., Eastbound towards Syria. Arthur.

Evans listened as Yosef expanded David's horizons with nonsense, content to let his hat remain low. He could only hope that his short attempts to tutor the boy were working and perhaps David was now thinking about learning in new ways. The boy was something of a sponge when it came to soaking up information. Matthew had seen it too. Now, as with every student Evans had ever tutored, some other teacher of an alternate school of thought was offering up a new fruit of enlightenment.

Evans should have pegged Ibrahim as a kabbalist nut sooner. The tells were all there: touch of crazy, touch of hippy. And while Yosef didn't strike Evans as belonging to the knock-off Los Angeles *Kabbalah* scam groups that attracted the likes of movie stars and pop musicians, even the "legitimate" scholars who studied the medieval practice of Jewish mysticism needed to be called to the mat as soon as they started talking about a hidden mystical oral tradition passed down from Adam and Eve. Evans had researched this junk years ago for Wyatt, before the tough times. He'd dived deep into the *Zohar* and other such alleged mystical texts. Back when the research had been peculiar and fun, and the terrible pay hadn't mattered. When he had needed an escape from reality and grief and Wyatt had provided it.

Evans had forgotten about Wyatt's fascination with *Kabbalah*. Medieval Jewish mysticism was just not something that appealed to him. It made about as much sense as praying for where to dig. Back in the day, Wyatt had even been a member of one of those Knights Templar revival groups for people too strange to be asked to join a proper and legitimate secretive society like the Masons or Shriners. It was all just drinking clubs with different names anyway, much like Lewis' Inklings. Retro-speculative wish-fantasies inspired by medieval fiction. Nothing at all like the silly notions that modern fiction authors had put into people's heads about such groups. *Thank you very much, Dan Brown.*

"As above, so below..." How many times had Evans heard Wyatt say something like that? It was all nonsense. And why shouldn't it be? It had been created by medieval Jews in search of a new revelation after the scattering of their people, amidst the powerful rise of Christianity, which was piggybacking on many of their traditions.

The alleged "discipline" of *Kabbalah*'s 'Tree of Life' centered around engaging in ways of thinking to join with God. But it had very little to do with the symbolic tree of the same name from the Genesis story, aside from a few loose symbolic connections. Mostly because top to bottom was not the only way to approach the 'Tree.' Evans wondered if Yosef would bother to explain to David the opposite path, the 'Path of the Serpent.' Notably, the kabbalist's path of redemption. He had long ago read that this second path meant *"opening the paths between Sephiroth in the consciousness of the Kabbalah Magician,"* or some such thing.

Yes—that was it. 'Path of the Serpent' practitioners believed that rising up from the base of the 'Tree' from Earth to the Crown was a way to open up the higher levels of human awareness and potential. It supposedly meant becoming "one with God." One could thus tap into the powers of creation for one's private use. *Not exactly "Thy will be done on Earth as it is in Heaven"!* This stuff was twelfth-century superstitious nonsense. The fundamental problem with that sort of magical thinking was that it turned God into some kind of sock-puppet with your hand up his backside. Pray hard enough and

God will answer your prayers, your way. That had long been Wyatt's way of thinking.

The so-called "Christian" Kabbalists were the worst of all. Compared to them, Wyatt was just a harmless Evangelical sycophant with too much imagination. A *Kabbalah* enthusiast with Templar fantasies. Truth-seeking Crusaders had discovered this new teaching and been enraptured by what they mistook for ancient knowledge, so they adopted it and adapted it to something vaguely Christian. This was just one of their many errors. When the real historical Templars encountered the Islamic Dome of the Rock in medieval Jerusalem, they mistook it for the long-gone Jewish High Temple and named themselves for it. But then, what did one expect of Middle Age lords and farmers exactly? The world still hadn't forgiven Christianity for the misguided path of death and destruction that were the Crusades.

The Enlightenment didn't brand them the Dark Ages because they were dark, Evans repeated to himself. The early *Kaballah* was just one example of that slippery slope toward the so-called Enlightenment. Rabbi Yosef was obviously a Wyatt Aarons-brand Christian Kabbalist shill, which was very good to know. *Wyatt hand-picked this entire team. Mustn't forget that.*

Satisfied with his inner tirade, Evans reseated his hat and settled in to eavesdrop. It was becoming an interesting and useful habit.

"Our earliest written scripture began in a language that was Proto-Hebraic," Yosef was saying. "We now know more about the origins of Hebrew today than at any point in history. It is unlocking some very interesting secrets about the thinking of the first Semitic peoples. Last year I worked on the team that successfully decoded the hidden meanings of Proto-Sinaitic symbols and it is now fully translated."

Evans cocked his ear. *What's the man talking about?* Proto-Sinaitic consisted of pictograms much like Linear-A. Who studied that? There was so little of it in existence that most scholars hadn't been willing to agree that it was a legitimate written language until it had been matched up to early Hebrew by a fringe few with nothing better to do. Ancient writing was all the time being "decoded" by self-declared "experts" in the field, resulting in various levels of gibberish. Everyone wanted to be a Ventris, Smith, or Chadwick, achieving fame by decoding a language. But the reality was that it was an incredibly rare accomplishment, and exceedingly difficult to do. What was this rabbi playing at?

Yosef blathered on. "We now know with near certainty that Abraham's people did not speak the language of biblical Hebrew. And Moses certainly did not write in it. Proto-Sinaitic, on the other hand, is much older, and it is entirely possible that Moses essentially invented writing as we think of it."

David glanced at Evans questioningly, encountering his one open eye. *Busted!* Evans afforded David a subtle head shake. While true that the modern alphabet was derived from the same language family, to say that Moses invented writing was absurd. Cuneiform was thousands of years older than even pictographic Hebrew. Moses was almost certainly a highly educated individual, so he might have "invented" a new way of thinking about language using phonetic sounds, but even that was a stretch. It was the sort of nonsense logic that had Adam and Eve speaking Hebrew—or worse, Latin—to God in the Garden on the sixth literal day of creation.

Evans pulled his hat lower and snuggled back into the plush chair. He watched out of a half-closed lid as David set his jaw and pulled out his phone. The plane had a connection, and kid-internet had been happily using it for hours now. Soon his new pupil would piece together everything Evans had just thought through. Knowing this gave him a perverse little pleasure.

Yosef kept right on going, undaunted. "The *Alefbet* is the Hebrew name for the letters, so named for the first two, as with English. What is perhaps not so obvious is that the *Aleph*, as we think of it, changed much from the time of Moses. Yet remarkably, the sounds and meanings themselves changed very little. Do you have it there?" This last gave David a start. The Hebrew scholar was fully expecting David to hand over his phone.

"Uh, yea. I guess. One sec?" The teen tapped the glass rectangle a few more times and handed it over.

Yosef plugged the phone into his chair somehow, then tapped the monitor they'd been using. The information on David's phone appeared for them all to see. Matthew lifted a bushy eyebrow. Even David looked surprised at this trick. The infernal technology was showing off again, and this man was full of surprises.

Not his first flight with the company, Evans surmised.

On the screen was the Wikipedia entry for the Hebrew letter *Aleph*. There was both a modern stylized font and a more traditional script to the right of it.

Yosef made a deep throaty noise of pleasure and continued his lesson via the larger touch screen. "Yes, good."

"This is an ancient symbol for that first letter," Yosef said. "It is the silent consonant from Babylonian times. But the older symbol looks like this." He tapped the screen a few times and found a symbol Evans also recognized well enough.

"It's a sideways A," David stated the obvious.

"Very nearly," Yosef agreed. "This is Middle Hebrew, a transitional stage from which our modern Roman letter also evolved."

And the first letter of all Semitic abjads, Evans silently countered. Not everything was a Greek *Alpha-Bet*, after all. The other Abrahamic religions in the Middle East also used the old Arabic alphabet's first four letters: A, B, J, and D, whence the term *abjad.* This wasn't Proto-Sinaitic at all, but Phoenician. The origin of nearly all *phonetic* writing—whence the name! Evans was about to pipe up and say as much, but the man beat him to it.

"However," Yosef continued with a little hand wave, "if we go even further back in time, we will come to our real starting point. I will now show you the original *Aleph* in a language from before even the Canaanites. Perhaps you'll see the resemblance?"

The internet couldn't save him this time, so Yosef drew on the screen with his finger again. As the man had promised, it was a pictograph, in what was indeed generally regarded as Proto-Sinaitic.

"A longhorn?" David conjectured, like a good Texan.

"Close. This is the Ox's Head, the original symbol that became the *Aleph.*"

Evans scowled and shifted, planting his fist firmly back on his cheek. *Back to early pictograms, eh?* He was curious to know what his new pupil had retained.

David pounced right on it. "Okay, so what was there to translate? A symbol is a symbol, whatever sound it represents. This is pretty much like our modern alphabet, isn't it? Phonemes or whatever."

Evans smiled inwardly. *Good lad!* One should always check sources. And David was spot on. Just like Ugaritic cuneiform, the phonetic sounds were what mattered, not the symbols.

"Ah, it might seem so. But that's where we modern men would be wrong. You see, just as Hebrew scripture has four layers of meaning, every Hebrew letter has four meanings too. First, it has its name, such as *Aleph.* Second, it has the phonemic sound, as you say. In this case, the *Aleph* is silent and usually carries a vowel. Next, each letter has a numeric value, critical to numerology and mathematics. *Aleph* is 'one.' And finally, it has a symbolic meaning embedded into its deepest roots. The ox head is the symbol of 'strength' or 'power', 'leadership', and in its most perfect and ideal meaning,

'God'." The Rabbi paused to let this sink in. His audience of two was attentive, but otherwise inscrutable. "Our team recently finished translating all of the most ancient pictorial meanings. Just last year, we published our findings. It's very exciting."

"I don't get it," David admitted.

Yosef chuckled and pulled up a clean space for writing on the screen. With his finger, he traced out a word from right to left as one must with Hebrew. It adjusted itself into modern Hebrew text automatically, which was itself unsettling.

$$בָּרָא$$

"This is *BaRA*, typically translated as... Arthur?"

"'Create'," Evans provided reluctantly. He spoke through clenched teeth, not bothering to shift positions so much as a whisker.

"That's right," Yosef affirmed.

"But the older and more literal meaning is 'fatten'," Evans spat, not missing a tick. He allowed himself a wry partial smile behind his fist. It was a perfect example of how idiom changed the meaning of ancient words.

"Well, also true," The Hebrew scholar laughed, a little nervously perhaps. "So then, these letters are *Beyt*, *Reysh*, and *Aleph*." He pointed to each in turn, starting again from the right. "The vowels are not written, though here the sounds are indicated by these symbols for our modern sensibilities. A native reader would not use them any more than a native English user would write out phonics symbols for long and short vowels, but they will be helpful to us."

Yosef pointed to the symbols that looked like a squat capital *T* under the first two characters. The *Kamatz*. Yosef was right, of course. The vowel-marking symbols were a modern convention, mostly used by rookies and kids studying for their *bar-mitzvahs*. This one conveyed the 'ah' of the short *a* in English, but seriously, where was Yosef going with all this?

Yosef went on. "Looking deeply at the original symbols, we will also find that *Beyt* was written like so." He drew a new symbol.

$$ם$$

"The second letter of the *Alefbet*, and precursor of the modern B."

David spotted it. "It's sideways again. And Arthur, look, it's Uncle Sir Arthur's spiral."

Evans grunted. *Most common symbol in the ancient world.*

"And its true meaning," Yosef said with a twinkle. "The floorplan of a tent. A covering for the family, house, or even the preposition 'in', or 'inside'."

David was undoubtedly loving this. Matthew had again retreated, rather uncharacteristically, into quiet observation—but Evans knew that look. The priest was scrutinizing Yosef's every word. Understandably, this was not a subject Evans had covered in their biblical Hebrew tutoring sessions a decade ago. This was fringe stuff that nobody paid much attention to. Evans kept an eye on the newer publications regarding Semitics, but he hadn't heard anything about Yosef's book. *Probably self-published.* If this was the profound discovery that Yosef had mentioned, then there was nothing to worry about. A pictographic interpretation was a far cry from "cracking a language." This sort of exercise was old hat for the Oxford tutor of ancient literature and languages. He and David had done a similar exercise just yesterday.

Plus, Evans still craved that nap.

"Next in our word is *Reysh*, the R. We find it revealed as a man's head. It means first, top, or beginning."

Evans yawned noisily and returned to half-ignoring the conversation as Yosef drew it. *Yes, yes, 'beginning'.* That made sense. *And so shall I begin my nap within my own head,* he mused.

"And finally, our *Aleph*, to carry the final vowel," Yosef said.

Evans peeked despite himself while Yosef drew the ox head. The full picture now could be seen with both the ancient and traditional Hebrew letters.

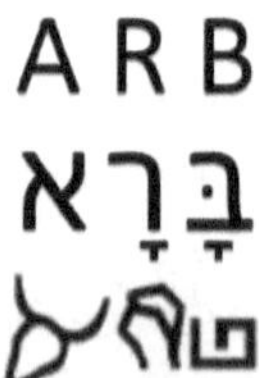

"There," Yosef declared. "Now David, would you kindly read this 'word' in full, or perhaps I should say, sentence?"

For a moment, David looked like a deer in headlights. Evans opened his mouth to bail him out and remind him that the word was pronounced *"bah-rah,"* but suddenly David's expression changed to delighted awe.

"Inside... began... God?" he whispered incredulously.

Yosef was pleased. "Very close, David. The ancient Proto-Semitic word for 'create' correctly means 'So began God,' just like the phrase which precedes it in Genesis 1:1. Many have suggested that the best translation of this verse is simply, *'First, Elohim began creating the Heavens and the Earth.'*" Yosef chuckled knowingly. "We can do this with every ancient Hebrew word there is. For example, the verb 'to-make' is *ASaH*. We now know it means, *'man has a need to separate and behold.'*"

Evans slowly lifted himself upright and stared, his blasted hat falling off yet again. He looked first at the screen and then at the trio, his grandson and his best friend sitting cross-legged before the rabbi like *Yeshiva* pupils. David gawked in wild-eyed wonder. Matthew's attention flicked to Evans, searching for confirmation or denial of all this from his old college tutor. Evans knew he couldn't do either. In his humble opinion, *"When God began to create the heavens and the earth,"* was a far better translation of the original Hebrew than what was found in most modern Bibles.

"Men 'make', you see, *ASaH*—but only God can *BaRA*, 'create'." Yosef turned to look Evans square in the face. "Now we know why. It is the very foundation of the natural order." The cherub was gone, replaced by a deadly serious and laser-focused colleague of ancient languages. It dawned on Evans that perhaps he'd been terribly wrong about this man.

"Every word?" Evans asked, dreading the answer. "You can't possibly be saying that this method is linguistically viable? That is to say, you can decode other words consistently into something meaningful by doing this?"

"Every word," Dr. Yosef Ibrahim affirmed, with no discernable tone of apology. He held his little black book out open to a page with hand-written notes. It was clear that every Hebrew letter was denoted there, along with the pictographic equivalent. Beside each was the further translation denoting Yosef's alleged original meanings. Evans fought the urge to take it and scrutinize it wholesale.

Aarons picked this man. He cannot be trusted, Evans reminded himself.

"Now, Arthur, shall we talk about what *Genesis* really says about Eden?"

Just then, the plane's altitude dropped slightly and the seat belt sign lit up. They would be landing soon.

"Ah," Evans croaked. "It seems we are out of time. I look forward to discussing it with you soon, Yosef." Mercifully, the Hebrew scholar accepted this. "You'd better find a place for your bag and buckle up, David. It's time we shifted our focus back to Wyatt's little hunt for Eden."

"Find a place for my bag?" David whispered under his breath. He looked across the aisle to his original chair, where his backpack had been abandoned some hours before. He stared at it like a stuffed dodo for a great long while.

"Uh, Arthur?" he finally breathed. "Can you pull up that last video from Mr. Aarons real fast? I need to check something."

XLIX

Chinese Airspace. 36,000 ft., Westbound towards Syria. Mel.

Mel casually tapped different windows on her screen. Each tap pulled up a larger version of the audio-video feed. It didn't bother her that the Dilmun team passengers didn't know they were being watched. What they didn't know could only help her. And thus, help all of them in the long run.

Drs. deMata and Pitman were engrossed in their workstations, working on innocuous information she already had seen. Dr. Lee was cocooned in his chair with a blanket, pillow, and eye mask. But two of the passengers had done something most curious. Dr. Evans' guests had abandoned their chairs and come to sit on the floor in front of Dr. Ibrahim.

Yet, Dr. Evans was ignoring them all, his hat pulled low. She couldn't tell if he'd properly fallen asleep or not, but she understood Dr. Evans a little better now. He had not hidden the journal away as she had thought he might, but he had also not engaged in the inflammatory conversations that exploded around him. Yet he had not ended them either. Evans was brilliant, rational, and eccentric, but so far, his humble streak seemed true enough.

Moreover, Mel was now fairly sure that Evans needed others to weigh his thoughts against. People to challenge him and take him out of his comfort zone. More than just "assistants," the boy and the priest were acting as his counsel of some sort. Mel knew as well as anyone that every computer needed its peripherals. Perhaps Evans' human peripherals were sifting the information he needed. Like software, they might process it for him and highlight the relevant data, just as Mel often got from her proprietary web spiders and digital filters.

Unfortunately, with the hidden cameras stationary and positioned for seated passengers, that meant that Mel could not watch the two floor-squatting rogues' faces, nor hear them through the noise-filtering directional mics embedded in the seats. She could only hear Dr. Ibrahim's side of the conversation, and it was most frustrating. At least that part would be recorded and automatically transcribed into the file. Perhaps she could have someone extrapolate the rest later if needed, time-consuming as that would be. It was an unanticipated problem with the cabin design. She was already brainstorming ways to fix it, but there was nothing to be done about it now.

Dr. Ibrahim was talking about Jewish traditions. No, he was referencing the *Kabbalah*. That was interesting. The man had been working with one of her Jerusalem teams for a while, but not in that area specifically. His file said he was a messianic rabbi, but what did that mean in actuality, and how did *Kabbalah* come into it? It was a set of legends she had not explored much of yet, but she knew how to fix that. She mirrored his work screen on her own, watching as he drew various things on a curious image which he was calling the "Tree of Life."

The sleep she had allowed herself earlier had been good. She couldn't remember the last time she'd given herself the luxury of four full hours of it. She almost felt sluggish now. Fortunately, her tea was boiling. She stood and poured herself a tall mug of steaming Indonesian Gold-Black. She savored the smell, anticipating the caffeine-rich beverage, then sipped. There were notes of sweet honey and caramel, then a smooth finish. It was divine.

From across her mobile office, she noted movement on one of the screens. She turned to see that Dr. Evans was now sitting up, a look of surprise on his face. Ibrahim must have said something important. So then, the American scholar had been listening after all. Mel smiled at the evidence that they were all interacting with one another so well. Regardless of their odd behavior, she had her human computers working in tandem now.

She glanced at the other plane's GPS readout. They were already dropping in speed and altitude. Everything was right on schedule.

L

On approach to Bassel al-Assad International Airport. Latakia, Syria. David.

The two Evanses stared at the screen as realization dawned.

"Play it again Arthur. Skip back to where he leaves the frame the first time.

That satchel, see? He goes off-camera with it. But when he comes out—"

"Yes, David. I see. Keep your voice down."

"The journal says the proof is 'hidden away.' Do you think—?"

The plane shuddered as its landing gear extended. David felt frustrated. The whole flight had been nothing but talk and theory and lazy conversation, but now they were out of time just when they needed it.

"I've no idea." Arthur felt around on the monitor until he got it to behave and power down. "But let's keep this little detail between us for now." He looked at David squarely, motioning toward the other chair.

David glanced toward the empty seat, Cat, and his abandoned bag. He wanted to catch Emma up on this new clue, but he suddenly wondered if his phone would even work after they left the plane. *Does Syria do data plans? Come to think of it, does Syria even do mobile phones?*

He and Emma been messaging off and on the whole flight. She'd decided that she was going to have their date with or without him, sending him dozens of pictures of Oxford sites all day long. He'd had to laugh because instead of pictures of the tourist sites, she'd sent him pictures of throngs of people, herself at the grocery store, a cup of tea at a coffee shop, a hallway at the shopping mall, among others. It was great. His favorite was the selfie with her arm around an invisible nobody in front of the phone store which had inspired the whole thing, himself glaringly absent from the picture. He was beginning to love her sense of humor. Apparently, he couldn't forget her even if he'd wanted to, which he didn't. But it might be about to end if there was no signal after the plane. Did he need to say goodbye?

He huffed in frustration and bolted across the aisle to his original chair. He snagged his bag, zipped it the rest of the way, and stuffed it under his chair with no small amount of difficulty.

"Welcome back," Cat said, punching his arm playfully.

David Evans was experiencing something he'd never felt before, and he was completely at a loss as to what to do about it. He was getting attention from two girls at once. This was no girl though. Dr. Catalina deMata was every bit the woman. From her two advanced degrees to her graceful physique, to whatever it was she did to her hair to make it look that good. He hadn't dared ask.

When the flight started, he'd been about neck-deep into his terrible Spanish before he'd realized there was something else happening with Cat. He'd told a joke, a pretty stupid one at that, but she had reached out and batted him on the arm, just like now. It was a playful gesture, but much to David's surprise, not an entirely innocent one. And he'd felt like an idiot for how long it had taken him to figure that out. Now, he didn't want to be rude, but he also felt weirdly awkward. Just what exactly had he gotten himself into by sitting down next to her? It was utterly unidentifiable to him. He had no frame of reference for this feeling, and it was freaking him the heck out. What was the big deal, then? He had no idea.

For the hours and minutes since then, he'd orbited around the question in his mind until it finally hit him. He wasn't used to getting attention from girls, but in just the last few days he'd been wallowing in it from every girl he'd met. He would need to develop a new social protocol strategy very quickly.

What he was slowly realizing now as he fumbled with the seatbelt, was that he was comparing this woman with her double Ph.D.'s, multilingual ability, and really impressive hair to Emma and vice-versa. Two girls he barely knew. One who he'd spent an afternoon in a museum with, and the other he'd be spending a summer with doing archeology. And flirting with in Spanish if he wasn't careful.

Seriously, what does Cat do to get her hair that shiny?

And that was the strangest part. David didn't know if he wanted to be spending the rest of the summer doing that. It wasn't just about looks. Objectively Cat was prettier and more put-together, though maybe not cuter in a girl-next-door way. But David had never focused much on looks anyway, it was something else. He was supposed to have spent the day with Emma and gotten the big private tour of Oxford for real. Instead, his England adventure had taken a sharp left turn. Or rather, a Middle Eastern one. It should have excited him. Instead, there was this weird stretching and he felt kind of guilty about it. It was all happening too fast. He took a deep breath and smiled. This adulting stuff was a real pain.

Cat was looking at him with big bottomless eyes. She'd asked a question he'd missed and was waiting for an answer. David shook his head as if waking from a dream.

"It means," she repeated in English, "Which College will you be a part of?"

"Oh. Um, honestly I don't know yet. I'm sorry, can you excuse me for a minute? I seem to have forgotten my bag."

Without stopping for an answer to his little white lie, he popped his seatbelt and sprang up. All in one swoop, he yanked his backpack from under the seat and headed towards the hideaway compartment where it had been briefly stowed at the beginning of the flight.

Forgotten my bag? That didn't even make sense! He was holding his bag. And given that the fasten seat belt sign had been on for a while, and since the plane already had out its landing gear, it was probably a terrible idea to be ignoring it. He had mere seconds to figure something out. Nobody stopped him, but Arthur did give him a disapproving glare.

David popped open the compartment and threw his bag in. Then, with his back to the others, he pretended to search around in it. As slyly as he could but as swiftly as he dared, he pulled his phone out of his hoodie. His heart skipped a beat. Emma had messaged him almost ten minutes ago, a long string ending with:

> Where'd you go?
> Did you start your Adventures
> without saying bye to me?
> Totes Jealous! :-(
> ;-p

While he'd been looking at that video with Arthur, she'd been trying to get him. Now the plane engines whined, and he could feel the aircraft slowing. His phone was supposed to be off. As quick as he could, he typed a reply.

> Literally landing in Syria now! O.o
> Turning phone off so I don't crash
> the plane or whatever.
> I'll message you if I can after I do
> some archeology and stuff.

He powered off the phone and glanced up. Cat was waiting for him to finish so they could resume their conversation. He shoved the backpack back into place and shut the cabinet, then stumbled his way back towards his chair. For half a second, he was tempted to go back and sit next to Arthur. Instead he popped his headphones in and laughed nervously as he found his original seat. At the same moment, the wheels found the ground and the engines roared to put on the brakes as the plane screamed to a stop on the runway.

Cat did a little sarcastic clap for his gymnastics. "You will do this every time?" she ribbed.

He smiled awkwardly and did a little ironic bow, instantly regretting it. He popped out the earbuds given that there was no reason to have them in with the phone turned off. In all, his plan could have gone better, but at least he'd seen Emma's message in time to reply to it.

What was it Dr. Pitman said about paradigms? Same data, different conclusions? Okay, yea. It was time for a new social paradigm. There was no reason he couldn't be friends with more than one girl. A good start would be getting to know Cat better.

"So, uh, you ever been to Syria before?"

LI

Chinese Airspace. 36,000 ft., Westbound towards Syria. Mel.

Something was eating at Mel. She had spied on the team until the last possible moment, when Dr. Evans' trio had finally deplaned. Now, she was watching the archived video of those last minutes again.

The professor, the priest, and the boy were the last to leave the cabin by just under five minutes, and if that wasn't suspicious enough, the majority of that was spent in a huddle with bowed heads and whispers she could not hear on any of the feeds. Had the three planned something based on new information she missed? The whole last few minutes of the flight, both Evans and the boy David had acted strangely. Mel never allowed herself paranoia, but something in her brain insisted that there was more to it. She ran the video back a second time, allowing it to go much further than before.

As the plane began its landing approach, David had started to get up, then sat back down. The Evanses then pulled out Dr. Evans' monitor for the only time on the whole flight. While others were putting their electronics away, the professor was getting his out. She ran it back again and turned up the volume.

"—that video log from Mr. Aarons again? I want to check something."

She watched as the Evans boy replayed Wyatt Aarons' last transmission, then ran it back and paused it exactly as she had done upon first seeing it. What was he doing? Certainly, they knew about the raven emblem already? It was in the file notations. There must be something else. Mel froze the first recording and pulled up the Aarons video log in a second window. She synced them and played both, cranking up the volume even more.

"That satchel, see? He goes off-camera with it. But when he comes out—"

"Yes, David. I see. Keep your voice down."

"The journal says the proof is 'hidden away.' Do you think—?"

Mel thrilled. She had overlooked the disappearing satchel too. She smiled at her youngest human computer.

She trusted her people, they were a family, but she still couldn't take chances with Dr. Evans just yet. Wyatt Aarons had kept his secrets and entrusted those secrets to his first partner instead of to her. And now Dr. Evans was keeping things close to his chest too. She would need to pass these observations on to her uncle as soon as possible.

But first, some celebratory tea.

LII

Bassel al-Assad International Airport. Latakia, Syria. David.

David was reeling. Yesterday he had walked the ancient streets of Oxford, England. Today, he was in Syria, riding in an APC. So, you know, a pretty typical day for a guy like him. *Said no one, ever!*

Well, technically it wasn't an APC, but it was "armored" and "carrying personnel" so that was good enough, David decided. Namely, it was carrying Rabbi Yosef, Arthur, Father Matthew, and himself. The vehicle was kind of like a Humvee knock-off, but with ridiculous little windows you couldn't look through and a ton of passenger space. And while there was a visual feast of tech and accessories on every surface, air conditioning didn't seem to be one of them. David wasn't sure if it was hotter inside or outside of the vehicle, but he'd quickly ditched his hoodie and was now using it as makeshift padding.

"It's a Russian GAZ-TIGR," a soldier named Rogers told David proudly. "Nearly identical to a Hummer in all the ways that matter."

David did not ask how an American soldier who knew all about Russian military vehicles had come to work for a Chinese mega-company's private military. Or in which order. It was safer that way.

Like Miss Chen had promised, the vehicles came pre-installed with four armed men who met David and the team at the airport. They called themselves guards, but they looked more like special-ops mercenaries to David. The small squad even had its own commander. He was a chisel-faced barbarian whose badge read Raskolnikov but he announced himself as "Colonel Ivan" in a thick Eastern European accent. David wasn't going to argue. Colonel Ivan was a brick of a man who looked like he could break most of them in half without much effort. At the moment, Ivan was arguing with an airport guard about their paperwork, and his Arabic was about as good as the other man's Russian.

Rogers explained how this TIGR had been converted to a troop transport, while the other was more of a standard cargo design. Otherwise, they were a matched set clad in a digital desert gray-brown camo. Dr. Pitman and Cat were in the other vehicle along with two of the soldiers and everyone's bags. Rogers sat in the front of this one watching Ivan, while David and the other three passengers fidgeted in the back, awkwardly facing one another. Oh, and sweating. Lots of sweating. This part of the world had been in drought for years apparently, at least according to the internet. Not that he could check it now, his data connection had vanished after leaving the plane, just as he'd feared.

Why the TIGRs didn't have proper air conditioners he had no idea. Or real windows for that matter. The little slot in the wall was hardly any taller than the width of his phone. David supposed it all had something to do with Russian design, glass, and warzones. He didn't own a car, but a third-generation Texan still knew the importance of a climate-controlled vehicle. So far, Texas had nothing on Syria in the hot-and-arid department. Summers here had to be unlivable. David decided to be thankful for the solid metal plates that blocked the sun where passenger windows should have been, even if it was like riding inside a pizza oven. He started thumbing through e-books to kill time and get his mind off of it. It didn't work.

"All right Yosef," Arthur said after the uncomfortable silence had gone on entirely too long. He was twisting his hat into an unnatural shape. "Let's hear it. What does the Bible really say about Eden?"

Oh, yea! And Hebrew has secret meanings! David kept thinking about every "Unlocking the Bible code—secrets revealed!"-type advertisement he'd ever seen, and that *Ancient Aliens* TV show that had inspired all the memes. Not to mention about a thousand YouTube clips he'd watched about Atlantis, Stargates, and crop circles over the years. He craved to consult the internet for answers.

Rabbi Yosef extracted his little black book, and with no preamble broke into a series of guttural phrases that sounded like Klingon.

It was Father Matthew who translated, reciting in English from memory yet again. "'So God created man in his own image, in the image of God he created him; male and female he created them.'"

"You have a mind for memorizing scripture, Matthew." Yosef was impressed.

"Occupational hazard," he replied, chuckling. Yosef joined him.

"That is from the sixth day," Yosef explained, "when God made mankind. That is chapter one, verse twenty-seven. Not to be confused with the story of Adam and Eve."

"Sorry, what?" David asked. "Isn't that the same thing?"

"Ah," Matthew said, "I might know where you are headed with this, Yosef. David, why don't you use your phone to search for the first biblical appearance of the name 'Adam'?"

Yosef nodded approvingly. With great joy, David thumbed the Bible app icon and entered the search term. The results were confusing.

"But the name Adam doesn't appear until..." He double-checked. It had to be wrong. "Verse 2:20? 'But for Adam, there was not found a helper fit for him. So, the Lord God caused a deep sleep to fall upon the man, and while he slept took one of his ribs and closed up its place with flesh. And the rib that the Lord God had taken from the man he made into a woman and brought her to the man.' That's the first time his name is actually mentioned?"

"It is this word *Adam* that is causing all of the difficulty, you see." Yosef pronounced it *"Hah-dem,"* which was cool. "Perhaps we could write it?" He flipped through his little black book until he found a mostly blank page at the end of a chapter. Yosef frisked himself with his other hand and glanced around the massive truck's interior but came up empty of any sort of pen.

David could see that the book had dozens of notations in the margins and between the lines of every page. Little pictographs and English letters alike had been scrawled there, all similar to what Yosef had drawn on the screen before. Whole sentences were squeezed into the book's margins, ancient pictographic words drawn then translated into whole phrases of meaning. It looked like some madman's memoirs. Mr. Aarons' journal had looked perfectly sane and normal by comparison.

Arthur cleared his throat and handed the man the golf pencil he'd been keeping in the spiral of his little notebook. With a great smile, Yosef focused on the page and wrote a Hebrew word into it. Over it, he put the normal Latin letters.

M D A
אדם

David instantly recognized the first one, even remembering to start on the right. "That's *Aleph*, the silent consonant again. The A in *Adam*. Once the vowel sound is attached, I mean."

"Excellent, yes. And *Adam* is also related to the words *adom*, 'red', and *adamah*, 'earth.' *Adam* accurately signifies mankind, as I believe Arthur mentioned before. They are all spelled similarly in Hebrew, but have different pronunciations, depending on the vowels applied."

"Okay," David said, nodding slowly. The recent series finale of *Battlestar Galactica* popped into his head. He wasn't supposed to watch it, but a friend of his owned the DVDs. The last season they'd downloaded and watched together. Admiral Adama, the Cylons, and the series' enigmatic final scenes suddenly made way more sense. *Spoiler alert, after five seasons on the run, they all made it to Earth.* The big ironic twist was that the series turned out to be set in the remote past, ancient history, rather than the far future. David now realized that the admiral's name, Adama, had been chosen purposefully to imply a connection to *Genesis*.

"Now, let us look at the more ancient pictographs." Yosef moved the pencil again.

"What does it mean?" David asked. "God-something, right?" He remembered the first symbol's meaning, but the other two were new.

Yosef did his smile-blink-nod thing. "Recall that *Aleph* can also mean 'God,' or sometimes just 'power' as we have discussed." He pointed to the second letter, the Hebrew D. "This is ancient *Dalet*. It is the door or path—illustrated here as a tent flap. And these ridges are *Mem*. The image is of water, but it also represents blood or chaos."

David could see the M there with its extra ridge. He instantly thought of the flood and Noah's family with all the animals floating above a drowned world as torrential rain wiped out all other life. *Water, blood, chaos? Yea, that made sense.* He put it all together as a chill ran down his spine. "Adam, God's powerful door to bloody chaos?"

Yosef laughed. Arthur made a duck face. Father Matthew looked thoughtful and said, "Perhaps 'First through the door of Chaos' might be a more accurate theological statement?"

David nodded agreeably, since the others obviously liked this second answer better.

Outside, someone shouted in Arabic and was answered in kind by a much closer voice. Ivan's shouts joined in. After a while of this, the chatter went back to normal levels of arguing.

"Might I?" Matthew asked, holding his hand out to receive the book. He thumbed through it and quickly found the page where Yosef had drawn the individual pictographic Proto-Sinaitic "words" and defined them in a little chart. Sticking a thumb there, Matthew began turning back and forth and back again. His intensity was a little scary. In a moment's pause, David snapped a picture, allowing him to look at the chart properly.

"Now, as to Eve," Yosef brought David's attention back. "We should consider the significance of Adam's side."

"God took Adam's rib and made Eve," David shrugged. "We just read it."

"The word is *tsela*," Yosef supplied. "'Rib' is valid, but 'rib-cage' is far more appropriate. Everywhere else the word is used in the Torah, it is architectural. Wing of a building, side of the temple, that sort of thing. No, this passage is clear. Adam, the archetype for mankind, has a dream-vision where God tells him that his mate should be his equal in the work they were to begin. One flesh, metaphorically."

David was stunned by this idea.

Arthur cleared his throat. "The creation story of Adam and Eve is not our only point of focus here. Shall we return to the matter of Eden? Context notwithstanding, how does this help us?"

"Ah," Yosef said, drawing it out into four or five syllables. "It is all a matter of function."

Name	Pictograph	Meaning
Aleph		Ox/strength/leader/God
Bet		House / "in"
Gimmel		Foot/camel/pride
Dalet		Tent door/pathway
Hey		Lo!/Behold!/"The"
Vav		Nail/peg/add/"And"
Zayin		Plow/weapon/cut off
Chet		Tent wall/fence/separation
Tet		Basket/snake/surround
Yod		Arm & hand/work/deed
Kaf		Palm of hand/to open
Lamed		Staff/goad/control/toward
Mem		Water/chaos
Nun		Seed/fish/activity/life
Samekh		Hand on staff/support/prop
Ayin		Eye/to see/experience
Pey		Mouth/word/speak
Tsade		Man on side/desire/need
Qof		Sun on horizon/behind
Resh		Head/person/first
Shin		Eat/consume/destroy
Tav		Mark/sign/covenant

David was about to ask what that meant, but heavy footsteps were approaching. Colonel Ivan got in, slammed the door, and pushed the ignition button. The vehicle had no keys. David added that to the list of weird features on this not-a-Hummer APC.

"I should have flown helicopter," Ivan spat. "This is not very trusting place."

It took about five minutes before the little convoy hit the first roadblock.

LIII

Latakia, Syria. Route 1, northbound to Ras-Shamra. Arthur.

Evans still didn't know if Yosef was insane or just clever. But if nothing else, his ideas about the Proto-Sinaitic pictographs were wildly excellent abstractions with intriguing possibilities. It was going to take a lot more than a chart with some doodles, however, to convince Evans that phonetically based Hebrew was derived from a much simpler and far older logographic precursor language.

Matthew had begun happily fact-checking the man's little black book against scripture, while David was letting his imagination take charge as usual. Joseph would have a field day with the man, Evans suspected. Perhaps starting with the New Testament and Jesus' thoughts on the matter. Or maybe he'd just ask the rabbi to step out of the vehicle without telling the driver to stop. That idea made Evans smile a bit.

Only, his brain kept circling back to that thing that Yosef had said, *"It's all a matter of function."* Evans didn't want to take that bait, but the truth was that functional ontology was one of his all-time great pet theories. Did Yosef somehow know this?

Finally, Evans couldn't take it anymore. As casually as he could, he said "So, Yosef, did I understand correctly that you said something about the function of Eden's inhabitants?"

"Ah yes," Yosef cooed like a serene hippy, closing his little black book. "First, God made mankind. I shall use your word, Arthur. 'And Powers fattened the human in his image. In the image of Powers, he fattened him. Male and female he fattened them.' That is how 1:27 might be translated."

BaRA, fatten, create, Evans translated in his head, nodding.

"Each time," Yosef said, "God declares it *tobh*. Most English translations translate this 'good.' Yet to write that God declared his creation 'good' is slightly misleading. A better translation—"

"Functional," Evans and Matthew said together, eying each other conspiratorially. Arthur caught David doing a double-take.

He had discussed this topic with Matthew too many times to count. There had always been a chessboard between them, rather than hot Syrian air. And the priest's definition of 'functional' diverged wildly from Evans' own. But there was no denying that this rabbi was about to enter Evans' wheelhouse.

"Only," Matthew added right on cue, "it is not entirely fair from an implicit standpoint. There is no other Hebrew word for 'good,' at least not in the Greek *kalos* versus *agathos* sense. We are tied to that dichotomy in our Western thinking." It was his standard rebuttal.

David mouthed a *"what?"* to Matthew, who leaned in. "Aesthetics versus practicality," The priest told him. "Pleasing as opposed to useful, if you will."

David nodded. "Okay, different kinds of 'good'. Got it."

"Ah, but isn't that the very point?" Yosef asked, accepting the argument. "Each time in chapter one that God creates, He declares it to be both: both beautiful and functional. The sun is functional for giving day and night cycles. The animals are functional for filling the land and sea. And man is functional for his purpose too."

"To tend the Garden," Matthew said, nodding. "We're gardeners. I gave a sermon along those lines recently. And the function of a garden is to provide both food and beauty."

"True, we are gardeners. But moreover, we are priests," Yosef said. Evans couldn't help but notice the irony of this, a rabbi telling a man wearing a clerical collar that he was a priest. But the unconventional holy man didn't stop there. "The Garden was largely self-sufficient. It was apart from the rest of man's territory and made special for God to reside with his creation. To rest on the seventh day. It is from this holy place that the all-important trees of the Garden sprang, including the Tree of Life. It was no ordinary garden, but a holy place."

David looked at Evans knowingly. Yosef had been teaching the boy about the Kabbalistic Tree of Life, but he suspected they were both thinking about the final journal message Evans had chosen not to share with everyone. *'You were right about Nûh and the tree after all...' Blasted Wyatt.*

"In the pictographic Hebrew, Eden translates as, 'see and know the door to life.'"

Rabbi Yosef looked straight at David, making sure he wasn't leaving him behind. Evans gave it about even odds at this point. Matthew offered the black book to David for help. Tentatively, the teen took the pencil too and consulted a photo he had evidently taken of the chart. A minute later, he wrote his best guess and held it up for all to see.

Yosef smiled and congratulated him. "Even your word 'fatten' is helpful, Arthur. Such ancient knowledge indicates that the material of the universe was brought into existence first, and then organized by God to have a function.

And what greater blessing to ancient man could there be than a fat garden, fat animals, fat children, and a fat wife? It is the perfect word in many ways."

"Yes, interesting," Evans lied. It was time to poke the bear and see how far Yosef was willing to take this. "So, I suppose then, that Adam was appointed a higher function than his primitive ancestors."

"Uh, what?" David stammered. "Arthur, how could the first person have ancestors?" The boy was getting bolder. Hopefully, that also meant he was beginning to think critically about such things.

"He couldn't" Evans replied. "Unless he wasn't 'first' in the way most people think. I told you before that the epic myths of Genesis are neither science nor history. We are told that Adam was made from the 'dust of the earth,' that's fine. The word for 'dust' is *aphar*, it's used in dozens of other places in the Bible, often to describe people. It refers to their mortality. It also means 'ashes,' as from a funeral pyre. Many scholars would agree that the historical man we think of as Adam was not necessarily the first human. The Eden story is quite probably, well, let's call it a sequel to the Genesis 1 creation myth, originating from a slightly different oral tradition."

David looked like he'd just been told his dog had died.

"Come now, Arthur," Matthew chided sweetly. "You do recall that the horse typically precedes the cart?"

Evans harumphed, but didn't argue. David had proven he could handle complex thinking without needing someone to build a scaffold first, but Matthew did have a point: they were getting off-topic again.

"*Aphar*, dust. Spelled *Ayin, Pey, Reysh*," Yosef affirmed, undaunted by the two old friends' banter. "Literally, from the pictographs: 'watch the scattering of those who came first.' A clear allusion to Adam's ancestors, who were not self-aware in the philosophical and religious sense. A rudimentary mankind, created by *Elohim*-Powers on the sixth day. Long dead ancestors from whom Adam and Eve were born. Equal one to another, but separate from the rest. A marriage made functional by God, in his personal garden, which perfectly suited the first self-aware couple."

Evans was stunned. This man should not be agreeing with him.

David went to work on the word. His fingers dizzily flicked and resized the image on his screen as he went from symbol to symbol between the written text and his digital version of the chart. Finishing, he held the book up again.

"All right, I'll bite," Evans said. "If that is so, then also the days, the *Yom*, of Genesis must similarly be 'eras.' Eons, even."

"The work that secures the chaos," Yosef translated without missing a tick. Evans smashed the symbols together in his head as David wrote. All this shouldn't be working, but it was. David flashed the book as Yosef nodded.

Evans pondered the implications. "We aren't told the literal time it took in the text because the storyteller didn't know. Evening and morning would just be words indicating chaos and order, darkness and light, ignorance and knowledge. Or perhaps the amount of time simply doesn't matter."

"Huh?" David asked. "But, what about the seven days?"

Matthew lifted an eyebrow questioningly as the truck bounced through a rough patch of road. His old student knew him too well. Matthew was remarkably open-minded about new ideas, but he did have his limits, especially when it came to too-quickly rethinking scripture. Except Evans was well past entertaining the priestly side of Matthew right now. He was having too much fun.

"That does all fit," Evans acknowledged, ignoring them both. "If it's proved true, it could change everything we know about the early Semitic people, scripture, and frankly most ancient language groups." He scanned the ceiling of the TIGR as if he could see through to the dome of heaven itself, continuing to think aloud. "Could the early Israelites have had a rudimentary written language after all? I've long suspected that *Genesis* was just like all of the other ancient texts. Ancient creation stories are always about describing a functional ontology, not a material one. And you are suggesting an even older, corroborative meaning exists in the original pictographs on a word-to-word level! But then, why not? Moses would have studied the concept of hieroglyphics if anything, and such a practice would predate any later idiomatic elements imposed upon it by the compilers of *Genesis*. That alone could unlock, well, who knows what. Good lord, could it really be so blasted simple?"

"That's simple?" David snorted under his breath.

There was a long silence, broken finally by a gentle whisper from Yosef. "And so too must we now follow the 'Path of the Flaming Sword.'" Evans blinked a half-dozen times and turned to Yosef, not sure what he meant. He'd used that familiar phrase a few times now, having to do with the Kabbalistic Tree of Life. But Yosef was obviously implying something more now.

"*Genesis* 1-3 is about God giving extravagantly with only a few restrictions," Yosef explained. "It is his very nature. Whereas man's nature is to take and to try to be the center of order. It is the very root of our dysfunction, and why we often fail. The Hebrew word is *chata*, to miss. The modern word for this is 'sin.' Adam and Eve chose themselves over God, and in doing so they became dysfunctional, no longer worthy to be priests of the Garden. Thus, Eden lost its purpose too, and they were exiled from orderly paradise to the chaotic earth."

"The Path of the Serpent," Evans stated mindlessly. "The map of man's fall from paradise." He reached out to David for Yosef's little annotated Bible. "May I keep this for a while, Yosef?"

"Certainly. I suspect we will need it if we are going to find your Dilmun."

Evans wasn't sure what that was supposed to mean, but David dove on it. "Mr. Aarons thinks that the Tree is a map! If one path takes you farther from paradise, then he must think the Path of the Flaming Sword has to be the way back in?"

Yosef bowed. "That is my suspicion, yes."

Evans was dumbfounded. This was just too much. Wyatt's ridiculous conclusions aside, Yosef's research on Paleo-Hebrew might show promise. If supportable, it was the missing piece of what Evans had always thought must be true. The *Genesis* epic really could be about the function of creation and the subsequent dysfunction in which the world still abided. *Chaos and order reframed.* Evans was tickled by the mountains of potential research this simple idea unlocked.

However... he frowned. An alternative reading of Genesis was decidedly unlike Wyatt. It had no place in a young-Earth biblical literalist's worldview. *So, why would he have recruited Yosef?* Evans was missing something, and it was something incredibly important.

But a short minute later, Evans forgot about Wyatt's wild fantasies and everything else. He was too busy mumbling through *Genesis* in Hebrew with little gasps of childlike surprise and delight. As the TIGR rumbled on towards the ruins of Ugarit, Evans flipped back and forth between the translation chart, the text, and Yosef's margin notes, reading far more deeply than he had ever thought possible. He didn't even notice a few minutes later when the vehicle slowed and stopped for yet another of the interminable military checkpoints.

LIV

Ras-Shamra Ruins. Ugarit, Syria. David.

Most of the day was already gone when the military truck finally rumbled and bounced its way past the outskirts of Latakia. France may not have wanted to see their passports, but Syria sure did. Again, and again, and again... Thus, a twenty-minute drive had dragged into a ten-hour circus show, and the sun had set well and proper by the time David finally set foot in Ugarit. The whole process had truly driven home where David now was. Everybody knew that there had been political problems, wars, and scandals in this part of the world since before he was born, but did people really understand it while watching TV from the couch and complaining about the president's foreign policy? David felt certain that they had just accomplished something big just by making it to this place.

He only wished he could actually see it. Standing on the edge of the dusty patch where their camp was soon to be, David tried to make out some features of the ancient city, but the headlights of the super-trucks and a portable halogen made it impossible to see anything. Two more guards greeted their four, and they all began breaking out supplies and equipment with military efficiency. Sometime in the last day or so, everything they might need had been delivered to the dig site. Crates and footlockers were stacked everywhere around a wrecked little camping tent and firepit that somebody else had recently used here. With a start, David realized that it must be Mr. Aarons' former campsite.

A few minutes later, he thrilled when he saw that a communications tower was being cranked up into the sky. So then, Miss Chen was not making the same mistakes twice. And Arthur wasn't making Mr. Aarons' mistakes all over again, either. He had already given instructions that he wanted to take three of the armed guards down into the ruins with them. The other half of the troops would have the upgraded camp assembled when they got back, and then they could all get caught up on sleep. It couldn't be safer.

But not everyone was as eager to go dashing into the ruins as David. Dr. Pitman quickly fell into loudly advising the troops as to where the tents and supplies should go, based on some plan that only he understood. The old guy was a firecracker, but nobody else had a strong enough opinion or desire to stop him. People were already calling bunks and rummaging around for supplies, but David didn't care about any of that. He shoved his phone into his pocket and walked around a low rise to get away from the chatter and headlights.

As his eyes adjusted, David saw a dark maze of ruins sprawled out even further than he'd imagined. Above him was a silvery dome of innumerable stars and a half-moon doing its best to light it all up for him. It was unbelievably magical. The excavated part of the city looked like something akin to trench warfare. It was all sunken passages, tiny walkways, and roofless rooms open to the air like courtyards. Except that it was ghostly empty. An arched entrance gate set in the old city wall gaped impressively nearby. As a little cloud passed in front of the moon and the shadows deepened, the stone archway seemed to mouth an ancient, *"Welcome, weary traveler,"* frozen in time.

David sighed a deep and contented sigh. This was his first step onto a real archeological dig site. He was beginning to understand Arthur's passion. This ancient-world stuff was tantalizing.

"All unpacked?" Arthur said, stepping up beside him like a ninja.

"Nah, I guess I left my bag in the truck. I'll do it later, I wanted to see this."

Arthur put a hand on David's shoulder. "Me too," he whispered. The two Evanses stood at the rim of the ruins for a moment and drank it in. David found his imagination filling in what time and ancient enemies had torn down. He could see the broken and war-torn ancient city rebuilding itself before him, and roads bustling with people. This moment would not come again, so David embraced it.

"*Ras-Shamra* means 'fennel head' in Syrian," Arthur said reverently. "It's a sixty-five-foot mound over there somewhere. But now the whole site is known by the name. The ancient people who lived here simply would have called it Ugarit."

"I can smell the sea. And are those goats?" David began to slowly wander toward one of the roofless passages. Sure enough, a handful of snoozing goats startled and bounded away.

"It may be little more than a goat-grazing hill now, David, but Ugarit was the central hub of this part of the world four thousand years ago. It was the New York City of its era. It was never a technological superpower like Knossos and the so-called Minoans, but Ugarit was an important cultural center of art and languages and a major economic center for Canaan. The last great stop before sailing out into the Mediterranean. The first port before venturing into the mountain passes that led to Mesopotamia. Everyone in the ancient world knew of this place. But it was locked away by dirt, modern political borders, and time until a short lifetime ago. Countless academics, researchers, and historians in the last eighty years have desired to stand where we are now."

"Like Mr. Aarons?"

Arthur frowned and ignored the question. "One of the greatest finds of all mankind was found right here. Do you recall that Ugaritic cuneiform is unique because it is phonetic?"

"Yea, the little hash marks represented sounds instead of ideas. Like the alphabet."

"Like the Hebrew *Alefbet*, technically, but yes. It was the libraries here that contained that previously unknown cuneiform script. Plus, an entirely new mythological and religious literature from the Canaanite perspective. Not to mention archives dealing with all aspects of the city's political, social, economic, and cultural life. Scads of new information about *Ba'al* worship."

"Oh, yea," David remembered, "Mr. Aarons was digging around in a *Ba'al* temple, right? Oh, and the Atra-Hasis tablets, you said they were found right here too."

"Quite right. And that temple is where we need to go. Don't forget the plan."

The statement jarred David back to the here and now. The journal said that Mr. Aarons found the other translation tablet fragment down in these ruins. That was the true goal here. And if it really did have a transcription in Linear-A, then he was standing near the key that could make Uncle Sir Arthur's archive readable. Much like the Ugaritic library had been. It was a lot of "ifs," but Arthur was right, they could be on the verge of decoding all the earliest secrets of Minoan Crete. That was kind of exciting.

But first things first. They needed to get down into the tunnels and find Mr. Aarons' stashed bag in the darkness of the dig before anyone else figured out it was there. Assuming it was still there. David's mind flashed to the dozens of untranslated tablets back at the museum, and he wondered for the millionth time what secrets might be hidden in plain sight, just waiting for the right lingual key to unlock them.

Arthur took a deep breath of the searing night air. He must have been thinking something similar because he said, "Come along David, I'm tired of waiting. Let's get a little closer to this marvelous place."

*   *   *

"So, I heard you use the word 'ontology' earlier," David said.

The Evanses stood in a little sunken courtyard that had once been a building. Trenches led away in nearly every direction. For some reason, it reminded David of the Lamb and Flag Passage, right before that gunman showed up. Just stone walls and an infinite sky. Arthur was scrutinizing a large rock that might have once been a column.

"Yes, that's right," Arthur replied over his shoulder, his answer about as helpful as usual.

"It's just that you said something about 'functional ontology' in the truck, but I couldn't figure out what you meant, and I can't look it up until they finish hooking up the tower." David pulled his phone out of his pocket to indicate that Syria had no data network out here in the boonies, but Arthur wasn't looking at him. "It's been bugging me."

"Ah, I see. Well essentially it means 'the way things work,' but in that usage—*Genesis*, I mean—ontology would indicate a description of creation, while the functional element has to do with intent or purpose for doing a thing." Arthur dusted the rock with his handkerchief. "That's opposed to 'material ontology', which is a more scientific approach describing the makeup of a thing."

"So, what you mean is, that *Genesis* isn't so much about how God made the world..." David searched for the words.

"...as it is about why he did so." Arthur finished for him, finally looking up. "Precisely. I keep telling people that the library we call the Bible contains no science books. History texts, yes, but *Genesis* isn't history either. Well, not its early chapters, anyway. And not as we think of history, even then."

David thought back to Galileo, Einstein, the Big Bang, and Father Matthew's assertion that Arthur didn't take *Genesis* literally. Maybe this functional ontology stuff was the reason. "So, why did God create then? You know, according to *Genesis* or whatever."

"Ah. Well, that's fairly easy. Yosef said it. Each thing he makes, he assigns a job. The sun is to mark the day, the moon is to mark the night, the animals are to fill the earth, and mankind is meant to tend the Garden and commune with God. Put another way, he was bringing order out of chaos by declaring things to function a certain way, as only he could."

"Rabbi Yosef also said we were supposed to be priests."

"Indeed. Moses told Israel that they were meant to be a nation of priests. As such, Eden was far more than just an archetypal sacred garden, it was the first Temple of God. Even Solomon understood that. His temple was styled to look like a garden, a direct reference to the temple communion that Adam and Eve enjoyed at the beginning. It's a wonderful story understood that way. Especially compared to other ancient texts where the gods are petty and vengeful and make the Edenic garden for themselves. Utnapishtim's garden is in fact an anomaly, in that he is gifted it as a reward for his obedience. In most creation stories, mankind is an afterthought, a mistake, or a divine accident." Arthur cleared his throat. "Until *Genesis*, that is."

"Okay." David nodded, accepting the first idea for now. "Only, I've been thinking. Noah, Utnapishtim, Atra-Hasis. You said that Nûḥ was just another name for him in Arabic. And so, I was like, how do we know whether one story is older than another, anyway? Didn't they all get passed down by mouth until Moses wrote it in the Old Testament, er, *Torah*? I mean you keep talking about this Utnapishtim guy and Dilmun. But maybe, I don't know, I just don't see how the Bible could be a myth that we are still expected to believe. And now there's all this hidden meaning stuff in it. What are we supposed to believe anyway? Where do we even start?"

It had the potential to be a word-flood of mythic proportions. For a moment, David wasn't sure he could stop, but realizing it, he shrugged, sighed, and shoved his hands into his jeans. He waited for some kind of answer from his wizard slash Oxford tutor. An answer that David wasn't sure his grandfather could give.

Arthur took a few paces toward a larger pile of rubble, chewed his lip for a second then frowned. He pushed his glasses back up onto his nose, straightened his hat, and scratched his beard, every one of his time-buying tells. The bleats of the goats were all David could hear. Not even a wind to rustle the scrubby grass on this hot dry night. Finally, Arthur spoke.

"Many scholars have asked those questions, David. Supposing the flood was a real event, then one or more of the accounts must have borrowed from any of the others. But how could we know which came first? Does *Genesis* retell the *Gilgamesh* account with a monotheistic twist? Did the Babylonians pervert the 'true' oral story of Noah's ark into a polytheistic form by writing it down with different details? Or perhaps, many centuries later, the tradition of Moses canonized it and restored it after a fashion via the Hebrew tradition? Did Moses truly have a written language, or were these stories reverse-engineered after contact with the Babylonians during the Great Exile? How so, if that was when they finally began using what we think of as ancient Hebrew? These are good questions."

David tensed. His every fiber was willing Arthur to continue. To actually answer a question instead of posing any more. Then, to his great surprise, his wizard did.

"There was a time when I was in favor of a literal biblical reading, but not anymore. Now, I think of it this way. Much of the Bible was literature long before it was scripture. Especially the oldest parts. And the further we go back, the more mythological it seems to be."

"'Myth is not a dirty word?'" David surprised himself by echoing.

Arthur nodded. "What we must understand is that the story of Adam and Eve is not a creation myth in the strictest sense. It is a—"

"—sequel, you said."

"Right. The story of the placement of Adam in the Garden isn't anything like the world-creation myths. Not even the other ones compiled together in the Bible."

"Uh, okay. How many are there?" David asked dubiously. The last time Arthur had said something like this, he'd learned that hundreds of alternate flood myths existed.

"Some scholars put the count at as high as six in *Genesis*, but that's neither here nor there. We need to understand that the elements of Adam and Eve in Eden appear elsewhere. In other and much older myths from the same part of the world. They truly are archetypal. And ancient man would have instantly understood the symbolism of those elements in any telling."

"Yea. Like the Flood myths."

"Correct. It is true that the thematic elements of the snake and the tree, a walled garden, the woman tempted, and the complicit man, are near-universal. Though they often appear after the flood, as in the *Gilgamesh* epic."

David furrowed his brow thoughtfully, but Arthur didn't pause.

"The thing to remember David, is that before Adam and Eve were expelled from Eden, they were placed in it. Perhaps even came upon it. And doing so was their figurative waking up into what we would consider civilization. The balance of the natural and the civilized. The iconic importance of a walled garden or planted orchard. The chaotic feminine and the orderly masculine archetypes in balance. It's the whole point of the Eden story. That all had to happen first, before the balance was thrown off the first time. Before the functional order began to lapse back into dysfunctional chaos."

"The first time?" David's mind whirled. "As in, eating the forbidden fruit of knowledge inevitably led to the first apocalypse—Noah's flood?"

Arthur forced a weak smile. "Or maybe the point is that the coveting of the knowledge was the true original sin, and the expulsion from Eden was itself the first apocalypse. Either way, it was a disruption of what God had declared functional. In that, Yosef has a very good argument. One I've made many times myself, frankly."

David was dumbfounded. He considered asking Arthur which kind of 'good' he meant, but Emma posing in front of that perfect Venus and Cupid statue popped into his head for some reason. *Which kind of good had that been?* He wasn't sure. Could it be both? David crossed his arms grumpily and sighed. "So how long has it been since you believed in the *Genesis* stories? Literally, I mean."

Arthur cleared his throat and looked at the sky. David followed his gaze. Even in Texas, he had never seen so many stars. He could imagine reaching up and touching the Milky Way. "Don't get me wrong David, when we first found the Doomsday... anomaly, in '77, I was almost positive we'd found the Ark of Noah. Honestly, that connection is why I stuck around for so long. In case we found what we were hoping for, some sort of writing that pre-dated *Gilgamesh* and authenticated *Genesis*."

"Yea. Proto-Indo-European or whatever."

"That's right."

"But why does it matter? Dad always said that if it was in the Bible it was good enough for us." It felt a little weird to take his dad's side.

"That certainly sounds like Joseph." Arthur chuckled nervously. "But literally true? No, not at the expense of common sense." He cleared his throat. "All right, listen. It's not always that simple. You see, with absolutely no disrespect meant towards your father or the other millions of people who think likewise and purchase his books, it is important to understand how valuable our ancient stories are. How deep they go. The full degree to which such stories encode the wisdom of our ancestors is unclear. Perhaps they even resonate with the hard knocks of evolution. It's entirely probable that we story-told ourselves into our very existence around the first campfires."

It was the second time David had heard Arthur say that. "Fireside theory."

"Yes, but it's more than just a theory about human evolution. The class of stories that deal with religious elements are those which deal with the deepest issues of human life. Good and evil, chaos and order. Mankind's told, retold, and distilled myths contain every lesson that has ever been passed on by those who failed forward into what we are now. It's what being human means. Or rather, the stories are about what being human means. We ignore them, or god forbid edit them, at our great peril. And when we do, well, we must learn the lesson again from scratch."

"'There have been many apocalypses,'" David mumbled. "Yea, I remember."

Arthur smiled thinly. "Yes."

"So, you don't believe the Ark ever really existed."

Arthur sighed. "No David, I do not. Thirty years ago, I was sure we'd found it, but I need more now. You see, in the end, the best evidence that the Doomsday anomaly was the genuine Noah's Ark came from a cramped, miserable, taxi ride." His words were thick with sarcasm, and he spat the last two out like a profanity one does not say in polite conversation.

David stood by in a way that he hoped was encouraging. A moment later, Arthur the wizard-bard plopped himself down onto a flat-ish bit of rubble and began his tale.

"It was August of 1977 when we touched down in Istanbul that first time."

LV

Ras-Shamra Ruins. Ugarit, Syria. Arthur.

Evans had long ago abandoned his youthful dreams of ever setting foot in Ras-Shamra. With his own spotty history, no traditional research team had wanted him taking up space anywhere. Not when his comparatively slow translation work could be done from a desk. His place had always been back at the Ashmolean, while the "proper" archeology happened elsewhere. *It still is*, he realized. Nothing about this expedition was traditional or proper at all.

Maybe finally being in Ras-Shamra had done something to Evans, but he decided it was time to come clean. David was as ready as he was going to be after his crash course in ancient cultures. Evans could only hope the boy had been paying attention.

"First, you must understand this, David," he began. "Turkey has a long-held fiercely secular posture, especially when it comes to political and religious neutrality. Yet, things were still a lot different in that part of the world than they are today. No cell phones or internet obviously, but no gas stations or tourists either. That Istanbul flight was the worst one of my life. I'll just say, 'engine fire' and leave it at that."

This won a smile from David. So far, so good.

"We had to take a rusty bus to Ankara, followed by an antique train to Erzurum. This alone consumed the first three days, and we were still not yet to Dogubeyazit, the closest village to where the anomaly was supposed to be. So, if you can imagine it, we were hungry, we stank, and we were in foul moods.

"Finally, when we reached Erzurum, we used some of our limited funds and just hired a blasted taxi. Wyatt pantomimed to the driver until the poor fellow finally understood to take us to a hotel in Dogubeyazit, but the fact is that Eastern Turkey was both remote and dangerous. Perhaps even more so today given the various wars in the neighborhood. As the only two white men for hundreds of miles, it did not take long for us to become notorious. Very few people spoke any English. Even fewer knew anything about a group of scientists who had checked out a random pile of rocks in the mountains nearly two decades prior."

"The *Time Magazine* team, you mean. From that article you keep in the myster—in your wooden chest."

"The same."

"So, what did you guys do?"

"Well, Wyatt, being the man of faith that he was, did the only thing he knew to do. He prayed about it. I must admit I joined him. He said a prayer that the taxi would stall where we should begin looking."

"You're kidding?" David was laughing, thank goodness. "So, what happened?!"

"Well, believe it or not, the taxi stalled."

"No way."

"Yep. Three times, in fact. Each time, Wyatt and I exited the car, we set up a pile of rocks, prayed again, and continued on. Eventually, we made it to the hotel, where we slept harder than I ever remember sleeping—except for maybe a night train from Barcelona to Paris one time. But as I recall, the train had far fewer bugs."

David started to laugh again but was startled by something tugging on his shoe. Neither of them had noticed the baby goat approach and start nibbling on David's laces. The teen broke into a wide smile. "Well hello there, little guy. Are you hungry?" He rooted around in his hoodie and produced a bag of crushed airplane biscuits. Eighty-five degrees at night and he was still wearing the thing. Evans just didn't understand young people.

"The point is this, David. In Wyatt's way of thinking, if you prayed hard enough and with enough faith, God would do what you asked. Like a vending machine. Punch in the right code, put in enough currency, out comes a bag of crisps. And since the taxi stalled in three locations, we set out the next day to investigate the first of the three piles of rocks. We walked perpendicular to the road until we came across something significant. We were simply relying on our belief in miracles. Blind faith and all that."

"I think I believe 'all that' too, actually. But what did you find?" The goat nibbled a bit of biscuit from David's hand.

"Well, the truth is, we found several interesting things. But to Wyatt, they were all of supreme biblical and archeological significance. There was an ancient vineyard that claimed to be the oldest in the region. Then, massive, vaguely egg-shaped stones with a hole through the top which Wyatt said could only be anchor stones from the ark. Those were later analyzed by proper experts who declared them to be made of local basalt. Which, as I understand it, is not found within five hundred miles of Mesopotamia, where Noah would have necessarily chiseled the things. One expert later declared them to be pagan gravestones. He noted that the carved holes tended to perfectly frame the peak of modern-day Ararat when you looked through them. But, that was all after my time."

"Oh." David didn't sound very convinced.

"Last of all was the anomaly proper. A big dirty hill with a rather odd shape. But it was our last day, and we could do little more than look around and marvel."

"You found it based on the pile of rocks. Wow."

"Indeed. It took us a year before we could go back. This time we were after proper scientific data. Again, it wasn't my job, and I never could prove it, but I later suspected Wyatt of somehow manipulating or faking those results. It always seemed like he knew exactly where to take the sample, or how much trouble he could make with the locals just short of getting us banned from the site. We never did manage to secure a digging permit to excavate properly, and I don't think Wyatt ever forgave them for that. Ultimately, he drilled core samples anyway and smuggled them home. Pitman's lab was the one that analyzed them. The truth was that Wyatt's reputation for miracles and faith notwithstanding, he was a hot-tempered and stubborn man who didn't like being called out or blockaded on his work. He and I nearly came to blows some dozen or so times. More than once I walked away from him entirely, just to keep from saying something I'd regret. Until the time I finally did, and never went back." It occurred to Evans that he still owed Wyatt a punch in the nose for dragging him into all this.

"I—I didn't know any of that." David's face was full of compassion now. Another of Karen's tricks. He was also petting the goat. Evans tried not to think about wild goat germs but failed.

"Some ark hunters accused Wyatt of simply having too vivid of an imagination. They claimed that he just dreamed up his largely-circumstantial evidence. As his partner, I caught a lot of that fallout too. But I stood up for him, for years, even when I wasn't sure about my personal beliefs anymore. He seemed to have enough faith for both of us."

"Yea, I kind of saw some of that on the web. Search strings starting with Mr. Aarons' name aren't very flattering." David thought for another second, then asked, "So was he lying? Is that why you left?"

"Well, I suppose that's the only reason I stayed by his side for so long and kept going back. He wasn't lying, and he wasn't making it up. I watched the samples get pulled from the site myself. I watched them photographed, labeled, and mailed to the lab. Some of them I personally smuggled out of the country in my luggage, if I'm honest. But it was when the results for the corings came back with extremely high levels of pure iron that I left."

At first, David's expression was unchanged, but then Evans saw it hit him like a brick wall. His jaw dropped as he figured it out. Hesitantly, he said what he knew to be true, each word unraveling the entire story like a loose thread on a cloth. "Because, iron. Duh. There wasn't any iron used in Noah's day. It was, I dunno, the Bronze Age or something."

"Technically, the Bronze Age didn't even start until about the 34th century B.C., but you've hit the iron nail on the head regardless. Point of fact, the earliest Iron Age did happen here in the Near East, but not until about 1200 B.C. Man did not start working iron until at least 4,000 years after the flood by anyone's timeline. Raw iron and other alloys can, however, occur quite naturally in volcanic areas, and the Ararat region is most certainly that. The anomaly itself visibly sits in an old lava bed. Wyatt's first explanation was that the mineral-rich lava flow must have been what preserved his Ark. Next he argued that Noah must have miraculously invented iron-smithing, thousands of years earlier than anyone else. The lab results laid out a very different scenario."

Evans paused to clear his throat. "You see David, the problem always is that when you are looking for miracles, you tend to find them. Even when they aren't there. An undisciplined imagination is a dangerous thing."

"Yea, I get it. So then, did Mr. Aarons fake it? Pretend to have visions or something? Planted evidence maybe?"

"No, I honestly don't think so. Wyatt Aarons is a hothead, a dreamer, and a religious nut, but he wasn't a crook or a charlatan—not when I knew him. I don't think the problem was the data, it was how he was interpreting it." Evans paused. He could feel the dusty cobwebs of old thoughts being swept away. Was he honestly still defending Wyatt after all these years? "You know David, I truly think he saw what he wanted to see so badly, that he started to believe his own propaganda. He later claimed to discover other biblical sites too. Sodom and Gomorrah, the foundation of the tower of Babel and whatnot, and I honestly don't recall what all else."

"Yea. That stuff is all over his website. He's got a YouTube channel even. But how did he manage all of it? I mean, he's just one guy."

Wyatt had a website? *Oh, dear lord.* "It was always the same. He prayed or had a vision or both. That's essentially why I left. I couldn't handle the crazy anymore. Not to mention spending a week in a Turkish prison cell because he decided to drill without permits. My career never really recovered from the fallout of being absent for the start of term that year." *Why did I say that?* David must be getting to him. Evans shrugged apologetically, adding, "but I make do."

"I think I get it. But I still don't understand one thing."

Evans tilted his chin, waiting for the question to come, seriously doubting that it would truly be the last one.

"If Mr. Aarons is so obsessed with biblical archeology, then why all this

Dilmun, 'Nûḥ and the tree' stuff? I mean, why not just follow the description of the Bible? He could have looked in Mesopotamia for Eden instead of poking around in old Syrian ruins for some other version a thousand miles away, like the Atra-Hasis. You know, like those old riverbeds Dr. Pitman showed us."

Evans fidgeted and cleared his throat. "Ah, yes. Well, I'm afraid that detail is probably all my fault. Wyatt was looking for Utnapishtim because he was looking for Noah. Once I started working with him, I convinced him that the other stories most likely referred to the same events, just with different details with different names. I finally convinced him that the Bible's version must have been transmitted first through an oral tradition. I laid out the theory that the story was passed on by Noah's three sons, Shem, Ham, and Japheth, to their own sons. This would explain the different versions of the story to the Hamites and Japhetites, including the Sumerian and Akkadian versions we call *Gilgamesh*, and finally to Moses through the line of Noah's son Shem." Evans leaned back on his stone slab and sighed. "It's old research. The name Atra-Hasis isn't just on one tablet found in Ugarit. It also appears on one of the Sumerian king lists as the name of a king of Shuruppak, a region in Mesopotamia. And from an era long before they claimed the flood happened. It means 'Important Man,' and might very well be a title. I wrote a paper all about it. Wyatt read it and hired me."

"Oh, that paper," David said, remembering Dr. Pitman's rather sarcastic mentioning of it on the plane. "Okay, so there really could be a connection to Utnapishtim. Why Shem specifically though?"

"Well, it would have to be Shem. As in Shem-ites. Semites, rather. The whole region was Semitic after all. That's why Yosef's Proto-Sinaitic connection is so staggering. If those pictographs have been translated, it could connect cultures in ways we never realized was possible, much like Ugaritic did for Hebrew and Akkadian cuneiform."

"Oh," David said. In the low light, he looked older somehow. "So, you convinced Mr. Aarons that the *Genesis* version was first because of the alphabetic connection. Because it looked Mesopotamian, but was phonetic. And even if that part of *Genesis* was told as stories and written down later, the Babylonian version would still have to have been the one that deviated from the original, if the Bible's version was first. That's why Mr. Aarons thinks you were right about with 'Nûḥ and the tree,' isn't it?"

Evans smiled weakly. "Yes. And he seems to think he can prove it." He sighed. "Wyatt and I fought like cats and dogs about so many of the details. For example, I wanted to try searching a different hill altogether at one point at a place called Mt. Cudi. It's the name of the Ark's landing site, as recorded in the *Quran*. But Aarons vetoed that one immediately and wouldn't budge.

He refused to believe that anything in a Muslim holy book could be right. Even though, ironically, it is closer to the Genesis version than any other ancient source, including the *Atra-Hasis*. The *Quran* is technically Semitic too, though the Islamic tradition stems from some rather significant differences, such as Ishmael rather than Isaac being the son of Abraham who was spared by God on the altar."

"I guess it's one thing to compare Babylonian or Canaanite sources, but another to tap Islam," David considered.

Evans grunted. "Well, to Wyatt's credit, the others are all far, far older. The *Quran* was written at the beginning of the fifth century. That's A.D.—a non-starter in his opinion. And in mine too, but for the interesting tidbits smattered about within the *Quran* that some scholars have identified as written versions of local—but very ancient—stories and folklore."

"*Tradents?*"

"Indeed. Nevertheless, *Gilgamesh* remains the oldest written record discovered to date, so that's why Wyatt is willing to chase after Dilmun and always has been. The moment he realized it could be a slightly distorted written account of an even older oral tradition about a real, historical Nûḥ, nothing else mattered."

"Like *The Chaldean Account of Genesis*," David breathed. "Oh, man."

There it was—the truth. Evans nodded, regret hanging heavy on his face. "George Smith's misleading title when he first published *Gilgamesh* in English, yes. And thirty years ago, I hung my hat on the idea behind that title. Back then, Wyatt's certainty was so contagious that I started to believe my nutty hypotheses too. It's no great wonder that all these years later, Wyatt is still searching for Eden by looking for references to Dilmun, here in ancient Ugarit."

"Well, at least you guys didn't go off chasing after Islamic scripture."

"Oh, don't be so quick to judge, David. All faiths have some bit of truth in them, it's just easier to spot it in some than others. As they say, even a broken clock is right twice a day. For example, the Islamic name of God is etymologically derived from the same tradition as the Hebrew one."

"It is? Do you mean... *Allah?*" David whispered the Arabic name for God like a swear he wasn't allowed to say.

"Yes. 'El' is the Hebrew prefix that means God. 'Al,' 'El,' and 'Il' all mean the same thing in different Semitic languages. It's your silent consonant again, merely carrying a different vowel. Yosef's right about that much, unquestionably."

"'El'? Like *Elohim*? Oh man."

"Yes. And *Dani'el, Jo'el,* or *Isra'el,* just to name a few. It's in the word

Aleph, for Pete's sake. It's the first letter in all Semitic scripts. Even the ancient custom of *Ba'al* worship is connected. Etymologically, that is. Thus, the blasphemy and whatnot. *Ba'al Zebub* comes to mind."

Evans watched David make the connections in his head before he replied. "So, the silent consonant that was originally an ox pictograph. The one that means power and strength and in its pure form, God." The teen opened his mouth to say more, but nothing came forth for a long moment. Evans braced himself for anything. "No wonder the ancient Israelites had a problem with worshipping golden calves," he finally said. For some reason this was funny, and the Evanses shared a chuckle. Then, the real question came. "So, just how are we supposed to separate the myths from the history, Arthur? Is it even possible?"

Pastor Joseph Evans' son was green, idealistic, and entirely too full of imagination, but he was no fool. The pieces were all coming together for David finally, whether he realized it or not. And now, the foundation was laid for the strange paths that always seemed to stretch out before a Wyatt Aarons™ brand Bible quest.

"David. It takes much focus and arduous work to spot the myths and discern truth from fiction, in any pursuit, be it gods, gardens, or translating ancient pictographs. Most especially, to discern and accept the truths we don't want to find, and discard the fictions we most fervently desire to believe. Wyatt could never do that. Alas, Sir Arthur never did either. We must do them one better."

Evans didn't have all the answers. But one thing he did know for certain was that it always took time to work those answers out logically. And to keep fantasies and dreams from getting in the way. He leaned in a bit. "We might be in the wrong place for Eden, but we are definitely in the right place to pick up Wyatt's trail."

A sublime quiet fell over the ruins. Even the distant clatters and shouts of the camp abated. Finally, David spoke. "Hey, Arthur, if Mr. Aarons found a translation tablet relating to Uncle Sir Arthur's work in Crete, then why did that guy with the gun come after us? The same guys were after Mr. Aarons on the video too, right? I mean, why go to all this trouble for a journal that might unlock a dead language from Crete? What do a bunch of revolutionaries care about that? Mesopotamia is the other direction, isn't it?"

There it is. The same question that had been troubling Evans ever since he realized their Oxford attacker had the same raven tattoo as the men who'd attacked and robbed them in Turkey, thirty years ago. The same worn by the policemen who detained them in holding cells for over a week afterward. He'd give a hundred-to-one on Aarons' gunmen here in Ugarit having the same ink, though their raven-emblazoned armbands seemed evidence enough of a connection.

Footfalls alerted the Evanses that the others were finally coming. David's little goat friend leaped away in the general direction of the little herd's bleating.

"Cheers, gentlemen!" Matthew boomed. "Ryan and Yosef have opted to stay behind for the first expedition, but we are to carry on with their blessings. Literally, in the latter case."

Evans felt his shoulders relax a bit. *No Pitman?* That was some small relief, at least. And he had three guards as requested. *Splendid.*

"I don't know what the men with the raven tattoos are after," Evans answered, "but I don't think they are just a bunch of Kurdish freedom fighters. I need more data. What do you say we find out together?"

David grinned so wide, Evans could have counted his teeth. "Deal!"

LVI

Ras-Shamra Ruins. Ugarit, Syria. David.

From the moment David scrabbled down into the exposed passages of Ras-Shamra, the same thought kept popping into his head. He had been in this situation at least a hundred times before. Around his dining room table, that is. He just couldn't seem to wipe the massive smile from his face. No kobolds or rat-men here, but it was still an amazing feeling to be in a real ancient maze, on a quest, and facing unknown challenges. David felt more alive than he ever could have imagined.

The place where Mr. Aarons had been accessing the unexcavated tunnels was well hidden. David was already standing in front of it before he spotted the rough wooden hatch latched to a spike with a flimsy padlock. This was stuck on the side of a huge hillside, and David realized that the hill itself must be covering part of the massive complex of unexcavated ruins here. Whole sections of some palace temple had been buried here ages ago, and no true doorways were yet exposed to it.

Colonel Ivan extracted a key and swiftly removed the lock, throwing the hatch wide. The rabbit hole behind it revealed a large crack in a stone wall. This was undoubtedly where Mr. Aarons had broken through, but David couldn't shake the feeling that just about anything could be down there.

Single file they squeezed in. Beyond the irregular crack was a rickety stool meant to be used as a step, but everything was pitch black a few feet beyond that. The team's footfalls echoed in the dark, an odd combination of crunching sand and boots on stone. Two of the guards had large black guns mounted with powerful flashlights which they quickly switched on. The tight beams cut the darkness like bayonets through an old curtain. The whole thing made David feel more like a burglar than an amateur archeologist, and only a little guilty that he was enjoying it.

Cat dug in her pack and pulled out two more flashlights. "Here, Dr. Evans, take my spare torch," she said with a mysterious little smile.

Thanking her, Arthur fumbled with it in the dark, momentarily blinding himself as his thumb found the switch. David kicked himself for not grabbing one from the supplies too. *This would be a terrible time to get eaten by a grue!* He whipped out his phone, thumbed on the flashlight app, and began using it as a humble light source of his own.

It was refreshingly cool in the tunnels. David had been sweating nonstop since arriving in this scorched country. Even the sunless night was hot. The whole area was going to be an unbearable oven when dawn came again. But for now, it was classic, almost stereotypical dungeon crawl time. *Or should that be archetypal?*

"No evidence of anyone breaking in?" Cat asked the guards.

"No," Ivan stated. "No one is come here since attack."

Attack? For a moment his brain flashed to grues again, but then it struck David that somewhere in this cluster of tunnels were the bloodstained floors where Mr. Aarons' guards had been taken down. It was not a reassuring thought. A chill ran down his spine. *Yep, surprisingly cool in here.* He was glad he'd had the foresight to bring his hoodie.

Arthur and Cat disagreed only slightly before deciding which direction to go. She turned out to be right, and before very long the little procession came to an archway with an unlit lantern and a can of kerosene nearby. *"Aarons' much-preferred light source to flashlights,"* Arthur had explained. In the man's final panicked rush from the room, Mr. Aarons would have blown past this lantern. No time to light it and walk the path they had just come by. It hadn't occurred to David until now that the archeologist had fled into total darkness. It was pretty impressive.

Something glinted nearby. "Hey Arthur, over here."

Arthur cast his beam towards David's voice revealing a small alcove with a silent generator. Numerous power cords snaked off into the darkness where a short hallway gave access to a series of small doors lightly decorated in the quintessential Canaanite style or something.

"The libraries of Ugarit," Cat breathed, charging off into the darkness. "I will not go far."

With a quick prompting, David gave the starter a few tugs, but it wouldn't turn over. Undaunted, he tucked away his phone and grabbed a nearby can of fuel. A minute later the generator roared to life and a light glowed from one of the arches. It was the last doorway before the hallway ended in collapsed rubble.

"I suppose that's our room. Nice work, David." Arthur clicked his flashlight off and started towards the new light.

Cat popped back out of a different door. "Most of these rooms are inaccessible. They will have to be excavated. It is the work of a lifetime!" There was excitement in her voice like David had not heard before. It was contagious.

*   *   *

The moment had come to put their plan into action. The room was larger than it had looked on the screen. Two of the guards stayed behind on Arthur's word, but everybody else came into the light. The story here was self-evident. Even if he hadn't seen the video footage, David would have guessed that the site had been hastily evacuated and then ransacked.

"Don't touch anything, David," Arthur said, a little too loudly. "If there are tablets here, they are some of the oldest written records on Earth. We wouldn't want your first trip to be tainted with any unfortunate accidents."

David smiled. It was a clever lie, even if Arthur needed a few acting lessons. They both knew what he had to do, but it meant everyone needed to forget about David for a minute. In one sentence Arthur had done just that.

"You got it, Arthur," he said to his wizard, suppressing a smile.

The single lampstand was about David's height and only lit half the room. Even with that, it made for a stark contrast of light and shadows everywhere. There was a tight row of columns down each side of the room, and beyond those, only streaks of light in the darkness. Father Matthew walked straight to a column and caressed it. He was soaking in the marvels of this place too.

The remains of ancient shelves and broken pots could be seen everywhere, the only things left of a once well-organized set of records. Much of the room was empty now but in one dark corner, a haphazard pile of tablets and little sculptures still awaited careful exploration. David was suddenly reminded of the storage room at the Ashmolean. To his surprise, the ancient Phoenicians didn't seem quite so strange and foreign anymore.

Next to the lamp was a completely modern mess. Papers, small equipment, and a black leather-bound Bible were scattered about on the floor. Nearby was an upside-down folding table and rickety chair where Mr. Aarons had obviously worked. Arthur headed to the overturned table and flipped it.

Cat headed for the middle of the room and began examining three ultra-modern cabinets. They were some sort of stackable crates, interlocking, and they even had wheels. The setup reminded David of his dad's tool cabinet in the garage back home. Joe was a tool junkie and had about three cabinets and various footlockers full of them in their massive garage.

But Cat had recognized the crates for what they were, they held trays for carefully packing-out artifacts from places like this. He watched her extract a foam-lined drawer and cover her mouth in a silent gasp. Full of tablets or little sculptures no doubt. An anthropologist's dream. Not that she could read them like Arthur. *Could she?*

David suddenly felt a knot in his stomach. Something about this whole scenario didn't feel right. It wasn't just the organized looting of the ancient world financed by the company, though that was certainly part of it. Something else about the room was wrong. He looked again towards the place where Arthur was starting to poke around in the scattered paperwork. His wizard scooped up Mr. Aarons' papers and started sorting them into little piles. The table wasn't in the video. This made sense, the laptop had been sitting on it.

Obviously though, someone had come and taken the portable computer with its little onboard camera, albeit not for many hours after. Miss Chen's notes had mentioned this fact, but the significance of this detail hadn't clicked until David stood there looking at it. Nobody had come back down here, or so Colonel Ivan said. But the laptop had definitely been removed and the table overturned. If nothing else, the video it had recorded made it to the company somehow, so whoever had swiped it had also ransacked the room. Either that, or somebody was lying, or else very misinformed.

Had the second intruders been looking for the bag? Had they found it? Who were they? *Could someone still be in here?* The last thought gave him a dark shiver. There were missing pieces and David didn't know what they were. He needed to find Mr. Aarons' satchel.

David glanced at the inky darkness beyond the pillars. It was the direction Mr. Aarons had gone in his last moments in the room, and where David needed to go. That corner of the room had collapsed at some point in the palace's history. One of the columns there was crumbled and the ceiling slanted off into the darkness. It made sense how Mr. Aarons could have hidden a bag back there, and why he'd chosen to try. But it also might make finding it all the harder. Given that someone had come looking for it, that might be a good thing.

That bag was in there somewhere. His gut told him so.

Everyone else was focused on their own thing. Even Colonel Ivan was scrutinizing the stonework of the arched ceiling. This was David's moment. Back on the plane, Arthur had decided that discretion was the right strategy moving forward, at least until they knew for sure what was in Mr. Aarons' ditched satchel. Arthur was probably just being paranoid, but David had that feeling his wizard was up to something again.

David quickly stepped over the shadow line and beyond the colonnade. He reminded himself that there was no such thing as grues. It didn't help. If this had been all a game, and Arthur his wizard, David suddenly knew which class he was playing. It made him smile. *Rogue stealth-check successful! Now, to check for traps and steal a hidden bag of loot.*

No big deal. Seated with his gaming friends around his parents' kitchen table, he'd done it a hundred times before.

LVII

Aleppo, Syria. Mr. Suit.

In front of a bustling café nestled into the Al-Zarab Souk, a little motorcycle waited for the man in the suit. It was a Honda that at some point in its life would have been described as red. Duct tape, rust, and several spot-welds held it together now. A tatty helmet hung from the handlebar. The man thought of his shiny new Multistrada, abandoned now in some police lock-up in Oxfordshire, and mumbled a curse. He was not in the Western world anymore.

This was Aleppo, one of the great old cities of the world. Crossroads of major trade routes for at least four thousand years, ruled over by six major empires. The man took a deep breath of the hot-sweet night air and sighed it out slowly. He could just smell the spices and dyes from the nearby stalls brought in from India. Shopkeepers were lowering the wooden shutters for the day, but by sunup, silks from Iran, carpets from Turkey, and other precious goods would hang on every vertical surface again. The entire walking street would be a giant kaleidoscope for the senses, swarming with shoppers, tourists, beggars, and pickpockets.

A few streets over, a call for the *'Isha Adhan* began out of one of the tall minarets, the fifth and final prayer before retiring. The faithful bustled and hurried to their duty. *Some things never change.* An old memory tugged at the back of his mind.

It occurred to him how very close he was to his birthplace. The mountains to the north were the border, and beyond it a road that could easily take him there. The thought surprised him. He had no desire to go home. *Do I?* Was "home" even the right word?

The man in the suit shrugged his shoulders, but the old twitch did not calm him now. His holster was empty. He felt weakened. With a sneer, he walked into the café to find a place to urinate. The men's toilet was nothing more than a water pipe running along a back wall with a drain in the floor, but it was functional. He would have greatly enjoyed spending tomorrow in the Hammam al-Nahasin men's bathhouse, working out his stresses. It had been a major tourist draw in the old city since the thirteenth century, but he didn't have the luxury of a wasted day. His phone might ring, and he couldn't be caught with his trousers down when it happened.

As his bladder emptied, he considered how tomorrow would go. On his little bike, it would be slightly more than a three-hour ride down to the dig site, plenty of time to enjoy the countryside. Tomorrow night, he would sneak into the research team's camp, commit whatever act of mayhem, theft, or fear needed to be accomplished, and then make his escape. Dr. Evans wouldn't know what hit him. It would then be a simple matter of clamping down on the academics, in whatever way necessary to end it. His mentor would know. Others could provide the required resources. A phone call. Maybe two? The family had sleepers like himself all over the world. *We are everywhere,* he reminded himself. *We are watching.*

Soon the world could be his playground again, once this whole business with Wyatt Aarons and his ex-partner was worked out. Syrian women were like caged tigers. That could be fun. Or perhaps the United States? New York City had always beckoned to him. How wonderful it would be to set foot on American soil. Someday, perhaps. Today he was working.

Remember who you are.

The man in the suit returned to the bike. The stained and yellowed helmet the anonymous brother had left for him smelled like a wet goat. He was about to ditch it in favor of feeling the wind on his face when he felt his lapel buzz. He extracted his phone with a thrill and mashed the answer button. He cringed slightly at the lingering pain from Dr. Evans' shoe.

"Speak."

"Change of plans, boy. I need you in Ras-Shamra by sunrise."

A minute later, the man in the suit slid his phone back into his jacket and slapped the nasty-smelling helmet down onto his head. It was a good thing that the speed limits in this country were more like suggestions, seeing as he would be ignoring them.

Things were getting very interesting again.

LVIII

Ras-Shamra Ruins. Ugarit, Syria. David.

Aside from the muffled footfalls of David's companions, and the low hum of the generator down the hall, the ancient library was eerily silent. Arthur broke the spell, providing cover for David's movements.

"It was in a room like this that the Atra-Hasis tablet was discovered in the 1920s," he began. "After a farmer accidentally plowed into an ancient tomb, a group of French archaeologists came. They brought seven camels, one donkey, and some burden bearers to the hill known by the locals as Ras-Shamra. After a week at the site, they discovered a whole cemetery. In those graves, they found Egyptian and Phoenician art and artifacts side by side. They soon found some Mycenean and Cypriot materials too. The team quickly surmised that the whole ancient world came here to buy and sell."

David moved like a thief through the shadows, careful not to trip over a loose stone or a crumbled chunk of ceiling. He found the wall almost immediately with his hand, the cold stone surprising him even though he was looking for it. Using it as a guide, he moved quickly towards the collapsed back corner where Mr. Aarons had gone in with a bag that never came out. If the bag was just lying there in the dark, then maybe it was nothing. Or maybe it was just full of Mr. Aarons' dirty socks.

But David didn't believe that for a second. His gut told him that they were on the verge of something big. *"I had proof,"* The journal had said. Not "have," but "had." And if Mr. Aarons' bag was stuffed back in the dark here somewhere, he probably thought it was the key to finding Eden.

"Soon thereafter," Arthur continued, "one of the greatest archeological finds in history was discovered. Pancaked floor to ceiling was the footprint of the old temple. But amazingly well-preserved in its library were what we now call the Ugaritic texts. They included a variety of scripts, Summero-Akkadian syllabic cuneiform, the native alphabetic cuneiform, Hurrian writing, Egyptian hieroglyphs, Hittite hieroglyphs, and even some Minoan syllabary. It's a staggering variety of languages. These rooms must be an annex, you see. Not a part of the main library. Records, perhaps. Treaties and whatnot, as opposed to histories and literature." David smiled. Arthur had scoured every page of Mr. Aarons' journal. He knew full well what was found in this strangely preserved room.

Cat made a throaty growl. Maybe she resented someone else giving the archeology lesson, or maybe Arthur had missed something she thought important, but she was way too focused on the items in the crates to do anything about it. It occurred to David that there was a better than fair chance the translation tablet pieces were somewhere among the cataloged and stored artifacts. Cat could be holding one right now. But Arthur would have to see to the crates—David's job was in the shadows. He took another silent step, his hand still tracking the rough wall. Suddenly, the angle leaned away, and David's foot slid up against a massive pile of rubble. He'd found the collapsed part of the room.

David felt around but could find no bag. It was all stones and rubble that had poured in from a crack in the ceiling and wall, untold centuries ago. *What would Mr. Aarons have done?* David imagined himself being hunted, scared, and with only moments to choose. There wasn't much to climb on, but maybe there was just enough? Mr. Aarons was tall and skinny, so David would have to compensate. He searched for a foothold and found one, then another. He smiled and pulled himself onto the pile of debris with a quiet grunt. The broken wall jutted out like a little platform here, inviting him forward. *This has to be right!*

As David wiggled himself up onto the slab, Arthur continued his impromptu lecture. Though David could no longer see the others, his wizard's voice was an anchor beyond the dark.

"It is worth noting that in antiquity, when parts of the city fell due to earthquake or disuse, they simply built over it. Quite a common practice at that time. Helpful for archeology, but as you see, not always practical."

David cringed. Arthur probably hadn't meant to draw attention to the collapsed end of the room where David was delving, but perhaps his grandfather's mind had wandered to the dark aisles regardless. David froze, not daring to move a single trembling muscle for fear of dislodging even a pebble.

"I say, what did finally happen to this place, Arthur?" Father Matthew sounded very far away. David wasn't sure whether the priest meant the city or the room, in ancient times or recently. If the latter on both counts, the answer was simple. Mr. Aarons happened to this room. Crammed into a crack in the wall under a ton of loose stone and dirt while looking for a bag that might not be there at all, that answer seemed kind of obvious.

Arthur must have assumed the former on both counts though, because without any pause at all he replied. "I suppose the short answer is that they disappeared in about 1200 B.C. Wiped out, along with other civilizations all up and down the coast, by a nation known only as the Sea Peoples. For what it's worth, that corresponds roughly with the entry of Israel into Canaan, but as they say, history is written by the victors. And nobody else claimed that one."

"The Sea Peoples?" Cat chided. "You are not being serious. That part of the roof likely fell in at the same time as the passage that separated this part of the palace from the rest. An earthquake is much more likely to explain what happened here than an ancient battle between petty kings. Give me time and I will find out."

The banter shifted. Matthew chuckled, but in here his laughter rumbled like the Kool-Aid man. It masked a little shower of debris as David resumed his climb.

"There were five cities here across five millennia," Cat continued, taking over the lecture. "The earliest hearths were found with flint and bone tools. This means it was a pre-pottery culture, only later joined by farmers who used both stone and pottery vessels. The second and third city levels contained finely painted pots, the last was devastated by fire. But it was the rebuilt fourth city that expanded into the rich commercial center you speak of. This included economic exchanges with the 12th Egyptian dynasty. The final iteration of this place happened around 1600 B.C.E. It is what contained fortifications, temples, and your palace, including this room."

"And tell me, is there evidence that the Israelites did them in, do you think?" Matthew asked.

Cat did not hesitate. "Nonsense. There has been absolutely no archeological evidence for a biblical Exodus, much less some large-scale conquest of the area by twelve tribes of nomads. Phoenicia was one of the great empires of the world, no lowly city-state. The biblical Moses is obviously a hero legend, written much later by a culture that didn't understand the realities of the region half a millennium before. It is a national origin fable about an angry god's deliverance of the persecuted, written by a people resentful of their much later exile in Babylon. Probably, in an attempt to incite revolution."

Even in the dark, David winced and closed his eyes. What was she talking about? Moses wrote the early books. Even if he didn't do it literally with that *tradent* thing, he at least was responsible for delivering the Ten Commandments, the law, and the rest of the early history of the Israelite people. He even took a census in the boring books David had never bothered to read. Cat couldn't possibly think a priest didn't know that. Then again, maybe she didn't know that.

"Well, we are standing in the land of Canaan," Father Mathew mused. "And while the Old Testament tells us that God changed his original judgment upon the sinful generation of the Exodus at Moses' behest, I do wonder how many times he delayed his justice for Ugarit before their end came? Perhaps the finger of God pushed this particular city down, if you catch my meaning. Judgment eventually comes to us all, Dr. deMata. Even if it is not always the light-and-sound-show of Jericho."

"The Bible is a collection of cultural myths. It is not history, it is fables and poetry," Cat said with finality.

"St. Augustine wrote on those same ideas sixteen centuries ago," Matthew added helpfully. "It was a work of multiple volumes and many subjects, but as one example, he entitled a chapter 'Of Paradise, that it Can Be Understood in a Spiritual Sense Without Sacrificing the Historic Truth of the Narrative Regarding The Real Place.' Quite the, er, page-turner."

Matthew passed between the lamp and David's side of the room, his shadow jumping the spaces between one column and the next. David blinked and resumed inching up the rubble pile. To his surprise, he was already at the top.

"St. Augustine points out," Matthew continued, "that as with any book, whether it's history, fiction, neither, or both, we must be ever careful not to worship the words themselves, for to do so is to fall into the trap of fanatic Biblicism. We are instead encouraged to worship the author of life, trust his salvation, and learn from the events which the divinely-inspired Holy Books describe. That is the unifying belief of the believer, after all. To us, scripture is not merely a history-altering tome, but a collected understanding of lynchpin events in history about which much has been written." The echo of Matthew's soothing voice faded. "I paraphrase, of course," he finished.

Cat made a noise like a deflating balloon, so Arthur jumped in. "Er, yes. Right then. You are probably both right. Most credible biblical scholars now agree that much of the early Bible was written down later. But a deep reading of the Books of Moses also leads us to the inevitable conclusion that Israel believed Yahweh gave and took away. Humans aren't the ones in charge of what chaos and cataclysms come. He is, and we must never forget it."

When mankind gets too enlightened, an apocalypse happens. David was starting to appreciate that idea. The roof was lower at this end of the room and sloped away, but between the rubble pile and the ceiling, he could feel a narrow gap. With only one option left, he plunged his arm into the opening.

"We are in charge of our own blasted selves, which is hard enough," Arthur continued. "Come to think of it, that's the unifying theme of the library we call the Bible. And never forget, Dr. deMata, those fables, letters, histories, and poems were literature first. Long before they were ever canonized as scripture. You must not dismiss them out of hand."

David wasn't sure how Cat and Matthew could both be right though. If it was all fantasy and fables, what was the point? Then again, Matthew had said that even real people could be legendary. David didn't have time to ponder the idea of a legendary-real Moses right now. Maybe Arthur was just saying things to buy him time. He was about to abandon the whole dark climb and rethink his strategy when his fingertips caught on to something long and flexible.

A strap! The bag! David had it. As carefully as he could, he pulled the leather satchel out of the gap. It was surprisingly heavy, but also kind of soft. He lowered himself a few inches and found another foothold. He was coming down at a different angle, but there was nothing he could do about it. A handful of tiny debris clattered down the pile, but the others didn't seem to notice.

"Either way, I'm doubtful we will find the answer to that question here," Arthur said. "Looking at these pages of loose notes, it seems like Wyatt was trying to translate some things. But it does mean I'm right about one thing. This room was a library of records. A very unusual one at that. I've never seen so many ancient languages in one place."

David twisted away from the pile, clutching the satchel with one hand. He tried to lower it down to the ground by the strap, but it was a few feet short. He shifted to one foot to recenter himself, leaving the bag to dangle below him against the rubble, but he felt something give way under the makeshift foothold. Everything shifted and he was going down with it, like it or not. With only one free hand, David had to choose between himself or the bag to take the fall. Instinct took over—he released the bag, his hand flashing out for a new handhold but finding only loose rubble.

David slid down the pile in a massive cloud of dust and dirt, small rocks and debris pelting him. A large stone bounced way too close to his leg and clattered across the floor. His tailbone complained, and there would probably be a scrape and bruise or two, but nothing bad. More important though, the bag had only slid a few feet before flopping over on its back, dusty but no worse for wear.

With his agility check failed and his cover blown, David coughed and extracted himself from the shadowy rubble. He resisted the urge to kick Mr. Aarons' leather satchel and picked it up instead. He stepped squinting into the lamplight with a big cheesy thumbs-up. As his vision readjusted, he smiled at Arthur and froze. What he saw made no sense.

Everyone was staring, but not at David. Colonel Ivan had everyone's full attention. All three of the armor-clad Mao Sien paramilitary team were in the room now. The large men blocked much of the light and cast long shadows onto the entrance wall, making the room feel absolutely tiny. But it was Arthur who was clearly the most surprised. The colonel had him in a headlock and was holding his little black pistol against Arthur's temple.

"Careful, boy." Ivan growled. "Give over bag. Move slow."

LIX

Ras-Shamra Ruins. Ugarit, Syria. Arthur.

There was a great clatter of rubble and an audible "Oof!" from the darkness. Before he could move, the other two Mao Sien guards burst into the room. Evans opened his mouth to calm them, to call out and make sure David was alright, he wasn't sure, but was surprised to find he could do neither as his vision had blurred and his breath caught. He instinctively brought his hands to his neck, only to discover a meaty arm constricted around it. Something cold and metallic was poking into his temple.

A moment later, David emerged from between two columns covered in ancient dust and sand, his hair even wilder than usual, but otherwise apparently unhurt. Wyatt's overstuffed leather satchel was thrown over the teen's shoulder, and he was beaming as though he had just been named stroke of a four-man boat team after beating Cambridge at the Great Britain World Championship Squad. *So much for subtlety then.*

"Careful, boy. Give over bag. Move slowly." So, Ivan was the owner of the meaty arm. That made sense.

Wait, no it doesn't! None of this makes sense!

One of the other soldiers stepped forward, his large semi-automatic weapon pointing menacingly in David's general direction. The third soldier extended his other hand for the leather satchel, making a hand-it-over motion, but David stood paralyzed. Only his eyes moved, darting about like a wild animal's, searching the room for some explanation of his own.

Evans tried to speak but still couldn't. He slapped the meaty arm and it relaxed slightly, allowing him a much-needed breath. His flattened hat plopped to the ground as he felt the blood rush back to his brain. He was not embarrassed to gasp aloud. The stale dusty air now tasted deliciously sweet.

"Give it to him," Evans coughed.

And good lord, don't you dare get shot. Karen would skin me!

But David stayed frozen. Evans hardly noticed Ivan's other hand put the weapon away and pluck Wyatt's journal from his coat pocket.

"The bag," Evans wheezed desperately. "Give him what he wants."

Less than a day in Syria, and they were being robbed just like Doomsday all those years ago, this time by their own guards. Everything had gone south, but he had no idea at what point. Was Wyatt behind this? Guns weren't his style, but then it had been decades, and people changed. But why take the journal? That had to be the key, but why would the company's hired guns suddenly do this? Were they under higher orders? Had this been a complicated setup by Mel Chen from the start? Had Evans played his hand too close to the chest by not sharing everything in Aarons' journal?

He needed to focus. They didn't have time for him to sort it all out. Evans had vowed not to make Wyatt's errors, but he'd evidently made all different ones instead. *Blast it all.* He flicked his gaze to Ivan's meaty red arm. No raven tattoo. *That's something, at least.* His mind continued to race as David slowly handed over the bag to their former guard. No, none of this made any kind of logical sense, and there were far easier ways to steal a bag. Somebody was making this up as they went along, and that meant he would have to do the same.

Matthew and deMata were being held in check by the third guard. Matthew had plopped onto the work stool, and deMata stood frozen by the artifact crates. The priest did not look amused, but he also didn't look scared. Matthew was no small man, and no stranger to competitive boxing in his college days. But Matthew also knew better than to bring a fist to a gunfight. He furrowed his brow at Evans in an unhelpful expression that could have meant anything from *"Do you have a plan?"* to *"This is a fine mess you've gotten us into."*

"You don't have to do this," Evans said to the hot breath on the back of his head. "We'll cooperate. Perhaps if you explain—"

The arm flexed around his neck again. Though not as tight this time, Evans still lost the ability to finish the thought.

"Belt up," the huge Russian snarled in his ear.

"Is it there?" Ivan asked the man now digging around in Wyatt's laundry. Everyone watched as a pair of dubiously stained briefs and a crumpled button-up shirt fell to the floor.

"This must be it, colonel," the man replied. In the high-contrast shadows, all Evans could make out was the silhouette of a dinner plate lifted a few inches into the air. *What the blazes is that?* Clay tablets weren't circular, they were rectangular.

"*Davai,*" Ivan spat smugly. "Take these to Pitman now. We gather other artifacts and meet you back at camp." He tossed the man the journal. The man playing soldier extracted a wadded undershirt from Wyatt's bag and wrapped the dinner plate in it.

Evans felt sick. His ears were hot and his breathing ragged, but it wasn't from the arm around his neck. They'd been led like a dog on a leash and done all the real work like hired hands. He'd been watched and baited the whole time, and he'd been too stupid to see it. Did Mel not trust him? To be fair, they were technically sneaking around and had in fact hidden things from her, but for good reason, right? Heart pounding in his ears, Evans couldn't even hear himself think.

The soldier dropped the limp satchel with a *whump* and left. Ivan half-shoved and half-tossed Evans towards the table where Matthew mercifully caught him. The colonel grunted, pointing with his wide chin towards the cargo containers. "Take all of those ones in crates also, just for to be sure. You four, pack it up. I want everyone seeing the stars after ten minutes. We are leaving after three."

Pack it up? Evans had no clue why Pitman would want to do that, but in learning it, an idea formed. This man was the muscle. He'd been told to come down here and look for a tablet, but he didn't know which one. David's actions had tipped him off to the satchel. Then, seeing that Wyatt had already done the grunt work by collecting numerous other artifacts, the meathead must have decided to take every tablet Wyatt had touched at some point just in case. Ivan had no idea what Pitman was after! These men were idiots. Strong, choking, well-armed idiots.

And that was their edge. There was a chance that the all-important fragment they were after was still in the bag.

"Yes, of course, Colonel," Evans said as sincerely as he could manage, dusting himself and smoothing his coat to no discernible effect. "It will take us a few minutes to secure these drawers. deMata, if you would assist me here?"

Evans' mind began working overtime. Dozens of scenarios played out in his head and were methodically eliminated when they ended in bullets, flailing about in the dark, or both. He glanced around for the two flashlights. His sat unlit on the table. deMata's was perched on a stone slab, also off. *Both in the opposite direction from the door, blast it all.* It came down to one thing. Evans needed to convince these men that he was still the one in charge here. However, this was considerably challenging since Evans didn't know why he wasn't. This mercenary gorilla was obviously under orders.

How does one negotiate with a gorilla, precisely? Have the most bananas?

A short minute later the bolts and latches on the crates were secure. Matthew began wheeling the first one across the room, the lithe deMata close behind with the second. She was quite a bit stronger than she looked.

"David, would you mind grabbing this third one?" Evans asked over his shoulder as he threw the last latch.

But an instant after he said it, he knew he'd made an error. Ivan and the other guard turned, seeing what Evans had caught at the edge of his vision. Only a pair of dirty underwear and a crumpled shirt gave any evidence that the bag had been there moments ago.

"Find him!" Ivan barked to the other man.

But before either of them could take a step, a mechanical hum that Evans had long since adjusted to and stopped hearing abruptly died. A moment later, the room faded to pitch black.

LX

Ras-Shamra Ruins. Ugarit, Syria. David.

David desperately hoped that he was doing the right thing. Crouching a few paces from the now-silent generator, he heard someone rush past him in the darkness. His best guess was that it was one of the mercenaries, but he couldn't be sure. It could have been anybody but Cat blowing by.

A second later, the figure flipped on his light with a click, and the LED beam burst into the hallway from the end of his submachine gun. That meant the soldier named Dolan. Captain Rogers had left a while ago with an artifact, so only Colonel Ivan, Cat, Matthew, and Arthur were still in there. At four to one, David decided to risk it. He whipped around the corner and down the hall on memory and touch alone, then stuck out a hand and found the edge of the right doorway. His other hand flashed into his pocket and extracted his phone, which he turned on automatically.

Thin pale light cast into the room from the screen, but it was enough. He could make out the glowing forms of four people and the three shoulder-high crate stacks. Unfortunately, it also lit David up like a target, and the closest glowing form had a distinct Colonel Ivan shape to it.

"Do not move, boy," the shadow said, whipping his sidearm toward David. Ivan was not playing around, but it was as far as he got.

From behind one of the rolling storage crate stacks, a sixth of a ton of growling Englishman collided with him like a freight train. They both went down. A sickening smack of fist on face, and the gun clattered away, stopping a few feet from David. Suddenly they were on St. Giles again, in front of the yellow façade of the Eagle and Child Pub. That guy in the suit dropping to the ground clutching his crotch, his gun skittering away.

In a flash, David grabbed Ivan's pistol and pointed it at its prone owner. He willed his hands to stop shaking, but they didn't obey. It was his first time pointing a gun at anything that wasn't made of paper at the end of a range. Mr. Aarons' bag was askew, the strap digging into his neck, but he dared not adjust it.

"David," a faraway voice said. "David, please give me the gun now." David looked at Arthur without comprehension. *Where had he come from?* He blinked. Colonel Ivan lay still, knocked unconscious by a nearby Matthew. Cat stood frozen by the door, and Arthur was holding his hand out.

"Someone is coming!" Cat said in a stage whisper.

David handed the gun to Arthur and ducked behind a column. To his horror, he realized his phone was still shoved unlocked and lit into his hoodie pocket. He fumbled for it and thumbed it dark. A moment later, Dolan was back, his beam of light beating him into the room by a few seconds.

"Sir, I didn't see any—" The sharp-eyed Irishman stopped short at the sight of his commander sprawled on the floor. He held his beam there for a moment too long, then began swinging it wildly around the ink-black room.

"There are four of us and one of you, young man," David heard Father Matthew say from somewhere in the dark. "I recommend that you think this through."

There was an eerie silence, broken only by the crunch of Dolan's boots. David watched the beam of light retreat to a safer position.

"Your commander will be fine," Matthew continued. "It's not the first time I've knocked a fellow out." A pause. "Admittedly, it has been a few years, and usually in the ring.”

The shadows shifted again as Dolan slowly scanned the room but found no one.

“This must be a simple misunderstanding of some sort.” Arthur now. He was nearby.

Dolan whirled towards David’s side of the room. Why hadn’t the soldier replied?

Arthur spoke again, closer this time. “Perhaps we can put our weapons down and discuss this?”

“Our weapons?” Arthur was either being very clever or very stupid. Would his grandfather kill a man? David had no idea. He felt like he was about to burst apart.

“Let’s all go upstairs and sort this out with administration, what do you say?” Matthew soothed, now from the back of the room. They were moving around.

Suddenly, David felt hands on his shoulders and a beard at his cheek. He could smell Arthur’s sweat and feel his fear. “Go now,” his grandfather whispered. “Follow deMata. Find a side alcove and wait.”

David instantly understood the plan. They were sneaking out one at a time, Cat was already out. He was next, then one of the others would follow. If they shot the guy, David supposed he would know it. A pistol made a very different sound than the semi-automatic the other man carried. Even when echoed down a buried hallway.

David nodded, realized how silly that was, and started to reply, but swallowed it instead. Arthur squeezed his shoulder once and moved away. David stood stupidly for a moment and then went. He was not as silent as he’d hoped, but either Dolan didn’t notice or didn’t care because he didn’t follow.

Once out of the door, David broke into a run.

*   *   *

David bolted down the hallway by the necessary light of his phone. He heard a *“Psst!”* from a side passage he hadn’t even realized was there and ground to a stop. Whirling, the meager beam fell on Cat pressed up against a wall of the dark passage. She clutched her unlit flashlight like a melee weapon, ready to ring somebody’s bell.

“Took you long enough!”

“Sorry,” David whispered. “I didn’t know the plan.”

They shared a nervous laugh and a relief-filled hug, but both froze in mid-embrace. Ragged gunfire of an automatic weapon echoed down the hallway, shaking loose dust from the ceiling.

"Arthur, no!" Without thinking, David launched himself back down the corridor, no longer caring about what his sound or light might give away. He ignored Cat's angry whisper-shouts to stop and come back.

"Arthur!?" he shouted, feeling unexpected tears well up. One more corner. "Arthur, where are—"

David slammed into a wall of meat, bounced, and hit the floor with an audible *thwack*. His phone slid away, and his elbow shot pain to his fingertips. He wheezed, the air gone from his lungs.

"I say, steady on, David!" Father Matthew stretched out his hand to help him up.

"Arthur!" David managed. "Where's Arthur?"

"Good lord, David, what's all the fuss about?" Arthur stepped out of the darkness from behind the priest. He was ineffectually trying to unflatten his dusty fedora while juggling their second flashlight.

"I heard gunfire! It was the guard's gun." He grabbed Matthew's hand and allowed himself to be wrenched up. He felt something pop in his elbow and it felt better. "I thought..."

"Ah," Arthur said. Then, "Oh, I see. Yes, well, the young man's gun went off when Matthew clocked him, you see. Must have had his finger on the trigger. Bad form really. But then, what can one expect from a hired baboon?"

David grabbed Arthur and squeezed, just as Cat had done to him moments before. This time though, it was much more awkward, for Arthur at least.

"Um, yes. Thank you, David," Arthur mumbled. "Now, if you don't mind, I'd like to be out of here before those men wake up in the dark." He stooped towards Mr. Aarons' forgotten lantern and picked up a matchbook. Arthur struck a match and a moment later bright flickering light lit up the ancient hallway.

"And just where did you leave our Cat?" Father Matthew asked, turning to David. Only then did David notice the automatic weapon slung over the priest's shoulder. Matthew lowered it and flipped on the flashlight, adding his beam to Arthur's glow. The contrast between the clerical collar and Rambo pose amused David. Just how different might things have gone for Mr. Aarons if he'd had Father Matthew? Suddenly Arthur's choice to have the priest along didn't seem so far-fetched.

"She's this way," David said, rubbing the feeling back into his elbow. "And I think she's figured out how Mr. Aarons got out. There's a place where this part of the complex connects to somewhere else."

"Well then, I suppose we aren't done following in Wyatt's footsteps just yet then. Lead on." Arthur glanced down at David's side as he turned. "Wait a tick, is that Wyatt's satchel? Well done, my boy! Well done indeed."

LXI

"What do you mean, 'attacked?' Who attacked you!?"

Mel was furious. Upon landing at the airport in the pre-dawn darkness, she had been immediately whisked to one of the Russian GAZ-TIGRs on semi-permanent loan from the Syrian military. She'd instructed the driver to waste no time getting her to the Ugarit basecamp and so far, they had managed to plow through most of the roadblocks. Due to the newly erected tower, she could also video chat with the commander of their security contingent, so Mel checked in.

She instantly regretted it.

The sweaty red face of Colonel "Ivan" Raskolnikov filled the screen. He quickly explained the unexpected turn the expedition had taken after just one trip into the Ras-Shamra ruins. The huge man had a split lip and a lump that was turning colors. And nothing he was telling her made any sense.

"Your eggheads do this," Raskolnikov replied with measurable disgust. "They ambush us in darkness, take lights and guns and run like cowards." He gestured dramatically. Behind him, Mel glimpsed another man in the same tent seated on a supply crate and holding his head with a bag of something frozen. Connor Dolan, former IRA she recalled. The pair looked as if they'd fought one another armed with two sacks full of rocks.

"We did not realize how very trained they were, or we would have done things differently."

"Trained?" *In what, ancient insults?* Mel held it together long enough for him to explain. After regaining consciousness an hour ago, Raskolnikov had kicked Dolan awake. They'd swept the dig area for the team as best they could in the dark, but finally were forced back up to the mobile camp.

The whole situation was completely unfathomable.

"And just why exactly was it that you felt the need to rob our academic team in the first place?" she asked, dreading the answer.

Raskolnikov looked genuinely surprised and confused. It was not a good look for him. "There was... security concern."

She waited for him to elaborate. He didn't.

Mel took a deep breath and let it out slowly. She needed more data. She needed to talk to her man on the inside if there was to be any hope of finding out what was truly going on.

"Thank you, Colonel," she said, smiling sweetly. "You have been very helpful. Put Dr. Pitman on, please. I want to speak with him."

Yes, Uncle Ryan would know what was happening. It was why she had inserted her old family friend in the first place, after all.

Raskolnikov started to obey, but heavy footfalls and a series of shouts came through from outside the tent. Ivan stood to investigate just as one of the other guards burst in through the flap. Carlos Rogers, ex-Marine.

"Sorry to interrupt, Colonel, but somebody just took off in one of the turtlebacks."

"Who?" the Colonel demanded.

"LT says it was the priest. He drove about a half-klick down to the old wall and picked up the old man and the kids."

LT—Lieutenant Li Yao, former PLA Special Operations Forces.

"Well, go stop him!"

"Can't, sir. The other one was—" Maddeningly, the call dropped. She poked the screen to redial.

Dr. Evans was stealing trucks now? Was it possible that she had misjudged the old tutor? It made no *Èr bǎi wǔ* sense at all. Or did it? Her mind latched onto a stray thread of an idea. The man's pattern was to run away from his problems, which would mean he was scared. But if so, then just what was he running from?

Her phone refused to reconnect. Something was wrong.

The first slivers of sunrise could be seen peeking out from behind the distant eastern hills. At least some things in life were unchanging. The ever-moving sun would be well into baking the countryside by the time she made it to the mobile basecamp.

LXII

Unnamed road, northwestern Syria. David.

"This road should be good for a while," David said. He had been providing navigation courtesy of his GPS map app while they worked to ditch the other truck. They'd long abandoned the freeway and now skulked the hilly back roads in their Russian Humvee wannabe. So far it seemed to have worked, though they were effectively going in circles. They'd passed the same abandoned bus frame three times and skirted the same highly suspicious blockade twice.

Being back in the TIGR reminded David that they were still in a regime-held closed country known for its revolutionary insurgent groups, except now heading away from the false safety of the basecamp. The awareness would have made him sweat if he wasn't already drenched with it.

Matthew was driving, thank goodness. David was moderately surprised at how well he was doing it too, considering Oxford was a "walking town" and Syrians drove on the normal side of the road, instead of the English backwardness. It was weird to see something so familiar in a place so foreign. Only a handful of vehicles were out on the roads, but at one point they were forced to stop the truck for a long tense minute to let a goat shepherd and his herd pass. In all, Father Matthew had proven to be full of surprises. The scientist-priest's past was still mostly a closed book to David. Though after seeing the way the Anglican priest had subdued their guards, extracted them from the little library dig-site, crept to the basecamp, and then subsequently "borrowed" a vehicle, David was beginning to wonder if it had something to do with the English military. There was a new intensity to the priest that David would not have predicted.

Cat sat in the other rear bucket seat, firing off questions one after another in an attempt to understand what had just happened. The whole set-up made David feel like they were little kids in the back seat during some family road trip. Being swallowed up by the TIGR's huge interior didn't help. It was a strange feeling.

"So, where are you suggesting we go then?" Cat demanded.

Arthur wrenched himself around to look back at them. His gray hair was a mess under his hat and he was unsuccessfully cleaning his glasses with his shirt. But there was a twinkle in the old wizard's eye that could not be denied. Arthur's brain was in high gear dealing with being on the run in the outskirts of northwestern Syria. *Is Arthur having actual fun?* For some reason, this realization helped David relax.

"Trusting a team was a mistake," Arthur said aloud, answering a question nobody had asked instead. "Mel Chen set us up."

Matthew didn't reply but supplied a weak head bob of encouragement. Then Arthur answered the actual question.

"We need to hide somewhere before that other truck finds us again," Arthur repeated, for what felt like the sixtieth time. "Perhaps there's a barn or something somewhere..."

It was a terrible plan. Worse than Arthur's last terrible plan that hadn't worked. Or had it?

David replayed the scenario in the stage of his mind. Arthur had made a point of censoring his reading of the journal to the group on the plane. He had mentioned the broken tablet, though not its significance as a possible translation key. They had kept their discovery about the bag a secret, but it hadn't mattered. Why not? Dr. Pitman had used deadly force to take the translation tablet for himself, but, why? They were all on the same team, he would have found out about it soon enough. And more importantly, how had he known about the bag at all? Had he spotted it on the big screen when everybody else missed it? That was too many unlikely coincidences that David didn't swallow for a second.

Or maybe the mere existence of Mr. Aarons' journal had panicked Dr. Pitman into acting. If Mr. Aarons' new partner had a falling out with him like Arthur in the '80s, maybe Dr. Pitman didn't want the man found. Pitman had lectured passionately for an hour about the dead rivers in various parts of modern Iraq. Perhaps the archeologist had not accepted the topographer's satellite image river theory, and this was all some complicated revenge scheme.

There were other possibilities too. Maybe the partners hadn't disagreed. Maybe they were still working together, and the company was just a means to an end. But then, why had the journal been sent to Arthur at all? There was no way to know any of it for sure. Too many missing pieces. Not to mention, their guards had been weirdly clueless. The tablet fragment was a broken rectangle, not that circular frisbee thing they had pulled from the bag. That was not a tiny error.

"It was round," David said aloud, grabbing the all-but-forgotten satchel from the center kiosk where he had tossed it an hour ago.

"What's that?" Arthur cocked his head back slightly. He was still smearing his greasy lenses to no effect.

"The tablet that Captain Rogers took out of the bag was round. Not a triangular fragment like the rubbing in the journal."

"Yes, that's right." Arthur agreed. "Wyatt had the page marked out for a second rubbing of the other half, but he hadn't transferred it yet."

"What rubbing?" Cat asked suspiciously.

"Oh, oh I say!" Arthur twisted around again to look at them. David was already unlatching the front buckles that held it closed. "Carefully, David."

It was a silly request. David had slid down the rubble and run the halls of one of Ras-Shamra's libraries with this bag. He'd climbed from the dark trenches with it, stealthed to the edge of the city, and finally thrown himself into a vehicle, all at Arthur's command. He could handle opening the thing.

Arthur said it again anyway. "Open it carefully."

Ever so gingerly, David lifted the flap and peeked inside. He worked his way one layer at a time through Wyatt Aarons' dirty laundry, tossing a probably cleanish sock at Arthur to use as a slightly superior glasses-wiper. As Arthur wiped and replaced his glasses, David extracted an empty waterskin, a discolored toothbrush, some loose papers, and a pair of shorts. Other items emerged before he finally came up with a tiny but surprisingly heavy chunk of clay. David knew instantly what it was. What it had to be.

Cat gave a little gasp then leaned in, her hand covering her mouth like an excited schoolgirl. Arthur let out the breath he had been holding for a little too long. Exactly as Arthur had theorized, the tablet had a small bit of Ugaritic along the broken edge at the top. It then switched to the never-translated Linear-A across the diagonal break. The ragged edge lined up perfectly with what he remembered from the journal rubbing of the top part.

"Here, David. I'll take it."

David didn't argue. He supported the artifact with a tee-shirt and handed the fragment up. Arthur cradled it as carefully as a grandfather might hold a newborn, then after a moment the old wizard cautiously turned it over. What Arthur saw on the backside startled him so much that he nearly dropped the tablet onto the floorboard.

"Good lord!" he said aloud. "This—no, it can't be!" David grabbed the back of the driver's seat and launched himself towards the front, so he could see whatever it was that Arthur was disbelieving.

"What is it, Arthur?" Matthew probed, barely glancing away from the road. David could see that the backside of the tablet also had something on it, but it was different.

"Double-sided tablets were fairly common in the ancient world," Arthur whispered, awestruck. "Even the *Epic of Gilgamesh* was done that way across some eighteen different tablets. Though that was Akkadian of course, a whole other family of cuneiform."

David couldn't wait for Arthur's mouth to catch up with his brain. "Is there another language on it?" he prompted.

But David knew the answer already. The backside was not like the stylized pictures of Linear-A, they were way earlier, more like actual pictures. Almost like Rabbi Yosef's Proto-Sinaitic. Three languages, just like on the Rosetta Stone. Suddenly Mr. Aarons' various journal entries about Uncle Sir Arthur's Archive made way more sense:

I had proof...

"Just like the seal stones you showed me at the Ashmolean," David affirmed. "That's neat." He crashed back into his seat with satisfaction.

"Oh, it's more than neat, David," Arthur whispered reverently. "This tablet is even more valuable than we thought. It's quite possibly the keystone to not just one language, but two. And by the looks of it, an incredibly ancient one." His excitement suddenly was overtaken by a wave of strange rage. "Or rather, it would be if we had the blasted journal and the infernal rubbing of the top half!"

David wasn't sure what Arthur meant. He looked to Cat for help, but she was elbow deep in the satchel herself now, digging around in it like a little girl looking for the last piece of candy in her Halloween bag. Again, David felt like they were the silly kids in the back seat who had just missed something important the adults were talking about.

"Don't you see?" Arthur spat through gritted teeth, "This is the find of the century! Except it's worthless." He was Saruman the White again, only this time the anger wasn't at David. "Without the journal we can never translate it. We need the top half of the blasted tablet!"

David slumped, defeated. Of all the things he had taken pictures of, why hadn't he archived the journal too? If it came down to that, he was going to feel truly guilty about it. A whole civilization's language left untranslated because he hadn't thought to take a few pictures? A million "what ifs" tugged at him from every direction.

"Aha!" Cat exclaimed, proudly. "Dou you mean this top half?"

David stared. It had not occurred to him that Mr. Aarons would hide both halves together. Relief washed over him, and in an instant, Arthur's frustration evaporated too. With a shaking hand, he took the clay fragment from her and carefully aligned it to the bottom half. It fit perfectly but for a few ancient chips. At least, David hoped they were ancient. Regardless, few clay tablets in the world had fared better over the intervening millennia, if David's opinion meant anything.

"Arthur," Matthew pondered, "I can't help wondering what exactly it was that our misguided guards took from the bag."

"It was round," Arthur restated dismissively. "It was too dark to see it clearly, but ancient tablets are rectangular."

David laughed to himself. Why were they talking about some oversized coaster Mr. Aarons had kept in his bag? They'd gotten lucky that the guards didn't know what they were looking for.

"I got a pretty good look at it when the guard took it out," he said. "It looked practically new, like shiny brown porcelain or something. It definitely had symbols on it like those ones, but they were in a spiral." David held his hand out for the empty satchel. Cat slowly handed it to him, eying him questioningly.

"Sorry, what?" Arthur stammered accusingly. "Like these?" He flipped the ancient tablet back to the pictographic side.

David nodded hesitantly. "Exactly like those. I remember the little shield, and the guy with the mohawk, and that funny little r-shaped feather thingy." He began shoving the extracted laundry, papers, and Mr. Aarons' other junk back into the now-unimportant satchel.

The TIGR rumbled as the road became gravel. Arthur's jaw dropped.

"Are you sure it was a spiral?" Cat demanded, her tone betraying deep suspicions.

David nodded again. "Why? Does that mean something? Oldest symbol in the world or whatever, right?" *What was it Arthur said about spirals the other day? Something about mazes and chaos?*

"Good lord," Arthur whispered, "It couldn't be, could it?"

LXIII

Ras-Shamra Basecamp. Ugarit, Syria. Mel.

"Do you have it yet?" Mel demanded.

Standing in the door of the tent, she gazed up with disgust at the useless coms tower looming large over the hills and scraggly trees. Colonel Raskolnikov sucked violently on a cigarette as he swore into an open metal casing at the base of the tower, shouting various orders to someone Mel couldn't see.

"Almost there ma'am," her military tech reported from within the tent, "Everything on our end is working, far as we can tell, but we are only getting a trickle of the bandwidth we should be. Nowhere near enough for anything useful. Central is running diagnostics too, but they think it might be a problem with the satellite itself. Some sort of glitch in the software. We are trying to shunt things through one of the other satellites, but it's not exactly flipping a light switch in this part of the world. It doesn't help that we can't even talk to each other in real-time."

Mel turned, forcing calm into her voice. "Can we track them at least?"

"No ma'am. The GPS tracking system for all company vehicles in our section is down too."

"All of it?"

"Yes, ma'am. It's on the list, but they are telling me that the whole grid in our sector is out. It is likely just an unrelated side-effect. Apologies."

Mel slapped the door flap closed and fumed. No comms of any sort? A carload of runaway scholars and no way to track them? There was no way that was an 'unrelated side-effect.' The good news was that Dr. Pitman had gone after them, the bad was that he had done it so quickly he hadn't taken any of the men with him. But why?

According to Raskolnikov, Dr. Pitman was the one who had ordered the security alert to begin with, meaning that her intel about Aarons' stashed bag had paid off, but it didn't explain the obvious need to act quickly. It almost seemed suspicious. Could Pitman and Evans somehow be working together? It would be possible if it was anyone else but Uncle Ryan. It was maddening that she couldn't simply call him for an explanation. *What's the missing piece?* Mel was overlooking something critical. She took a deep breath and let it out slowly. She needed to think.

GPS units were ridiculously simple technology. Using satellite signals everyone had access to, the little tracker triangulated its position against a pre-loaded map. Easy. Going the other way was a bit more complicated. The trackers on her vehicles also pinged out a signal that her satellites could see, which meant tracking software. Which wasn't working.

This meant that the very two vehicles she needed to find, along with a few hundred others, were untrackable due to a convenient "glitch" in her software. *Can't be a coincidence.* This meant that Dr. Evans had not only stolen a car from her and disrupted comms, but somehow targeted the GPS network in the process. How any of that could even be the least little bit possible she could not comprehend. Someone with high-level access and technical ability had planned this. Evans was a textbook technophobe. He'd easily been the least technologically competent individual at basecamp. Such an operation was decidedly not in his skillset.

Another thing that vexed her was how Dr. Evans had been such a deep pain to recruit. She'd burned a well-placed—if eccentric—employee, called in favors, and puppeteered the good professor by finding his particular leverage. The man had even demanded a scholarship for his grandson and a donation to a church, of all things! He could forget about those now. This hadn't been a cheap exercise. Not that it was about the money, but the man was proving to be a real liability. Had he manipulated her that thoroughly?

The rational part of Mel's mind intruded, reminding her of something. If the scholar had perceived a serious threat in the form of the Colonel and his men, then perhaps it made sense for the professor to have run. She should have considered Evans a flight risk; it was his pattern, after all. Though how anyone on the team had overcome two highly trained armed guards was still anybody's guess. Colonel Raskolnikov's best answer was that they had been "ambushed in the dark." It did not compute. The man was ex- *Spetsnaz*. Dr. Evans was a gray-bearded professor with a fondness for tweed. And for that matter, how does an Anglican priest manage to steal a military vehicle in broad daylight from a guarded camp?

Mel sighed. She needed tea for this to work properly.

That little thread of doubt she'd felt before dangled again, teasing her doubts. This time, she tugged at it. Because, as silly as it would be, she could just as easily go the other way with these facts. Uncle Ryan had access to the satellite software. With a little time and premeditation, he could probably have disabled parts of the comms and GPS grid himself. There were several valid reasons why he could have been trying to get at Wyatt Aarons' work before Dr. Evans, but also a non-zero chance that Pitman could be colluding with his old partner, or else had stolen Aarons' work for his own ends. In that scenario, the problems would not be a glitch, but *bona fide* sabotage.

But obviously, all of that was impossible. It didn't compute, not after all the machinations that had brought them to this moment. She'd enlisted Pitman—Uncle Ryan—to manipulate Mr. Suit. She'd brought him out of retirement for this. He was family, and Uncle Ryan cared about finding Aarons as much as she did. Those had all been her decisions. Her choice of who to involve. *Hadn't it?* The creeping doubt lingered, and Mel was a little less sure of herself now.

The thing about it all was that Pitman had been with Mao Sien since the beginning, and a consultant to Chen Global long before that. Pitman was the one who first introduced Mel to Wyatt Aarons, not to mention dozens of other employees. Pitman had always been one of her father's closest advisors, in an era when an American geologist who spoke five Middle Eastern languages was an invaluable resource to her father's international oil empire.

When Mel was just a little rich girl jet-setting around the world with her powerful father, Uncle Ryan always had a hug and a candy for his favorite adopted niece. Dr. Pitman was an asset. Had *always been* an asset. If there was one thing she could rely on, it was that Uncle Ryan was on her side. He was so much more than just one of her favorite human computers. He was so well-established that he predated the standard HR protocols and screenings. He had helped establish them! Pitman was the one person she could trust implicitly.

The import of this little detail suddenly loomed large, like jumping out of a plane and then remembering to pack a parachute. Her sentimental blind spot stood out like wine on new satin. What did she categorically know about the man? Everything! Nothing?

Emotions always change the equation.

Mel stepped to her technician and put her hand on his shoulder. "Write a message to central, please. Have them check the logs for anything Dr. Ryan Pitman has accessed in the last forty-eight hours. Plus, I need a full background report on him. Everything."

"Ma'am?"

"You heard me. I want them to go deep, and I want access to it the exact minute that comms are restored."

Mel fell into a chair with her mind racing, hoping to her bones that she was wrong. Her heart pounded like a drum. It was going to be a very busy day.

LXIV

Unnamed road, northwestern Syria. Arthur.

Evans scanned the fragmented tablet in front of him, straining against the inevitable idea that had come to him. He ran a finger across the stamped symbols on the back of the translation tablet. It was bad form to touch it, but there wasn't much to be done about it.

"Not mind readers," Matthew reminded him.

"What? Oh, right." Evans pushed his glasses up. "The spiral is one of the most ancient symbols known to man. Nearly every culture in the world has used the spiral shape symbolically. It has represented everything from the mystery of life and birth concealed in the woman's womb, to the coiled chaos serpent who hid in the garden at the beginning of time. It is chaos and order intertwined. Tiamat and Abzu and all that. The terrible enlightenment born of the knowledge of good and evil. As in the Adam and Eve myth, actually."

"What are Tiamat and Abzu?" David asked, but Evans didn't have time to explain the Mesopotamian pantheon right now. He waved the question away, set the reunited tablet fragments down on the central kiosk, then twisted himself to look at the back seat.

"How much do all of you know about something called the Phaistos Mystery Disk?"

David shrugged and shook his shaggy head, but deMata gave Evans a death stare.

"That sounds vaguely familiar," Matthew said. "Not coming to me I'm afraid."

"You can't be serious," deMata said, her voice dripping disbelief.

Evans looked at her directly, prompting her to sigh, roll her eyes and say more.

"It is a fifteen-centimeter disk of fired clay that was found in the Aegean palace of Phaistos on the island of Crete," she provided with a touch of venom. "Allegedly dating to the middle or late Minoan Bronze Age, around two thousand B.C.E. It is covered on both sides with a spiral of stamped symbols that have never been properly translated. Very few examples of the pictographs exist elsewhere—a few seal stones, a highly degraded metal ax, that sort of thing."

Evans' hunch was right. The girl's practicum work and entire focus of study had been in Phaistos researching alleged fakes. Of course she would know all about the Mystery Disk, it was the most famous Minoan fake of all. *Young, but brilliant,* he reminded himself.

"Ah yes," Matthew decided. "I daresay I saw a program on the telly about it once. A strange mystery that one."

"Not for lack of trying, mind you," Evans stated. "The translation part, I mean. Scholars have spent years studying the Disk to no avail."

"I have studied the Disk completely," deMata stated with finality.

That was true. Evans now had a creeping feeling about the real reason Wyatt had picked this young scientist for his team. Confirming it would require some tact. Theories abounded about the Phaistos Disk, each more outlandish than the last. There was something about the enigmatic pictographs pressed into that clay spiral that sparked people's crazier theories.

The Disk was segmented into sixty or so "phrases," indicating probable word groups or phonetic clusters. Some said it was an early board game. Others, an astronomer's chart. Speculative translations abounded, including everything from a hymn to a forgotten goddess to literal pictographic nonsense like some child's practice clay tablet. The problem was that the Phaistos Disk was double-sided, expertly crafted, yet completely unreadable.

Experts loved to punt to mystery when they didn't understand something. The "Mystery Disk" of Phaistos might as well be Exhibit A.

And the Spanish girl-genius, admirably, believed none of it.

"The Phaistos Mystery Disk is nothing more than modern fakery," deMata declared.

Well, that's sorted then, Evans didn't say.

"It was the same symbols," David assured them, pointing at the broken tablet. "The Disk was stamped with them. I'm sure of it."

"Let's not jump to conclusions, David," Evans warned him, turning toward the back seats again. "We don't know that for sure." But even as he said it, he second-guessed himself. His mind was already creaking into action and calling up the symbols he knew to be on the untranslatable Disk.

"Uh, yea Arthur, I'm pretty sure we do." David held his phone up.

The screen was slowly loading a composite image of both sides of the clay disk in question. "This is exactly what that guard pulled from the bag. I remember this."

The still-growing image showed a side-by-side illustration of the front and back of the famous Mystery Disk of Crete. The one and only Phaistos Disk.

"Give it a second to finish, it's being ridiculously slow," David said, handing over the device. As of yet within the range of Mel's tall tower, David had simply pulled it up as the first hit of hundreds on an image search. Kid-internet had struck again.

Evans felt the shiver return. It took over his body, turning into a full-blown excited shake all the way to his fingertips. It was the work of a moment to confirm that the digital pictographs were the same as the broken tablet before him. It wasn't hard, even blasted Wyatt had clearly spotted the connection.

"I do not understand," deMata said. "The Phaistos Disk is kept on display at the archaeological museum of Heraklion. It is a large draw for many tourists. It is never taken out and all requests for taking of samples or even close-up scrutiny are denied regularly. I know, I have tried multiple times. Wyatt Aarons could not have gotten it, and especially not to Syria. Absolutely not, it is impossible."

"Actually," David said, holding up a wrinkled-up piece of white computer paper. "I think I know the answer to that too."

Evans looked over his glasses at the crumpled paper. The revelation was staggering in its simplicity: "Thank you for your eBay purchase," he read aloud. "Please don't forget to rate your seller for your purchase experience of 'Authentic high-quality replica of Phaistos Mystery Disk.'" He blinked, looking over the frames at the kids in the back seat. "You can buy replicas of ancient artifacts on the internet?"

David laughed. "Arthur, you can find anything on the internet, assuming you know where to look and are willing to pay shipping. And it looks like Mr. Aarons had a copy of the Phaistos Disk sent to himself by some private courier the week before he went missing." He was scanning another crumpled sheet now. "And he paid a lot more for the shipping than he did for the Disk, it looks like. Yikes!"

"Wyatt thought the Phaistos Mystery Disk was translatable?" Evans heard himself croak. It was the missing piece that brought this wild goose chase suddenly into focus.

Wyatt had hand-selected his Dilmun team. Dr. Catalina deMata was a Phaistos Disk specialist and skeptic. "Rabbi" Yosef Ibrahim had been selected for his unconventional new research and theories in translating ancient pictographs. Pitman had been working with Aarons for decades, providing him with all kinds of scientific and pseudoscientific fuel for his fire. *Mustn't forget that Wyatt had been trying to get Mel to recruit me for months.* Evans finally understood what this expedition was all about.

"I've been a ridiculous fool. This was never about translating Linear-A. I doubt Wyatt even recognized three distinct languages on his tablet. Wyatt thought I could translate the blasted Phaistos Disk!" It was ludicrous. It reeked of deplorable scholarship. Every bone in Evans' body screamed at him with good, healthy, academic skepticism to back away now.

The others were attuned to Evans' every syllable and twitch. Matthew even risked a few glances away from the road, as unsettling as that was. It all made Evans feel especially twitchy.

"Arthur," Matthew gently probed. "Could you? Translate it?"

Evans looked up from the spiral image on the phone and blinked about seven times. He thought it through aloud.

"Well, there is quite a high reciprocity of the symbols between the Disk and the tablet. And given that there is a readily available translation for a known contemporary language on said tablet—"

"Arthur..." Matthew warned, sternly.

"Good lord, then! Yes, I quite probably could." *This is a bad idea.*

There was a moment of stunned silence, then the vehicle burst into wild chatter, the other three all talking and asking Evans a dozen questions at once.

Evans held up his hand for silence. Using David's phone to motion to the two tablet fragments, he clarified, "But it will take me some time for even the most rudimentary pass. Not to mention I would need access to three or four libraries back home if I should hope for any sort of accuracy." Their disappointment was palpable. "Er. But that doesn't mean I can't give it the old Oxford try..." He blinked at them. No one dared reply.

"So, does anyone have a blasted pencil? I'd like to get cracking."

LXV

Unnamed road, northwestern Syria. David.

"But if Mr. Aarons was looking for Eden, uh, Dilmun, he must have thought it was somewhere in Mesopotamia, right?" David yawned, staring at some pelicans diving for food. "You know, fertile crescent and all that?"

All morning Cat and he had been trying to piece together the various clues they had gathered, but for David, guessing at the strange mind of Mr. Aarons was proving to be about as easy as understanding Arthur's translation work. He couldn't shake the feeling they'd missed something important.

Matthew had pulled to a stop at the end of a dirt road hours ago that morning. It wasn't exactly hiding, but in a way, it was much safer than driving in circles. They were now parked on a little overlook, mostly hidden by scrubby trees and sad little desert bushes. David could see the ocean breaking on a rocky beach not far below. He was fighting the urge to go down there and swim in the ocean, swimsuit or not. But even more striking was the steep side of a mountain sloping dramatically down to the sea.

Cat called it Mt. Aqra. Apparently, the ancient people here had worshiped it as the home of their gods. And no wonder, it was astounding. The birds made another dive. Matthew was taking a bio break, something they had all done a few times now.

"That Pictographic-Hebrew table again?" Arthur requested.

Arthur was not paying attention to their conversation at all. He had tuned out hours ago, mumbling to himself in ancient languages with the occasional "Oh!" or "Hmm." All the while he scribbled strange nonsense into the little spiral notebook he had taken notes in before. This work was supplemented with scratch paper from Mr. Aarons' bag, and even some blank sheets torn from a Russian-language military manual. The broken tablet sat in the kiosk near Arthur for easy access, and every so often he would ask for David to pull up one of two images on his phone. The Phaistos Disk obviously, and rather grudgingly David noted, the translation page from Rabbi Yosef's little black book.

David unlocked and handed him the phone for about the thirtieth time that hour. The sly candid photo of Yosef's Proto-Sinaitic pictograph chart made David happiest. Without it, Arthur probably couldn't have bridged the tablet and the Disk. Whatever method he was using, Arthur now seemed to be translating the fragmented tablet at a record pace. It was all quite impressive, if completely unintelligible. David had not thought about the necessity of translating that part first before Arthur could move on to the Phaistos Disk. What David had thought of was to thoroughly photograph the tablet fragments, like he should have done with the journal rubbing when he'd had the chance.

Cat yawned. David's mind had wandered, but hers hadn't. "According to the Hebrew myths, Eden was east of Israel. But in truth, we already know from much archeological evidence that the nation of Dilmun was on the coast of the Persian Gulf. Then there is no mystery at all. They are simply not the same legend."

"Oh yea, Arthur did say that Dilmun was a real ancient country, named for Utnapishtim's city.

Cat sighed, "Yes. Or more likely it was the other way around, an origin story for the capital of a self-important nation. It is only the location of the garden city of Dilmun that is a mystery. If it ever existed at all. But there is no doubt that the land of Dilmun was along the northwestern coast of the Persian Gulf."

David was dubious. "But then why would Mr. Aarons think there was some kind of connection between Dilmun and Crete or the palace at Phaistos? It's not even the same ocean." He decided to risk an interruption. "Hey Arthur, did Uncle Sir Arthur discover the Phaistos Disk?"

To David's surprise, Arthur's answer came right away. "No, he never worked at Phaistos. That was a competitor. His great rival, arguably. An

Italian archaeologist by the name of Luigi Pernier. A man who wasn't very well known until he discovered the Disk at Phaistos frankly."

"Because of Émile Gilliéron," Cat teased.

Arthur merely grunted assent.

"Who?" David looked back and forth between his wizard and the Spaniard. She was the one who answered.

"Pernier's assistant," she said. "He was a very good artist and half of a father-son team. Together they almost single-handedly brought the Aegeans to the world."

"But I thought that Uncle Sir Arthur did that?" It was meant at Arthur, but he was busy scratching his chin with the pencil and back to scowling at his literal pile of notes.

"Uncle?" Cat was also perplexed, but for very different reasons. "Are you saying that the famous English archeologist Sir Arthur Evans is your uncle?"

"Well, technically his, not mine." David clarified with a little puff of his chest. "Actually his great-uncle, if you want to get even more technical." Arthur's family pride was beginning to rub off on him.

Cat's lips tugged into a mischievous smile. "Then you might be interested to know that Gilliéron also became the chief restorer for Sir Arthur Evans at the Palace of Minos in Knossos."

David was pondering this when he noticed Arthur glance toward Cat suspiciously. But she was at the wrong angle in the seat behind him to see.

"For over three decades Gilliéron worked with his son and partner, also named Émile." She began. "They created reproductions of frescoes and other artifacts for Sir Arthur Evans. The Gilliérons are now recognized as contributing many illustrations to Arthur Evans' four-volume book, *The Palace of Minos at Knossos.* Some of the most famous reconstructions by the Gilliérons include the Priest-King fresco, the Ladies in Blue fresco, and their painting of the throne room at the Palace of Minos."

"Wow," David said. "That's really impressive." Cat's ability to rattle off the titles was impressive too. He'd be hard-pressed to remember the titles of more than five or six of the art pieces he had seen just the other day. David had never thought about what it must have been like doing archeology back then without easy digital photography. A project like Knossos would have taken, what? Decades? He had no idea.

"Yes, it is," Cat said conspiratorially. "A little too impressive, some have said." David hadn't expected that. He did expect Arthur to now jump in and defend Uncle Sir Arthur or explain it away, but his wizard was already back into the translation. Except, his pencil was upside down and his ear was cocked towards them. Nope, Arthur was up to something again. David bit his tongue and waited.

"The Gilliérons were known forgers," Cat pronounced definitively. "It has been said that much of the so-called Minoan art we have today is a complete fabrication. Pieces made from the mind of a greedy father and son's workshop."

A moment passed and then Arthur spoke without looking up. "Actually, a lot of people have said that."

"I am one of them," Cat announced proudly. "I wrote a book about it." Had Arthur baited her? If so, she'd taken it and she wasn't stopping. "I believe that the duo fabricated much of what they found for the sake of the dueling archeologists Evans and Pernier." She said. "Probably even more than we realize. Their copies were so good that they often were mistaken for the originals. That is a fact. Perhaps it is because those alleged originals were also faked."

"They faked stuff? And they worked with Uncle Sir Arthur? Hey Arthur, is that true?"

Arthur merely grunted noncommittally. Whatever it was that was bothering him, it apparently wasn't the accusations of forgers working with his idolized uncle. Either way, David was still on his own in the conversation.

After a few moments of nothing, Matthew returned to the TIGR and did a few pushups against the driver's side. The vehicle didn't so much as wobble. After finishing his set, he returned to his seat with a sigh. "Still not a soul around." He informed them. Arthur grunted again.

"I have often believed that the Phaistos Disk was a forgery," Cat declared after a few more moments of nothing. Clearly, she wasn't dropping the subject.

She flipped her dark hair back and folded her arms across the top of her chest defiantly. She did defiant well. She had shed her trendy jacket for the tank top underneath some time ago. Now her cheeks were flushed and her lips a perfect shade of red. A light sheen of sweat made her look just like an action movie lead. Had she snuck some lipstick on when David wasn't looking? It seemed unlikely.

"For example," she continued in the same haughty tone, "the clay spiral Phaistos Disk was deliberately baked. Not incidentally baked like many other tablets found at the palace at Phaistos."

"Incidentally baked? What does that mean?" David felt himself being sucked in by Cat, but he didn't know what else to do.

"Simply that all of the other tablets were not baked in a kiln or fired on purpose, but rather by an accident. Pernier determined that an earthquake had caused a collapse in Phaistos, followed by a fire. Set off by oil lamps, you understand? The roof would have been wooden, so there was plenty of fuel. Centuries later when the ash and mud were cleared away, many rectangular tablets with real Aegean writing were recovered because of this accident."

"But the Phaistos Disk was baked on purpose?"

"That is correct. And also, the Disk survived not only the same fire, which had preserved the genuine artifacts, but somehow also survived a great fall from the second story where it was kept." She pursed her lips and veritably purred. "A nearly impossible set of circumstances, and the real mystery of the Disk."

"Bah, we don't know any of that for certain," Arthur weighed in, still not really helping or even looking up. "Phaistos was strange. They found no clerical records of anything there. Those 'real artifacts' were fragments of scrap clay with a few scattered pictographs. Total chaos. Guesswork at best."

"We know many things," Cat countered. "The ruins of Crete are in a shamble for a reason. The layers are all mixed up. Volcanic ash and sea creatures are where they should not be. When I worked there, we found cattle bones mixed with volcanic pumice dating definitively to 1600 BCE, the year of the explosion at Santorini. It led us to conclude that a great tsunami was the cause. Fifty kilometers wide, and perhaps thirty meters high, their entire navy would have been wiped out in a few minutes."

Arthur considered this. "It's plausible. The Minoans had no city walls. Their entire defense was based on their advanced armada of ships. Anything not nailed down would have washed right into the valleys and out the other side of the island."

"Oh yea, we talked about that," David realized. "The Minoans disappeared. Arthur called it one of archeology's great mysteries. But that theory that makes it sound more like the sinking of Atlantis,"

Arthur broke in from the front seat. "You are not the first to suggest it, but there are a lot of reasons Crete does not fit the Atlantis myth." He returned to his translation, muttering to himself, and did not elaborate.

David laughed. "Nice."

Cat shot him a sly glance of approval. then continued her narrative. "Soon, the Mycenean Greeks swept in from the north. They burned, pillaged and sacked everything. Within a generation, there was no trace of the Aegean culture. That is why the Gilliérons made and sold reproductions to museums and private collections all over the world. There were not enough originals. Since then, the National Museum in Athens has had a gallery entirely devoted to their alleged replicas of the Greek Bronze Age."

"And yet," Arthur countered, "despite scrutiny of validity, and questions of forgery, those reproductions remain valuable representations of ancient artistic achievements to this day." He sounded completely disinterested compared to Cat, who had been getting more into it each time she spoke. "The Gilliérons created replicas of metal artifacts based on molds of the original masks, weapons, and vessels. Their extrapolations of incomplete works have proven quite valuable to students of Minoan art for over a century."

"That's quite interesting indeed," commented Matthew. He was reclining sideways in the driver's seat, but there was a mediating tone there too.

David looked around, comparing everyone's disposition. Values were being weighed in with every word, even with the seemingly casual banter. He suddenly wondered what a verbal spark might do to set off the real differences that lay under the surface. Arthur and Cat had seemed to be unified in their opinions about Eden and Dilmun on the plane, but now Arthur was testing her, and David didn't know why. Only, if it wasn't about Sir Arthur, then what was it? David's imagination ran wild.

"Valuable?" Cat scoffed. "The Gilliérons created full-scale 'copies' of Minoan frescoes on watercolor paper from only tiny fragments. They made elaborate three-dimensional reconstructions in plaster form from shards. Both of which have been proven to be wildly inaccurate. Yet their imaginings still can be found in many art texts!"

Arthur made a harrumphing noise that sounded very horse-like. "Even the Ashmolean has plaster copies, Dr. deMata."

It does? David suddenly wondered which of the marble pieces he had admired, weren't. Certainly not the Greek statues? Then again, it's not like he'd noticed.

"Archeology is a lengthy process. It is an iterative exercise that requires much research, humility, and time." This last word he emphasized with a glance over his shoulder and across his glasses. It made him look both scholarly and every bit his sixty-five years.

Cat puckered her lips and waved the idea away dismissively, which made her seem decidedly untraditional or stuffy, and every bit the sassy-but-brilliant teenage girl she was. David swallowed hard and focused on her reply.

"This is obvious. It does not change the very suspicious fact that by 1911, the Gilliérons had a literal catalog of antiquities from Crete. It consisted of over one hundred and forty-four reproduction pieces, which could be manufactured in Germany by the Wurtemburg Electro Plate Company. And, we must not forget that before the elder Gilliéron ever began his career as an archaeological artist, he had already designed commemorative postage stamps for the inaugural Olympic Games of 1896 and 1906, and even served as an art tutor for the royal family of King George I. A brilliant artist makes for an excellent forger."

David was awed by her knowledge, and a little jealous of her memory. No wonder she already had so many degrees under her belt.

"Hogwash," Arthur said, coolly and conclusively. "Of course, Sir Arthur and Luigi Pernier hired royal-caliber artists. They were top-notch professionals. Emile Senior was an archaeological illustrator in Athens for Heinrich Schliemann long before he worked in Crete. That is simply how it was done back then. And as for the mistakes that were made along the way, well, that just proves the authenticity of the whole story."

"Then why is the Phaistos Disk the only artifact with those specific markings? There would have to be a great deal of other artifacts with them if it was to be believed."

"There are a few," Arthur said. "The Arkalochori Ax comes to mind. It shares a handful of the symbols here."

"Fifteen," Cat said with absolute finality. "Of course, I know it. That desiccated bronze ax is an even worse fake than that thing. And the symbols are only similar, not matching."

David was intrigued. He automatically grabbed his phone to look this ax up, then remembered with a wince that they were out of service range.

"Perhaps so," Arthur said agreeably, "But if the Disk is a forgery, then the Gilliérons certainly knew a lot more about pictographs and ancient syntax than they ever let on. Because this is astounding."

Everyone waited for Arthur to finish, but he didn't, only going back to mumbling to himself and scratching out notes on random papers. With a start, David realized that Arthur had moved on from his work with the translation tablet and was now zoomed in on the image of the Phaistos Disk again. He was already working on Mr. Aarons' theory and was miles ahead of them all as far as what he now knew. Was that Arthur's game? Was he keeping Cat distracted so he could work on the Disk? Just what exactly had he discovered? David felt a surge of adrenaline and fought the urge to demand that Arthur tell them everything he knew so far. But the last thing he wanted to do was foil his wizard's cunning plan.

"I will be sure to send you a copy of my dissertation when we get back to a civilized place, Dr. Evans," Cat finished, crinkling her nose at the back of Arthur's chair.

David smiled at her weakly.

She of course smiled back, only hers was different. It wasn't that the smile made David uncomfortable, exactly. It was more like the realization that it didn't make him uncomfortable made him uncomfortable. He was working this out in his head when he realized he wanted to get Emma caught up on things. But his internet had cut out as soon as they got far enough away from

Miss Chen's tower, and he didn't know when, or if, he might get it back. Plus, Arthur once again had his phone.

That was probably all that was bothering David. He always felt so cut off when his phone was out. Plus, he was hungry. They hadn't eaten a decent meal since the plane. He grinned. He was in a stolen Russian TIGR, on the run in rural Syria, pinned on a rocky outcrop overlooking the Mediterranean, with limited supplies, and no foreseeable way to get home, but his biggest problem was that he was stuck talking to a brilliant drop-dead gorgeous girl who was interested in him... yet he wanted a Coke. Horror of horrors, he might be forced to look at the scenery some more, engage in scintillating conversation, or go for a walk. Plus, that rocky shoreline was still calling to him, if they were here much longer he wouldn't be able to contain himself, lack of swimsuit notwithstanding.

*   *   *

Sometime later, David was munching on a truly horrible protein bar from a scrounged-up MRE and thumbing through his Ashmolean guidebook. Cat was asleep. He was glad to have snagged a few hours of uncomfortable sleep himself, but he was about done with this sitting around stuff. Far in the distance, he watched a dark-skinned young shepherd hurry his herd along the root of the scraggly mountainside parallel to the beach. David was just about to make up an excuse to go out and try to feed a goat when Arthur finally spoke.

"I have it," his wizard announced. "It's not perfect, but it will serve."

LXVI

Unnamed road, northwestern Syria. Arthur.

Evans gazed out the window at the sea he hadn't properly looked at all day. His scientific mind was playing tug of war with near-giddy amazement. He couldn't believe what he now held in his hands. Evans' work over the last few hours was rough, ugly, and unquestionably full of errors, but he had still translated the untranslatable. It would take unfathomably more work to do it right. Decades, even. But for now, he had something approximating a working field translation.

Lacking his real library, Evans had resorted to searching the library of his mind instead. To his surprise, he'd found this rather effective. As his mental books opened one by one, dozens—hundreds even—of word origins and language parts spilled out and connected up in ways he'd never considered before. The mental archive of his very real books was more complete than he realized, and it was a surprisingly imaginative application of the information in a way he had never considered.

It was also not lost on him that it was precisely what David had been doing from the moment he had laid eyes on the boy, albeit from a much different data set. Evans looked down at the flimsy little notebook in his hands. Stray notes about an aborted field team in front, and wonderful and substantially significant ancient secrets in the back.

Long ago, the mostly-genial competition between Luigi Pernier and Sir Arthur had gone decidedly in Uncle Arthur's favor with but one small exception: The Mystery Disk of Phaistos. Most texts didn't even mention the Phaistos Palace in more than a parenthetical, footnote, or stray comment. To this day, the site remained unexcavated and practically unknown but for the Disk itself, which was one of the greatest tourist draws in Crete. Not to mention the cash cow of the museum in Heraklion, on the other side of the island. The Knossos side of the island, where people actually went. The Disk was like the Mona Lisa to Paris' Louvre. The David to Florence's Academia. The Rosetta Stone to London's British Museum.

Thinking of these things reminded Evans of how they had gotten into this situation. Thanks to Wyatt-blasted-Aarons of all people, Evans had been given the key to translating the spiraling pictographs of the Phaistos Disk. The one significant artifact that Uncle Arthur had not been a party to discovering. The irony was scathing. He realized with a start that if he played his cards right, this rectangular clay Rosetta Stone—No, that was wrong. This little Ras-Shamra Translation Tablet could be the centerpiece of the Ashmolean's tablet collection. Little sparks of memory brought him images of the museum's old Minoan display. Only instead, it would be placed front-and-center in the newly remodeled building. Bigger and better than even Elisabeth had ever imagined it.

Evans held in his hands the key to the fame and fortune that he had once craved. It should have overjoyed him. Yet, he couldn't seem to access the feeling. The reason was completely practical. He was well aware that the tablet, and the Disk it correlated to, both represented a lifetime's work. A work that he simply no longer had the years to pursue.

Or was there more to it? Yes, there was an emotion there. A rather silly one. And painted on its face was Wyatt Aarons.

This wasn't Evans' discovery at all. It was Wyatt's.

Again.

The coals that had been burning low and light in his chest since that blasted journal appeared in his mailbox glowed brighter, and then they caught and blazed. *Devil take it, Wyatt Aarons! You cannot have this! You will neither defame nor claim Sir Arthur's legacy!*

Other, less polite thoughts followed.

"Arthur?" David looked worried. "Everything okay?"

Evans realized he was gritting his teeth and seething at the spiral notebook in his hands. He must have looked like a madman to his companions, who had all been quietly watching him, waiting for him to say something.

"Yes David, my apologies. I was just considering our next move," he lied.

The others didn't understand his love for Uncle Arthur. How could they? David was too young to have a calling yet. Matthew's was from God, and the precocious girl genius was brilliant but inexperienced. None of them had his years of scholarship, patience, and reasonable dedication to the field that he himself had shown. He had given his life to the University, to the Ashmolean, and to Sir Arthur.

Evans was tempted to toss the translation tablet out the window and be done with it. To go home to his flat and his books and his office and attend to his duties with the Colleges.

No, that wasn't true either. What Evans truly wanted was to make Wyatt look like the lucky bumbling amateur he was. He wanted to present the stories of ancient people like Uncle Arthur's Minoans to the world. To hear Wyatt's confession of apology from his own crooked mouth, saying that Evans had been right, and he had been wrong. Wrong about that blasted mountain in Turkey. Wrong about the fool's quest that was Noah's Ark. And most of all, wrong about the old weasel's own foolish and arrogant pride.

David eyed Evans from the back seat, his expression full of questions that Evans didn't have the answers to. No, that was wrong too. Evans had a translation, even if it was a rudimentary one. He now knew more information about the message recorded on the Disk than anyone on the planet. A message which had been obscured for some thirty-five hundred years or more. And now, given what he understood that message to be, he was willing to wager it was quite a bit older even than that. *If only I knew what to do about it.*

It was then that a strange and unexpected calmness came over him. Evans' emotions fell away like some old husk. Not Karen's green eyes this time, or guilt over a promise to her. Not an imaginary Elisabeth. Not even fear of a man in the suit with a gun. No, this time it was the memory of Wyatt Aarons' penned words coming back to him from the journal. The words that had started this whole thing were now etched into his memory. Evans knew exactly where to go from here. The Disk was precisely the sort of thing they had dreamed about finding all those decades ago on Doomsday. By god, had Wyatt actually gotten something right?

"'I'm sending you this journal so you will understand,'" Evans said aloud.

David leaned in. "'As it was in the days of Noah?'"

"'It's time for us to be vindicated for Doomsday.'" Matthew and David finished together, much to deMata's surprise.

She looked around, unsure what inside joke or reference she had missed. It only served to remind Evans how very badly this whole research expedition was being run. His team lacked even basic information about the journal and Wyatt's nutty theories.

Only... *is that my own fault?* A disturbing notion, to say the least.

"How far north have we come?" Evans asked.

"We are just a few miles south of the border," David said. He had taken charge of navigating hours ago, courtesy of his phone superpowers.

"Good. We need to get across it."

"The border?" Matthew asked incredulously. "Arthur, do you mean that you want to cross into Turkey?" Evans looked at him stoically. He loathed silly and obvious questions and Matthew knew better. "Do you at all mind if I ask why?" the priest probed.

"Because Wyatt clearly understood that the broken tablet was the key to decoding the Phaistos Disk," Evans said with certainty. "And now that I know what the Disk says, I also know precisely where he will have thought it would lead him. Even the first phrase would have been enough, and I'm positive he had that much figured out."

"Doomsday?" David breathed as if saying it too loudly might accidentally trigger the end of the world.

"Lead us?" Matthew wondered. "Whatever can you mean? What does a bit of clay from Crete have to do with a rocky hill in Turkey? Just what exactly does that thing say, Arthur?"

Evans wasn't sure where to start. Wyatt had always been a nut and this was abhorrent fieldwork by any rational standard, but given the context, perhaps the rational thing was to simply be out with it. This was not the time for skepticism. It was time to settle the score with Wyatt and save their own skins.

"First, you must understand that it has long been suspected by some scholars—including myself, I suppose I should own—that the Phaistos Disk might be another diluvial narrative recorded in the tradition of Atra-Hasis.

Based on the Semitic syntax indicators alone—"

Everyone was looking at him. David was eying him suspiciously.

"Arthur," Matthew interrupted gently. "Layman's terms, if you please?"

"Ah, yes. Sorry." He flipped through his spiral notebook for the visual, where he had transcribed the pictographic phrases across multiple pages. "The first symbol here is a boat, see? And there is the symbol for waters, yes?"

Dr. deMata frowned, but David lit up. "It's practically the same symbol from the seal stones at the museum, and that's like the merchant boat you showed me." Then, "Oh, and a man's head. It's another story of the Ark, isn't it Arthur? Is it a new flood myth?"

There was a pregnant pause while Evans realized that only now was everyone catching up to where he had been hours ago.

"What? Yes, of course it is." Evans couldn't imagine why this was so difficult. He had just said exactly that. "But that's not the most interesting part. There are forty-five different signs on the Disk, too many for them to constitute a phonetic alphabet. Too few for them to constitute a truly ideographic script, as is the case with say, Chinese—or so it has been argued. This observation has led numerous scholars to deduce that the Disk's script is syllabic, as is Linear-B, Greek, Latin, and so forth. But it turns out that the sixty-one phrases aren't words at all. They're more like sentences. It's quite simplistic, and it's a bit odd that the Disk reads from right to left starting in the center and working out, given the context of the late paleolithic pictographs, and I have to wonder—"

"Arthur..." Matthew cajoled.

"I'm getting to it," Evans protested, but nobody was buying it. "Oh fine. It's a migration history, blast it all! It translates as something like a path or road, depicting their people on a journey of some kind. I'll need more time and access to a library to translate it properly of course, but from what I can interpret here it says roughly, 'The road where the sword of fire branches out from the city of the great flood's Important-Man.' It's the translated name of Atra-Hasis, you see? Clearly an allusion to Nûḥ with some interesting and uniquely Semitic symbols woven in. Biblical ones, even."

"The sword of fire like that of the angel who guards the door to Eden?" Matthew provided. "Arthur, that's marvelous!"

"The Path of the Flaming Sword!" David gasped. He had gone completely white and was quoting Yosef's *Kabbalah* nonsense.

"Er, well, yes. That translation would technically work also, I suppose." Evans had not thought of it quite that way and wasn't too fond of the idea. He tried to think of some way to defuse it, but it was no use. Everyone started talking at everyone at once.

*   *   *

"There isn't much more to this road, Arthur," Matthew finally said. "It appears that we are almost at the border crossing." As they crested a hill, a massive yellow sign rose to meet them saying, "Yayladagi Border Gate, 5 Kilometers" in English, with the equivalent in Turkish and Arabic.

"Well, you may need to turn off then. Find a safer way to cross over." Evans had no desire to try to explain to the *ipso-facto* border authorities why they were headed this way in a stolen Russian military vehicle while trying to cross the border into Turkey, illegally, and without paperwork. Not to mention the two also-stolen deadly weapons that were just laying the on the floorboard.

"I doubt that would be wise," Matthew warned. "It appears that we have reacquired our tail. They are about a kilometer behind us."

The kids jumped to a window slot, but Evans didn't have to look to know Matthew would be right. There was going to be no safe road.

At that moment, a random bit of trivia that had been nagging at Evans for the last hour finally came to him. In ancient Sumerian mythology, the deity known as 'the wielder of the flaming sword who ensured the most perfect safety' was called *Asaruludu*. The same god had also been known as 'the beautiful shining one who illuminates the path.' It was a name which Christian mythology had associated with another being entirely. As Evans had said to David when they were in a much safer place, the 'bringer of light' was, in Matthew's circles, more commonly referred to by his Latin name.

"Devil take it," Evans sighed, "Fine. Pull across the highway to that dirt road over there, Matthew. We can try to lose them in the countryside again. Don't stop, even if it's the good guys."

Then, as an afterthought, he added, "Whoever that is."

LXVII

Junction of Route 4 and Route 1. Northwestern Syria. Mr. Suit.

In a little nothing town near where the twisting eastern road fed into the highway, the man in the suit waited. The voice on his phone had said that the scholar was making for the border. The man had chosen his spot well. From here, he could see where the road ended at the border gate, and aside from little nothing offshoots, there was nowhere else to go.

Finally, he saw an unmistakable desert-brown GAZ-TIGR crest the hill. He would let it pass, then follow. *Easy.*

To the man's amusement, the Russian vehicle did not slow but turned sharply left off of the little freeway, fishtailing onto a dirt road that ran roughly parallel to the border. From the corner of his eye, the man in the suit spotted the second truck now coming over the hill. Evans was on to them then. So be it. It was time for the backup plan, and he was the backup plan.

As the man in the suit gunned his little toy motorcycle to life, he sighed. It felt incredibly good to be free and on the open roads again, even on this ratty thing. But this next part would have been so much easier with the Ducati. He leaned into the wide bend and opened up the throttle, keeping sight of his target. Inside would be Dr. Evans and the other company people who had run. It was strange to think that he had been similarly employed just a few days prior. But that time was past, it was time for the man in the suit to cement his true loyalties. There was more than one kind of ambush.

The TIGR sent up a massive dirt cloud that made it difficult to work with any precision. Any hope of using the cover for stealth would be fruitless, Dr. Evans would hear him approaching well in advance. It didn't matter. The man in the suit had a score to settle with Evans and that boy. The pain in his hand and head were gone, but that wasn't the point. He would not forget that kick to the crotch any time soon either. Perhaps a tooth for a tooth would suffice if the opportunity arose. Not that there were any plaster busts nearby.

Maybe a rock? He smiled and leaned in for a fraction more speed.

The man in the suit entered the dirty cloud and zoomed right out of it past the 4x4. The front passenger was unmistakable. Dr. Evans was shuffling papers around and giving muddled instructions to the driver. A moment later he heard the second military truck roar up behind them. This was his cue, it was time to begin the game.

He crossed to the right and slowed the bike a bit, allowing the truck to catch up and perhaps give the driver the idea to pass. He eased in beside Dr. Evans' passenger window and waited for the old man to see him. It was confusion at first, but when the man reached up and pulled off his sunglasses with a smile, the old tutor's expression turned to surprised fear. Everyone in the car started shouting, and the big hairy driver floored it. The man on the bike replaced his glasses and gunned the little motorbike again, keeping pace beside them.

In his mirror, the man saw the second truck close in on their bumper and slam into them. It wasn't enough to seriously affect either of the war vehicles, but it was enough to make the leader swerve away into the oncoming lane. An old truck full of chickens veered into the ditch to avoid catastrophe. The Syrian driver screamed and raised an angry fist out of his window at what must have seemed to him like the crazy Russians making his life difficult again.

Evans and company recovered and zoomed forward. Adrenaline surged as the man in the suit prepared for what must come next. He opened the bike up and drew in close to his target. He could touch the side with but a flick of his arm. It was now or never. He lifted off of the seat and leaned into his intent, lashing out for the tiny back passenger window to use as a foothold. In one swift motion, he drew himself onto the roof and clutched there, even as the bike fell away from under him. It skidded and tumbled away, the second TIGR steering wide to miss it. This was a tough week for motorcycles.

The man in the suit reached down and wrenched open the passenger door, then using its weight for leverage, expertly twisted himself down and into the vehicle like a snake. Without warning and with one leg still hanging from the vehicle, he was suddenly wrestling with a tiny and feminine-soft body that smelled of Spanish saffron, cumin, and an undertone of pine. She screeched and shouted and swore at him in Spanish. He kicked himself inside the rest of the way, using his weight and an elbow to pin her against the seat without apology. Then the Evans boy was trying to pull him away and fists started flying. Only a second or so later everyone felt the jolt of the other vehicle ramming into one side of the bumper. The door slammed shut and a strange sensation of weightlessness came as the 4x4 spun around, fishtailed off of the road, and skidded to a stop.

The man in the suit had expected this possibility and so was first to recover. He threw the door open, dragging the struggling woman with him by her dark hair and long neck. In another life not too long ago, she would have been a worthy conquest using only slippery words, but that time was over. He jerked her roughly to demonstrate his power, but she kept fighting until he tightened his hold.

Everyone else piled out. The mountainous driver dodged as the second TIGR slid to a stop behind the first. In one swift motion, the giant vaulted across the hood and landed in front of the man in the suit. Dr. Evans' friend in the clerical collar was very quickly becoming a problem. The man ached for his lost pistol, but a hostage was a hostage, and he'd chosen well. He squeezed her until she squeaked, and the big man stopped short, accepting the threat.

The man considered his position. The Syrian sun beat down on them all equally. The horizon was nothing but a haze of dry heat waves, making the rocky foothills dance. The girl was threatening him and pulling at his arm, but she was no match for his raw power and strength. Everyone was talking at once at him, but he didn't waste his breath. He was the distraction. A few more seconds of this and it would be over.

In his periphery, the man spotted the boy. Young Evans was coming in for another ambush, just as he had in front of the pub. But this time the man in the suit was ready for him. Shifting his weight, he kicked out and connected square in the teenager's chest. The kid went sprawling toward the ditch, knocked flat on the desert sand. Not quite a shot to the crotch, but it would do. The boy didn't move again until Dr. Evans rushed to his side and helped him up, but both wisely kept their distance.

Suddenly the man felt a sharp slashing pain on his cheek. He instinctively tightened his grip on the woman but found himself clutching only her arm. She had already twisted away with one and broken his hold with the other, leaving only a few strands of silky black hair behind in the process. He locked onto her wrist like a vice and swiped his cheek with his free hand. It came away bloody. The little Spanish witch had scratched him. She kicked and twisted and broke free the rest of the way, bouncing and shouting to rejoin the others. He let her.

There was nothing more to do. It was over. The man in the now bedraggled suit watched helplessly as everyone hurried back into their vehicle. It peeled away in a cloud of sand and dust before the doors were even shut. He growled a curse and straightened his dusty coat as he watched them go. He would inevitably have to face some righteous wrath for failure, and he would deserve it.

"Well? Are you going to get in, or stand around like an idiot and bleed?"

Standing by the large door, the familiar old man was grinning at him as if everything was perfectly normal. Dr. Ryan had always been old, but he looked veritably ancient now. His pale skin was nothing but wrinkles. Over his shoulder was a fully automatic SMG with a flashlight attachment. What Dr. Evans had been doing with that killing tool he could only guess, but at least they hadn't tried to use it. Regardless, the old man's gleaming smile could only mean one thing, and it was very good. The distraction had worked well enough.

The clever sneak raised his clenched fist. From it dangled a leather satchel. He brought the satchel close and threw it open, digging through laundry and other items until he was forced to give up. Whatever it was Dr. Ryan was looking for wasn't there. The man in the suit braced himself for a torrent of violent anger, but instead, the old man shook with laughter, tossing the bag into the truck. The whole situation struck the man in the suit as entirely absurd, but he dared not say anything about it.

"What is down this no-name road?" Dr. Ryan asked once the man had taken the passenger seat.

The man in the suit was trying to staunch the blood from his cheek with an old shirt from the satchel but having only limited success. He looked into the stern face of the man he had first met as a pathetic wretch on the streets of Şırnak. Dr. Ryan was one of the two American men who had changed his life. He and Mr. Wyatt had given him as close a thing to a family as he had ever known. Role models both, and first of a very long line of teachers and benefactors. All part of the long path which had helped him understand what having a true mentor meant. The man in the suit smoothed the sleeve of his now stained coat and looked at Dr. Ryan.

Remember what you are.

"The northwestern foothills and the coast," he replied flatly. "It likely loops back to the highway in a few kilometers."

"Good," Dr. Ryan replied. "They won't fall for the same trick twice, but unless I miss my guess, they are going to try to cross over again. The Doc has picked up a trail, and we are going to follow him. It's like I always say, boy, you gotta study people. They are like clocks, predictable."

The man in the now ruined suit nodded. He had assumed Dr. Ryan planned to stop Dr. Evans at all costs. It had not occurred to him that they might let Evans go further down the path before trying again. What a fool he was. He mustn't forget that they were playing a long game, and his role in these events was now critical. His family was counting on him, and his place was by Dr. Ryan's side now more than ever. He would adapt also. It was what he did. He would not be caught off guard again.

Remember who you are. Who you really are.

"Yes, certainly," the man in the suit apologized, shifting uncomfortably in his seat. His foot kicked something on the floorboard. Looking down, he saw a tan spiral disk about the size of a pie pan. Into it had been pressed dozens of little pictures of men and crops and boats further divided into segments. He reached to pick it up and was surprised when it was taken from his hands.

"Don't play with that boy, we might still need it."

The American carefully wrapped it in the now-bloody tee-shirt and set it in the large central kiosk of the TIGR. A very familiar-looking leather journal and an unfamiliar Makarov PM semi-automatic pistol already lay there. A black PP-2000 submachine gun was also wedged between the panel and the seat.

"I stole you a new gun." Dr. Ryan handed the pistol over, smiling warmly. "I'm keeping the big one. I don't suppose you still have that shoulder holster I sent you way back when?"

"Yes, Dr. Ryan. It has not left my side."

"Well then, aren't you full of surprises? C'mon, once the Doc is out of the country, we'll have better control. Let's see if that bike of yours survived. I need to make a few calls."

"As you wish, Dr. Ryan."

"And knock off the 'Dr. Ryan' crap, would you? It's irritating. You're a grown man for god's sake."

"Yes, Dr. Pitman. My apologies."

"Much better."

*   *   *

An hour later the man in the ruined suit watched from his hiding place as the academics pulled into the waiting area at the border crossing. They left the motor running while they waited, a wise but unnecessary precaution this time.

LXVIII

Yayladagi Border Gate. Syria-Turkey Border, Syria. David.

Arthur decided that being in a crowd of people when crossing the border would be safer, though that remained to be seen. Not that it was a bustling port of entry or anything. More like an afterthought by somebody who realized the road went off to somewhere in not-Syria.

David was surprised to see the total lack of security at the crossing, given all the roadblocks Syria had presented them so far. Two officers on the Syrian side, a booth with a sad little gate, and an oversized cattle chute with a concrete theme were all that separated them and three other cars from Turkey. At the moment, one of the border guards was arguing with a truck driver about his paperwork, and the other leaned back in a chair somewhere between apathy and sleep. David supposed that Syria wasn't nearly as worried about people leaving as they were about their own internal political problems. The incoming sides were another story altogether, as a small army was heavily policing a short line of delivery trucks full of who knows what. This part of the world was so alien in so many ways, but some things were the same everywhere.

That's not to say that the outgoing waiting area was empty of people. A small crowd of merchants, guides, and other hopefuls were lined up against a concrete retaining wall. David's stomach growled at the smell of something sizzling on a funny-looking grill Arthur called a *brazier*. A few vendors approached the truck hoping to make a sale and David caved, buying two of the oily meat strips from a little girl and downing them in four bites. The rest of the sellers crowded in as soon as word spread that the vehicle was filled with Americans who had money, even though that wasn't strictly true.

The sweltering heat was starting to get to them all. Their clothes were drenched with sweat and the TIGR smelled like a monkey house. At least they had been lucky enough to steal the vehicle with some of their bags still in the back. Or had Father Matthew done that on purpose? Cat's bag was back at camp, and she complained about it off and on until it devolved into quiet frustration. David felt bad for her, but there wasn't anything he could do about it except promise to loan her a shirt. He half suspected her mood had more to do with Arthur and the Disk anyway. Even level-headed Father Matthew had a forced tone in his voice now. But none of that mattered to David. All he could think about was Dr. Pitman and the man in the suit.

It was clear that the tattooed gunman had somehow followed them from Oxford and was working with Dr. Pitman. Which meant Arthur was right, the whole thing had been Miss Chen's setup from the beginning. But the funny thing was, through luck or providence they still had the translation tablet fragments. They had been safely hidden in David's bag and stowed in one of the TIGR's many compartments for hours. Different underwear to keep it company for a while. So either the geomorphologist still hadn't known what he was really after, or he hadn't realized fast enough that the translation tablet fragments were already out of the bag. The only thing the attackers would have for their trouble was Mr. Aarons' dirty laundry and a couple of guns Arthur had wanted to get rid of anyway.

And yet, no further attacks had come. Maybe they had tried and simply not considered scouting the border gate, but now too much time had passed.

David still had that strange feeling in his gut that there was something they had all missed. Arthur knew all of this but was refusing to discuss it further, which in its own way made everything worse. Every minute that passed Arthur grew more irritable and cantankerous, which had a debilitating effect on everyone's morale. The tension was thick enough to cut with a knife and getting worse.

Matthew finally broke the silence with a perfect distraction. "Arthur, what do you say that we take this moment of calm for you to properly tell us what that Phaistos Mystery Disk is all about?"

David hadn't forgotten about the Disk in all the excitement, but he was beginning to learn Arthur's timetable on these things. And the more he got to know Matthew, the more David understood why Arthur's best friend was good for his grandfather's overall quality of life. He seemed to be the only one who could kick Arthur into gear when he was being difficult. David held his breath and willed his wizard to take the suggestion.

"Yes, all right," Arthur decided. "But you'll have to bear with me, this is a rudimentary translation at best. These phrases are not as cut and dry as Proto-Sinaitic or Ugaritic cuneiform. If not for the Semitic syntax I doubt I could have done it at all."

David coughed to suppress a laugh. He had recently been exposed to both of those ancient languages, however briefly. He hadn't perceived either of them to be anything close to "cut and dry." But his grandfather was something of an ancient language super-genius, whether Arthur realized it or not. If he said the Phaistos Disk translation was tricky, then he meant it.

Even though his first pass had taken less than a day while in a parked truck helped only by random photos while being run through a related but obscure ancient pictographic language.

David decided not to interrupt.

"There are only four archetypal stories from the ancient world," Arthur said thoughtfully. "Genres, if you like." He seemed to be waiting for objections, but getting none, continued. "There is the creation myth, of course, usually involving some deity or another bringing chaos into order. Second is the flood myth, in which the order reverts to chaos for a time before it is restored, and whichever iteration of Nûḥ happens to correspond to the particular morality of the society telling it. Then there is the lineage catalog, usually focusing on a specific line of kings or semi-divine mortals who did a great deed or founded the society. And finally, there is the giving of the law either by the divine, one of the god-kings, or some other prophetic individual."

"All four of which are found in the books of Moses," Father Matthew observed. "The first three before Genesis 11."

"True," Arthur agreed hesitantly. "Which is why, first and foremost, we should look at the first ten chapters of Genesis as a collection of epic myth stories. In terms of genre, I mean." Arthur's mind was wandering already.

"And the Disk?" Cat had been strangely silent about the Phaistos Disk for a while now. Based on her tone, she was clearly still dubious about the whole thing. But she still caused Arthur to focus.

"Ah yes," Arthur pushed his glasses up and consulted his notes.

To cut his reliance on David's phone, Arthur had sketched each of the Disk's segments into his spiral notebook. The overall result was a rough-looking little notepad that only Arthur seemed to understand. But it was also a notepad that held the secrets of the Phaistos Disk decoded after untold ages. David had taken pictures of every page and picture of that too, making his phone a good candidate to be the single most important smartphone in all of archeology. It was now happily charging in the rear kiosk through a complicated series of adapters and cords that David had worked out, which was a comfort of a different sort.

"So then," Arthur began, "the Disk is interesting because it contains two of those stories, and they are relegated quite precisely to each of the two sides, which is remarkable. Someone planned very well what they wanted to press into that clay spiral, without an inch to spare."

"Which two?" Cat asked, suspiciously.

"Nûḥ is one, right Arthur? You said there was a boat and the symbol for water?"

"Flood myth, yes," he corrected, "And based on the pictographs alone, it is a candidate for being the oldest one yet discovered. Older even than the Atra-Hasis or the most ancient Gilgamesh stories."

"And the other?" Cat demanded.

"Well, the flip side is a lineage tale of sorts. The origin story of a couple that their nation must have deemed important.

"A couple?" David asked. It seemed weird.

"Nations come from tribes, tribes from families, and families from couples. Yes."

"Adam and Eve come to mind," Matthew said.

"Well yes, a bit," Arthur admitted, "but this one is much less detailed than that, and there are other figures mentioned too. It's more of a tribal genealogy, starting when this couple met, after the flood event, but I'm not sure if these are their names or just descriptions." He held up his transcription and flipped between two pages. One series was a head with a mohawk next to a circle full of dots, the other a woman with various plants and animals.

"As far as I can tell, this name means "Important-Man" and the other something like "Kitchen-Wife.""

"Kitchen-Wife?" Cat mused. "That is what you are going with? You do realize that kitchens didn't exist, and cooking wasn't necessarily done by wives, no?"

"Well, yes, of course. But what more desirable quality to an ancient fisherman would there be than a good cook to make his wife?"

"I could think of a few things." Cat raised a mildly suggestive eyebrow at David, then stuck out her tongue toward Arthur's general direction. Arthur failed to notice either.

"The stories are intertwined, however, and in a rather interesting way." Arthur flipped between pages in his little book, comparing some of the repeated images. "Plus, it jumps around a little, which is unusual. It seems that these people are survivors of the flood. Much like Nûḥ and his wife, his sons, and their wives, in the Genesis version. The interesting part is nearly always the differences, which in this case is on the backside."

David cringed a bit. He was still getting used to the idea that there were other versions than the biblical flood story, but his curiosity was too strong to resist.

"Arthur, didn't you say there was an ale-wife in *Gilgamesh*?"

Arthur flipped pages in his little makeshift book for a moment and then cleared his throat. "Yes." Then, without elaboration or so much as a "once upon a time," he began. Everyone else was silent while he spoke. The chattering of merchants and the truckdriver's frustrated arguing in Arabic were his backdrop.

"'When the flood came, only one ship loaded animals. One family went. Went with livestock and clothing. Behold! The sea covers the livestock! Houses fall onto people. It happens. The flood happens!'" His reading was surprisingly dramatic.

Arthur had a storytelling voice? Cat looked at David with something between wonder and disbelief. David couldn't help but meet her gaze. Her eyes were gorgeous even with her smeared mascara. He shrugged back.

"Some of this might be past tense," Arthur apologized. "Happens, happened? I'm not sure yet. 'Trees fall!'" he continued undaunted. "'But one ship is loaded greatly. Behold! The sea covers the animals. The animals wash away. Struck by the...'" Arthur paused, then decided which word to commit to.

"'Struck by the sea monster.'"

David and Cat shared a silent surprised laugh. *Sea monster?* David mouthed. It was too much to hear his wizard speaking like this! He sounded like Nicholas Cage at a poetry jam. But David decided he liked it. Where had this Arthur been this whole time?

"'Behold!" Arthur bellowed again. A flourish with his hand this time. "The sea covers all creatures. The sandal-maker, the kitchen-wife, they swim like fish toward the lands of the very rich.'" He broke character again. "Actually, that might literally be 'the high hills,' or maybe 'mountain?'" he mumbled. "If the rich lived on the hillsides..."

Matthew cleared his throat, subtly pulling Arthur back.

"Ah, quite right, yes. Let's see." He continued his reading. "'Then, from the high hills, the great ships from the Important-Man divided—' he paused again, puzzling out his various notations.

"*Atra-Hasis* means 'important man.'" David noted, taking advantage of the lull. "Is the guy with the Mohawk Nûh?"

"Well, yes," Arthur said without looking up. "But not as we typically think of him. Perhaps a better title would be 'king?' Though if that translation is applied, then..." Arthur paused again, then took a little breath. "Oh, I see now! The circular shield is the city he rules over." He looked up and smiled, pleased with himself over this. "The kingly hairpiece can convey the important-man element without a modifying declarative attached to the—"

Matthew cleared his throat again. Arthur smiled up at him weakly. "Sorry, where was I?"

"'Great ships,' I believe," the priest said.

"Ah, yes. 'The great ships from the other branch of the good king came from the city. Ships with sides made of reeds. From this war came death. Famine. They barely escaped the attack. This was our own very important house, with leather-sided ships. Behold the first child! His branch-house—' No, scratch that, sorry. It's more like, 'Our house of wood comes from the great flood's good king.'" His pencil danced across the notebook even as he spoke. "Which, I suppose we could call the authority of Nûh. See, this symbol here designates the good-important-man as a High-King, different from the others that come later."

David craned his neck to see. The symbols meant nothing to him, but he didn't care. It was still the wildest thing he'd ever witnessed.

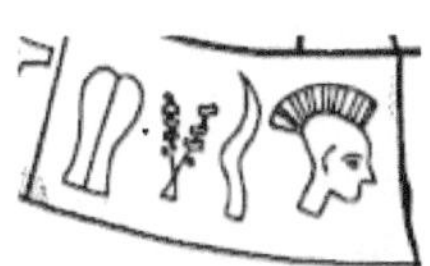

"And that's the last phrase," Arthur said with finality.

"It falls apart a bit at the end," Matthew noted. "What, pray-tell is the significance of a 'house of wood?'"

Again, David supposed that only Arthur's best friend could get away with that kind of criticism under such unfriendly circumstances.

"Well isn't it obvious?" Arthur puffed. "A wooden house would be high technology in those days, and the mark of true wealth for a king to have that much wood to spare."

Arthur mumbled something else about it still being a rough translation, but David didn't care. The linguistic connections his wizard was making on the fly were remarkable. David hadn't known the first thing about ancient languages just a few days ago, but he still understood the impossible thing Arthur had just managed. The pride he felt in his grandfather swelled, and he let it spill out in the form of a huge grin.

"And what does the other side say?" Cat demanded.

David thrilled. *That was only half?* Arthur had said the back was the interesting part. David was bursting to hear it.

"I beg your pardon," Matthew interrupted, changing the subject. "It appears as if we are being waved forward by that man over there. Mind your P's and Q's, everyone."

LXIX

Ras-Shamra Basecamp. Ugarit, Syria. Mel.

Mel had co-opted one of the freshly installed computer stations hours ago, for all the good it had done her with comms down. Then finally, after an insufferably long day, the connection to her network was reestablished. She still lacked the ability to track her vehicles, but in two quick breaths, she was finally logged in to her personal interface and reconnected to the world.

Dozens of notifications wanted her attention, but she singlemindedly swept them all away. Just as she had requested, the results of the deep search on Ryan Pitman was waiting for her. Also, as requested, it was exhaustively thorough.

She quickly tapped through the first pages of familiar information. It contained a CV and other documents, photos, and company reports. These she swiped past quickly, slowing her pace only when she got to the older materials. As she had expected, there was a great deal of information involving Aarons and Pitman at Durupinar.

AKA "Doomsday" mountain.

AKA Dr. Evan's secret shame.

The pictures and articles were numerous. One of the soldiers had made her a cup of tea from something he found in the supplies. She appreciated the gesture, if not the flavor. She drank it off regardless and refilled it twice before she finally found something.

It was a black and white picture that finally caught her eye, part of a full-page spread from a Turkish newspaper. The image depicted a ceremony atop a mountain, presided by the Turkish Government and attended by a small crowd. The auto-generated translation of the article indicated that it was the official opening of the Noah's Ark Monument Visitor Center in the early '90s. Kneeling over a just-sacrificed goat—a local tradition like the West's ribbon cutting—was a young Wyatt Aarons. And standing next to him was his second partner, the man who had replaced Dr. Evans, Dr. Ryan Pitman.

AKA her late father's trusted friend.

AKA her Uncle Ryan.

AKA her last-minute addition to the Dilmun team.

AKA her insurance.

AKA my glaring mistake?

Ryan Pitman looked just as she remembered him during the time he had worked for her father. His face was younger, smiling. He was mostly bald and distinctively wrinkled. The man had always looked so respectably old. But it was a tiny detail in the candid photo-op that had caught her attention. She zoomed in. Pitman's arm was outstretched in a handshake of congratulations with the Turkish officiate. The evidence in the little digitized photo couldn't have been more damning if it had been written out in actual words and letters. Even with the pixelated distortion of scanned newsprint, she knew a raven tattoo when she saw it. Mel Chen had been out-played since before she'd even begun the game. But at least she now knew why, if not exactly how.

Uncle Ryan is one of them!

She had to find a way to track her lost team members. If only the vehicles' geolocators were working, but no, she needed another answer. Mel sat and sipped her plain and simple tea until a plain and simple idea presented itself. What a fool she had been. One of those vehicles did have a working geolocator on it, of a sort.

She closed the file and pulled up a comms window to her people. "I need you to track the location of a phone for me. It was recently placed onto our private network under the name David Evans. Also, lock out Dr. Ryan Pitman's access to everything. Codes, passwords, all of it. Blacklist him and set up a special worldwide search centered on his last known location northbound from Ras-Shamra. Find him. Use every available resource. I want to know the second you get a hit on either one."

Mel leaned back in satisfaction, this chaos quelled for the moment at least. She had a plan, and the whole internet was working for her again. Besides, this Russian-style tea wasn't half bad, considering the circumstances. Maybe someone could hunt up a cinnamon stick for her. That would be lovely.

LXX

European Route E91. Northbound, Turkey. David.

"Very happy you are now. I am the best tour guide money buys!"

The Kurdish man who had waved them over now sat smiling and babbling from the floorboard in the back of the TIGR with Arthur's rucksack. He didn't seem to care that there was no chair for him, simply ecstatic that the four Westerners had hired him for their driving tour into Turkey. David was just glad the guy spoke okay English. Arthur's Kurdish was about two decades rusty and had never been more than passable to begin with, or so he claimed.

Their new Turkish Guide had not hesitated. He'd simply motioned them out of the lane and held up a hand for them to stay put, then trotted off and argued with the men controlling the Turkish gate for a few seconds. He came back to collect some money, not caring that it was a mix of American Dollars and British Pounds for the briefest second. Then, to David's surprise, he hopped inside. The border guards waved them through without so much as a glance at a passport or a question about their business in Turkey. At this rate, where would they all be this time next week? Australia?

With their escape plan back in gear again and the border a few miles behind them, Arthur nodded, reseated his bedraggled hat, and flipped his little spiral notebook to the second part of his translation. "Now then, the other side of the Disk begins with: 'Understand this about the war. Remember the wood-before. Before our side-wood.' Wait, oh I see now, it's wealth again.

The wood is reserved for the prestigious. So, it would be: "Remember the wealth before, Before our side-wealth. Understand this. Behold the first wealth.'"

"Family," Cat interrupted. "It's neither wealth nor sticks. You were right the first time, only it is not 'house of wood,' or 'branch-house,' it is more like a 'house-branch.'"

"Oh! Like on a family tree," David affirmed, "A house branch is uncles and nephews and all that. "

Arthur considered it, sucked on his pencil thoughtfully, then made some notes in his spiral book. He consulted the scratch paper and flipped around a bit. It was maddening. Then finally, looking up from his notes he said, "Actually, that's rather insightful and fits quite nicely. Thank you, Dr. deMata."

David beamed. Cat gave him a wry little smile. Maybe she was coming around to the idea that the Disk could be translated after all. Or was that just for him? He wasn't sure anymore.

"'Remember the war,'" Arthur began again after a few moments of mumbling. "'Remember our... ancestors. Before the family tree split.' Yes, that's quite good. 'The Important-Man.' That's Nûḥ again, of course. 'He is made an important god-king! Number three from a woman. Oxhide. Behold! Another god-King. He fathers Oarman with the leather boat. Behold! He is a god-King.' This is the genealogy part you see," Arthur explained, looking up.

David found this amusing. Apparently, everybody got to be a god-king in the ancient world, including Noah. With a start, he remembered something Arthur had said days ago about the 'mythologically real' King Gilgamesh. *"He was deified after he died."*

"'And that one...' meaning King Oarman, I suppose." Arthur paused, again searching for the right word in English. "I don't know, perhaps, 'fosters?' 'Oarman fosters that one who is related to our ancestor.' I suppose we could say great-great-grandfather or patriarch maybe? 'Behold the God-King! He fathered Oarman.'"

Arthur looked up at this point, slightly befuddled. "And this is where it gets confusing, but perhaps with the idea of family? 'Storm! Behold! The most important men come from our,' uh, let's go with, 'side of the family. A second family of important men. A family of God-kings! Important men with a woman.' Frankly, I have no idea what that is supposed to mean, unless it's a wife or a daughter."

Shrugs and head shakes passed between everyone, then Arthur smiled weakly and cleared his throat. He was at the end and it was time for the great crescendo.

"'The great sea monster caused the great flood!'" he all but shouted, "'Our family is taken, they board their livestock. The animal flood happened! Our house is important!'"

David glanced around at the others, expecting more. "Is that all of it? The whole thing?"

Arthur lowered his notes and looked up over his glasses. "Technically there's one more phrase, but I think it's just another name. A signature perhaps. Something like 'King Goes-to-War.' Perhaps that's an indication that the war that was mentioned was over finally. Whatever it was that caused them to flee in their leather-sided boats."

"Now that's a cracking good finish," Matthew stated. "I suppose that King Oarman was rather important to them. Seeing as they wanted to connect him to Noah and whatnot. It's a shame we don't know more."

Arthur closed his little book and shrugged. "Yes, he was probably some well-known local king of the day. It's rare enough to have a complete tablet, though. Keep in mind, that everything will need to be verified, starting with the Ugarit translation tablet. We will need to bring Yosef in on it of course to verify my—our—interpretations, but it won't stop us from publishing. Not this hasty field translation, of course, that's madness, but the interpretation process is more than enough to keep a room full of scholars busy for the next few decades. I'm sure they'll be happy to pick apart every word and write whole essays on why I'm wrong with my translation. Perhaps, Dr. deMata, you would like to have the first honor?"

Cat smiled devilishly, but David knew it was all in good fun. So this was Arthur in a good mood. He'd never seen his wizard so happy.

"That's pretty amazing Arthur," David said genuinely, but something still didn't sit right as he mulled the story over. Maybe it was just the idea of different Noah stories getting to him again. He wasn't sure he'd ever get used to that. "So, the first side is a flood account, and the backside is a lineage of one of Noah's sons and how there was a third-generation war?"

Arthur nodded. "Yes. The war was between the reed-boat people and the leather-boat people. Both who claimed to be the descendants of Nûḥ, if you are right about the family construct. It would have to be Shem's line, I suppose. Then at some point, the leather-boat branch of the family sailed away in fear from the reed-boat men and settled somewhere else. Given where the Disk was found, perhaps it's even an early account of the first settling of Crete from the mainland. Wouldn't that be something?"

Cat was tapping her perfect teeth with one manicured nail. Whatever she was thinking, her gears were turning.

"And what about the thing you said before, Arthur? 'The road of the sword of fire branches out from the city of the flood's Important-Man,' or something?"

"Ah," Arthur blanched. "I may have been taking that a bit too literally. Likely, it is a metaphor to describe the war. You see, here is the first phrase, and again here?" He pointed to the transcribed drawings in his notebook. It sure looked to David like a man and an ancient cudgel or something, but who was he to argue? More than once it appeared right after a boomerang thing too.

David grabbed his phone and pulled up the high-res image of the Disk Arthur had been working from.

"If I had to guess," Arthur continued, "the Disk was likely a record of this fearful retreat by the leather-boat people, and a plea for everyone involved to remember the flood event. Someone, this King-Goes-to-War person perhaps, wanted to recognize their common ancestry. To remind them that if the houses continued to war, the sea monster might well see fit to destroy both seafaring branches all over again."

"That's incredible, Arthur." David meant it. "Chaos leads to apocalypse, right?"

"Indeed," Arthur agreed.

David was about to ask for more about the sea-monster part, but Matthew beat him with a more practical question. "And just how did you translate it all so fast, Arthur? Even for you, that's quite remarkable."

"What? Oh, well that was quite easy, once I figured out the syntax."

"The syntax?" Cat asked suspiciously.

"Well yes, it's quite extraordinary really. As I started to say, the images are not phonemic at all as many have theorized, but entirely pictographic and representational. Frankly, it's not a very complex language. Their written vocabulary seems to be quite limited. This must be quite early in its development. I shall have to thank Rabbi Yosef if we ever see him again. These symbols are very, very old. A clear precursor to the same Proto-Sinaitic that Yosef and his team cracked. I can't speak to his beliefs on all that medieval *Kabbalah* silliness, but his Proto-Sinaitic checks out. The Disk's syntax is practically a straightforward ancestor to Old Ugaritic and Lydian. There are only twenty-two symbols in the later Proto-Sinaitic, so memorizing them wasn't particularly difficult, and it made the recognition of these earlier transitional pictographs essentially a matter of cross-referencing with the translation tablet Wyatt discovered. We extrapolated a bit on the symbols I didn't have a reference for as you know, but that's something I can work on later when I get back to my library."

Cat was staring at Arthur incredulously, her jaw slack in a very unladylike fashion. David tried to swallow a smile as he shook his head at his wizard's massive humblebrag. Arthur hadn't liked Yosef very much. Obviously, a day made a world of difference to an ancient languages tutor when he discovered that someone's translations worked.

"What?" Arthur asked, looking from one to another of the others for a clue.

"I daresay Arthur," Mathew soothed, "that you are one of the few people on the planet who would consider memorizing an entire ancient language in an afternoon to not be particularly difficult." Arthur blinked and looked around. David nodded his agreement then broke into a huge smile.

"Well, technically it was two," Arthur grumbled, adjusting his coat.

The car burst into laughter for a subjective minute while Arthur sat by grumpily. The laughter defused the excitement, and everyone deflated a little. They were perfectly exhausted, all except for their new guide who was all eyebrows and teeth. The local man sensed the lull in the conversation and pounced on it.

"Much of Noah you speak! You maybe are want to see the Noah's Ark? Is a very long drive but is museum and visitor center there. Is near Durupinar! Very famous! American archeologist Wyatt Aarons had discovered it on Doomsday Mountain. I will take you!"

"I've seen it," Arthur said flatly, much to the man's great disappointment. "But yes, by all means, please take us to Wyatt Aarons' Ark."

The guide's expression exploded into wondrous joy, but something scratched at the back of David's mind. Going to Doomsday just felt—wrong— somehow. Arthur had literally just unpacked an uncountable number of clues, but they were going to the ark why, on a hunch? It felt way too much like running away.

LXXI

Ras-Shamra Basecamp. Ugarit, Syria. Mel.

Colonel Raskolnikov burst into the Rabbi's tent as though he was storming a beachhead. Mel entered gracefully a moment later and waved for the hulk to sit down. Raskolnikov relaxed into a formal "at ease" position.

"My apologies Dr. Ibrahim, I hope we did not disturb you in prayer or meditation." It was a polite and very obvious lie. The very surprised Yosef Ibrahim stood by his bunk in mid-dress, his arms precariously frozen halfway into a billowy shirt.

"M-Miss Chen?" Mel glanced at the man's naked forearm. No tattoos, that was good at least. Yosef stood awkwardly for another moment, then shrugged the shirt on the rest of the way. "I was told you had arrived," he stammered, "it is a pleasure." He bobbed his head in a little polite gesture then continued buttoning his shirt. "Am I needed with the rest of the team finally?"

"The team has gone," she stated bluntly. "While you have been enjoying the amenities of my basecamp's mobile shower, I have been trying to track them."

Ibrahim looked confused, then startled. "Gone? Do you mean they have not yet returned?"

"That's right. I was hoping you could tell me why I just tracked one of my vehicles crossing the border into Turkey?"

"Turkey?" His surprise seemed genuine. "Well, that's fabulous! Though I'm saddened that they chose to begin without me."

"It was a bit rushed," Mel said, nonplussed. If this man was playing games with her, she was not amused. But he wasn't trying to lie either, which was interesting. "And just what is it they have chosen to begin?"

The rabbi moved to his shoes and started working them on. "Ah, I suspect they have found the starting point of the path."

"The path? What path?"

"It is called the Path of the Flaming Sword. It is the path to Eden, hidden by God from all mankind except to those worthy of finding it. Arthur and I spoke at length about the subject on the plane. He must have found a clue and felt that haste was necessary. I am sad to not be a part of it, but perhaps it is for the best." He grabbed his vest from a hook and deflated onto his cot.

Mel considered the one-sided conversation. So, Yosef's little lecture with

Dr. Evans' companions squatting on the floor had been for Evans' benefit after all. The professor hadn't shown any indication of listening until the subject had changed to ancient languages, but Yosef had seen through it. This rabbi was subtle but shrewd. Mel admired both of those qualities.

"And just where is this path?"

"Why, no one knows. That's the very point. It is not a place as much as a metaphysical journey of the spirit. It is a way of looking at life. In the Kabbalistic Tree of Life, the destination is the Crown Sephirot. Heaven itself. The starting point, however, is less clear. It is the city of the divine king, so in many ways, it is the very thing that Mr. Wyatt Aarons was looking for. That's why he contacted me through the company directory in the first place, you see. He claimed to have a theory related to my Proto-Hebraic translation work. He asked that I come to be on the Dilmun team and perhaps translate some of his findings. And so, here I am. Though, he is not."

His facts on this last part checked out at least. Aarons had done exactly that, and she had the digital paper trail to prove it. "The city of the divine king?" Mel's love of legends threatened to eclipse the task at hand, she shoved it away and focused. This was about her team. "Does such a place exist on Earth?"

The rabbi laughed. "Unquestionably. Hundreds of them. Especially in the ancient world. Most kings, pharaohs, and Caesars claimed some form of divinity. Many called themselves a 'son of god.' Though, if I had to pick one city, I suppose I would argue for Jerusalem as the greatest of them all, many times over. However, I do not think that is what you mean."

"Then why pray-tell are they headed north into Turkey? There is nothing up there but goats and Kurdish insurgents unless you count Dr. Evans' old work at—"

She stopped. What a fool she had been. It was logical for Dr. Evans to run for familiar territory. He spoke the language, he understood the people, there were reasonable airports, no military roadblocks, and friendliness toward Americans, for starters. Who knows, Dr. Evans might already know where this city of the divine king was or have even zeroed in on Wyatt Aarons and now be headed to rescue him.

Yes, it made perfect sense that Dr. Evans had run. Ryan Pitman was her man, so to Evans' mind, Mel had betrayed them. And given that Wyatt Aarons had sent Evans his private journal, she couldn't rule out the possibility that the two had been colluding all along.

Mel had a headache. She needed damage control, and fast.

"Thank you, Dr. Ibrahim, you have been incredibly helpful. Please consider yourself on retainer for the time being, and continue to enjoy the amenities of this camp as long as you like."

"Certainly, yes, thank you, any time. Blessings be upon you."

But Mel was already to the tent flap with the Colonel in step behind her. The rabbi would have to sort out his own confusion. *Perhaps a grant would help? A foundation dedicated to the study of ancient Semitic languages?* She filed that idea away for another day.

"Colonel, please contact your Russian friends at the Bassel Al-Assad airbase that doesn't exist. Your countrymen were kind enough to loan us the TIGRs; while there is no need to mention that we have misplaced them, I would very much like one of their helicopters to retrieve them. Something long-range and fast. I want you flying it."

Raskolnikov didn't say a word, he just quirked a half-smile, stomped out his cigarette, and stomped off toward the coms tent.

Mel only hoped Ivan had time to spring whatever trap the traitor Pitman had set before the professor blindly bumbled into it.

LXXII

European Route E91. Northbound towards Antakya, Turkey. Arthur.

Evans felt much better now that they were out of Syria. Turkey was a country slightly wider than Texas, except a great deal more mountainous by orders of magnitude. They were smack in the middle of its southern parts, and Doomsday Mountain lay on the far east side of those twisting inhospitable roads. The further east his little cadre traveled those mountainous trails, the farther from civilized parts and Westernized cities they would be too. Just finding gas would be a challenge. This was not going to be an easy road trip, but at least they had slipped through Mel's fingers, a perfectly logical reason to go to Wyatt's Ark. Plus, it would give him days of wonderful alone time with the translation tablets.

Evans' time with Wyatt had ended in that ridiculous prison cell in the shadow of Ararat. But that didn't preclude an additional week trying to get home. Another horrible bus ride, that miserable train, and a few days in the

Istanbul embassy had given him enough time to stew and swear he would never return to this godforsaken land. Then, when he finally made it back to sane and civilized parts, Evans had only just begun his struggle to keep any sort of job within the University. It had taken years to rise to the level of respected inter-college tutor he'd eventually settled into. Never in his wildest imaginings could he have thought that he would neglect that post and be traveling this part of the world again. And it was all Wyatt's fault, wherever the devil he was.

Though he had to admit, the roads had improved significantly since the 1980s. They had already put some good miles behind them on whatever mostly-empty Turkish highway this was. Once again, Evans considered the strange company he was keeping this time. An ancient language scholar, two teenagers, and a priest? It was like the beginning of a bad joke. And that was not even counting their new Kurdish guide squatting in the floorboards, providing endless facts about the scenery outside. At least he spoke English, thank the lord. Things seemed to be looking up at last. Or so Evans deeply hoped.

"Dr. Evans," deMata's accented voice sang out from behind him, "Can you explain how a pictographic Hebrew precursor language came to be written on a clay disk on an island in the middle of the Mediterranean?"

Evans wasn't sure what she was getting at. Everything they were doing was maddeningly bad form, and they were well into the land of wild speculation at this point. He was quite sure he had no idea whatsoever and said as much.

"Because," she continued, her voice thick with unspoken accusations, "when the Minoans of Crete disappeared, the Mycenaean people arrived, took their writing and other elements, and evolved it. Linear-B is a proto-Greek language. There is no connection to the Semitic language or culture."

Evans had no answer for her, given that she was supposed to be exactly right. On the other hand, as long as they were speculating wildly, if pictographic languages of the Minoans were a wholly different language family than Linear-B, then it would go a long way to explaining why no one had ever been able to translate the former by attempting to reverse-engineer the latter. Perhaps much like the Minoan flush toilets, the island's Mycenean usurpers had simply never been able to understand how it worked.

Matthew broke in. "Could there be a connection between your legendary Sea Peoples and the Minoans of Crete? As I recall, you said that those same Sea Peoples were responsible for wiping out Ugarit in the end, did you not? Do you think there might perhaps be a connection to our Phaistos Disk? Considering the section in the story about boats migrating away from war and whatnot."

Evans pondered this. It made some sense. Quite a bit, in fact. He had his own private opinions regarding the mysterious seafaring race referred to only as the "Sea Peoples," but he had long held a pet theory that perhaps they were the people who had eventually tamed and settled Crete. No way to prove it, of course; his feeble attempts to make those connections stick had been more tenuous than Uncle Arthur's Minotaur theories. Thus, he had relegated such thinking to the realm of chess games with his best friend and general imaginative nonsense. But the dates did fit, however roughly, and Matthew had an interesting point about the war theme. Not a normal flood-myth motif by any means.

"You mentioned Sea Peoples before," David ventured. "Who were they?"

"A myth," the girl answered before Evans could formulate a different one. "They are a fable. A morality tale to teach vigilance to societies vulnerable to sea attack."

"Fable?" Evans heard himself say, more defensively than he'd intended. He twisted sideways in his giant seat so that the kids in the back could see him. "Nearly every coastal nation from 2600-1000 B.C. wrote about them in fear. Meanwhile Troy, Agamemnon, Jericho, and even the Minoans, or rather Aegeans, who lived where your Phaistos Disk was found, were all believed to be the stuff of legends until great scholars like Heinrich Schliemann and Sir Arthur Evans changed the way we look at myths. Some myths are true, Dr. deMata. Or at least based on a seed of truth. I see no reason why the legend of the Sea Peoples, the Israelite Exodus, or even the flight of the Lydians might not also be true." Evans felt a little silly arguing with a teenager, but he had swallowed about enough of her sass and veiled accusations for today. Prodigy or not, Evans wasn't going to take any more lip from the rude little Castellana with her intolerance for myths and legends. He just hoped David wouldn't mention his recent scathing criticism of Uncle Sir Arthur's overblown faith in Greek myths.

Come to think of it, he wasn't sure why he was defending the position at all. Yet there was a limit to his graciousness when it came to Sir Arthur and the ancient stories that were his bread and butter. The all-but-forgotten tour guide smiled encouragingly at him from the back.

"Lydians?" David tried again. "That sounds familiar." The boy's insatiable hunger for knowledge was always drawing Evans out, but not this time. The Lydian tales were a further pet theory of his about the origin of the Sea Peoples, but David could just wait until term and read about the plight of Lydia himself.

"Oh, good lord," Evans gasped, his mouth catching up with his brain. "The Lydians!"

Somewhere in the back of his head, he had already made the connection. Now, to the core of his being, he knew it was a piece of the puzzle. He sat with his mouth open as his conscious mind raced to catch up with what his subconscious must have been working out for the last few hours. He'd simply been so preoccupied with the what of the translation, that he hadn't bothered to consider the why or how of the Phaistos Disk's content.

DeMata eyed him suspiciously from the back seat with crossed arms, waiting for him to explain himself. But Evans wasn't even sure where to start. He wasn't an expert in the modern stuff like Greek mythology, and he was sure he would jumble it up if he tried. He grunted, closed his eyes, and took himself to his mental library instead.

"Lydia and Ugarit are the same place," he faltered. "The former became the latter, eventually taking over the whole coast up to Turkey. But there is a legend, dating from a time well earlier, that says half of the Lydians left. They took to the sea after a famine."

"Famine?" Matthew wondered. "Like in your translation, Arthur? 'From this war came death. Famine. They barely escaped the attack,' I believe you said."

Blast Matthew and his memory for verse. He probably had the whole thing memorized already, and Evans wasn't even remotely finished translating it properly.

"Wait a minute," David interjected. "I do know this. They played games, right? There was a famine, and every other day they ate, but on the days they couldn't they played games to pass the time. It saved them, and finally, after years of that or whatever, they had some big contest. Then, half of them got into boats and left, never coming back because they went and kickstarted the Greek civilization or something." He looked around at Evans and then deMata for confirmation, finding only surprise in both. "Is that right?"

"That's pretty spot on, David," Evans said, impressed. "Where did you learn that?" He doubted that the somewhat obscure writings of Herodotus had been part of David's homeschool studies, no matter how eccentric Karen's curriculum might have been.

"A Ted Talk video I saw a few months ago." The teen proclaimed. "There was this game designer who did one about *World of Warcraft* and worldbuilding. She talked about the Lydians, gaming, and how it saved their civilization. It was all pretty epic. Some ancient historian wrote about it, I think."

Evans wasn't sure what half of that meant, why war would make the world better, or who this game designer named Ted was, but he didn't fight it. The way David accessed his imagination for making rational connections was astounding. Insight came through many pathways, he supposed. "Herodotus," he clarified. "The historian's name was Herodotus."

"The Father of History himself!" Matthew pondered aloud. "I didn't know that particular legend. Very interesting."

"Hold on," David continued, clearly still processing something out. "If the Minoans of Crete were responsible for the Greek civilization, but the Lydians also split off and eventually became the Greeks, then does that mean that it was the Lydians who settled in Crete and became the Minoans?"

Again, David looked from deMata to Evans for his error, but Evans couldn't think of one straight off.

"I suppose that timeline fits," Evans said. "Though it's based on quite a bit of speculation and circumstantial evidence from later writings across at least three very different cultures."

Evans allowed this new idea access to his mental library. He guided the Lydians toward the relevant books of his mind and let them have their way once more. There might well be something to connect the cultures, if he could just think of it. This time when the books opened they stayed aloft. No need for a table in one's mind of course. Evans even pulled pages out, tacked them to a wall of nothingness, and arranged them into categories. He cringed at the idea of destroying books, reminding his logical self that it was just a mental exercise and he should calm down.

And so, he sat like that for a minute, or maybe an hour, tearing books apart as one concept kept bubbling up over and over, demanding to be addressed, until there was a stack of imaginary pages piled high with the obscure little idea repeating over and over.

"The labrys," he finally said with equal parts certainty and surprise.

"The double-sided crescent ax?" deMata asked. "What of it?"

"It's one of the great images of Crete," Evans said. "It mirrors the shape of the bull horns, yet also is a symbol of the divine feminine. It is even associated with the snake-goddess of the Mycenean usurpers. And worth noting perhaps, one of the very few other examples of the Disk's language can be found on what I believe you called the 'desiccated old bronze ax' unearthed in Arkalochori cave."

DeMata scowled, but Evans couldn't let himself be distracted now.

"Regardless, before any of that, the labrys was undeniably Lydian." He turned to David so fast and intensely that he saw the boy jump. "David, will you pull that image of the Disk up again?"

As David did so, Evans turned to a blank page and sketched a proper labrys for all to see.

"See here?" Evans said, awkwardly zooming in to the digital spiral on the phone. "This symbol for family—the one I thought was a branch at first. It is similar to a double-sided stick, like a slingshot Y-shape. It's a rudimentary labrys. You had it right David, it means family-tree."

"*Dios mio,*" deMata breathed. "Family, branch, woman?"

"A Tree of Life," David whispered. "But like a family tree."

Evans couldn't manage much more than a nod. He hadn't thought of that. He let the young anthropologist's sassy-but-brilliant mind catch up and finish the thought for him.

"The labrys symbolizes very many things to us today," She said, reaching out for the notepad. "It was a pagan symbol and is used by modern feminists to symbolize the power of womanhood. But it is also one of the most ancient symbols of the Greek world," she continued. "We do not know its true origin. It always accompanies goddesses, and was probably the symbol for the mythological *arche*, the beginning of creation to the Greeks."

"*Mater-arche,*" Evans provided. "Matriarchy. 'The mother who creates.' 'Archeology' and 'archaic' are also etymologically linked. Of course, the labrys often referred to the Achaean people symbolically as well. A sort of generic term for the Greeks used by poets like Homer." After he said it, Evans heard it. *Arche-aeans?*

DeMata nodded and shivered as if to shake the rest loose. "There is one exception to the goddess connection."

Evans racked his brain but it didn't come.

"*Zeus Labrayndeus,*" she provided, softly.

"Zeus of the Labrys ax! Of course!"

DeMata nodded to Evans, clearly having heard what she was hoping to. "It was an image worshiped by an ancient cult in western Turkey."

"In Lydia?" David asked.

"Yes," Evans and deMata agreed.

The ancient city of Labraunda was as far again to the west as Doomsday

Mountain was east, but at least there were fewer mountains and freedom-fighting rebel groups that way. Should they go west instead? The wrong decision would cost them a week or more.

"Zeus was the father of the gods, wielding the power of the feminine goddess," deMata explained. "More than a contradiction, it would have been a deep blasphemy to the worshipers of either god. Yet, it existed."

David soaked this in. Evans could see the gears of the boy's mind turning wildly. Evans was glad to have someone else to give the lesson, even if it was a somewhat unlikely tutor. Or perhaps it was precisely the right one? deMata was young, beautiful, and brilliant. It was the most natural thing in the world, when he really thought about it. Even the Greeks would have been hard-pressed to find a better model for a muse of knowledge and beauty than this young woman. He smiled and thought of Elisabeth, the exotic, brilliant, and alluring young Englishwoman he had courted and loved. Still loved. Every bit the muse in her own right, frankly.

"But that is not the only time the Greeks and Lydians supposedly connected through womanhood," deMata continued. "According to the mythology, there was a Lydian queen named Omphale, said to be the daughter of the river Lardanos. Heracles, the son of Zeus, was required to serve her for a time as penance for an act of violence."

"Serve?" David asked. "What, like a slave?"

"Honestly, yes," deMata said. "Some accounts say he was forced to do the labor of a woman and even dress as one, as well as perform sexual favors." David turned a shade redder. DeMata did not. "But Heracles also conquered Omphale's enemies. He slew a river serpent and captured the simian trickster people. Eventually, she wed him."

"Wow," David said, coughing a little. "Mobs, ape-men, a boss fight, then marrying a goddess at the end? Sounds like a great tabletop scenario." Evans didn't get the joke but deMata snickered for him.

"Aren't there accounts that tell of a son born to Omphale and Heracles?" Evans probed, his Herodotus creeping back in fuzzy formlessness.

"Yes," deMata replied. "Various names were given to the son of Heracles by the Lydian woman. But many point to a Heraclid dynasty of kings who ruled Lydia for an age thereafter."

"Right!" Evans said, remembering. The book of his mind snapped into his hand from the imaginary place against his baseboard at home. "And one of those Heraclean kings was Ninus, founder of Ras-Shamra."

"Wow," David said again. "You guys are making me dizzy. Next, you'll be telling me there is a Greek version of the flood myth and all this Noah's Ark flood stuff was really just a retelling of Heracles."

Evans and deMata looked at each other nervously, neither wanting to be the one to say it. She broke first. "His name was Deucalion." She explained. "He was the king of Crete before his son Idomeneus succeeded him and led the kingdom into the Trojan War."

David shook his head in disbelief, but there was nothing to be done. Evans felt like he'd just asked David to swallow an Ark full of animals and drink it down with an ocean's worth of floodwater. But there was no going back now. The kid was getting an entire university education dumped on him in a weekend.

"According to one version," Evans clarified, "Deucalion was the son of Minos and the grandson of Zeus. Making him Heracles's nephew, technically. To survive the flooding, he built an ark and landed in Greece, founding it."

"Minos? As in Minoan?" But it was clear that David already knew the answer. "It all connects back to Noah's ark, doesn't it? All of it. It's a story so deep everybody had a version, they just kept changing the names, dates, and place of landing to be their particular land."

There was a pregnant silence as everyone processed what had just happened.

"But if that's the case," David thought aloud, "then Mr. Aarons was wrong. This path of the flaming sword isn't about the Doomsday mountain Ark at all. We'd need to go west to Lydia. Or what about Crete? I mean, that's where the Disk was from, after all."

If he was honest, Evans was rather pleased with this idea. And not just the part about proving Wyatt wrong. He thrilled at the idea of walking where Sir Arthur had done his famous work, seeing the restored Knossos Palace, and searching for clues on Crete instead of following Wyatt on some wild goose chase.

"What do you want to do, Arthur?" Matthew asked. "West and east are in opposite directions, I think you'll find. Psalm 103 comes to mind." Matthew, with his dry wit, being clever again.

"Crete is, of course, an island," Evans thought aloud. "And the land of Lydia was up the far northwest coast of Turkey. If we went to either, I suppose we would be better off jogging over to the coast and finding a proper boat than trying to drive any of it."

The coast of Turkey bent west then doglegged north along the part of the Mediterranean known as the Aegean Sea. Odysseus' ancient stomping ground was an elongated embayment filled with islands and framed by Greece, Turkey, and Crete. The TIGR was still quite close to the sea, if relatively far away from the land of Labraunda proper. It wasn't Crete, but if the clues truly were leading them to Lydia then perhaps it was time to find alternate transportation and ditch the not-so-subtle war truck. Evans' head hurt.

"Coast? Boat!" The guide said excitedly. "Yes, yes! Let us go to my cousin's hotel in Antakya! It is not far! Then tomorrow I will take you to Samandaği and we will hire the very finest of boats. You will see."

Cousin? David mouthed to deMata, laughing.

"Hospitality is very important in the Middle East," she answered. "And a real bed sounds nice."

"If I might be so bold, Arthur," Matthew cooed wryly, "we are nearly out of petrol and we already switched to the reserve tank some time ago."

Ah, so that was it. Reality was rearing its chaotic head through Matthew's voice of reason.

But it still snapped Evans out of his temporary insanity. Turkey was a large and dangerous country with far more problems than provinces. No need to create more. He sighed.

"Very well sir," he said to the guide. "Direct us to Antakya if you please. We can decide on our final destination later."

"Ejder!" the man said enthusiastically, already pulling out his phone to make the arrangements. The man's name, Evans realized. They hadn't bothered to learn it. *I didn't, anyway.*

"What are all those places?" David asked.

"Well, Samandaği is named for the mountain of St. Symeon," Evans explained. "*Dagi* and *Dagh* both mean 'mountain,' you see. Lots of those around here. It was a famous port city in the Middle Ages. And you've heard of Antakya I'm quite sure, though probably by its Western name. It was an important Roman river-city long before the crusader knights ever used it as a staging area and started building castles. To medieval man, it was always called Antioch."

"I pray we find a warmer welcome than the crusaders," Matthew joked. Evans didn't find it funny.

LXXIII

Antakya, Turkey. Mr. Suit.

The man in the suit stood watch. He hadn't expected to be back "home" in Turkey so soon. Or more accurately, to be back home in Kurdistan. Modern political borders were small irritations at best for his people. His was a cultural nation that spanned three countries and generally ignored most modern political barriers. A people that hailed from a time well before recorded history. And he had just crossed back into his people's ancient lands.

It also felt like Syria had chewed him up and spat him out. The scratches on his cheek burned where the little Spanish witch had scratched him. New aches and bruises nagged at him, and his wrist was wrenched again from his dive onto a moving vehicle. He even fretted like an old woman over the bloodstains on his lapel when Dr. Pitman was not looking. He shrugged his shoulders and felt the weight of his new pistol calm him.

One phone call to the loyal brothers and they had a plan. Dr. Pitman had driven faster than was safe along those twisting back roads. He was playing things close to the chest, but the man in the ruined suit wouldn't have dared to say anything. He had learned that lesson long ago as a small starving boy. He smiled at the distant memory, forgetting the insignificant pains of today.

*　　*　　*

In Şırnak, he had been born and abandoned by a loveless mother. In Şırnak, a little boy in rags had first seen the Americans. The two men had crossed the street near the alleyway where he was sleeping. Their English was what first caught his attention. The boy watched with fascination as the two white men were welcomed into a small house. He had never seen an American before, much less two. The local man reached out and shook the hands of the outsiders, laughed at some shared joke, then invited them in.

Curiosity got the better of the boy, and he crept up onto the barred window to peer in. The meeting happened in broken Kurdish and some English, but he knew only some words of the latter. It became immediately clear that the man who owned the house was an important man in town. The boy didn't know the man's name but knew that the house belonged to a person who commanded respect, knew things, and could get things. It was also the first time the boy ever saw the raven tattoo.

The boy in the rags watched the three men eat a meal fit for kings. A motherly woman as beautiful as a queen served them with grace and hospitality unlike any the boy had ever witnessed. He shook with anticipation, his mouth watering at the smells of the feast and yearning for a taste. He hoped they would leave some for him. He would check their garbage later and find out. The feast kept his tiny attention, but it was the wealthy look of the white men that emboldened him to act foolishly.

The boy followed the pair of American Southerners all afternoon. Finally, in the crowded open market, he tried to take the bald man's cloth bag and failed. In a flash, the man snatched the boy's wrist and pulled him to his tiptoes. The surprising raw strength of the balding American shocked him as much as anything. And then, that tattoo again, peeking out at him from the American's dirty sleeve.

"Well now, what do we have here? Look, Wyatt, it's a job applicant for that valet position we have available."

"Poor kid. He looks hungry." The man pantomimed eating. "You hungry there, son?"

*   *   *

Eventually, the boy would learn the meaning of their words as the story was retold to him a hundred times. Stories had power, just as names had power. He learned that the men were Ark hunters, not the first to visit Şırnak. The ancient name of his birth town had been Sehr-i Nuh, he now knew. Words in the old tongue, claiming this "the village of Noah." And why not? It was located deep in eastern Turkey, near the place of Noah's landing recorded in the holy books. Later, the name morphed into Sernah, and finally Şırnak — although various businesses in the city had kept the original name. Oblivious Bible-tourists and scholars hosted by Şırnak University sometimes passed through on their way to Mt. Ararat and elsewhere. They often slept comfortably under the large and faded Sehr-I Nuh Otel sign, ignorant of the scathing irony. All of this now amused the man in the suit greatly.

But those two men had been different. They took that boy in rags to places he never could have dreamed, and what followed changed him forever. They had led him to a real family after all. What squalor would he be in now, if not for the family? Would he even be alive? He owed everything to them, and this was his opportunity to finally repay that debt. To show them what he was really made of, no matter the personal cost. He pulled his stained sleeve down over the edge of his own tattoo and shrugged his shoulders.

Remember who you are. Remember what you are.

Here, on a not-so-different Turkish market street, the city bustled with ancient commerce, deep culture, and long-lived history. The vendors and tourists were going about their day, obliviously reenacting the ancient dance of cultures in this part of the world. This was Antakya, the seat of the medieval crusader kingdoms. Western invaders brought their Western ideas to the same lands that had given birth to Christianity a thousand years prior. But without warriors, weapons, and citadels, what was a holy kingdom?

And so, the West had brought their knights with broadswords, built their castles, and erected a city wall that still stood behind this market street. The city had adapted, even after that short-lived crusader kingdom fell and the Westerners retreated with their stolen treasures. The man smiled so as not to delve too deep into his own familiar hypocrisy. He loved the West. He had hoped to go even further into it. If not for his mentor, the family, and his current assignment, he might be standing in the streets of New York or Los Angeles right now. But that time would come. Today, he was working.

Finally, the vehicle he waited for came down the bustling market street. By a stroke of incredible luck, it stopped. He straightened, all thoughts of the past, future, and his bloody suit instantly forgotten. He watched his targets exit their stolen Russian TIGR and stretch.

Dr. Evans was a man he'd mostly known by reputation and habits until a few days ago. Yet he now grasped that Evans was the same man he had been sent to Oxford to handle if such a need should ever arise. His mentor had explained it all. The family had been watching Dr. Evans carefully for years. Decades, really. It made the man in the suit proud to be a part of that complex clock. The family had grown. They were everywhere now, guarding every gate and watching every market road, preparing for what was soon to come. Moves ahead of every other player.

The Antakya locals conspicuously ignored the military vehicle. The tourists on the street, not so much. The Oxford tutor's whole operation was about as subtle as a band of 11th-entury medieval crusader knights riding up with polished armor and sharpened swords to "liberate" the already-Christian Armenians. Soon everyone in this town would know of the modern invaders in their overblown military vehicle.

Dr. Evans emerged, straightened his hat, and drank in this ancient city at the threshold of the east and west. Dr. Evans understood this place. He was a knight worthy of Antakya. His companions came around next to him and also stood in awe. They had added a local guide to their number, five strong now. From his hidden vantage point, the man in the suit permitted himself a sneer at the little Spanish witch. His cheek burned at the memory of their last encounter.

Much has changed in Kurdistan in three decades, Dr. Evans, he imagined saying. *We have grown. We are strong. We are ready.*

LXXIV

Antakya, Turkey. David.

When their guide Ejder touted the extravagant luxury and hospitality of his cousin in Antioch, David had imagined a series of interconnected goat shacks. But as they crested the hill onto a bustling metropolis in a valley surrounded by mountain peaks and sweeping knolls, David discovered just how wrong he'd been. A mere glimpse was enough for him to spot a mix of modern and medieval, exploding in color and life. England had been backwards, but this place was inside-out crazy and he wanted pictures. *So many pictures.*

"It is called the Grand Palace," Ejder proclaimed proudly as they pulled up to the tall and sparkling hotel on one of the high hills. The place looked like something out of Vegas, completely over the top and opulent, but with an Ottoman theme. It was all fountains and columns and glass against gleaming white stucco and stone.

Straight away Arthur went in to see about rooms, but David wasn't ready to go inside yet. Admittedly, the appeal of clean sheets and a real bed beckoned them all, but David was tired of sitting, tired of theorizing, and he definitely didn't want to sit around in a hotel while Arthur made decisions about tomorrow. Not when there was an alluring Turkish town to explore today! And from this side of the hotel, he could see just about all of it.

A million roofing tiles on a thousand ancient row houses, all twisted together by tiny little cobblestone streets. Minarets of half a dozen mosques poked out of this, but he also spotted the domes of as many Christian churches too. There were also sprawling parks and modern skyscrapers shoving the rest aside for modern commerce and lavish living. Through it all, a river twisted like a huge snake, spanned by stone arch bridges that had to be a thousand years old, maybe more. It was like the Western world had slammed up against the Eastern one, and they'd settled on an arrangement without an inch to spare. David's imagination exploded with possibilities.

"The Bishop reminded me once that we all ultimately worship something." Matthew stepped up beside David. "Whether it be God, tradition, science, wealth, or even ourselves, there is no corner of the world where we will not find some form of religion."

"I was kind of thinking the same thing," David agreed. "It's weird to see so many religions all smashed together here. No wonder Arthur says that the old stories and ideas got traded around. Just looking at that city makes me think of chaos serpents and walled gardens, with, you know, Gilgamesh, Utnapishtim, and the snake who shed his skin to steal the Tree of Life, Satan tempting Eve, all that stuff."

"Quite so!"

"Well, except Arthur said Satan was a Western idea, so maybe not him."

Matthew chuckled in his deep-chested guffaw. "As with many others, Arthur and I have agreed to disagree on that point, so I'll not belabor it. But I will say this—Satan has always been called the father of lies, the enemy, the tempter, and the great deceiver. The original Hebrew word means 'accuser' or 'adversary,' and as a name, Satan has always referred to that specific entity whose very nature it is to do and be those things." Matthew paused, decades of remembered friendship visible through his eyes, then continued gently. "Despite what Arthur might say, he knows that each man must face the adversary in his own way, as even Christ did. We can be certain that those who do not call the devil by one of his many names are tempted in no lesser way. In scripture, the list of men tempted by Satan is quite long. Job, King David, Peter, Paul, Ananias. I dare not try to list those tempted by their fellow men and women. No, temptation is universal, but the devil is in the details, if you'll excuse the pun. And needs must that the first man and woman are at the top of our proverbial list—Ark, garden, or otherwise."

David nodded, wondering what sorts of temptations an Oxford-educated, married, Anglican priest faced.

"So, I've always wondered, why did God do it? To Adam and Eve, I mean. Wasn't it kind of a setup? 'One rule guys, don't push the big red button that I'm putting right here in front of you.'"

"An excellent question, David. Before we try to answer it, let's consider another. Would you say that sin is often a matter of passion and not merely an ill-chosen decision?"

"Well, yea. Sure. Temptation is universal like you said."

"Then perhaps it is unfair to call Adam and Eve's sin a mere 'decision' in that regard. Should we not also recognize the passions involved?"

"Yea, sure. But why does it matter?"

"Well, Eve is often vilified in their story, but it went rather badly for Adam also. Once the deed was done, he couldn't even stay loyal to her in betrayal. When God showed up asking his questions, Adam said 'The woman you put here with me—she gave me some fruit from the tree, and I ate it.' He blamed Eve for doing it, blamed God for making her, and lied about the whole thing all in one breath. At least Eve had a somewhat reasonable excuse. She was tempted by the embodiment of chaos, deception, and temptation itself. I'd challenge anyone to do better."

There was a mischievous twinkle in Matthew's kind eyes. David couldn't help but smile.

"But also recall that Eden is a story of hope, not blame. Things are the way they are in this world because of things that happened long before you and I came along. The message of the whole Bible is that creation will be restored to perfection again someday, and we will get to experience it unspoiled by our selfish natures. We need only embrace that promise, and live for it. In that sense, we might even say that Adam and Eve are role models."

David screwed up his face in doubt. Was Matthew playing some sort of trick?

The priest put his hands up in mock surrender. "I only mean, David, that those two overcame their dysfunction, accepted each other's flaws, started over, and made it. Despite all manner of family dramas, they stuck together till the end. Would that we could all do as well as Adam and Eve in that regard." David shook his head a little in wonder, trying to absorb and appreciate this new perspective. "And on that note," Matthew decided, "I suppose I should go fetch the luggage from the truck."

As Matthew turned to go, Cat nudged David from his other side. Just how long had she been standing there, anyway?

"Should we go see what is down there?" she suggested, nodding toward the beautiful, chaotically-balanced city. There was mischief in her eyes that matched David's own burning curiosity. He was ready to say yes to whatever Antakya had to offer them. *Within reason, anyway.*

"Definitely. I'll just go tell Arthur real quick."

Cat shrugged and followed.

*   *   *

Arthur was still stumbling his way through bad attempts at Turkish and worse attempts at politeness at the front desk when they found him. Ejder was there, apparently helping in some fashion.

"Arthur, we are going to check out the town. Be back later, 'kay?"

Arthur grunted a vowel in David's direction, continuing his failing negotiations.

"Um, is that a yes?"

"It will be everything fine!" Ejder injected way too enthusiastically. "My cousin will give all the very best bedroom!" This was followed by a string of Turkish that there was no hope of deciphering toward the irritated man behind the desk. In an instant, the man plastered on a big professional smile and turned back to Arthur, full of new helpfulness. Then, turning to David and Cat, Ejder whispered, "And now I will show you my town!"

Cat raised an eyebrow and snuck David a "you can't be serious" smirk. David wasn't thrilled at the idea of a chaperone either, but it was a fair compromise. At least the guy was hilarious to watch.

"Come! Come!" their impassioned city guide added, shoeing them toward the lobby door. "The greatest bazaar of all the world is very close by! You will see!"

A Turkish bazaar? That sounded absolutely amazing. Besides, they had Ejder, and like he'd said, *"It will be everything fine!"* How could somebody argue with that?

Down the street a bit, David spotted Father Matthew extracting some critical part from the engine of the TIGR. He closed the hood and grabbed their bags from inside the vehicle before he spotted them. He lifted his chin questioningly.

Cat gave a little patronizing wave as David cupped his hands and called out, "Arthur knows!" then gestured toward town with a big thumbs up. *Responsibility? Check.*

With a fresh smile, David pushed all thoughts of Father Matthew, Arthur and hotel rooms away and vowed to have fun soaking in every second of this ancient place. Only a few days ago, Turkey had seemed like a far-off country where his mysterious questing grandfather had once had archeology adventures that sent David's imagination soaring. Now, he was an apprentice wizard in that same far-off land, with no clue as to what tomorrow would bring.

Or, for that matter, the next ten minutes.

LXXV

Uzun Çarşı Bazaar, Antakya, Turkey. David.

David cocked his head and tried to decipher the huge sign identifying an unassuming entrance to the Uzun Çarşı market crammed between two highly questionable buildings. Ejder noticed and provided a helpful translation.

"'Long Bazaar,' it reads. It is a great hallway full of everything. Like American mall-shop, as old as the very city. This is the heart of the city. Everything you may possibly want is here! A place where the local lives a daily life also. Many famous and traditional restaurants are at the narrow side-paths of Uzun Çarşı. Come! Come! Only the best food I will get for you."

Cat and David grinned at each other in disbelief even as the man plunged into the crowd. They followed, passing under the large aluminum arch and into the ancient brick and stone of the shopping center. It was too surreal. There was no way David was missing this.

"After food," Cat told him, "you are helping me shop. I want new outfits, a bag, shampoo and toothbrush, and fresh underwear." To David's shock, she shoved her manicured hand down into her bra. For a moment he was worried about what kind of visual she was about to provide until she came up with a wad of Euros in a little silk pouch. "I need clean clothes!" There was an air of desperation in her tone.

David gave her a goofy relieved smile. He hadn't gone shopping with a girl for clothes before. Well, except for his mom, but that didn't count. He thought again of his canceled date in Oxford and decided to embrace the now. After all, they weren't here alone. How much trouble could they get into, really?

"Come! Best food, come!" Ejder beckoned again, a few yards away.

He padded past stalls, kiosks, and carts with countless salesmen touting stacks and walls of tapestries, beautiful carpets, and other handmade goods, classy, trashy, and everything in between. The whole market was some ancient cobblestone road now covered by an anachronistic vaulted roof of stained clear plastic on a rusty metal frame. Long rows of store after store had become the walls, and in that way, it really was like a mall, but there were fountain courtyards every so often, and whole free-standing buildings were swallowed up inside the now-covered market. David lost count of the dark and narrow alleyways that snaked off into who knows where. Peddlers, pickpockets, and hundreds of tourists from everywhere imaginable strode past. It was wonderful.

Edjer pulled Cat away from hand-woven bags and fine silks more than once and refused to let David buy anything edible until they emerged onto a spot where the road split. Here, it was nothing but food stands, carts, shops, and a handful of restaurants. The smell was overwhelming to David's growling stomach. Little braziers, stone and clay stoves, and other open fires were everywhere.

First, Ejder led them to a counter where a man handed them each a massive strip of greasy meat on a kabob and pointed them to a park-style picnic table. It smelled absolutely delicious and tasted even better than the one David had bought at the border gate. Cat handed him hers in disgust, citing vegetarian reasons, so he unapologetically ate her kabob too.

Cat didn't have to go hungry though. Ejder next brought a huge plate of hummus and some kind of eggplant stuff with fresh vegetables and stacks of flatbread. The man kept going back and forth bringing various meats, fruit and vegetable dishes, sauces, and more until David forced him to stop, fearing that he wouldn't be able to pay their host back with the mix of American and British bills he had. But Ejder never asked for any money, and David began to wonder just how much Arthur had overpaid their guide in the first place. The exuberant man's final presentation was to fill a large sheet of paper with Turkish delight, fold it over, and hand it to them with a wink.

"This is the best meal I've ever eaten," David mumbled to Cat and Ejder through a mouth full of savory whatever.

"See!" The man declared, throwing his arms wide. "Ejder knows the best food." His pocket buzzed, and their guide whipped out a little Nokia straight out of 2004. The rapid language that burst forth from the man seemed almost violently vulgar to David's ear.

David pulled his phone out and glanced at it. He had a signal and data! But, no messages. He had completely lost track of what time it was in the West, so he decided not to worry about it.

"Apologies!" Ejder said, a moment later. "I must go settle things with my cousin. He has arranged the very best room for you all but desires to see me. We must respect family, no? You will be fine here." This last wasn't a question evidently, because a moment later the young people were alone.

David looked at Cat and gulped. *Room?* Just how many would they be getting? Cat met his gaze and smiled mischievously, a world of potential past her dark eyes. *Dad is going to literally kill me,* he thought for the millionth time.

Swallowing so hard it hurt, David hit the button on his phone to put it away, but as it went to black, he noticed something and brought it back up. The image of the Phaistos Disk was still there, zoomed in to the last phrase of grouped symbols Arthur had been working on. It was the boomerang-man-weapon combo, the one Arthur had said was the signature, someone named "King Goes-to-War."

"Cat? What did you think of Arthur's Disk translation?" he asked haltingly.

She raised an eyebrow but said nothing, crunching into a huge red apple.

"It's just that I think he may have messed one really important part up. He kept saying 'important-man,' for the shield symbol and the mohawk guy, right?" David showed her the images. "But then, Arthur changed the shield to 'city.' But, I was thinking that if the important man was Noah then the mohawk guy could just be him... Because Atra-Hasis means 'Important Man,' right? And the other day he told me that Utnapishtim means basically the same thing."

Cat's eyes went wide. "Well? Do not stop there."

It was all coming out at once as a derailed mess that felt ridiculous, but David was committed now. "What I mean is that Arthur said 'important' like a half-dozen times in his reading. But if he got the word 'war' from the first phrase about going off with the sword and shield, then I was thinking, there might be this entire other possibility of how to translate the last phrase, the signature part, into something else, based on Arthur's words alone. One that doesn't have the word war in it, but the word city instead?"

She crossed her arms under her chest, raised an eyebrow, and smiled invitingly. "Something like, 'Follow the Path of the Flaming Sword to the city of the important man?'"

"Yea, something like that," David squeaked.

He must have been staring at the apple pretty hard because Cat laughed and held it out. "We can share. Trade me for the phone?"

*   *   *

The two young adults talked about translation, art, fashion, and archeology for hours. They even compared notes on Crete and explored various theories about the great mystery of the disappearing Minoans, including debunking Atlantis, ancient aliens, and how it would all make a great tabletop RPG scenario, because, why not?

The conversation hardly waned even as she haggled for clothes and supplies and a new bag, which David carried for her even as she continued to add more to her new wardrobe. He didn't mind, he hardly noticed the weight at all.

Cat surprised David with her Arabic. One shopkeeper surprised them both with his Spanish. Nearly everybody spoke some English, which was surreal. As quickly as possible, Cat found a place to change and made a show of throwing her old clothes away. It seemed a bit extreme to David, but it was funny. Then again, he tended to wash his jeans about once a month, so what did he know. Her new outfit was tight shorts and an even tighter shirt, which he thought he probably should disapprove of on some objective level, but utterly failed to do so. It looked completely natural on her, even if she did stand out a bit among the locals.

Or, you know, a lot.

They happily lost themselves in the side passages and hidden shops that the crowds passed by unnoticed. Eventually, Cat had a half-dozen outfits, including some that were much more modest. David took a million pictures and posted the best ones for people to see when they woke up. They both quickly lost track of time, and only stopped when the crowds thinned to nothing and the shopkeepers began politely shoeing them away so that they could close up. David was surprised to look up through the roof and see a starry night. It was only then that the duo realized they had no idea which way was out. They began walking and laughing through the empty bazaar, searching for any familiar landmark or someone to ask but finding neither.

"Where is it?" asked a lightly accented voice from behind him.

They both whirled, Cat let out a small cry of surprise. The man in the suit stood, gun out, friendly smile, a ragged copy of his former self under the painted wooden sign of the Eagle and Child, and with three new painful-looking scratches down his cheek.

"Where is what?" David stammered, now an imitation of Arthur in the same memory.

"No games," The man cooed. "The constables are not nearly as responsive nor understanding in this place. Please tell me, where is the tablet hidden? Your vehicle? A bag? Your hotel room?" This last he said with a certain menace. A threat.

Arthur! The tablet was in fact in their room, inside David's bag presumably, but he wasn't going to tell this man that.

But he didn't have to, his face had already given it away. The man's smile grew wider, and with his free hand, he withdrew a little phone and flipped it open.

David didn't hesitate. Uttering a shout worthy of a *kung fu* master from an 80s martial arts film, he threw Cat's full new bag at the man's arm. It unbalanced him just enough that he went to one knee on the cobblestone.

Cat decided her bag wasn't as important as her life, so she grabbed David's arm and half ran, half pulled him around a twisting corner before his brain could catch up to his legs.

When it finally did, David saw hanging strings of lights in a little square he thought he recognized.

Cat's long legs quickly outpaced David's. She beat him to the square and dodged a little fountain. David curved his run and they met up just as they entered another side passage. If memory served, it was the one they had used an hour ago when they'd first found the little courtyard. Or so he hoped.

The man's shouts told David that he was not far behind. He risked a glance and saw the man vault the fountain effortlessly. This wasn't going to work, they needed a better plan, but the narrow ancient street was nothing but stonework, brick, and steel shutters.

"Come ba-ack," The man called in a sing-song voice, "There is nowhere you can run."

David knew it was true, but Cat was noticeably faster than him, maybe faster than their pursuer.

"We have to split up," David shouted. "Get back to the hotel. You have to warn them!"

The only way that he and Arthur had gotten away last time was by splitting up. The man had chosen Arthur that time, the slower target. Maybe it would work again. All he needed was a place to hide

They sped past an uneven place in the alley that took the path at an odd angle. Beyond it was a fork, bisected by a dirty yellow restaurant. But David recognized it. They were in the courtyard where they had eaten, a million years ago that afternoon, and there were a half-dozen other paths out, two of which were the main thoroughfare of the Uzun Çarşı.

"Go that way," David barked, even as he split the other way. He could hear the echoing footfalls of the man in the suit. There was no way they would make it out before he came in.

David weaved through the wooden benches and tables toward the nearest path, a smaller, darker one. He only hoped that it went somewhere that wasn't a dead-end, but maybe the darkness could keep him from bullets too. This time he didn't turn as he rocketed into the shadows, but the man's feet told him that Cat was safe. He, however, was now in serious trouble. The man was close.

David had always hated running. One of the best things about homeschooling, in his opinion, was the total lack of requirement to take physical education or team sports. He was now questioning his decision in that regard because even if the man couldn't shoot him in the relative darkness, he would only have to aim for the ragged panting breaths to hit his mark.

A sudden inspiration hit David. *In roleplaying games, you play to your strengths. Or, rather, your stats.* So, what were they? He could never outrun this man, he had no weapon or shield, but he had the shadows. Without a second to spare, David dodged into a wooden stall with his first-ever baseball slide. He failed terribly—scraped up his arm, tore his pants, and felt the pain shoot back into his elbow—but he made it.

The sellers had taken their wares home, but the smell of spices lingered behind the little wooden counter. David felt a sneeze coming on, but he swallowed it, holding his breath for two reasons. The man in the suit shot past, the sound of his shoes fading, then stopping. He took a few halting steps, then started walking back towards David.

"Where are you, little man?" He taunted. "You cannot hide. Tell me where the tablet is, and you will survive this." A stack of something that sounded like baskets fell into the street.

This hiding place was terrible. The man would find him if he stayed here, hear him if he didn't, and maybe even shoot him in the silhouette of light in the courtyard as he went. He pushed himself up on shaking arms and crouched into a runner's starting position. It was now or never.

"*Oye, gilipollas!* You lose someone?"

Cat? She hadn't followed the plan at all then. David could see her unmistakable silhouette standing at the entrance of the passage for the briefest moment before she flashed away. The man in the suit hesitated but must have decided that the target you can see was better than the one you can't and took off after her.

David stayed until he couldn't feel his heart in his ears anymore, then slunk away, feeling about as unheroic as a level one rogue could. He followed the main path out, then ran as fast as his body would let him toward the gleaming multicolored lights of the Grand Palace Hotel, praying that the others were okay.

LXXVI

Grand Palace Hotel, Antakya, Turkey. Arthur.

Evans was exhausted. The moon was shining brightly through the hotel window when he finally had a chance to sit down. The teens hadn't returned yet, but seeing as they had a local guide, Evans had not given it a second thought until now. He'd expected them to return before dark, but then he hadn't explicitly said it either. Perhaps Evans would need to have words with Ejder in the morning about his expectations in regards to his new ward.

As soon as he sorted out exactly what those were, of course. He shouldn't have let them go at all, but he'd been distracted, and by the time he realized what had happened, it was too late. Matthew had not been pleased, to say the least, but his friend was overreacting. Antioch was a tourist destination, not a war zone.

Then again, it was unlikely that they were going to see anything this close to civilization for a while. Why not let the kids have some fun? Young love was an irreplaceable thing after all, and even though the love of a lifetime was superior in almost every way, what it had in stability it sometimes lacked in pure unbridled excitement. In all though, David truly was a good kid. Chances were, David had gone to help deMata shop for replacement necessities, and that was a task Evans would not ask any young man to endure. It was a pretty clear indicator of David's state of mind though, and it would be just a matter of time before deMata got her claws into him, assuming tonight hadn't sealed that deal. Then, lord only knew what sort of trouble there might be.

Evans massaged his temple. *Trouble,* that was the theme of the day. The details of the room, suitable payment, ordering room service, and arranging special laundry amenities all while hunting down Ejder's alleged cousin, had taken entirely too long to get sorted. Language difficulties aside, it was almost like the hotel people were being obtuse on purpose.

After a strained disagreement with Matthew about apparently letting the kids and their guide go to town—which Evans didn't exactly remember having done—the men spent the rest of the evening discussing their next move. With a large map of Turkey and his pencil, Evans spent several hours optimizing which horrible roads might be the least horrible should they choose to go easterly to Durupinar or westerly to Labraunda. He had decidedly abandoned the silly ideas of going to Crete on some leaky boat-for-hire. He would love to see and walk the ruins of Knossos Palace, but the Disk was undeniably Semitic. Spoils of war from Ugarit, certainly. Even Wyatt had figured that out. It just made sense.

Wyatt wasn't the first to theorize that the Phaistos Disk contained a flood myth. Dozens of scholars had proposed it based on the water and boat symbology that David had recognized in seconds. But Evans was the first who was equipped to prove it. Regardless, if there was a path to be followed, he may well have just found the coded instructions on where to go if they could figure it out.

Ah, but he did love a good ancient riddle. And if it did lead to Dilmun, could Wyatt somehow be there waiting as the journal had said? What Evans would not be doing was praying for a taxi to stall, or for a divine sign of where to dig. That much one could be sure of. He just needed the right starting point, and that had to be Noah's landing. To Wyatt, that could only be Doomsday mountain in Turkey.

Trying to discern the mind of Wyatt Aarons was enough to drive a man to madness. Or possibly to drink. Evans was happy that Islamo-conservative Turkey had remained a secular country with a great drinking tradition. He was never one for wines or that fruity *Raki* that was touted with such pride, but a nice Turkish beer or three at the hotel bar had helped him swallow his looming tasks of tomorrow.

Thank you, Ottoman Empire, he toasted each time. Uncle Arthur would forgive him for that, given the nature of the quest they now seemed to be on. He just hoped the rest of academia never found out about the sloppy science and leaps of logic they had all used to get this far.

Finally in his room and much more relaxed, Evans tossed his hat onto the bed and scratched his filthy head. He then slung his sweat-stained coat across a plush armchair and began tugging down his pants. This suite had a shower and he couldn't wait to take an embarrassingly long one. Evans had expected there to be some reasonable accommodations in Antakya, given the blasted tourist trap that it was. What he had not expected was to finally be set up in the royal suite.

Their hotel room, or rather rooms, had a connecting communal living area off the main entry. The open floorplan included a furnished "American kitchen" and breakfast nook, as well as a sitting area with a colossal flat screen television on one wall. In front of this was a delightfully plush-looking couch and matching armchairs. This central room also led out onto a wide private rooftop balcony appropriately equipped for a large cocktail party. There was even a bathroom with a full sink and bathtub next to the kitchen, a luxury most English hotels did not provide. An ornate Turkish rug finished each room. In truth, the whole royal suite was like something one expected to see on one of those "profiles of the rich and notorious" television programs Elisabeth had always enjoyed watching.

He draped his overshirt across the chair only to watch his spiral notebook unceremoniously fall out of the breast pocket onto the fancy rug. He stooped and groaned to pick it up, every muscle hurt to the bone from sheer tiredness and lack of sleep.

In the end, Ejder had proven to be on the level about being the owner's cousin, despite running off with the kids. The room cost more than all of them probably had in cash combined, but the owner assured him credit account numbers were fine and had insisted that they take the upgrade for their troubles, giving them what may or may not have been a discount. By that point, Evans had stopped caring. He just wanted a bed and a bath no matter the cost. Tomorrow they could finalize their plans with a clear head and a full stomach courtesy of a Turkish breakfast buffet.

Matthew had pointed out that two beds did not divide equally among four people when one of them was female, so the compromise he'd suggested was that one of the two rooms go to the Evanses and that he would settle for the central room's fold-out couch. This was how the second room became deMata's entirely. Or would, as soon as the kids got back.

A furious pounding sounded on the outer door, signaling that very event.

"Can you get that?" Evans called to Matthew. The pounding didn't stop, and he could just hear David's frantic voice out in the hall.

Evans tucked the spiral notebook into his undershirt pocket and grumbled an incomplete thought about doing everything himself. He stepped out of the bedroom just as Matthew yanked the door open. The boy exploded into the suite in a flurry of arms and words, pausing only for a moment when he saw his grandfather standing there in nothing but his black socks and underclothes.

"Slow down my boy, slow down. What are you saying? Wait a tick, where is Dr. deMata?"

"That's what I'm trying to tell you. The man who ambushed us back on the road is still following us! He chased us in the bazaar, and we got split up. He knows about the tablet and the hotel! We have to get out of—"

An explosion outside rocked the windows and floor and brought everyone up short. The glass wall between them and the rooftop cracked in three places, pictures went askew, and small bits of decor fell to the floor.

The Evanses stared at one another stupidly for a long moment, then bolted for the sliding door in the glass wall of the common room. Matthew was three steps ahead, threw the glass door open, and was already leaning over the edge of the dark balcony when they got there. Evans could hear fear-filled shouts from the street far below.

The three men stared down, unbelieving, at a burning vehicle. It lit up the quad and every other building on the street in flickering reds and yellows. A large truck belched dark smoke from the car bomb that had just turned it into scrap on wheels. *A military truck,* Evans realized. *Wait! Our military truck!* The Russian 4x4 would not be taking them anywhere now.

"David, go get our bags," he urged. "Quickly now."

There was no time for the boy to obey. The door to the suite splintered open and three men charged in. They were unmistakable. Camo pants and jackets, black masks that covered all but their eyes, and automatic machine guns. These last they gestured menacingly at Evans and company, shouting angry commands. But it was the other small detail that was most concerning to Evans. Each of them wore the matching armband with the all too familiar black raven on a red and white background.

More than fear or surprise, there was an overwhelming sense of irritation for Evans. They were hundreds of miles from the eastern provinces where insurgents such as these made their hideouts, and yet, bad pennies and all that. Evans was never going to get his shower now.

"What do you want?" Evans demanded. He pushed David forcibly back against the parapet despite their being on the fourteenth floor.

A rapid string of Kurdish was the reply.

"Go inside and get down, David," Evans translated as he started moving toward the room himself. "We are being robbed." There would be no rushing these men with a sucker-kick to the crotch. That was death. Then under his breath, *Oh please let us simply be robbed!*

David wisely complied, finding the floor in front of the couch. Matthew entered last and dropped to one knee near the television. He put his hands behind his head with a stone-faced scowl. Evans took an armchair, having no desire to squat on a tile floor. The men spread out, talking angrily to one another and waving their guns around for effect, but never lowering them.

A long minute later, a fourth man stepped into the room escorted by deMata. She was dressed like a streetwalker now, her outfit entirely inappropriate for the Middle East, even in a place like Turkey. For a moment, Evans thought the man was a security guard here to assist. Understandable, since the olive-skinned man wore a suit and held a handgun. Evans opened his mouth to praise the girl for her assistance, then it registered. DeMata wasn't escorting anyone, the man in the suit was holding onto her by the back of the neck. But at least he hadn't left her for dead, so that was something.

The man in the suit was all smiles despite having a nasty scabby gash along his cheek. It looked quite painful. He steered deMata a few steps and shoved her roughly into the room hard enough for her to go down. She scrambled toward the place where David huddled against a wall and seethed cold hatred at the invaders. Evans didn't blame her a bit. They were a full set of prisoners now.

"Hello again, Dr. Evans," the man in the suit sang out. "Once more, you have something that does not belong to you."

LXXVII

Grand Palace Hotel, Antakya, Turkey. David.

David froze while the man in the suit casually roamed the room like a hotel inspector making his rounds. The stains and rips in his ruined outfit detracted a bit from David's mental image. First, the man ran a hand across the ornate wallpaper. Then it was a finger across the slick marble countertop. Finally, he picked up a crystal and gold vase full of decorative beads and scrutinized it.

"You have expensive taste, Dr. Evans," the gunman said. "I can appreciate that." To everyone's surprise, he opened his hand, letting the vase fall to the tile floor in a million little shards. He stepped toward the three masked men. The string of Kurdish that followed could only have been instructions. Two of them broke away, one to each bedroom. The man in the suit looked at the third one and said in English, "Thank you Ejder, you've done the family proud today."

David's heart quickened as their former guide pulled down his facemask and smiled. "Thanks be to you, brother! Welcome home." There was no mistaking Ejder. The man who had gotten them across the border was now holding a gun on them. The one who had sat by smiling while they casually worked out their next moves in the car, had offered to take them deep into the mountainous countryside, had gone to the bazaar with David and Cat and fed them such amazing food, and who had recommended Antakya for gas and lodging and proclaimed the hospitality of his family's hotel in the first place.

David suddenly felt completely basic in a very non-sarcastic way.

"That one has a phone," Ejder informed the man in the suit.

The man nodded, walked over to David, and held his hand out. Grudgingly David produced it, teeth clenched hard enough to hurt. He was mad enough to explode, no car bomb required.

One of the gunmen reemerged from the bedroom. He was carrying David's backpack in one hand and Arthur's open rucksack in the other. Their verbal exchange was quick and needed no translation. This was game over, the end of their party's adventures. If they were lucky, David and the others would live to tell about it.

Then, another person David didn't expect walked through the door. Dr. Pitman didn't stop to inspect the furnishings or break décor. He crunched past the broken glass, instantly sized up the room, and gestured toward Cat.

"What the blazes are you doing, boy? Have you no manners?" Then, "No, of course you don't."

For a horrible moment, David thought Dr. Pitman was talking to him until the man in the suit holstered his pistol and roughly yanked Cat up onto the couch. The man in the suit stared at David then jerked his head sideways as if to say, *"Couch, idiot!"* David scuttled up next to Cat and sat.

"You ok?" David whispered. She gave him a quick but insincere nod. Then to his great surprise, snatched his hand and squeezed hard.

With them resituated off of the floor, Dr. Pitman set down a gun David hadn't even noticed, but now instantly recognized as one of the flashlight-mounted SMGs from the dig. The geomorphologist began rummaging through their bags. He quickly rifled through Arthur's rucksack, not finding anything of interest, and moved on to David's backpack. David watched his spare jeans and only clean shirt plop out onto the glass fragments. Next his white earbuds painfully bounced onto the floor, followed by his Ashmolean guidebook. Finally, Pitman came up with his prize. His grin was a madman's as he unwrapped the translation tablet fragments from yesterday's tee-shirt.

"He had this too," the man in the suit said, stepping forward with David's phone. What he got from Dr. Pitman was a look of deep disdain. The old man grabbed the phone and tossed it into David's open backpack.

David let out a breath he didn't know he'd been holding. There was hope—Dr. Pitman didn't know what was on his phone!

"What do you need to begin translating these, Doc?" Pitman demanded, kicking David's laundry aside.

There was an awkward silence nobody dared break. Of all the things David would have expected Dr. Pitman to say, that was not one of them. Interestingly, the man in the suit looked genuinely surprised too. Predictably, so did everyone else in the room whose face was not behind a mask.

Arthur mumbled an answer, but David couldn't understand it.

"What?" Pitman demanded.

"I said I've already done it!" Arthur spat. He looked completely unhinged. Wild-eyed, wild-haired, and half-naked, David's wizard looked like a mad homeless indignant hippie after an all-night bender. Assuming Oxford even had those.

"You've already finished? That's absurd."

"Try me," Arthur growled. He glanced subconsciously at the little spiral notebook sticking precariously out of his undershirt pocket. Too late, Arthur realized his error.

The bald old man doubtfully plucked the spiral notebook up. As he thumbed through it, his mouth split, and David could see every one of the old man's perfect gleaming teeth. If it was a smile, it was the creepiest one he had ever known. Dr. Pitman placed the tablet fragments into his satchel and felt around for something else. *Mr. Aarons' satchel,* David realized off-handedly.

"Well then, how about you take a crack at this next?"

Pitman drew out the unmistakable spiral circle of the Phaistos Mystery Disk. Mr. Aarons' bag, the two translation tablet fragments, and the novelty ceramic disk copy had all been reunited. And probably the stolen journal too, David suspected.

"That thing?" Arthur squeaked. "It's a century-old forgery, don't you know? The real one, I mean."

What was he doing? Could Arthur seriously hope to lie about the Disk now? A closer look at Arthur's notes would out that story pretty fast, but David wasn't going to be the one to blow it.

"Don't play games with me, Doc. I know you saw this thing come out of Aarons' bag back at Ugarit." He slapped at the satchel for emphasis. "And I also know you've started working it into your theories." He pointed his chin at their ex-guide, Ejder.

The local man bobbed his head wildly in confirmation. Just how much had Arthur said in front of their alleged guide about the real translation of the Disk? David suddenly wasn't sure.

"Wyatt thought this thing was the key to finding Dilmun, and once you translate it, I am going to show the entire world the difference between fairy tales and real history. You mark my words Doc, I will find Eden right where Genesis says it is. And I will use any and every scientific tool and technology at our hands to do it, from rocket ships to submarines. Then we'll see who the real believers of this world are."

"Luigi Pernier wasn't very well known until he discovered the Disk at Phaistos." Arthur stammered. "He was about to pack it all in and go home when his assistant—and I use the term lightly—conveniently 'found' the disk. That man was Émile Gilliéron, a well-known forger and expert craftsman and artist." Cat's words coming out of Arthur's mouth. "Wave guns at me all day, you old fossil. I won't, can't, and never will be able to ascribe meaning to that worthless trash. It's been utterly untranslatable and forever will be. If you don't believe me, then perhaps you'd like to do some real research for a change. I recommend starting with Dr. deMata's dissertation on the subject."

Cat's hand was like a vice. She raised it to her chest, taking David's with it. Her eyes narrowed, but she said nothing. Arthur just held his poker face. David almost believed the whole thing himself.

As for Dr. Pitman, it was unclear if he was buying what David's wizard was selling, but a deep rumble caught the geomorphologist's attention. It sounded like someone was mowing the lawn with a supersized riding mower. Then it got louder and even louder still. Dr. Pitman pocketed the notebook, then tossed the Disk into David's open bag with a smack of ceramic against plastic and glass that made David cringe. The old man stepped towards the cracked glass wall and scanned the starry night.

"Do we have a helicopter?" Pitman demanded loudly of Ejder.

The answer was a fearful headshake no. The man in the suit quickly agreed.

Helicopter? Who was flying a helicopter? Seconds later David had his answer. The chaotic street noises were drowned out by the thumping of whirling blades. A floodlight bathed the balcony in light, followed by a no-nonsense white and gray military helicopter that landed with a massive jolt literally a few meters from the door. It vibrated the whole suite, cracked the concrete patio, and shattered most of the already weakened glass, but the rooftop held. The copter was twice the size of the one they had ridden into France in, some part of David's brain noted.

David could barely take in what was happening. Their masked captors dove for the side rooms, the man in the suit falling back to behind the kitchen counter. Then, the last remaining pane of the glass wall exploded followed by the TV, and David realized someone was shooting. Dr. Pitman was uselessly firing on the helicopter from behind an overturned chair. It was quickly joined by sustained fire from the other big guns out of the bedroom windows.

Arthur lunged behind his armchair. Cat realized they had best do something similar and stood, taking David with him. They climbed the back of the couch and pressed flat against the wall. A painting fell, but David ignored it. If he could have climbed the wall and clung to the ceiling like Spiderman, he would have.

Dr. Pitman didn't stop until the clip was empty. He fumbled with a second clip, snarled in frustration, then fell back to the kitchen with the man in the suit and thrust the gun at him for help.

A second later the other automatic gunfire stopped too. Reloading or just waiting? There was no way to know. With the glass wall gone, the vehicle's blades were blowing tiny shards, dust, and other debris into the ruined room. Then Matthew was shouting something about the helicopter door. David forced an eye open, and indeed the vehicle's side door gaped wide. Just inside, a large man in desert fatigues was gesturing wildly for everyone to run to him. The whole thing was like something out of an old '90s action movie, safely happening to somebody else. Except, not.

"Go!" Arthur shouted, waving furiously.

David turned to Cat to say something heroic, but she was already halfway to the shattered window. Matthew dove across the room toward her, crouch-running as fast as he could and using his body as a living shield. In a few short seconds, they were both halfway across the terrace, then aboard.

The pilot jumped back to his chair and the blades doubled their speed. David and Arthur exchanged looks, then scrambled to follow. Suddenly, David realized what he had forgotten. He whirled and danced back towards the wrecked common room and his bag.

"Don't, David!" Arthur shouted. "Pitman has the fragments!"

David didn't answer. He just stooped, grabbed his floppy backpack, and bolted back to the helicopter like a relay runner. When David finally hit the vehicle's hard floor he gasped for breath and lay there, clutching his bag closed. A moment later he pulled himself into a chair, phone in hand, victorious glee on his face.

The pilot didn't wait. The blades screamed, and the flying behemoth took flight again. Matthew slid the door closed just before gunfire from a bedroom window raked across the helicopter's side. He breathed a quick prayer and scanned for a chair. The copilot seat was available, so he stumbled to it. Arthur began shouting questions no one could hear.

"Headset!" the pilot mouthed back, twisting around and pointing at his own gear.

To his horror, David instantly recognized the man flying the helicopter. Arthur did too, and while the man's discolored goose egg and crusty lip were something of a disguise, being choked by someone probably made them pretty memorable. But if Colonel Ivan was planning on kidnapping them, he was planning on rescuing them first, and that was good enough for David. As soon as Arthur had his headset and mic positioned, he began demanding answers.

"There was a problem with, ah, chain of command," Ivan stated simply. "It is corrected." Arthur looked to everyone for some kind of answer, but of course, they had nothing. "Miss Chen sends apology. She explains everything when are getting back to camp."

"How the devil did Miss Chen know where we were?" Arthur squeaked. "Not that I'm ungrateful or anything."

"Twitter," the Russian man replied.

David looked sheepishly down at his phone. He could not have felt more awkward if it had just been declared a murder weapon in an important case. He deftly thumbed his weapon of destruction off and shoved it deep into his hoodie pocket.

"You also charge expensive room in hotel to company account," Ivan continued. "I saw the fire, came right away. No hesitation."

It was Arthur's turn to go white. David covered his mouth and they both shared a silent laugh as the helicopter tore into the velvet night. Some vigilante spies they were!

"Arthur?" Father Matthew's voice came through the headset from the front passenger seat a second later.

"Yes, Matthew, what is it?"

"Are you aware, my good man, that you have forgotten your trousers?"

LXXVIII

Grand Palace Hotel, Antakya, Turkey. Mr. Suit.

The man in the ruined suit stood by silently as Dr. Pitman raged.

"That stupid woman continues to destroy everything that she touches!"

The old man stalked across the ravaged presidential suite and stooped, swooping up Dr. Evans' abandoned travel bag for the second time. He tossed it into the armchair where the scholar had been sitting.

"Her incessant obsession with mythology is a disgrace to Dingxiang Chen's legacy! If her father had known the lengths his daughter would go to squander the resources it took him a lifetime to build, he would roll over in his ornate little grave!"

Dr. Pitman threw open the bag and started tossing more shirts and underclothes onto the glass-strewn floor. It was an exercise in futility.

"That woman believes every little story she hears," he seethed, "and throws a fortune away every time she wants a glass of tea or a glimpse at some old ruin. If my great friend Ding had realized how deep her betrayal to his own values went, I daresay he would have made some very different decisions in his will, I tell you what!"

A toiletry kit hit the ground and a toothbrush bounced away under a chair.

"Her father should have left his god-forsaken empire to me. Can you imagine what we could do with those resources working entirely for us?"

The man in the ruined suit lifted his chin once, a non-committal gesture. This was not the time to file an opinion. He shrugged his blood-stained suitcoat, letting the holstered gun under his arm comfort him. This situation had gone from bad to worse, but he had to trust that this was only a minor setback to the agenda. Pitman was acting rashly now. Abandoning his shadows had been a risky move.

A distant siren squealed as terrified shouts and various bangs and slams continued to drift up from below.

Without a doubt, they had kicked the anthill, and this event would draw all kinds of unwanted attention. It was sloppy. He hated sloppy. Had Wyatt Aarons' disappearance unhinged Pitman more than even he realized? He must trust his mentor's wisdom now more than ever.

"Nothing else here," Dr. Pitman declared, tossing Dr. Evans' now-empty bag into a corner.

Every item left by the travelers after their impressive egress was now strewn about the room. But they were only things found in any random tourist's bag. Then, contrary to his own words, Pitman swept up some papers that had come out of Dr. Evans' bag, folded them, and placed them into the leather bag with the other spoils he had taken. Whatever else Dr. Pitman was doing, he was respecting the archeology. Something about that struck the man in the suit as ironic, but he filed these details away regardless.

People are clocks to be studied, he reminded himself.

"The Disk is gone." Ejder quietly remarked to the man in the suit.

The man in the suit nodded. The round tablet had ended up in the boy's near-empty bag, yet he had bolted back into mortal danger to retrieve it. So then, Evans had understandably lied about the Disk's importance.

Dr. Pitman was still ranting. "Eden is not meant for Mel Chen. She is in every way unworthy, doesn't even believe in Genesis. Dilmun? What a load of crap. Read the book, I say! It's time to take that woman's little empire down." He turned to the man in the suit with a burning intensity. "And I'm tired of dealing with her military vehicles and helicopters. We need to fight fire with fire. Mobilize, get this insurgency started early before all Hell rains down on us."

A chill ran down the man in the suit's spine. He understood precisely what Dr. Pitman was suggesting. His part of the world had been fighting for freedom from oppressive regimes and invaders since the beginning. His people had been conducting guerrilla warfare to protect their ancient lands for millennia. Persian swords then, Western-made assault weapons now. Did this man from the United States, whom he had known and respected for so long, really understand the implications of what he was saying?

It was a full decade into the twenty-first century now, and the man in the suit's expensive education had served him well. He understood that this part of the world was on the brink of boiling over at any moment, with regimes, dictatorships, and religious factions muddying who the righteous and wicked truly were. The fanatics had brought political and military forces to a head in his homeland like never before. But they were no fools either. They were well-trained military specialists with complicated plans ready to play puppeteer, Khalif, or messiah, as needed.

And to the east? The Kurdish "rebels" he called brothers protected much more than just land. It was their very way of life, religion, and culture that was at stake. The lands of Kurdistan had never known any real political borders. Yet in recent decades, his people had begun policing roads and border-crossings and posting silent watchmen further and further afield. The world had changed, and the family had changed with them. Even the American military had recently provided training, gear, and weapons for his people as a bulwark against common enemies. It was ironic, and he did so love the Americans and the idealistic Western bubble they lived in. No awareness of the very real struggles of his people, his family.

It came down to this: The Middle East was a powder-keg, primed and ready to blow. All it would take would be one wrong spark to ignite it. When that happened, well, it would be a veritable springtime for whichever side came out on top. Dr. Pitman knew all this. There was no way he couldn't. But he was angry. Understandably so, and he was, after all, still a Westerner. *But there is a reason for all that is happening,* he reminded himself. *It just needs to play itself out.* His mentor knew what he was doing. The man in the suit stowed his doubts and smiled inwardly.

"Find someone to clean this mess up and meet me downstairs," Dr. Pitman said to Ejder, suddenly. He picked up a dusty brimmed hat laying among Dr. Evans' things and turned it in his hands. "And tell your cousin not to whine about the damage. These artifacts are more valuable than you, your family, and this whole ridiculous hotel."

Ejder's eyes narrowed, but he nodded once in acknowledgment.

Dr. Pitman then turned to the man in the suit. "And as for you, find me something you can fly."

"Fly?" It wasn't a question of being able to, it was simply surprising. Did Dr. Pitman expect to be able to follow them? They had no idea where the others had gone. Did they?

"Don't ask questions, boy. Find a way to get us in the air. If Doc Evans and his little band aren't running scared it will be a miracle, and I'm getting tired of chasing that man. He was obviously lying about the Disk, but there's no stopping him from telling Chen what he knows now. That woman is not worthy of our secrets, so it's time to cut this snake off at the head. I have a plan, but it's going to take everybody we have. Plus, it's a long dang way to Doomsday from here, and I really don't want to drive it." The man in the ruined suit said nothing, but a look of mild nervous surprise crossed Dr.

Pitman's face. Clearly, he'd said more than he'd meant to. He covered it by adding, "Not that I have to explain myself to you." He cleared his throat and popped his new hat onto his bald head. "Now, if you are done asking stupid questions and wasting time, how about you go do your job?"

"Yes, Dr. Pitman, my apologies."

Remember who you are. Remember what you really are.

There was an airport a few miles out of town. Ejder would have a cousin or a brother-in-law to take care of their needs. The family always did. The man in the suit motioned for Ejder to come. The sooner they both obeyed, the better it would be for everyone.

The sound of emergency vehicles and angry shouts would likely not die down for about an hour, a decent distraction. He would have them long gone by then.

LXXIX

Mao Sien AW101 Merlin Helicopter. 14,000 ft. Southbound over South-Central Turkey. David.

As the helicopter knifed through the darkness, away from Antioch and back towards Syria, David flipped through his photos, lost in his thoughts. He couldn't believe he was on his second ride on one of these things in just a few days. Something about his life had taken a strange turn.

So far, he had crawled around in an ancient library, helped uncover the key to two languages, found a Mystery Disk that turned out to be another flood myth, and discovered that the Path of the Flaming Sword might be a real ancient trail leading to Eden. And that was just the academic stuff. He'd been held up, shot at, and chased down, been in a car chase, ambushed, held captive, and even made crazy escapes in Russian military vehicles. What's more, David realized, he liked it. His tabletop adventures had nothing on this real stuff.

"Hey, Arthur?" David said, his reverie sparking something important that had been shoved aside in all the chaos. "You said that the circle with all the dots meant 'city,' right?" There was some uncertainty in his voice. "On the

Disk, I mean."

"What's that, my boy?" Arthur replied through the shared channel.

David cleared his throat and tapped at the phone again, zooming in on the last segment of the Disk. He turned the little screen for Arthur to see the phrase he had called a signature.

"So," David faltered, "Cat and I were talking about it, and it's just that in your translation of the Phaistos Disk earlier, you said the thing about the 'important-man.' But then you changed it as you were reading. You said that the mohawk-head guy could mean 'important-man' or 'king' on its own. You also said that the circle thing meant 'city.' But then you kept saying 'important' a bunch more anyway."

Arthur stared at David like he had a circle with seven dots drawn on his forehead.

"Yea, so, I got to thinking, that maybe the other places where you said 'important' might actually be the word 'city?' And that since you changed it in the middle, maybe you weren't thinking about how that symbol is really on there—.

"Seventeen times." Arthur finished for him. "Good lord. What an amateur mistake! Well spotted, David." He patted his hand along his underclothes, entirely forgetting he was mostly undressed, and his little notebook lost. He sighed, removed his glasses, and began massaging the bridge of his nose with the other hand.

There was more, but David wasn't sure if he should say it. Cat looked at him questioningly. She already knew the rest and if he didn't say it, she probably would. After a few seconds, David cracked.

"So, we were thinking, what if you took your original translation of that last phrase as being 'the Path of the Flaming Sword' and put it together with the other idea. That it really is 'the city of the important-man?' You know, Atra-Hasis or Utnapishtim or whatever."

Arthur dropped his glasses.

"Ivan," he finally croaked. "Would it be possible to make a call to Miss Chen right now? Satellite shortwave or somesuch?"

Colonel Ivan grunted. Arthur's strange notions about technology notwithstanding, their pilot made the call.

*   *   *

Without warning, Arthur's voice broke back in on the group channel. "All right everyone, it took some convincing, but Mel understands why we need to go west."

West? David couldn't believe it. They were going home? It was over? That couldn't be. He started to stammer out one of these questions, but Matthew beat him to it like the disembodied voice of God from his seat in the front.

"She's financing some new goals then?"

"Yes. Same terms, new objectives. And thanks to our pilot here, we will be there by morning."

David thrilled. It wasn't over after all. It could only mean one thing. "So, are we going to Lydia? To Zeus of the Labrys ax?"

"Goodness, no. Not after what you just said."

"What I said? What did I say?"

"The last line of the Disk. You were right David, it's no signature. The best translation is, 'Follow the Path of the Flaming Sword to the city of the Important-Man.' The path is real."

Cat caught David's eye. There was a shared excitement there that he could practically grab hold of. *The path is real!*

Arthur started thinking aloud again. "Mel was a bit wary of such a leap, considering the resources that have already been invested in Ugarit. But I managed to convince her that such measures will be unnecessary moving forward, especially since we have the Colonel here. I'm done with teams. No one knows where we are going, and Pitman will almost certainly be expecting us to fall back and regroup. But Wyatt was on the trail of the Minoans, and unless I miss my guess, that's the real starting point."

"The real starting point?" Matthew asked, enthusiastically.

"Yes, Rabbi Yosef's starting point. For the Path of the Flaming Sword, you see. The Disk is telling us to look for a holy city of a divine king with a connection to the important-man. Nûḥ, as David has reminded us. But there was only one great city in the ancient Mediterranean world that fit that description, and it was just up the road from where the blasted Disk was kept."

A jolt of understanding hit David. Arthur had called Knossos the greatest city in the ancient world. Kings of the ancient sea and inventors of flush toilets or whatever, and just across the short part of the island from Phaistos. Ugarit might have been the New York, but Knossos was the Los Angeles. It was no wonder Arthur was so chipper suddenly. They were going to Crete!

"If Yosef's theory is right," Arthur continued, "then the Disk is an ancient map that will somehow point the way to Dilmun. If I can translate the Disk this easily using just Yosef's work and the Ras-Shamra translation tablet, then so can others. Yosef is the one Wyatt picked to do it in the first place, after all. We can't know who to trust anymore, but we have to assume that Pitman has the journal, knows about the Disk, and he took the translation tablets too of course. But if we are lucky, then maybe he doesn't know what he has." In a flash, Arthur's mood flipped. He realized he was literally grinding his teeth. "But either way, we can't let Pitman have this. We must get to Knossos and use our advantage to beat him to Nûḥ's city first."

So, Mr. Aarons' second partner was trying to stop Arthur from following the path. No wonder everything had blown apart so quickly. Maybe Dr. Pitman was worried Arthur might debunk the Doomsday find, or maybe he just wanted the glory of finding Dilmun all for himself, but whatever the reason, he was obviously in league with the tattooed guys and was not afraid of shooting anybody who got in the way. It was just like Mr. Aarons wrote—finding Noah's city could really be a vindication for Arthur. Maybe even a partial vindication for Uncle Sir Arthur, too.

Only for some reason, all of this gave David an uneasy feeling. His wizard was acting weird.

"Arthur," David ventured, "How do we know that the starting point isn't Phaistos or somewhere else on the island? I mean, that's where the Disk was found, right?"

Cat met David's eyes again and she nodded.

"The word *Knossos* literally means knowledge, David," Arthur explained. "Sir Arthur wouldn't have doubted my theory for a second. It's entirely possible that the Disk was taken to Phaistos as a means of protecting or hiding it. Or for that matter, as the spoils of war or something similar."

Cat harrumphed. "The Minoans did not fight among themselves like petty city-states. They were the center of trade and culture for the entire world. The very fact that your translation tablet had two parallel languages of Crete in a place like Ugarit is proof of their mighty merchant navy. We should go to Phaistos. To where the Disk was found."

Arthur soured even more. David knew his wizard agreed with these facts, he'd said the same thing himself the other day. But there was something else going on too, and David felt in his gut what it was. For Arthur, this was now about vindicating Uncle Sir Arthur. It wasn't about finding Mr. Aarons anymore, it was about beating him. In one way of thinking, anyway.

Arthur and Cat began a tense academic debate on the better destination, but David's thoughts turned to something else that had bothered him for a while. His imagination swirled with images of the Minoans from the museum. He recalled the seal stone pictograms he'd held in his actual hand. The translation tablet that Mr. Aarons found, and Arthur had so deftly translated.

There was Rabbi Yosef's breakthrough work on Proto-Sinaitic pictographs. And it all connected to the Phaistos Disk, which wasn't a forgery any more than it was a board game. As Arthur was now willing to admit, the Disk was a spiraled message with encoded directions for the path to Noah's city. But they were missing something, David just knew it!

Images of other spirals popped into his head. The overgrown maze at St. Giles, tucked into the crook of the busy twisted street. The Proto-Sinaitic symbol for 'B,' *Beyt*. The spiral on one of those same Minoan seal stones hidden away up in the Ashmolean archive room, tiny versions of the double-sided spiral of the Phaistos Mystery Disk itself. What was it that Arthur had said? The spiral had represented everything from the mystery of life and birth to the snake who hid in the garden at the beginning of time.

David's mind raced to make connections. He imagined the pictographic *Mem*, the M with the extra ridge that looked like the waves of an ocean, or maybe a snake too. Rabbi Yosef's translation page said it meant 'chaos' or 'water' or both, the crashing seas of Noah's storm tossing the old man and his family in the massive ark of his own technological making. The natural wiping away of everything by God, a clean slate for creation. A consequence of sin, like Adam and Eve's expulsion from the Garden for eating the fruit offered by that snake. The fruit of knowledge of good and evil, that is. Knowledge of order and chaos perhaps?

Mem, spiral, chaos, nature... Ancient man believed chaos was represented by the female and that order was seen as male. Nature female. Culture male. Adam and Eve. They became what they had eaten: knowledge of good, evil, chaos, and order. All because of the snake, probably Lucifer. The 'bringer of light,' of enlightenment, and with it, apocalypse.

No! David realized with a start. *Not a snake, but a serpent!*

"Chaos serpent!" David exclaimed. The others stopped talking and stared at him. "Arthur, you said the spiral was one of the oldest symbols. That it's a chaos serpent coiled and ready to strike or something, like in the garden of Eden, or in Gilgamesh when the snake steals the Tree of Life from him?"

Only the *thrum-thrum-thrum* of the helicopter blades answered him at first, then Cat caught it too. "The Phaistos Disk is a spiral because it represents chaos? Perhaps its inner knowledge is hidden?"

"Yes!" David exclaimed. "Which means it can't be Knossos. Knowledge is the opposite of chaos, it brings order to it. Maybe the Palace at Phaistos was a place of celebrating chaos? Didn't you say there were no records kept there?"

"It was the principal place of the snake priestesses," Cat said. "Phaistos was known for its cult of the mother goddess."

David thrilled. "Snakes and women? Those are both chaos symbols! I, um,

I mean archetypally. Adam was civilization, and Eve was nature. Right?"

"Like Tiamat," Arthur said, flatly—a slow nod forming. "Etymologically related to the Hebrew words *taum*, 'chaos' and *tohu*, 'waste.'"

"Tiamat and Abzu. You said that before only, you never said what Tiamat and Abzu actually were, and I couldn't exactly google it."

"Didn't I? Well, Tiamat was the great chaos serpent who lives at the bottom of the sea. It's from the Sumerian creation myth, the Akkadian *Enuma Elish*. Her lover was Abzu, the freshwater dragon whom the younger gods murdered to usurp his lordship of the universe. Enraged, Tiamat gives birth to the first dragons. She makes war upon her treacherous first children, only to be slain by Marduk, god of storms. Marduk then forms the heavens and earth from her corpse."

Cat and David looked at each other quizzically, then back to Arthur, waiting for him to explain the connection to *Genesis*. Father Mathew cleared his throat into the mic. It seemed to snap Arthur into gear.

"Order from chaos, you see. Tiamat is the first and greatest of the chaos serpents. *Leviathan, Lotan, Tannim.* She is nearly every whale, sea-serpent, behemoth, snake, dragon, and jackal that made it into the Bible."

"There are dragons in the Bible?" What insanity was Arthur talking about this time?

"Jackal?" Cat laughed in equal measure of disbelief.

"'Listen! The report is coming'—" Matthew offered, using his scripture-quoting voice. It sounded even more godlike over the headset. "'A great commotion from the land of the north! It will make the towns of Judah desolate, a haunt of jackals.'"

"Jeremiah 10:22," Arthur affirmed. "But in the King James translation, a much more appropriate word is used."

Matthew accepted the challenge. "'Behold, the noise of the bruit is come, and a great commotion out of the north country, to make the cities of Judah desolate, and a den of dragons.'" *Just how many versions does this priest have memorized, anyway?*

"Chaos serpents are everywhere in the Bible if you know where to look," Arthur continued. "*Exodus, Deuteronomy, Nehemiah, Isaiah...*" He faltered. "*Lamentations?*"

David was amazed. He'd definitely never heard this in Sunday School. He felt a sudden, perverse desire to throw that little fact in his dad's face the next time he complained about the evils of D&D.

"Quite right," Matthew affirmed. "And you will recall that Malachi also refers to the *Tannoth*, plural. And John's *Revelation* of Christ must not be overlooked, nor must we forget *Genesis*." The two men had talked about all of this before, David realized.

Arthur waggled a thankful finger in the air. "The Leviathan in the *Book of Job* reflects the older Canaanite *Lotan*, a primeval monster defeated by the god Hadad. Parallels to the role of Mesopotamian Tiamat defeated by Marduk have long been drawn in comparative mythology. And as I said, *Tohu*—chaos or formlessness in Old Hebrew—is clearly related. It's all right there in the first few lines of *Genesis*. Chaos, waters, firmament. Even Noah's 'springs of the great deep' have a connection to poor Abzu's murder, after a fashion. After which there was only chaos once more."

"Then why the jackals?" Cat asked.

"Translation choice," Arthur shrugged. "Scholars have, er, pragmatically interpreted the chaos serpent as referring to other predatory creatures better known to zoology since the beginning. Choices such as the crocodile, great whales, and named sea monsters like Leviathan are generally understandable, if lamentable. But no aquatic substitution worked for land-locked Jerusalem, so a local animal was chosen. It's deeply ironic. We modern folks miss the pattern of the sea dragon in *Genesis*, earth dragon in *Job*, sky dragon in *Jeremiah*, and fire dragons in *Numbers*—if we aren't paying very close attention. And that's just off the top of my head."

David beamed. *There are dragons in the Bible!* He'd had no idea about any of that, but he couldn't have set it up better if he had. "The Bible is not a science book!" he blurted, parroting Arthur's words back to him.

"Indeed," Arthur nodded. "The point for these writers was not the biological reality of dragons, but rather the enigmatic reality that an ancient, unknown chaotic force was coming, or had arrived. Things so terrible and unimaginable that—at least in Jeremiah's time—when all was done, there would remain only dragons living in Jerusalem. It was a powerful literary symbol."

"For what it's worth," Matthew added, "Jeremiah was right. The conquest of Israel and great exile was pretty horrific, as we are told by others later."

"Of course, not all the dragons are bad," Arthur added. "Isaiah's vision of the *Seraphim* comes to mind."

"I thought *Seraphim* was a sort of angel?" deMata countered.

"Well, yes," Arthur agreed, "but the literal translation would be 'fire serpent.' The six-winged creatures in Isaiah's vision are fundamentally chaos dragons too. One essential point being that they serve the Lord, just as chaos must. You see, the point of a symbol is to show deeper truth than some literal object or event can."

"In the case of *Isaiah*," Matthew explained, "the purpose for all those wings was to demonstrate that even the most terrifying creatures cannot look upon Him, are naked before Him, and cannot walk on His holy ground. Small wonder Isaiah was terrified."

"Is that why Satan is depicted as a snake in Eden?" Cat asked, "because he was a fallen fire serpent?"

"Certainly not," Arthur answered. "Technically, the serpent in Eden is never identified as Satan. And Satan is never identified as an angel. That's all medieval Christian mythology. But I think even those insights might be missing the point."

David smiled. He had heard this one before. It was nice not to be at the receiving end this time, but thanks to Matthew, he also knew that Arthur's was not the only reasonable perspective.

"I think perhaps what Arthur is implying," Matthew clarified, "is that it takes the coming together of order and chaos to give meaning to creation. Apologies, it's something Yosef and I spoke about on the plane. 'A complex phenomenological approach, not a simple practical one.' That's the thrust of it at any rate. Or perhaps Isaiah's prophetic words are more appropriate? 'I form the light and create darkness. I make peace and create evil. I the Lord do all these things.' We mustn't conflate chaos with evil, is I believe the point here Arthur, is it not?"

That's from the Bible, too? Not for the first time, David seriously wondered if his understanding of the Bible and its God was entirely too shallow.

Arthur grunted. "Isaiah's not wrong. *Genesis* says that God used chaos to form the world by putting it in order. It's an idea far older than Moses, I assure you."

"'And the earth was without form, and void.'" Matthew rumbled. "'And darkness was upon the face of the deep. And the Spirit of God moved upon the face of the waters... And God said, let there be a firmament in the midst of the waters, and let it divide the waters from the waters.' Order from chaos indeed."

Arthur waggled a finger. "Quite right. To name something is to give it a function and take away its unknown qualities. And we too are allowed to bring order to chaos by naming things. It was the power given to Adam, the animal-namer. The lion, the bear, the snake, the bird of prey, we collect these creatures of death into zoos to amuse children because we no longer fear them. We would likewise steal the power of the dragon if we could somehow classify it taxonomically. Which is, of course, entirely impossible. That's why the dragon remains such a powerful image even today. And yet, the God of *Genesis* is the God of the chaos serpent too. The very structure of *Genesis'* opening chapter is about the true word spoken by God which brings order out of the chaos. The naming, the days, it's all quite orderly. Plus, this concept of ordered chaos is a truer reading of the spiral's most deep and ancient meaning."

"'In the beginning was the Word, and the Word was with God, and the Word was God.'" Matthew quoted. "John's opening lines."

"Yes," Arthur agreed, smoothing out his beard. "*Logos* is the word used there. A philosophical insight from the ancient Greeks. That's full circle on the idea."

David's mind was spinning. There was something just out of his grasp that he couldn't see. Yosef had said that there were four levels of interpretation, the Hebrew letters for 'paradise' derived from the acronym PRDS. Four words that stood for the simple, the alluded to, the instructive, and the mystical meanings. *Could that be true of the Disk too?*

"It's a code," David blurted. "You said the language of the Disk is Proto-Semitic or whatever, right? Well, then there's got to be a deeper meaning to the Disk. The plain reading is the first level that you already did Arthur, but the second level is supposed to be an allusion. You know, symbolism?" He felt like an idiot lecturing these three Oxford scholars on symbolism, but he braved it. "It's just that the big symbol is right there. It's obvious if you know it. The chaos spiral—the serpent—it must represent something, right? The place to start maybe? I mean, the thing is literally called the Mystery Disk."

Arthur looked dubious. Cat was deep in thought, her brow furrowed. David wished that Matthew was visible, so he could maybe help out with more than words on the headset.

"It is the Labyrinth," Cat said, without a shred of doubt.

"Pardon?" Arthur stammered.

David couldn't tell if he hadn't heard or hadn't believed what he'd heard. But there was no doubt in David's mind the moment she'd said it. *Labrys ax, Zeus Labrayndeus? Labyrinth? That's gotta be it!*

If the starting place was on Minoan Crete, then the Disk had to be pointing to the most famous spiral of all, King Minos' Minotaur Maze.

LXXX

Mao Sien AW101 Merlin Helicopter. 14,000 ft. Southbound over South-Central Turkey. Arthur.

"You can't possibly be serious," Evans stammered. "Even if it was remotely plausible that the Disk intended the Cretan Labyrinth as the starting point, we wouldn't have any idea how to go about locating it. Sir Arthur went to his grave believing that the Greek myths of a Minotaur's Labyrinth stemmed from the mazelike palace at Knossos. It only affirms my assertion that it should be our target."

"No," deMata said firmly.. "The Palace at Knossos is wrong in every way. I am sorry. Your grand uncle's theories were formed with only half the clues. As David has guessed, the work at Phaistos reveals the rest. Phaistos was indeed a place for the worship and celebration of chaos, motherhood, nature, and sexual liberation." She spoke each word with a sense of pride and ownership that none of the men in the car could have managed. "It was made for the greatest of festivals."

"Yes, yes," Evans agreed dismissively, "but listen everyone, even a chaotic Phaistos is no more the answer than an orderly Knossos. Spirals aren't just about chaos—they're about the balance between chaos and order together. Without a definitive place to start, this exercise is pointless. Perhaps your labyrinth is a place located somewhere in between." Evans couldn't believe he was allowing himself to become sucked into this fantasy. "Why don't you consult a map on that phone of yours, David?"

"The alphabet is the place to start," David stated matter of factly. He whipped out his phone, but not to access his map software. "Arthur, it's been right in front of us the whole time. Mr. Aarons was giving us the biggest clue he could think of, but also one that nobody else would possibly understand. Only, it's not the alphabet, it's the *Alefbet*! The first two letters are the clue."

"What are you talking about David? What clue?"

David zoomed in on the first two letters of the little chart and they passed the phone around.

Name	Pictograph	Meaning
Aleph		Ox/strength/leader/God
Bet		House / "in"

"In the house of God?" Evans ventured, putting the words together in one of the more obvious ways. "What of it?"

"No," David said. "I mean, yes... but not the God of *Genesis*. In this case, I'm pretty sure it's more about the symbols. Look at the shapes. It's a cattle head and a spiral. A spiral, Arthur."

DeMata caught where David was going and gave a little gasp. "It is the bull of Crete and a chaos spiral." She decided in an instant.

David looked around expectantly, "Guys, it's a bull and a spiral! A maze? In Crete? With a bull?"

Matthew began chuckling from the front.

DeMata covered her mouth. A string of muffled Spanish slipped out. Evans didn't need to fully understand it to know it was quite profane. "The Labyrinth of the Minotaur," she finally squeaked. She launched herself at David and hugged him in her excitement. "It is right there, hidden into the very words we use to name the alphabet. I do not believe it!"

"Yes," David managed. "Mr. Aarons was trying to point us to the Labyrinth. This proves it."

Evans scowled, not comfortable with the implications of any of this. The boy was completely lost in his wild fantasies, clearly. Worse, Matthew and the girl genius were going along with it.

He spoke hesitantly, working out how to debunk this nonsense properly. "Listen, the *aleph* 'strong cattle' symbol is an incredibly ancient word for a god. Given the connections between pictographic Minoan and Proto-Sinaitic that we have made today, it stands to reason that the bull-worship of Crete could stem from the old Canaanite bull-worship cults, but that still doesn't tell us which palace the Labyrinth myth was based on—if it even existed. All we have are highly contaminated Greek myths written down centuries later. We would need much more to even begin puzzling it out than a few coincidental symbols." Evans capped off his speech with a firm nod. *Silliness settled.*

"I know precisely where the Labyrinth is." deMata stated, oblivious to Evans' mental distress. Her voice had the same deadly seriousness as before. "But it is not at a palace."

A little cough from Matthew came through the headset. "Pardon?"

"I know right where the Labyrinth of Crete is said to be. Every local person in southwestern Crete does."

"What?" Evans and David said together. Evans punctuated the question by blinking a dozen or so times.

"I studied the ruins at Phaistos while living in Gortyna for over a year. There is an ancient quarry cavern nearby that has been called the Labyrinthos Caves for longer than anyone can remember. It is what you might call a, a public secret? It is sealed now, but I have a colleague who has taken me inside many times."

"Quarry cavern?" Evans stuttered. "Are you talking about the legend of the Gortyn Labyrinth?" This was too much. DeMata nodded proudly, causing another horrible thought to stack itself on top of Evans' already precarious collection. "Oh, dear lord." The helicopter's restraints went taut against Evans' chest as he tried to sit up and failed. "Did you ever publish anything about it?"

DeMata looked uncertainly at the crazy old man with no pants, challenging her laurels yet again. David mercifully came to the rescue.

"Wyatt Aarons!" he exclaimed. "Cat, did you ever talk to him about that Labyrinth? Something that you wrote and maybe he read? Like a paper?"

"Well, yes." She said, slowly. "I published a piece on the Gortyn Labyrinth a few years ago while I studied there. It was a silly throw-away article about how the Gortyn Labyrinth is a local legend. People have known of it since at least the twelfth century, but few are allowed down anymore. Not since the Nazis blew it up. But Wyatt Aarons wrote to me that it was inspiring, whatever that is supposed to mean. Some emails later, and he put me onto his team."

Evans clasped his hands together and leaned back, not caring about the goofy smile that was taking over his face. David beamed no less foolishly. There were still questions on the edge of deMata's lips, but Evans waved for her to hold on to them. "Whether it's the right place or not is irrelevant. It's what Wyatt thought was right. Ivan, take us to the town of Gortya in Crete."

"Dragons, secret codes, the Minotaur, labyrinths, and now Nazis too?" David laughed. "This is officially better than any tabletop module ever."

Evans gawked at his grandson in disbelief. He was beginning to wonder who had in fact dragged who into this mess. "Yes," he offered with the thickest of sarcasm, "After all, we simply need to solve an ancient riddle, navigate the Minoan Labyrinth, and perhaps confront a Minotaur, before beginning the nice simple 'Path of the Flaming Sword.' Perfectly normal archeology."

Worse, the boy's strange humor was rubbing off on him.

Blasted Wyatt Aarons.

LXXXI

Ras-Shamra Basecamp. Ugarit, Syria. Mel.

Mel swirled the black Assam tea in front of her with a cinnamon stick and sighed. One of her men had scrounged it up for her in town. She would have to increase his pay.

Dr. Evans was safe, and she now understood everything that had happened. Her newest human computer hadn't betrayed her—he had protected everything they were doing. Dr. Evans had isolated himself from her contaminated network. Despite being lied to, betrayed, attacked, chased, robbed, and threatened by guerilla rebels, the man was a consummate professional. Far better than Wyatt Aarons had behaved when faced with similar opposition.

Or was she being too critical of her favorite employee? Aarons had been the most regular, most loyal, and most appreciative of all her teams—even though he'd long insisted on being a one-man show. Every one of her employees had their quirks and eccentricities. If Wyatt Aarons had sent her the journal, would they be in as good of a position as they now were? Would she have even recognized its true value? Dr. Evans' translation skills were undoubtedly some of the best in the world. However, she had seriously underestimated his drive and determination to follow this mystery to the end. Aarons hadn't.

Moreover, Wyatt Aarons' impulsive actions had brought them further than she could have imagined. He had exposed an ancient trail of clues that Dr. Evans had now persuaded her could very well lead to the original objective of the Dilmun team, the city of Noah itself. Additionally, Aarons had inadvertently exposed the traitor Pitman and his connection to this insurgent group with the raven emblem. It was everything she could have wanted.

And Mel always got what she wanted.

She took a long swig of the local black tea and swallowed hard. There was still the matter of what to do about "Uncle" Ryan Pitman, but it could wait until he popped his head up again. If he was smart, he would go to ground hard and not come up for a very long time.

The terminal chimed, indicating a new video connection coming in. Automatically, she answered it. A strange image appeared on the screen. It looked like a bad picture of a cork bulletin board dedicated to random Noah's

Ark facts. One sheet of paper had a drawing of a long ovoid egg shape with labels like "rock intrusion," "horizontal beams spaced evenly," and "central corridor." Another was a boat-shaped cutaway with arrows and measurements meant to illustrate something she couldn't quite discern. The words were in Turkish also. Though she couldn't read it herself, she assumed they were translations of the same.

Next to all this, was a framed lightbox that contained a wide-angle photo of what could only be the Doomsday Mountain site. The Noah's Ark monument where the damning evidence of Pitman had been snapped. This was no coincidence, but what did it mean? She reached out to tap the image and pull up the metadata to find out, when a shape darted past so fast that she jerked her hand away. This wasn't an image, it was video! *Live video*, she quickly realized.

She maximized the window. The subtle shifting of pixels from the outside light established in her mind what she already knew, even before another bird could zoom by. What she had too quickly assumed was a lightbox was, in fact, a window in the wall of the building on which the corkboard was mounted. As the true scale of what she was seeing unfurled in her mind, a chill ran down her spine.

She tapped the screen a few times and confirmed her fears. The video was being streamed from one of her computers. One that had been logged missing only recently, Wyatt Aarons' laptop. The last of her suspicions locked into place. It was inarguably a complete and total trap, but Pitman had also just foolishly tipped his hand.

Mel considered her options, then pulled up a second com window. "I'm going to need another helicopter, something fast, delivered here right away. A pilot also. Promise our Russian friends whatever they want, there is no time to negotiate. Also, I'll be going dark for a while once it gets here, so don't worry about me."

*   *   *

Ten minutes later, Mel was geared up in black tactical gear. She walked in silence with four armed men for two short miles northwest. They passed out of the stony ruins, through a scrubby glade, past a field filled with perfect rows of olive trees, then finally stopped at a little bay by the sea. She stood and watched the waves crash upon a breakwater. Someone had cleverly placed it to protect the farmland from the unpredictable Mediterranean. It was all quite beautiful.

Now it was time for Mel to become a breakwater, to absorb the destructive energy that Ryan Pitman had released. She needed to protect her other assets, to become an antivirus program among her human computers.

Shortly, she heard her helicopter. It had crocodile camouflage with Russian markings and a prominent red cross painted on its sides.

"That's an Mi-35M Hind E," Captain Rogers said, impressed. "Export version of an Mi-24, and with a Medivac configuration. Extra tanks for extra range."

"Extra tanks are good, we need that. But is it fast?"

"Second fastest in the world, Ma'am."

"That will do," she smiled.

The flying tank hovered near the beach and they all clipped in. It rose, and her borrowed pilot turned widely over the bay before pointing the nose north toward Turkey. Mel checked her phone for messages one last time, then tossed it out the still-open door. It dropped and disappeared into the frothy sea. Mel settled in for the flight. She was in the thick of it now, just like she'd wanted.

And Mel always got what she wanted.

LXXXII

Mao Sien AW101 Merlin Helicopter. Westbound toward Gortyna, Crete. Arthur.

Evans was only half paying attention to the conversation the others were having about Sir Arthur's island. His mind was racing, and he wasn't used to feeling this way. What was it, ambivalence? Yes, that was it, Dr. Arthur M. Evans of Oxford was of two minds.

It was all because of Wyatt, of course. Evans had been telling himself that he had no choice but to follow the path because Wyatt would have tried to do it, but surely that was nonsense. Wyatt was probably kidnapped by the raven-tattooed insurgents and stuck in a hole somewhere, assuming he wasn't dead. It might have been an attempt to collect on an old vendetta, but why? Not after all these years. No, Wyatt had gotten too close to their secrets again. The same secrets Evans was now chasing. It stood to reason then, that the best way to find these men was to find out what they were protecting. If nothing else, it would draw them out.

So then, why were they now heading to the Mediterranean? He had drawn them out, hadn't he? This felt like running away. And that was where the other half of his mind was entrenched. Sir Arthur's island. Crete. Back to Europe. Running away was good! Hang Wyatt and his kidnapped self. They would be safe here. He felt almost giddy.

"The Greeks called it *Megalonisi*," deMata shouted into her headset. "It means 'The Big Island.'" Out of the window, Evans could see the coast of that big island. It loomed so large as to not look like an island at all, even from up here. The speed at which the military helicopter had crossed more than a quarter of the Mediterranean was positively mind-boggling. *More miracles of flight.*

"I can see why!" David shouted back. "And that water is so blue!" The teen had been attempting to take photos through the window with only limited success, but it had not affected his enthusiasm.

"Most of what we know of Crete comes from the Greeks," deMata continued. It was going to be Evans' same lesson reframed, then. Time to see if David had been paying attention. "Their mythology was often little more than war propaganda, but fascinating nonetheless. For example, classical tales tell us that Gortyna was the site of one of Zeus' many affairs, a myth which features the Princess Europa."

"Europa?" David asked, "As in Europe? Like how the Minoans were the first Europeans?"

"Correct," the feisty girl-genius confirmed. "It gives some weight to the claim that the civilization of the European continent was born on the island of Crete. A colossal statue of Europa sitting on the back of a bull was discovered at the amphitheater in Gortyna in the nineteenth century. And many coins have been found with Europa's representation on the back, showing that the people honored Europa as a great goddess. And so, disguised as a bull, Zeus abducts Europa from Lebanon and they have an affair under a *platanus* tree, a family of trees still seen today in Gortyna."

"Bull?" David said, excitedly. "Like the Minotaur, and the pictographic symbol for God, eh Arthur?" His face was a few shades redder, whether from excitement at the connection or shock over the details, Evans couldn't guess.

Evans just smiled and nodded stupidly. He had stated repeatedly that the Proto-Sinaitic symbol David was referring to was an ox, but he didn't have the will to argue right now. He had refrained from mentioning the particulars of the sexual encounter with the Minotaur's bull father and witch mother. He doubted that the open-minded Spaniardess would even notice such boundaries. This was a different myth, one he'd forgotten till she mentioned it. But there was no debating that the kingdom of Minos was tied to the symbol of the strong and fecund ox or bull. Evans was still working out whether to change the subject when deMata soldiered on unabashedly.

"Following their love affair," she said, with a little shoulder shake, "three children were born. Sarpedon, Rhadamanthys, and Minos. It was these who became the kings of the three Aegean Palaces in Crete."

"And Minos founded the Minoans! Nice." David was a few shades redder, but undoubtedly still holding his own.

Evans felt a smile tug at the edge of his mouth. There was more than one reason that the symbol of chaos was considered by ancient man to be female. How many a man had lost his mind when he became close to a smart and pretty girl? Evans was no classical mythology expert, but he knew the Minoan stories probably as well as Uncle Arthur had known them. And if the boy didn't, Evans suspected that the curvaceous Spaniard would make a far better Greek lit tutor than Evans ever could.

"This is the southern coast," deMata continued. "The Palace of Phaistos is not at all far from Gortyna. It lies to the southwest, on the east end of Kastri hill and the Mesara plain. We will not quite reach the Palace, but perhaps we can go together soon."

David nodded drunkenly as the helicopter banked into a turn. A moment later, the beaches were behind them and the craggy hills and mountains grew. Impossible ravines and slopes dared them to find a place to land without disastrous results. Evans began to second guess his earlier ideas about retreating to western civilization here.

"There!" deMata finally exclaimed, pointing to a distant point on the horizon. "That is Mt. Psiloritis, the highest mountain in Crete. On its slopes is the Kamares cave, a religious cult center for Phaistos and the whole Mesara Plain. Gortyna is not far now."

Out the window, Evans could see the mountain in question. It loomed beautifully over the hills and twisting valleys with nothing but sheep trails. "This whole place is filled with mountain passes and cave systems," Evans growled, finally finding a wedge into the conversation. "I would hate to get lost down there."

"Yes," deMata agreed. "but that is exactly where we must go."

"We are landing east of Gortyn City," Colonel Ivan announced. "Is closest I can land to quarry road. After, I must find helipad with fuel."

The quarry road that led to the alleged Minotaur's Labyrinth. It gave Evans a shiver. There was a big gap between the facts and what they were about to do, but to follow Wyatt Aarons, they had left the world of rational peer-reviewed scientists behind long ago. This was the Wyatt he remembered—fringe scholarship all the way. What would Sir Arthur have said about this?

With a start, Evans realized that he probably would have jumped at the chance to come.

"Adolf Hitler sent the Nazis to search the Labyrinth," deMata said, "but even they were not able to map the depths very far. They used many tons of concrete to turn it into a bunker, then took a dangerous amount of munitions and other materials deep into the tunnels. When they eventually abandoned it at the end of the war, they detonated their own ammunition dump. It caused irreparable damage to the site and many cave-ins."

A chill ran down Evans' spine. *How many have sought that hoary old chestnut, the Labyrinth, and been consumed by their obsession?* It was no laughing matter.

"Then, one morning in 1961," deMata cheerily continued, "the locals were awakened by a grand series of explosions from deep underground. Investigation revealed that treasure hunters had tried to blow a hole in what they believed to be a hidden chamber. They failed terribly. The accident left four people dead, and the entrance to the complex has been shut by order of the Greek army ever since. The Labyrinth Cave simply disappeared from public sight. Unto now, the cave is still closed, and entering it is strictly forbidden to the public. But as I said, I know someone who I believe can get us in."

"Who?" Evans groused. "How?" In this precise place, searchers had died trying to unlock the secrets under Gortyna, as deMata had so casually explained. That could not happen today. Today, he had to be Theseus.

"A professor I assisted during my studies has been permitted to work in the caverns and map it. Colonel Ivan, can you connect another phone call? I will tell you the number."

A short private-channel conversation was conducted in rapid and excited Greek, and the details were readily squared away. Evans noted no change in wide-eyed David as the girl giggled her goodbyes to the man on the other end of the line. She did so with a clear familiarity he hadn't anticipated.

"Nikolaos will meet us with a car after we land." deMata declared, as the helicopter's whir changed, and they spiraled their way down to the spot Colonel Ivan had chosen.

Nikolaos? Evans wondered. *Who the devil is Nikolaos?*

*   *   *

Ten minutes later, Evans and company stood by the road and listened to their helicopter fade into the sky. Ten more, and a swarthy dark-haired young Oxonian Evans did not know drove up in a compact car with a bicycle mounted on the back. Dr. Nikolaos Andino hopped out and was greeted with more Greek and a kiss on each cheek by their Spanish guide. The kiss lingered just a little too long for mere greeting, in Evans' opinion.

Matthew gave a sideways glance and Evans knew his suspicions were shared. In any language, it was clear that this man was more than just a colleague. Had David even noticed? University folks were one of the world's more sexually liberated populations, at least by reputation. And when you combined that with lonely research in remote locations for years on end, well... it wasn't something Evans had ever been interested in, but there had been one or two propositions along the way.

Dr. Andino spoke a few more hushed words, then to Evans' surprise, handed deMata the keys. They both laughed, she kissed him again, and he removed the bike while she took the driver's seat. Evans suddenly realized he was the only one in the group not moving towards the little car. He quickly followed David to the back seat, and Matthew squeezed his bulk into the front.

On the back seat was a tightly folded and expensive-looking Greek outfit straight out of 1978. The pants had a characteristic gaudy zipper and felt inlay. An ostentatious belt with an oversized buckle and a colorful shirt were included. There was even a suitcoat with immense buttons to complete the horrible ensemble. But it was better than spelunking in one's boxers, so Evans grunted and wiggled himself into the borrowed designer slacks. It was a tight fit on the waist, and he had to roll the pant legs a few times, but it would be serviceable.

Evans chose not to dwell on what deMata might have said to get a man she hadn't seen in months to so quickly abandon his car and a spare outfit. *Or perhaps it was repayment for some favor rendered in the past?* He wiggled the silk shirt into place, but let the coat lie. *Best not think about it.* He was just grateful to be clothed again.

"I see you found your little gift from Dr. Andino," deMata laughed, peeking at him in the rearview mirror. "Was I right that you are similarly sized?"

Evans nodded as politely as he could manage.

And then they were off, deMata at the wheel, the mysterious stranger waving to them as he began pedaling the few kilometers or so back to town. Matthew ducked awkwardly as his head bounced against the ceiling of the little toy car.

"The entrance to the Labyrinth is only a short way up this little mountain range," deMata stated. "There is sometimes a night guard, but Dr. Andino gave me the gate combination. Once inside, we will have as much time as we need. We can use any lights and equipment we want, so long as we put it back after."

Evans busied himself with shirt buttons and trying to thread a belt while seated. It took a few miles. David watched him, but something about the youth's expression made it seem that his thoughts were somewhere else entirely.

"What is it, David?" Evans softly asked.

David's eyes flicked up and his mouth thinned into a line. "It's my phone's battery," he whispered. "I don't have a way to charge it anymore."

Evans considered this and nodded. The little smartphone had been surprisingly helpful so far. A bit of order in their chaos, in a sense. But soon to be subject to chaos itself, evidently. It didn't escape Evans' attention that the only available copy of his notes was on the blasted thing.

There was silence for some minutes except for the straining of the little engine as the overloaded car struggled up each hill. Mercifully, Matthew's recitation voice broke it.

"'And he went down into that doleful gulf, through winding paths among the rocks, under caverns, and arches, and galleries, and over heaps of fallen stone. And he turned on the left hand, and on the right hand, and went up and down, till his head was dizzy; but all the while he held his clue. For when he went in, he had fastened it to a stone and left it to unroll out of his hand as he went on. And it lasted him till he met the Minotaur, in a narrow chasm between black cliffs.'"

Charles Kingsley's able retelling of *Theseus*, Evans realized. Spoken aloud, as all myths rightly should be, courtesy of Matthew's remarkable gift for recalling massive passages. Evans didn't know he'd kept that one, but it didn't surprise him either. Chances were, Matthew had the whole volume tucked away in some corner of his remarkable mind.

"Well-chosen, Matthew. Quite apt." It occurred to Evans that these words did not sound much like the description of a complicated temple complex but did fit the description of a mountainous quarry cavern quite well. He decided not to mention it. The kids needed no further encouragement of their silly notions.

"Thank you, Arthur," his best friend replied. "Coincidentally, does anyone happen to have brought along a considerable length of twine?"

LXXXIII

Cessna Skyhawk. On approach to Yukarıçarıkçı, Iğdır Province, Turkey. Mr. Suit.

"You want me to land on that?" the man in the suit shouted over the whine of the little turboprop engine.

Dr. Pitman laughed. "You've been away too long, boy! This airfield is brand new. Everybody up here is quite proud of it." It was unclear how much sarcasm the old man intended.

"That landing strip is mostly dirt," the man stated calmly. "Those are construction vehicles. This airfield is not open."

The man saw nothing whatsoever to be proud of. There was a skeleton of a building at one end of the unfinished runway. Some kind of communication tower stood, and a great deal of fencing protected the shoddy assets of the construction company. It was early enough yet that he didn't see any people, but he couldn't be sure. He checked his cynicism and held his tongue to avoid saying something foolish.

"That's the entire point, boy," Dr. Pitman assured him. "Nobody knows we're here. It took years to get the permits, but soon we'll open this airport to the people. A real airport! Tourists, imports and exports. It'll be grand. People will be swarming to see evidence of the real Noah."

The man in the ruined suit was doubtful, but he smiled encouragingly. He readied the plane for an approach to the half-airport while Dr. Pitman kept talking to himself much as he had the entire flight.

"I have to admit boy, you flew this tin can alright. You may look Muslim, fancy yourself Christian, and act pagan, but I invested well in you. We'd have been driving mountain roads all week. No way we could have beat Mel here."

The last was true at least. They had just flown the full length of Kurdistan. From a socio-political point of view, this wide plain was situated in one of the poorest regions of Turkey. Iğdır Province was squashed in against the borders of Armenia and Iran, and home to less than two hundred thousand people. Most of Kurdistan was that way. People spread out over thousands of square miles, or else crammed into little concrete stink-hole towns of mostly Kurdish farmers and shepherds. And the government was building them airports? What madness drove that? Though honestly, he knew the answer perfectly well. The man in the suit's eyes flicked to the massive snow-capped peak dominating the horizon. He understood the significance of that mountain better than most. How strange to think of the time, money, and lives wasted in pursuit of that silly peak now called Ararat. All because of ancient stories that modern man was incapable of deciphering properly.

How I love these wonderful Westerners!

The dangerously short runway grew bigger. The man circled the plateau once, dropping his speed for approach. No control tower yet, just the one tall antenna. He was just going to land as he pleased.

"What is that antenna?" he asked.

"Cell tower." Pitman was dripping with pride. "There are hundreds all through these mountains now."

The man in the suit blinked in disbelief. Cellular service? This was the middle of nowhere by anyone's standards. But apparently, they were building cell towers now too. What else would he find here? Two decades ago, when he had been a pathetic street rat in Şırnak, Kurdish nationalism had been a dream more than anything. His town had grown some by the time he'd left for school in Istanbul, but for these provinces to be worthy of an airport? The revolution truly was close at hand. The family had been busy.

Or perhaps he had been away too long. Had he gone soft in the Western world? He only hoped that this runway would prove safe enough to think about it later. As Dr. Pitman grumbled complaints and clutched the passenger seat, the little Skyhawk fought the earth and won. The plane slowed at his command and growled to a stop, coming far closer to the end of the dirt strip than he would have preferred. The cloud of dust that resulted, obscured everything from ground to shack to hillside.

The man in the suit hopped out of the plane and looked around before Dr. Pitman even unbuckled. It was profoundly quiet. Almost peaceful. The dust settled, and the distant craggy mountains greeted him like old friends. He pulled off his polarized glasses and let the sun's warmth hit him on his already sweaty face. From the ground, he now saw a little tin-roof carport attached to the side of the shack. In it, a vintage VW microbus held together with spot welds and rust sat waiting for them. The letters T-A-X-I were spray-stenciled on it, none quite aligned with the others. That was more like it.

Yes, I am home, he decided.

"What are you standing around for?" Dr. Pitman walked up and pocketed his phone. "It's a tough drive, and we need to be there first for this plan to work. Get moving, boy."

"Yes, Dr. Pitman."

Remember who you are. Remember what you really are.

LXXXIV

Gortyn Labyrinth. Gortyna, Southern Crete. David.

David and the others found no guard on duty, only an ominous "No Trespassing" sign in various languages posted by the military to warn them off. Cat flipped the numbers on a rusty bike chain lock, and the chain-link fence creaked wide.

A few minutes later, they came to a gash in the mountainside that split it like a wide crooked mouth. Under it, an iron frame was wedged into the rock. Barring this was a large iron gate on hinges that leaned into the mountainside, locked with a numerical padlock. Cat quickly dispensed with it too, and Father Matthew assisted in unlatching and carefully hefting the wrought iron door to rest against the wall. It let out a dull moan, and then the entrance to the Labyrinth of Gortyn was open to them.

"It used to be bigger, until the Nazis destroyed the old entrance," she said. Then, with no hesitation at all, Cat disappeared into the hole.

This was it. *"Doleful gulf," here we come!*

David peered into the entrance. Rusty metal rungs jutted from old concrete, daring him downward. It was the second time recently that David had begun his day by crawling into a hole in the ground. He thought about all of the things that had happened since the ruins at Ugarit. Once again, it felt like a different life. Oxford seemed like a strange dream, and Dallas—well, that was where some little kid had lived, not him.

He dropped down from the third rung and landed harder than he expected. The ground here was dirty, thick with gritty dust and sand. Just who was he trying to impress, anyway? Cat held her hand out with a sly smile and he suddenly knew the answer to his question. A twinge of excitement washed over him. It was adventuring time again.

David had been without a phone connection since Antioch. He still had not updated anybody on the newest events. Without his charger, who knew if he'd even get a chance to. Everyone at home probably thought he was just waking up in a plush Turkish bed and about to go down to an exotic continental breakfast with figs or Turkish Delight or something. His stomach rumbled, and he pushed the idea away, focusing on where he was.

There was a smell David couldn't quite identify here. Something between cave and concrete parking garage, and maybe a hint of campfire. Impulsively, he pulled his phone out and scanned the strange surroundings with its light. He could see stone walls crudely cut by ancient hand tools. It was not the organized and smooth machine-dug tunnel network of a modern mine. Rather, it had been carved with no plan he could identify. Only a few paces away, one passage ended in collapse, while others shot off into utter blackness.

But overlaying all of this was a modern concrete layer, ironically broken and cracked in ways that the ancient tunnels seemed to have effortlessly shrugged off. Seventy-year-old cement beams and whole slabs of ceiling lay flaked and broken on the floor. Everywhere, rubble was jaggedly strewn like the broken bones of an ancient creature who had lost its fight with time. A mangled train rail led from a bricked-over passage to nowhere at all, hinting at some other forgotten use of the place not so long ago. As he adjusted to the dark, David realized that brightly-colored graffiti covered nearly every surface. To his shock, a massive spray-painted swastika dominated a nearby wall.

"Put it away," Arthur whispered, stepping down from the last rung.

David obeyed. It was stupid to waste the phone's batteries on something like this anyway. Even with battery saver mode on and all connections off, it was just smarter to leave it powered down. For the millionth time, he thought of his charger and slew of adapters that had been abandoned in the ravaged hotel room. Until they could find their way to a town, their only source of Arthur's notes, the images of the tablet fragments, and everything else were available for a few hours more. Except for the ceramic copy of the Phaistos Disk that happened to still be in his mostly-empty backpack, he supposed.

"Over here," Cat said, indicating some footlockers and other supplies nearby. Surreally, they were marked "University of Oxford School of Archeology," part of Dr. Andino's special efforts to map the place. Cat drew out an armful of powerful flashlights, some other tools and supplies, and a thin three-ring binder.

David shrugged his bag on properly and took one of the lights. Arthur mumbled a "thank you," under his breath as he flicked on a light of his own. The beam lit up the blood-red Nazi emblem in full. Arthur grunted his multi-layered disapproval.

"Amateur explorers," Cat explained. "People used to come down here all of the time before World War II, until the army closed it off. Now it takes a little more finesse to get in, and local rumor is that sometimes people don't come back out. But that's probably not true anymore. There are also stories of an alternate entrance somewhere, which I suspect might hold some truth."

David wasn't so sure. Security in this place was a bike chain and a padlock. He was no criminal mastermind, but he was pretty sure that a bolt cutter would do the trick for any would-be explorer with a spray can. Not exactly the most challenging "lockpick" roll ever.

"Looters and thrill-seekers also come," Cat said, reading his mind. "The boldest thrill-seekers use tags and symbols to mark the way. Then they make and sell highly questionable maps with the same symbols. It's a dangerous business. Also, the local shepherds know all of the paths and valleys of these hills. Some can be bribed to share certain secrets, but they are not very fond of academics." Then, motioning with her light to the swastika, "I suppose that one is someone's idea of recognizing history."

"That's recent?" David realized, suddenly wondering when spray paint was invented.

Cat nodded. "It is worse than I remember. People simply can't resist going into caverns and tunnels to leave their mark. Every major city in the world has a secret underground, and also a community that lives and plays in it. The Paris Catacombs have graffiti dating back to the French Revolution. The best parts are not on the public tour, though straying off—not to mention defacing the walls—is quite illegal."

David got the feeling Cat was speaking from personal experience. The pockets of underground ruins at Ras-Shamra had seemed dangerous at the time, but the truth was that most of that ancient city was open to the elements now. There was an earthy deepness here that issued from the heart of a mountain, and it chilled him.

David's imagination drifted to *The Fellowship of the Ring*. That fictional party had delved through the Mines of Moria, but frankly, their journey hadn't ended very well. This was no tabletop dungeon delve of course, and they were no mere wizard, priest, rogue, and sorceress searching for loot. There was a real danger of being lost forever down here in the deep darkness. David looked to his wizard, wearing somebody else's clothes and scowling into the various dark tunnels. Like Gandalf, he seemed to be thinking, *"I have no memory of this place."* David couldn't help but grin.

"I thought you said this place was unmapped?" Arthur said instead, stepping up next to Cat. She was thumbing through various laminated sheets in the binder that could only be a series of maps.

"Well, it is," she said, tentatively. "Much of it, anyway. The story behind this is strange also. The first foreign visitor we know of came in 1415. He wrote of 'endless corridors' and 'galleries, entangling one another and all of which seem to come back to the place where they began.' There is a legend that this place is unmappable. Perhaps that is the origin of it. A silly superstition, obviously."

David gulped and wondered what his own skill modifier might be to explore this place with no map.

"He fared better than the next visitor though," she went on, strangely chipper. "In 1680, Bernard Randolf advanced no more than one hundred meters in a single hour, judging by the ball of yarn he used to mark his trail. He reported only that he saw many bats."

Matthew hummed thoughtfully. He was having to duck rather dramatically just to stand in this part of the entryway. For once, David was glad for his particular lack of height.

"And speaking of the French Revolution, Louis XVI even sent spies here for some clandestine reason, just before he lost his head. And yet another legend speaks of a portion of the crown jewels of France having been whisked away to Crete by one of Marie Antionette's servant girls, in an attempt to purchase her lady's safe passage elsewhere. Given that the servant also lost her head, some have suggested that the treasure is still down here somewhere."

David thrilled, but Arthur simply stared at her impatiently, waiting for her to get to the point. This amused David more than anything.

"So, yes, there have been many maps. Some more accurate than others." She turned a page David could not see. He moved closer. "This one is from 1821, by a man from Prague named Franz Sieber. It was drawn by his French partner, which is probably why it is not in Czech or German. This is a copy of what was considered the definitive map for many generations."

She flipped the page again as David stepped up. On it was a simple line drawing showing dozens of passages and rooms. It looked like a madman's idea of a rabbit warren. The labels amused him. Things like "the altar," "meeting room," "table," and "hole of the cat."

"There was not another good map until the 1980s," she continued. "Only then could the full damage done by the Nazis begin to be understood. These tunnels are now collapsed, here, and here. But we can go around." Cat traced her finger in a rough s-shape, stopping at a point furthest away from the entrance. "The university mapping project has been expanding and improving on these maps for some time now, using lasers, echolocation, and other methods with extreme precision. We—they," Cat corrected herself, "have already found three major errors of orientation on the nineteenth-century map. More exciting, they have nearly doubled the overall size of the Labyrinth from the old maps. There is a large series of previously unknown chambers and tunnels on a level that extends below this one. Or so I have been told."

"I see," Arthur stated flatly. "And you don't happen to have that map around here somewhere, do you?"

Cat shrugged. "It is all on the computer in the lower camp." She flipped to an incomplete computer-drawn printout. "The way down is here. It is where we should go first. These maps are quite sufficient to get us there." She straightened. "But, as I said, I have been here before. You have nothing to worry about." She tucked the binder under her arm and crossed them, daring anyone to argue.

Arthur stared at her, sputtered, and accepted it, mumbling something about "infernal technology" and a "blasted pencil." Matthew gave David a knowing wink.

"What do you mean, 'unknown chambers?'" David asked, stifling a laugh at Arthur's expense.

Cat nodded. "They were walled off. No one is sure by whom precisely. The stones were very old, but the mortar tested as more modern. Only a few centuries at best. It was suggested that an earthquake or one of the larger explosions may have collapsed the wall and revealed the lower sections. A bit of luck, I suppose."

A few centuries is modern? David again surveyed the crude graffiti slathering the crumbling concrete walls. Every generation had contributed something to this place, though not all for the better, it would seem. A very rude, if well executed, nude bent and peeked into a narrow passage trailing off into the darkness. *No, not nude.* he decided. *That one is naked.*

Below the paint were a few strange cylinders hiding in the shadows. They looked like giant bullets the size of his lower leg. Stepping closer and squinting, David could see that there were a dozen or so large crates stacked inside the narrow tunnel, some of which had broken open, revealing more of the giant bullets.

"Do not touch those, they are not safe." A beam of light came from behind him, lighting up the dark passage.

David blinked, fully understanding what Cat meant. The German lettering and Nazi insignia on the crusty munitions boxes said it all. The artillery piece they were meant to load must have been massive, and this particular hallway was full of them. Too many to count, but enough to make David want to be anywhere else right now.

Matthew cleared his throat. "I say, everyone," he whispered, "I think I hear something—"

A loud metal groan from the entrance cut him off. Everyone whirled and froze as the rusty gate above slammed shut. The noise echoed away down the dark corridors. For a moment, David wondered if the wind had somehow blown the heavy metal door over, but that didn't even make sense. They had left it pinned open by its own weight against the angled interior wall of a cave. A moment later he knew the answer when a silhouette flashed past the opening and the sound of the latch and click of a padlock followed. The missing guard was not so missing after all.

"Hey there!" Father Matthew shouted, already moving. He launched himself at the ladder and was up in less time than it had taken David to fall off of it, but it didn't matter. "It's locked," the priest affirmed, rattling the iron. "Cheers, friend!" he tried. "We are with the University! Ox-ford!" he annunciated.

Matthew reached and twisted to check the padlock closer. From the disgusted way he dropped it, David knew it was not the same lock as before. This one would require a real key they didn't have.

"No good," Matthew declared. "We have quite a pickle."

"He did that on purpose," Arthur decided. "Someone knows we are here." Then, turning to Cat, he added, "There is another entrance you say? Perhaps you could guide us to it?"

Cat stared at Arthur wordlessly and shook her head. "We never found another. Some of the older maps reference sealed entrances, but so far we have found nothing." She flipped through the binder and slapped her hand on a random map. "We need to use what we have to get to the deep research camp. We can access a better digital map there."

Arthur took the binder and shone his flashlight on it. David leaned in. It was the 1821 French one done for the guy named Sieber. Even as a printed copy, it was amazing. The hand-drawn tunnels and rooms had labels in a fancy foreign hand. It was meticulously detailed for such a small thing, but that wasn't the element that screamed out at David. In the margins on every side, corner, and top of the old map were numerous spiral designs of every shape and size. Only they weren't just designs—they were most definitely labyrinths!

Someone else had made these same connections almost two hundred years ago, only they hadn't been carrying a Phaistos Disk in their backpack. It was the key, David felt it in his very bones now. He reached for his phone to snap a picture of the map for his own use, but stopped himself, sighing.

Somehow, it would be okay. This had to be the right place.

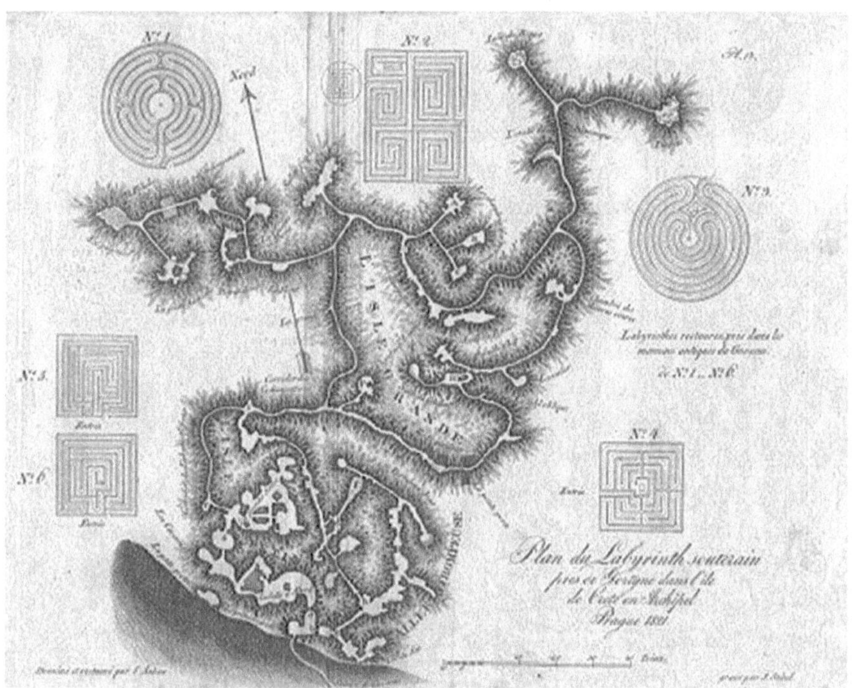

LXXXV

Gortyn Labyrinth. Gortyna, Southern Crete. Arthur.

This can't possibly be the right place, Evans decided immediately.

He tried to listen as deMata finished her retelling of the legend of Theseus and the Minotaur to her new pupil, but his mind kept wandering. David did ask some questions here and there, and Matthew supplied the occasional quote of epic verse, but Evans chose to remain silent. The reality of their predicament had sunk in. He was less concerned at the moment with solving the age-old mysteries of the Labyrinth than finding a way out of this dark and dangerous old quarry.

Evans' own cautionary words to David in the ruins of Ras-Shamra came back to him. *"It takes much focus and arduous work to spot the myths and discern truth from fiction in any pursuit, be it gods, gardens, or translating ancient pictographs. Wyatt never could do that. Alas, Sir Arthur never did either. We must do them one better."*

He sighed. This is where Wyatt's clues had led them. Fantasy or not, they were on the "right" track. Even not feeling right, seemed right. It had that all too familiar sensation of being on a Wyatt Aarons brand myth quest. It was something he hadn't felt in a dog's age. The more Evans thought about it, the more insane this idea seemed. Not that he was worried about Minotaurs of course, but the chaos serpent had many forms, and the devil was in the details. And right now, food, drink, light, and freedom were genuine concerns. Though not necessarily in that order.

DeMata insisted that there was a basecamp near the point at the furthest reaches of her map. She'd promised a generator, lights, and much more besides. At the time, it had seemed like a good plan. But now, as they delved deeper into the mountain, Evans began to wonder if they had doubled back. He'd swear that some of these twisting passages and chambers he had seen already. Either way, they had been walking for hours and his ridiculous borrowed pants were starting to chafe.

"Daedalus was the architect of the Labyrinth," deMata was saying. "It is said that he based the design on the Egyptian Labyrinth."

"There's an Egyptian Labyrinth?" David marveled.

"It is lost, but well attested. All but destroyed in Roman times, though some claimed to find the small part that remained as recently as the seventeen-hundreds."

"If this place was the Labyrinth of Minos," Evans interrupted. "Then it was nothing like the Egyptian Labyrinth. Egypt's was built as a series of temples with adjoining rooms. According to Herodotus at any rate."

"Herodotus again?" Matthew asked. "He made it around then, didn't he?"

"The same." Evans hoped that nobody would grill him on the man beyond that, given his Greek history was still rather fuzzy. His ancient Egyptian and labyrinth lore, however, were other matters entirely. "It is said that even the pyramids were surpassed by the Labyrinth of Egypt. A monument built by the twelve provincial kings of Egypt to themselves, it was twelve mazelike palaces with a central court surrounded by fifteen hundred rooms. All of this was sunk into the ground, intertwined, and completely covered in stone slab roofing, an unheard-of technique in ancient times. And if that was not enough, a precisely matching duplicate of the entire complex was then built atop the first, so that the one foolish enough to wander into it might have no idea if they were above or below without first crossing to the other."

"Doubtful," deMata said. "Such legends are all the same. A grain of truth is exaggerated over generations until they become nonsense. Much like this place, the truth is quite different from the fiction."

"Regardless," Evans continued, overemphasizing the word. "Such a description might lend a bit of favor to Sir Arthur for picking Knossos as his preferred location for the Cretan version. His palace is precisely that description. And he spent his life uncovering the innumerable rooms that surrounded one particular central courtyard."

"Or perhaps that theory prevails so strongly in the popular imagination because of Sir Arthur Evans' personality and privileged position, rather than any real science?" deMata taunted.

Evans puffed. "If you are saying that this quarry is a great and dirty hole, then I agree with you. I have yet to be convinced we are acting logically here, except insofar as we seem to be following Wyatt Aaron's illogic." He barely stopped himself punctuating this last comment with a sarcastic snort. "On quite a separate matter: do we know how long these flashlights will last?"

"This is the place," deMata declared, ignoring him.

Evans girded himself and drew in a great breath to begin a speech about sloppy archeology and bad scholarship, maybe with a side helping of respecting one's elders. But before he could, deMata disappeared behind a broken wall. The others quickly followed, and Evans was alone.

"Come on, Arthur," David's head popped back to say. "This is where the old map ends! We really don't want to get separated down here!"

Oh. This was the place. Evans released the breath, pushed his glasses up, and trudged over to the hole. It was as deMata had described. The crumbling wall was ages older than the twentieth-century concrete near the entrance, but also not anywhere as old as other elements original to the quarry. Someone in antiquity had walled off half of the maze and it had been subsequently breached in recent decades. It was intriguing, frankly.

He stepped through and was immediately disoriented. A series of tunnels met here, a high-ceilinged, almost cylindrical chamber. Every passage began with a stone arch. Some stretched down at a steep angle, others up, while still others continued into darkness. The whole thing reminded him of a medieval crypt of the sort found under any of a thousand churches in the world, but for one major difference. The enigmatic adornments here were spraypainted, representing all levels of artistic skill. He turned to the wall they had passed through to see if it was also an archway and physically jumped.

A vicious snarling Minotaur with drooling jowls and blood-red eyes towered over him. Worse yet, it wore a Nazi S.S. commander's uniform, ripped where the muscles of the creature had compromised it. The thing even sported a little German officer's hat with the signature double lightning bolts of the notorious *Schutzstaffel.*

"Wild, huh?" David said at his ear, making him jump again. "Can you imagine how long it took them to paint that? And all the way down here. Like, what if you run out of a certain color or something?"

Evans stared at the anachronistic graffiti monster for another moment, then turned. "Which way did the others go?"

David darted into the downward-leading passage stenciled with pink flowers and green vines, his backpack bouncing jauntily as he went. Evans sighed and followed, nearly tripping on a loose stone before catching up to the exuberant girl-wonder and the others. No, they were not acting logically at all.

"Pardon me," Evans said, sweetly as he could muster, "But if this lower section is where the old map ends, then just how exactly are we going to keep from being lost? We must have walked a mile in these tunnels so far. As we don't know if another exit even exists, I don't fancy spending the rest of a very short life in the darkness here."

"We think the lower level is every bit as extensive as the upper one, similar but in slightly different configurations," deMata replied, not at all addressing his concerns. "Once it is all mapped, then we will know more, but until then we must see how much data the computers have compiled so far. It is not far now."

As if by some stage magician's trick, they emerged into an exact duplicate of the chamber they had just left. Architecturally at least, for there was no crumbling wall with a Nazi Minotaur here, just an overwhelming variety of different vandalism in all manner of languages and colors.

"See Arthur? Maybe it is like the Egyptian Labyrinth. If the upper level and the bottom level are copies of each other, then maybe all we have to do is look for the differences. As above, so below?"

Evans grunted. He felt frustrated, tired, and out of control. He needed something to focus him, and regretted—not for the first time—that it wasn't going to be a pint. If only that snake Pitman hadn't taken his notes. He considered the possibility of looking at David's virtual version on the phone again but quickly dismissed it. It was selfish and a bad use of resources without any real plan. They already had one dreadful plan to navigate the bottomless horror of this place, which was one bad plan too many.

A step or two ahead, Matthew stopped and turned. As if sensing his friend's distress, he put a hand on Evans' shoulder. Somehow, it calmed him. "Perhaps now would be a good time to discuss the meditative purpose of a labyrinth?" the priest quietly suggested.

For a moment Evans was unsure what his best friend meant, but then it occurred to him that a little meditation was perhaps precisely what everyone needed. Or at least, a distraction was what he needed, and that was good enough.

"Yes, yes. The meditative labyrinth." He tried to sound enthusiastic. "One path, leading from the entrance to the center. Always twisting, often switching back, but never dead-ending or leading to a false choice. Not to be confused with a maze, mind you. You see, first and foremost, a labyrinth is a tool for minfulness, guidance, and enlightenment. To walk one is a deceptively long spiritual journey, yet the choice to abandon that journey is always present too."

"But Arthur," David said, "this place is nothing like that. There are tons of dead-ends and false trails. I mean, if it were straightforward, then we could just walk, um, straight forward. Even this room is literally nothing but identical choices."

"Precisely," Evans said pointedly. "This place is a maze. And yet, we plunge forward." He didn't hide his irritation.

"False choices," deMata stated. "Not identical. None of these doorways go anywhere."

"Really?" David said, turning in a circle. "None of them?"

"Yes. Other than the ways in and out, that is. The research camp is this way. Everything we need to make a plan is just through there." She started towards one of the spraypainted arches.

But David didn't follow. Instead, he shrugged his backpack off just enough to extract the Disk then held his flashlight over it. "You know Arthur, I still can't shake the feeling that this thing is supposed to guide us. Rabbi Yosef's layers of meaning, or whatever?"

Evans considered the troublesome ceramic replica of the Mystery Disk that David held in his hands. He had lost the priceless Ras-Shamra translation tablet, his real notes, and even Wyatt's ridiculous journal, but not this blasted thing. *No, of course not.* There were a million replica disks in the world. *Just our luck.*

Evans smiled in spite of himself and clasped his hand on the boy's shoulder. A cheap imitation of Matthew, but better than nothing.

It did not have the intended effect. David was caught off balance as the backpack shifted from his shoulder towards the flashlight. The Disk slipped from his other hand, turned end-over-end then thumped loudly into the thick layer of dust on the floor.

"Oh, no. Terribly sorry," Evans mumbled, as both he and David stooped to pick up the Disk at the same time. David stuck a finger under one end and lifted. But instead of scooping it up, he was forced to dodge Evans' own attempt at helping. The Disk flipped on its edge and plopped back down.

"Oh, dear lord," Evans sighed, resigning himself to leaning on a large flat stone rather than risk a third entanglement. "Is it broken?"

David laughed and tried the operation again. This time he squatted on his heels and lifted the ceramic circle away effortlessly. Suddenly the teen's snickering caught in his throat. Evans feared the worst until he realized that David wasn't even looking at the Disk. He was staring at the two deep impressions it had left behind.

"More light, please?" was all the teen said.

Immediately, Matthew shone his beam at the floor, followed a moment later by deMata. Evans juggled his light on too, though the change was negligible. The imprint looked vaguely like a sideways figure-eight or infinity symbol. First one side of the Disk, then the other edged in next to it.

"As above, so below," David breathed. "It's so simple."

"Oh, dear lord," Evans breathed to himself, bringing three fingers to his temple.

"What is it, David?" Matthew prompted. "What do you see?"

David looked up, but it was Evans that he turned to. The boy's eyes were ablaze.

"I know how to read this map."

LXXXVI

Gortyn Labyrinth. Gortyna, Southern Crete. David.

"It's not literal," David began. "It's like Rabbi Yosef said, there are embedded layers of meaning. The paradise acronym, right? PRDS?"

"*Pshat, Remez, Drush, Sod*," Arthur provided. "What of it?"

"Yea, that! Well, we have the simple meaning of the Disk, right? The translation you did of the new flood myth and the list of kings on the other side." The others accepted this. "And we found this place with the allusion of the spiral, which is the ordered chaos idea."

There was not as much acceptance this time. Cat nodded confidently, but Arthur made his fish face.

"Go on, David," Matthew encouraged.

"So that leaves the instructive and mystical interpretations. A map would be instructive, but there aren't really any instructions in the text. So, I was thinking, what if the Disk really was a map of this place, like the margin designs on the 1820s map?"

"The Franz Sieber map?" Cat asked, glancing at the binder tucked under her arm. "He added those ancient designs to sell more copies of his book, nothing more."

"No," David insisted. "Sieber and his partner were on to something. Listen, Arthur basically just said that looking for a literal map in the shape of a spiral would be a failure to understand the mystical importance of a labyrinth. The point is not that you can't make a wrong turn, it's that you shouldn't. You know, in life or whatever."

"I don't, um…" Arthur couldn't find words to finish.

"Look," David said. "The Disk made an impression in the dirt. It's a mirror image, a stamp of the other, like the seal stones back in the museum. But that doesn't matter. It's when it flipped over that it hit me. See this part of the Disk? This little dashed line where the passages sort of dovetail to the edge in an L-shape. It's like we are supposed to flip the thing over or something." He pointed to the edges of the images in the dirt. "It's weird. There's no reason for it to be shaped like that."

Nobody said anything. They didn't understand.

David huffed and without warning erased the impression with his hand. He carefully rotated the Disk and laid it down in the dirt again. Then, as carefully as he dared, he lifted it up and flipped the Disk over. Only this time, he was careful to make sure that the edge of the flip was precisely on what Arthur had identified as the "end" of the passage where the spiral stopped. The result was undeniable. The ends lined up.

Matthew was the first to say it. "By Jove. I daresay they connect, Arthur."

"Yes, I can see that."

"See guys, it's not just one spiral..." David waited with bated breath.

"...It is two." deMata finished. "Undeniably so."

"Cat, you said that this place had two levels, right? That the top part was almost identical in size to the bottom?"

She nodded. "Well, this Disk is the same, and the connecting point is just like this place. There are two connected rooms that look alike and seem to go nowhere, except to lead either up or down to the rest of the Labyrinth."

Matthew smiled and a low rumbling chuckle came out of him. Did he understand? David wanted so badly to make everyone see. If they could only use a little imagination, they would.

He tried again. "If this really is the Minotaur's Labyrinth, then there's no exit, right? Maybe the way we came in used to be blocked or walled off or something, like Cat said. That makes only one way out or in, except it's hidden. Because the upstairs and downstairs both seem almost the same. But the Disk is telling us that none of that matters. It's the connecting point that gives us all the information we need, and we found it. We are in it. It's this room."

Arthur blew a long breath past his lips, then gently spoke as one might to a small child. "David, you're presuming too much. It's an interesting coincidence admittedly, but there is nothing at all that points to the Disk as a map in the way you suggest. There would have to be something more for it to be useful in any practical sense. Something like a symbol from the Disk marking a certain passage, or something in the translation which indicates that this crossover location has some kind of importance. Maybe a phrase or a symbol near your connecting point..."

Arthur stopped and leaned in towards the imprint. Then, not willing to believe his own eyes, he grabbed the Disk itself and flipped it over until the final phrase was in front of him. The very phrase David had pointed out an alternate translation for.

Arthur looked over his glasses at it and then back to the imprint. "It's backwards," he croaked.

David looked at Arthur dubiously. Obviously it was backwards, it was an imprint. Because, duh.

"What I mean to say is that it reads from right to left this way, just like a Semitic language should. But it's pictographic, so the meaning doesn't change, just the script direction."

David hadn't thought of that, but he watched the last of Arthur's doubts fall away.

"Follow the Path of the Flaming Sword to the city of the important man," Cat remembered. "I do not follow."

"It's the last phrase after a flip," David pointed out, "the dotted line where the Disk connects to the other side. One spiral goes all the way around the Disk exactly once before reaching it, but it ends right next to the connection point too. It's like the old symbols for the labyrinth, the ones on the Sieber map. A real labyrinth has only one path, but is all about false endings and switchbacks before finally reaching the center. That's the key, see?"

They didn't see.

"Okay, look, the Disk really is a map, it's just that the instructions are super simple. Who knows how much more unmapped stuff there is, or how much has collapsed that used to be here. The full layout of this cave or mine or whatever doesn't matter, only this room and the one above it does. If somebody walks the metaphorical path of the Disk, then the spirals would cross over at the point of the flip, see? Three times, actually, before finally ending there on those dotted lines." He tapped the edge of the Disk. "Before ending here, in this room! There must be a secret somewhere that points the way to Dilmun. And it has to be hidden somewhere right in front of us."

"*Drush*, the instructive interpretation," Matthew clarified. "Bravo, David. Now, just what shall we do about it?"

"We must try all of these archways, of course," Arthur breathed. "If it is true, then there is something here that literally everyone before us has missed."

*   *   *

Cat and Matthew ran through an archway to the research camp. They quickly returned with more supplies including fresh flashlight batteries, eight water bottles, and much to David's dismay, more MREs and a box of protein bars. A few minutes later everyone was searching a different archway. They scanned every inch for some clue that might have been missed by any explorer not actively looking for it.

Cat quickly eliminated one dead-end, then Matthew called out a "no-go" from another false ramp. They all met back in the middle and tried again until there was only one set left.

"Could it be in the other room above?" Cat suggested.

"I guess," David said. "But I have a hunch that it is on this level somewhere. The phrase about the path is at the end of the genealogy of the Kings. That's the second story, which makes me think it's the underside here too."

"I chose which side to read fairly arbitrarily, David," Arthur said. "I wouldn't take too much stock in it."

But David was sure. Something about the translation's ending hadn't sat right, and he was convinced that there was a clue in it that Arthur had missed. But first, they had to find that passage. This was the starting point of the Path of the Flaming Sword. He just knew it.

"Over here, everyone!" Matthew bellowed.

They rushed to the archway where he stooped pointing at yet more graffiti. An unmistakable lime green labrys shape had been sprayed just inside the passageway by some unknown tagger. David didn't hesitate. He plunged into the opening with his flashlight tearing at the darkness.

"That can't possibly be helpful," he heard Arthur say behind him. "All of this graffiti is new."

Only a few dozen steps in, David realized Arthur was right. A natural wall kept him from going further. Dejected, he leaned against the side, not wanting to report his failure. Was this really just his imagination getting the better of him? He was following modern spray-paint to try to find the secrets of the Minotaur's maze! It was tabletop fantasy stuff, not archeology. He sighed. Adventuring was easier around the dining room table. What he wouldn't give for a real-life observation check or an ancient bardic knowledge roll right now. He cast his flashlight around one more time, just to be sure.

"David? What did you find?" Cat called, much louder than she needed to.

He opened his mouth to relay his disappointment, but stopped as a shadow shifted. He took a step just to make sure. Carved at the end of the tunnel in the natural stone was a spiral petroglyph. Only, this one looked old.

Really old.

"Hang on," David called back, "I have something." He leaned in and ran his fingertips across the ancient petroglyph, imagining what it might mean. Should he push it? Would the walls start closing in if he did? Or the ceiling produce spikes and start collapsing? His hand shook with nervousness.

Breathing hard David turned and leaned back, but instead of the wall, he found himself stumbling for balance. Where the side of the tunnel should have been, only empty space met his hand. Here the wall ended abruptly, and the rest of the stone was a few feet further back than it looked.

David's shadow appeared as the light doubled. "What is it, David?" Arthur said from just behind him.

"There is a hidden switchback here," David whispered. "Just like in the old labyrinth drawings. I just about missed it. And look, here on the wall."

"A spiral," Arthur gulped. "I don't believe it."

Arthur squeezed past David and edged forward. David watched his wizard's left half disappear behind the rock like a bad stage magician.

"Well done, David. Let's gather the others and see where your secret tunnel leads, shall we?"

LXXXVII

Gortyn Labyrinth. Gortyna, Southern Crete. Arthur.

Evans hated eating crow as much as the next person, but he hated being lost and dead in the dark more. He only hoped that this narrow, hidden passage actually led somewhere. Preferably, to an exit.

"I see something," David called back. "It's a room."

Evans breathed a little sigh of relief and picked up the pace. When he emerged, David and deMata were standing next to a large flat stone in the middle of a small room. Evans first assumed the monolith had fallen in from the ceiling like so many others they'd passed on their deep journey, but as he drew closer, he realized it was no accident. The top of the slab was level and covered with a repeating circular pattern. Worked into the pattern, there was a deep carving in the center, a perfect and unmistakable double-headed ax.

"It's big," David said. "Big enough to lay a real ax into."

"Good lord," Evans whispered. "You are exactly right. There must have been some sort of ceremonial labrys laid into this depression." He was instantly reminded of the bronze Arkalochori Ax with its fifteen pictographs similar to the Disk, found in a cave not—*what?—thirty miles from here?* That familiar chill worked its way down his spine again.

"It's the fourth interpretation," David declared. "*Sod*—the mystical dimension. I just know it."

Evans bit his tongue. The boy's wild imagination had gotten them this far, they might as well see where it goes.

"A labrys," Matthew said, stepping up. "Well, I say."

"There is another passage here," deMata said, scanning the far wall. "I will see where it goes."

Matthew and Evans exchanged a wordless nod and the priest followed after her. Turning back, Evans watched David extract the Disk and set it next to the Labrys carving.

"Look Arthur, the curve of the blade is the same size as the Disk." David dug a bit of grime out of the stone with his finger, then to Evans' great surprise, slotted the Disk into the leftmost blade. It fit perfectly, though Evans couldn't understand how a circle could fit into an ax shape.

"Okay," Evans said tremulously. "Now what?"

"Flip it," David suggested, "Trust me, Arthur."

David stood by and grinned as Evans carefully did so, using the carving as a guide. The replica slotted perfectly into the groove of the blade socket as it stood on end. It then leaned effortlessly into the other side, the act of flipping vertically covering the shape of the right ax blade.

"I see it now," Evans marveled. "The circular pattern continues in slight relief just above the labrys shape. It allows the Disk to slot in above the inset arc of the blade." Even as he said it, he lifted the Disk and slotted it into a third circle just above the ax blade, again marveling as it formed the upper line of the labrys shape. Then, he repeated the flip one last time on the horizontal axis. A subtle lip in the carving guided the Disk into the final position, completing the ritual and the full shape of the ax. Four circles, like a four-leaf clover. Four alignments outlining the ancient Labrys shape. Four flips, and four interpretations of the Disk. David was right. This was no coincidence.

"I think, David, that this would be the moment to ignore the limits of technology, and take some pictures with your infernal device?"

The boy immediately powered up his phone and gleefully took pictures of the room, the passage, and the stone ax from every angle and orientation. It was strange to see him taking so many pictures in total silence. Now that Evans thought of it, this was the first real moment he'd had alone with the boy since their starlit conversation in the Ras-Shamra ruins. Such moments had been altogether few and far between since David had disrupted his life.

And yet, where would he be without his grandson's creativity and imagination? *Shot dead for a book? Stuck in some Syrian prison cell? Wandering alone in a dark labyrinth?* No, chances are he would be at home sipping tea, or at one of the pubs enjoying a good book and a better bitter. They were here because David's uncanny ability to crack the clues had gotten them to see myths in a way that even Sir Arthur would have appreciated.

A strange feeling washed over Evans as the camera's flash lit the room again and again. Here, deep in a Cretan mountain in the heart of King Minos' Labyrinth, looking at the stone labrys on the altar before him, something felt deeply wrong. Sure, he knew he had been mistaken about this place, but that wasn't it. Every symbolic element here lined up, and the carving in the stone, the Disk, the map-like clues, and the very layout of the Labyrinth's center all seemed to confirm the method David had used to find this spot. But in the end, it was all veritably pointless.

Ah yes, that was it! Why put the clue after the solution? Otherwise, what was the reason for the third and fourth flips at all? Was it merely to outline the shape of the ax head?

Again, Evans felt as though David had triggered a profound impact on his thinking. The rusty gates of his imagination creaked open again, and a sea of facts collected and connections made over a lifetime of study took shape as his personal library. The books of his mind threw themselves open and the pages collated and reorganized in ways that he had never considered, cross-referencing, connecting, and coalescing around all of these new facts and paradigms.

The ancient pictographic language of the Minoans of Crete was real and readable. They had been the forgotten children of Lydia who escaped to sea, only to become the most advanced European civilization at the time. Then, they were wiped out in one grand blow by some unknown catastrophe, taken out by a volcanic tidal wave, if Dr. deMata's data had any merit, as he suspected it did. A veritable Atlantis, as David had once suggested.

Evans shook the crazy out of his head and centered himself. A handful of days working for Mel Chen and he was already sounding like Wyatt. No, this table must have had a purpose beyond recording a myth or being a coded map of where and how to find this room. And if so, then such a purpose would be the reason why one might seek out this room, chaos disk in hand. Perhaps with David's photos, time to do some proper research, and the help of the University's Dr. Andino and his maps, they could eventually figure out that purpose.

Except that then, standing in the secret room of the Minoan Labyrinth, Dr. Arthur Evans suddenly knew exactly how to read the hidden fourth meaning of the Disk. Elegantly simple. Wonderfully hidden. It took his breath away, but he would need his blasted notes to confirm it.

"Do you think anybody else has discovered all of this?" David asked between camera flashes. Evans couldn't answer, but he didn't have to. The others emerged back into the chamber chattering wildly.

"I do not believe it," deMata said, excitement in her voice. "This passage leads to another hidden switchback, which emerges into a place I recognize. The locals call it the 'Little Labyrinth.' There are old stories about how the two caverns are connected, but until now I thought they were only that. We have passed almost entirely through the mountain."

"Wait a tick," Evans croaked. "There's a 'little labyrinth' in this infernal mountain, too? And we didn't start with it?"

Matthew rumbled the undertone of a laugh. "Come along, Arthur, let's get out of this 'infernal' mountain. Dr. deMata says that it's only a bit further beyond that to an exit."

*   *   *

They emerged from a strange little crack in the wall behind a curtain of rock. It was so well hidden that Evans never would have seen it without knowing he had just emerged from it.

"This is how the locals have been getting in," Cat said. "Look here."

Sure enough, there was a subtle labrys spraypainted at the edge of the stone curtain. It was just enough of a clue to tip off someone with an illicit vandal map as to the secret way forward. Even the deepest portions of the Labyrinth had been tagged with signs and codes this way. Perhaps the various Nazi emblems were little more than trail blazes now, regardless of the so-called artist's original intent.

"The vandals have been coming into the Little Labyrinth, then using the connection to go into the big one," she laughed snidely. "So much for our secret room. I will need to tell Dr. Andino his computer equipment is not so safe as he thinks. But he will be very excited."

Evans smiled, knowing that the others wouldn't see it in the dark. "I doubt they came with the Mystery Disk in hand when they did it, though. It was happenstance and curiosity that led generations of explorers here, not ancient mysteries."

"I see light!" David said, excitedly.

"Once we are out, there is a road that connects back—"

Everyone froze. A Greek soldier with fatigues and an assault rifle moved across the entrance, his features kicked into stark contrast by the blinding whiteness outside.

"That is the man who locked us in," Matthew informed them. "He must have surmised we could only come out this way."

"It is crime to come here and deface our tunnels," the guard said authoritatively. "You persons are to be arrested now." His Greek accent was thick enough to cleave with a double-sided ax.

"You do not understand," deMata began. "We are with the University. Dr. Andino can explain everything." Nothing, so she tried again in Greek.

But the man's chance to reply was cut short. A large shape loomed behind the little guard and a meaty white arm grabbed him around the neck, yanking him fully into the daylight. The gun clattered to the ground even as the soldier slapped at his attacker's arm. Everyone stood in shock for a moment, then Matthew rushed out to pick up the weapon. Something about the whole situation felt strangely familiar.

"Stay here!" Evans ordered the teenagers. He hurried into the light to see Colonel Ivan holding the guard in the same stranglehold he had used on Evans at Ras Shamra. A signature move apparently, not that Evans was complaining this time. Matthew stood by, mild amusement on his face as he checked the gun and removed the clip.

"You are gone for a day," Ivan stated. "I come looking for you. There is man skulking with weapon."

"Yes. Right. Good work. Thank you?" Evans wasn't sure what else to say. Just how long had they been down there in the dark?

"Ah, not to worry then," Matthew said wryly, "but if you don't mind me asking—Arthur, do you have a plan?"

Evans scanned the guard. He was just a local man doing his job. He had obviously mistaken them for the same vandals who had been entering and tagging the old quarry for some time. He couldn't have known otherwise.

Then, as the man struggled and spat, Evans saw the tattoo. An impossible raven peeking out of the man's sleeve. The emblem of a Kurdish freedom-fighter guerilla force on a Greek army guard. It made no blasted sense!

Until, with sudden clarity, it did. Evans understood. The raven, the Disk, the stone labrys. It all connected. How could he have been so obtuse? Evans swallowed hard.

"Let him go, Ivan."

Doubtfully, the Russian soldier released his hold on the local man. The guard gasped, flailed, straightened his shirt, and glared at them all.

"I say, Arthur, I'd prefer not to shoot anyone today."

"Don't worry, Matthew. Nobody is shooting anyone. David, will you bring out the Disk please?"

With the strangest look, David pulled the Mystery Disk from his backpack.

The guard's eyes narrowed.

Evans addressed the man directly. "I know we are not the first to come here. Perhaps we aren't even the first to walk the Path of the Flaming Sword. But without a translation of the Disk, I don't see what good it would do them."

At this, the guard straightened and crossed his arms, all anger gone. "Continue."

"The translation?" David muttered, turning the Disk to look at it. "What does the translation have to do with anything?"

Evans cleared his throat. "Ah, well, yes. Sir, as my colleagues here can attest, I have already done so."

The guard inclined his chin, eyes locked on Evans. *No, not guard,* Evans realized. *Guardian.*

"The spiral is the symbol of chaos," Evans continued, "but it is also a symbol for order. Moreover, it is a deep symbol for temptation, for the serpent, the feminine, the womb, and for the idea of mystery itself. And, apparently, for the Labyrinth of Crete. With a bit of imagination and logic, it led us here. The Minoans knew these symbols well, as did their enemies and usurpers, and I suspect, as do you, my friend." No one so much as twitched. "But the Labrys is also a symbol of these same things and more besides. Both are inextricably linked to the idea of a labyrinth, to danger, to the eternal unknown, fate, and apparently, of a kingdom that became divided."

"The story on the Disk," David realized.

"Yes, or at least of the simple reading." Evans cleared his throat. This next part was risky. If he was wrong—

"When I translated it, I simply ignored those two places on the Disk where the cells angle off towards the edge, as I'm sure I was meant to. But the stone labrys shows us the true reading, doesn't it? If we flip the Disk a few times as we read it, at just the right place in each of the two stories, I wager that we are going to discover something quite remarkable."

David looked at Evans with a certain wildness, then down at the Disk in his hand. Crazed wonder erupted onto his face.

"You have what you came for, Professor Evans." The guardian's accent dropped by an order of magnitude. "Which means it is time for you to leave this place. Please, allow me to escort you to your car."

Just a tutor, Evans didn't say. But he understood the man's meaning well enough regardless. And he was quite happy to oblige. It wasn't every day one passed through a mountain.

LXXXVIII

Doomsday Mountain. Ağrı Provence, Turkey. Mel.

The Russian chopper sliced its way across the Turkish countryside until it reached its target. It was all quite serene from the air. Except for the occasional town, this part of Ağrı was nothing but rolling hills and intertwining valleys as far as she could see. Except for one very strange almond-shaped rock formation, the Doomsday Anomaly. Allegedly, the remains of Noah's true Ark.

The pictures did not do it justice. From the air, Mel could see the obvious boat shape formed by the outside curves of the Ark. Even the rock walls that jutted further up looked distinctively like the petrified ribs of a ship. There was also something peculiar about the way the interior mound of the little plateau bulged and cracked, something in the shape that reminded her of a medieval motte-and-bailey castle.

Mel had no problem imagining how the gigantic vessel might have looked as Noah and his family abandoned it so long ago. She had read all the various theories about how it had navigated the rivulets as the flood drained, dropped anchor three times, came to rest, and was eventually brought by a mudslide to this final resting place.

She easily saw now how it might have snagged, split, and impaled itself on the large stone outcropping that still jutted up in the middle of the odd old boat. She could now see the ancient volcanic flow, the dark rock splitting on either side of the ark and continuing on. As the floodwater drained away, the remarkable boat had stayed here, preserved for the long centuries by that same mineral-rich volcanic soil and mud until fate, time, nature, man, or perhaps even Wyatt Aarons' God, had intervened. Looking at it from the air, she could believe any or all of it.

Perched above the ark was a little building of red-washed plaster, mud, and tin. This was the Information Center and Museum, and the location of the window from which Pitman had flaunted her stolen laptop. From the glorified shack on the hill, a little lane wound off toward a nearby town in the next valley. This, little as it was, was the glory of Turkey's Ark National Park. Mel had no time for tourism, but she could think of no more poetic place for this little game of cat and mouse to end.

She spotted two figures making their way from the sad little building down to the Ark. Even with the helicopter's obvious approach, the duo did not waver. Mel was willing to play. She gave an order and they circled once, then hovered above the plateau. Mel adjusted her assault gear, clipped in, and joined her four mercenaries in repelling down.

An incredibly amused Ryan Pitman waited for her just in front of the stone outcropping. His shirttails blew wildly in the artificial wind, but the black machine gun over his shoulder was unmistakable. Mel's former employee Mr. Suit stood next to him, his expensive coat billowing out like a sail. Only, his whole outfit was horribly torn and stained, and he had some nasty-looking slashes on his face as well. Dr. Evans had indeed been busy.

So, there were two traitors then. Mel had no time to sort it out. Battered and bloody or not, the Turkish man had a cold hard intensity that Mel was impressed with, despite herself. And Pitman was still flashing her his million-dollar smile, which meant they hadn't sprung his trap just yet. The two men had fooled her incredibly well, she would have to be equally careful. As the ops team circled up around them, the helicopter returned to the sky. A strange quiet settled on the mountain and a Zen-like breeze wafted over the plateau, cutting the blistering heat ever so slightly.

"Drop the guns please," Mel said.

Mr. Suit looked at Pitman, but he did not get so much as a sneer in return. At least Pitman could still do maths. He slowly lowered his stolen machine gun to the ground by the strap. Mr. Suit raised an eyebrow then locked eyes with Mel as he tossed his gun into the dirt just in front of her. She hadn't brought a personal weapon, four armed military guards seemed more than enough, but she stooped for the little black pistol and shoved it in her belt anyway. One of her men grabbed the more deadly of the two weapons and slung it over his shoulder. So that was that, then.

"Hello, Uncle Ryan. I would have liked to see you on better terms, but you have been quite busy."

"Your terms, you mean," Pitman laughed. "Where's Doc Evans?"

"No," she said flatly. "You lied, you get me."

Now the sneer came. "Since when do you do your own dirty work? Oh no matter, but you're wrong. I never lied."

Mel took two steps, grabbed the shriveled old man's arm, and jerked violently at his long shirt sleeve. The sweat-stained white cotton tore, and the button popped, revealing the raven tattoo beneath. She stared at him coldly, daring him to deny what was literally on his body.

He somehow broke into an even wider smile. "You got me," he shrugged. It sounded childish, a little boy caught with his hand in the cookie jar. It made her sick.

"Where is Wyatt Aarons? Do your people have him somewhere?"

Pitman looked genuinely surprised. "What are you talking about, kiddo? Of course not. If I knew where he was, we wouldn't be having this conversation. Shoot, we wouldn't be in this whole mess to begin with."

"Then what is the meaning of this..." she searched for the word, "Betrayal!?" Her voice was louder than she intended. She brought it back down. "Why did your Brotherhood of Ravens attack Aarons in Ugarit in the first place? If you knew something, I would have supported you fully. And why put this man in Oxford? Was it simply to watch Dr. Evans?" She waved accusingly at Mr. Suit, then lasered back in on Pitman. "And how did you ever come to be a part of it in the first place? You're no Kurdish nationalist. You're from Arkansas!"

"'Brotherhood of Ravens?' Oh, I like that." He turned to Mr. Suit. "Let's use that. Write it down or something." Mel couldn't believe how glib Pitman was being. Did he not understand all the things that had been put into motion because of his arrogant selfishness? Instead of being an important node in her network of human computers and a solution to her problems, he had become the living worm in the software. This man had caused a catastrophic failure in the very system she had trusted him to protect. That he had helped her to design! The irony was beyond scathing.

"As for you, kiddo, don't talk to me about betrayal. Not after what you have done with your father's legacy."

This surprised her. "You don't get to call me that anymore, Pitman." Hot anger was creeping into Mel's face. "And don't you dare speak to me of my father. He was your friend. He loved you in a way you can't possibly understand after the things you have done. You never lied? You lied to my father every day you pretended to be his friend."

Pitman's backhand caught Mel completely off guard, sending her sprawling into the scattered rocks and topsoil that concealed the ancient Ark.

Every one of Mel's men stepped forward, guns at the ready. Captain Rogers shouted a question she didn't fully hear, ready to end this with blood if necessary. Pitman just stood there, sourly looming over Mel. She raised a hand to hold her men off. There was silence again, except for the pulsing in her ears. She touched her stinging lip. A tiny smear of blood came away on her shaking hand.

"Ding was my dearest friend. But you, Melanie—you've become a force of destruction. Can't you see it? Everything you touch becomes tainted. Did you really think we would allow some starry-eyed little girl with an inheritance and an agenda to destroy everything we've built and protected? You have already squandered half of Dingxiang Chen's business fortune. The loyal fools

you've appointed to run your companies never knew your father like I did."
He paused to tip his hat and wipe the sweat from his bald head. "Or do you
even look at the financial reports anymore? Mao Sien? What a joke. Your silly
obsession with mythology is a disgrace to Dingxiang Chen's name. You find
all these hack experts like Wyatt and Doc Evans, then spend billions for them
to search the world for fantasies in leather airplane seats and overpriced
military vehicles. Then when they find something, you twist the biblical
realities of science and history into whatever form happens to suit your own
little personal—"

Mel's conscious mind didn't catch up to what happened next until after
she heard the gunshot. First, she saw the blood spreading on Pitman's torn
white shirt, then the deep surprise spreading on his wrinkled white face.
Finally, she looked down in confusion at the smoking pistol in her
outstretched hand.

Only then did she realize what she had done.

LXXXIX

*Mao Sien AW101 Merlin Helicopter. 14,000 ft., Eastbound over the
Mediterranean. Arthur.*

The helicopter blades sounded the way Evans' mind felt. "Can we try her
again?" he asked Ivan through the headset.

"Apologies Dr. Evans. Central is saying Miss Chen is 'off-grid.' I will try
later." Realistically, it was all he could ask of the man, but it didn't make it any
less frustrating.

"Arthur," David said haltingly, "You told that guard you know the mystical
reading of the Disk. Is it true?"

Technically it wasn't true. Technically it was just a half-baked theory. But
technically—all things considered—this was as good a time as any to test said
half-baked theory.

"Hand me that copy of my notes, please. The Disk too."

David grinned and promptly obeyed. He powered up the phone and
helpfully found the photos of Evans' notebook before handing it over.

Evans took a deep breath and focused. "It starts pretty much like my original reading," he began, "so I suppose I will start there." All eyes were on him. Even Matthew had chosen to relegate himself to the back with the rest of them this flight. "Though some of the meanings will need to change contextually, especially the pronouns, given the nature of this translation and the iconographic nature of the language—"

Matthew cleared his throat in that way he did when he wanted Evans to get on with it.

"Ah, quite right. 'When the flood came, only one ship loaded animals. One family went aboard. They went with livestock and clothing. Behold! The sea covered the livestock. Houses fell onto people. It happened. The flood happened. Trees fell.'" Evans glanced up, but never had an Oxford tutor recited to a more attentive audience. He blinked and looked over his glasses to continue. "'But one ship was greatly loaded. Behold! The sea covers the animals. The animals wash away, struck by the sea monster!'"

"Chaos serpent, right?" David interrupted. "The dragon Tiamat, or whatever."

Evans shrugged and accepted the change. He wouldn't submit it for publication that way, but with artistic license and all that, it would do fine here. "'The animals wash away, struck by the chaos serpent. Behold! The sea covers all creatures. The sandal-maker and kitchen-wife swam like a fish, toward the high mountain where the rich people lived.'" He paused. This was the place where the Disk reached the edge with the strange dog-leg. Evans now needed to ignore the remaining text, flip it and begin again on the other side. He took another deep breath, swiped a few times with only minor difficulty to another photo, and flipped the Disk over. He began anew in the middle, hoping he was right.

"'Understand this about our war. Remember the great-great grand-*mother* of our nation.'"

"What!?" deMata and David demanded in unison. Evans didn't stop. Better to let the text speak for itself.

"'Understand this. Behold the first family-nation. The important-man is made a God-king in his city. Then, a third child is born: and *she* was called Oxhide.'"

"What!?" The teens interrupted again.

"Arthur, are you serious?" David asked, "Is it actually talking about women instead of Noah and his sons?"

Evans quirked the edges of his mouth but did not break stride. This was the good part. "'Behold Oxhide, the divine-*queen*, for she birthed Oar-*ess* Leatherboat. Behold, she was a divine queen too. And from the line of our great-great-grandmother. Behold the divine-queen who *mothered* Oar-*ess*.'"

No interruptions this time from the kids, only stunned silence. Mathew still had his tongue though.

"Oh, I say. That is something now, a matriarchal genealogy. As I recall, Arthur, Jewish Orthodoxy still practices it, does it not?" Matthew was being humble again.

"Yes. Supposedly has its roots in the oral tradition of Moses and the law. Most ancient texts make very little mention of women by name, but the Old Testament is full of them. Genesis describes three patriarchs of Israel: Abraham, Isaac, and Jacob, but we are also given four matriarchs: Sarah, Rebekah, Rachel, and Leah. If Yosef were here, he could tell us more, I'm sure."

"So, according to the Disk, it seems that our 'kitchen-wife' mothered a parallel line of divine-matriarchs not spoken of in scripture?"

"I'd say it's a distinct possibility, Matthew. Especially given what comes next."

"The Minoans were matriarchal," deMata said, her face lighting up. "That is significant also."

"Yes, all interesting connections." Until recently, Evans might have argued the merits of these points, but he had reached the second edge. He flipped the Disk back to the side he had started with, and careful to pick up where he'd stopped, resumed his reading.

"'Then, from the high mountain, the great ships from the other family branch came. The male cousins of our good *queen's* house. They had warships with sides made of reeds. And from this war came death and famine. They barely escaped the attack with our leather-sided ships. So, remember the first child,' er, '*daughter*, of our family. *She* was born after the Great Flood to the important man.'"

"Oaress was their Queen!" David said, putting it all together. "It's not about a king at all. She saved them from a sneak attack from their stronger cousins up the river by running away. And she was the granddaughter of Oxhide, the first baby born after the flood, a girl. To Noah's—what? Second wife? Oh man, that's more than just new, that changes the whole story."

"Yes," Matthew grumbled. "Changes it quite a bit I would say."

"Why does it matter?" deMata asked.

"Only that if there were other survivors of the flood, then 'Father Noah' might not be everyone's father. Bit of a theological pickle for some, I'd wager." Matthew said with admirable calmness.

"Bah, we are still talking about myths," she chided. "You can't seriously think—"

DeMata stopped as Matthew innocently straightened his clerical collar. Why he was still wearing the thing Evans had no idea, but it did the job. "Occupational hazard," Matthew smiled.

"So, what happened?" David thought aloud, "How's it end now?"

There was only one passage left. Evans flipped the Disk the final time and translated the outside line with all of this new context. "'Destroyers of crops, behold. From the important-man's city, our generation also came. A second branch of city-*queens*! A family of divine-*queens*! From the important-man's city, this woman's family-branch begins again. The great sea beast caused the great flood! Our relatives were taken aboard, they boarded their animals too. The rest of creation flooded. But the important city of our ancestors remains.' And I believe you all know the last line."

David nodded. "'Follow the Path of the Flaming Sword to the city of Noah,'" he said. It was close enough.

"Tiamat was female," deMata observed, no small amount of pride bleeding through. "Just as the sea creature that caused the flood was female."

David looked around, not quite understanding.

"Oh, dear." Matthew thought aloud. "Arthur, could this all perhaps be the very origin of the snake-goddess cult on Crete?"

"I suspect you are both right," Evans affirmed. "This story is an encoded message to something like a matriarchal goddess-cult. It was the natural female chaos deity that wiped out the male civilization. The Nûḥ figure used a boat, but one of the rich women survived the flood by swimming to a high point. At first, I thought the sandal-maker and kitchen-wife were two people, male and female respectively. But part of the secret is that they were one and the same. I'd conjecture that 'sandal-maker' was a somewhat prestigious job for a woman of the day. So, after the cataclysm, Nûḥ married her and made her his 'kitchen-wife,' maybe even changing her name. Then, she bore him a daughter. It may have been a necessary union, but probably something of a demotion in status for her to go from business owner to the second wife of an old man. Perhaps that alone was enough for the family to split. Who knows?"

DeMata snorted. "And Sandal-Maker's descendants worshiped her as a goddess. That's some justice for her at least, after the men tried to kill everyone."

If ever there lived a liberated and capable woman who would sail off and start her own country, Evans supposed deMata would make a good candidate.

He cleared his throat and continued. "Three generations later, symbolically at least, they were at war. The 'orderly' patriarchy in their advanced boats against the 'natural' matriarchy in their leather ones down the coast somewhere. The women-led tribe fled out to the sea, and apparently to

Crete, thus establishing the most advanced civilization on earth, and ultimately giving birth to Europe. Maybe it was the origin of the flight of the Lydians myth, as told by those who stayed behind."

"I told you Europa was a goddess," deMata added flippantly.

"Or maybe it was something more like the Mycenean colonization of an island already emptied, ravaged by a catastrophe," Evans mused. "No way to be sure. Of course, like any other flood myth, this story almost certainly isn't strictly true, but the instructive and moral point holds. Figuratively I mean— that's the important part. This is a secret story about the success of their female ancestors against superior technology, written so that those who did not know the secret would not understand its true meaning. Not to mention, a warning about not letting it all happen again."

"When mankind gets too enlightened or comfortable, an apocalypse occurs," David marveled.

Evans nodded soberly.

"So where is it?" deMata asked. "This reading is interesting, but it still does not tell us where the 'Important City' of Noah, your Dilmun, actually is, or where to continue this Path of the Sword."

"Actually, Dr. deMata, it does. Twice." Evans pushed his glasses up from his nose and handed the phone and Disk back to David.

David began shoving everything back into his bag but then froze.

"The high mountain," he breathed, "The men in reed boats attacked the leather boat women from upriver. It was the place where the rich people lived before the flood. Noah must have built a town there since it was a place that didn't flood. But that could be anywhere."

Evans ran his dirty fingers through his dirtier hair. "*Cudi Dagi*," he said flatly. It's talking about Mt. Cudi. The mountain I first suggested to Wyatt that we search for the Ark on, all those years ago."

"Do you mean to say," probed Matthew, "that it is not on Doomsday Mountain after all?"

"Hold on, wasn't that the landing site named in the *Quran*?" David asked, clearly wanting Evans to deny it.

"Some call it *Judi Dagh*, or Mount Judi with an *i*, but it doesn't especially matter. It is an incredibly ancient name that means 'mountain of the nomads.' It's the highest hill in a range known locally as the 'high mountains' that overlook the Mesopotamian plain in Urartu. That is to say, Ararat. They are the literal mountains of Ararat. To the ancient Semitic world, that could be the only possible place where the 'high mountain' could be."

Matthew spoke with his scripture-quoting voice. "I say! 'And the waters prevailed so mightily on the earth that all the high mountains under the whole heaven were covered. The waters prevailed above the mountains, covering them fifteen cubits deep.' Could it truly be the location, Arthur? Plainly there the whole time? It would certainly solve a certain biblical math problem regarding fifteen cubits of water, eh David?"

But David wasn't listening. "Judi with an i?" he said slowly. The teen's face was twisted into raw confusion. "Does that have anything to do with Judi Bell?"

Evans felt the blood drain from his face. "What did you say?"

David stammered to get it out. When it came, it came in a torrent. "There was this little box, in the Mystery Chest in the attic—well, I called it that—and it looked just like the chest in your flat back in Oxford, except it had this massive stack of handwritten love letters in a little box, and pictures of this woman named Judi Bell who looked like Amelia Earhart or whatever, and other pictures of some little girl, and Dad told me not to get into it, but I used to sneak up there and go through it, only this last time the box with all the letters was gone so I just thought..." He ran out of words. "Sorry. It's stupid. Forget it." The boy looked like he was about to throw up.

Matthew stretched his hand out to David's shoulder. He looked to Evans with an odd questioning smile. The old tutor's heart caught in his throat. He had not expected this, and yet, it made perfect sense. Full circle, he supposed.

"No, David, you are exactly right. I had forgotten that my school chest's old twin was still up there in the Texas attic, but undoubtedly it would be. I left it there so very long ago now."

David stared at him with his mother's green eyes, an animal in a trap. "You put it there?"

Evans shrugged noncommittally. "Except, that adventurous woman's name wasn't Judi Bell. She was Gertrude Bell, a truly great and famous Englishwoman of the nineteenth century. She was a writer, world traveler, political officer, administrator, and archaeologist at a time when women did not do such things. She explored, made maps, and became highly influential to British imperial policy-making. Hers is a sad story with an unfortunate ending, but her journals are magnificent. And she became, notably, the first person to report sighting Noah's Ark on Mount Judi."

"What?" David managed. "How?"

"I can't imagine how young you must have been when you saw those pictures, David. Karen sent me Gertrude's letters quite a few years ago. It was a delight to have it all again. And to think, it was in that second chest all along? That explains so much."

"But, Arthur! Why was there a trunk in our attic with all this Bell person's letters and stuff at all? I mean, how did you get it in the first place? What is going on with you!"

Evans laughed. A genuine shoulder-shaking that surprised even himself. "It was my father's attic long before it was your childhood home, David. I had a perfect right to store my things there. And as for the letters, I acquired them from that little girl herself. She was the unintended product of Gertrude Bell's, uh, relationship with a married man. It was a very different time then. A pregnant mistress was much too scandalous for a proper English gentleman I'm afraid. They came to a financial arrangement, which was not out of the ordinary in those days. Gertrude loved him greatly, and she exchanged those love letters for many years thereafter, often sending him updated photos of her travels, and of her beautiful daughter whom she named Caroline."

David shook his head, still not understanding.

"As I said, Gertrude Bell's is a sad story. She eventually gave the girl up, sent her to one of the best finishing schools for young ladies in London, and resumed her fieldwork. Eventually, Caroline married well and had a daughter of her own. I suppose that is when her father presented himself, or at the very least returned her mother's letters to her. In time, Gertrude's granddaughter was even accepted to the University of Oxford, which is of course where I come in. I encountered that remarkable young lady as a classmate, having myself just come to England to study." Evans felt a mix of joy and sadness at the memory. "I never met Gertrude obviously, but Caroline was a dear sweet lady. And her lovely young daughter and I became the very best of friends. Eventually, I learned of her grandmother's unusual quest for the Ark all those years before, and I daresay it even sparked my first interest in the subject. We swore that one day we would go there together and retrace her grandmother's steps, solve the mystery. Unfortunately, we never had the chance."

David pursed his lips into the beginning of a whispered "wha—," but nothing more came out.

"The little girl in the pictures was my mother-in-law, Caroline Bell, before she took her husband's name. Your great-grandmother, David. The granddaughter's name was Elisabeth. She was your grandmother. And I daresay, something of a divine queen herself. Though admittedly, I'm a bit biased."

XC

"Help him," the man in the ruined suit heard someone say. "Now!"

It was the woman he now knew to be Melanie Chen, his former employer. She still held his gun. He only hesitated for a moment, then knelt on the ground beside Dr. Pitman.

There was a bemused surprise on the old man's face. It almost masked the pain. The man in the ruined suit had always admired Dr. Pitman for his ability to read people and get what he wanted from them. From the moment they had first met, the American scientist had never seemed out of control of anything.

Until now.

People are like clocks to be studied. Resources to be consumed.

Now the old man who had taught him these ideas lay bleeding into the dirt, his pilfered hat beside him. How quickly things can change.

"He needs a surgeon," the man told Chen truthfully.

He had been trained in basic battlefield first aid during his time with the Turkish Air Force, but short of binding the wound, there was not much he could do. Dr. Pitman would need a real doctor to remove the bullet this crazy woman had put into his side. And from the angle she had fired it, he wouldn't be surprised if his gut had been perforated in the path.

"This isn't gonna go how you think, Melanie," Dr. Pitman said to the sky, still holding onto his clenched smile. Then, "You might want to get down, boy."

As if on cue, there was a shout from the fringes of the little plateau. Sackcloth coverings pulled away and a dozen or so men with guns popped up from their hiding places on both sides of the hill. They wore the black masks and armbands the man in the suit knew so well. Dr. Pitman's loyal soldiers rose out of where the plateau's edge met the jutting stone walls with wild ululations. Before anyone could react, they braced their guns on the rocks and the shooting started.

The man in the suit hit the dirt reflexively, more surprised by this turn of events than Chen's little mercenary team. Dr. Pitman had been keeping secrets from him after all. And because of it, things were getting complicated again.

His military training kicked in. He assessed the situation in less than a breath. They were boxed in. The attackers had the better position, but the assault team was better equipped and much better trained. As well as their much more accurate weapons, they also wore bullet-proof armor. Plus, it was highly likely that none of the men in the shadows of the rock were older than twenty. The chances of them doing something foolish were high. There was a low outcropping here if he could get behind it. But it was wide, and that was not an easy task unless he abandoned Dr. Pitman. There was one other factor too. It seemed that the ambushers were trying very hard not to hit their leader. This last was something he knew he could use.

The man in the ruined suit scrambled on the ground next to the prone Pitman. He shed his spoiled suitcoat, then grabbed the fallen man's hat, shoving it onto his own head. A sloppy impromptu disguise if ever there was one, but hopefully it would suffice. The corporate soldiers squatted low, formed up, laid down cover fire, and fell back from the shootout like clockwork. Bullets kicked up dirt and one or two even thudded against armor. One of the soldiers took a hit in the leg and a bloody gash opened up. The wounded mercenary cried out in pain, but it only fueled him. Chen shouted orders into her vest and almost immediately the distant whir of their Mi35 helicopter grew louder. She had an exit strategy.

Then, the pattern of gunfire changed. As the attackers popped up like over-eager gophers, the soldiers began to snipe at them with precise and deadly aim. It only took a few near misses and one bullseye for the attackers to rethink their strategy.

Half dragging, half helping, he got Dr. Pitman a few feet further away from the others and the target zone of fire. The man in the hat wasn't the only one to notice the attackers' reluctance to shoot the wounded man though. No sooner had he managed this small victory than the mercenary captain barked an order and the soldiers formed up around him with lightning speed. The man's way to the outcropping was blocked as the little squad unabashedly used the two unarmed and unarmored men for cover.

So much for a fair fight. The man in the hat laughed. It was precisely what he would have done.

The attackers stopped firing, not sure what to do about this new development. Some scrambled for a better angle, exposing themselves to even more return fire from Chen's people. But it didn't matter. For a moment the man wasn't sure why the gunfire kept echoing until a cloud of dirt hit him, and he realized that Chen's egress had arrived. It came down close, creating a hovering wall between the attackers and the mercenaries.

"Go!" Chen shouted. With a whoop, her men snapped up and ran crouching to the helicopter.

The way it hovered only feet above the rocky hill was impressive. Had he been the pilot, the man in the hat would not have attempted such a maneuver, even without a firefight. With their targets blocked, the rebels decided it was time to charge. With banshee screams and more gunfire, they stupidly vaulted up and over and ran toward the helicopter.

Then Chen truly surprised him. With his gun still in her hand, she growled, "Get him in there. Now!"

With a smile, the man complied. He hoisted Dr. Pitman onto his shoulder with a grunt, feeling hot blood that was not his soak through his thin shirt. Dr. Pitman was limp, but the man didn't stop to see if he was just passed out or already dead. In a few hard steps, they were below the copter's open side.

The attackers closed in, happily filling their bigger, hovering target with holes. If they hit one of the fuel tanks, it would be all over. There wasn't time to think about it. With a visceral growl, the man in the hat found the strength to heft Dr. Pitman over to the hovering beast's floor, just as it veered away by a few feet and set down hard. The man ducked forward to avoid possible decapitation, and the limp old man dropped and bounced in rather roughly.

One of Chen's mercenaries hoisted the old man and strapped him into a seat, lolling head, sticky blood and all. Another soldier scrambled for some surprisingly appropriate medical supplies. Medevac helicopter, the man remembered. Maybe Dr. Pitman had a chance after all.

Regardless, the man in the hat was done here. He had obeyed Chen, and Dr. Pitman's fate was now out of his hands. If he could fall back to the edge of the plateau, then maybe he could leave in safety, make a call, and formulate a plan. For now, he just needed to avoid getting shot, friendly fire, or otherwise. He chucked the twice-stolen hat at Dr. Pitman like a frisbee and watched it bounce off him. Turning to scramble away on his hands and knees, he came face to face with his forfeited gun again. Chen squatted at the other end.

He considered relieving her of it, but the soldiers behind him kept him from trying it. Before either of them could speak, one of the men shouted out from the Mi35.

"Ma'am, we have a problem! Our Russian dusty just caught a bullet. We aren't going anywhere."

Realization dawned. *The pilot was shot?* This changed everything. No wonder he had set the helicopter down so fast and hard. The man in the bloody white shirt smiled.

"I can fly it," he told his gun confidently, his eyes flicking up to meet Chen's. "I can fly."

"Yes. Yes, you can." she realized. "But why should I trust you?"

Two of the rebels had decided to come around to the other side. A series of bullets raked just above the man and Chen's heads and they both squatted reflexively. One of the mercs fired two quick shots from the door and the two insurgents went down.

"Because you need to get Dr. Pitman out of here, and I can do it. But most importantly," he flashed his perfect smile, "I know where Wyatt Aarons is."

Chen's expression hardened, then she made her decision.

"I have the utmost faith in your abilities."

XCI

Mao Sien AW101 Merlin Helicopter. 14,000 ft. over Şırnak Provence, Turkey. Eastbound toward Mt. Cudi. David.

"Did you know there is a town down there called Batman?" David chuckled into the mic. "We practically just flew over it."

Nobody responded. They were all in foul moods. The novelty of flying in something as exciting as a helicopter had long since worn off after their second Mediterranean crossing in as many days. David powered off his phone and sat in silence. He only had a little bit of battery left anyway, and the helicopter had its own GPS.

"That is your mountain," Ivan barked a few minutes later. "If you wish to land, I see place, but there is also people."

Instantly, all boredom left David. As the military helicopter circled once and slowed, David could see a small settlement at the base of the large hill. Dozens of people scrambled out of colorful buildings like ants to watch them land. They weren't exactly being subtle in their arrival, but what else was there to do?

The most obvious building was a huge, rectangular-ish structure nestled into a crook between two rolling hills. It looked like stonework to David, with maybe a grass bundle or stick roof. Far more like a big wall built by shepherds than any sort of thing from Noah's time. And nothing like the Doomsday "amoeba" from the LIFE magazine article that had sparked Mr. Aarons' Ark quest in the first place. This whole thing seemed a bit surreal, and not at all as David had imagined. He wondered if the others were having similar thoughts.

"What's going on down there?" Matthew asked, to himself as much as anyone else.

"It's too late for the Kurdish new year, but Revolution Day is around this time as I recall," Arthur said.

"Revolution Day?" Asked David.

"It's a bit like an Independence Day, Fourth of July, or Cinco de Mayo if you like. Except here it was when the Turkish and Ottomans began their war of independence at the tail end of World War I."

"Oh, well that's good, right? People are way friendlier on holidays." David observed.

David could see Arthur weighing the decision. It had not been an easy trip. The helicopter had required refueling twice, and that was no simple proposition in this part of the world. With Mel's resources and credentials working for them they'd managed, crossing borders with minimal issues, but they were all exhausted, hungry, dirty, hadn't changed clothes in days, and stretched very thin on patience. So, as they finally hovered over their target, Arthur deliberated.

David knew what his wizard must be thinking. On the one hand, it was the best, maybe only shot they would have of exploring the place. But on the other, they had not expected to encounter people, much less a village's worth. And especially not having a festival possibly celebrating the defeat of the West.

Only days ago, his grandfather's strange and mysterious past had been dark waters he knew nothing of. Now he was plunged so deeply into that abyss of impossible things that no one back home would ever believe him. He hardly believed it himself. And yet, here they were, landing on a desolate mountaintop in south-central Turkey, looking for Noah on the highest peak of the lowest mountain range in the area known as Urartu on practically every map. *The 'high mountains' of Ararat.*

But, if this was the right place, then something was very, very wrong with the whole thing. They were supposed to be landing near what might be the lost city of Noah. Dilmun. Eden? So why were there people down there, and why were they having a party?

"Do it," Arthur said. "It's time to put this nonsense to bed."

*   *   *

A herd of goats scattered as Ivan brought the helicopter down in a cloud of dry hot dust.

A minute later, everyone gathered what few things they had. Matthew whispered a prayer. Colonel Ivan holstered a sidearm. The contrast of these both comforted and unnerved David for very different reasons.

Another minute and a winding line of people could be seen approaching them. David realized there was a trail in the direction of the structure, made by the goats, maybe. As the little caravan drew closer, David was shocked to realize that he recognized them. Or at least, he recognized what they were. They wore matching camo pants and jackets and black face wraps that covered all but their piercing black and white eyes. Glimpses of olive skin were visible, and they each carried a deadly-looking assault rifle. This last was a horrifying detail that almost kept David from noticing their matching armbands of red, white, and black. Or more precisely, a black raven on a red and white background. It was all just like Mr. Aarons' final video log.

"Well, I suppose we are in the right place," Arthur said rather flippantly.

"Stand behind us," Matthew warned, holding up his hands in peace to the half-dozen guerillas. It looked to David like a surrender. He realized with a shock that it was.

Ivan was strung so tight he looked like he was fully ready to kill something, but he watched Arthur intently for a cue that wasn't coming as his jaw moved back and forth.

David reeled. How had these guys beaten them here? What insane sort of organization had this much clout? He suddenly remembered thinking the same thing about Mel Chen and wondered if they had all been outplayed again somehow. If this were one of his tabletop games, he might have accepted such a twist, but this just didn't make any sense. David started to say as much, but unbelievably, Arthur cut him off with another of his random little lectures.

"So, I've been thinking, there are different theories about the origin of the word *Kurd*," Arthur began. "According to one theory, it originates in Middle Persian as *kwrt*, a term for 'nomad or tent-dweller.' After the Muslim conquest of Persia, this term was adopted into Arabic as *Kurd*, and was used specifically to speak of the nearby nomadic tribes."

"Arthur, is now really the time?" Father Matthew began.

"However, the land of *Karda* is mentioned on a Sumerian clay tablet dated to the 3rd millennium B.C. It states that this area was inhabited by 'the people of Su,' who dwelt here in the southern regions of Lake Van. The philological connection between *Kurd* and *Karda* is uncertain, but the relationship is considered possible. Other Sumerian clay tablets refer to the people who lived in the land of Karda as the *Qarduchi* and the *Qurti*. Plus, *Karda* and *Qardu* are both etymologically related to the Assyrian term *Urartu* and the Hebrew term *Ararat*."

The men were dangerously close now, a string of rapid shouts David didn't understand carried across the scraggy hilltop to them. But David's attention was divided between them and Arthur.

"They have had many names throughout the many eras," he continued, "but I've been a terrible fool. I all but said it before. *Cudi Dagh* literally means 'high mountain of the nomads,' and the Kurdish nomads have always been known as 'the people of the High Mountain of Urartu.' *This* mountain. They are literally named for Cudi. They are the people of the high mountain. The word itself is so old as to have lost any contemporary context."

Everyone but Ivan stared at him questioningly. They were about to die, and Arthur was giving etymology lessons.

"But, don't you see? The West did the same thing. It's the Kurds from whom the mountains took the name *Cardu*, then *Gardu*, and eventually the Greeks as we know them turned it into the Mountains of *Gordyae*. It's the only logical answer to all this."

"Arthur," Matthew chided, "How were we possibly to know that? And what precisely, my good man, is your point?"

"From the Labyrinth of Gortyna to the mountains of Gordyae?" Cat breathed. The rest she rattled off so fast that David could hardly follow it. "Why, the Gordian Knot itself might well be an elaborate metaphor for the Labyrinth and our Path of the Flaming Sword also. Even the city of Gordium lies on the ancient road between Lydia and Babylonia, to the northwest of here. It can't be a coincidence."

Arthur scratched his beard thoughtfully. "If that was true, then I suppose Alexander the Great's fabled 'cutting of the Gordian Knot' could have symbolically pointed to the disruption of that very route between Crete and Mt. Cudi. Certainly, the Greek military apparatus must have created a significant shift of political power in the region, cutting ties as it were."

"Oh yes, was he also hunting the Ark?" Cat quipped sarcastically.

But there was no more time for discussion. The men of the mountain were here, all angry shouts and gesturing weapons. David couldn't believe how calm Arthur was being about it all.

"Please hand me your bag, David. Everyone, relax and smile."

David relaxed as much as he could manage. His wizard had a plan. He watched as Arthur slowly unzipped the bag and extracted the Disk, tossing the mostly empty bag over his shoulder into the helicopter.

Teeth clenched, Matthew asked, "Can you understand them?"

"Yes," Arthur said. "My Kurdish is pretty rusty, but it will suffice. Everyone raise your hands, please. They will probably search us. Ivan, they will most certainly take your sidearm. Please let them." The look the Russian soldier gave him could have melted lead. "Try to think of yourselves as guests, and these men as our personal guards."

"Is that what they are saying?" Cat asked.

"No," Arthur said. "You don't want to know what they are saying."

*   *   *

As Arthur predicted, the gunmen did a thorough search of everyone. They confiscated Colonel Ivan's gun, along with a second gun from his belt and large combat knife from his leg that David hadn't realized he was carrying. They took various other items of concern to them, some gum and other snacks, a book of matches also from an MRE, and most painfully, David's phone again. They got a little handsy with Cat, but she faked a casual dismissal of it everywhere except in her deadly eyes.

On Arthur's orders, Ivan was instructed to stay with the helicopter. David could tell that it was a toss-up for the man between his self-imposed guard duties to them and to their only way home, but in the end, he complied with Arthur. The ark-hunters were then led along a little goat path towards the direction of the large stone structure David had seen from the air.

Now that he was closer, David could understand the layout better. What he had mistaken for a town was a series of tents thrown up in and around cobblestone ruins. The whole setup reminded him of an open market or booths at the State Fair. David also thought he could detect where a courtyard had once been. A few people milled about in local outfits, and somewhere a flute played accompanied by singing. Many stopped and stared, but if these were simple farmers and shepherds, then they were wearing their colorful Sunday best. And there were kids there too, who stopped their game of tag to stare at the visitors from the west, giggling and jabbing one another.

Then there were the smells. A dozen different exotic foods hit his nostrils all at once. His stomach twisted, reminding him how long it had been since eating real food. Army rations still did not count, especially Russian ones. He spotted a dozen braziers with skewers of meat, something that looked like dumplings, and he most definitely detected flatbread and about a million different spices and fruity concoctions he could only guess at. It was a feast for every sense and his mouth watered just thinking about it.

David forced himself to focus on other things. He could now see the details of the large stone structure. It still looked like a highly organized pile of rocks more than anything else. It had no real mortar or foundation that he could tell, but it was incredibly well-crafted. Each stone was fitted perfectly with the next.

"That wall..." David whispered.

"It looks like Scottish drystone," Matthew said. "Quite well done."

"Older technique than that, I assure you," Arthur muttered.

"But, it's the background from some of the old pictures, Arthur. The Judi, er, Gertrude Bell pictures from the Mystery Chest—"

David didn't need to know Kurdish to understand the order the man in the mask gave him. The butt of the rifle in his back punctuated it just fine.

Yes, sir. Not talking, he thought, even as Arthur gave him a wordless warning to the same end. But there was more there too. An affirmation. This was *that* wall. The same one his great-great-grandmother Gertrude Bell had stood in front of so long ago. The thought thrilled him to his core.

A well-groomed older man in ornate clothes stepped out of a doorway. He had deep wrinkles and laugh lines on his clean-shaven face, complementing his broad gleaming smile. He wore a head wrap of beautiful twisted silks and a matching cloth belt, wrapped around him many times, plus an ornate vest and some very traditional-looking middle-eastern pants. Over all of this was a handcrafted leather piece that looked to David like some kind of belt-suspender combo with dozens of little pouches lined along it. Yet, in a way, the man looked every bit as grandfatherly as anyone might hope to.

"We've been expecting you, Dr. Evans," the man said with an excellent Middle Eastern and British-blend accent that surprised David greatly. The man threw his arms wide, and for a moment David thought he might try to hug Arthur. Instead, he barked a command to their masked captors with a scowl.

The other men lowered their guns into what David supposed was meant to be a non-threatening posture for people wielding fully automatic weapons of war. But the men's razor-sharp attention never wavered.

"Ah," Arthur stuttered, pushing up his glasses and extending a hand. "Call me Arthur. I would say I'm pleased to make your acquaintance sir, but I'm afraid you have us at a disadvantage."

The old man laughed, clasping Arthur's hand firmly with both of his, shaking vigorously. He did not try to hide his faded raven tattoo.

"And you will please call me Ashti." The two men stood studying each other for a moment, hands clasped. Only, Ashti seemed to be waiting for something. "You do not recognize me," he finally said, a shade of disappointment evident in his tone.

Arthur hesitated. He blinked a few times, and then his jaw dropped, his free hand rising to his eye. "You!?"

The other man laughed uproariously, and some of his comrades even joined him. David didn't get the joke.

"Good lord, but you got old!" Arthur declared. "But then, I suppose I have too after almost thirty years."

David looked to Matthew for a hint at what might be happening, but the priest shrugged in bemusement.

"The last time I saw you, I was chasing you down an alley in Dogubeyazit. You didn't speak the Queen's English then."

"The first is true," the man agreed. "Though my English was better than I might have let on. I was selected to study abroad shortly after our first meeting." Ashti stuck his thumbs under the suspender things. "I took a degree from Cambridge in 1993."

Arthur's shock was palpable, but he held it together admirably. "Ah, yes. It's a fine school. Fine. You know, it took three weeks for my eye to return to normal color again. You have an excellent right hook."

"It's no longer what it was, I assure you," the old Kurd laughed. "Still, no need to test it today. Come—the festivities are starting soon."

"Festivities?" David mouthed to Cat, who had her arm hooked under his. She only shook her head in equal confusion.

A long low rumble rolled out across the mountaintops. It took David a surprised few seconds to realize that it was thunder. In the far distance, he could see dark clouds approaching far beyond the rolling mountains.

"And it would seem," Ashti added, "that our prayers for rain have also been answered. It is a sign of good things. Quickly now, let us get inside Nûḥ's sanctuary. Dayik is looking forward to speaking with you and wishes to show you something that will no doubt answer your many questions."

David and Cat traded looks of thrilled wonder. *Could it really be?*

A small crowd had gathered, but with a mere gesture from Ashti, men, women, and children crowded in from every direction holding various items, trinkets, and ornamentation. David was sure they would begin trying to sell these things to them, but to his great surprise, they didn't. They began draping the scholars in elegant cloth sewn with bells, offering hats and simple handmade bracelets and necklaces, asking nothing in return beyond an embrace or a pat or a squeeze on the arm.

Then to David's greater delight, the fantastic-smelling food arrived in wooden bowls and cups. He took everything he could hold, stuffed his pockets full of fruit and nuts, even letting Matthew be his third hand. His stomach growled audibly in utmost appreciation.

"Well now," Matthew said flippantly, "one might think that had the potential to be awkward."

David had to laugh. He was really growing fond of British wit. And yet, he still couldn't believe what was happening. *Nûḥ's sanctuary? Prayers for rain? Just what is this place?* The first few notions that popped into his mind were completely impossible. Or so he would have thought, only a few unbelievable days ago.

David took a long swig of a white drink tasting vaguely of yogurt and almond, and a huge bite of the meat strip on a stick that was dripping oil onto his hand, his new favorite thing ever. It was pure Edenic perfection either way.

And hey, bonus—we aren't prisoners, apparently!

XCII

Nûh's Sanctuary. Mt. Cudi, Şırnak Provence, Turkey. Arthur.

Dayik? That means 'mother,' Evans realized. "How did you know we were coming, Ashti?" he asked their host.

"An associate sent word that a small group was beginning the path. We put the pieces together and knew to expect you. Though you arrived much faster than I would have thought possible."

"Your Labyrinth guardian," Evans marveled. "Of course."

Ashti's words were light. "In the old days, it would have taken much longer for someone to unravel the clues and do the research necessary to find their way here. I suspect you cheated a bit, sir."

Evans lifted an eyebrow. "Well, to be fair, most of my research was done four decades ago. But in all truth, I didn't do it alone." He instantly knew how true his statement was. Where would they be without David's wild imaginings? Matthew's strength and unswerving faith? Even deMata's cynical young brilliance and experience? *Not standing here, certainly.* "But I must ask—Ashti, how the devil did your people send word of anything? I mean this isn't exactly a major rail stop." Evans glanced at the small crowd still milling around them and the multitude of others scattered all around the nearby structures. *On the other hand...*

The local man casually reached into his voluminous cloth belt and extracted a little phone. "We have mobile service on most of the high hills now! It is quite exciting."

Evans was flabbergasted. Somewhat predictably David lit up, juggled the goat kabob he had been wolfing, and reached for his phone, only to remember that it had been taken.

"And the deadly force?"

"Ah, apologies. That was not meant for you. It was..." Ashti chose his words carefully, "for another."

He means Wyatt, Evans realized. They were guarding themselves against predatory archeology. He would need to be very careful about what he said in this place. These were the people who had attacked Wyatt in Ras-Shamra. Video evidence didn't lie. It was highly likely that these people had him stuck in a hole somewhere, perhaps on this very mountain. A stray thought occurred to Evans and he voiced it. "You said you were chosen to go to Cambridge. Just who exactly chose you?"

The man laughed. "All will be explained, Dr. Evans. Come, it is not my place today. That is for Dayik."

Ashti shooed the gunmen away like children and led the scholars through a short tunnel in the dark stonework. It jogged sharply first one way, and then the other.

A doorless entry, Evans realized. *Just like the floorplan of the tent depicted in the pictographic letter Beyt. Just like the Gortyn Labyrinth's hidden switchback.*

Inside, the place was much larger than Evans had expected. It was the thick layer of rugs that he noticed first. Every inch of the floor was covered in dozens, perhaps more, of enormous Turkish carpets. Each one had intricate geometric and floral patterns of all colors. No two were alike, but in this uniqueness, they all went together.

The carpets met around great wooden posts, designed to hold up smaller crossbeams and a roof of long thatch bundles thicker than a man. They were packed so tight that no light penetrated from outside. Small ornate tin lanterns lit what little Evans could see, casting pockets of light in otherwise deep shadows. This was because the walls were the same windowless thick stonework as outside, and judging by the depth of the entryway, they were a good ten or twelve feet thick at least.

Though most of the interior was empty space, two dozen crude backless benches were scattered about, enough to seat maybe a hundred people. But there were far fewer bodies than that here. Some were gathered around a poet reciting a verse. A few lounged and laughed, while still others sat in quiet contemplation, meditation, or prayer. Despite all the component elements being entirely different, the overall effect reminded Evans of the little stone church of St. Giles, or even Matthew's St. Michael at the North Gate, in its own simple way. This was a true sanctuary in more ways than one, albeit more on scale with a small cathedral. Yet even the word *basilica* seemed much too modern for this place.

"I must apologize," Ashti said. "But the rest of you will need to stay here and enjoy the festival." The man motioned to the benches. Matthew frowned, but Evans gave him a wordless nod of assurance. This was Ashti's show now. *'His roof, his rules,' and all that.* They were in too deep for anything else and if this was a trap, then he was far beyond stupidly wandering into it.

"I'll see you all soon," Evans said for the benefit of the others.

He watched as the three made their way to one of the benches. David lowered himself onto it and gave Evans one of Karen's slightly worried looks and a weak smile before cracking open a pomegranate to share with deMata. In two breaths, the others had shifted focus to the celebrations around them.

As Evans followed the jolly Ashti, he drank in celebrations around him. He remembered these people. Of course, that wasn't strictly true. Evans had spent most of his time with Wyatt Aarons a few hundred miles away, at the feet of the modern Mount Ararat. But Evans remembered the culture. Little things had brought bits of it scampering back. These carpets, the traditional outfits, the smell of local delights cooking, and the slight undertone of goat throughout. And most of all, the *Dengbej* musician in the corner reciting what he now recognized as a traditional oral *lawj* epic-poem in the forbidden Kurdish language. One of an unknown number of ancient stories that had literally never been written down.

And then Evans understood. He still didn't know what festival this might be, but it certainly was not Revolution Day. That was a Turkish holiday; these people were Kurdish, through and through. The name of this celebration didn't matter. The Kurds had known political and cultural repression as deeply as any group in the world. In Turkey, Iran, Iraq and Syria alike, there had been various extensive campaigns at forced assimilation, attempting to wipe them out. The Kurds had even been forbidden to speak Kurdish in public. They had been forced to change their names to local ethnic names if they wanted a job or to enroll their children in school. Their books, music, and clothing were considered contraband and they'd had to hide these things in their homes. If the authorities found anything Kurdish, they could even be imprisoned, and many had been.

But there were no such restrictions being observed here. It was no wonder they guarded this place with armed militants. The Westerners were witnessing the celebration of a culture older than some silly border disputes by modern militaries and governments. It was a deep festival of being, identity, and life itself. Whatever this festival was, it was far, far older than any modern holiday, religious or otherwise. Probably far older than all of Oxford. As these things passed through his conscious mind, in his gut Evans was quite sure he would be safe. These were good people. Real people. Not just faceless freedom fighters or guerilla soldiers, but hosts who had offered their hospitality in an ancient sacred tradition that was oldest of all. Quite possibly as old as the mountains themselves.

Ashti put his arm on Evans' back, steering him in the low light toward the front of the place. In a church, it would be the choir or altar, he supposed. And then to Evans' surprise, his jolly guide disappeared behind another fold in the thick wall. Evans followed him through the little passage into, for lack of a better term, the apse.

Standing there meditatively by a small lamplit table was an old woman, beautifully serene. She wore a long-sleeved jacket over a great flowing gown and cloth belt. Her complimentary Kurdish hat was ornamented with colored stones, beads, and gold.

Many Kurdish people groups are matriarchal, Evans' brain reminded him offhandedly, for whatever good it might do him.

This elegant grandmother was *Dayik*, and even before she spoke, Evans understood that he was in the presence of a queen.

"You are most welcome here, Dr. Evans," Dayik said in thinly accented English. It had the musical quality of one who had acquired it in India. "All faiths are welcome here."

"Um, yes. Thank you." He managed. Then remembering himself, "*Merhaba,*" he added with a respectful nod. "You are these people's leader, aren't you?"

Dayik laughed. "Today, I am. And so much the better for you!"

Evans felt his expression go blank. He had no idea what she was getting at.

"It is providential that you have found your way here during Festival. I do not think that the guardians would have received you quite so hospitably otherwise." There was a mischievous twinkle in the matriarch's eyes.

Evans considered their masked gun-toting welcoming party and smiled back weakly. He had never crashed a religious festival before, and he wasn't at all sure how one was supposed to act after doing so. Evans suddenly felt ridiculously underdressed. *Or overdressed?* Either way, Dr. Andino's Greek clown suit was contributing greatly to his sense of self-consciousness.

"You are here to see the Ark, Dr. Evans," Dayik stated plainly. There was no hint of a question in her words.

Evans choked back a gasp. "Please, call me Arthur," he croaked. "With apologies, Dayik, I am—" he swallowed hard— "only trying to find a missing man for my employer. An amateur archeologist with whom I worked some time ago."

"You will not find Wyatt Aarons here," she stated flatly. Her bluntness surprised Evans, and it must have shown on his face because she softened again. "There are things in motion now, Arthur, which cannot be stopped. Your employer, Melanie Chen, has begun her own path. We cannot interfere."

Evans was flabbergasted, but Dayik seemed unphased by his silence. With a chuckle, she turned back to the little table and knelt beside it, tucking her hand under the corner of one of the magnificent Turkish rugs.

"Come," she said.

At first, Evans wasn't sure what she was doing, or what she expected him to do, but as she folded the corner of the rug back and then another under it, he saw what could only be described as a tiny hatch. At her word, he hauled it up and peered into the inky blackness below. A smell he could not quite identify tickled his nose. It reminded him of standing over the Egyptian mummies at the Ashmolean and the very old books at the Bodleian all at once.

"After you, please," Dayik said, passing over the only tin lantern in the room.

As Evans held the little lamp over the hole, he saw jutting flat stones resembling footholds leading down into a shaft. He gingerly stepped down onto one and was pleased to feel it take his weight quite firmly.

One step at a time he lowered himself into the hole, until a perfectly smooth cobblestone floor came into view. He found himself in a small stonework room nearly identical to the one he had left above, except for the lack of carpet, furniture, and other décor. As above, a curtain of stone hid a passage to somewhere else in the darkness. He suddenly felt like he was back in the Gortyn Labyrinth, a horrible thought.

"As above, so below," he grumbled, frowning over the possible implications. A moment later Dayik stepped down beside him.

"There is a niche that way where you can place the lamp, but you will find another lamp over there. Please light it first."

Evans did as he was told, finding a kindling stick with which to transfer the fire. The niches were darkened with smoke above and smoothed to a curved polish on the sides and bottom. He had seen such wear only in monasteries and churches still in use from the days of the Roman Empire. *Just how old is this place?*

As he was doing this, Dayik moved to the only other feature in the room. It looked like a farmhouse window shutter, completely out of place down a secret hole hidden below a great stone temple in the middle of nowhere on a mountain in southeast Turkey. It took everything Evans had not to scoff audibly at the absurdity of it. With ceremonial grace, a few head bobs, and a whispered prayer, Dayik unclasped a little latch and pulled the shutters open.

In the dim light from the two lanterns, all Evans could see was more darkness. Did Dayik expect him to now crawl up and over the little opening into an adjoining chamber on his hands and knees? Was this to be his fate then, sealed away in a dark hole? Perhaps Wyatt Aaron's corpse awaited him on the other side of this wall.

But as he stepped closer, Evans realized that the darkness was not nothingness, but a deeply blackened *something*. He was looking at an exposed interior wall deeply aged and coated with a pitch-black substance. This was the source of the mummy-book smell. The thick varnish was cracked and hardened, but it was very apparent that the wood it was meant to preserve had successfully been shielded for quite some time.

Yes, Evans thought with bated breath. *Quite some time indeed.*

XCIII

Nûh's Sanctuary. Mt. Cudi, Şırnak Provence, Turkey. David.

Low rolling thunder shook the beams of the temple and its great roof of bundled reeds. David and the others watched from their uncomfortable bench as the festival was quickly moved inside. More lanterns were brought to life, and soon the place was filled with light and noise. The whole cavernous room became a sea of dancing, laughing people, music, and song. Even the animals were herded inside. It was the most marvelous thing David had ever witnessed.

"This is amazing," he said, "but what are they even celebrating?"

"I have no idea," Matthew replied, "But it is quite lively, is it not?"

There was an ancient element to it that David couldn't quite place. It was foreign, sure, but what wasn't around here?

Cat had been writhing to go be anthropological since the moment they had arrived. Now that the cultural festivities had come to them, she was practically bursting with pent-up energy and not even listening to him and Matthew at all.

A group of jangling young women wiggled by the bench-sitters, each one reaching out to them to stroke a head, a shoulder, a hand, and even a beard, much to Matthew's surprise. Then as the last girl passed them, instead of a caress she seamlessly transitioned into a perfect impression of a moonwalking Michael Jackson, motioning for Cat to join her. Cat couldn't resist any longer. Within moments, she was danced away into the crowd. David and Matthew looked at each other and burst into laughter.

"We humans are not so different at the end of the day," Matthew remarked. "I suspect it is because people need their rituals."

David was just glad he hadn't been asked to join too. He was a lot of things, but 'dancer' was not one of them.

"Father Matthew, will Arthur be okay? Should we really have let him go in alone?"

Matthew considered it for a moment, then nodded confidently. "Arthur knows what he is doing, and I daresay that he has waited his whole life for this moment. But it is possible that the Arthur we know may not return from this place at all."

A brief moment of panic and fear shot through David. Was Arthur in danger? He tensed reflexively as if to make a break for it. Not that he would have known where to go. But no, Matthew was still quite calm, so David relaxed a little too.

"As I have said before, we all worship something. For Arthur, his faith has long been rooted in the rational. I daresay he has been greatly challenged in this regard as of late."

"Multiclassing his reason with imagination, you mean?"

Matthew snorted wryly. "Indeed. And I suspect you have contributed more than a little to that process." The priest's amused expression was not betraying any of Arthur's secrets, but David sensed that Matthew had enough stories to tell him about his grandfather to last until David graduated from university. *Probably longer.* He wanted to hear them all.

"Arthur may surprise us before it is all over," Matthew mused. "He does have his ways."

Another dancing crowd swept in between them and Cat. She wiggled away, and melted into the crowd.

"What is faith, Father Matthew? I've always thought it was about believing in something really hard, but now I'm not so sure anymore."

"Yes, well. The writers of the New Testament had much to say to their fellow Christians on the matter of faith, David. The author of the letter to the Hebrews begins by calling it 'the substance of things hoped for, the evidence of things not seen.'" Matthew shifted to his scripture voice. "'For these all died in faith, not having received the promises, but having seen them afar off, and were persuaded of them, and embraced them, and confessed that they were strangers and pilgrims on the earth.' He says this about the rather long list of faithful who came and went before Christ's time. His chief point is that if their faith were not well-founded, they would not have been able to live as they did. It seems that biblically, 'believing' or 'having faith' means living as if a particular claim is true in the absence of definitive concrete evidence, even though one may have deep doubts." He cleared his throat and gently shook his shaggy head. "Though that's not to say we don't have any at all. I happen to believe that we have evidence in abundance."

"The gospel of creation," David remembered.

Matthew rumbled ascent and gave David's shoulder another of his characteristic squeezes.

David had only just begun to understand Matthew's philosophy. Arthur spoke of chaos and order all the time, while Matthew talked of imagination and the rational. But David was beginning to wonder if it might just be two different ways of saying the same thing. Sure, there was probably a right way to integrate faith and logic. And a wrong one too. Even Arthur had said as much in his own way, with his criticism of Uncle Sir Arthur and Mr. Aarons taking myths too literally. But maybe it was more than that? Maybe it was a code by which everyone should live their lives, with the inverse just as true. Maybe everybody could do with a little ordered imagination coupled with a little chaotic rationality. He thought of his dad and laughed. *Yea, right.*

David pushed his philosophizing aside and scanned the area where Cat's dancers had led her. She was now examining the clothing of a local girl not much younger than herself. Only, something about it was wrong. There was a clinical way she examined the sewn-on ornaments, the fabric, the belt. She clutched at the blouse with borderline rudeness. Instead of sharing the moment with the girl and admiring her dress, Cat was studying her apparel as if she were a European runway model. The girl-genius was feeding her personal faith in learning, anthropology, fashion, or whatever, oblivious to the person in front of her.

David liked Cat. She was fun, and he could imagine having a lot more fun with her. But, as Matthew might say, her imagination was untrained. *Or maybe mistrained?* Anyway, it seemed bent in a different way than his own. She'd nurtured her skepticism to investigate conspiracies.

David turned to Matthew again. The priest was cheerfully drinking in the festivities around him. He tapped his large shoe to the beat of a nearby instrument and the accompanying vocals that David wasn't even sure were words.

"Matthew, Arthur believes in evolution. Do you?"

Matthew turned. "So, it's no holds barred today then? Very well." The priestly man of science thought for a moment. "Arthur does, yes. And before you ask it, no, he does not see any conflicts biblically. To him, the function of creation is not marred by the process used by the creator to do it. It might even be enhanced by it, if we understood what the fall of Adam would be in that context."

"Like what? Some kind of slow unraveling of mankind to have free will over millions of years, instead of that divine set-up with a forbidden tree?" David's words surprised himself. "I guess that could make the choice pretty meaningful."

Matthew waved a presentative hand and gave the same broad smile David had received when they first met. "You will do just fine at Oxford my boy. Just fine indeed."

"You didn't actually answer my question."

"Correct, I did not. Nor will I. But I will say that I have faith that it is of little consequence to God's people. The simplest ideas about the sun being at the center of our solar system are now universally accepted. The geocentric model has been debunked, dispelled, and discarded. Today, Christians see such medieval notions as nonsense. It took some work, but eventually we came to understand that heliocentrism does not change the core truths of the universe, of its creator, nor of our position with respect to Him. Including, one might note, the unhappy fact that we are—from our own perspective—still at the center of our own respective universes. Metaphorically, that is."

David took it from there. "You're saying that someday, believers might not even question evolution, but it wouldn't change anything about our need for a real relationship with God, because we'll be just as prone to egocentrism as we've always been? Yea, I could see that. Science and faith are not enemies. You said that when we first met."

There was a long pause filled with music and dancing. David again scanned the crowd for Cat, but didn't spot her. "So, what do you think Arthur is doing, anyway?" David pressed. For a moment, he didn't think Matthew was going to answer.

"Whatever it is David, I will be satisfied to have been given the chance to come this far. 'Blessed are those who have not seen and yet have believed.'" In Matthew's words was a reverential delight for the unknown, for possibilities and potential. But it was more than that. The priest seemed quite happy not to know all of the answers. He seemed strangely satisfied with the existence of the unanswered mystery itself.

"Jesus said that," David said. "After he, you know, resurrected."

"To Thomas the Doubtful, yes. I've always considered him my favorite of the disciples." Matthew didn't elaborate. He didn't really have to.

"Arthur needs more than that, though. That's what you're saying?"

"Perhaps. Or perhaps he is simply wired for a different mode of faith. To some of us, it is enough to simply believe and act. For others of us, the path is more complicated."

"You said 'us' both times, Father Matthew."

The scientist-turned-priest smiled innocently. "Did I indeed?" he rumbled. "Now then, on to other matters. I can't help but notice that we seem to have mislaid our Cat."

XCIV

Mel had her men take turns holding a gun on Pitman for every long minute of their flight. The old man drifted in and out of consciousness, but her medic said he was as stable as he could be under the circumstances. They burned through the auxiliary tanks, but she would not let Mr. Suit put down.

Not to get Pitman to a hospital.

Not to avoid the storm that had come up from the gulf.

Not for anything.

She wouldn't, perhaps couldn't. They were just too close to where Mr. Suit swore they needed to go.

When they finally reached their target, Mel couldn't believe it. Out of the haze of the storm, a multi-story offshore platform loomed out of the ragged sea. Metal pipes, cranes, towers, and machinery competed for every inch of space against the angry sky. Most insanely, CHEN GLOBAL was emblazoned in enormous red letters in English and Chinese on the side.

This wasn't just any oil rig; it was *her* oil rig. One of dozens in the Persian Gulf that her father had built not so long ago. These were the pillars that held up the foundation of her father's empire. One of her many inherited assets.

There was no activity on the rig. An inactive platform meant a skeleton crew at best, and the lower decks would be quite empty.

Except for the other obvious possibility. Had Pitman and his brotherhood been so bold as to invade and occupy a company asset? *Were they using it to hold Wyatt Aarons?* The very thought made her blood boil.

No one came out to meet them. The Russian chopper dropped onto the helipad, but Mel didn't wait for it to power down. "Get the wounded down to medical, but don't take your eyes off either one."

She tossed her headset into the chair and hopped down to the deck. She crouch-ran to the metal stairs leading to the narrow maze of walkways of the work level, not caring that she was being soaked to the bone. She could see lights on in the bridge, the enclosure for electronics that controlled the complicated machinery on the rig floor and nearly everything else. As a little girl, it had been her favorite room on these things. Her father had always called it the "doghouse." She'd loved that. But she wasn't a little girl anymore, and this wasn't her father's rig. The answers were in that room.

She burst in with one hand on her pistol. What she saw brought her up short. Wyatt Aarons sat cross-legged in a comfortable looking chair. He was clean, his white beard freshly trimmed, and happily drinking a steaming mug of the dirty water Americans call coffee. His arm was in a sling, but otherwise, he looked better than she had ever seen him. Aarons looked up startled from the black leather Bible he was reading, then closed it and stood with an enormous smile.

"Mel? How wonderful to see you. I was getting a might tired of this place." He stepped forward as if to give her a great big one-armed hug. "Can you believe this merciful rain? I didn't even hear you land."

Mel shoved him away at his center of gravity, and the Bible plopped onto the floor. Before he had a chance to properly recover, her pistol was out and aimed at his head.

"Talk or die, Mr. Aarons."

Aarons blinked rapidly, half-risen from the deck and not daring to move further. "Now Mel, calm down. You don't want to do this. It's not whatever you are thinking. How 'bout some coffee?"

"I think Ryan Pitman is trying to take over my company. I think his brotherhood is staging a revolution and wants my father's empire to finance it. And I think you are not nearly as missing as you would have everyone think!"

Aarons processed this. "Well, all right then. Maybe it is what you think. But there's more to it than that. Quite a bit more."

"Then explain it to me."

Aarons laughed nervously. "I—I'm not real sure where to start."

*   *   *

Three-fourths of a conversation later, Mel still only felt like she had a slim grasp on this mess Aarons had gotten them all into. Faced with an apparent conspiracy against his life, Aarons had involved Evans in a desperate toss over the wicket to try and save the research. Then, he'd used some off-grid company connections, slick words, and a few favors to go to ground—or more accurately, to sea. He had been hopping rigs and boats for weeks now, recovering, collecting data, and most of all, hiding from Pitman and his men.

"But why an oil rig? And why one of mine? There are a thousand better places the credentials we gave you could have allowed you to go. You didn't have to hide from me."

Aarons opened his mouth to explain, but his expression shifted to surprised shock.

"Yes," came a smug voice from the door. "That will do nicely. Why don't you tell Melanie just why you hid everything from her?"

Mel whirled. The bedraggled Mr. Suit was already inside, and in the door stood the bandaged and bloody Ryan Pitman. He was as pale as a ghost under his soggy hat, but he carried one of her soldiers' automatic weapons regardless. She quickly did the math, trying to figure out how any of this could be possible, but it came down to a simple reality. She had underestimated Uncle Ryan again. He hadn't been near as hurt or subdued as he had let on.

We do such foolish things when we are angry. And Mel was absolutely outraged.

Mr. Suit stepped forward and took back his pistol with grim and expressionless efficiency. He then stepped aside, allowing his master some room to work. Suddenly the control room felt very crowded.

"I told you this wasn't going to go how you think, kiddo. But this is even better than I imagined. Wyatt, your Doc Evans turned out to be a real pain in my side. He's one slippery guy."

Then the next thing Pitman said made no sense at all. Taking a step towards Aarons he cooed, "I was beginning to think I'd never find you. And I sure didn't think Melanie would take me right to you. But I guess you won't be hiding behind her anymore, huh Wyatt?"

Aarons said nothing.

"Now," Pitman chided, "talk or die, Wyatt."

XCV

Evans and Dayik stood in silence together for a very long time. The seasoned tutor was afraid to say anything. Afraid that any words he said would be inadequate, inappropriate, or both.

"This is the only place where the first structure can still be seen," Dayik told him. "When Nûh landed in these mountains, it is said that he built an altar to his God."

Evans snorted. "Yes, it is written too." He looked at the old woman. Her expression remained unchanged. "Uh, apologies. My grandson must be rubbing off on me."

A hint of a smile tugged at the corner of her mouth. "He used what he had. Stones, debris..."

"The ark," Evans said, thinking aloud. Dayik bowed her head in affirmation. "But you can't possibly be saying that Nûh built all of this? Even with the help of his family, it would be the work of a lifetime. And a few other lifetimes besides."

"You are quite correct. Everything that is above is part of the new temple. And even much of what you see there has been replaced and rebuilt over the course of many millennia. The roof is quite new though, only a century or so."

Evans had to smile at this. He appreciated a culture that considered a dozen decades to be recent times. It dovetailed in nicely with his own particular sentiments.

"But the deepest and holiest parts," she continued, "have not changed in a very long time. You now stand in Nûh's original temple to God."

"Dayik, please forgive me for asking, but I must. Which flood story is true?"

For the first time, the old woman looked directly at Evans. He got the feeling that she was searching for something inside him, though he had no inkling what. He looked back, holding the gaze an uncomfortably long time. He squirmed a bit at such intimate candor but saw only grandmotherly kindness behind her eyes.

Finally, she spoke. "The faithful don't need proof, Arthur. But their faith is strengthened by symbols."

Evans felt his face screw up in disgust. This woman was kind, elegant, and clearly as well-educated as Ashti, but she sounded like Wyatt Aarons. He took a step back and scowled. Was this a trap of a different sort? Was Dayik testing him? It was Doomsday Mountain all over again. He could not be sucked into this.

"With apologies, Dayik, the truth does matter. There is an objective reality, and the universe abides by it. Science does work, ma'am, and thanks to its methods, mankind has gotten rather good at distilling fact from fiction. History is real, and myths are stories that speak to it. But the stories can't all be true." Evans considered the geological tests that had debunked Doomsday. What would a simple carbon dating test come up with, if a sliver of Dayik's old wood wall was tested? *Best not mention that.* Bad enough that he was lecturing this woman in her own temple.

But Dayik was already turning away. The kind old woman's face fell in sadness as she slowly moved to the ancient shrine. So, he'd blown it then.

To Evans' surprise, she did not close the shutter. Instead, she lifted out a small object wrapped in beautiful red silk, stitched with gold thread.

"If you truly feel that way, then you should have left things alone. You should never have begun the path." She looked at him strangely. "But I do not believe you. We gave you and your partner what you wanted thirty years ago. Yet, here you are." *She means Wyatt!* Evans realized. *She's talking about Doomsday and Wyatt's blasted Ark park museum.* "For most people, Arthur, it is enough to see what they want to see."

"We weren't after the Ark this time, Dayik. We were after Wyatt Aarons," he stammered. It felt like a lie, though he knew it wasn't. "But everything we found led us here, regardless."

"After all you have seen, read, and done, Arthur, do you still not understand? This place must be protected. Time and family have kept it and remembered it with stone. The new temple above conceals the one below. No single person or government's ambition is worth endangering that."

But Evans did understand. This mountain was these people's deepest truth. Their heritage. The West had no right to it. For these people, taking out Wyatt had been self-preservation. He wanted to say as much, but instead, he heard himself ask, "Wait. You gave us Doomsday? How?"

Dayik chuckled. "Your Doomsday-ark is a very old decoy. It was made by Western crusaders in the Middle Ages, during the brief time when these lands were ruled over by Western kings. It was a clumsy, but effective, ruse to protect what the Temple Knights found here. They understood their countrymen well. It was constructed so that pilgrims might have a place to go and worship without disturbing the sanctity of this place. And now, thanks to you, Wyatt Aarons, and the Turkish government, it will do so again for quite some time, as a national park."

A medieval decoy? This Kurdish matriarch was talking about the Knights of Solomon's Temple in Jerusalem, the real historical Knights Templar. *More nonsense—it has to be! Although…* if anybody in that era stood to make a profit off of Western gullibility, it would have been the Templar. It wouldn't have been the first time folks had capitalized on faith through the sales of fake relics. Nor the last. There were enough finger bones of the "true apostles" out there to fill an Olympic swimming pool or three. Evans shook his head in disbelief. "But that still doesn't make any sense, Dayik. How could you give us Doomsday? Wyatt said it was a miracle that guided us to Doomsday. The blasted taxi broke down, for Pete's sake. I was there."

"Yes," she smiled. "Your taxi driver was very adept at improvising. It may interest you to know that he was my father. He was always quite proud of that day when he convinced you the car was broken. Three times it was. His story always centered on the three times."

"Improvising? But he didn't even speak English—oh, dear lord." Ashti's words came back. *"My English was better than I might have let on."* Evans couldn't believe it. What was the real truth? Which one was the lie? It made his head hurt. "What rubes we were. But Dayik," he faltered, "if it was all lies, what is true then? Any of it?"

Dayik looked at him with deep empathy, and maybe a little pity too. "This was once Nûḥ's chamber. That much is real. He slept and prayed here. Later, he wrote." She paused to let it sink in, there in the dark silence.

"Wrote?" Evans squeaked. "Wrote what?" It was preposterous. Noah didn't have a written language. That much simply could not be true.

Dayik didn't answer. Instead, she uncovered the object she had been cradling in her hands and gingerly tilted it towards Evans. Instantly, he recognized it was a clay tablet in remarkably good condition. It was roughly egg-shaped, no bigger than David's phone. Looking closer, he saw not letters or cuneiform, but a string of unmistakable pictographs connected by lines. The icons had been pressed into the ancient clay by small carvings. Like Sir Arthur's seal stones at the museum, and the blasted Phaistos Disk. But even that wasn't the worst of it. The symbols were aligned in a rudimentary zig-zag pattern, much like the Kabbalistic Tree of Life's alleged paths.

No. Exactly like the Tree of Life. A chill ran down his spine. He realized he was shaking his head in denial. "That's not possible!"

"It is a map," Dayik explained, although he had not asked. "Of many things, truly. See, the eleven chambers of the first temple are connected in a path. One to another to another. The further one goes in, the closer one gets to the holy of holies. It is a rite that only the high holy man performs once a year. Today is not that day."

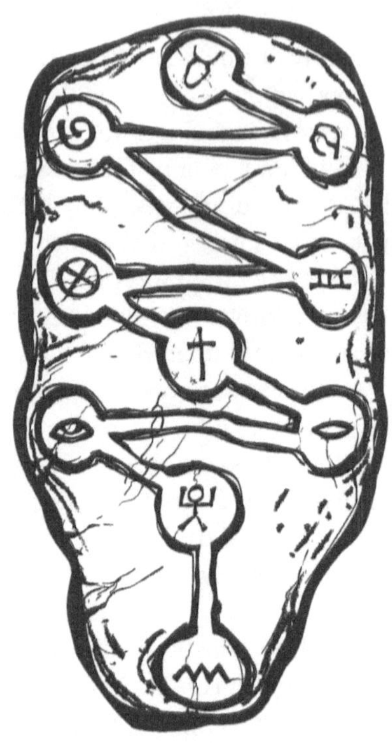

Evans glanced at the dark passageway leading into the darkness. *Eleven chambers? A path?* Did that mean ten more impossible treasures? Ten more mind-boggling truths? He looked at the tablet again. She had erred, though. There were only ten symbols.

The whole thing was too much. He stared for a moment longer, then nodded and turned away, bracing himself against the wall. Dayik covered the tablet in silk again and reverently replaced it in the shrine alcove next to the ancient wood.

There existed a floorplan of Noah's temple to God? The Tree of Life was a map? Evans felt like he was falling into a bottomless pit. It was all just a little too perfect and it defied logic, scholarship, and everything else. Or... *is that the point?* A tiny thought took root and began to grow. Archeology was never this clean. That was their mistake. It seemed so obvious suddenly. This was another setup. Doomsday wasn't the only forgery made to fool pilgrims.

But he wasn't fool enough to call her on it, either. Better to play his part and walk away. "Thank you for showing me this, Dayik," Evans said, as professionally as he could muster. "I think I understand you now." Dayik paused, sizing him up for the second time. He did his best to look serene and inspired. It wasn't particularly convincing, but it would have to do.

"You may have misunderstood me before, Arthur, when I said that the faithful don't need proof." Her eyes pierced into him. "For I did not mean that the literal truth does not matter. I meant that people almost always understand a symbolic truth first."

Evans wasn't sure what she was getting at. *Why isn't this conversation over?* Why wasn't she content with any of his answers?

"Stories are the oldest thing in the world Arthur. Before anything else, there were the stories. And within those, the symbolic truth has always been the deeper truth. Even when the facts and details of the story are lost in time and the elements of the story change, the greater importance and truth behind the story remain. Such stories give purpose. Purpose gives power. And such power testifies to the truth of the story."

"Yes, humans very likely story-told ourselves into existence. Oh, dear lord." Evans swallowed hard. It was a line he had given his students a thousand times, a lesson more familiar to him than his own telephone number, whatever that was. "You are talking about archetypes. Symbolic truths passed on through various iterations of the same story. Fireside theory."

Dayik bowed again, slower this time.

So, Evans was to be convicted by his own lessons then. He decided to embrace it. "The details of the story will reflect the culture that tells it," he began. "The story of biblical Noah is the story of faith, courage, and obedience to God that leads to salvation amidst apocalyptic chaos. Of Yahweh's great mercy and forgiveness. Of his unending love. That's the only part that really matters. Not the location of the Ark, or how many people survived the flood, or if it was a literal global event that is or isn't scientifically provable."

She gave a third and final bow, her point now made.

"Why show me this, Dayik?" he demanded. "What makes you think I will keep your secrets?"

Dayik laughed. It was the light and happy laugh of a grandmother. "These are not secrets, Arthur. Everyone who looks for this place the right way eventually finds it. Whether they come to this mountain as you have or not. This sanctuary is private, sacred, hidden, but it is not a secret."

Evans shook his head, hearing the words but not understanding their meaning. He thought of Gertrude Bell, who had come here not so long ago. Had she looked for this place 'the right way?' *What does that even mean?* Had Gertrude stood in this hidden chamber, too? Even Dayik could not be old enough to remember so long ago.

Besides, talking to this woman was just like talking to Wyatt. *Nonsense wrapped in faith wrapped in miracles.* The team had found none of the things they had set out to find. Not Aarons, not Dilmun, not even an easy paycheck or an uncomfortable bunk in a tent at the Ras-Shamra ruins. Everything had gone wrong from the moment they had stepped on Mel Chen's plane. Even the translation tablet and his original notes were long gone.

"Just where is Eden, Dayik?" he blurted. "Or maybe it's Dilmun, or Pardes, or Nûḥ's city? If Noah made a map of the Tree of Life, then he must have known. The Path of the Flaming Sword was always supposed to be instructions on how to find the way back to God, to His temple. To Eden. But the clues led us here, and this is no walled garden. But if Noah knew where Eden was, he might have returned there after the flood, built a wall, and started an orchard. That's what other legends tell us." Evans was as certain of it as anything he had ever been in his life. "Noah knew. And if he built this place, then it was to show later generations how to get there. Maybe he even did it so other flood survivors would know where to go to follow his family."

"I cannot answer your questions, Arthur. But I hope that someday you find your paradise. You may even realize that it has been in front of you for a long time." There was no malice or anger in her words, only kindness and hope and a touch of sadness.

Behind her, an imaginary Elisabeth ran a hand along the ancient wood with great delight. Only it wasn't Elisabeth at all, it was her grandmother Gertrude, in her day here as young as the wife Evans had lost but still loved with every inch of his heart. "And Wyatt? Did he get too close to these hidden things? Is that why your people took him out?"

Dayik closed the wooden shutter. She did not deny the accusation, but she did not show any signs of remorse either. For a moment, Evans was worried he had pushed it too far. Sealed his fate. But the old woman only pressed her lips together grimly.

"I do not know where Wyatt Aarons is, Arthur. If I did, I would tell you." If it was a lie, it was a darn good one. Evans felt a little embarrassed for his bold thick-headedness.

"Thank you, Dayik. Let's go back up, please. I should gather my people and leave this place. I have found out what I wanted to know and seen more than I ever thought possible."

"As you wish," she agreed impishly. "But, as an honored guest on a festival day, I have a small favor to ask of you first."

XCVI

Nûh's Sanctuary. Mt. Cudi, Şırnak Provence, Turkey. David.

Matthew and David walked the perimeter of the temple as best they could, dodging crowds and avoiding stepping between performers and their audience. The musicians slowed, transitioning from percussion to flutes, but with just as much of the tambourine-like things as ever. Almost everyone held one and they seemed to be the music's constant timekeeper.

Some of the crowd dodged them, having never seen a real-life hairy giant before. Others did the opposite. In all, it was not a casual stroll, but it was fun. Cat, however, was nowhere to be seen.

"Father Matthew, do you think Noah actually built all this? Or maybe his descendants? Is this place, you know, Dilmun?"

"I really couldn't say, David." The amount of quiet enthusiasm in the priest's voice was still palpable.

"So, what about Adam and Eve?" David pressed. "If the *Epic of Gilgamesh* stuff is even partly true, then does *Genesis* tell things in the wrong order? Did the flood happen first? Like, did Moses choose to reverse the stories to make a point? I mean, c'mon, this mountain is the one named in the..." he shifted to a whisper, "*Quran*. Not the Bible. At least not specifically. So what's real? How can we know?"

"We all have choices we must make, David," he said. "To believe or not believe, to go and do or to stay and do something else. To face our dragons or let them lie in dark caves. Some people think that if one suggests the Bible is not factually true down to every word, then it denotes a lack of faith. Some fear that such a view will undermine all the rest of the Holy Scripture. But I think that may be missing the point of those first stories. Do you recall what questions God asked Adam and Eve in the Garden just after they had sinned?"

David thought about it and nodded. He had just reread those passages recently. "He asked them where they were, then, asked who had told them they were naked."

"Has that ever struck you as a bit odd?" David wasn't sure what Matthew was getting at. Fortunately, the priest answered his own question. "He is God after all. He knows everything. He already knew those answers. But instead of being angry, violent, or striking them dead straight away, he explains to them the full consequences of their choice, and what they would be losing. It was the knowledge they sought, and they instantly regretted having it.”

Another small line of girls danced by David in colorful dresses, shaking their ornaments and noisemakers, adding a surreal quality to the intermittent thunder outside. But Cat was not with them.

“But, why didn’t God tell them sooner? Maybe if he’d explained it all, they would have chosen differently?”

“Perhaps he couldn’t. Perhaps that’s what it means to eat from the Tree of the Knowledge of Good and Evil. If such a tree truly existed, then one could argue that evil necessarily existed before Adam and Eve came to understand it. Chaos certainly did, as Genesis records that it was the material of creation. Or, perhaps it was the potential for evil to exist that the tree represents. Potential is the point of this whole universe, you know. To be made a gardener, an animal-namer, and given a proper freedom to disobey, is to be made a co-creator with God, after a fashion. Lewis said that. Tolkien too. In that way, perhaps the serpent was right.”

David looked at Matthew dubiously. “What do you mean?”

“You recognize, of course, that following something called The Path of the Serpent up a sacred tree has very uncomfortable associations for most Westerners. But we must remember that there is more than one way to become ‘like God.’ The one we often think of is Adam’s method, whereby he sought to make himself ‘like God.’ The other is by being conformed to the image of he whom Paul names the Second Adam—Christ. We mustn’t conflate the Serpent’s Path with the Pilgrim’s Progress. Even if they tread the same ground in the same order, the journey’s manner and the motives make, shall we say, worlds of difference. It is the distinction between humbly seeking the source of true light, or seeking to become enlightenment and thus self-sufficient from God.”

“Wow, I never thought of it all that way before.”

“No one is a villain in their own story David. In our individual minds, we’re all unsung heroes.” Matthew put his heavy arm around David’s shoulders and squeezed. “Now, I for one believe Scripture to be inspired, true, and accurate. Unlike some, I simply do not need scientific proof of the flood, Noah’s ark, or Eden to make these stories any more meaningful than they already are.”

David slowly nodded. It was less cut and dry than his dad’s biblical literalism, but somehow, coming from Father Matthew, it also seemed better thought out. Less antagonistic or defensive, maybe. He couldn’t really say why. *Maybe it’s the accent?* David felt a strange peace fall on him, despite the literal thunderstorm outside and the swirling storm of celebrations inside.

Matthew cleared his throat. “Oh, but I do go on, don’t I? Apologies for the sermon, my boy. Occupational hazard.”

XCVII

Mel's mind crunched the data as only a human computer could. What could Pitman *possibly* mean by, *"I was beginning to think I'd never find you?"* Pitman had worked with Aarons for decades. Only, it was clear now that he was also in command of the tattooed men. The tattooed men had attacked Aarons. Aarons had chosen to run but involved his first partner, not Pitman. And not her. Wyatt himself had now confirmed all of these things.

But if Pitman hadn't known Aarons' location, then how had his lackey, Mr. Suit, figured it out? None of it made sense. She was cut off from her people and her tech, frustrated, angry, and powerless. Pitman had been faking at least some of his injuries, but for how long? Were her soldiers dead? Most important of all, why was Wyatt Aarons hiding from his former partner? Someone *had* to be lying.

Lightning flashed, and the heavens broke. A fresh torrent of rain began, so thick that she could no longer see the metal decking out the window. Everyone was looking at Wyatt. They were still waiting for his explanation. He glanced at his Bible on the floor but did not move.

"'The wise men shall be put to shame; they shall be dismayed and taken; behold, they have rejected the word of the Lord, so what wisdom is in them?'"

"What are you blathering about?" Pitman asked, unamused.

"Jeremiah," Aarons said gently as if reminding him. "It's about men like you, Ryan."

Pitman laughed. "You and your smug Bible-thumping. God won't help you now, Wyatt. You have about three seconds to convince me why I shouldn't just shoot you and let Him have you."

"Because, Ryan, you've forgotten why we did the things we did. It wasn't for fortune and glory, it was out of faith and obedience. The Day of the Lord is upon us, Ryan. I know you see it, too. The moral fiber of the world is changing back to what it was like in the time of Noah. Why do you think God allowed the Path of the Flaming Sword to be revealed in this late hour? It's a miracle from Heaven, a final chance in these last days to gaze upon the wonderous things written of in scripture, before God wipes the slate clean once and for all. Ryan, my friend, there isn't much time. I've come to fear for your soul, too."

"My soul? Please! I'm pulling the mask of respectability off of this world's science. I'm going to find out where Melanie has Evans stashed, and I'm going to make him finish what you started, just to prove that you've started chasing fairy tales. I'm doing God's work. I'll show the world that every literal word of *Genesis* is true, whether the fools up on that Turkish mountain like it or not. If you don't want to be a part of that mission anymore, then I will be God's divine messenger by myself. I don't do 'faith quests' anymore Wyatt. I serve a higher calling."

"'Higher calling?' Listen to yourself, Ryan. You're on a path of darkness and greed, and you're sucking a bunch of kids into it with you. You gave them weapons of war. They killed people, Ryan! Those Ras-Shamra guards were just guys trying to feed their families. And your revolutionaries shot me, too! Nearly killed me. You have dangerous ideas, and the Lord will not let you succeed. Darkness can't serve the light, no matter the motive. Ends don't justify means—you know that!"

Pitman stepped closer to Aarons, right up into his face. He stuck the large gun into the man's thin gut, but there was nothing Mel could do about it. Not with Mr. Suit's pistol still on them all. She agreed with Wyatt in one regard, though: They needed a miracle about now.

"Most new ideas seem stupid and dangerous," Pitman admitted. "But some of them are vital. We need to set aside the myths and lies of modern science and focus on the real science laid out in Genesis. This is about finding the true origin of mankind. Real science is the key to unlocking the Bible. I will prove those fools who write the textbooks and run the universities wrong with cold hard facts, not by chasing after ridiculous myths like your damnable Dilmun and that twisted Gilgamesh trash. How can you not see that after all your years hunting fables?"

"That's not how faith works, Ryan. You are risking everything the family has protected for thousands of years."

"If we don't take risks, we're all going to die," Pitman sneered. "So what if a few fall along the way? This is a holy war. People die in wars. Noah took risks and saved his whole family while the rest of the world drowned. If we stay in our current mode of fear, then when all Hell breaks loose, we'll go down too! The family taught us that."

Last days? Holy war? 'The family?' What were these men even talking about?

"It's Hell I'm worried about with you, Ryan." Then, glancing down at Pitman's bloody side, Aarons softened. "Come now, you're clearly hurt. Let Mel's people take care of you, and we can all sit down together like civilized folks and talk this through. We need to be patient, and not do anything we'll regret. The family taught us that too.”

Something wasn't right. Had Mel heard correctly? A horrible thought occurred to her, prompting a reflexive step forward. Pitman whirled with his machine gun, but Mel wasn't after him. She jerked Aarons' sling away from his shoulder. It fell away from his arm and he sucked in a breath of sharp pain, but there, indisputably, was the same raven tattoo that had caused her so much trouble from the start. Aarons froze wordlessly for a moment, then closed his eyes and pressed his lips together sadly.

Pitman hooted at Mel with terrible amusement. “You didn't know? Oh, but of course you didn't! Everybody keeps secrets from Mel Chen. Wyatt, me, that fool Evans. Shoot, even handsome here was what I wanted you to think he was.”

Mel's eyes flicked to the battered and bloody Mr. Suit, standing by like a trained attack dog, simply waiting for the order to kill.

“But don't you worry. After I deal with Wyatt, I'll find Doc Evans and his little entourage and make him do the job I gave him to do. I'll make him translate every tablet and carving in Ras-Shamra if I have to. I'll rip apart the ancient world until we have real proof. Then, after I reveal Eden, the world will know the truth, and I'll be the one who shows them. One last chance for men to know how wrong they are before God slams the book shut on this pathetic world forever.” He turned to Mr. Suit. “I may even let you hunt down Evans, boy, if you think you can manage it this time.”

Mel shook. She didn't know who to be more furious at. She couldn't think straight.

We all make such poor decisions when we are angry.

“It's people like you, kiddo, that have turned scripture into myth. But I've played you like a fiddle. Every move you made was because I wanted it. I even made you think calling me out of retirement was your idea. You were never cut out to run your father's companies. All you ever wanted was to chase legends and spend Ding's money. You're a failure, Mel. Your computers are a crutch and a liability for smart men like me to exploit. Your little empire's going to crumble unless I choose to prop it up.”

Pitman waved the gun in the general direction of the door—everything around them now evidence of his claim—then leaned in for a mock whisper. “The way I did for your father. With Ding's empire and a private army behind me, I'll do anything I want.”

A second more and Mel probably would have tackled Pitman and risked the bullet, but she didn't have a chance. Mr. Suit's pistol shifted, and Mel felt herself being grabbed by Aarons' good arm. Her first instinct was to struggle, to avoid becoming Wyatt's hostage, but then she saw where the pistol was aimed.

"Drop the gun, Dr. Ryan," Mr. Suit said. "I'm ending this."

"What the blazes are you doing, boy?" Pitman hissed. "Don't be a fool. This man is a misguided lunatic. You don't have to protect him anymore. Think of the new brotherhood we're building. Everything we have worked to achieve. The revolution has already begun. No more of this 'family' and 'mother' nonsense. It's time to cut down anyone who stands in our way. This coward's just not worth it."

With the last two words, Pitman whirled, his gun came up to hit Mr. Suit, shoot him, or both, but Mr. Suit deftly blocked it. Both guns roared in the little metal room. Bullets raked holes in the roof and glass showered down from a high monitor. But Mr. Suit wrenched the SMG away, sucker-punched Pitman in the nose, and in an instant was wielding both weapons. Pitman fell and landed in a slump under the wide viewing window sheeting with rainwater.

"Oh, Ryan, no!" Aarons said. "God have mercy." Blood was already oozing in a dark stain from a new wound in Pitman's shoulder and his unmistakably broken nose.

"*Nǐ shì shénme dōngxi*, Wyatt Aarons!" Mel screamed. "What is going on here? What is this *sǐ bù yào liǎn huài dàn* even talking about, and why do you have that thing on your arm? You can't be one of them. You were attacked by them!"

"I think we should tell her, son," Aarons said. "I reckon she's earned it, don't you?"

Mr. Suit shrugged one shoulder. "As you wish, my mentor."

XCVIII

Nûh's Sanctuary. Mt. Cudi, Şırnak Provence, Turkey. David.

Neither the rain nor the festival was showing any signs of letting up. In fact, it seemed to David that the former had only made the latter more jubilant. Nobody seemed to care about the various leaks and drips all around that were soaking into the carpets. He still counted at least three separate songs being played and sung in various parts of the cavernous hall. And every time he thought he had seen all the varieties of flute or drum and lute, another would appear.

Matthew was sitting on the floor and clapping along with a group of children who were greatly amused by the big white man with his fluffy brown head and funny clothes. David leaned against a post near one of the tin lamps, still passively scanning for Cat.

He and Matthew had walked the full length of the place twice, but she was nowhere to be found, so they decided to return to the spot where she had left them and let her come back on her own. David couldn't shake the feeling that perhaps this was all a complex ruse, designed to pick them off one by one. It was the sort of thing he would have tried in one of his tabletop games.

Then, by some cue David missed, every musician in the place stopped playing. Some did so in mid-chord, and the chanters of poetry and storytellers also cut themselves short. Every head in the place turned towards the front end of the room where Arthur had disappeared behind the wall some time ago. There was motion there, but David could not see beyond the many wrapped and ornamented heads. People from all over the temple started grabbing lamps and moving toward them, drawing up in a rough semi-circle around the front.

A moment later and Matthew was beside him, having been forced to his feet by the rush of bodies.

"Can you tell what's happening?" David whispered, but Matthew shook his head. Impulsively David hopped onto a bench, so he could see over the heads.

The whole crowd erupted in an explosion of shouts, percussion, and jingling ornamentation. As the cheer died down, the instruments fell into a rhythm. From the edge of the semi-circle, a musician began to bellow out a song with one of the lute-guitar things. Or maybe chant was a better word. Whatever was going on, this guy was singing about it.

Next, A magnificently dressed old woman stepped from behind the wall and into the middle. She wore a marvelous flowing gown decorated with gold. She was escorted by a man in equally lavish clothes of mostly blacks and reds, but also with golden trim including all the accessories. The man's gray beard was fuller than most of the men there though. His flashes of skin were paler too.

Matthew suddenly began laughing. His deep hearty hoots made David want to laugh too, though he wasn't sure at what. Then, he did a double-take as he realized that the man in black was Arthur. He had ditched his horrid Greek suit and upgraded to a Kurdish traditional costume. It was as nice as any man's there, however outrageous he looked in it. Arthur even had the headwrap turban-thing and doubly big cloth belt wrapped and tied at his stomach like Ashti's. Arthur looked amazing, but he also stood with a certain horrified nervousness.

For the millionth time, David reached for his phone and cringed. Another lost opportunity.

Arthur produced an ornately beautiful length of fine cloth from his belt and offered it to the old woman. She hesitated then snatched it away. She caressed it and examined it before placing it onto herself like a shawl. Instantly she slumped, as if in a trance. Arthur then did a little crouching sidestep all the way around her, then again, and also a third time.

It took everything David had, not to burst into uproarious laughter. Though if he had it was unlikely anyone would have noticed.

Ashti emerged from the crowd and joined the woman and Arthur. He looked Arthur in the face and stomped the ground in time to the beat. Each step drove Arthur back a little further until he was at the edge of the crowd. The musician emerged from the crowd on the other side as he continued his song. Half storyteller, half holy man, he was only slightly less ornamented than the other two, but it was no less magical. Ashti danced his way back to the old woman and took up her hand, kissed it, then stood next to her, facing the chanter, while she lay limp on the floor.

David suddenly understood what was happening. "It's a love story!"

"Yes, my boy," Matthew shouted back, "I do believe it is."

Arthur looked for a break in the tightly packed crowd, having apparently finished his duties of giving the bride away. He glanced around and spotted Matthew's tall head with great relief. Not finding any other way out of the circle, he took a deep breath and plunged into the crowd, worming his way over to them. Every man woman and child he pushed past caressed his head, shoulders, and chest like fans at a rock concert. The chanter started waving his hands and gesturing wildly as the beat picked up and flutes dominated. The old woman opened her eyes and stood. She then moved away in fear, doing a well-rehearsed dance of her own. She was spry for a grandmother. The woman twirled the long silken cloth in an undulating circle around her. It looked like someone drowning, perhaps stuck in a whirlpool. That's when it clicked.

"Hold on," David whisper-shouted. "It's not just any story. It's *Genesis*."

"That's right," Arthur said, finally reaching them, and slapping away the last few grabby hands. "Well, more of a verse from an epic poem, and a very old one at that. However, now that my horrible part in it is done, I would very much like to go before any of these folks decide that their hospitality has been sufficient and develop ideas about the Western intruders. Where is deMata?"

"We're not entirely sure," Matthew said, a bit of concern coming through.

"We hoped that perhaps she had found you?"

Arthur shook his head and frowned. "No, Dayik—the, uh, matron of these people—took me to a place deep below this temple. She said it was hidden and private but not a secret, whatever the devil that's supposed to mean."

As he said this the beat shifted, and Ashti began to yo-yo towards and away from his mock-lover like some invisible force was keeping them apart. David tore himself from the distraction, giving Arthur his full attention.

Matthew cocked an eyebrow, encouraging Arthur to go on. "Why did she do that?"

"She showed me a wooden wall black with pitch and age. And she also showed me a very old tablet of the Mesopotamian style with a series of paleolithic pictographs. She claimed that both were made by Noah himself. A segment of the original Ark and an Eden map respectively, if you can believe it."

"A map to Eden?" Matthew was incredulous. "I say, Arthur, that's rather astonishing."

"Yes, it is. But not a map *to* Eden—so much as a map *of* Eden, highly symbolic in style. At least, I think that's what it's meant to be."

"Was it really Noah's Ark?" David asked in starry-eyed wonder. "Is the actual Ark buried below this place?"

"I don't know David. I don't think so."

David's hopes sunk, but not entirely. "Then, if it's not a secret, we have to get a photo of it. We have to make them give back my phone and take a picture of it so you can show people. And of the tablet too so you can translate it. If it's real, then this is a really big deal."

"There's no need for any of that David," Arthur said, gently. "You already have a picture of the tablet, in a way. Besides, I will never forget those symbols for as long as I live."

David didn't understand. How could he already have a picture of it? Even if he'd still had his phone, he certainly didn't have a picture of whatever was down in a secret chamber in the temple of Noah, in the mountains where his Ark had landed. It was insane!

A deep silence fell in the room as Ashti finished his dance and the chanter's song died away. David couldn't help but turn and look. Dayik was completely motionless on the ground again, this time in a swirl of cloth. One of the roof leaks was falling so near her body that she was becoming quite wet. For a second, David wondered if she had really fallen by accident. Then, ever so slowly, one of the musicians began to thump on one small drum. It sounded like a heartbeat. Felt like one.

With each beat, Ashti moved ever closer to the woman until he was close enough to kneel beside her. Slowly, one beat at a time, he took her hand and coaxed her up, taking her cloth mantle upon himself. As he did, a second drum joined the first and the chanter cried out a great command. A shouted word that thrust them together. The couple stood next to one another and embraced. Two heartbeats beating in time.

"It's Sandal-Maker," David whispered, "Noah's second wife. He just saved her from the flood."

"Of a sort," Arthur agreed. "And elements of Adam and Eve as well, though not in the sequence you might expect."

At that point, the play shifted into something else and the music picked up again. Ashti motioned towards the cirle of people and led the woman to them, interacting with those they could reach.

"Is it over?" David wondered.

"Not yet," Arthur said. "He is presenting his bride to the people now."

"Oh, ok," David acknowledged, pondering the implications of there being a people to present her to. He could see now that people were handing her things, and in turn, she was helping some of them in small ways, adjusting one girl's jewelry here, filling a glass from a little pitcher there, repositioning two people in what might have been a matchmaking act and to which the crowd laughed and cheered.

Finally, the crowd closed in, shouts of approval and encouragement from one and all, and in one fluid motion after another, the couple danced for a surprisingly long minute, before stepping apart and into a recognizable posture for a marriage ceremony. Facing one another, the bride and groom acted out a brief ceremony as the chanter resumed his narration. It culminated in Ashti moving Arthur's former cloth from his shoulders to over the woman's head. No longer a shawl, it was now a veil. All quite beautiful, even if David didn't know a word of ancient Kurdish.

"That's the *Shara Buk*," Arthur explained. "They're married now."

The three westerners watched in silence as the crowd rushed in with great fervor and escorted the couple out in much the same way they had manhandled Arthur earlier. Finally, with great jubilance the audience broke to all parts of the room, and the various different celebrations began anew with even greater vigor than before. David had a feeling that this party was going to go on all night, maybe longer.

"Arthur, my good man," Matthew asked coyly, "am I right in thinking that you just played the part of the tempting serpent?"

Arthur frowned. "I would prefer if we called it a 'force of chaos' and left it at that."

Matthew and David burst out laughing. David stopped only because he spotted Cat coming towards them, her face shining with excitement. She was hardly recognizable, ornamented from head to toe in necklaces, silks, and other jangly things. He waved her over.

"Oh, thank heavens," said Arthur. "Now maybe we can get out of here."

As they pushed their way out, David saddled up beside Father Matthew. There were a million things still bugging him, but one especially had been popping up the most. "Matthew, what about all that *Kabbalah* stuff? I mean, it gave us clues that we couldn't have gotten here without. Could there really be some kind of ancient mystical knowledge passed down from Adam that we have forgotten with all of our modern church stuff?"

The priest chuckled knowingly. In his scripture voice, he said, "'The words of the wise are like goads, their collected sayings like firmly embedded nails given by one shepherd. Be warned, my son, of anything in addition to them. Of making many books there is no end, and much study wearies the body.'"

"*Proverbs*?"

"*Ecclesiastes*. Let us not forget, David, that the search for forbidden knowledge is what got mankind into trouble in the first place. Just because there is some truth in a thing, does not mean that it is fully true, nor that it is beneficial to us. Perhaps it's best if we humans let certain sleeping serpents lie, eh?"

David pictured Adam and Eve hiding, naked and afraid after realizing their sin, but blaming it all on the chaos serpent. They'd been faced with the temptation to disobey God, to take the forbidden wisdom on offer from it and because of that choice, mankind was forever separated from perfect paradise.

For some reason this took David's mind back to the supposedly nude Greek statues in the Ashmolean, and the picture with Emma mimicking the pose of the little Venus. His imagination sparked, and he realized a connection he'd been working on subconsciously for days now. Among all of those nude statues, the Venus had been singularly naked and afraid, just like Eve. Afraid for her son, afraid of some unknown chaos, afraid of what might come next.

David smiled, nodded at Matthew, and set aside his other unanswered questions for some later day.

*   *   *

David reluctantly followed the others out of the stone structure. So it was going to be goodbye to his phone and everything on it after all. That was just great. At least the relative quiet and cool of the mountaintop was surprisingly refreshing. The rain had not even turned the parched ground to mud, but David could smell the clean scent of ozone and moistened stone. Two young goats played in a patch of nearby scrub, clearly enjoying the first rain they had ever known. As David ruminated over these things, Cat jingled up beside him.

"Not the craziest party I have been to, but it's up there." She nudged David mischievously. "You would not believe what I had to trade for this blouse, but traditionally, the locals don't wear anything under it anyway."

David didn't have a chance to process what she meant, much less respond. As they rounded the corner of the great drystone wall towards the goat path that led back to the helicopter, the raven-emblazoned armed guards were already waiting for them.

XCIX

Chen Global Oil Rig MG38, Northwest Persian Gulf. Mel.

Mel slapped Wyatt Aarons as hard as she could and watched him stagger back into his chair. Mr. Suit surged to grab her, but Aarons stopped him.

"I deserved that. It's all right."

The gunman tucked his pistol into a shoulder holster, ominous without his coat. He tucked the SMG's magazine in his belt, emptied the chamber, then set the weapon of war aside with disgust. Pitman looked deathly pale. Aarons moved to stand over him. Mel wasn't sure if the geomorphologist was even conscious, but he would not fool her twice. Not ever again.

Aarons sighed and subconsciously caressed his tattoo with a thumb. He shook his head sorrowfully. "Oh Ryan, you can't convince people that God exists with science," Aarons said. "Not with Arks or genetics or logic problems or satellites. Belief comes first. People will always believe what they want to believe and see what they want to see, even if it's a pile of rocks or nothing at all. You know I've always done what I do to show people that the Bible's full of history. Real, true, and accurate. And I know you believe that to your core too, but our work was meant for the people who understand and want to marvel at the miraculous things that they already know to be true. Those who will stand in awestruck wonder before the Creator, the Savior of the faithful, the Rock of faith. Those with shallow faith, well, they'll always be fooled by the flawed philosophical promises that science offers. We need biblical truth, not man's imperfect science."

Aarons sighed again, and turned toward the door where the curtain of rain marked the edge of the tempest outside. "You'll never find Eden your way, Ryan. I don't understand what happened to you. You don't have faith in anything anymore except yourself, your satellites, and your laboratory tests. But God doesn't work that way. He has always dealt in miracles first. *Genesis 1:1* is the greatest miracle of all. If you can believe that, then you can believe anything that comes after it. We don't need man's science to shoehorn proof into anything."

Suddenly Mel had the strange feeling that Aarons wasn't just talking to Pitman, but to her too. Only, that wasn't entirely fair. Mel had never claimed to believe in any of the things that she and her teams hunted for. She hired people from all faiths, religions, and creeds. Mostly, she just loved finding things that people said couldn't and shouldn't exist. Her people were explorers, pioneers, engineers, poets, and even priests, uncovering the hidden myths of the world. Networked to her resources, they became human computers, making connections that no one else in the world had been able to make before. Thanks to her vision. Because of her dream. Because of her faith in humanity. Just as Aarons had always done. *Hadn't he?* Why should it matter if her faith wasn't in Wyatt Aarons' God? Faith was all the same, anyway. It wasn't like she was searching for any sort of meaningful eternal answers or anything. Aarons' accusations made no sense. She smiled. Her anger was fading. She was starting to think clearly again.

"Where are my men?" She asked Mr. Suit sweetly.

"Locked in the accommodation level. They are fine."

"In that case—" she stopped, distracted by motion on the floor. "Wyatt—!"

Against all probability, Pitman surged forward, bloody and crazed. The old man dove at Aarons and both men sailed out onto the metal walkway that connected the bridge to the rest of the platform.

Before Mel could even think about moving to the door, Mr. Suit was through it. He slammed into Pitman's bloody shoulder, tearing him away from Aarons and knocking him hard enough for the old man's hat to gust up and plop onto the decking a few feet away. Pitman howled, pivoted and hit the railing hard. Rain splattered on his bald white head.

Then, to Mel's horror, he kept going.

She rushed to the rail to peer down past the stinging rain into the waves crashing against the enormous pillars of the rig but saw no sign of Pitman.

"Oh, Ryan, why?" Aarons cried out. He was hardly audible over the downpour.

The three stood for a long time as the storm raged, watching the churning waters of the Persian Gulf, but Pitman was gone. The sea had swallowed him.

Finally, Aarons spoke. "As above, so below, my old friend. You should have listened to Dayik."

"Mr. Aarons," Mel shouted, blinking the water away, "you and I need to have a very serious talk about your future in my company."

*   *   *

"Ryan and I found the family a long time ago," Aarons said, once they were inside again and slightly drier. "Or I should say, they found us. In time, we were inducted, took our vows, received our tattoos. But Ryan was never content. He always wanted to sell the family's secrets, monetize them, turn them into an ideology. He would have seen them distilled, packaged, and exploited for the weak-minded."

Mel looked at Aarons sideways. Had she misunderstood these men so completely? "Why did he do it? I would have given Ryan anything he asked for. He lacked for nothing."

Aarons sighed. "Power. Knowledge. Jealousy... call it what you want Mel, but I've known Ryan since a time when you were still wearing diapers. I figured out a while back that he was never satisfied with anything. Always needed more. I'm not sure if he really was hoping to convince people the Bible is true or not, but I'm now very sure he was trying to convince himself." Aarons tugged pensively on his little white beard. "When we started working together, he told me he had an old friend wanting to foot the bill for everything, so I signed on and let your father Ding, and then you, finance my work for a while. I realized too late that he needed you and I both out of the way to make good on his real plan, taking over your father's company. Thing is, I was sworn to let him reap the consequences for his own actions. It's the family's way of doing things, you understand?"

Mel shook her head.

"It's an old tradition." He took a breath. "Ancient. But, when Ryan got wind I was putting a team together in Ugarit and he wasn't on it, I guess he finally decided to strike out at me directly. I knew then that I needed a new plan. Something Ryan wouldn't think of."

"Dr. Evans?"

"The one and only," Aarons smiled, slicking his ivory hair back. Water dripped from the point of his little white beard. He looked at Mr. Suit with sincere admiration. "And some backup. Ryan was trying to divide the family. Has been for years. He gathered a small contingent loyal to his new ideas. His new 'brotherhood,' I suppose. Bunch of idealistic kids, sadly. But I couldn't take the chance of who to trust. You were just too close to him, Mel, I knew that. Heck, Ryan introduced us. But I guess he had other ideas about you. I'm truly sorry I couldn't warn you or do more to help."

"What happens now, Mr. Aarons?"

"Well, now that he's gone, the insurgents will return and repent, the family will forgive them, and everything will fall back in line with the old ways." Aarons turned again to Mr. Suit. "Won't they, my friend?"

Mr. Suit was leaning against a wall with his arms crossed. He glanced at Aarons through hollow eyes, but his subtle nod was for Mel's benefit.

Aarons sighed. "You did what you had to do son, no one is going to hold that against you. Remember who you are. What job you were sent to do. The family put you in an impossible position, and that will not be forgotten. You have fulfilled your vows, and they will accept your choices."

Mr. Suit nodded again with solemnity, this time for Aarons. "Yes. My duty to the family is fulfilled. Miss Chen has become the witness to Dr. Pitman's betrayal of the family."

Suddenly, Mel understood. She understood family better than anything. It wasn't just about blood. It was about a shared dream. A network of minds working together for common goals. No wonder Aarons had never quite fit in with the Mao Sien corporate family—he already had one. Perhaps that was even why her Uncle Ryan had done what he did. Perverse as that loyalty to her father had become, perhaps to Ryan it hadn't been a betrayal at all. A software glitch with conflicting data sets that had almost crashed the network.

Even her Mr. Suit had answered to another family first, one that had clearly put him into a no-win situation between two father-figures. What outcome had they hoped for? Perhaps that he would act as mediator between them? A judge?

One thing was certain though. Mel needed to completely overhaul her HR screening process. She was already thinking of certain human computers who would be perfect for that task.

"Speaking of Arthur," Aarons continued, "just where in the world have you hidden my old dig partner? I really thought he would be the one to find me, once Ryan made his move. We have some real catching up to do."

"Ah," Mel hesitated. "I must confess, I'm not entirely sure. Last I heard, he was headed for Crete."

Aarons broke into a wide smile. "Well, that's fantastic! I'm sure he'll be fine then, so long as Ryan's revolutionaries don't know where he is either. Now, if you don't mind, Mel, I need to make a call. I reckon the family will want to know what's happened here."

Mel strode to one of the control panels on the bridge and fired up the ship-to-shore. She had a few calls to make too. The rain was letting up, she noted. Out the window, she could see the edge of the storm on the horizon, and beyond that, a faint rainbow.

Mel turned to Mr. Suit. "Consider your contract reinstated. Go free my men. No more gunplay today, please." He turned toward the door. "And one more thing," she added sweetly, "find the galley. I need a cup of tea."

C

Mt. Cudi, Şırnak Provence, Turkey. David.

Everyone's hands were as high as they could go. Arthur's stuttering attempts at Kurdish were cut short by quick commands from the masked men. The conversation didn't seem to be going anywhere productive.

Far up the hill, David watched their Russian pilot straighten. Colonel Ivan tossed a cigarette to the ground and stomped it out. As he started their way, the steel-hard man reached around behind himself and withdrew yet another pistol. His third by David's count, stashed in the helicopter somewhere. It would have been funny if he weren't literally outgunned six to one by assault rifles.

"My friends," a voice called out from behind them. "I did not expect you to depart so quickly. The evening has only just begun, and you are our guests of honor."

Arthur turned and visibly relaxed, as Ashti stepped up and let loose a long string of angry-sounding words. He was still wearing his ornate costume from the little one-act play, but David noticed an odd detail. He also held a little flip-phone, which he quickly tucked away.

The gunmen lowered their weapons, though David wouldn't have called it relaxed exactly. Only then did David let out a breath he didn't realize he'd been holding.

"Apologies, everyone!" Ashti insisted. "They were only following orders."

"Let me guess," Arthur said, "not meant for us, but for another."

Ashti smiled widely and threw his arms open. "Quite right, Dr. Evans. Quite right."

"Ashti, thank you for your hospitality, it is truly appreciated, but Dayik has given us what we needed. And as I said to her, it is time for us to go. The West is not ready for the things you protect here. I understand that now."

A moment later Ivan arrived, snorting like a bull and ready to bend guns and rip off heads or something. The guards snapped to attention, but Arthur halted Ivan with palms held up in peace. David had to hand it to the man—he was very good at taking orders from whoever he thought was in charge. Once that person had become Arthur, the mercenary colonel had been quite handy to have around.

Ashti's expression became very serious, and he nodded to Arthur. "We have allowed outsiders to join our family in the past, but each time we have let them make their own choices. It is our way. This has been such a time for us. I am sorry you were forced to become involved. But the arbitrator has made his decision. It is now over, and we know which path has been chosen."

He glanced down to the pocket where he had stashed his phone and patted it. "Dr. Ryan Pitman has had an accident at sea. He did not survive. You will have no more trouble from us, I swear it upon my blood and the things we protect here."

The old Kurd looked to each of the four Oxonians in turn. It was quick, subtle, but there was meaning there—a personal connection that gave David a quick shiver. Then, as if it was the most natural thing in the world, Ashti's smile returned. "So please, permit me to walk with you back to your helicopter?"

*   *   *

A few minutes later they were strapping in as Ivan prepped for takeoff. Out of the voluminous yards of material Ashti was using as a belt and his many-pocketed leather vestment, he extracted the confiscated guns and combat knife. He handed them to the highly suspicious and slightly surprised Colonel Ivan, then quickly returned the rest of their things that had been taken.

"And this is yours, Mr. Evans?"

It took David a second to realize that Ashti was talking to him. But once he spotted the phone he didn't hesitate. "Yes sir! Thank you."

Relief washed over him and he suddenly felt a little homesick. No, not homesick. It wasn't Texas he missed. Sure, he was beyond thankful to have his phone again and get connected back to something familiar, to let his mom and friends know he was okay. To beg his dad not to be mad at Arthur, and explain everything that had happened. But more than any of that, he longed to be back in Oxford. To have his interview, be selected by a college, move into a dorm. To begin his own adventure.

He looked around himself and laughed. *Yea, because ancient ruins, the Labyrinth, masked gunmen, and maybe Noah's temple or whatever aren't exciting enough!*

As they lifted away David thumbed it on, determined to find that signal Ashti was using while he still could. He was unsure who exactly to message first, or how long he would have to do it. He supposed it should be his mother, but it might just be simpler to post a public message on Twitter or something. As the amazing little device finished connecting, it buzzed to let him know that he had a string of messages. But one was particularly strange, a voice message from an unknown caller only a few minutes ago.

He stuck it under his headset and played it, not believing his ears. It was distorted, but understandable.

"Dr. Evans, this is Melanie Chen. I have located Wyatt Aarons. He will meet you in Bahrain in five days. The company will arrange whatever you need. Use the following number to make contact as soon as you possibly can..."

"Uh, Arthur?" David shouted into the mic. "You are not going to believe this!"

David watched as his wizard listened to the message, went from surprise to incredulity, then broke into the strangest laughter ever.

"What's happened Arthur?" Matthew asked, "Is everything all right?"

After Arthur recovered and wiped away the tears, he explained. "Bahrain is a kingdom on the northwestern edge of the Persian Gulf. It's little more than a tiny archipelago centered around an island. One of the smallest countries in the world, in fact. But it is literally in the footprint of the ancient Kingdom of Dilmun." He paused for a moment, then added, "I'm glad Wyatt is alive, because I am going to kill him myself."

There was an awkward silence until Matthew began his own deep laugh, Arthur started back up again, and the others couldn't help but join.

"What now Arthur?" Matthew asked.

"Dilmun," Arthur said, firmly. "Kingdom of Bahrain. I owe Wyatt-infernal-Aarons a punch in the nose."

He's joking, David decided. *Probably.*

CI

Evans hired a taxi to shuttle them over to Wyatt's island hotel.

"Overlooking the cerulean blue Arabian Sea, amidst the fresh ocean breeze, lays the Dragon Hotel and Resort. Visible from everywhere on the island, it is the first and only luxury property on the Amwaj Islands of Bahrain."

Or so David had recited from the hotel's website.

Frankly, it was all one big overblown inconvenience as far as Evans was concerned. He'd been half-tempted to walk, since he could see the blasted thing. But the series of little islands connected by bridges would probably be more trouble than it was worth, and it was still infernally hot. It was precisely what he had come to expect from Wyatt Aarons. So, David, Evans, and his bad attitude got into the taxi.

At least they had come by far more civilized paths this time, even stopping for a few days in Istanbul. There, Evans had acquired some sensible clothing and a much-needed toothbrush. David took innumerable pictures of the Hagia Sophia and other such marvels, playing tourist in the former capital of the world. Replacement passports and paperwork had been waiting for them at the British Embassy. How Mel Chen had managed that one, Evans had decided not to question. If he'd had her kind of access all those years ago in that cell in Erzurum, things might have gone quite differently.

Truly, the world has changed.

With their ridiculous adventuring over, Matthew was kind enough to accompany deMata back to Western civilization. He'd cited a great need to return to his "flock," so they had all parted with heartfelt goodbyes.

"I'm sorry about deMata, David," Evans finally said. "I know that you were becoming close."

David looked up from his phone and blinked a few times. "Okay?"

"What I mean to say, David, is that sometimes a relationship feels like the right thing, but it can easily be... Er, what I mean to say, is that you have to understand that there are a lot of factors to attraction. You can't always trust that friendship will turn into... other things." Evans had been trying to figure out how to breach this subject with David all day. Even Adam hadn't gotten companionship right the first time, by some accounts. He shook his head, shelved that one. The story of Lilith was probably not best suited to conveying teenage romance advice.

"Arthur," David said, ever so slowly, "did you think that I was... romantically interested in Cat?"

It was Evans' turn to be confused. "Weren't you? I daresay that she has a lot to be interested in. It's only natural."

"What? No." The youth flushed slightly. "I mean, sure, she's nice and attractive or whatever, but she's not a very stable person. I mean, I don't want to talk bad about her behind her back, but she acts a little too old for me, too impulsive, and I think the only thing she truly believes in is herself, you know?"

"Oh, I don't know about all that, er..." Evans began, but he knew David was right. At least in aggregate.

"I'm not trying to be mean, Arthur. I'm sure we will stay good friends and all. But she has, well, different ideas about certain things." He turned another shade redder.

Evans was flabbergasted. He muttered a few indistinct vowels and cleared his throat. He would have to congratulate Karen. The boy was doing better than Evans had done against the heart's call in his youth. Though how in the world David expected to be friends with her was beyond him. He started to say something to that effect, but David was already back on his phone, and Evans realized the answer.

"They've landed in Paris, by the way. She's taking the train to Madrid tonight, and Father Matthew's flight to London boards soon."

Evans could only smile and nod. The ability of young people to connect with everyone and consider them friends never ceased to amaze him. It just wasn't his world anymore.

"Also, mom wrote you a pretty big email. She wants you to call her when you get a chance."

Evans grimaced sheepishly. This hadn't been the start of summer that Joe and Karen had envisioned for David. Come to think of it, it hadn't been the one he had envisioned either. Evans was going to have to pay the piper soon. But for the first time in a very long time, he wasn't completely dreading it. It might be nice to talk to Joe, clear the air. He had a fair bit to say this time. The kids had done well with David. Very well indeed, and it was only fair for them to know it.

David took a picture through the taxi window. Twisting island roads, mazelike waterways, and tall bridges made up much of the tiny island kingdom. Every inch of water's edge seemed to have something moored to it. It was the western edge of the Persian Gulf out there, pretty much smack in the middle of the long side. This part of the world had been the staging area for many a war, ancient, modern, and otherwise. But it was still beautiful, Evans had to admit.

"Is this place really Eden?" David asked. "Dilmun, I mean."

"It's undeniably part of the ancient nation of Dilmun," Evans replied. "But as for whether their capital city is still waiting to be found—or for that matter had anything to do with Nûḥ—well, that's up for debate. It certainly fits many of the known variables. But capitols change, cities rise and fall, become lost and buried, and the earth tends to guard its secrets well. As you will recall, the sea levels of the world are a lot higher than they used to be. This whole cluster of islands would have been more like a mountain range some dozen millennia ago. There was certainly no capital city on these peaks, despite the urban oddity you see here today."

"Like grandpappy's ax?"

Evans was taken aback. "Er. I don't think the Lydian labrys has any real connection to Dilmun, David."

"No, Arthur," David laughed. "I mean it's like the old saying, 'This is grandpappy's ax, we've replaced the handle five times and the head twice.' Maybe Nûḥ did build a walled city where he thought Eden used to be. Then, at some point, way later that city gets named Dilmun, the country gets named after it, and then the capital gets moved inland or something as the sea levels rise. Wash, rinse, repeat."

Evans smiled goofily. "You know David, you have a remarkably intuitive mind."

"Thank you, Arthur," the teen said with mock seriousness and a not-entirely-horrible English accent. "It's a family trait, you see."

Evans gave the boy a friendly snort. "Still, it's not a bad theory overall. It's highly likely that Nûḥ's city, Dilmun, and Eden never were the same place, just a similar archetypal lost paradise that moved legendary locations as man migrated outward from Mesopotamia. Rituals can last long after the reasons for them have been forgotten, and our stories can re-evolve out of them. Even if an ancient myth was somehow literally and wholly true, stories first and foremost are representations of the way our ancestors behaved, and those myths are the way they passed that knowledge to us. It's a deep part of being human that we must never neglect, even if none of the details of the stories are objectively factual."

"You can't be serious, Arthur! After everything we've done, you still don't think at least some of it has to be true? I mean, you saw part of Noah's Ark, his clay tablet. You translated untranslatable things."

Evans crossed his arms grumpily. "All I'm saying is that for ancient man, thinking about his actions, representing them, and constructing morality stories about those representations were probably the first thing that separated him from the animals. Fireside theory is almost universally accepted now. Such an ability to tell stories is knowledge of good and evil, almost by definition. These patterns of thought are our heritage of collective conscience, morality, choice, and even the concept of 'sin' in its rawest form. That's partly what makes the Adam and Eve story archetypal."

"'We story-told ourselves into existence.' Okay, I think I get what you mean now. Ancient wisdom stories are... well, ancient wisdom stories. But what about the 'original sin' part? Evil isn't some metaphor. Creation fell when they ate the fruit—archetypically, or whatever? The Bible is pretty clear on that process."

"Oh? Are you certain? Which is more plausible, that man ruined all of God's good world with one act of sin, or that we merely ruined it for ourselves by following the allure of enlightenment?"

David screwed up his face in disbelief. "So, you still think *Genesis* is just wrong?"

"Oh no, not at all. You must never fall into that trap. The Bible is a representation of the lived experience and cultures of profoundly influential individuals across multiple millennia. That it has a plot and consists of mostly historical accounts is perhaps the most remarkable thing about it."

"Hm, that's what Father Matthew said."

"Yes, I imagine he did. Who do you think taught him that idea?"

David looked at Evans sideways. "Okay Arthur, but Father Matthew also said he didn't need any proof to know that scripture was true and accurate." There was a question behind David's words that he didn't ask, and a touch of concern too.

"Well, Matthew is right to say what he believes. The Bible is the greatest library ever collected. But the great and ancient stories in the first ten chapters of *Genesis* are special. In some sense, truer than reality even, because they might well be an archetypal abstraction. We just don't know. I presume that is what Dayik meant when she said that Nûḥ's tablet was a map of many things. It's a map of our minds too."

David scrutinized him suspiciously. "So just what is the point of those early *Genesis* stories, then? What do they mean, you know, archetypally?"

"Ah, that one is easy." Evans waggled a finger so the words would come. "Creation and flood myths are the great lens through which cultural values are expressed in every culture, from antiquity even to today. Epic myths in the truest sense. But the biblical version is unique. Unlike most myths, God didn't create because he was lonely, needy, careless, or vindictive. Nor did he later wipe out mankind because they were loud, or he was petty. He didn't save Noah because he needed someone to worship him or make him food offerings. Other ancient myths cast the biblical versions into stark contrast. Adam and Eve were cast out of Eden because they made a selfish choice. Noah was saved for his faith because he 'walked with the Lord' and chose to obey. I suppose each is a story about faith and salvation first and foremost, but these things all hinge on the choices humans make. No theology needed, these stories shout the point loud and clear as literature alone. Choice is the grand theme of the biblical library."

"Did Matthew get that from you too? He said almost the same thing the other day."

Evans felt himself blush under his merciful beard. "No, David, that one I took from him."

David simply grinned.

"That we Westerners look to *Genesis* as containing a literal story of a worldwide flood at all shows our modern bias," Evans continued. "To insist on scientific or historical proof, before accepting the moral truths in a morality story, is very telling about our ideals. It's a bit sad that we westerners have missed the deeper symbolic truth in our quest for Noah's presumed literal boat. The ancient flood myths are a chorus of stories so old, so true in a far deeper way, that to use geology or archeology to try to prove or disprove them is simply beyond our reach. Eden is the same, I'm afraid."

"But Arthur, if the purpose of the early *Genesis* stories is to set the record straight against parallel ancient stories, then why does it matter if it is literal or not? Who's to say it isn't?"

"Well, that's precisely the point, isn't it? Blind faith can get us into trouble. But, as I have recently been reminded, having no faith is oftentimes much worse. But then, what do I know? I'm no theologian." Evans removed his glasses and began rubbing them with his brand-new handkerchief. "I'm often told that my ideas lack a deeper faith."

"Just the humanities guy?" David asked mischievously.

Evans chuckled. "Just the humanities guy."

"And Noah's map to Eden? That's probably not real then either. Literally, I mean."

"*Of* Eden," Evans corrected. "No. I'm fairly convinced it can't be. Remember David, if you go looking for myths, you'll find them."

"Confirmation bias, yea. Like Uncle Sir Arthur and Mr. Aarons with their archeology."

"That's right. It's like Rabbi Yosef said: Eden has always been a mythical symbol for God's first temple, his dwelling place among men in his perfect creation. The ten Kabbalistic *sephirot* like mercy, understanding, wisdom, are a wonderful symbolic depiction of God's interaction with man. When the path was disrupted, mankind became disconnected from God. We lost Eden, if you will. But like any other symbolic tool, we shouldn't take it too literally."

"I thought it was eleven," David said.

"What's that now?" Evans replaced his glasses so he could hear better.

"Rabbi Yosef said it was eleven." The teen began flipping through the hundreds of images on his phone, then held it up. "See? Eleven *sephirot*."

"Ah, I see the problem." The old tutor scratched his cheek. "I had forgotten that Yosef showed you an image with the depiction of the eleventh. That's quite common."

"The missing point in the center is called *Daath*, right? Yosef said it meant knowledge or whatever."

No doubt about it, David was a quick study. "That's right. It's the hidden point on the path that crosses over the abyss threshold, the dividing line between God and creation. Not all representations show it, but it is quite a good symbol. In some sense, it is the key to understanding the whole grand and silly teaching of the Kabbalistic Tree of Life. Yosef didn't tell you that the tree works both ways. The 'Flaming Sword' you know, it is the return to Edenic holiness. But let's not forget that the second path is called the 'Path of the Serpent' and goes the other way. It represents the fall of man. Thus, when not shown, *Daath* represents that same impassible barrier to God we were just talking about. Sin itself, you see. It's why the Kabbalistic Tree doesn't really work as a religious guide." David's eyes asked the question for him. "We can't puppet God, David. 'As above, so below,' is nonsensical wishful thinking. It is built upon the idea that if we become holy enough, or pray hard enough, we can align ourselves with Heaven and get what we want. It's what children do at Christmas to get presents from Santa Claus."

"Yea," David said. "I was kind of thinking the same thing when Yosef explained it the first time."

"Which is, of course, the very reason why God expelled Adam and Eve in the story. They chose self-determination over God's one rule, broke the connection, and metaphorically tried to side-step the eleventh symbol. They listened to the bad advice of the chaos serpent because they wanted access to divine knowledge, but inadvertently cut themselves off from Eden forever. If the Tree of Life were somehow a map of Eden, then I suppose that central hidden point would represent the location of the forbidden Tree of Knowledge in the middle of the garden itself—"

Evans gasped, the final pieces falling into place in his mind.

It couldn't really be that simple. Could it?

CII

Manama, Kingdom of Bahrain. David.

"Arthur? You okay?" David's wizard was as white as when he'd first seen Mr. Aarons' journal in The King's Arms Pub all those long days ago.

Arthur cleared his throat and his voice dropped to a reverent monotone. "Utnapishtim sent Gilgamesh to the bottom of the sea with rocks strapped to his feet."

"Yea?"

"The sea near the coast of his garden, Dilmun."

"Okay…"

"This sea. This coast. This nation."

David's face lit up. "Oh yeah, right."

"And he sent him down to recover…?"

"The Tree of Life. The other tree that Adam and Eve were allowed to eat from." He looked at the Kabbalistic image on his phone again. "Which is what this thing is called. But it was stolen by a snake, er, chaos serpent in that story."

"And the *Cudi-Nûḥ* tablet only had ten icons, but even Dayik said there were eleven. She was giving me a clue. How could I be so blind? It's like she said, 'You may realize you've had Eden all along.'"

"Arthur, what are you talking about? Are you saying you solved it?"

Arthur nodded, clearly not believing it all just yet. "Pitman's satellite data, the biblical account, Gilgamesh, the *Cudi-Nûḥ* tablet. It all fits together perfectly, despite literally thousands of years of separation, by any measure."

David tried again. "So, you know where Eden is? Actual old, original Eden?"

"The Kabbalistic Tree of Life has always been called a map to paradise. I just didn't realize how literal it was meant to be."

"But Arthur, what was on that tablet anyway? I never saw it."

"Ah, quite right." Arthur eyed David's phone dubiously. "Can you draw on that thing?"

David switched apps in a heartbeat. "You bet I can!"

Moments later, they'd reconstructed a crude image of Noah's tablet.

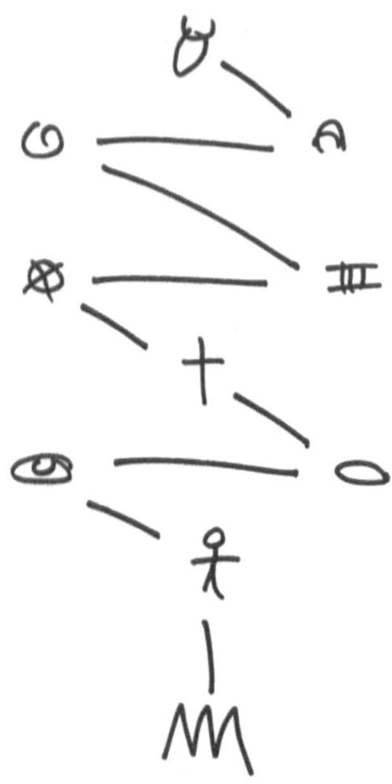

"So, what's it say?" David asked.

"Give it a try, David. You have everything you need."

David hadn't expected Arthur to throw to him, but with a few quick taps, he was flipping back and forth between Yosef's translation page and his new drawing, and he realized that he did have everything. He haltingly tried to put the words together with some sort of meaningfulness.

"*God-began-inside-separate-surround...* Or maybe that should be *snake*? Actually, it kind of looks like the word for *city* on the Phaistos Disk. The one we thought meant 'important' at first?"

"You're doing fine. Keep going."

"*Covenant-word-experience-see-chaos*? Um. Sorry, Arthur, I'm not seeing it."

"I might try it this way. 'God created, then entered the walled garden of the serpent. His covenant spoken, he looked upon it, and declared that it was chaos.'"

"Arthur, that's almost *Genesis*. Except that God called creation *good*, uh, 'functional' or whatever, not 'the serpent's garden.' But Father Matthew did kind of say that chaos could have been built in from the start, so maybe it's not that weird?" David felt his resolve crack. "Oh man, it's like the spiral symbol, chaos and order intertwined. Order comes from chaos. Stuff loses power when we name it, but it needs the chaos so that it can exist. Like how if the serpent was supposed to be in the garden from the start, then it was his job to tempt Eve." He paused. "Dad would so hate that."

Arthur nodded. "And if we insert the hidden *sephirot—*"

"Oh yea, right." David talked it out. "So, the hidden word is 'knowledge' and it would have to go between 'enter' and 'wall,' I guess. So, 'God created, then placed knowledge into the walled garden of the serpent?' Is that right?"

"Close enough," Arthur affirmed. "That sequence is the lightning flash of creation. The Path of the Flaming Sword." His smile turned strange. "Now go the other way, translate the Path of the Serpent."

David blinked a few times. He wasn't sure what Arthur meant. You can't translate something backwards, it just wouldn't work. He tried anyway, starting on the other end and talking it out again. "Chaos-behold-see-speak-covenant-garden-separate..." David gasped. "The last three symbols!"

Arthur nodded. "Yes. It's the pictographic version of *bara*, 'to create.' The one that literally means 'in the beginning, God.' It does not escape my attention that it is above the abyss threshold. Now, put it all together if you can."

David could. "Waters of chaos, behold, experience, and speak the covenant. The Garden is separated. In the beginning, God?"

"Yes. Or perhaps the last phrase is, 'Enter and begin again with God,' or maybe even, 'Enter the Ark, Godly man. Though that one is a stretch, admittedly."

"Woah, sick. It's another flood myth."

"And a creation myth. The second is the unmaking of the first, just as the *Genesis* version tells us. A fresh start."

"So, what does it all mean, Arthur?"

"Well, a few things I suppose. First, that the original Path of the Flaming Sword doesn't end at Mt. Cudi—it starts there. If the old walled garden of paradise was known to Noah, then he almost surely tried to go back. Maybe to see what had survived. He couldn't have written of it being separated away unless he saw it for himself."

"Like how Utnapishtim and his wife went to the garden of Dilmun after the flood and gained the secret of eternal life. That's where Gilgamesh found them. Oh man, I'd forgotten!"

"Good connection. It also means that the *Cudi-Nûḥ* tablet must be a map of an incredibly large and ancient fertile valley garden. Natural walls. A lush river delta. Where four rivers meet and become one. *Genesis* names them, two are gone now. But after the time of Noah, the world's sea levels rose significantly. Maybe it was the last Ice Age melting or leftovers from the flood, it doesn't especially matter. The point is that certain valleys would have filled with water just as you said, submerging old cities, Eden included. Except, if some sort of natural dam broke, it would have done so very, very fast. A literal deluge from the waters of the earth. It would have been apocalyptic to anyone living there."

"Well, where is it? Let's go!"

"We can't."

"What? Why not!?"

"Because of the last thing the tablet tells us. The city of Dilmun might well have been established on the high hills of Eden's border, on the fringes of whatever little part of the garden remained. But not all the water receded. Eden is still at the bottom of the sea." Arthur swallowed hard. "This sea."

"The Persian Gulf?"

The old wizard nodded slowly, meeting David's eyes with a rabid intensity. "I think the Tree of Life is a map of the Gulf basin. What used to be a great deep valley where the four biblical rivers met. It must have been a true paradise before the sea took it. And Nûḥ's map pinpoints the exact spot where the Tree of the Knowledge of Good and Evil once grew."

"Under the hidden eleventh *sephirot*. Unbelievable."

"Unbelievable indeed, David. An invisible spot, right in the middle of the Gulf. Hidden, but not secret."

"So, the map is real?"

Arthur hesitated, apparently unsure how to answer. "I don't know, David. If not, it's a pretty impressive fake. Dayik claimed that Wyatt's Ark was a medieval hoax. Perpetrated by the actual Templar Knights, if you can believe that. I doubt we'll ever know the objective truth of either one, but perhaps it doesn't matter.

Ever so slowly David broke into a barely restrained maniacal laugh.

"David?"

"Arthur!" The teen said between gasps. "Don't you see? Iron!"

Arthur didn't see. He shook his head, brows furrowed.

"Your Doomsday samples came back positive with medieval-age worked iron, right? You said so yourself."

Arthur's jaw dropped, thunderstruck. David could practically see the gears grinding in his wizard's head. "And the *Kabballah* is medieval too, right? Maybe it comes from Noah's map. Because, why not?"

They both sat looking at each other for a minute with goofy smiles. The full implications of it were—actually, David had no idea what the full implications were.

Finally, after a long minute of this, Arthur spoke. "There is a third consideration if the Nûḥ map tablet is genuine and not another Templar hoax. It's that Wyatt could be right about Noah having a written language. And that's deeply disconcerting."

David couldn't stop grinning like a madman. "Okay. So, how can we know? What do we do?" He felt ready to strap rocks to his feet and dive into the gulf right away.

Arthur pushed his glasses up. "Well, I certainly know what I plan to do about it, and just in the nick of time too. We seem to have arrived. Let's keep this little theory to ourselves for a while, eh?"

Out of the taxi window, Bahrain's internet-famous luxury Dragon Hotel loomed. By design, it was shaped quite a bit like some great undulating serpent. It boasted great ridges on the high roof and its great glass sides reminded David of silvery-blue scales. It was as if Tiamat herself had risen and flopped herself atop this no-longer-a-mountaintop island.

Very appropriate, David decided. His poor wizard was going to have to face one more dragon after all.

CIII

Dragon Hotel, Amwaj Island, Kingdom of Bahrain. Mr. Suit.

The man in the suit watched as Dr. Evans and the boy approached the umbrella-covered table. His mentor had good taste. Every room in the luxurious beachfront hotel was a suite. It had everything from gorgeous views to an infinity pool, and the best views were unquestionably poolside. Even now, he could see a few American girls laying out towels to sunbathe.

Later, perhaps. He was working.

His new suit felt good against his skin. As before, his personal requirements had been filled to the letter by Mel Chen, so he had honored Mr. Wyatt's wishes and accepted his old job back. After a fashion at any rate. *What she didn't know...*

People are clocks to be studied. Resources to be consumed.

Or perhaps that second idea was flawed? It had ended badly for Dr. Pitman. His ambition and greed had consumed him in the end.

Oh, the lies we tell ourselves.

The man in the suit would need to think about all that later. Right now, he was working.

He took off his sunglasses so as not to appear aggressive to the good doctor. Given the long dry scabs on his face, it was the best he could do. As the old tutor approached, the man in the suit tossed a now-familiar fedora onto the table.

"I was seriously planning on punching you in the nose, Wyatt, but evidently somebody beat me to it." Evans pulled out a chair and sat, his young protégé doing the same. The kid eyed the man in the suit suspiciously. The man couldn't blame him, all considered.

"It's fantastic to see you after all these years, Arthur," Wyatt Aarons said. "You look quite well."

"Whatever it is you want, Wyatt, the answer is no."

"Oh, Arthur, give me a chance. Things are different now."

Dr. Evans snorted, finally noticing his hat. He snatched it up and examined it with confusion before fitting it squarely on his head with obvious contentment. Again, the boy gave the man in the suit an icy glare. He just smiled back and winked.

"What happened to your arm?" The good doctor pointed his chin at Aarons' sling.

"Oh, a bullet took a chunk of me back at Ugarit. It's almost healed."

Dr. Evans scoffed loudly. "I didn't think bullets could hit you, Wyatt. You are losing your touch."

"The Lord works in mysterious ways, my old friend." Mr. Wyatt's tone shifted slightly. "I still want you on the team, Arthur. Mel is doubling her original offer for what you did. She says you can name your price moving forward."

"I'm not joining any more of your teams, Wyatt. Forget it." The tutor scowled.

"Eden is out there, Arthur. God wants us to find it!"

"You're lying to yourself, Wyatt."

"Oh Arthur, don't you see? The world is full of the Devil's lies. But God led you to the true ark, just like he led me and Ryan all those decades ago. It was to show us the truth. But you had to follow the path yourself. To see Noah's temple for yourself. That's how it works. If I had just told you what I knew, you never would have believed me. Besides, I took an oath a long time ago that I will not break. Everything I did, I did in faith."

The man in the suit watched as his mentor pulled the sling back and revealed his raven tattoo.

"What?" the teenage Evans exclaimed. He tensed and half stood like a creature hunted and about to bolt for his life.

Dr. Evans shook his head and laughed. "I should have known." The old tutor took his glasses off and rubbed the bridge of his nose. "So, you've known about Mt. Judi for years. Which means you knew Doomsday was a hoax too. And of course you acted in faith, Wyatt. That's what you always do."

Then, to the man in the suit's surprise, Dr. Evans replaced his glasses and looked straight at him. "And you. You shot at me! Not to mention all those innocent bystanders on the Broad."

The man smiled innocently and shrugged one shoulder. "I shot a book and a window, Dr. Evans. If I had wanted to put a bullet in you, I would have. Rest assured, you were never in real danger. Nor was anyone else."

"Somehow, I think that might be worse," Evans growled. "You were never after the journal at all, were you? You just goaded me into this little adventure with violence."

The man in the suit sat back in his chair and crossed his arms. *No need to muddy the waters with complicated details.* People saw what they wanted to see, and that was enough. He had concluded his job as arbitrator, watched, assisted, evaluated, and finally acted. His mentor had been right: The family had understood.

Dr. Evans sucked his teeth, shook his head, then turned back to his old partner. "But see, here's the problem Wyatt. There's no blasted way that you cracked the Phaistos Disk, connected the dots to Gortyn from Lydia, or solved the riddle of the Labyrinth. It took four of us to manage it on the ground, five counting Yosef's work. You cheated. I don't know how, but you and Pitman did an end-run around the maze and just skipped to the finish."

Mr. Wyatt put his good hand up in mock surrender, a gesture that reminded him disconcertingly of Pitman's performance on the *Mao Sien* jet. "You got me, Arthur. My path was different. I'm glad that Ugarit worked out, but I'm afraid I don't know what you are talking about if I'm honest. The family keeps secrets from me too. It's their right. I do know that there are many paths to Noah's sanctuary, though. That's one thing that's not a secret. Honestly, I was hoping those translation fragments would unlock the secrets of the Disk and reveal the path to Dilmun, but it doesn't surprise me that it took you to Mt. Judi instead. All things considered, it makes sense though."

The man in the suit's mentor waited for a comment from Dr. Evans, but none came.

"So, now that you have seen Noah's tablet for yourself, Arthur, tell me. Did you translate it? Do you know where Eden is?"

Dr. Evans merely sat with his arms crossed, scowling. The man in the suit smiled inwardly. The Oxford scholar was an open clock to him, and this clock was never going to agree. Dr. Evans' decision was made long ago. But his mentor was up to something, and he was interested to learn what.

"It's out there, Arthur," Aarons enticed, despite getting no answer to his questions. "I still have Ryan's satellite scans, and while I was hopping around on Mel's oil rigs, I gathered enough data on the gulf floor to corroborate his facts. Motivations notwithstanding, Ryan found some really good candidates for the Gihon and Pishon riverbeds, up near the coast of Iraq. I've talked to the American military, and they're giving us permission to work down in the allied free zone. Saddam had that whole southern marsh area drained off to force the locals out, which means that things will be exposed that haven't been seen for five thousand years at least. I'm thinking if we start in ancient Eridu, work our way south—"

"No, Wyatt," Dr. Evans cut in. "Not in another five thousand years. Not now, not ever. No more war zones. No more adventures. Can't you see that Eden is just not meant to be found? *Genesis* calls it guarded for a reason. If God hasn't already told you this in one of your visions, then I'm telling you now. No."

Tick tock, the man in the suit told himself.

"Oh, Arthur, don't answer right away, think it over. The family doesn't care about Eden. It's like I said before, when we find it, you can be vindicated for all that bad press over Doomsday! Now, I got you a nice luxury suite here at the hotel. Once you're rested, we can spend a few days getting a plan together."

"Come on, David, we're done here."

Aarons sighed in frustration. "Do you remember what Noah did after the Ark landed, Arthur?"

Dr. Evans stood and reseated his hat, but answered anyway. "He made a sacrificial offering, Wyatt. Then, he got drunk and passed out naked. I can't say as I blame him given everything else he'd just seen and done. I could go for a pint myself, frankly."

Aarons' face lit up. "That's right! Only a few days after God reset the world, his most faithful man had already screwed up again. Sin was still around. Nakedness was still a thing. But you know who found him? His son, Arthur. His middle son. Folks get that wrong, but everywhere the Bible says his sons' names it's Shem, Ham, and Japheth. In that order."

Dr. Evans blinked, cocked his head, and pushed his glasses onto his nose. "Where are you going with this, Wyatt?"

"You know what happened next. The other two shielded their eyes and covered Noah up. And when he woke up, he realized what had happened. He put a curse on Ham and demoted him to third son, bringing Japheth up to number two."

"I'm not sure that's exactly how that story goes."

"Now a lot of folks wonder what sin it was that Ham did," Wyatt continued as if Dr. Evans hadn't spoken. Some of the theories are real disturbing. But that's missing the point, see? It's right there in the story. He did nothing, Arthur. Nothing at all. He walked away and made fun of his father to his brothers. But Japheth didn't do that. He helped Shem cover Noah up, and did so while looking the other way. It's not a story about what Ham did, it's about what Japheth did to honor his father, despite being the youngest member of the family."

The man in the suit was amused. His mentor had set the trap. Dr. Evans' face showed it too.

"Ryan was Ham, Arthur. He saw God's ancient secrets and wanted to expose them to the world. Prove the miracles with science, something he believed in even more than God's own words. He mocked our Heavenly Father, and he went and lost his birthright. But now that birthright is falling back to you. Won't you help me find and protect the truth?"

Aarons wasn't talking about Melanie Chen's corporate team, then. He was offering his old partner a chance to join the family. Suddenly, the man in the suit understood why they were really here.

"I suppose that makes you Shem, then?" Dr. Evans mused, his eyes squeezed shut. "Wyatt, you are still an arrogant nincompoop. But at least you aren't an evil one. I'm sorry, but that's just a story about honoring your father. It has nothing to do with you and me. My answer is still no."

"Is *Genesis* still just literature to you, Arthur? Have you no faith left?"

"No. Quite the opposite. But I'm not about to punt to miracles either."

"But don't you see, Arthur? It's meant to be. God wants us to work together again."

"Wyatt, I didn't want to have to say this, but I just don't believe you. You knew too much. You gave too many clues not to know what we would find. Archeology doesn't work that way. And in the end, I just don't have enough faith in you to know whether you faked the whole blasted thing. Or maybe it's all some ancient decoy, like that infernal mountain of yours, which would mean that it fooled you too. The whole thing is much too neat and tidy. No. My answer is no. Once and for all. I've got more important things in my life now than some silly quest for Eden. Things—people—that I've been ignoring for much too long. Best of luck, though."

As Dr. Evans said this, he turned and put his hand on the teenager's shoulder. The kid looked over at him and smiled. And at that, the Evanses walked back to their taxi.

All for the best really, in the man in the suit's opinion. Dr. Evans wouldn't be any more trouble now. Ashti could be satisfied about that. Meanwhile, there was still much to learn from Mr. Wyatt. Very much indeed. It would be interesting to see what he did next.

The man in the suit glanced at the pool and smiled. After all, the possibility of failure was half the fun.

Remember who you are.

Remember who you really are.

EPILOGUE

David keyed in the code to the little room Arthur called his office, then held the door open for Emma.

"Hey Arthur, I brought you a sandwich."

David set the plate down next to a stack of papers and smiled. Among the pages were photos that he had printed for his wizard just the other day. On top was a close-up of one of the pieces of the Ras-Shamra translation tablet. Unsurprisingly, Arthur had scribbled notes all about the Linear-A section in a brand-new lined notebook. The ancient languages expert had hardly come up for breath in days.

"So, do you mind if I take Emma to see Uncle Sir Arthur's archive?"

Arthur grunted noncommittally. His nose remained buried in a thick old book.

"Don't forget you're meeting Rabbi Yosef for dinner to talk about his new foundation grant thing."

"Mmm, yes. Quite right."

"And by the way, my application to Magdalen College was approved, so I'll finally be moving out of your flat next week. Before term officially starts, I mean. Did you know that they still have like a hundred acres of grounds? It's nuts."

"Well done, David," Arthur said, still not looking up.

"Thanks, Arthur," David called. "We'll be in the back." He gestured toward the door to the magical dark room where the off-display collections were kept.

Emma plunged excitedly into the history-smelling darkness. She elbowed David mischievously in the ribs as he stepped in beside her. "So, this is where you and Arthur stow your family skeletons, huh?"

"Yep. Just wait till you see Uncle Sir Arthur's portrait. I like his mustache most."

Emma laughed. David loved that laugh.

As the self-closing door clicked shut, he barely heard Arthur call out:

"Wait a tick. David! Who the devil is Emma?"

About the Author

Adam "Doc" Brackin is an English teacher, writer, gamer, storyteller, and Christian apologist, though not necessarily in that order. He lives in Dallas, TX with his wife and son. Visit him online at:

www.adambrackin.com

About the Illustrator

Randall Worley pastors an intentionally multiethnic church and has a passion for teaching the Bible. He lives in Plano, Texas with his wife and a much-too-large collection of tabletop games.

www.ingramcontent.com/pod-product-compliance
Lightning Source LLC
Chambersburg PA
CBHW032105310726
48972CB00001B/105